MISS MARPLE

"Miss [ ] really believe you know the truth."

"Well, dear," said Miss Marple, "it is much easier for me sitting here quietly than it was for you—and being an artist, you are so susceptible to atmosphere, aren't you? Sitting here with one's knitting, one just sees the facts. Bloodstains dropped on the pavement from the bathing dress hanging above, and being a red bathing dress, of course, the criminals themselves did not realize it was bloodstained. Poor thing, poor young thing…"

AGATHA CHRISTIE

"The champion deceiver of our time!"   —*New York Times*

The most popular mystery writer of all time, Agatha Christie achieved the highest honor possible to a woman in Britain when she was made a Dame of the British Empire.

AGATHA CHRISTIE

MISS MARPLE

THE COMPLETE SHORT STORIES

BERKLEY BOOKS, NEW YORK

The stories appearing in this volume have all been
previously published in the following books by Agatha
Christie: *The Tuesday Club Murders, The Regatta Mystery
and other Stories, Three Blind Mice and Other Stories,*
and *Double Sin and Other Stories.*

This Berkley book contains the complete
text of the original hardcover edition.

MISS MARPLE: THE COMPLETE SHORT STORIES

A Berkley Book / published by arrangement with
G. P. Putnam's Sons

PRINTING HISTORY
Dodd, Mead edition published 1985
Berkley trade paperback edition / November 1986

ISBN: 0-425-09486-3

BERKLEY®
Berkley Books are published by The Berkley Publishing Group,
200 Madison Avenue, New York, New York 10016.
The name "BERKLEY" and the "B" design are
trademarks belonging to Berkley Publishing Corporation.

PRINTED IN CANADA

20 19 18 17 16 15 14

CONTENTS

FROM THREE BLIND MICE

FROM DOUBLE SIN

THE
TUESDAY
CLUB
MURDERS

The Tuesday Night Club

"U nsolved Mysteries."

Raymond West blew out a cloud of smoke and repeated the words with a kind of deliberate self-conscious pleasure.

"Unsolved mysteries."

He looked round him with satisfaction. The room was an old one with broad black beams across the ceiling and it was furnished with good old furniture that belonged to it. Hence Raymond West's approving glance. By profession he was a writer and he liked the atmosphere to be flawless. His Aunt Jane's house always pleased him as the right setting for her personality. He looked across the hearth to where she sat erect in the big grandfather chair. Miss Marple wore a black brocade dress, very much pinched in round the waist. Mechlin lace was arranged in a cascade down the front of the bodice. She had on black lace mittens, and a black lace cap surmounted the piled-up masses of her snowy hair. She was knitting—something white and soft and fleecy. Her faded blue eyes, benignant and kindly, surveyed her nephew and her nephew's guests with gentle pleasure. They rested first on Raymond himself, self-consciously debonair, then on Joyce Lemprière, the artist, with her close-cropped black head and queer hazel-green eyes, then on that well-groomed man of the world, Sir Henry Clithering. There were two other people in the room, Dr. Pender, the elderly clergyman of the parish, and Mr. Petherick, the solicitor, a dried-up little man with eyeglasses which he looked over and not through. Miss Marple gave a brief moment of attention to all these people and returned to her knitting with a gentle smile upon her lips.

Mr. Petherick gave the dry little cough with which he usually prefaced his remarks.

"What is that you say, Raymond? Unsolved mysteries? Ha—and what about them?"

"Nothing about them," said Joyce Lemprière. "Raymond just likes the sound of the words and of himself saying them."

Raymond West threw her a glance of reproach at which she threw back her head and laughed.

"He is a humbug, isn't he, Miss Marple?" she demanded. "You know that, I am sure."

Miss Marple smiled gently at her but made no reply.

"Life itself is an unsolved mystery," said the clergyman gravely.

Raymond sat up in his chair and flung away his cigarette with an impulsive gesture.

"That's not what I mean. I was not talking philosophy," he said. "I was thinking of actual bare prosaic facts, things that have happened and that no one has ever explained."

"I know just the sort of thing you mean, dear," said Miss Marple. "For instance Mrs. Carruthers had a very strange experience yesterday morning. She bought two gills of pickled shrimps at Elliot's. She called at two other shops and when she got home she found she had not got the shrimps with her. She went back to the two shops she had visited but these shrimps had completely disappeared. Now that seems to me very remarkable."

"A very fishy story," said Sir Henry Clithering gravely.

"There are, of course, all kinds of possible explanations," said Miss Marple, her cheeks growing slightly pinker with excitement. "For instance, somebody else—"

"My dear Aunt," said Raymond West with some amusement, "I didn't mean that sort of village incident. I was thinking of murders and disappearances—the kind of thing that Sir Henry could tell us about by the hour if he liked."

"But I never talk shop," said Sir Henry modestly. "No, I never talk shop."

Sir Henry Clithering had been until lately Commissioner of Scotland Yard.

"I suppose there are a lot of murders and things that never are solved by the police," said Joyce Lemprière.

"That is an admitted fact, I believe," said Mr. Petherick.

"I wonder," said Raymond West, "what class of brain really succeeds best in unravelling a mystery? One always feels that the average police detective must be hampered by lack of imagination."

"That is the layman's point of view," said Sir Henry drily.

"You really want a committee," said Joyce, smiling. "For psychology and imagination go to the writer—"

She made an ironical bow to Raymond but he remained serious.

"The art of writing gives one an insight into human nature," he said gravely. "One sees, perhaps, motives that the ordinary person would pass by."

"I know, dear," said Miss Marple, "that your books are very clever. But do you think that people are really so unpleasant as you make them out to be?"

"My dear Aunt," said Raymond gently, "keep your beliefs. Heaven forbid that I should in any way shatter them."

"I mean," said Miss Marple, puckering her brow a little as she counted the stitches in her knitting, "that so many people seem to me not to be either bad or good, but simply you know, very silly."

Mr. Petherick gave his dry little cough again.

"Don't you think, Raymond," he said, "that you attach too much weight to imagination? Imagination is a very dangerous thing, as we lawyers know only too well. To be able to sift evidence impartially, to take the facts and look at them as facts—that seems to me the only logical method of arriving at the truth. I may add that in my experience it is the only one that succeeds."

"Bah!" cried Joyce, flinging back her black head indignantly. "I bet I could beat you all at this game. I am not only a woman—and say what you like, women have an intuition that is denied to men—I am an artist as well. I see things that you don't. And then, too, as an artist I have knocked about among all sorts and conditions of people. I know life as darling Miss Marple here cannot possibly know it."

"I don't know about that, dear," said Miss Marple. "Very painful and distressing things happen in villages sometimes."

"May I speak?" said Dr. Pender smiling. "It is the fashion nowadays to decry the clergy, I know, but we hear things, we know a side of human character which is a sealed book to the outside world."

"Well," said Joyce, "it seems to me we are a pretty representative gathering. How would it be if we formed a Club? What is today? Tuesday? We will call it The Tuesday Night Club. It is to meet every week, and each member in turn has to propound a problem. Some mystery of which they have personal knowledge, and to which, of course, they know the answer. Let me see, how many are we? One, two, three, four, five. We ought really to be six."

"You have forgotten me, dear," said Miss Marple, smiling brightly.

Joyce was slightly taken aback, but she concealed the fact quickly.

"That would be lovely, Miss Marple," she said. "I didn't think you would care to play."

"I think it would be very interesting," said Miss Marple, "especially with so many clever gentlemen present. I am afraid I am not clever myself, but living all these years in St. Mary Mead does give one an insight into human nature."

"I am sure your cooperation will be very valuable," said Sir Henry, courteously.

"Who is going to start?" said Joyce.

"I think there is no doubt as to that," said Dr. Pender, "when we have the great good fortune to have such a distinguished man as Sir Henry staying with us—"

He left his sentence unfinished, making a courtly bow in the direction of Sir Henry.

The latter was silent for a minute or two. At last he sighed and recrossed his legs and began:

"It is a little difficult for me to select just the kind of thing you want, but I think, as it happens, I know of an instance which fits these conditions very aptly. You may have seen some mention of the case in the papers of a year ago. It was laid aside at the time as an unsolved mystery, but, as it happens, the solution came into my hands not very many days ago.

"The facts are very simple. Three people sat down to a supper consisting, amongst other things, of tinned lobster. Later in the night, all three were taken ill, and a doctor was hastily summoned. Two of the people recovered, the third one died."

"Ah!" said Raymond approvingly.

"As I say, the facts as such were very simple. Death was considered to be due to ptomaine poisoning, a certificate was given to that effect, and the victim was duly buried. But things did not rest at that."

Miss Marple nodded her head.

"There was talk, I suppose," she said, "there usually is."

"And now I must describe the actors in this little drama. I will call the husband and wife Mr. and Mrs. Jones, and the wife's companion Miss Clark. Mr. Jones was a traveller for a firm of manufacturing chemists. He was a good-looking man in a kind of coarse, florid way, aged about fifty. His wife was a rather commonplace woman, of about forty-five. The companion, Miss Clark, was a woman of sixty, a stout cheery woman with a beaming rubicund face. None of them, you might say, very interesting.

"Now the beginning of the troubles arose in a very curious way. Mr. Jones had been staying the previous night at a small commercial hotel in Birmingham. It happened that the blotting paper in the blotting book had been put in fresh that day, and the chambermaid, having apparently nothing better to do, amused herself by studying the blotter in the mirror just after Mr. Jones had been writing a letter there. A few days later there was a report in the papers of the death of Mrs. Jones as the result of eating tinned lobster, and the chambermaid then imparted to her fellow servants the words that she had deciphered on the blotting pad. They were as follows: 'Entirely dependent on my wife . . . when she is dead I will . . . hundreds and thousands . . .'

"You may remember that there had recently been a case of a wife being poisoned by her husband. It needed very little to fire the imagination of these maids. Mr. Jones had planned to do away with his wife and inherit hundreds of thousands of pounds! As it happened one of the maids had relations living in the small market town where the Joneses resided. She wrote to them, and they in return wrote to her. Mr. Jones, it seemed, had been very attentive to the local doctor's daughter, a good-looking young woman of thirty-three. Scandal began to hum. The Home Secretary was petitioned. Numerous anonymous letters poured into Scotland Yard all accusing Mr. Jones of having murdered his wife. Now I may say that not for one moment did we think there was anything in it except idle village talk and gossip. Nevertheless, to quiet public opinion an exhumation order was granted. It was one of these cases of popular superstition based on nothing solid whatever, which proved to be so surprisingly justified. As a result of the autopsy sufficient arsenic was found to make it quite clear that the deceased lady had died of arsenical poisoning. It was for Scotland Yard working with the local authorities to prove how that arsenic had been administered, and by whom."

"Ah!" said Joyce. "I like this. This is the real stuff."

"Suspicion naturally fell on the husband. He benefited by his wife's death. Not to the extent of the hundreds of thousands romantically imagined by the hotel chambermaid, but to the very solid amount of £8000. He had no money of his own apart from what he earned, and he was a man of somewhat extravagant habits with a partiality for the society of women. We investigated as delicately as possible the rumour of his attachment to the doctor's daughter; but while it seemed clear that there had been a strong friendship between them at one time, there had been a most abrupt break two months previously, and they did not appear to have seen each other since. The doctor himself, an elderly man of a straightforward and unsuspicious type, was dumbfounded at the result of the autopsy. He had been called in about midnight to find all three people suffering. He had realized immediately the serious condition of Mrs. Jones, and had sent back to his dispensary for some opium pills, to allay the pain. In spite of all his efforts, however, she succumbed, but not for a moment did he suspect that anything was amiss. He was convinced that her death was due to a form of botulism. Supper that night had consisted of tinned lobster and salad, trifle and bread and cheese. Unfortunately none of the lobster remained—it had all been eaten and the tin thrown away. He had interrogated the young maid, Gladys Linch. She was terribly upset, very tearful and agitated, and he found it hard to get her to keep to the point, but she declared again and again that the tin had not been distended in any way and that the lobster had appeared to her in a perfectly good condition.

"Such were the facts we had to go upon. If Jones had feloniously administered arsenic to his wife, it seemed clear that it could not have been done in any of the things eaten at supper, as all three persons had partaken of the meal. Also—another point—Jones himself had returned from Birmingham just as supper was being brought in to table, so that he would have had no opportunity of doctoring any of the food beforehand."

"What about the companion," asked Joyce—"the stout woman with the good-humoured face?"

Sir Henry nodded.

"We did not neglect Miss Clark, I can assure you. But it seemed doubtful what motive she could have had for the crime. Mrs. Jones left her no legacy of any kind and the net result of her employer's death was that she had to seek for another situation."

"That seems to leave her out of it," said Joyce thoughtfully.

"Now one of my inspectors soon discovered a significant fact," went on Sir Henry. "After supper on that evening Mr. Jones had gone down to the kitchen and had demanded a bowl of corn-flour for his wife, who had complained of not feeling well. He had waited in the kitchen until Gladys Linch prepared it, and then carried it up to his wife's room himself. That, I admit, seemed to clinch the case."

The lawyer nodded.

"Motive," he said, ticking the point off on his fingers. "Opportunity. As a traveller for a firm of druggists, easy access to the poison."

"And a man of weak moral fibre," said the clergyman.

Raymond West was staring at Sir Henry.

"There is a catch in this somewhere," he said. "Why did you not arrest him?"

Sir Henry smiled rather wryly.

"That is the unfortunate part of the case. So far all had gone swimmingly, but now we come to the snags. Jones was not arrested because on interrogating Miss Clark she told us that the whole of the bowl of corn-flour was drunk not by Mrs. Jones but by her."

"Yes, it seems that she went to Mrs. Jones's room as was her custom. Mrs. Jones was sitting up in bed and the bowl of corn-flour was beside her.

" 'I am not feeling a bit well, Milly,' she said. 'Serves me right, I suppose, for touching lobster at night. I asked Albert to get me a bowl of corn-flour, but now that I have got it I don't seem to fancy it.'

" 'A pity,' commented Miss Clark—'it is nicely made too, no lumps. Gladys is really quite a nice cook. Very few girls nowadays seem to be able to make a bowl of corn-flour nicely. I declare I quite fancy it myself, I am that hungry.'

" 'I should think you were with your foolish ways,' said Mrs. Jones.

"I must explain," broke off Sir Henry, "that Miss Clark, alarmed at her increasing stoutness, was doing a course of what is popularly known as 'banting.'

" 'It is not good for you, Milly, it really isn't,' urged Mrs. Jones. 'If the Lord made you stout he meant you to be stout. You drink up that bowl of corn-flour. It will do you all the good in the world.'

"And straight away Miss Clark set to and did in actual fact finish the bowl. So, you see, that knocked our case against the husband to pieces. Asked for an explanation of the words on the blotting book Jones gave one readily enough. The letter, he explained, was in answer to one written from his brother in Australia who had applied to him for money. He had written, pointing out that he was entirely dependent on his wife. When his wife was dead he would have control of money and would assist his brother if possible. He regretted his inability to help but pointed out that there were hundreds and thousands of people in the world in the same unfortunate plight."

"And so the case fell to pieces?" said Dr. Pender.

"And so the case fell to pieces," said Sir Henry gravely. "We could not take the risk of arresting Jones with nothing to go upon."

There was a silence and then Joyce said, "And that is all, is it?"

"That is the case as it has stood for the last year. The true solution is now in the hands of Scotland Yard, and in two or three days' time you will probably read of it in the newspapers."

"The true solution," said Joyce thoughtfully. "I wonder. Let's all think for five minutes and then speak."

Raymond West nodded and noted the time on his watch. When the five minutes were up he looked over at Dr. Pender.

"Will you speak first?" he said.

The old man shook his head. "I confess," he said, "that I am utterly baffled. I can but think that the husband in some way must be the guilty party, but how he did it I cannot imagine. I can only suggest that he must have given her the poison in some way that has not yet been discovered, although how in that case it should have come to light after all this time I cannot imagine."

"Joyce?"

"The companion!" said Joyce decidedly. "The companion every time! How do we know what motive she may have had? Just because she was old and stout and ugly it doesn't follow that she wasn't in love with Jones herself. She may have hated the wife for some other reason. Think of being a companion—always having to be pleasant and agree and stifle yourself and bottle yourself up. One day she couldn't bear it any longer and then she killed her. She probably put the arsenic in the bowl of corn-flour and all that story about eating it herself is a lie."

"Mr. Petherick?"

The lawyer joined the tips of his fingers together professionally. "I should hardly like to say. On the facts I should hardly like to say."

"But you have got to, Mr. Petherick," said Joyce. "You can't reserve judgment and say 'without prejudice,' and be legal. You have got to play the game."

"On the facts," said Mr. Petherick, "there seems nothing to be said. It is my private opinion, having seen, alas, too many cases of this kind, that the husband was guilty. The only explanation that will cover the facts seems to be that Miss Clark for some reason or other deliberately sheltered him. There may have been some financial arrangement made between them. He might realize that he would be suspected, and she, seeing only a future of poverty before her, may have agreed to tell the story of drinking the corn-flour in return for a substantial sum to be paid to her privately. If that was the case it was of course most irregular. Most irregular indeed."

"I disagree with you all," said Raymond. "You have forgotten the one important factor in the case. *The doctor's daughter*. I will give you my reading of the case. The tinned lobster was bad. It accounted for the poisoning symptoms. The doctor was sent for. He finds Mrs. Jones, who has eaten more lobster than the others, in great pain, and he sends, as you told us, for some opium pills. He does not go himself, he sends. Who will give the messenger the opium pills? Clearly his daughter. Very likely she dispenses his medicines for him. She is in love with Jones and at this moment all the worst instincts in her nature rise and she realizes that the means to procure his freedom are in her hands. The pills she sends contain pure white arsenic. That is my solution."

"And now Sir Henry, tell us," said Joyce eagerly.

"One moment," said Sir Henry, "Miss Marple has not yet spoken."

"Dear, dear," she said. "I have dropped another stitch. I have been so interested in the story. A sad case, a very sad case. It reminds me of old Mr. Hargraves who lived up at the Mount. His wife never had the least suspicion—until he died, leaving all his money to a woman he had been living with and by whom he had had five children. She had at one time been their housemaid. Such a nice girl, Mrs. Hargraves always said—thoroughly to be relied upon to turn the mattresses every day—except Fridays, of course. And there was old Hargraves keeping this woman in a house in the neighbouring town and continuing to be a Churchwarden and to hand round the plate every Sunday."

"My dear Aunt Jane," said Raymond with some impatience. "What have dead and gone Hargraves got to do with the case?"

"This story made me think of him at once," said Miss Marple. "The facts are so very alike, aren't they? I suppose the poor girl has confessed now and that is how you know, Sir Henry."

"What girl?" said Raymond. "My dear Aunt, what *are* you talking about?"

"That poor girl, Gladys Linch, of course—the one who was so terribly agitated when the doctor spoke to her—and well she might be, poor thing. I hope that wicked Jones is hanged, I am sure, making that poor girl a murderess. I suppose they will hang her too, poor thing."

"I think, Miss Marple, that you are under a slight misapprehension," began Mr. Petherick.

But Miss Marple shook her head obstinately and looked across at Sir Henry.

"I am right, am I not? It seems so clear to me. The hundreds and thousands—and the trifle—I mean, one cannot miss it."

"What about the trifle and the hundreds and thousands?" cried Raymond.

His aunt turned to him.

"Cooks nearly always put hundreds and thousands on trifle, dear," she said. "Those little pink and white sugar things. Of course when I heard that they had had trifle for supper and that the husband had been writing to someone about hundreds and thousands, I naturally connected the two things together. That is where the arsenic was—in the hundreds and thousands. He left it with the girl and told her to put it on the trifle."

"But that is impossible," said Joyce quickly. "They all ate the trifle."

"Oh, no," said Miss Marple. "The companion was banting, you remember. You never eat anything like trifle if you are banting; and I expect Jones just scraped the hundreds and thousands off his share and left them at the side of his plate. It was a clever idea, but a very wicked one."

The eyes of the others were all fixed upon Sir Henry.

"It is a very curious thing," he said slowly, "but Miss Marple happens to have hit upon the truth. Jones had got Gladys Linch into trouble, as the saying goes. She was nearly desperate. He wanted his wife out of the way and promised to marry Gladys when his wife was dead. He doctored the hundreds and thousands and gave them to her with instructions how to use them. Gladys Linch died a week ago. Her child died at birth and Jones had deserted her for another woman. When she was dying she confessed the truth."

There was a few moments' silence and then Raymond said:

"Well, Aunt Jane, this is one up to you. I can't think how on earth you managed to hit upon the truth. I should never have thought of the little maid in the kitchen being connected with the case."

"No, dear," said Miss Marple, "but you don't know as much of life as I do. A man of that Jones's type—coarse and jovial. As soon as I heard there was a pretty young girl in the house I felt sure that he would not have left her alone. It is all very distressing and painful, and not a very nice thing to talk about. I can't tell you the shock it was to Mrs. Hargraves, and a nine days' wonder in the village."

The Idol House
of Astarte

And now, Dr. Pender, what are you going to tell us?"
The old clergyman smiled gently.

"My life has been passed in quiet places," he said.
"Very few eventful happenings have come my way. Yet
once, when I was a young man, I had one very strange and
tragic experience."

"Ah!" said Joyce Lemprière encouragingly.

"I have never forgotten it," continued the clergyman. "It
made a profound impression on me at the time, and to this
day by a slight effort of memory I can feel again the awe and
horror of that terrible moment when I saw a man stricken to
death by apparently no mortal agency."

"You make me feel quite creepy, Pender," complained Sir
Henry.

"It made me feel creepy, as you call it," replied the other.
"Since then I have never laughed at the people who use the
word atmosphere. There is such a thing. There are certain
places imbued and saturated with good or evil influences
which can make their power felt."

"That house, The Larches, is a very unhappy one," remarked Miss Marple. "Old Mr. Smithers lost all his money
and had to leave it, then the Carslakes took it and Johnny

Carslake fell downstairs and broke his leg and Mrs. Carslake had to go away to the south of France for her health, and now the Burdens have got it and I hear that poor Mr. Burden has got to have an operation almost immediately."

"There is, I think, rather too much superstition about such matters," said Mr. Petherick. "A lot of damage is done to property by foolish reports heedlessly circulated."

"I have known one or two 'ghosts' that have had a very robust personality," remarked Sir Henry with a chuckle.

"I think," said Raymond, "we should allow Dr. Pender to go on with his story."

Joyce got up and switched off the two lamps, leaving the room lit only by the flickering firelight.

"Atmosphere," she said. "Now we can get along."

Dr. Pender smiled at her, and leaning back in his chair and taking off his pince-nez, he began his story in a gentle reminiscent voice.

"I don't know whether any of you know Dartmoor at all. The place I am telling you about is situated on the borders of Dartmoor. It was a very charming property, though it had been on the market without finding a purchaser for several years. The situation was perhaps a trifle bleak in winter, but the views were magnificent and there were certain curious and original features about the property itself. It was bought by a man called Haydon—Sir Richard Haydon. I had known him in his college days, and though I had lost sight of him for some years, the old ties of friendship still held, and I accepted with pleasure his invitation to go down to Silent Grove, as his new purchase was called.

"The house party was not a very large one. There was Richard Haydon himself, and his cousin, Elliot Haydon. There was a Lady Mannering with a pale, rather inconspicuous daughter called Violet. There was a Captain Rogers and his wife, hard riding, weather-beaten people, who lived only for horses and hunting. There was also a young Dr. Symonds and there was Miss Diana Ashley. I knew something about the last named. Her picture was very often in the Society papers and she was one of the notorious beauties of the Season. Her appearance was indeed very striking. She was dark and tall, with a beautiful skin of an even tint of pale cream, and her half-closed dark eyes set slantways in her head gave her a curiously piquant oriental appearance. She had, too, a wonderful speaking voice, deep-toned and bell-like.

"I saw at once that my friend Richard Haydon was very much attracted by her, and I guessed that the whole party was merely arranged as a setting for her. Of her own feelings I was not so sure. She was capricious in her favours. One day talking to Richard and excluding everyone else from her notice, and another day she would favour his cousin, Elliot, and appear hardly to notice that such a person as Richard existed, and then again she would bestow the most bewitching smiles upon the quiet and retiring Dr. Symonds.

"On the morning after my arrival our host showed us all over the place. The house itself was unremarkable, a good solid house built of Devonshire granite. Built to withstand time and exposure. It was unromantic but very comfortable. From the windows of it one looked out over the panorama of the Moor, vast rolling hills crowned with weather-beaten Tors.

"On the slopes of the Tor nearest to us were various hut circles, relics of the bygone days of the late Stone Age. On another hill was a barrow which had recently been excavated, and in which certain bronze implements had been found. Haydon was by way of being interested in antiquarian matters and he talked to us with a great deal of energy and enthusiasm. This particular spot, he explained, was particularly rich in relics of the past.

"Neolithic hut dwellers, Druids, Romans, and even traces of the early Phoenicians were to be found.

"'But this place is the most interesting of all,' he said.

'You know its name—Silent Grove. Well, it is easy enough to see what it takes its name from.'

"He pointed with his hand. That particular part of the country was bare enough—rocks, heather and bracken, but about a hundred yards from the house there was a densely planted grove of trees.

" 'That is a relic of very early days,' said Haydon. 'The trees have died and been replanted, but on the whole it has been kept very much as it used to be—perhaps in the time of the Phoenician settlers. Come and look at it.'

"We all followed him. As we entered the grove of trees a curious oppression came over me. I think it was the silence. No birds seemed to nest in these trees. There was a feeling about it of desolation and horror. I saw Haydon looking at me with a curious smile.

" 'Any feeling about this place, Pender?' he asked me. 'Antagonism now? Or uneasiness?'

" 'I don't like it,' I said quietly.

" 'You are within your rights. This was a stronghold of one of the ancient enemies of your faith. This is the Grove of Astarte.'

" 'Astarte?'

" 'Astarte, or Ishtar, or Ashtoreth, or whatever you choose to call her. I prefer the Phoenician name of Astarte. There is, I believe, one known Grove of Astarte in this country—in the North on the Wall. I have no evidence, but I like to believe that we have a true and authentic Grove of Astarte here. Here, within the dense circle of trees, sacred rites were performed.'

" 'Sacred rites,' murmured Diana Ashley. Her eyes had a dreamy far-away look. 'What were they, I wonder?'

" 'Not very reputable by all accounts,' said Captain Rogers with a loud unmeaning laugh. 'Rather hot stuff, I imagine.'

"Haydon paid no attention to him.

" 'In the centre of the Grove there should be a Temple,'

he said. 'I can't run to Temples, but I have indulged in a little fancy of my own.'

"We had at that moment stepped out into a little clearing in the centre of the trees. In the middle of it was something not unlike a summer-house made of stone. Diana Ashley looked inquiringly at Haydon.

" 'I call it The Idol House,' he said. 'It is the Idol House of Astarte.'

"He led the way up to it. Inside, on a rude ebony pillar, there reposed a curious little image representing a woman with crescent horns, seated on a lion.

" 'Astarte of the Phoenicians,' said Haydon, 'the Goddess of the Moon.'

" 'The Goddess of the Moon,' cried Diana. 'Oh, do let us have a wild orgy tonight. Fancy dress. And we will come out here in the moonlight and celebrate the rites of Astarte.'

"I made a sudden movement and Elliot Haydon, Richard's cousin, turned quickly to me.

" 'You don't like all this, do you, Padre?' he said.

" 'No,' I said gravely, 'I don't.'

"He looked at me curiously. 'But it is only tomfoolery. Dick can't know that this really is a sacred grove. It is just a fancy of his; he likes to play with the idea. And anyway, if it were—'

" 'If it were?'

" 'Well—' he laughed uncomfortably. 'You don't believe in that sort of thing, do you? You, a parson.'

" 'I am not sure that as a parson I ought not to believe in it.'

" 'But that sort of thing is all finished and done with.'

" 'I am not so sure,' I said musingly. 'I only know this: I am not as a rule a sensitive man to atmosphere, but ever since I entered this grove of trees I have felt a curious impression and sense of evil and menace all around me.'

"He glanced uneasily over his shoulder.

" 'Yes,' he said, 'it is—it is queer, somehow. I know what you mean but I suppose it is only our imagination makes us feel like that. What do you say, Symonds?'

"The doctor was silent a minute or two before he replied. Then he said quietly:

" 'I don't like it. I can't tell you why. But somehow or other, I don't like it.'

"At that moment Violet Mannering came across to me.

" 'I hate this place,' she cried. 'I hate it. Do let's get out of it.'

"We moved away and the others followed us. Only Diana Ashley lingered. I turned my head over my shoulder and saw her standing in front of the Idol House gazing earnestly at the image within it.

"The day was an unusually hot and beautiful one and Diana Ashley's suggestion of a Fancy Dress party that evening was received with general favour. The usual laughing and whispering and frenzied secret sewing took place and when we all made our appearance for dinner there were the usual outcries of merriment. Rogers and his wife were Neolithic hut dwellers—explaining the sudden lack of hearthrugs. Richard Haydon called himself a Phoenician sailor, and his cousin was a Brigand Chief, Dr. Symonds was a chef, Lady Mannering was a hospital nurse, and her daughter was a Circassian slave. I myself was arrayed somewhat too warmly as a monk. Diana Ashley came down last and was somewhat of a disappointment to all of us, being wrapped in a shapeless black domino.

" 'The Unknown,' she declared airily. 'That is what I am. Now for goodness' sake let's go in to dinner.'

"After dinner we went outside. It was a lovely night, warm and soft, and the moon was rising.

"We wandered about and chatted and the time passed quickly enough. It must have been an hour later when we realized that Diana Ashley was not with us.

" 'Surely she has not gone to bed,' said Richard Haydon.

"Violet Mannering shook her head.

" 'Oh, no,' she said. 'I saw her going off in that direction about a quarter of an hour ago.' She pointed as she spoke towards the grove of trees that showed black and shadowy in the moonlight.

" 'I wonder what she is up to,' said Richard Haydon, 'some devilment, I swear. Let's go and see.'

"We all trooped off together, somewhat curious as to what Miss Ashley had been up to. Yet I, for one, felt a curious reluctance to enter that dark foreboding belt of trees. Something stronger than myself seemed to be holding me back and urging me not to enter. I felt more definitely convinced than ever of the essential evilness of the spot. I think that some of the others experienced the same sensations that I did, though they would have been loath to admit it. The trees were so closely planted that the moonlight could not penetrate. There were a dozen soft sounds all round us, whisperings and sighings. The feeling was eerie in the extreme, and by common consent we all kept close together.

"Suddenly we came out into the open clearing in the middle of the grove and stood rooted to the spot in amazement, for there, on the threshold of the Idol House, stood a shimmering figure wrapped tightly round in diaphanous gauze and with two crescent horns rising from the dark masses of her hair.

" 'My God!' said Richard Haydon, and the sweat sprang out on his brow.

"But Violet Mannering was sharper.

" 'Why, it's Diana,' she exclaimed. 'What has she done to herself? Oh, she looks quite different somehow!'

"The figure in the doorway raised her hands. She took a step forward and chanted in a high sweet voice.

" 'I am the Priestess of Astarte,' she crooned. 'Beware how you approach me, for I hold death in my hand.'

" 'Don't do it, dear,' protested Lady Mannering. 'You give us the creeps, you really do.'

"Haydon sprang forward towards her.

" 'My God, Diana!' he cried. 'You are wonderful.'

"My eyes were accustomed to the moonlight now and I could see more plainly. She did, indeed, as Violet had said, look quite different. Her face was more definitely oriental, and her eyes more of slits with something cruel in their gleam, and the strange smile on her lips was one that I had never seen there before.

" 'Beware,' she cried warningly. 'Do not approach the Goddess. If anyone lays a hand on me it is death.'

" 'You are wonderful, Diana,' cried Haydon, 'but do stop it. Somehow or other I—I don't like it.'

"He was moving towards her across the grass and she flung out a hand towards him.

" 'Stop,' she cried. 'One step nearer and I will smite you with the magic of Astarte.'

"Richard Haydon laughed and quickened his pace, when all at once a curious thing happened. He hesitated for a moment, then seemed to stumble and fall headlong.

"He did not get up again, but lay where he had fallen prone on the ground.

"Suddenly Diana began to laugh hysterically. It was a strange horrible sound breaking the silence of the glade.

"With an oath Elliot sprang forward.

" 'I can't stand this,' he cried, 'get up, Dick, get up, man.'

"But still Richard Haydon lay where he had fallen. Elliot Haydon reached his side, knelt by him and turned him gently over. He bent over him, peering in his face.

"Then he rose sharply to his feet and stood swaying a little.

" 'Doctor,' he said. 'Doctor, for God's sake come. I—I think he is dead.'

"Symonds ran forward and Elliot rejoined us walking very slowly. He was looking down at his hands in a way I didn't understand.

"At that moment there was a wild scream from Diana.

" 'I have killed him,' she cried. 'Oh, my God! I didn't mean to, but I have killed him.'

"And she fainted dead away, falling in a crumpled heap on the grass.

"There was a cry from Mrs. Rogers.

" 'Oh, do let us get away from this dreadful place,' she wailed, 'anything might happen to us here. Oh, it's awful!'

"Elliot got hold of me by the shoulder.

" 'It can't be, man,' he murmured. 'I tell you it can't *be*. A man cannot be killed like that. It is—it's against Nature.'

"I tried to soothe him.

" 'There is some explanation,' I said. 'Your cousin must have had some unsuspected weakness of the heart. The shock and excitement—'

"He interrupted me.

" 'You don't understand,' he said. He held up his hands for me to see and I noticed a red stain on them.

" 'Dick didn't die of shock, he was stabbed—stabbed to the heart, and *there is no weapon*.'

"I stared at him incredulously. At that moment Symonds rose from his examination of the body and came towards us. He was pale and shaking all over.

" 'Are we all mad?' he said. 'What is this place—that things like this can happen in it?'

" 'Then it is true,' I said.

"He nodded.

" 'The wound is such as would be made by a long thin dagger, but—there is no dagger there.'

"We all looked at each other.

" 'But it must be there,' cried Elliot Haydon. 'It must

have dropped out. It must be on the ground somewhere. Let us look.'

"We peered about vainly on the ground. Violet Mannering said suddenly:

" 'Diana had something in her hand. A kind of dagger. I saw it. I saw it glitter when she threatened him.'

"Elliot Haydon shook his head.

" 'He never even got within three yards of her,' he objected.

"Lady Mannering was bending over the prostrate girl on the ground.

" 'There is nothing in her hand now,' she announced, 'and I can't see anything on the ground. Are you sure you saw it, Violet? I didn't.'

"Dr. Symonds came over to the girl.

" 'We must get her to the house,' he said. 'Rogers, will you help?'

"Between us we carried the unconscious girl back to the house. Then we returned and fetched the body of Sir Richard."

Dr. Pender broke off apologetically and looked round. "One would know better nowadays," he said, "owing to the prevalence of detective fiction. Every street boy knows that a body must be left where it is found. But in these days we had not the same knowledge, and accordingly we carried the body of Richard Haydon back to his bedroom in the square granite house and the butler was dispatched on a bicycle in search of the police—a ride of some twelve miles.

"It was then that Elliot Haydon drew me aside.

" 'Look here,' he said. 'I am going back to the grove. That weapon has got to be found.'

" 'If there was a weapon,' I said doubtfully.

"He seized my arm and shook it fiercely. 'You have got that superstitious stuff into your head. You think his death was supernatural; well, I am going back to the grove to find out.'

"I was curiously averse to his doing so. I did my utmost to dissuade him, but without result. The mere idea of that thick circle of trees was abhorrent to me and I felt a strong premonition of further disaster. But Elliot was entirely pig-headed. He was, I think, scared himself, but would not admit it. He went off fully armed with determination to get to the bottom of the mystery.

"It was a very dreadful night, none of us could sleep, or attempt to do so. The police, when they arrived, were frankly incredulous of the whole thing. They evinced a strong desire to cross-examine Miss Ashley, but there they had to reckon with Dr. Symonds, who opposed the idea vehemently. Miss Ashley had come out of her faint or trance and he had given her a strong sleeping draught. She was on no account to be disturbed until the following day.

"It was not until about seven o'clock in the morning that anyone thought about Elliot Haydon, and then Symonds suddenly asked where he was. I explained what Elliot had done and Symonds's grave face grew a shade graver. 'I wish he hadn't. It is—it is foolhardy,' he said.

" 'You don't think any harm can have happened to him?'

" 'I hope not. I think, Padre, that you and I had better go and see.'

"I knew he was right, but it took all the courage in my command to nerve myself for the task. We set out together and entered once more that ill-fated grove of trees. We called him twice and got no reply. In a minute or two we came into the clearing, which looked pale and ghostly in the early morning light. Symonds clutched my arm and I uttered a muttered exclamation. Last night when we had seen it in the moonlight there had been the body of a man lying face downwards on the grass. Now in the early morning light the same sight met our eyes. Elliot Haydon was lying on the exact spot where his cousin had been.

" 'My God,' said Symonds. *'It has got him too!'*

"We ran together over the grass. Elliot Haydon was unconscious but breathing feebly and this time there was no doubt of what had caused the tragedy. A long thin bronze weapon remained in the wound.

" 'Got him through the shoulder, not through the heart. That is lucky,' commented the doctor. 'On my soul, I don't know what to think. At any rate he is not dead and he will be able to tell us what happened.'

"But that was just what Elliot Haydon was not able to do. His description was vague in the extreme. He had hunted about vainly for the dagger and at last giving up the search had taken up a stand near the Idol House. It was then that he became increasingly certain that someone was watching him from the belt of trees. He fought against this impression but was not able to shake it off. He described a cold strange wind that began to blow. It seemed to come not from the trees but from the interior of the Idol House. He turned round, peering inside it. He saw the small figure of the Goddess and he felt he was under an optical delusion. The figure seemed to grow larger and larger. Then he suddenly received something that felt like a blow between his temples which sent him reeling back, and as he fell he was conscious of a sharp burning pain in his left shoulder.

"The dagger was identified this time as being the identical one which had been dug up in the barrow on the hill, and which had been bought by Richard Haydon. Where he had kept it, in the house or in the Idol House in the grove, none seemed to know.

"The police were of the opinion, and always will be, that he was deliberately stabbed by Miss Ashley, but in view of our combined evidence that she was never within three yards of him, they could not hope to support the charge against her. So the thing has been and remains a mystery."

There was a silence.

"There doesn't seem anything to say," said Joyce Lemprière at length. "It is all so horrible—and uncanny. Have you no explanation yourself, Dr. Pender?"

The old man nodded. "Yes," he said. "I have an explanation—a kind of explanation, that is. Rather a curious one—but to my mind it still leaves certain factors unaccounted for."

"I have been to seances," said Joyce, "and you may say what you like, very queer things can happen. I suppose one can explain it by some kind of hypnotism. The girl really turned herself into a Priestess of Astarte, and I suppose somehow or other she must have stabbed him. Perhaps she threw the dagger that Miss Mannering saw in her hand."

"Or it might have been a javelin," suggested Raymond West. "After all, moonlight is not very strong. She might have had a kind of spear in her hand and stabbed him at a distance, and then I suppose mass hypnotism comes into account. I mean, you were all prepared to see him stricken down by supernatural means and so you saw it like that."

"I have seen many wonderful things done with weapons and knives at music halls," said Sir Henry. "I suppose it is possible that a man could have been concealed in the belt of trees, and that he might from there have thrown a knife or a dagger with sufficient accuracy—agreeing, of course, that he was a professional. I admit that that seems rather far-fetched, but it seems the only really feasible theory. You remember that the other man was distinctly under the impression that there was someone in the grove of trees watching him. As to Miss Mannering saying that Miss Ashley had a dagger in her hand and the others saying she hadn't, that doesn't surprise me. If you had had my experience you would know that five persons' account of the same thing will differ so widely as to be almost incredible."

Mr. Petherick coughed.

"But in all these theories we seem to be overlooking one essential fact," he remarked. "What became of the weapon? Miss Ashley could hardly get rid of a javelin standing as she was in the middle of an open space; and if a hidden murderer had thrown a dagger, then the dagger would still have been in the wound when the man was turned over. We must, I think, discard all far-fetched theories and confine ourselves to sober fact."

"And where does sober fact lead us?"

"Well, one thing seems quite clear. No one was near the man when he was stricken down, so the only person who *could* have stabbed him was he himself. Suicide, in fact."

"But why on earth should he wish to commit suicide?" asked Raymond West incredulously.

The lawyer coughed again. "Ah, that is the question of theory once more," he said. "At the moment I am not concerned with theories. It seems to me, excluding the supernatural in which I do not for one moment believe, that that was the only way things could have happened. He stabbed himself, and as he fell his arms flew out, wrenching the dagger from the wound and flinging it far into the zone of the trees. That is, I think, although somewhat unlikely, a possible happening."

"I don't like to say, I am sure," said Miss Marple. "It all perplexes me very much, indeed. But curious things do happen. At Lady Sharpley's garden party last year the man who was arranging the clock golf tripped over one of the numbers—quite unconscious he was—and didn't come round for about five minutes."

"Yes, dear Aunt," said Raymond gently, "but he wasn't stabbed, was he?"

"Of course not, dear," said Miss Marple. "That is what I am telling you. Of course there is only one way that poor Sir Richard could have been stabbed, but I do wish I knew what caused him to stumble in the first place. Of course, it might have been a tree root. He would be looking at the girl, of course, and when it is moonlight one does trip over things."

"You say that there is only one way that Sir Richard could have been stabbed, Miss Marple," said the clergyman, looking at her curiously.

"It is very sad and I don't like to think of it. He was a right-handed man, was he not? I mean to stab himself in the left shoulder he must have been. I was always so sorry for poor Jack Baynes in the War. He shot himself in the foot, you remember, after very severe fighting at Arras. He told me about it when I went to see him in the hospital, and very ashamed of it he was. I don't expect this poor man, Elliot Haydon, profited much by his wicked crime."

"Elliot Haydon," cried Raymond. "You think he did it?"

"I don't see how anyone else could have done it," said Miss Marple, opening her eyes in gentle surprise. "I mean if, as Mr. Petherick so wisely says, one looks at the facts and disregards all that atmosphere of heathen goddesses which I don't think is very nice. He went up to him first and turned him over, and of course to do that he would have to have had his back to them all, and being dressed as a brigand chief he would be sure to have a weapon of some kind in his belt. I remember dancing with a man dressed as a brigand chief when I was a young girl. He had five kinds of knives and daggers, and I can't tell you how awkward and uncomfortable it was for his partner."

All eyes were turned towards Dr. Pender.

"I knew the truth," said he, "five years after that tragedy occurred. It came in the shape of a letter written to me by Elliot Haydon. He said in it that he fancied that I had always suspected him. He said it was a sudden temptation. He too loved Diana Ashley, but he was only a poor struggling barrister. With Richard out of the way and inheriting his title and estates, he saw a wonderful prospect opening up before him. The dagger had jerked out of his belt as he knelt down by his cousin, and almost before he had time to think, he drove it in and returned it to his belt again. He stabbed himself later in order to divert suspicion. He wrote to me on the eve of starting on an expedition to the South Pole in case, as he said, he should never come back. I do not think that he meant to come back, and I know that, as Miss Marple has said, his crime profited him nothing. 'For five years,' he wrote, 'I have lived in Hell. I hope, at least that I may expiate my crime by dying honourably.' "

There was a pause.

"And he did die honourably," said Sir Henry. "You have changed the names in your story, Dr. Pender, but I think I recognize the man you mean."

"As I said," went on the old clergyman, "I do not think that explanation quite covers the facts. I still think there was an evil influence in that grove, an influence that directed Elliot Haydon's action. Even to this day I can never think without a shudder of The Idol House of Astarte."

Ingots of Gold

I do not know that the story that I am going to tell you is a fair one," said Raymond West, "because I can't give you the solution of it. Yet the facts were so interesting and so curious that I should like to propound it to you as a problem, and perhaps between us we may arrive at some logical conclusion.

"The date of these happenings was two years ago, when I went down to spend Whitsuntide with a man called John Newman, in Cornwall."

"Cornwall?" said Joyce Lemprière sharply.

"Yes. Why?"

"Nothing. Only it's odd. My story is about a place in Cornwall, too—a little fishing village called Rathole. Don't tell me yours is the same?"

"No. My village is called Polperran. It is situated on the west coast of Cornwall; a very wild and rocky spot. I had been introduced a few weeks previously and had found him a most interesting companion. A man of intelligence and independent means, he was possessed of a romantic imagination. As a result of his latest hobby he had taken the lease of Pol House. He was an authority on Elizabethan times, and he described to me in vivid and graphic language the rout of

33

the Spanish Armada. So enthusiastic was he that one could almost imagine that he had been an eyewitness at the scene. Is there anything in reincarnation? I wonder—I very much wonder."

"You are so romantic, Raymond dear," said Miss Marple, looking benignantly at him.

"Romantic is the last thing that I am," said Raymond West, slightly annoyed. "But this fellow Newman was chock-full of it, and he interested me for that reason as a curious survival of the past. It appears that a certain ship belonging to the Armada, and known to contain a vast amount of treasure in the form of gold from the Spanish Main, was wrecked off the coast of Cornwall on the famous and treacherous Serpent Rocks. For some years, so Newman told me, attempts had been made to salve the ship and recover the treasure. I believe such stories are not uncommon, though the number of mythical treasure ships is largely in excess of the genuine ones. A company had been formed, but had gone bankrupt, and Newman had been able to buy the rights of the thing—or whatever you call it—for a mere song. He waxed very enthusiastic about it all. According to him it was merely a question of the latest scientific, up-to-date machinery. The gold was there, and he had no doubt whatever that it could be recovered.

"It occurred to me as I listened to him how often things happen that way. A rich man such as Newman succeeds almost without effort, and yet in all probability the actual value in money of his find would mean little to him. I must say that his ardour infected me. I saw galleons drifting up the coast, flying before the storm, beaten and broken on the black rocks. The mere word galleon has a romantic sound. The phrase 'Spanish Gold' thrills the schoolboy—and the grown-up man also. Moreover, I was working at the time upon a novel, some scenes of which were laid in the sixteenth century, and I saw the prospect of getting valuable local colour from my host.

"I set off that Friday morning from Paddington in high spirits, and looking forward to my trip. The carriage was empty except for one man, who sat facing me in the opposite corner. He was a tall, soldierly-looking man, and I could not rid myself of the impression that somewhere or other I had seen him before. I cudgelled my brains for some time in vain; but at last I had it. My travelling companion was Inspector Badgworth, and I had to run across him when I was doing a series of articles on the Everson disappearance case.

"I recalled myself to his notice, and we were soon chatting pleasantly enough. When I told him I was going to Polperran he remarked that that was a rum coincidence, because he himself was also bound for that place. I did not like to seem inquisitive, so was careful not to ask him what took him there. Instead, I spoke of my own interest in the place, and mentioned the wrecked Spanish galleon. To my surprise the inspector seemed to know all about it. 'That will be the *Juan Fernandez*,' he said. 'Your friend won't be the first who has sunk money trying to get money out of her. It is a romantic notion.'

" 'And probably the whole story is a myth,' I said. 'No ship was ever wrecked there at all.'

" 'Oh, the ship was sunk there right enough,' said the inspector—'along with a good company of others. You would be surprised if you knew how many wrecks there are on that part of the coast. As a matter of fact, that is what takes me down there now. That is where the *Otranto* was wrecked about six months ago.'

" 'I remember reading about it,' I said. 'No lives were lost, I think?'

" 'No lives were lost,' said the inspector; 'but something

else was lost. It is not generally known, but the *Otranto* was carrying bullion.'

" 'Yes?' I said, much interested.

" 'Naturally we have had divers at work on salvage operations, but—*the gold has gone, Mr. West.*'

" 'Gone!' I said, staring at him. 'How can it have gone?'

" 'That is the question,' said the inspector. 'The rocks tore a gaping hole in her strong-room. It was easy enough for the divers to get in that way, but they found the strong-room empty. The question is, was the gold stolen before the wreck or afterwards? Was it ever in the strong-room at all?'

" 'It seems a curious case,' I said.

" 'It is a very curious case, when you consider what bullion is. Not a diamond necklace that you could put into your pocket. When you think how cumbersome it is and how bulky—well, the whole thing seems abolutely impossible. There may have been some hocus-pocus before the ship sailed; but if not, it must have been removed within the last six months—and I am going down to look into the matter.'

"I found Newman waiting to meet me at the station. He apologized for the absence of his car, which had gone to Truro for some necessary repairs. Instead, he met me with a farm lorry belonging to the property.

"I swung myself up beside him, and we wound carefully in and out of the narrow streets of the fishing village. We went up a steep ascent, with a gradient, I should say of one in five, ran a little distance along a winding lane, and turned in at the granite-pillared gates of Pol House.

"The place was a charming one; it was situated high up the cliffs, with a good view out to sea. Part of it was some three or four hundred years old, and a modern wing had been added. Behind it farming land of about seven or eight acres ran inland.

" 'Welcome to Pol House,' said Newman. 'And to the

Sign of the Golden Galleon.' And he pointed to where, over the front door, hung a perfect reproduction of a Spanish galleon with all sails set.

"My first evening was a most charming and instructive one. My host showed me the old manuscripts relating to the *Juan Fernandez*. He unrolled charts for me and indicated positions on them with dotted lines, and he produced plans of diving apparatus, which, I may say, mystified me utterly and completely.

"I told him of my meeting with Inspector Badgworth, in which he was much interested.

" 'They are a queer people round this coast,' he said reflectively. 'Smuggling and wrecking is in their blood. When a ship goes down on their coast they cannot help regarding it as lawful plunder meant for their pockets. There is a fellow here I should like you to see. He is an interesting survival.'

"Next day dawned bright and clear. I was taken down into Polperran and there introduced to Newman's diver, a man called Higgins. He was a wooden-faced individual, extremely taciturn, and his contributions to the conversation were mostly monosyllables. After a discussion between them on highly technical matters, we adjourned to the Three Anchors. A tankard of beer somewhat loosened the worthy fellow's tongue.

" 'Detective gentleman from London has come down,' he grunted. 'They do say that that ship that went down here last November was carrying a mortal lot of gold. Well, she wasn't the first to go down, and she won't be the last.'

" 'Hear, hear,' chimed in the landlord of the Three Anchors. 'That is a true word you say there, Bill Higgins.'

" 'I reckon it is, Mr. Kelvin,' said Higgins.

"I looked with some curiosity at the landlord. He was a remarkable man, dark and swarthy, with curiously broad shoulders. His eyes were bloodshot, and he had a curiously furtive way of avoiding one's glance. I suspected that this was the man of whom Newman had spoken, saying he was an interesting survival.

" 'We don't want interfering foreigners on this coast,' he said somewhat truculently.

" 'Meaning the police?' asked Newman, smiling.

" 'Meaning the police—*and others*,' said Kelvin significantly. 'And don't you forget it, mister.'

" 'Do you know, Newman, that sounded to me very like a threat,' I said as we climbed the hill homewards.

"My friend laughed.

" 'Nonsense; I don't do the folk down here any harm.'

"I shook my head doubtfully. There was something sinister and uncivilized about Kelvin. I felt that his mind might run in strange, unrecognized channels.

"I think I date the beginning of my uneasiness from that moment. I had slept well enough that first night, but the next night my sleep was troubled and broken. Sunday dawned, dark and sullen, with an overcast sky and the threatenings of thunder in the air. I am always a bad hand at hiding my feelings, and Newman noticed the change in me.

" 'What is the matter with you, West? You are a bundle of nerves this morning.'

" 'I don't know,' I confessed, 'but I have got a horrible feeling of foreboding.'

" 'It's the weather.'

" 'Yes, perhaps.'

"I said no more. In the afternoon we went out in Newman's motor boat, but the rain came on with such vigour that we were glad to return to shore and change into dry clothing.

"And that evening my uneasiness increased. Outside the storm howled and roared. Towards ten o'clock the tempest calmed down. Newman looked out the window.

" 'It is clearing,' he said. 'I shouldn't wonder if it was a perfectly fine night in another half-hour. If so, I shall go out for a stroll.'

"I yawned. 'I am frightfully sleepy,' I said. 'I didn't get much sleep last night. I think that tonight I shall turn in early.'

"This I did. On the previous night I had slept little. Tonight I slept heavily. Yet my slumbers were not restful. I was still oppressed with an awful foreboding of evil; I had terrible dreams. I dreamt of dreadful abysses and vast chasms, amongst which I was wandering, knowing that a slip of the foot meant death. I waked to find the hands of my clock pointing to eight o'clock. My head was aching badly, and the terror of my night's dreams was still upon me.

"So strongly was this so that when I went to the window and drew it up, I started back with a fresh feeling of terror, for the first thing I saw, or thought I saw, was a man digging an open grave.

"It took me a minute or two to pull myself together; then I realized that the grave-digger was Newman's gardener, and the 'grave' was destined to accommodate three new rose trees which were lying on the turf waiting for the moment they should be securely planted in the earth.

"The gardener looked up and saw me and touched his hat.

" 'Good morning, sir. Nice morning, sir.'

" 'I suppose it is,' I said doubtfully, still unable to shake off completely the depression of my spirits.

"However, as the gardener had said, it was certainly a nice morning. The sun was shining and the sky a clear pale blue that promised fine weather for the day. I went down to breakfast whistling a tune. Newman had no maids living in the house. Two middle-aged sisters, who lived in a farmhouse near by, came daily to attend to his simple wants. One of them was placing the coffeepot on the table as I entered the room.

" 'Good morning, Elizabeth,' I said. 'Mr. Newman not down yet?'

" 'He must have been out very early, sir,' she replied. 'He wasn't in the house when we arrived.'

"Instantly my uneasiness returned. On the two previous mornings Newman had come down to breakfast somewhat late; and I didn't fancy that at any time he was an early riser. Moved by those forebodings I ran up to his bedroom. It was empty, and, moreover, his bed had not been slept in. A brief examination of his room showed me two other things. If Newman had gone out for a stroll he must have gone out in his evening clothes, for they were missing.

"I was sure now that my premonition of evil was justified. Newman had gone, as he had said he would do—for an evening stroll. For some reason or other he had not returned. Why? Had he met with an accident? Fallen over the cliffs? A search must be made at once.

"In a few hours I had collected a large band of helpers, and together we hunted in every direction along the cliffs and on the rocks below. But there was no sign of Newman.

"In the end, in despair, I sought out Inspector Badgworth. His face grew very grave.

" 'It looks to me as if there had been foul play,' he said. 'There are some not over-scrupulous customers in these parts. Have you seen Kelvin, the landlord of the Three Anchors?'

"I said that I had seen him.

" 'Did you know he did a turn in gaol four years ago? Assault and battery.'

" 'It doesn't surprise me,' I said.

" 'The general opinion in this place seems to be that your friend is a bit too fond of nosing his way into things that do not concern him. I hope he has come to no serious harm.'

"The search was continued with redoubled vigour. It was

not until late that afternoon that our efforts were rewarded. We discovered Newman in a deep ditch in a corner of his own property. His hands and feet were securely fastened with rope, and a handkerchief had been thrust into his mouth and secured there so as to prevent him crying out.

"He was terribly exhausted and in great pain; but after some frictioning of his wrists and ankles, and a long draught from a whisky flask, he was able to give his account of what had occurred.

"The weather having cleared, he had gone out for a stroll about eleven o'clock. His way had taken him some distance along the cliffs to a spot commonly known as Smugglers' Cove, owing to the large number of caves to be found there. Here he had noticed some men unloading something from a small boat, and had strolled down to see what was going on. Whatever the stuff was it seemed to be a great weight, and it was being carried into one of the farthermost caves.

"With no real suspicion of anything being amiss, nevertheless Newman had wondered. He had drawn quite near them without being observed. Suddenly there was a cry of alarm, and immediately two powerful seafaring men had set upon him and rendered him unconscious. When next he came to himself he found himself lying on a motor vehicle of some kind, which was proceeding, with many bumps and bangs, as far as he could guess, up the lane which led from the coast to the village. To his great surprise the lorry turned in at the gate of his own house. There, after a whispered conversation between the men, they at length drew him forth and flung him into a ditch at a spot where the depth of it rendered discovery unlikely for some time. Then the lorry drove on, and, he thought, passed out through another gate some quarter of a mile nearer the village. He could give no description of his assailants except that they were certainly seafaring men, and, by their speech, Cornishmen.

"Inspector Badgworth was very interested.

" 'Depend upon it that is where the stuff has been hidden,' he cried. 'Somehow or other it has been salvaged from the wreck and has been stored in some lonely cave somewhere. It is known that we have searched all the caves in Smugglers' Cove, and that we are now going farther afield, and they have evidently been moving the stuff at night to a cave that has been already searched and is not likely to be searched again. Unfortunately they have had at least eighteen hours to dispose of the stuff. If they got Mr. Newman last night I doubt if we will find any of it there by now.'

"The inspector hurried off to make a search. He found definite evidence that the bullion had been stored as supposed, but the gold had been once more removed, and there was no clue as to its fresh hiding-place.

"One clue there was, however, and the inspector himself pointed it out to me the following morning.

" 'That lane is very little used by motor vehicles,' he said, 'and in one or two places we get the traces of the tyres very clearly. There is a three-cornered piece out of one tyre, leaving a mark which is quite unmistakable. It shows going into the gate; here and there is a faint mark of it going out of the other gate, so there is not much doubt that it is the right vehicle we are after. Now, why did they take it out through the farther gate? It seems quite clear to me that that lorry came from the village. Now, there aren't many people who own a lorry in the village—not more than two or three at most. Kelvin, the landlord of the Three Anchors, has one.'

" 'What was Kelvin's original profession?' asked Newman.

" 'It is curious that you should ask me that, Mr. Newman. In his younger days Kelvin was a professional diver.'

"Newman and I looked at each other. The puzzle seemed to be fitting itself together piece by piece.

" 'You didn't recognize Kelvin as one of the men on the beach?' asked the inspector.

"Newman shook his head.

" 'I am afraid I can't say anything as to that,' he said regretfully. 'I really hadn't time to see anything.'

"The inspector very kindly allowed me to accompany him to the Three Anchors. The garage was up a side street. The big doors were closed, but by going up a little alley at the side we found a small door that led into it, and that door was open. A very brief examination of the tyres sufficed for the inspector. 'We have got him, by Jove!' he exclaimed. 'Here is the mark as large as life on the rear left wheel. Now, Mr. Kelvin, I don't think you will be clever enough to wriggle out of this.' "

Raymond West came to a halt.

"Well?" said Joyce. "So far I don't see anything to make a problem about—unless they never found the gold."

"They never found the gold certainly," said Raymond, "and they never got Kelvin either. I expect he was too clever for them, but I don't quite see how he worked it. He was duly arrested—on the evidence of the tyre mark. But an extraordinary hitch arose. Just opposite the big doors of the garage was a cottage rented for the summer by a lady artist."

"Oh, these lady artists!" said Joyce, laughing.

"As you say, 'Oh these lady artists!' This particular one had been ill for some weeks, and, in consequence, had two hospital nurses attending her. The nurse who was on night duty had pulled her arm-chair up to the window, where the blind was up. She declared that the motor lorry could not have left the garage opposite without her seeing it, and she swore that in actual fact it never left the garage that night."

"I don't think that is much of a problem," said Joyce. "The nurse went to sleep, of course. They always do."

"That has—er—been known to happen," said Mr. Petherick, judiciously; "but it seems to me that we are accepting facts without sufficient examination. Before accepting the testimony of the hospital nurse, we should inquire very closely into her bona fides. The alibi coming with such suspicious promptness is inclined to raise doubts in one's mind."

"There is also the lady artist's testimony," said Raymond. "She declared that she was in pain, and awake most of the night, and that she would certainly have heard the lorry, it being an unusual noise, and the night being very quiet after the storm."

"H'm," said the clergyman, "that is certainly an additional fact. Had Kelvin himself any alibi?"

"He declared that he was at home and in bed from ten o'clock onwards, but he could produce no witnesses in support of that statement."

"The nurse went to sleep," said Joyce, "and so did the patient. Ill people always think they have never slept a wink all night."

Raymond West looked inquiringly at Dr. Pender.

"Do you know, I feel sorry for that man Kelvin. It seems to me very much a case of 'Give a dog a bad name.' Kelvin had been in prison. Apart from the tyre mark, which certainly seems too remarkable to be coincidence, there doesn't seem to be much against him except his unfortunate record."

"You, Sir Henry?"

Sir Henry shook his head.

"As it happens," he said smiling, "I know something about this case. So, clearly, I mustn't speak."

"Well, go on, Aunt Jane, haven't you got anything to say?"

"In a minute, dear," said Miss Marple. "I am afraid I have counted wrong. Two purl, three plain, slip one, two purl—yes, that's right. What did you say, dear?"

"What is your opinion?"

"You wouldn't like my opinion, dear. Young people never do, I notice. It is better to say nothing."

"Nonsense, Aunt Jane; out with it."

"Well, dear Raymond," said Miss Marple, laying down her knitting and looking across at her nephew. "I do think you should be more careful how you choose your friends. You are so credulous, dear, so easily gulled. I suppose it is being a writer and having so much imagination. All that story about a Spanish galleon! If you were older and had more experience of life you would have been on your guard at once. A man you had known only a few weeks, too!"

Sir Henry suddenly gave vent to a great roar of laughter and slapped his knee.

"Got you this time, Raymond," he said. "Miss Marple you are wonderful. Your friend Newman, my boy, has another name—several other names in fact. At the present moment he is not in Cornwall but in Devonshire—Dartmoor, to be exact—a convict in Princetown prison. We didn't catch him over the stolen bullion business, but over the rifling of the strong-room of one of the London banks. Then we looked up his past record and we found a good portion of the gold stolen buried in the garden at Pol House. It was rather a neat idea. All along that Cornish coast there are stories of wrecked galleons full of gold. It accounted for the diver, and it would account later for the gold. But a scapegoat was needed, and Kelvin was ideal for the purpose. Newman played his little comedy very well, and our friend Raymond, with his celebrity as a writer, made an unimpeachable witness."

"But the tyre mark?" objected Joyce.

"Oh, I saw that at once, dear, although I know nothing about motors," said Miss Marple. "People change a wheel, you know—I have often seen them doing it—and, of course they could take a wheel off Kelvin's lorry and take it out through the small door into the alley and put it on to Mr. Newman's lorry and take the lorry out of one gate down to the beach, fill it up with the gold and bring it up through the other gate, and then they must have taken the wheel back and put it back on Mr. Kelvin's lorry while, I suppose, someone else was tying up Mr. Newman in a ditch. Very uncomfortable for him and probably longer before he was found than he expected. I suppose the man who called himself the gardener attended to that side of the business."

"Why do you say, 'called himself the gardener,' Aunt Jane?" asked Raymond curiously.

"Well, he can't have been a real gardener, can he?" said Miss Marple. "Gardeners don't work on Whit Monday. Everybody knows that."

She smiled and folded up her knitting.

"It was really that little fact that put me on the right scent," she said. She looked across at Raymond.

"When you are a householder, dear, and have a garden of your own, you will know these little things."

The Bloodstained
Pavement

I t's curious," said Joyce Lemprière, "but I hardly like telling you my story. It happened a long time ago—five years ago to be exact—but it's sort of haunted me ever since. The smiling, bright, top part of it—and the hidden gruesomeness underneath. And the queer thing is that the sketch I painted at the time has become tinged with the same atmosphere. When you look at it first it is just a rough sketch of a little steep Cornish street with the sunlight on it. But if you look long enough at it, something sinister creeps in. I have never sold it, but I never look at it. It lives in the studio in a corner with its face to the wall.

"The name of the place was Rathole. It is a queer little Cornish fishing village, very picturesque—too picturesque perhaps. There is rather too much of the atmosphere of 'Ye Olde Cornish Tea House' about it. It has shops with bobbed-headed girls in smocks doing hand-illuminated mottoes on parchment. It is pretty and it is quaint, but it is very self-consciously so."

"Don't I know," said Raymond West, groaning. "The curse of the tourist bus, I suppose. No matter how narrow the lanes leading down to them, no picturesque village is safe."

Joyce nodded.

"There are narrow lanes that lead down to Rathole and very steep, like the side of a house. Well, to get on with my story. I had come to Cornwall for a fortnight, to sketch. There is an old inn in Rathole, the Polharwith Arms. It was supposed to be the only house left standing by the Spaniards when they shelled the place in fifteen hundred and something."

"Not shelled," said Raymond West, frowning. "Do try to be historically accurate, Joyce."

"Well, at all events they landed guns somewhere along the coast and they fired them and the houses fell down. Anyway, that is not the point. The inn was a wonderful old place with a kind of porch in front built on four pillars. I was just settling down to work when a car came creeping and twisting down the hill. Of course, it would stop before the inn— just where it was most awkward for me. The people got out—a man and a woman—I didn't notice them particularly. She had a kind of mauve linen dress on and a mauve hat.

"Presently the man came out again and, to my great thankfulness, drove the car down to the quay and left it there. He strolled back past me toward the inn. Just at that moment another beastly car came twisting down, and a woman got out of it, dressed in the brightest chintz frock I have ever seen, scarlet poinsettias, I think they were, and she had on one of these big native straw hats—Cuban, aren't they?—in very bright scarlet.

"This woman didn't stop in front of the inn but drove the car farther down the street toward the other one. Then she got out and the man, seeing her, gave an astonished shout. 'Carol,' he cried, 'in the name of all that is wonderful. Fancy meeting you in this out-of-the-way spot. I haven't seen you for years. Hello, there's Margery—my wife, you know. You must come and meet her.'

"They went up the street toward the inn side by side, and I saw the other woman had just come out of the door and was moving down toward them. I had had just a glimpse of the woman called Carol as she passed by me. Just enough to see a very white powdered chin and a flaming scarlet mouth, and I wondered—I just wondered—if Margery would be so very pleased to meet her. I hadn't seen Margery near to, but in the distance she looked dowdy and extra prim and proper.

"Well, of course, it was not any of my business, but you get very queer little glimpses of life sometimes, and you can't help speculating about them. From where they were standing I could just catch fragments of their conversation that floated down to me. They were talking about bathing. The husband, whose name seem to be Denis, wanted to take a boat and row around the coast. There was a famous cave well worth seeing, so he said, about a mile long. Carol wanted to see the cave, too, but she suggested walking along the cliffs and seeing it from the land side. She said she hated boats. In the end, they fixed it that way. Carol was to go along the cliff path and to meet them at the cave, and Denis and Margery would take a boat and row round.

"Hearing them talk about bathing made me want to bathe too. It was a very hot morning and I wasn't doing particularly good work. Also, I fancied that the afternoon sunlight would be far more attractive in effect. So I packed up my things and went off to a little beach that I knew of—it was quite the opposite direction from the cave and was rather a discovery of mine. I had a ripping swim there and I lunched off a tinned tongue and two tomatoes, and I came back in the afternoon full of confidence and enthusiasm to get on with my sketch.

"The whole of Rathole seemed to be asleep. I had been right about the afternoon sunlight—the shadows were far more telling. The Polharwith Arms was the principal note of my sketch. A ray of sunlight came slanting obliquely down and hit the ground in front of it and had rather a curious effect. I gathered that the bathing party had returned safely, because two bathing dresses, a scarlet one and a dark-blue one, were hanging from the balcony, drying in the sun.

"Something had gone a bit wrong with one corner of my sketch and I bent over it for some moments, doing something to put it right. When I looked up again there was a figure leaning against one of the pillars of the Polharwith Arms, who seemed to have appeared there by magic. He was dressed in seafaring clothes and was, I suppose, a fisherman. But he had a long dark beard, and if I had been looking for a model for a wicked Spanish captain, I couldn't have imagined anyone better. I got to work with feverish haste before he should move away, though from his attitude he looked as though he was perfectly prepared to prop up the pillars through all eternity.

"He did move, however, but luckily not until I had got what I wanted. He came over to me and he began to talk. Oh, how that man talked.

" 'Rathole,' he said, 'was a very interesting place.'

"I knew that already, but although I said so that didn't save me. I had the whole history of the shelling—I mean the destroying—of the village and how the landlord of the Polharwith Arms was the last man to be killed. Run through on his own threshold by a Spanish captain's sword, and of how his blood spurted out on the pavement and no one could wash out the stain for a hundred years.

"It all fitted in very well with the languorous, drowsy feeling of the afternoon. The man's voice was very suave and yet at the same time there was an undercurrent in it of something rather frightening. He was very obsequious in his manner, yet I felt underneath he was cruel. He made me understand the Inquisition and the terrors of all the things the Spaniards did better than I have ever done before.

"All the time he was talking to me I went on painting,

and suddenly I realized that in the excitement of listening to his story I had painted in something that was not there. On that white square of pavement where the sun fell before the door of the Polharwith Arms, I had painted in bloodstains. It seemed extraordinary that the mind could play such tricks with the hand, but as I looked over toward the inn again I got a second shock. My hand had only painted in what my eyes saw—drops of blood on the white pavement.

"I stared for a minute or two. Then I shut my eyes, said to myself, 'Don't be so stupid, there's nothing there, really,' then I opened them again, but the bloodstains were still there.

"I suddenly felt I couldn't stand it. I interrupted the fisherman's flood of language.

" 'Tell me,' I said. 'My eyesight is not very good. Are those bloodstains on that pavement over there?'

"He looked at me indulgently and kindly.

" 'No bloodstains in these days, lady. What I am telling you about is nearly five hundred years ago.'

" 'Yes,' I said, 'but now—on the pavement . . .' The words died away in my throat. I knew—I knew that he wouldn't see what I was seeing. I got up and with shaking hands began to put my things together. As I did so the young man who had come in the car that morning came out of the inn door. He looked up and down the street perplexedly. On the balcony above his wife came out and collected the bathing things. He walked down toward the car but suddenly swerved and came across the road toward the fisherman.

" 'Tell me, my man,' he said, 'you don't know whether that lady who came in that second car there has got back yet?'

" 'Lady in a dress with flowers all over it? No, sir, I haven't seen her. She went along the cliff toward the cave this morning.'

" 'I know, I know. We all bathed there together, and then

she left us to walk home and I have not seen her since. It can't have taken her all this time. The cliffs round here are not dangerous, are they?'

" 'It depends, sir, on the way you go. The best way is to take a man who knows the place with you.'

"He very clearly meant himself and was beginning to enlarge on the theme, but the young man cut him short unceremoniously and ran back toward the inn, calling up to his wife on the balcony.

" 'I say, Margery, Carol hasn't come back yet. Odd, isn't it?'

"I didn't hear Margery's reply, but her husband went on. 'Well, we can't wait any longer. We have got to push on to Penrithar. Are you ready? I will turn the car.'

"He did as he had said, and presently the two of them drove off together. Meanwhile, I had deliberately been nerving myself to prove how ridiculous my fancies were. When the car had gone I went over to the inn and examined the pavement closely. Of course there were no bloodstains there. No, all along it had been the result of my distorted imagination. Yet, somehow, it seemed to make the thing more frightening. It was while I was standing there that I heard the fisherman's voice.

"He was looking at me curiously. 'You thought you saw bloodstains here, eh, lady?'

"I nodded.

" 'That is very curious, that is very curious. We have got a superstition here, lady. If anyone sees those bloodstains—'

"He paused.

" 'Well?' I said.

"He went on in his soft voice, Cornish in intonation, but unconsciously smooth and well-bred in its pronunciation, and completely free from Cornish turns of speech.

" 'They do say, lady, that if anyone sees those bloodstains, there will be a death within twenty-four hours.'

"Creepy! It gave me a nasty feeling all down my spine.

"He went on persuasively. 'There is a very interesting tablet in the church, lady, about a death—'

" 'No, thanks,' I said decisively, and I turned sharply on my heel and walked up the street toward the cottage where I was lodging. Just as I got there I saw in the distance the woman called Carol coming along the cliff path. She was hurrying. Against the grey of the rocks she looked like some poisonous scarlet flower. Her hat was the colour of blood. . . .

"I shook myself. Really, I had blood on the brain.

"Later I heard the sound of her car. I wondered whether she, too, was going to Penrithar, but she took the road to the left in the opposite direction. I watched the car crawl up the hill and disappear, and I breathed somehow more easily. Rathole seemed its quiet sleepy self once more."

"If that is all," said Raymond West as Joyce came to a stop, "I will give my verdict at once. Indigestion, spots before the eyes after meals."

"It isn't all," said Joyce. "You have got to hear the sequel. I read it in the paper two days later, under the heading of 'Sea Bathing Fatality.' It told how Mrs. Dacre, the wife of Captain Denis Dacre, was unfortunately drowned at Landeer Cove, just a little farther along the coast. She and her husband were staying at the time at the hotel there and had declared their intention of bathing, but a cold wind sprang up. Captain Dacre had declared it was too cold, so he and some other people in the hotel had gone off to the golf links nearby. Mrs. Dacre, however, had said it was not too cold for her and she went off alone down to the cove. As she didn't return, her husband became alarmed and in company with his friends went down to the beach. They found her clothes lying beside a rock but no trace of the unfortunate lady. Her body was not found until nearly a week later, when it was washed ashore at a point some distance down the coast.

There was a bad blow on her head which had occurred before death, and the theory was that she must have dived into the sea and hit her head on a rock. As far as I could make out, her death would have occurred just twenty-four hours after the time I saw the bloodstains."

"I protest," said Sir Henry. "This is not a problem—this is a ghost story. Miss Lemprière is evidently a medium."

Mr. Petherick gave his usual cough.

"One point strikes me," he said, "that blow on the head. We must not, I think, exclude the possibility of foul play. But I do not see that we have any data to go upon. Miss Lemprière's hallucination, or vision, is interesting, certainly, but I do not see clearly the point on which she wishes us to pronounce."

"Indigestion and coincidence," said Raymond, "and anyway, you can't be sure that they were the same people. Besides, the curse, or whatever it was, would only apply to actual inhabitants of Rathole."

"I feel," said Sir Henry, "that the sinister seafaring man has something to do with this tale. But I agree with Mr. Petherick, Miss Lemprière has given us very little data."

Joyce turned to Dr. Pender, who smilingly shook his head.

"It is a most interesting story," he said, "but I am afraid I agree with Sir Henry and Mr. Petherick that there is very little data to go upon."

Joyce then looked curiously at Miss Marple, who smiled back at her.

"I too think you are just a little unfair, Joyce dear," she said. "Of course, it is different for me. I mean, we, being women, appreciate the point about clothes. I don't think it is a fair problem to put to a man. It must have meant a lot of rapid changing. What a wicked woman! And a still more wicked man."

Joyce stared at her.

"Aunt Jane," she said. "Miss Marple, I mean, I believe—I do really believe you know the truth."

"Well, dear," said Miss Marple, "it is much easier for me sitting here quietly than it was for you—and being an artist, you are so susceptible to atmosphere, aren't you? Sitting here with one's knitting, one just sees the facts. Bloodstains dropped on the pavement from the bathing dress hanging above, and being a red bathing dress, of course, the criminals themselves did not realize it was bloodstained. Poor thing, poor young thing!"

"Excuse me, Miss Marple," said Sir Henry, "but do you know that I am entirely in the dark still. You and Miss Lemprière seem to know what you are talking about, but we mere men are still in utter darkness."

"I will tell you the end of the story now," said Joyce. "It was a year later. I was at a little east-coast resort, and I was sketching, when suddenly I had that queer feeling one has of something having happened before. There were two people, a man and a woman, on the pavement in front of me, and they were greeting a third person, a woman dressed in a scarlet poinsettia chintz dress. 'Carol, by all that is wonderful! Fancy meeting you after all these years. You don't know my wife? Joan, this is an old friend of mine, Miss Harding.'

"I recognized the man at once. It was the same Denis I had seen in Rathole. The wife was different—that is, she was a Joan instead of a Margery; but she was the same type, young and rather dowdy and very inconspicuous. I thought for a minute I was going mad. They began to talk of going bathing. I will tell you what I did. I marched straight then and there to the police station. I thought they would probably think I was off my head, but I didn't care. And, as it happened, everything was quite all right. There was a man from Scotland Yard there, and he had come down just about this very thing. It seems—oh, it's horrible to talk about—that the police had got suspicious of Denis Dacre. That wasn't his real name—he took different names on different occasions. He got to know girls, usually quiet, inconspicuous girls without many relatives or friends; he married them and insured their lives for large sums, and then—oh, it's horrible! The woman called Carol was his real wife, and they always carried out the same plan. That is really how they came to catch him. The insurance companies became suspicious. He would come to some quiet seaside place with his new wife. Then the other woman would turn up and they would all go bathing together. Then the wife would be murdered and Carol would put on her clothes and go back in the boat with him. Then they would leave the place, wherever it was, after inquiring for the supposed Carol, and when they got outside the village Carol would hastily change back into her own flamboyant clothes and her vivid make-up and would go back there and drive off in her own car. They would find out which way the current was flowing and the supposed death would take place at the next bathing place along the coast that way. Carol would play the part of the wife and would go down to some lonely beach and would leave the wife's clothes there by a rock and depart in her flowery chintz dress to wait quietly until her husband could rejoin her.

"I suppose when they killed poor Margery some of the blood must have spurted over Carol's bathing suit, and being a red one, they didn't notice it, as Miss Marple says. But when they hung it over the balcony it dripped. Ugh!" She gave a shiver. "I can see it still."

"Of course," said Sir Henry, "I remember very well now. Davis was the man's real name. It had quite slipped my memory that one of his many aliases was Dacre. They were an extraordinarily cunning pair. It always seemed so amazing to me that no one spotted the change of identity. I suppose, as Miss Marple says, clothes are more easily identified than faces; but it was a very clever scheme, for although we suspected Davis, it was not easy to bring the crime home to him as he always seemed to have an unimpeachable alibi."

"Aunt Jane," said Raymond, looking at her curiously, "how do you do it? You have lived such a peaceful life and yet nothing seems to surprise you."

"I always find one thing very like another in this world," said Miss Marple. "There was Mrs. Green, you know. She buried five children—and every one of them insured. Well, naturally, one began to get suspicious."

She shook her head.

"There is a great deal of wickedness in village life. I hope you dear·young people will never realize how very wicked the world is."

Motive v. Opportunity

Mr. Petherick, the solicitor, cleared his throat rather more importantly than usual and beamed appreciatively over his eyeglasses.

"The story I am about to tell is a perfectly simple and straightforward one and can be followed by any layman."

"No legal quibbles, now," said Miss Marple, shaking a knitting needle at him.

"Certainly not," said Mr. Petherick.

"Ah well, I am not so sure, but let's hear the story."

"It concerns a former client of mine. I will call him Mr. Clode—Simon Clode. He was a man of considerable wealth and lived in a large house not very far from here. He had had one son killed in the war and this son had left one child, a little girl. Her mother had died at her birth, and on her father's death she had come to live with her grandfather who at once became passionately attached to her. Little Chris could do anything she liked with her grandfather. I have never seen a man more completely wrapped up in a child, and I cannot describe to you his grief and despair when, at the age of eleven, the child contracted pneumonia and died.

"Poor Simon Clode was inconsolable. A brother of his had recently died in poor circumstances and Simon Clode had generously offered a home to his brother's children—two girls, Grace and Mary, and a boy, George. But though kind and generous to his nephew and nieces, the old man never expended on them any of the love and devotion he had accorded to his little grandchild. Employment was found for George Clode in a bank nearby, and Grace married a clever young research chemist of the name of Philip Garrod. Mary, who was a quiet, self-contained girl, lived at home and looked after her uncle. She was, I think, fond of him in her quiet, undemonstrative way. And to all appearances things went on very peacefully. I may say that after the death of little Christobel, Simon Clode came to me and instructed me to draw up a new will. By this will his fortune, a very considerable one, was divided equally between his nephew and nieces, a third share to each.

"Time went on. Chancing to meet George Clode one day, I inquired for his uncle, whom I had not seen for some time. To my surprise George's face clouded over. 'I wish you could put some sense into Uncle Simon,' he said ruefully. His honest but not very brilliant countenance looked puzzled and worried. 'This spirit business is getting worse and worse.'

" 'What spirit business?' I asked, very much surprised.

"Then George told me the whole story. How Mr. Clode had gradually got interested in the subject and how on the top of this interest he had chanced to meet an American medium, a Mrs. Eurydice Spragg. This woman, whom George did not hesitate to characterize as an out-and-out swindler, had gained an immense ascendency over Simon Clode. She was practically always in the house, and many séances were held in which the spirit of Christobel manifested itself to the doting grandfather.

"I may say here and now that I do not belong to the ranks of those who cover spiritualism with ridicule and scorn. I am a believer in evidence. And I think that when we have an impartial mind and weigh the evidence in favour of spiritualism there remains much that cannot be put down to fraud or lightly set aside. Therefore, as I say, I am neither a believer nor an unbeliever. There is certain testimony with which one cannot afford to disagree.

"On the other hand, spiritualism lends itself very easily to fraud and imposture, and from all young George Clode told me about this Mrs. Eurydice Spragg I felt more and more convinced that Simon Clode was in bad hands and that Mrs. Spragg was probably an impostor of the worst type. The old man, shrewd as he was in practical matters, would be easily imposed on where his love for his dead grandchild was concerned.

"Turning things over in my mind, I felt more and more uneasy. I was fond of the young Clodes, Mary and George, and I realized that this Mrs. Spragg and her influence over their uncle might lead to trouble in the future.

"At the earliest opportunity I made a pretext for calling on Simon Clode. I found Mrs. Spragg installed as an honoured and friendly guest. As soon as I saw her my worst apprehensions were fulfilled. She was a stout woman of middle age, dressed in a flamboyant style. Very full of cant phrases about 'our dear ones who have passed over,' and other things of the kind.

"Her husband was also staying in the house, Mr. Absalom Spragg, a thin, lank man with a melancholy expression and extremely furtive eyes. As soon as I could, I got Simon Clode to myself and sounded him tactfully on the subject. He was full of enthusiasm. Eurydice Spragg was wonderful! She had been sent to him directly in answer to prayer! She cared nothing for money; the joy of helping a heart in affliction was enough for her. She had quite a mother's feeling for little Chris. He was beginning to regard her almost as a daughter. Then he went on to give me details—how he had heard his Chris's voice speaking—how she was well and happy with her father and mother. He went on to tell other sentiments expressed by the child, which in my remembrance of little Christobel seemed to me highly unlikely. She laid stress on the fact that 'Father and Mother loved dear Mrs. Spragg.'

" 'But, of course,' he broke off, 'you are a scoffer, Petherick.'

" 'No, I am not a scoffer. Very far from it. Some of the men who have written on the subject are men whose testimony I would accept unhesitatingly, and I should accord any medium recommended by them respect and credence. I presume that this Mrs. Spragg is well vouched for?'

"Simon went into ecstasies over Mrs. Spragg. She had been sent to him by Heaven. He had come across her at the watering place where he had spent two months in the summer. A chance meeting, with what a wonderful result!

"I went away very dissatisfied. My worst fears were realized, but I did not see what I could do. After a good deal of thought and deliberation I wrote to Philip Garrod who had, as I mentioned, just married the eldest Clode girl, Grace. I set the case before him—of course, in the most carefully guarded language. I pointed out the danger of such a woman gaining ascendency over the old man's mind. And I suggested that Mr. Clode should be brought into contact if possible with some reputable spiritualistic circles. This, I thought, would not be a difficult matter for Philip Garrod to arrange.

"Garrod was prompt to act. He realized, which I did not, that Simon Clode's health was in a very precarious condition, and as a practical man he had no intention of letting his wife or her sister and brother be despoiled of the inheritance which was so rightly theirs. He came down the following week, bringing with him as a guest no other than the famous Professor Longman. Longman was a scientist of the first order, a man whose association with spiritualism compelled the latter to be treated with respect. Not only a brilliant scientist, he was a man of the utmost uprightness and probity.

"The result of the visit was most unfortunate. Longman, it seemed, had said very little while he was there. Two séances were held—under what conditions I do not know. Longman was noncommittal all the time he was in the house, but after his departure he wrote a letter to Philip Garrod. In it he admitted that he had not been able to detect Mrs. Spragg in fraud; nevertheless, his private opinion was that the phenomena were not genuine. Mr. Garrod, he said, was at liberty to show this letter to his uncle if he thought fit, and he suggested that he himself should put Mr. Clode in touch with a medium of perfect integrity.

"Philip Garrod had taken this letter straight to his uncle, but the result was not what he had anticipated. The old man flew into a towering rage. It was all a plot to discredit Mrs. Spragg who was a maligned and injured saint! She had told him already what bitter jealousy there was of her in this country. He pointed out that Longman was forced to say he had not detected fraud. Eurydice Spragg had come to him in the darkest hour of his life, had given him help and comfort, and he was prepared to espouse her cause even if it meant quarrelling with every member of the family. She was more to him than anyone else in the world.

"Philip Garrod was turned out of the house with scant ceremony, but as a result of his rage Clode's own health took a decided turn for the worst. For the last month he had kept to his bed pretty continuously, and now there seemed every possibility of his being a bedridden invalid until such time as death should release him. Two days after Philip's departure I received an urgent summons and went hurriedly over. Clode was in bed and looked even to my layman's eye very ill indeed. He was gasping for breath.

" 'This is the end of me,' he said. 'I feel it. Don't argue with me, Petherick. But before I die I am going to do my duty by the one human being who has done more for me than anyone else in the world. I want to make a fresh will.'

" 'Certainly,' I said. 'If you will give me your instructions now, I will draft out a will and send it to you.'

" 'That won't do,' he said. 'Why, man, I might not live through the night. I have written out what I want here'—he fumbled under his pillow—'and you can tell me if it is right.'

"He produced a sheet of paper with a few words roughly scribbled on it in pencil. It was quite simple and clear. He left £5000 to each of his nieces and nephew and the residue of his vast property outright to Eurydice Spragg 'in gratitude and admiration.'

"I didn't like it, but there it was. There was no question of unsound mind; the old man was as sane as anybody.

"He rang the bell for two of the servants. They came promptly. The housemaid, Emma Gaunt, was a tall middle-aged woman who had been in service there for many years and who had nursed Clode devotedly. With her came the cook, a fresh buxom young woman of thirty. Simon Clode glared at them both from under his bushy eyebrows.

" 'I want you to witness my will. Emma, get me my fountain pen.'

"Emma went over obediently to the desk.

" 'Not that left-hand drawer, girl,' said old Simon irritably. 'Don't you know it is in the right-hand one?'

" 'No, it is here, sir,' said Emma, producing it.

" 'Then you must have put it away wrong last time,' grumbled the old man. 'I can't stand things not being kept in their proper places.'

"Still grumbling, he took the pen from her and copied his

own rough draft, amended by me, on to a fresh piece of paper. Then he signed his name. Emma Gaunt and the cook, Lucy David, also signed. I folded the will up and put it into a long blue envelope. It was necessarily, you understand, written on an ordinary piece of paper.

"Just as the servants were turning to leave the room Clode lay back on the pillows with a gasp and a distorted face. I bent over him anxiously, and Emma Gaunt came quickly back. However, the old man recovered and smiled weakly.

" 'It is all right, Petherick, don't be alarmed. At any rate, I shall die easy now, having done what I wanted to.'

"Emma Gaunt looked inquiringly at me as if to know whether she could leave the room. I nodded reassuringly and she went out—first stopping to pick up the blue envelope which I had let slip to the ground in my moment of anxiety. She handed it to me and I slipped it into my coat pocket and then she went out.

" 'You are annoyed, Petherick,' said Simon Clode. 'You are prejudiced, like everybody else.'

" 'It is not a question of prejudice,' I said. 'Mrs. Spragg may be all she claims to be. I should see no objection to you leaving her a small legacy as a memento of gratitude, but I tell you frankly, Clode, that to disinherit your own flesh and blood in favor of a stranger is wrong.'

"With that I turned to depart. I had done what I could and made my protest.

"Mary Clode came out of the drawing room and met me in the hall.

" 'You will have tea before you go, won't you? Come in here.' And she led me into the drawing room.

"A fire was burning on the hearth and the room looked cosy and cheerful. She relieved me of my overcoat just as her brother, George, came into the room. He took it from her and laid it across a chair at the far end of the room, then he came back to the fireside where we drank tea. During the meal a question arose about some point concerning the estate. Simon Clode said he didn't want to be bothered with it and had left it to George to decide. George was rather nervous about trusting to his own judgment. At my suggestion, we adjourned to the study after tea and I looked over the papers in question. Mary Clode accompanied us.

"A quarter of an hour later I prepared to take my departure. Remembering that I had left my overcoat in the drawing-room, I went there to fetch it. The only occupant of the room was Mrs. Spragg, who was kneeling by the chair on which the overcoat lay. She seemed to be doing something rather unnecessary to the cretonne cover. She rose with a very red face as we entered.

" 'That cover never did sit right,' she complained. 'My! I could make a better fit myself.'

"I took up my overcoat and put it on. As I did so I noticed that the envelope containing the will had fallen out of the pocket and was lying on the floor. I replaced it in my pocket, said good-bye, and took my departure.

"On arrival at my office, I will describe my next actions carefully. I removed my overcoat and took the will from the pocket. I had it in my hand and was standing by the table when my clerk came in. Somebody wished to speak to me on the telephone, and the extension to my desk was out of order. I accordingly accompanied him to the outer office and remained there for about five minutes engaged in conversation over the telephone.

"When I emerged, I found my clerk waiting for me.

" 'Mr. Spragg has called to see you, sir. I showed him into your office.'

"I went there to find Mr. Spragg sitting by the table. He rose and greeted me in a somewhat unctuous manner, then proceeded to a long discursive speech. In the main it seemed to be an uneasy justification of himself and his wife. He was afraid people were saying, et cetera, et cetera. His wife had been known from her babyhood upward for the pureness of her heart and her motives . . . and so on and so on. I was, I am afraid, rather curt with him. In the end I think he realized that his visit was not being a success and he left somewhat abruptly. I then remembered that I had left the will lying on the table. I took it, sealed the envelope, and wrote on it and put it away in the safe.

"Now I come to the crux of my story. Two months later Mr. Simon Clode died. I will not go into long-winded discussions. I will just state the bare facts. When the sealed envelope containing the will was opened it was found to contain a sheet of blank paper."

He paused, looking around the circle of interested faces. He smiled himself with a certain enjoyment.

"You appreciate the point, of course? For two months the sealed envelope had lain in my safe. It could not have been tampered with then. No, the time limit was a very short one. Between the moment the will was signed and my locking it away in the safe. Now who had had the opportunity, and to whose interests would it be to do so?

"I will recapitulate the vital points in a brief summary: The will was signed by Mr. Clode, placed by me in an envelope—so far so good. It was then put by me in my overcoat pocket. That overcoat was taken from me by Mary and handed by her to George, who was in full sight of me while handling the coat. During the time that I was in the study Mrs. Eurydice Spragg would have had plenty of time to extract the envelope from the coat pocket and read its contents and, as a matter of fact, finding the envelope on the ground and not in the pocket seemed to point to her having done so. But here we come to a curious point: she had the opportunity of substituting the blank paper, but no motive. The will was in her favour, and by substituting a blank piece of paper she despoiled herself of the heritage she had been so anxious to gain. The same applies to Mr. Spragg. He too had the opportunity. He was left alone with the document in question for some two or three minutes in my office. But again, it was not to his advantage to do so. So we are faced with this curious problem: the two people who had the opportunity of substituting a blank piece of paper had no motive for doing so, and the two people who had a motive had no opportunity. By the way, I would not exclude the housemaid, Emma Gaunt, from suspicion. She was devoted to her young master and mistress and detested the Spraggs. She would, I feel sure, have been quite equal to attempting the substitution if she had thought of it. But although she actually handled the envelope when she picked it up from the floor and handed it to me, she certainly had no opportunity of tampering with its contents and she could not have substituted another envelope by some sleight of hand (of which, anyway, she would not be capable) because the envelope in question was brought into the house by me and no one there would be likely to have a duplicate."

He looked round, beaming on the assembly.

"Now, there is my little problem. I have, I hope, stated it clearly. I should be interested to hear your views."

To everyone's astonishment Miss Marple gave vent to a long and prolonged chuckle. Something seemed to be amusing her immensely.

"What is the matter, Aunt Jane? Can't we share the joke?" said Raymond.

"I was thinking of little Tommy Symonds, a naughty little boy, I am afraid, but sometimes very amusing. One of those children with innocent, childlike faces who are always up to some mischief or other. I was thinking how last week in Sunday school he said, 'Teacher, do you say yolk of eggs is white or yolk of eggs are white?' And Miss Durston explained that anyone would say 'Yolks of eggs are white, or yolk of egg is white'—and naughty Tommy said: 'Well, I should say yolk of egg is yellow!' Very naughty of him, of course, and as old as the hills. I knew that one as a child."

"Very funny, my dear Aunt Jane," Raymond said gently, "but surely that has nothing to do with the very interesting story that Mr. Petherick has been telling us."

"Oh yes, it has," said Miss Marple. "It is a catch! And so is Mr. Petherick's story a catch. So like a lawyer! Ah, my dear old friend!" She shook a reproving head at him.

"I wonder if you really know," said the lawyer with a twinkle.

Miss Marple wrote a few words on a piece of paper, folded them up, and passed them across to him.

Mr. Petherick unfolded the paper, read what was written on it, and looked across at her appreciatively.

"My dear friend," he said, "is there anything you do not know?"

"I knew that as a child," said Miss Marple. "Played with it too."

"I feel rather out of this," said Sir Henry. "I feel sure that Mr. Petherick has some clever legal legerdemain up his sleeve."

"Not at all," said Mr. Petherick. "Not at all. It is a perfectly fair, straightforward proposition. You must not pay any attention to Miss Marple. She has her own way of looking at things."

"We should be able to arrive at the truth," said Raymond West a trifle vexedly. "The facts certainly seem plain enough. Five persons actually touched that envelope. The Spraggs clearly could have meddled with it, but equally clearly they did not do so. There remains the other three. Now, when one sees the marvellous ways that conjurers have of doing things before one's eyes, it seems to me that that paper could have been extracted and another substituted by George Clode during the time he was carrying the overcoat to the far end of the room."

"Well, I think it was the girl," said Joyce. "I think the housemaid ran down and told her what was happening and she got hold of another blue envelope and just substituted the one for the other."

Sir Henry shook his head. "I disagree with you both," he said slowly. "These sorts of things are done by conjurers, and they are done on the stage and in novels, but I think they would be impossible to do in real life, especially under the shrewd eyes of a man like my friend Mr. Petherick here. But I have an idea—it is only an idea and nothing more. We know that Professor Longman had just been down for a visit and that he said very little. It is only reasonable to suppose that the Spraggs may have been very anxious as to the result of that visit. If Simon Clode did not take them into his confidence, which is quite probable, they may have viewed his sending for Mr. Petherick from quite another angle. They may have believed that Mr. Clode had already made a will which benefited Eurydice Spragg and that this new one might be for the express purpose of cutting her out as a result of Professor Longman's revelations, or alternatively, as you lawyers say, Philip Garrod had impressed on his uncle the claims of his own flesh and blood. In that case, suppose Mrs. Spragg prepared to effect a substitution. This she does, but Mr. Petherick coming in at an unfortunate moment, she has no time to read the real document and hastily destroys it by fire in case the lawyer should discover his loss."

Joyce shook her head very decidedly.

"She would never burn it without reading it."

"The solution is rather a weak one," admitted Sir Henry.

"I suppose—er—Mr. Petherick did not assist Providence himself."

The suggestion was only a laughing one, but the little lawyer drew himself up in offended dignity.

"A most improper suggestion," he said with some asperity.

"What does Dr. Pender say?" asked Sir Henry.

"I cannot say I have any very clear ideas. I think the substitution must have been effected by either Mrs. Spragg or her husband, possibly for the motive that Sir Henry suggests. If she did not read the will until after Mr. Petherick had departed, she would then be in somewhat of a dilemma, since she could not own up to her action in the matter. Possibly she would place it among Mr. Clode's papers where she thought it would be found after his death. But why it wasn't found I don't know. It might be a mere speculation this— that Emma Gaunt came across it—and out of misplaced devotion to her employers—deliberately destroyed it."

"I think Dr. Pender's solution is the best of all," said Joyce. "Is it right, Mr. Petherick?"

The lawyer shook his head.

"I will go on where I left off. I was dumbfounded and quite as much at sea as all of you are. I don't think I should ever have guessed the truth—probably not—but I was enlightened. It was cleverly done too.

"I went and dined with Philip Garrod about a month later, and in the course of our after-dinner conversation he mentioned an interesting case that had recently come to his notice.

"'I should like to tell you about it, Petherick, in confidence, of course.'

"'Quite so,' I replied.

"'A friend of mine who had expectations from one of his relatives was greatly distressed to find that that relative had thoughts of benefiting a totally unworthy person. My friend, I am afraid, is a trifle unscrupulous in his methods. There was a maid in the house who was greatly devoted to the interests of what I may call the legitimate party. My friend gave her very simple instructions. He gave her a fountain pen, duly filled. She was to place this in a drawer in the writing table in her master's room, but not the usual drawer where the pen was generally kept. If her master asked her to witness his signature to any document and asked her to bring him his pen, she was to bring him not the right one, but this one which was an exact duplicate of it. That was all she had to do. He gave her no other information. She was a devoted creature and she carried out his instructions faithfully.'

"He broke off and said:

" 'I hope I am not boring you, Petherick.'

" 'Not at all,' I said. 'I am keenly interested.'

"Our eyes met.

" 'My friend is, of course, not known to you,' he said.

" 'Of course not,' I replied.

" 'Then that is all right,' said Philip Garrod.

"He paused, then said smilingly, 'You see the point? The pen was filled with what is commonly known as evanescent ink—a solution of starch in water to which a few drops of iodine has been added. This makes a deep blue-black fluid, but the writing disappears entirely in four or five days.' "

Miss Marple chuckled.

"Disappearing ink," she said. "I know it. Many is the time I have played with it as a child."

And she beamed round on them all, pausing to shake a finger once more at Mr. Petherick.

"But all the same it's a catch, Mr. Petherick," she said. "Just like a lawyer."

The Thumbmark
of St. Peter

"And now, Aunt Jane, it is up to you," said Raymond West.

"Yes, Aunt Jane, we are expecting something really spicy," chimed in Joyce Lemprière.

"Now, you are laughing at me, my dears," said Miss Marple placidly. "You think that because I have lived in this out-of-the-way spot all my life I am not likely to have had any very interesting experiences."

"God forbid that I should ever regard village life as peaceful and uneventful," said Raymond with fervour. "Not after the revelations we have heard from you! The cosmopolitan world seems a mild and peaceful place compared with St. Mary Mead."

"Well, my dear," said Miss Marple, "human nature is much the same everywhere, and, of course, one has opportunities of observing it at closer quarters in a village."

"You really are unique, Aunt Jane," cried Joyce. "I hope you don't mind me calling you Aunt Jane?" she added. "I don't know why I do it."

"Don't you, my dear?" said Miss Marple.

She looked up for a moment or two with something quizzical in her glance, which made the blood flame to the girl's cheeks. Raymond West fidgeted and cleared his throat in a somewhat embarrassed manner.

Miss Marple looked at them both and smiled again and bent her attention once more to her knitting.

"It is true, of course, that I have lived what is called a very uneventful life, but I have had a lot of experiences in solving different little problems that have arisen. Some of them have been really quite ingenious, but it would be no good telling them to you, because they are about such unimportant things that you would not be interested—just things like: Who cut the meshes of Mrs. Jones's string bag? And why Mrs. Sims only wore her new fur coat once. Very interesting things, really, to any student of human nature. No, the only experience that I can remember that would be of interest to you is the one about my poor niece Mabel's husband.

"It is about ten or fifteen years ago now, and happily it is all over and done with, and everyone has forgotten about it. People's memories are very short—a lucky thing, I always think."

Miss Marple paused and murmured to herself:

"I must just count this row. The decreasing is a little awkward. One, two, three, four, five, and then three purl; that is right. Now, what was I saying? Oh yes, about poor Mabel.

"Mabel was my niece. A nice girl, really a very nice girl, but just a trifle what one might call silly. Rather fond of being melodramatic and of saying a great deal more than she meant whenever she was upset. She married a Mr. Denman when she was twenty-two, and I am afraid it was not a very happy marriage. I had hoped very much that the attachment would not come to anything, for Mr. Denman was a man of very violent temper—not the kind of man who would be patient with Mabel's foibles—and I also learned that there was insanity in his family. However, girls were just as obsti-

nate then as they are now, and as they always will be. And
Mabel married him.

"I didn't see very much of her after her marriage. She
came to stay with me once or twice, and they asked me there
several times, but, as a matter of fact, I am not very fond of
staying in other people's houses, and I always managed to
make some excuse. They had been married ten years when
Mr. Denman died suddenly. There were no children, and he
left all his money to Mabel. I wrote, of course, and offered to
come to Mabel if she wanted me; but she wrote back a very
sensible letter, and I gathered that she was not altogether
overwhelmed by grief. I thought that was only natural, because I knew they had not been getting on together for some
time. It was not until about three months afterward that I
got a most hysterical letter from Mabel, begging me to come
to her, and saying that things were going from bad to worse
and she couldn't stand it much longer.

"So, of course," continued Miss Marple, "I put Clara on
board wages and sent the plate and the King Charles tankard
to the bank, and I went off at once. I found Mabel in a very
nervous state. The house, Myrtle Dene, was a fairly large
one, very comfortably furnished. There was a cook and a
house-parlourmaid, as well as a nurse-attendant to look after
old Mr. Denman, Mabel's husband's father, who was what is
called 'not quite right in the head.' Quite peaceful and well-
behaved, but distinctly odd at times. As I say, there was insanity in the family.

"I was really shocked to see the change in Mabel. She was
a mass of nerves, twitching all over, yet I had the greatest
difficulty in making her tell me what the trouble was. I got
at it, as one always does get at these things, indirectly. I
asked her about some friends of hers she was always mentioning in her letters, the Gallaghers. She said, to my surprise, that she hardly ever saw them nowadays. Other friends

whom I mentioned elicited the same remark. I spoke to her then of the folly of shutting herself up and brooding, and especially of the silliness of cutting herself adrift from her friends. Then she came bursting out with the truth.

" 'It is not my doing, it is theirs. There is not a soul in the place who will speak to me now. When I go down the High Street they all get out of the way so that they shan't have to meet me or speak to me. I am like a kind of leper. It is awful, and I can't bear it any longer. I shall have to sell the house and go abroad. Yet why should I be driven away from home like this? I have done nothing.'

"I was more disturbed than I can tell you. I was knitting a comforter for old Mrs. Hay at the time, and in my perturbation I dropped two stitches and never discovered it until long after.

" 'My dear Mabel,' I said, 'you amaze me. But what is the cause of all this?'

"Even as a child Mabel was always difficult. I had the greatest difficulty in getting her to give me a straightforward answer to my question. She would only say vague things about wicked talk and idle people who had nothing better to do than gossip, and people who put ideas into the other people's heads.

" 'That is all quite clear to me,' I said. 'There is evidently some story being circulated about you. But what that story is you must know as well as anyone. And you are going to tell me.'

" 'It is so wicked,' moaned Mabel.

" 'Of course it is wicked,' I said briskly. 'There is nothing that you can tell me about people's minds that would astonish or surprise me. Now, Mabel, will you tell me in plain English what people are saying about you?'

"Then it all came out.

"It seemed that Geoffrey Denman's death, being quite

sudden and unexpected, gave rise to various rumours. In fact—and in plain English as I had put it to her—people were saying that she had poisoned her husband.

"Now, as I expect you know, there is nothing more cruel than talk, and there is nothing more difficult to combat. When people say things behind your back there is nothing you can refute or deny, and the rumours go on growing and growing, and no one can stop them. I was quite certain of one thing: Mabel was quite incapable of poisoning anyone. And I didn't see why life should be ruined for her and her home made unbearable just because in all probability she had been doing something silly and foolish.

" 'There is no smoke without fire,' I said. 'Now, Mabel, you have got to tell me what started people off on this tack. There must have been something.'

"Mabel was very incoherent and declared there was nothing—nothing at all, except, of course, that Geoffrey's death had been very sudden. He had seemed quite well at supper that evening and had taken violently ill in the night. The doctor had been sent for, but the poor man had died a few minutes after the doctor's arrival. Death had been thought to be the result of eating poisoned mushrooms.

" 'Well,' I said, 'I suppose a sudden death of that kind might start tongues wagging, but surely not without some additional facts. Did you have a quarrel with Geoffrey or anything of that kind?'

"She admitted that she had had a quarrel with him on the preceding morning at breakfast time.

" 'And the servants heard it, I suppose?' I asked.

" 'They weren't in the room.'

" 'No, my dear,' I said, 'but they probably were fairly near the door outside.'

"I knew the carrying power of Mabel's high-pitched, hysterical voice only too well. Geoffrey Denman, too, was a man given to raising his voice loudly when angry.

" 'What did you quarrel about?' I asked.

" 'Oh, the usual things. It was always the same things over and over again. Some little thing would start us off, and then Geoffrey became impossible and said abominable things, and I told him what I thought of him.'

" 'There had been a lot of quarrelling, then?' I asked.

" 'It wasn't my fault—'

" 'My dear child,' I said, 'it doesn't matter whose fault it was. That is not what we are discussing. In a place like this everybody's private affairs are more or less public property. You and your husband were always quarrelling. You had a particularly bad quarrel one morning, and that night your husband died suddenly and mysteriously. Is that all, or is there anything else?'

" 'I don't know what you mean by anything else,' said Mabel sullenly.

" 'Just what I say, my dear. If you have done anything silly, don't, for heaven's sake, keep it back now. I only want to do what I can to help you.'

" 'Nothing and nobody can help,' said Mabel wildly, 'except death.'

" 'Have a little more faith in Providence, dear,' I said. 'Now then, Mabel, I know perfectly well there is something else that you are keeping back.'

"I always did know, even when she was a child, when she was not telling me the whole truth. It took a long time, but I got it out at last. She had gone down to the chemist's that morning and had bought some arsenic. She had had, of course, to sign the book for it. Naturally the chemist had talked.

" 'Who is your doctor?' I asked.

" 'Dr. Rawlinson.'

"I knew him by sight. Mabel had pointed him out to me the other day. To put it in perfectly plain language, he was what I would describe as an old dodderer. I have had too much experience of life to believe in the infallibility of doctors. Some of them are clever men and some of them are not, and half the time the best of them don't know what is the matter with you. I have no truck with doctors and their medicines myself.

"I thought things over, and then I put my bonnet on and went to call on Dr. Rawlinson. He was just what I had thought him—a nice old man, kindly, vague, and so shortsighted as to be pitiful, slightly deaf, and, withal, touchy and sensitive to the last degree. He was on his high horse at once when I mentioned Geoffrey Denman's death, talked for a long time about various kinds of fungi, edible and otherwise. He had questioned the cook, and she had admitted that one or two of the mushrooms cooked had been 'a little queer,' but as the shop had sent them she thought they must be all right. The more she thought about them since, the more she was convinced that their appearance was unusual.

" 'She would be,' I said. 'They would start by being quite like mushrooms in appearance, and they would end by being orange with purple spots.'

"I gathered that Denman had been past speech when the doctor got to him. He was incapable of swallowing and had died within a few minutes. The doctor seemed perfectly satisfied with the certificate he had given. But how much of that was obstinacy and how much of it was genuine belief I could not be sure.

"I went straight home and asked Mabel quite frankly why she had bought arsenic.

" 'You must have had some idea in your mind,' I pointed out.

"Mabel burst into tears. 'I wanted to make away with myself,' she moaned. 'I was too unhappy. I thought I would end it all.'

" 'Have you the arsenic still?' I asked.

" 'No, I threw it away.'

"I sat there turning things over and over in my mind.

" 'What happened when he was taken ill? Did he call you?'

" 'No.' She shook her head. 'He rang the bell violently. He must have rung several times. At last Dorothy, the house-parlourmaid, heard it, and she waked the cook up, and they came down. When Dorothy saw him she was frightened. He was rambling and delirious. She left the cook with him and came rushing to me. I got up and went to him. Of course, I saw at once he was dreadfully ill. Unfortunately Brewster, who looks after old Mr. Denman, was away for the night, so there was no one who knew what to do. I sent Dorothy off for the doctor, and cook and I stayed with him, but after a few minutes I couldn't bear it any longer; it was too dreadful. I ran away back to my room and locked the door.'

" 'Very selfish and unkind of you,' I said, 'and no doubt that conduct of yours has done nothing to help you since, you may be sure of that. Cook will have repeated it everywhere. Well, well, this is a bad business.'

"Next I spoke to the servants. The cook wanted to tell me about the mushrooms, but I stopped her. I was tired of these mushrooms. Instead, I questioned both of them very closely about their master's condition on that night. They both agreed that he seemed to be in great agony, that he was unable to swallow, and he could only speak in a strangled voice, and when he did speak it was only rambling—nothing sensible.'

" 'What did he say when he was rambling?' I asked curiously.

" 'Something about some fish, wasn't it?' She turned to the other.

"Dorothy agreed.

" 'A heap of fish,' she said. 'Some nonsense like that. I

could see at once he wasn't in his right mind, poor gentle-man.'

"There didn't seem to be any sense to be made out of that. As a last resource I went up to see the nurse-attendant, Brewster, who was a gaunt, middle-aged woman of about fifty.

" 'It is a pity that I wasn't here that night,' she said. 'No-body seems to have tried to do anything for him until the doctor came.'

" 'I suppose he was delirious,' I said doubtfully, 'but that is not a symptom of ptomaine poisoning, is it?'

" 'It depends,' said Brewster.

"I asked her how her patient was getting on.

"She shook her head.

" 'He is pretty bad,' she said.

" 'Weak?'

" 'Oh no, he is strong enough physically—all but his eye-sight. That is failing badly. He may outlive all of us, but his mind is failing very fast now. I had already told both Mr. and Mrs. Denman that he ought to be in an institution, but Mrs. Denman wouldn't hear of it at any price.'

"I will say for Mabel that she always had a kindly heart.

"Well, there the thing was. I thought it over in every as-pect, and at last I decided that there was only one thing to be done. In view of rumours that were going about, permission must be applied for to exhume the body, and a proper post-mortem must be made and lying tongues quieted once and for all. Mabel, of course, made a fuss, mostly on sentimental grounds—disturbing the dead man in his peaceful grave, et cetera, et cetera—but I was firm.

"I won't make a long story of this part of it. We got the order and they did the autopsy, or whatever they call it, but the result was not so satisfactory as it might have been. There was no trace of arsenic—that was all to the good—but the actual words of the report were that there was nothing to show by what means deceased had come to his death.

"So, you see, that didn't lead us out of trouble altogether. People went on talking—about rare poisons impossible to detect and rubbish of that sort. I had seen the pathologist who had done the post-mortem, and I had asked him several questions, though he tried his best to get out of answering most of them; but I got out of him that he considered it highly unlikely that the poisoned mushrooms were the cause of death. An idea was simmering in my mind, and I asked him what poison, if any, could have been employed to obtain that result. He made a long explanation to me, most of which, I must admit, I did not follow, but it amounted to this: That death might have been due to some strong vegetable alkaloid.

"The idea I had was this: Supposing the taint of insanity was in Geoffrey Denman's blood also, might he not have made away with himself? He had, at one period of his life, studied medicine, and he would have a good knowledge of poisons and their effects.

"I didn't think it sounded very likely, but it was the only thing I could think of. And I was nearly at my wit's end, I can tell you. Now, I dare say you modern young people will laugh, but when I am in really bad trouble I always say a little prayer to myself—anywhere, when I am walking along the street, or at a bazaar. And I always get an answer. It may be some trifling thing, apparently quite unconnected with the subject, but there it is. I had that text pinned over my bed when I was a little girl: *Ask and you shall receive.* On the morning that I am telling you about, I was walking along the High Street, and I was praying hard. I shut my eyes, and when I opened them, what do you think was the first thing that I saw?"

Five faces with varying degrees of interest were turned to
Miss Marple. It may be safely assumed, however, that no one
would have guessed the answer to the question right.

"I saw," said Miss Marple impressively, "the window of
the fishmonger's shop. There was only one thing in it, a
fresh haddock."

She looked round triumphantly.

"Oh, my God!" said Raymond West. "An answer to
prayer—a fresh haddock!"

"Yes, Raymond," said Miss Marple severely, "and there is
no need to be profane about it. The hand of God is everywhere. The first thing I saw were the black spots—the marks
of St. Peter's thumb. That is the legend, you know. St.
Peter's thumb. And that brought things home to me. I
needed faith, the ever-true faith of St. Peter. I connected the
two things together, faith—and fish."

Sir Henry blew his nose rather hurriedly. Joyce bit her lip.

"Now what did that bring to my mind? Of course, both
the cook and the house-parlourmaid mentioned fish as being
one of the things spoken of by the dying man. I was convinced, absolutely convinced, that there was some solution
of the mystery to be found in these words. I went home determined to get to the bottom of the matter."

She paused.

"Has it ever occurred to you," the old lady went on, "how
much we go by what is called, I believe, the context? There
is a place on Dartmoor called Grey Wethers. If you were
talking to a farmer there and mentioned Grey Wethers, he
would probably conclude that you were speaking of these
stone circles, yet it is possible that you might be speaking of
the atmosphere; and in the same way, if you were meaning
the stone circles, an outsider, hearing a fragment of the conversation, might think you meant the weather. So when we
repeat a conversation, we don't, as a rule, repeat the actual

words; we put in some other words that seem to us to mean exactly the same thing.

"I saw both the cook and Dorothy separately. I asked the cook if she was quite sure that her master had really mentioned a heap of fish. She said she was quite sure.

" 'Were these his exact words,' I asked, 'or did he mention some particular kind of fish?'

" 'That's it,' said the cook, 'it was some particular kind of fish, but I can't remember what now. A heap of—now what was it? Not any of the fish you send to table. Would it be a perch now—or pike? No. It didn't begin with a P.'

"Dorothy also recalled that her master had mentioned some special kind of fish. 'Some outlandish kind of fish it was,' she said.

" 'A pile of—now what was it?'

" 'Did he say heap or pile?' I asked.

" 'I think he said pile. But there, I really can't be sure—it's so hard to remember the actual words, isn't it, miss, especially when they don't seem to make sense. But now I come to think of it, I am pretty sure that it was a pile and the fish began with C; but it wasn't a cod or a crayfish.'

"The next part is where I am really proud of myself," said Miss Marple, "because, of course, I don't know anything about drugs—nasty, dangerous things I call them. I have got an old recipe of my grandmother's for tansy tea that is worth any amount of your drugs. But I knew that there were several medical volumes in the house, and in one of them there was an index of drugs. You see, my idea was that Geoffrey had taken some particular poison and was trying to say the name of it.

"Well, I looked down the list of H's, beginning He. Nothing there that sounded likely. Then I began on the P's, and almost at once I came to—what do you think?"

She looked round, postponing her moment of triumph.

"Pilocarpine. Can't you understand a man who could hardly speak trying to drag that word out? What would that sound like to a cook who had never heard the word? Wouldn't it convey the impression 'pile of carp?' "

"By Jove!" said Sir Henry.

"I should never have hit upon that," said Dr. Pender.

"Most interesting," said Mr. Petherick. "Really most interesting."

"I turned quickly to the page indicated in the index. I read about pilocarpine and its effect on the eyes and other things that didn't seem to have any bearing on the case, but at last I came to a most significant phrase: Has been tried with success as an antidote for atropine poisoning.

"I can't tell you the light that dawned upon me then. I never had thought it likely that Geoffrey Denman would commit suicide. No, this new solution was not only possible, but I was absolutely sure it was the correct one, because all the pieces fitted in logically."

"I am not going to try to guess," said Raymond. "Go on, Aunt Jane, and tell us what was so startlingly clear to you."

"I don't know anything about medicine, of course," said Miss Marple, "but I did happen to know this, that when my eyesight was failing, the doctor ordered me drops with atropine sulphate in them. I went straight upstairs to old Mr. Denman's room. I didn't beat about the bush.

" 'Mr. Denman,' I said, 'I know everything. Why did you poison your son?'

"He looked at me for a minute or two—rather a handsome old man he was, in his way—and then he burst out laughing. It was one of the most vicious laughs I have ever heard. I can assure you it made my flesh creep. I had only heard anything like it once before, when poor Mrs. Jones went off her head.

" 'Yes,' he said, 'I got even with Geoffrey. I was too clever for Geoffrey. He was going to put me away, was he? Have me shut up in an asylum? I heard them talking about it. Mabel is a good girl—Mabel stuck up for me, but I knew she wouldn't be able to stand up against Geoffrey. In the end he would have his own way; he always did. But I settled him—I settled my kind, loving son! Ha, ha! I crept down in the night. It was quite easy. Brewster was away. My dear son was asleep. He had a glass of water by the side of his bed; he always woke up in the middle of the night and drank it off. I poured it away—ha, ha!—and I emptied the bottle of eye drops into the glass. He would wake up and swill it down before he knew what it was. There was only a tablespoonful of it—quite enough, quite enough. And so he did! They came to me in the morning and broke it to me very gently. They were afraid it would upset me. Ha! Ha! Ha! Ha! Ha!'

"Well," said Miss Marple, "that is the end of the story. Of course, the poor old man was put in an asylum. He wasn't really responsible for what he had done, and the truth was known, and everyone was sorry for Mabel and could not do enough to make up to her for the unjust suspicions they had had. But if it hadn't been for Geoffrey realizing what the stuff was he had swallowed and trying to get everybody to get hold of the antidote without delay, it might never have been found out. I believe there are very definite symptoms with atropine—dilated pupils of the eyes, and all that; but, of course, as I have said, Dr. Rawlinson was very short-sighted, poor old man. And in the same medical book which I went on reading—and some of it was most interesting—it gave the symptoms of ptomaine poisoning and atropine, and they are not unlike. But I can assure you I have never seen a pile of fresh haddock without thinking of the thumbmark of St. Peter."

There was a very long pause.

"My dear friend," said Mr. Petherick, "my very dear friend, you really are amazing."

"I shall recommend Scotland Yard to come to you for advice," said Sir Henry.

"Well, at all events, Aunt Jane," said Raymond, "there is one thing that you don't know."

"Oh yes I do, dear," said Miss Marple. "It happened just before dinner, didn't it? When you took Joyce out to admire the sunset. It is a very favourite place, that. There by the jasmine hedge. That is where the milkman asked Annie if he could put up the banns."

"Dash it all, Aunt Jane," said Raymond, "don't spoil all the romance. Joyce and I aren't like the milkman and Annie."

"That is where you make a mistake, dear," said Miss Marple. "Everybody is very much alike, really. But fortunately, perhaps, they don't realize it."

The Blue
Geranium

W hen I was down here last year—" said Sir Henry
Clithering, and stopped.

His hostess, Mrs. Bantry, looked at him
curiously.

The ex-Commissioner of Scotland Yard was staying with
old friends of his, Colonel and Mrs. Bantry, who lived near
St. Mary Mead.

Mrs. Bantry, pen in hand, had just asked his advice as to
who should be invited to make a sixth guest at dinner that
evening.

"Yes?" said Mrs. Bantry encouragingly. "When you were
here last year?"

"Tell me," said Sir Henry, "do you know a Miss Marple?"

Mrs. Bantry was surprised. It was the last thing she had
expected.

"Know Miss Marple? Who doesn't! The typical old maid
of fiction. Quite a dear, but hopelessly behind the times. Do
you mean you would like me to ask her to dinner?"

"You are surprised?"

"A little, I must confess. I should hardly have thought
you—but perhaps there's an explanation?"

"The explanation is simple enough. When I was down

here last year we got into the habit of discussing unsolved mysteries—there were five or six of us. We each supplied a story to which we knew the answer, but nobody else did. It was supposed to be an exercise in the deductive faculties—to see who could get nearest the truth."

"Well?"

"Like in the old story—we hardly realized that Miss Marple was playing; but we were very polite about it—didn't want to hurt the old dear's feelings. And now comes the cream of the jest. The old lady outdid us every time!"

"But how extraordinary! Why, dear old Miss Marple has hardly ever been out of St. Mary Mead."

"Ah! But according to her, that has given her unlimited opportunities of observing human nature—under the microscope, as it were."

"I suppose there's something in that," conceded Mrs. Bantry. "One would at least know the petty side of people. But I don't think we have any really exciting criminals in our midst. I think we must try her with Arthur's ghost story after dinner. I'd be thankful if she'd find a solution to that."

"I didn't know that Arthur believed in ghosts?"

"Oh, he doesn't. That's what worries him so. And it happened to a friend of his, George Pritchard—a most prosaic person. It's really rather tragic for poor George. Either this extraordinary story is true—or else—"

"Or else what?"

Mrs. Bantry did not answer. After a minute or two she said irrelevantly:

"You know, I like George—everyone does. One can't believe that he—but people do such extraordinary things."

Sir Henry nodded. He knew, better than Mrs. Bantry, the extraordinary things that people did.

So it came about that that evening Mrs. Bantry looked around her dinner table (shivering a little as she did so, because the dining-room, like most English dining-rooms, was extremely cold) and fixed her gaze on the very upright old lady sitting on her husband's right. Miss Marple wore black lace mittens; an old lace fichu was draped round her shoulders and another piece of lace surmounted her white hair. She was talking animatedly to the elderly doctor, Dr. Lloyd, about the workhouse and the suspected shortcomings of the district nurse.

Mrs. Bantry marvelled anew. She even wondered whether Sir Henry had been making an elaborate joke—but there seemed no point in that. Incredible that what he had said could be really true.

Her glance went on and rested affectionately on her red-faced broad-shouldered husband as he sat talking horses to Jane Helier, the beautiful and popular actress. Jane, more beautiful (if that were possible) off the stage than on, opened enormous blue eyes and murmured at discreet intervals, "Really?" "Oh, Fancy!" "How extraordinary!" She knew nothing whatever about horses and cared less.

"Arthur," said Mrs. Bantry, "you're boring poor Jane to distraction. Leave your horses alone and tell her your ghost story instead. You know . . . George Pritchard."

"Eh, Dolly? Oh, but I don't know—"

"Sir Henry wants to hear it too. I was telling him something about it this morning. It would be interesting to hear what everyone has to say about it."

"Oh, do!" said Jane. "I love ghost stories."

"Well—" Colonel Bantry hesitated. "I've never believed much in the supernatural. But this . . .

"I don't think any of you know George Pritchard. He's one of the best. His wife—well, she's dead now, poor woman. I'll just say this much: she didn't give George any too easy a time when she was alive. She was one of those semi-invalids—I believe she really had something wrong with her, but whatever it was, she played it for all it was worth. She was capricious, exacting, unreasonble. She complained from morning to night. George was expected to wait on her hand and foot, and everything he did was always wrong."

"She was a dreadful woman," said Mrs. Bantry with conviction.

"I don't quite know how this business started. George was rather vague about it. I gather Mrs. Pritchard had always had a weakness for fortunetellers, palmists, clairvoyants—anything of that sort. George didn't mind. If she found amusement in it, well and good. But he refused to go into rhapsodies himself, and that was another grievance.

"A succession of hospital nurses was always passing through the house. Mrs. Pritchard usually becoming dissatisfied with them after a few weeks. One young nurse had been very keen on this fortunetelling stunt, and for a time Mrs. Pritchard had been very fond of her. Then she suddenly fell out with her and insisted on her going. She had back another nurse who had been with her previously—an older woman, experienced and tactful in dealing with a neurotic patient. Nurse Copling, according to George, was a very good sort—a sensible woman to talk to. She put up with Mrs. Pritchard's tantrums and nerve storms with complete indifference.

"Mrs. Pritchard always lunched upstairs, and it was usual at lunch time for George and the nurse to come to some arrangement for the afternoon. Strictly speaking, the nurse went off from two to four, but 'to oblige,' as the phrase goes, she would sometimes take her time off after tea if George wanted to be free for the afternoon. On this occasion she mentioned that she was going to see a sister at Golders Green and might be a little late returning. George's face fell, for he had arranged to play a round of golf. Nurse Copling, however, reassured him.

" 'We'll neither of us be missed, Mr. Pritchard.' A twinkle came into her eye. 'Mrs. Pritchard's going to have more exciting company than ours.'

" 'Who's that?'

" 'Wait a minute.' Nurse Copling's eyes twinkled more than ever. 'Let me get it right, *Zarida, Psychic Reader of the Future.*'

" 'That's a new one, isn't it?' groaned George.

" 'Quite new. I believe my predecessor, Nurse Carstairs, sent her along. Mrs. Pritchard hasn't seen her yet. She made me write, fixing an appointment for this afternoon.'

" 'Well, at any rate, I shall get my golf,' said George, and he went off with the kindliest feelings toward Zarida, the reader of the future.

"On his return to the house, he found Mrs. Pritchard in a state of great agitation. She was, as usual, lying on her invalid couch, and she had a bottle of smelling salts in her hand which she sniffed at frequent intervals.

" 'George,' she exclaimed, 'what did I tell you about this house? The moment I came into it, I felt there was something wrong! Didn't I tell you so at the time?'

"Repressing his desire to reply, 'You always do,' George said, 'No, can't say I remember it.'

" 'You never do remember anything that has to do with me. Men are all extraordinarily callous—but I really believe that you are even more insensitive than most.'

" 'Oh, come now, Mary dear, that's not fair.'

" 'Well, as I was telling you, this woman knew at once! She—she actually blenched—if you know what I mean—as she came in at that door, and she said, "There is evil here—evil and danger. I feel it." '

"Very unwisely, George laughed.

" 'Well, you have had your money's worth this afternoon.'

"His wife closed her eyes and took a long sniff from her smelling bottle.

" 'How you hate me! You would jeer and laugh if I were dying.'

"George protested, and after a minute or two she went on.

" 'You may laugh, but I shall tell you the whole thing. This house is definitely dangerous to me—the woman said so.'

"George's formerly kind feeling toward Zarida underwent a change. He knew his wife was perfectly capable of insisting on moving to a new house if the caprice got hold of her.

" 'What else did she say?' he asked.

" 'She couldn't tell me very much. She was so upset. One thing she did say. I had some violets in a glass. She pointed at them and cried out:

" ' "Take those away. No blue flowers—never have blue flowers. Blue flowers are fatal to you—remember that." '

" 'And you know,' added Mrs. Pritchard, 'I always have told you that blue as a colour is repellent to me. I feel a natural instinctive sort of warning against it.'

"George was much too wise to remark that he had never heard her say so before. Instead he asked what the mysterious Zarida was like. Mrs. Pritchard entered with gusto upon a description.

" 'Black hair in coiled knobs over her ears—her eyes were half closed—great black rims round them—she had a black veil over her mouth and chin—she spoke in a kind of singing voice with a marked foreign accent—Spanish, I think—'

" 'In fact, all the usual stock in trade,' said George cheerfully.

"His wife immediately closed her eyes.

" 'I feel extremely ill,' she said. 'Ring for Nurse. Unkindness upsets me, as you know only too well.'

"It was two days later that Nurse Copling came to George with a grave face.

" 'Will you come to Mrs. Pritchard, please. She has had a letter which upsets her greatly.'

"He found his wife with the letter in her hand. She held it out to him.

" 'Read it,' she said.

"George read it. It was on heavily scented paper, and the writing was big and black.

I have seen the Future. Be warned before it is too late. Beware of the full moon. The Blue Primrose means Warning; the Blue Hollyhock means Danger; the Blue Geranium means Death. . . .

"Just about to burst out laughing, George caught Nurse Copling's eye. She made a quick warning gesture. He said rather awkwardly, 'The woman's probably trying to frighten you, Mary. Anyway, there aren't such things as blue primroses and blue geraniums.'

"But Mrs. Pritchard began to cry and say her days were numbered. Nurse Copling came out with George upon the landing.

" 'Of all the silly tomfoolery,' he burst out.

" 'I suppose it is.'

"Something in the nurse's tone struck him, and he stared at her in amazement.

" 'Surely, Nurse, you don't believe—'

" 'No, no, Mr. Pritchard. I don't believe in reading the future—that's nonsense. What puzzles me is the meaning of this. Fortunetellers are usually out for what they can get. But this woman seems to be frightening Mrs. Pritchard with no advantage to herself. I can't see the point. There's another thing—'

" 'Yes?'

" 'Mrs. Pritchard says that something about Zarida was faintly familiar to her.'

" 'Well?'

" 'Well, I don't like it, Mr. Pritchard, that's all.'

" 'I didn't know you were so superstitious, Nurse.'

" 'I'm not superstitious, but I know when a thing is fishy.'

"It was about four days after this that the first incident happened. To explain it to you, I shall have to describe Mrs. Pritchard's room—"

"You'd better let me do that," interrupted Mrs. Bantry.

"It was papered with one of these new wallpapers where you apply clumps of flowers to make a kind of herbaceous border. The effect is almost like being in a garden—though, of course, the flowers are all wrong. I mean they simply couldn't be in bloom all at the same time—"

"Don't let a passion for horticultural accuracy run away with you, Dolly," said her husband. "We all know you're an enthusiastic gardener."

"Well, it is absurd," protested Mrs. Bantry. "To have bluebells and daffodils and lupins and hollyhocks and Michaelmas daisies all grouped together."

"Most unscientific," said Sir Henry. "But to proceed with the story . . ."

"Well, among these massed flowers were primroses, clumps of yellow and pink primroses, and—oh, go on, Arthur, this is your story."

Colonel Bantry took up the tale.

"Mrs. Pritchard rang her bell violently one morning. The household came running—thought she was in extremis; not at all. She was violently excited and pointing at the wallpaper, and there, sure enough, was one blue primrose in the midst of the others . . ."

"Oh!" said Miss Helier, "how creepy!"

"The question was: Hadn't the blue primrose always been there? That was George's suggestion and the nurse's. But Mrs. Pritchard wouldn't have it at any price. She had never noticed it till that very morning, and the night before had been full moon. She was very upset about it."

"I met George Pritchard that same day and he told me about it," said Mrs. Bantry. "I went to see Mrs. Pritchard and did my best to ridicule the whole thing, but without success. I came away really concerned, and I remember I met Jean Instow and told her about it. Jean is a queer girl. She said, 'So she's really upset about it?' I told her that I thought the woman was perfectly capable of dying of fright—she was really abnormally superstitious.

"I remember Jean rather startled me with what she said next. She said, 'Well, that might be all for the best, mightn't it?' And she said it so coolly, in so matter-of-fact a tone, that I was really—well, shocked. Of course I know it's done nowadays—to be brutal and outspoken, but I never get used to it. Jean smiled at me rather oddly and said, 'You don't like my saying that—but it's true. What use is Mrs. Pritchard's life to her? None at all, and it's hell for George Pritchard. To have his wife frightened out of existence would be the best thing that could happen to him.' I said, 'George is most awfully good to her always.' And she said, 'Yes, he deserves a reward, poor dear. He's a very attractive person, George Pritchard. The last nurse thought so—the pretty one—what was her name? Carstairs. That was the cause of the row between her and Mrs. P.'

"Now I didn't like hearing Jean say that. Of course, one had wondered—"

Mrs. Bantry paused significantly.

"Yes, dear," said Miss Marple placidly. "One always does. Is Miss Instow a pretty girl? I suppose she plays golf?"

"Yes. She's good at all games. And she's nice-looking, attractive-looking, very fair with a healthy skin and nice steady blue eyes. Of course, we always have felt that she and George Pritchard—I mean, if things had been different—they are so well suited to one another."

"And they were friends?" asked Miss Marple.

"Oh yes. Great friends."

"Do you think, Dolly," said Colonel Bantry plaintively, "that I might be allowed to go on with my story?"

"Arthur," said Mrs. Bantry resignedly, "wants to get back to his ghosts."

"I had the rest of the story from George himself," went on the colonel. "There's no doubt that Mrs. Pritchard got the wind up badly toward the end of the next month. She marked off on a calendar the day when the moon would be full, and on that night she had both the nurse and then George into her room and made them study the wallpaper carefully. There were pink hollyhocks and red ones, but there were no blue among them. Then when George left the room she locked the door—"

"And in the morning there was a large blue hollyhock," said Miss Helier joyfully.

"Quite right," said Colonel Bantry. "Or at any rate, nearly right. One flower of a hollyhock just above her head had turned blue. It staggered George, and of course, the more it staggered him the more he refused to take the thing seriously. He insisted that the whole thing was some kind of a practical joke. He ignored the evidence of the locked door and the fact that Mrs. Pritchard discovered the change before anyone—even Nurse Copling—was admitted.

"It staggered George, and it made him unreasonable. His wife wanted to leave the house, and he wouldn't let her. He was inclined to believe in the supernatural for the first time, but he wasn't going to admit it. He usually gave in to his wife, but this time he wouldn't. Mary was not to make a fool of herself, he said. The whole thing was the most infernal nonsense.

"And so the next month sped away. Mrs. Pritchard made less protest than one would have imagined. I think she was superstitious enough to believe that she couldn't escape her fate. She repeated again and again: 'The blue primrose—warning. The blue hollyhock—danger. The blue geranium—death.' And she would lie looking at the clump of pinky-red geraniums nearest her bed.

"The whole business was pretty nervy. Even the nurse caught the infection. She came to George two days before full moon and begged him to take Mrs. Pritchard away. George was angry.

" 'If all the flowers on that wall turned into blue devils, it couldn't kill anyone!' he shouted.

" 'It might. Shock has killed people before now.'

" 'Nonsense,' said George.

"George has always been a shade pigheaded. You can't drive him. I believe he had a secret idea that his wife worked the changes herself and that it was all some morbid, hysterical plan of hers.

"Well, the fatal night came. Mrs. Pritchard locked her door as usual. She was very calm—in almost an exalted state of mind. The nurse was worried by her state—and wanted to give her a stimulant, an injection of strychnine, but Mrs. Pritchard refused. In a way, I believe, she was enjoying herself. George said she was."

"I think that's quite possible," said Mrs. Bantry. "There must have been a strange sort of glamour about the whole thing."

"There was no violent ringing of a bell the next morning. Mrs. Pritchard usually woke about eight. When, at eight-thirty, there was no sign from her, Nurse rapped loudly on the door. Getting no reply, she fetched George and insisted on the door being broken open. They did so with the help of a chisel.

"One look at the still figure on the bed was enough for Nurse Copling. She sent George to telephone for the doctor, but it was too late. Mrs. Pritchard, he said, must have been dead at least eight hours. Her smelling salts lay by her hand on the bed, and on the wall beside her one of the pinky-red geraniums was a bright deep blue."

"Horrible," said Miss Helier with a shiver.

Sir Henry was frowning.

"No additional details?"

Colonel Bantry shook his head, but Mrs. Bantry spoke quickly.

"The gas."

"What about the gas?" asked Sir Henry.

"When the doctor arrived there was a slight smell of gas, and sure enough, he found the gas ring in the fireplace very slightly turned on, but so little that it couldn't have mattered."

"Did Mr. Pritchard and the nurse not notice it when they first went in?"

"The nurse said she did notice a slight smell. George said he didn't notice gas, but something made him feel very queer and overcome; but he put that down to shock—and probably it was. At any rate, there was no question of gas poisoning. The smell was scarcely noticeable."

"And that's the end of the story?"

"No, it isn't. One way and another, there was a lot of talk. The servants, you see, had overheard things—had heard, for instance, Mrs. Pritchard telling her husband that he hated her and would jeer if she were dying. And also more recent remarks. She said one day, apropos of his refusing to leave the house, 'Very well. When I am dead, I hope everyone will realize that you have killed me.' And as ill luck would have it, he had been mixing some weed killer for the garden paths the very day before. One of the younger servants had seen him and had afterward seen him taking up a glass of hot milk to his wife.

"The talk spread and grew. The doctor had given a certificate—I don't know exactly in what terms—shock, syncope, heart failure, probably some medical term meaning nothing much. However, the poor lady had not been a month in her grave before an exhumation order was applied for and granted."

"And the result of the autopsy was nil, I remember," said Sir Henry gravely. "A case, for once, of smoke without fire."

"The whole thing is really very curious," said Mrs. Bantry. "That fortuneteller, for instance—Zarida. At the address where she was supposed to be, no one had ever heard of any such person!"

"She appeared once—out of the blue," said her husband, "and then utterly vanished. Out of the blue—that's rather good!"

"And what is more," continued Mrs. Bantry, "little Nurse Carstairs, who was supposed to have recommended her, had never even heard of her."

They looked at each other.

"It's a mysterious story," said Dr. Lloyd. "One can make guesses, but to guess—"

He shook his head.

"Has Mr. Pritchard married Miss Instow?" asked Miss Marple in her gentle voice.

"Now why do you ask that?" inquired Sir Henry.

Miss Marple opened gentle blue eyes.

"It seems to me so important," she said. "Have they married?"

Colonel Bantry shook his head.

"We—well, we expected something of the kind—but it's eighteen months now. I don't believe they even see much of each other."

"That is important," said Miss Marple. "Very important."

"Then you think the same as I do," said Mrs. Bantry. "You think—"

"Now, Dolly," said her husband. "It's unjustifiable—what you're going to say. You can't go about accusing people without a shadow of proof."

"Don't be so—so manly, Arthur. Men are always afraid to say anything. Anyway, this is all between ourselves. It's just a wild, fantastic idea of mine that possibly—only possibly—Jean Instow disguised herself as a fortuneteller. Mind you, she may have done it for a joke. I don't for a minute think that she meant any harm; but if she did do it, and if Mrs. Pritchard was foolish enough to die of fright—well, that's what Miss Marple meant, wasn't it?"

"No, dear, not quite," said Miss Marple. "You see, if I were going to kill anyone—which, of course, I wouldn't dream of doing for a minute, because it would be very wicked, and besides, I don't like killing—not even wasps, though I know it has to be, and I'm sure the gardener does it as humanely as possible. Let me see, what was I saying?"

"If you wished to kill anyone," prompted Sir Henry.

"Oh yes. Well, if I did, I shouldn't be at all satisfied to trust to fright. I know one reads of people dying of it, but it seems a very uncertain sort of thing, and the most nervous people are far more brave than one really thinks they are. I should like something definite and certain and make a thoroughly good plan about it."

"Miss Marple," said Sir Henry, "you frighten me. I hope you will never wish to remove me. Your plans would be too good."

Miss Marple looked at him reproachfully.

"I thought I had made it clear that I would never contemplate such wickedness," she said. "No, I was trying to put myself in the place of—er—a certain person."

"Do you mean George Pritchard?" asked Colonel Bantry. "I'll never believe it of George—though, mind you, even the nurse believes it. I went and saw her about a month afterward, at the time of the exhumation. She didn't know how it was done—in fact, she wouldn't say anything at all—but it was clear enough that she believed George to be in some way responsible for his wife's death. She was convinced of it."

"Well," said Dr. Lloyd, "perhaps she wasn't so far wrong. And mind you, a nurse often knows. She can't say—she's got no proof—but she knows."

Sir Henry leaned forward.

"Come now, Miss Marple," he said persuasively. "You're lost in a daydream. Won't you tell us all about it?"

Miss Marple started and turned pink.

"I beg your pardon," she said. "I was just thinking about our district nurse. A most difficult problem."

"More difficult than the problem of a blue geranium?"

"It really depends on the primroses," said Miss Marple. "I mean, Mrs. Bantry said they were yellow and pink. If it was a pink primrose that turned blue, of course, that fits in perfectly. But if it happened to be a yellow one—"

"It was a pink one," said Mrs. Bantry.

She stared. They all stared at Miss Marple.

"Then that seems to settle it," said Miss Marple. She shook her head regretfully. "And the wasp season and everything. And of course the gas."

"It reminds you, I suppose, of countless village tragedies?" said Sir Henry.

"Not tragedies," said Miss Marple. "And certainly nothing criminal. But it does remind me a little of the trouble we are having with the district nurse. After all, nurses are human beings, and what with having to be so correct in their behaviour and wearing those uncomfortable collars and being so thrown with the family—well, can you wonder that things sometimes happen?"

A glimmer of light broke upon Sir Henry.

"You mean Nurse Carstairs?"

"Oh no. Not Nurse Carstairs. Nurse Copling. You see, she had been there before and very much thrown with Mr. Pritchard, who you say is an attractive man. I daresay she thought, poor thing—well, we needn't go into that. I don't suppose she knew about Miss Instow, and of course afterward, when she found out, it turned her against him and she tried to do all the harm she could. Of course, the letter really gave her away, didn't it?"

"What letter?"

"Well, she wrote to the fortuneteller at Mrs. Pritchard's request, and the fortuneteller came, apparently in answer to the letter. But later it was discovered that there never had been such a person at that address. So that shows that Nurse Copling was in it. She only pretended to write—so what could be more likely than that she was the fortuneteller herself?"

"I never saw the point about the letter," said Sir Henry. "That's a most important point, of course."

"Rather a bold step to take," said Miss Marple, "because Mrs. Pritchard might have recognized her in spite of the disguise—though of course if she had, the nurse could have pretended it was a joke."

"What did you mean," said Sir Henry, "when you said that if you were a certain person, you would not have trusted to fright?"

"One couldn't be sure that way," said Miss Marple. "No, I think that the warnings and the blue flowers were, if I may use a military term"—she laughed self-consciously—"just camouflage."

"And the real thing?"

"I know," said Miss Marple apologetically, "that I've got wasps on the brain. Poor things, destroyed in their thousands—and usually on such a beautiful summer's day. But I remember thinking, when I saw the gardener shaking up the cyanide of potassium in a bottle with water, how like smelling salts it looked. And if it were put in a smelling-salt bottle and substituted for the real one—well, the poor lady was in the habit of using her smelling salts. Indeed, you said they were found by her hand. Then, of course, while Mr. Pritchard went to telephone to the doctor, the nurse would change it for the real bottle, and she'd just turn on the gas a little bit to mask any smell of almonds and in case anyone felt queer, and I always have heard the cyanide leaves no trace if you wait long enough. But, of course, I may be wrong, and it may have been something entirely different in the bottle, but that doesn't really matter, does it?"

Miss Marple paused, a little out of breath.

Jane Helier leaned forward and said, "But the blue geranium and the other flowers?"

"Nurses always have litmus paper, don't they?" said Miss Marple, "for—well, for testing. Not a very pleasant subject. We won't dwell on it. I have done a little nursing myself." She grew delicately pink. "Blue turns red with acids, and red turns blue with alkalies. So easy to paste some red litmus over a red flower—near the bed, of course. And then, when the poor lady used her smelling salts, the strong ammonia fumes would turn it blue. Really most ingenious. Of course, the geranium wasn't blue when they first broke into the room—nobody noticed it till afterward. When nurse changed the bottles, she held the sal ammoniac against the wallpaper for a minute, I expect."

"You might have been there, Miss Marple," said Sir Henry.

"What worries me," said Miss Marple, "is poor Mr. Pritchard and that nice girl, Miss Instow. Probably both suspecting each other and keeping apart—and life so very short."

She shook her head.

"You needn't worry," said Sir Henry. "As a matter of fact, I have something up my sleeve. A nurse has been arrested on a charge of murdering an elderly patient who had left her a legacy. It was done with cyanide of potassium substituted for smelling salts. Nurse Copling trying the same trick again. Miss Instow and Mr. Pritchard need have no doubts as to the truth."

"Now isn't that nice?" cried Miss Marple. "I don't mean about the new murder, of course. That's very sad and shows how much wickedness there is in the world and that if once you give away—which reminds me, I must finish my little conversation with Dr. Lloyd about the village nurse."

The Companion

Now, Dr. Lloyd," said Miss Helier, "don't you know any creepy stories?"

She smiled at him—the smile that nightly bewitched the theater-going public. Jane Helier was sometimes called the most beautiful woman in England, and jealous members of her own profession were in the habit of saying to each other: "Of course Jane's not an artist. She can't act—if you know what I mean. It's those eyes!"

And those "eyes" were at this minute fixed appealingly on the grizzled elderly bachelor doctor who, for the last five years, had ministered to the ailments of the village of St. Mary Mead.

With an unconscious gesture, the doctor pulled down his waistcoat (inclined of late to be uncomfortably tight) and racked his brains hastily, so as not to disappoint the lovely creature who addressed him so confidently.

"I feel," said Jane dreamily, "that I would like to wallow in crime this evening."

"Splendid," said Colonel Bantry, her host. "Splendid, splendid." And he laughed a loud, hearty military laugh. "Eh, Dolly?"

His wife, hastily recalled to the exigencies of social life

(she had been planning her spring border), agreed enthusiastically.

"Of course it's splendid," she said heartily but vaguely. "I always thought so."

"Did you, my dear?" said old Miss Marple, and her eyes twinkled a little.

"We don't get much in the creepy line—and still less in the criminal line—in St. Mary Mead, you know, Miss Helier," said Dr. Lloyd.

"You surprise me," said Sir Henry Clithering. The ex-Commissioner of Scotland Yard turned to Miss Marple. "I always understood from our friend here that St. Mary Mead is a positive hotbed of crime and vice."

"Oh, Sir Henry!" protested Miss Marple, a spot of colour coming into her cheeks. "I'm sure I never said anything of the kind. The only thing I ever said was that human nature is much the same in a village as anywhere else, only one has opportunities and leisure for seeing it at closer quarters."

"But you haven't always lived here," said Jane Helier, still addressing the doctor. "You've been in all sorts of queer places all over the world—places where things happen!"

"That is so, of course," said Dr. Lloyd, still thinking desperately. "Yes, of course ... Yes ... Ah! I have it!"

He sank back with a sigh of relief.

"It is some years ago now—I had almost forgotten. But the facts were really very strange—very strange indeed. And the final coincidence which put the clue into my hand was strange also."

Miss Helier drew her chair a little nearer to him, applied some lipstick, and waited expectantly. The others also turned interested faces toward him.

"I don't know whether any of you know the Canary Islands," began the doctor.

"They must be wonderful," said Jane Helier. "They're in

the South Seas, aren't they? Or is it the Mediterranean?"

"I've called in there on my way to South Africa," said the colonel. "The Peak of Teneriffe is a fine sight with the setting sun on it."

"The incident I am describing happened in the island of Grand Canary, not Teneriffe. It is a good many years ago now. I had had a breakdown in health and was forced to give up my practice in England to go abroad. I practised in Las Palmas, which is the principal town of Grand Canary. In many ways I enjoyed the life out there very much. The climate was mild and sunny, there was excellent surf bathing (and I am an enthusiastic bather), and the sea life of the port attracted me. Ships from all over the world put in at Las Palmas. I used to walk along the mole every morning, far more interested than any member of the fair sex could be in a street of hat shops.

"As I say, ships from all over the world put in at Las Palmas. Sometimes they stay a few hours, sometimes a day or two. In the principal hotel there, the Metropole, you will see people of all races and nationalities—birds of passage. Even the people going to Teneriffe usually come here and stay a few days before crossing to the other island.

"My story begins there, in the Metropole Hotel, one Thursday evening in January. There was a dance going on and I and a friend had been sitting at a small table watching the scene. There was a fair sprinkling of English and other nationalities, but the majority of the dancers were Spanish; and when the orchestra struck up a tango, only half a dozen couples of the latter nationality took the floor. They all danced well and we looked on and admired. One woman in particular excited our lively admiration. Tall, beautiful, and sinuous, she moved with the grace of a half-tamed leopardess. There was something dangerous about her. I said as much to my friend and he agreed.

" 'Women like that,' he said, 'are bound to have a history. Life will not pass them by.'

" 'Beauty is perhaps a dangerous possession,' I said.

" 'It's not only beauty,' he insisted. 'There is something else. Look at her again. Things are bound to happen to that woman, or because of her. As I said, life will not pass her by. Strange and exciting events will surround her. You've only got to look at her to know it.'

"He paused and then added with a smile:

" 'Just as you've only got to look at those two women over there and know that nothing out of the way could ever happen to either of them! They are made for a safe and un-eventful existence.'

"I followed his eyes. The two women he referred to were travellers who had just arrived—a Holland Lloyd boat had put into port that evening, and the passengers were just be-ginning to arrive.

"As I looked at them I saw at once what my friend meant. They were two English ladies—the thoroughly nice travel-ling English that you do find abroad. Their ages, I should say, were round about forty. One was fair and a little—just a little—too plump; the other was dark and a little—again just a little—inclined to scragginess. They were what is called well-preserved, quietly and inconspicuously dressed in well-cut tweeds, and innocent of any kind of make-up. They had that air of quiet assurance which is the birthright of well-bred Englishwomen. There was nothing remarkable about either of them. They were like thousands of their sisters. They would doubtless see what they wished to see, assisted by Baedeker, and be blind to everything else. They would use the English library and attend the English church in any place they happened to be, and it was quite likely that one or both of them sketched a little. And as my friend said, noth-ing exciting or remarkable would ever happen to either of them, though they might quite likely travel half over the world. I looked from them back to our sinuous Spanish woman with her half-closed smouldering eyes and I smiled."

"Poor things," said Jane Helier with a sigh. "But I do think it's so silly of people not to make the most of themselves. That woman in Bond Street—Valentine—is really wonderful. Audrey Denman goes to her; and have you seen her in *The Downward Step*? As the schoolgirl in the first act she's really marvellous. And yet Audrey is fifty if she's a day. As a matter of fact, I happen to know she's really nearer sixty."

"Go on," said Mrs. Bantry to Dr. Lloyd. "I love stories about sinuous Spanish dancers. It makes me forget how old and fat I am."

"I'm sorry," said Dr. Lloyd apologetically. "But you see, as a matter of fact, this story isn't about the Spanish woman."

"It isn't?"

"No. As it happens, my friend and I were wrong. Nothing in the least exciting happened to the Spanish beauty. She married a clerk in a shipping office, and by the time I left the island she had had five children and was getting very fat."

"Just like that girl of Israel Peters," commented Miss Marple. "The one who went on the stage and had such good legs that they made her principal boy in the pantomime. Everyone said she'd come to no good, but she married a commercial traveller and settled down splendidly."

"The village parallel," murmured Sir Henry softly.

"No," went on the doctor, "my story is about the two English ladies."

"Something happened to them?" breathed Miss Helier.

"Something happened to them—and the very next day too."

"Yes?" said Mrs. Bantry encouragingly.

"Just for curiosity, as I went out that evening, I glanced at the hotel register. I found the names easily enough. Miss Marty Barton and Miss Amy Durrant of Little Paddocks, Caughton Weir, Bucks. I little thought then how soon I was to encounter the owners of those names again—and under what tragic circumstances.

"The following day I had arranged to go for a picnic with some friends. We were to motor across the island, taking our lunch, to a place called (as far as I remember—it is so long ago) Las Nieves, a well-sheltered bay where we could bathe if we felt inclined. This programme we duly carried out, except that we were somewhat late in starting, so that we stopped on the way and picnicked, going on to Las Nieves afterward for a swim before tea.

"As we approached the beach, we were at once aware of a tremendous commotion. The whole population of the small village seemed to be gathered on the shore. As soon as they saw us they rushed toward the car and began explaining excitedly. My Spanish not being very good, it took me a few minutes to understand, but at last I got it.

"Two of the mad English ladies had gone in to bathe, and one had swum out too far and got into difficulties. The other had gone after her and had tried to bring her in, but her strength in turn had failed and she, too, would have drowned had not a man rowed out in a boat and brought in rescuer and rescued—the latter beyond help.

"As soon as I got the hang of things I pushed the crowd aside and hurried down the beach. I did not at first recognize the two women. The plump figure in the tight green rubber bathing cap awoke no chord of recognition as she looked up anxiously. She was kneeling beside the body of her friend, making somewhat amateurish attempts at artificial respiration. When I told her that I was a doctor she gave a sigh of relief, and I ordered her off at once to one of the cottages for a rubdown and dry clothing. One of the ladies in my party

went with her. I myself worked unavailingly on the body of
the drowned woman. Life was only too clearly extinct, and
in the end I had reluctantly to give in.

"I rejoined the others in the small fisherman's cottage and
there I had to break the sad news. The survivor was attired
now in her own clothes, and I immediately recognized her as
one of the two arrivals of the night before. She received the
sad news fairly calmly, and it was evidently the horror of the
whole thing that struck her more than any great personal
feeling.

" 'Poor Amy,' she said. 'Poor, poor Amy. She had been
looking forward to the bathing here so much. And she was a
good swimmer too. I can't understand it. What do you
think it can have been, Doctor?'

" 'Possibly cramp. Will you tell me exactly what happened?'

" 'We had both been swimming about for some time—
twenty minutes, I should say. Then I thought I would go in,
but Amy said she was going to swim out once more. She did
so, and suddenly I heard her call and realized she was calling
for help. I swam out as fast as I could. She was still afloat
when I got to her, but she clutched at me wildly and we
both went under. If it hadn't been for that man coming out
with his boat, I should have been drowned too.'

" 'That has happened fairly often,' I said. 'To save anyone
from drowning is not an easy affair.'

" 'It seems so awful,' continued Miss Barton. 'We only arrived yesterday and were so delighting in the sunshine and
our little holiday. And now this—this terrible tragedy
occurs.'

"I asked her then for particulars about the dead woman,
explaining that I would do everything I could for her, but
that the Spanish authorities would require full information.
This she gave me readily enough.

"The dead woman, Miss Amy Durrant, was her companion and had come to her about five months previously. They had got on very well together, but Miss Durrant had spoken very little about her people. She had been left an orphan at an early age and had been brought up by an uncle and had earned her own living since she was twenty-one.

"And so that was that," went on the doctor. He paused and said again, but this time with a certain finality in his voice, "And so that was that."

"I don't understand," said Jane Helier. "Is that all? I mean, it's very tragic, I suppose, but isn't—well, it isn't what I call creepy."

"I think there's more to follow," said Sir Henry.

"Yes," said Dr. Lloyd, "there's more to follow. You see, right at the time there was one queer thing. Of course, I asked questions of the fishermen, et cetera, as to what they'd seen. They were eyewitnesses. And one woman had rather a funny story. I didn't pay any attention to it at the time, but it came back to me afterward. She insisted, you see, that Miss Durrant wasn't in difficulties when she called out. The other swam out to her and, according to this woman, deliberately held Miss Durrant's head under water. I didn't, as I say, pay much attention. It was such a fantastic story, and these things look so differently from the shore. Miss Barton might have tried to make her friend lose consciousness, realizing that the latter's panic-stricken clutching would drown them both. You see, according to the Spanish woman's story, it looked as though—well, as though Miss Barton was deliberately trying to drown her companion.

"As I say, I paid very little attention to this story at the time. It came back to me later. Our great difficulty was to find out anything about this woman, Amy Durrant. She didn't seem to have any relations. Miss Barton and I went through her things together. We found one address and wrote there, but it proved to be simply a room she had taken in which to keep some of her things. The landlady knew nothing, had only seen her when she took the room. Miss Durrant had remarked at the time that she always liked to have one place she could call her own to which she could return at any moment. There were one or two nice pieces of old furniture and some bound numbers of Academy pictures, and a trunk full of pieces of material bought at sales, but no personal belongings. She had mentioned to the landlady that her father and mother had died in India when she was a child and that she had been brought up by an uncle who was a clergyman, but she did not say if he was her father's or her mother's brother, so the name was no guide.

"It wasn't exactly mysterious, it was just unsatisfactory. There must be many lonely women, proud and reticent, in just that position. There were a couple of photographs among her belongings in Las Palmas—rather old and faded, and they had been cut to fit the frames they were in, so that there was no photographer's name upon them, and there was an old daguerreotype which might have been her mother or more probably her grandmother.

"Miss Barton had had two references with her. One she had forgotten; the other name she recollected after an effort. It proved to be that of a lady who was now abroad, having gone to Australia. She was written to. Her answer, of course, was a long time in coming, and I may say that when it did arrive there was no particular help to be gained from it. She said Miss Durrant had been with her as companion and had been most efficient and that she was a very charming woman, but that she knew nothing of her private affairs or relations.

"So there it was—as I say, nothing unusual, really. It was just the two things together that aroused my uneasiness. This Amy Durrant of whom no one knew anything, and the

Spanish woman's queer story. Yes, and I'll add a third thing: When I was first bending over the body and Miss Barton was walking away toward the huts, she looked back. Looked back with an expression on her face that I can only describe as one of poignant anxiety—a kind of anguished uncertainty that imprinted itself on my brain.

"It didn't strike me as anything unusual at the time. I put it down to her terrible distress over her friend. But, you see, later I realized that they weren't on those terms. There was no devoted attachment between them, no terrible grief. Miss Barton was fond of Amy Durrant and shocked by her death—that was all.

"But, then, why that terrible poignant anxiety? That was the question that kept coming back to me. I had not been mistaken in that look. And almost against my will an answer began to shape itself in my mind. Supposing the Spanish woman's story were true; supposing that Mary Barton wilfully and in cold blood tried to drown Amy Durrant. She succeeds in holding her under water while pretending to be saving her. She is rescued by a boat. They are on a lonely beach far from anywhere. And then I appear—the last thing she expects. A doctor! And an English doctor! She knows well enough that people who have been under water far longer than Amy Durrant had been revived by artificial respiration. But she has to play her part—to go off, leaving me alone with her victim. And as she turns for one last look, a terrible poignant anxiety shows in her face. Will Amy Durrant come back to life and tell what she knows?"

"Oh!" said Jane Helier. "I'm thrilled now."

"Viewed in that aspect, the whole business seemed more sinister, and the personality of Amy Durrant became more mysterious. Who was Amy Durrant? Why should she, an insignificant paid companion, be murdered by her employer? What story lay behind that fatal bathing expedition? She had entered Mary Barton's employment only a few months before. Mary Barton had brought her abroad, and the very day after they landed the tragedy had occurred. And they were both nice, commonplace, refined Englishwomen! The whole thing was fantastic, and I told myself so. I had been letting my imagination run away with me."

"You didn't do anything, then?" asked Miss Helier.

"My dear young lady, what could I do? There was no evidence. The majority of the eyewitnesses told the same story as Miss Barton. I had built up my own suspicions out of a fleeting expression which I might quite possibly have imagined. The only thing I could and did do was to see that the widest inquiries were made for the relations of Amy Durrant. The next time I was in England I even went and saw the landlady of her room, with the results I have told you."

"But you felt there was something wrong," said Miss Marple.

Dr. Lloyd nodded.

"Half the time I was ashamed of myself for thinking so. Who was I to go suspecting this nice, pleasant-mannered English lady of a foul and cold-blooded crime? I did my best to be as cordial as possible to her during the short time she stayed on the island. I helped her with the Spanish authorities. I did everything I could do as an Englishman to help a compatriot in a foreign country, and yet I am convinced that she knew I suspected and disliked her."

"How long did she stay out here?" asked Miss Marple.

"I think it was about a fortnight. Miss Durrant was buried there, and it must have been about ten days later when she took a boat back to England. The shock had upset her so much that she felt she couldn't spend the winter there as she had planned. That's what she said."

"Did it seem to have upset her?" asked Miss Marple.

The doctor hesitated.

"Well, I don't know that it affected her appearance at all," he said cautiously.

"She didn't, for instance, grow fatter?" asked Miss Marple.

"Do you know—it's a curious thing your saying that. Now I come to think back, I believe you're right. She—yes, she did seem, if anything, to be putting on weight."

"How horrible," said Jane Helier with a shudder. "It's like—it's like fattening on your victim's blood."

"And yet, in another way, I may be doing her an injustice," went on Dr. Lloyd. "She certainly said something before she left which pointed in an entirely different direction. There may be, I think there are, consciences which work very slowly—which take some time to awaken to the enormity of the deed committed.

"It was the evening before her departure from the Canaries. She had asked me to go and see her and had thanked me very warmly for all I had done to help her. I, of course, made light of the matter, said I had only done what was natural under the circumstances, and so on. There was a pause after that, and then she suddenly asked me a question.

" 'Do you think,' she asked, 'that one is ever justified in taking the law into one's own hands?'

"I replied that that was rather a difficult question but that, on the whole, I thought not. The law was the law, and we had to abide by it.

" 'Even when it is powerless?'

" 'I don't quite understand.'

" 'It's difficult to explain, but one might do something that is considered definitely wrong—that is considered a crime, even, for a very good and sufficient reason.'

"I replied dryly that possibly several criminals had thought that in their time, and she shrank back.

" 'But that's horrible,' she murmured. 'Horrible.'

"And then with a change of tone she asked me to give her

something to make her sleep. She had not been able to sleep properly since—she hesitated—since that terrible shock.

" 'You're sure it is that? There is nothing worrying you? Nothing on your mind?'

" 'On my mind? What should be on my mind?'

"She spoke fiercely and suspiciously.

" 'Worry is a cause of sleeplessness sometimes,' I said lightly.

"She seemed to brood for a moment.

" 'Do you mean worrying over the future, or worrying over the past, which can't be altered?'

" 'Either.'

" 'Only it wouldn't be any good worrying over the past. You couldn't bring back— Oh, what's the use? One mustn't think. One must not think.'

"I prescribed a mild sleeping draught and made my adieu. As I went away I wondered not a little over the words she had spoken. 'You couldn't bring back—' What? Or who?

"I think that last interview prepared me in a way for what was to come. I didn't expect it, of course, but when it happened, I wasn't surprised. Because, you see, Mary Barton struck me all along as a conscientious woman—not a weak sinner, but a woman with convictions, who would act up to them, and who would not relent as long as she still believed in them. I fancied that in that last conversation we had she was beginning to doubt her own convictions. I know her words suggested to me that she was feeling the first faint beginnings of that terrible soul-searcher— remorse.

"The thing happened in Cornwall, in a small watering place, rather deserted at that season of the year. It must have been—let me see—late March. I read about it in the papers. A lady had been staying at a small hotel there—a Miss Barton. She had been very odd and peculiar in her manner. That had been noticed by all. At night she would walk up and down her room, muttering to herself, and not allowing the people on either side of her to sleep. She had called on the vicar one day and had told him that she had a communication of the gravest importance to make to him. She had, she said, committed a crime. Then, instead of proceeding, she had stood up abruptly and said she would call another day. The vicar put her down as being slightly unbalanced and did not take her self-accusation seriously.

"The very next morning she was found to be missing from her room. A note was left addressed to the coroner. It ran as follows:

> I tried to speak to the vicar yesterday, to confess all, but was not allowed. She would not let me. I can make amends only one way—a life for a life; and my life must go the same way as hers did. I, too, must drown in the deep sea. I believed I was justified. I see now that that was not so. If I desire Amy's forgiveness, I must go to her. Let no one be blamed for my death—Mary Barton.

"Her clothes were found lying on the beach in a secluded cove near by, and it seemed clear that she had undressed there and swum resolutely out to sea where the current was known to be dangerous, sweeping one down the coast.

"The body was not discovered, but after a time leave was given to presume death. She was a rich woman, her estate being proved at a hundred thousand pounds. Since she died intestate, it all went to her next of kin—a family of cousins in Australia. The papers made discreet references to the tragedy in the Canary Islands, putting forward the theory that the death of Miss Durrant had unhinged her friend's brain. At the inquest the usual verdict of 'Suicide while temporarily insane' was returned.

"And so the curtain falls on the tragedy of Amy Durrant and Mary Barton."

There was a long pause and then Jane Helier gave a great gasp.

"Oh, but you mustn't stop there—just in the most interesting part. Go on."

"But you see, Miss Helier, this isn't a serial story. This is real life, and real life stops just where it chooses."

"But I don't want it to," said Jane. "I want to know."

"This is where we use our brains, Miss Helier," explained Sir Henry. "Why did Mary Barton kill her companion? That's the problem Dr. Lloyd has set us."

"Oh well," said Miss Helier, "she might have killed her for lots of reasons. I mean—oh, I don't know. She might have got on her nerves, or else she got jealous, although Dr. Lloyd doesn't mention any men, but still on the boat out— well, you know what everyone says about boats and sea voyages."

Miss Helier paused, slightly out of breath, and it was borne in upon her audience that the outside of Jane's charming head was distinctly superior to the inside.

"I would like to have a lot of guesses," said Mrs. Bantry. "But I suppose I must confine myself to one. Well, I think that Miss Barton's father made all his money out of ruining Amy Durrant's father, so Amy determined to have her revenge. Oh no, that's the wrong way around. How tiresome! Why does the rich employer kill the humble companion? I've got it. Miss Barton had a young brother who shot himself for love of Amy Durrant. Miss Barton waits her time. Amy comes down in the world. Miss B. engages her as companion and takes her to the Canaries and accomplishes her revenge. How's that?"

"Excellent," said Sir Henry. "Only we don't know that Miss Barton ever had a young brother."

"We deduce that," said Mrs. Bantry. "Unless she had a young brother there's no motive. So she must have had a young brother. Do you see, Watson?"

"That's all very fine, Dolly," said her husband. "But it's only a guess."

"Of course it is," said Mrs. Bantry. "That's all we can do—guess. We haven't got any clues. Go on, dear, have a guess yourself."

"Upon my word, I don't know what to say. But I think there's something in Miss Helier's suggestion that they fell out about a man. Look here, Dolly, it was probably some high church parson. They both embroidered him a cope or something, and he wore the Durrant woman's first. Depend upon it, it was something like that. Look how she went off to a parson at the end. These women all lose their heads over a good-looking clergyman. You hear of it over and over again."

"I think I must try and make my explanation a little more subtle," said Sir Henry, "though I admit it's only a guess. I suggest that Miss Barton was always mentally unhinged. There are more cases like that than you would imagine. Her mania grew stronger and she began to believe it her duty to rid the world of certain persons—possibly what is termed unfortunate females. Nothing much is known about Miss Durrant's past. So very possibly she *had* a past—an 'unfortunate' one. Miss Barton learns of this and decides on extermination. Later the righteousness of her act begins to trouble her and she is overcome by remorse. Her end shows her to be completely unhinged. Now, do say you agree with me, Miss Marple."

"I'm afraid I don't, Sir Henry," said Miss Marple, smiling apologetically. "I think her end shows her to have been a very clever and resourceful woman."

Jane Helier interrupted with a little scream.

"Oh! I've been so stupid. May I guess again? Of course it must have been that. Blackmail! The companion woman was blackmailing her. Only I don't see why Miss Marple says it was clever of her to kill herself. I can't see that at all."

"Ah!" said Sir Henry. "You see, Miss Marple knew a case just like it in St. Mary Mead."

"You always laugh at me, Sir Henry," said Miss Marple reproachfully. "I must confess it does remind me, just a little, of old Mrs. Trout. She drew the old-age pension, you know, for three old women who were dead, in different parishes."

"It sounds like a most complicated and resourceful crime," said Sir Henry. "But it doesn't seem to me to throw any light upon our present problem."

"Of course not," said Miss Marple. "It wouldn't—to you. But some of the families were very poor, and the old-age pension was a great boon to the children. I know it's difficult for anyone outside to understand. But what I really meant was that the whole thing hinged upon one old woman being so like any other old woman."

"Eh?" said Sir Henry, mystified.

"I always explain things so badly. What I mean is that when Dr. Lloyd described the two ladies first, he didn't know which was which, and I don't suppose anyone else in the hotel did. They would have, of course, after a day or so, but the very next day one of the two was drowned, and if the one who was left said she was Miss Barton, I don't suppose it would ever occur to anyone that she mightn't be."

"You think— Oh! I see," said Sir Henry slowly.

"It's the only natural way of thinking of it. Dear Mrs. Bantry began that way just now. Why should the rich employer kill the humble companion? It's so much more likely to be the other way about. I mean—that's the way things happen."

"Is it?" said Sir Henry. "You shock me."

"But of course," went on Miss Marple, "she would have to wear Miss Barton's clothes, and they would probably be a little tight on her, so that her general appearance would look as though she had got a little fatter. That's why I asked that question. A gentleman would be sure to think it was the lady who had got fatter and not the clothes that had got smaller—though that isn't quite the right way of putting it."

"But if Amy Durrant killed Miss Barton, what did she gain by it?" asked Mrs. Bantry. "She couldn't keep up the deception for ever."

"She only kept it up for another month or so," pointed out Miss Marple. "And during that time I expect she travelled, keeping away from anyone who might know her. That's what I meant by saying that one lady of a certain age looks so like another. I don't suppose the different photograph on her passport was ever noticed—you know what passports are. And then in March she went down to this Cornish place and began to act queerly and draw attention to herself so that when people found her clothes on the beach and read her last letter they shouldn't think of the common-sense conclusion."

"Which was?" asked Sir Henry.

"No body," said Miss Marple firmly. "That's the thing that would stare you in the face, if there weren't such a lot of red herrings to draw you off the trail—including the suggestion of foul play and remorse. No body. That was the real significant fact."

"Do you mean—" said Mrs. Bantry, "do you mean that there wasn't any remorse? That there wasn't—that she didn't drown herself?"

"Not she!" said Miss Marple. "It's just Mrs. Trout over again. Mrs. Trout was very good at red herrings, but she met her match in me. And I can see through your remorse-driven Miss Barton. Drown herself? Went off to Australia, if I'm any good at guessing."

"You are, Miss Marple," said Dr. Lloyd. "Undoubtedly

you are. Now it again took me quite by surprise. Why, you could have knocked me down with a feather that day in Melbourne."

"Was that what you spoke of as a final coincidence?"

Dr. Lloyd nodded.

"Yes, it was rather rough luck on Miss Barton—or Miss Amy Durrant—whatever you like to call her. I became a ship's doctor for a while, and landing in Melbourne, the first person I saw as I walked down the street was the lady I thought had been drowned in Cornwall. She saw the game was up as far as I was concerned, and she did the bold thing—took me into her confidence. A curious woman, completely lacking, I suppose, in some moral sense. She was the eldest of a family of nine, all wretchedly poor. They had applied once for help to their rich cousin in England and been repulsed, Miss Barton having quarrelled with their father. Money was wanted desperately, for the three youngest children were delicate and wanted expensive medical treatment. Amy Barton then and there seems to have decided on her plan of cold-blooded murder. She set out for England, working her passage over as a children's nurse. She obtained the situation of companion to Miss Barton, calling herself Amy Durrant. She engaged a room and put some furniture into it so as to create more of a personality for herself. The drowning plan was a sudden inspiration. She had been waiting for some opportunity to present itself. Then she staged the final scene of the drama and returned to Australia, and in due time she and her brothers and sisters inherited Miss Barton's money as next of kin."

"A very bold and perfect crime," said Sir Henry. "Almost the perfect crime. If it had been Miss Barton who had died in the Canaries, suspicion might attach to Amy Durrant and her connection with the Barton family might have been discovered; but the change of identity and the double crime, as you may call it, effectually did away with that. Yes, almost the perfect crime."

"What happened to her?" asked Mrs. Bantry. "What did you do in the matter, Dr. Lloyd?"

"I was in a very curious position, Mrs. Bantry. Of evidence, as the law understands it, I still had very little. Also, there were certain signs, plain to me as a medical man, that though strong and vigorous in appearance, the lady was not long for this world. I went home with her and saw the rest of the family—a charming family, devoted to their eldest sister and without an idea in their heads that she might prove to have committed a crime. Why bring sorrow on them when I could prove nothing? The lady's admission to me was unheard by anyone else. I let nature take its course. Miss Amy Barton died six months after my meeting with her. I have often wondered if she was cheerful and unrepentant up to the last."

"Surely not," said Mrs. Bantry.

"I expect so," said Miss Marple. "Mrs. Trout was."

Jane Helier gave herself a little shake.

"Well," she said, "it's very, very thrilling. I don't quite understand now who drowned which. And how does this Mrs. Trout come into it?"

"She doesn't, my dear," said Miss Marple. "She was only a person—not a very nice person—in the village."

"Oh!" said Jane. "In the village. But nothing ever happens in a village, does it?" She sighed. "I'm sure I shouldn't have any brains at all if I lived in a village."

The Four Suspects

The conversation hovered round undiscovered and un-punished crimes. Everyone in turn vouchsafed an opinion: Colonel Bantry, his plump amiable wife, Jane Helier, Dr. Lloyd, and even old Miss Marple. The one person who did not speak was the one best fitted in most people's opinion to do so. Sir Henry Clithering, ex-Commissioner of Scotland Yard, sat silent, twisting his moustache—or rather stroking it—and half smiling, as though at some inward thought that amused him.

"Sir Henry," said Mrs. Bantry at last, "if you don't say something, I shall scream. Are there a lot of crimes that go unpunished, or are there not?"

"You're thinking of newspaper headlines, Mrs. Bantry. SCOTLAND YARD AT FAULT AGAIN. And a list of unsolved mysteries to follow."

"Which really, I suppose, form a very small percentage of the whole?" said Dr. Lloyd.

"Yes, that is so. The hundreds of crimes that are solved and the perpetrators punished are seldom heralded and sung. But that isn't quite the point at issue, is it? When you talk of undiscovered crimes and unsolved crimes, you are talking of two different things. In the first category come all the crimes that Scotland Yard never hears about, the crimes that no one even knows have been committed."

"But I suppose there aren't very many of those?" said Mrs. Bantry.

"Aren't there?"

"Sir Henry! You don't mean there are?"

"I should think," said Miss Marple thoughtfully, "that there must be a very large number."

The charming old lady, with her old-world, unruffled air, made her statement in a tone of the utmost placidity.

"My dear Miss Marple," said Colonel Bantry.

"Of course," said Miss Marple, "a lot of people are stupid. And stupid people get found out, whatever they do. But there are quite a number of people who aren't stupid, and one shudders to think of what they might accomplish unless they had very strongly rooted principles."

"Yes," said Sir Henry, "there are a lot of people who aren't stupid. How often does some crime come to light simply by reason of a bit of unmitigated bungling, and each time one asks oneself the question: If this hadn't been bungled, would anyone ever have known?"

"But that's very serious, Clithering," said Colonel Bantry. "Very serious, indeed."

"Is it?"

"What do you mean, is it? Of course it's serious."

"You say crime goes unpunished, but does it? Unpunished by the law perhaps, but cause and effect works outside the law. To say that every crime brings its own punishment is by way of being a platitude, and yet in my opinion nothing can be truer."

"Perhaps, perhaps," said Colonel Bantry. "But that doesn't alter the seriousness—the—er—seriousness—" He paused, rather at a loss.

Sir Henry Clithering smiled.

"Ninety-nine people out of a hundred are doubtless of

your way of thinking," he said. "But you know, it isn't really guilt that is important—it's innocence. That's the thing that nobody will realize."

"I don't understand," said Jane Helier.

"I do," said Miss Marple. "When Mrs. Trent found half a crown missing from her bag, the person it affected most was the daily woman, Mrs. Arthur. Of course the Trents thought it was her, but being kindly people and knowing she had a large family and a husband who drinks, well—they naturally didn't want to go to extremes. But they felt differently toward her, and they didn't leave her in charge of the house when they went away, which made a great difference to her; and other people began to get a feeling about her too. And then it suddenly came out that it was the governess. Mrs. Trent saw her through a door reflected in a mirror. The purest chance—though I prefer to call it Providence. And that, I think, is what Sir Henry means. Most people would be only interested in who took the money, and it turned out to be the most unlikely person—just like in detective stories! But the real person it was life and death to was poor Mrs. Arthur, who had done nothing. That's what you mean, isn't it, Sir Henry?"

"Yes, Miss Marple, you've hit off my meaning exactly. Your charwoman person was lucky in the instance you relate. Her innocence was shown. But some people may go through a lifetime crushed by the weight of a suspicion that is really unjustified."

"Are you thinking of some particular instance, Sir Henry?" asked Mrs. Bantry shrewdly.

"As a matter of fact, Mrs. Bantry, I am. A very curious case. A case where we believe murder to have been committed, but with no possible chance of ever proving it."

"Poison, I suppose," breathed Jane. "Something untraceable."

Dr. Lloyd moved restlessly and Sir Henry shook his head.

"No, dear lady. Not the secret arrow poison of the South American Indians! I wish it were something of that kind. We have to deal with something much more prosaic—so prosaic, in fact, that there is no hope of bringing the deed home to its perpetrator. An old gentleman who fell downstairs and broke his neck; one of those regrettable accidents which happen every day."

"But what happened really?"

"Who can say?" Sir Henry shrugged his shoulders. "A push from behind? A piece of cotton or string tied across the top of the stairs and carefully removed afterward? That we shall never know."

"But you do think that it—well, wasn't an accident? Now why?" asked the doctor.

"That's rather a long story, but—well, yes, we're pretty sure. As I said, there's no chance of being able to bring the deed home to anyone—the evidence would be too flimsy. But there's the other aspect of the case—the one I was speaking about. You see, there were four people who might have done the trick. One's guilty, but the other three are innocent. And unless the truth is found out, those three are going to remain under the terrible shadow of doubt."

"I think," said Mrs. Bantry, "that you'd better tell us your long story."

"I needn't make it so very long after all," said Sir Henry. "I can at any rate condense the beginning. That deals with a German secret society—the *Schwartze Hand*—something after the lines of the Camorra or what is most people's idea of the Camorra. A scheme of blackmail and terrorization. The thing started quite suddenly after the war and spread to an amazing extent. Numberless people were victimized by it. The authorities were not successful in coping with it, for its secrets were jealously guarded, and it was almost impossible to find anyone who could be induced to betray them.

"Nothing much was ever known about it in England, but in Germany it was having a most paralyzing effect. It was finally broken up and dispersed through the efforts of one man, a Dr. Rosen, who had at one time been very prominent in Secret Service work. He became a member, penetrated its inmost circle, and was, as I say, instrumental in bringing about its downfall.

"But he was, in consequence, a marked man, and it was deemed wise that he should leave Germany—at any rate for a time. He came to England, and we had letters about him from the police in Berlin. He came and had a personal interview with me. His point of view was both dispassionate and resigned. He had no doubts of what the future held for him.

" 'They will get me, Sir Henry,' he said. 'Not a doubt of it.' He was a big man with a fine head and a very deep voice, with only a slight guttural intonation to tell of his nationality. 'That is a foregone conclusion. It does not matter, I am prepared. I faced the risk when I undertook this business. I have done what I set out to do. The organization can never be gotten together again. But there are many members of it at liberty, and they will take the only revenge they can—my life. It is simply a question of time, but I am anxious that that time should be as long as possible. You see, I am collecting and editing some very interesting material—the result of my life's work. I should like, if possible, to be able to complete my task.'

"He spoke very simply, with a certain grandeur which I could not but admire. I told him we would take all precautions, but he waved my words aside.

" 'Some day, sooner or later, they will get me,' he repeated. 'When that day comes, do not distress yourself. You will, I have no doubt, have done all that is possible.'

"He then proceeded to outline his plans, which were simple enough. He proposed to take a small cottage in the country where he could live quietly and go on with his work. In the end he selected a village in Somerset—King's Gnaton, which was seven miles from a railway station and singularly untouched by civilization. He bought a very charming cottage, had various improvements and alterations made, and settled down there most contentedly. His household consisted of his niece, Greta; a secretary; an old German servant who had served him faithfully for nearly forty years; and an outside handy man and gardener who was a native of King's Gnaton."

"The four suspects," said Dr. Lloyd softly.

"Exactly. The four suspects. There is not much more to tell. Life went on peacefully at King's Gnaton for five months and then the blow fell. Dr. Rosen fell down the stairs one morning and was found dead about half an hour later. At the time the accident must have taken place, Gertrud was in her kitchen with the door closed and heard nothing—so she says. Fräulein Greta was in the garden, planting some bulbs—again, so she says. The gardener, Dobbs, was in the small potting shed having his elevenses—so he says; and the secretary was out for a walk, and once more there is only his own word for it. No one had an alibi—no one can corroborate anyone else's story. But one thing is certain. No one from outside could have done it, for a stranger in the little village of King's Gnaton would be noticed without fail. Both the back and the front doors were locked, each member of the household having his own key. So you see it narrows down to those four. And yet each one seems to be above suspicion. Greta, his own brother's child. Gertrud, with forty years of faithful service. Dobbs, who has never been out of King's Gnaton. And Charles Templeton, the secretary—"

"Yes," said Colonel Bantry, "what about him? He seems the suspicious person to my mind. What do you know about him?"

"It is what I knew about him that put him completely out of court—at any rate, at the time," said Sir Henry gravely. "You see, Charles Templeton was one of my own men."

"Oh!" said Colonel Bantry, considerably taken aback.

"Yes. I wanted to have someone on the spot, and at the same time I didn't want to cause talk in the village. Rosen really needed a secretary. I put Templeton on the job. He's a gentleman, he speaks German fluently, and he's altogether a very able fellow."

"But, then, which do you suspect?" asked Mrs. Bantry in a bewildered tone. "They all seem so—well, impossible."

"Yes, so it appears. But you can look at the thing from another angle. Fräulein Greta was his niece and a very lovely girl, but the war has shown us time and again that brother can turn against sister, or father against son, and so on, and the loveliest and gentlest of young girls did some of the most amazing things. The same thing applies to Gertrud, and who knows what other forces might be at work in her case? A quarrel, perhaps, with her master, a growing resentment all the more lasting because of the long faithful years behind her. Elderly women of that class can be amazingly bitter sometimes. And Dobbs? Was he right outside it because he had no connection with the family? Money will do much. In some way Dobbs might have been approached and bought.

"For one thing seems certain: Some message or some order must have come from outside. Otherwise, why five months' immunity? No, the agents of the society must have been at work. Not yet sure of Rosen's perfidy, they delayed till the betrayal had been traced to him beyond any possible doubt. And then, all doubts set aside, they must have sent their message to the spy within the gates—the message that said, 'Kill.' "

"How nasty!" said Jane Helier, and shuddered.

"But how did the message come? That was the point I

tried to elucidate—the one hope of solving my problem. One of those four people must have been approached or communicated with in some way. There would be no delay—I knew that; as soon as the command came, it would be carried out. That was a peculiarity of the *Schwartze Hand*.

"I went into the question, went into it in a way that will probably strike you as being ridiculously meticulous. Who had come to the cottage that morning? I eliminated nobody. Here is the list."

He took an envelope from his pocket and selected a paper from its contents.

"The butcher, bringing some neck of mutton. Investigated and found correct.

"The grocer's assistant, bringing a packet of corn flour, two pounds of sugar, a pound of butter, and a pound of coffee. Also investigated and found correct.

"The postman, bringing two circulars for Fräulein Rosen, a local letter for Gertrud, three letters for Dr. Rosen, one with a foreign stamp, and two letters for Mr. Templeton, one also with a foreign stamp."

Sir Henry paused and then took a sheaf of documents from the envelope.

"It may interest you to see these for yourself. They were handed me by the various people concerned or collected from the wastepaper basket. I need hardly say they've been tested by experts for invisible ink, et cetera. No excitement of that kind is possible."

Everyone crowded round to look. The catalogues were respectively from a nurseryman and from a prominent London fur establishment. The two bills addressed to Dr. Rosen were a local one for seeds for the garden and one from a London stationery firm. The letter addressed to him ran as follows:

My Dear Rosen—Just back from Dr. Helmuth Spath's. I saw Edgar Jackson the other day. He and

Amos Perry have just come back from Tsingtau. In all Honesty I can't say I envy them the trip. Let me have news of you soon. As I said before: Beware of a certain person. You know who I mean, though you don't agree.—Yours,

Georgina.

"Mr. Templeton's mail consisted of this bill which, as you see, is an account rendered from his tailor, and a letter from a friend in Germany," went on Sir Henry. "The latter, unfortunately, he tore up while out on his walk. Finally we have the letter received by Gertrud."

Dear Mrs. Swartz—We're hoping as how you be able to come to the social on friday evening. the vicar says has he hopes you will—one and all being welcome. The resipy for the ham was very good, and I thanks you for it. Hoping as this finds you well and that we shall see you friday I remain

Yours faithfully,
Emma Greene.

Dr. Lloyd smiled a little over this and so did Mrs. Bantry. "I think the last letter can be put out of court," said Dr. Lloyd.

"I thought the same," said Sir Henry, "but I took the precaution of verifying that there was a Mrs. Greene and a church social. One can't be too careful, you know."

"That's what our friend Miss Marple always says," said Dr. Lloyd, smiling. "You're lost in a daydream, Miss Marple. What are you thinking out?"

Miss Marple gave a start.

"So stupid of me," she said. "I was just wondering why the word Honesty in Dr. Rosen's letter was spelled with a capital H."

Mrs. Bantry picked it up.

"So it is," she said. "Oh!"

"Yes, dear," said Miss Marple. "I thought you'd notice!"

"There's a definite warning in that letter," said Colonel Bantry. "That's the first thing caught my attention. I notice more than you'd think. Yes, a definite warning—against whom?"

"There's rather a curious point about that letter," said Sir Henry. "According to Templeton, Dr. Rosen opened the letter at breakfast and tossed it across to him, saying he didn't know who the fellow was from Adam."

"But it wasn't a fellow," said Jane Helier. "It was signed 'Georgina.'"

"It's difficult to say which it is," said Dr. Lloyd. "It might be Georgey, but it certainly looks more like Georgina. Only it strikes me that the writing is a man's."

"You know, that's interesting," said Colonel Bantry. "His tossing it across the table like that and pretending he knew nothing about it. Wanted to watch somebody's face. Whose face—the girl's? Or the man's?"

"Or even the cook's?" suggested Mrs. Bantry. "She might have been in the room bringing in the breakfast. But what I don't see is . . . it's most peculiar—"

She frowned over the letter. Miss Marple drew closer to her. Miss Marple's finger went out and touched the sheet of paper. They murmured together.

"But why did the secretary tear up the other letter?" asked Jane Helier suddenly. "It seems—oh, I don't know—it seems queer. Why should he have letters from Germany? Although, of course, if he's above suspicion, as you say—"

"But Sir Henry didn't say that," said Miss Marple quickly, looking up from her murmured conference with Mrs. Bantry. "He said four suspects. So that shows that he includes Mr. Templeton. I'm right, am I not, Sir Henry?"

"Yes, Miss Marple. I have learned one thing through bitter experience. Never say to yourself that anyone is above suspicion. I gave you reasons just now why three of these people might after all be guilty, unlikely as it seemed. I did not at that time apply the same process to Charles Templeton. But I came to it at last through pursuing the rule I have just mentioned. And I was forced to recognize this: That every army and every navy and every police force has a certain number of traitors within its ranks, much as we hate to admit the idea. And I examined dispassionately the case against Charles Templeton.

"I asked myself very much the same questions as Miss Helier has just asked. Why should he, alone of all the house, not be able to produce the letter he had received—a letter, moreover, with a German stamp on it. Why should he have letters from Germany?

"The last question was an innocent one, and I actually put it to him. His reply came simply enough. His mother's sister was married to a German. The letter had been from a German girl cousin. So I learned something I did not know before—that Charles Templeton had relations with people in Germany. And that put him definitely on the list of suspects—very much so. He is my own man—a lad I have always liked and trusted; but in common justice and fairness I must admit that he heads that list.

"But there it is—I do not know! I do not know . . . And in all probability I never shall know. It is not a question of punishing a murderer. It is a question that to me seems a hundred times more important. It is the blighting, perhaps, of an honourable man's whole career . . . because of suspicion—a suspicion that I dare not disregard."

Miss Marple coughed and said gently:

"Then, Sir Henry, if I understand you rightly, it is this young Mr. Templeton only who is so much on your mind?"

"Yes, in a sense. It should, in theory, be the same for all four, but that is not actually the case. Dobbs, for instance—suspicion may attach to him in my mind, but it will not actually affect his career. Nobody in the village has ever had any idea that old Dr. Rosen's death was anything but an accident. Gertrud is slightly more affected. It must make, for instance, a difference in Fräulein Rosen's attitude toward her. But that, possibly, is not of great importance to her.

"As for Greta Rosen—well, here we come to the crux of the matter. Greta is a very pretty girl and Charles Templeton is a good-looking young man, and for five months they were thrown together with no outer distractions. The inevitable happened. They fell in love with each other—even if they did not come to the point of admitting the fact in words.

"And then the catastrophe happens. It is three months ago now, and a day or two after I returned, Greta Rosen came to see me. She had sold the cottage and was returning to Germany, having finally settled up her uncle's affairs. She came to me personally, although she knew I had retired, because it was really about a personal matter she wanted to see me. She beat about the bush a little, but at last it all came out. What did I think? That letter with the German stamp—she had worried about it and worried about it—the one Charles had torn up. Was it all right? Surely it must be all right. Of course she believed his story, but—oh, if she only knew! If she knew—for certain.

"You see? The same feeling: the wish to trust—but the horrible lurking suspicion, thrust resolutely to the back of the mind, but persisting nevertheless. I spoke to her with absolute frankness and asked her to do the same. I asked her whether she had been on the point of caring for Charles and he for her.

" 'I think so,' she said. 'Oh yes, I know it was so. We were so happy. Every day passed so contentedly. We knew—we both knew. There was no hurry—there was all the time in the world. Some day he would tell me he loved me, and I should tell him that I, too— Ah! But you can guess! And now it is all changed. A black cloud has come between us— we are constrained, when we meet we do not know what to say. It is, perhaps, the same with him as with me . . . We are each saying to ourselves, "If I were sure!" That is why, Sir Henry, I beg of you to say to me, "You may be sure, whoever killed your uncle, it was not Charles Templeton!" Say it to me! Oh, say it to me! I beg—I beg!'

"I couldn't say it to her. They'll drift farther and farther apart, those two—with suspicion like a ghost between them—a ghost that can't be laid."

He leaned back in his chair; his face looked tired and grey. He shook his head once or twice despondently.

"And there's nothing more can be done, unless—" He sat up straight again and a tiny whimsical smile crossed his face. "—unless Miss Marple can help us. Can't you, Miss Marple? I've a feeling that letter might be in your line, you know. The one about the church social. Doesn't it remind you of something or someone that makes everything perfectly plain? Can't you do something to help two helpless young people who want to be happy?"

Behind the whimsicality there was something earnest in his appeal. He had come to think very highly of the mental powers of this frail, old-fashioned maiden lady. He looked across at her with something very like hope in his eyes.

Miss Marple coughed and smoothed her lace.

"It does remind me a little of Annie Poultny," she admitted. "Of course the letter is perfectly plain—both to Mrs. Bantry and myself. I don't mean the church-social letter, but the other one. You living so much in London and not being a gardener, Sir Henry, would not have been likely to notice."

"Eh?" said Sir Henry. "Notice what?"

Mrs. Bantry reached out a hand and selected a catalogue. She opened it and read aloud with gusto:

" 'Dr. Helmuth Spath. Pure lilac, a wonderfully fine flower, carried on exceptionally long and stiff stem. Splendid for cutting and garden decoration. A novelty of striking beauty.

" 'Edgar Jackson. Beautifully shaped chrysanthemum-like flower of a distinct brick-red colour.

" 'Amos Perry. Brilliant red, highly decorative.

" 'Tsingtau. Brilliant orange-red, showy garden plant and lasting cut flower.

" 'Honesty—' "

"With a capital H, you remember," murmured Miss Marple.

" 'Honesty. Rose and white shades, enormous perfect-shaped flower.' "

Mrs. Bantry flung down the catalogue and said with immense explosive force:

"Dahlias!"

"And their initial letters spell 'Death,' " explained Miss Marple.

"But the letter came to Dr. Rosen himself," objected Sir Henry.

"That was the clever part of it," said Miss Marple. "That and the warning in it. What would he do, getting a letter from someone he didn't know, full of names he didn't know. Why, of course, toss it over to his secretary."

"Then, after all—"

"Oh no!" said Miss Marple. "Not the secretary. Why, that's what makes it so perfectly clear that it wasn't him. He'd never have let that letter be found if so. And equally he'd never have destroyed a letter to himself with a German stamp on it. Really, his innocence is—if you'll allow me to use the world—just shining."

"Then who—"

"Well, it seems almost certain—as certain as anything can be in this world. There was another person at the breakfast table, and she would—quite naturally under the circumstances—put out her hand for the letter and read it. And that would be that. You remember that she got a gardening catalogue by the same post—"

"Greta Rosen," said Sir Henry slowly. "Then her visit to me—"

"Gentlemen never see through these things," said Miss Marple. "And I'm afraid they often think we old women are—well, cats, to see things the way we do. But there it is. One does know a great deal about one's own sex, unfortunately. I've no doubt there was a barrier between them. The young man felt a sudden inexplicable repulsion. He suspected, purely through instinct, and couldn't hide the suspicion. And I really think that the girl's visit to you was just pure spite. She was safe enough really, but she just went out of her way to fix your suspicions definitely on poor Mr. Templeton. You weren't nearly so sure about him until after her visit."

"I'm sure it was nothing that she said—" began Sir Henry.

"Gentlemen," said Miss Marple calmly, "never see through these things."

"And that girl—" He stopped. "She commits a ˙cold-blooded murder and gets off scot-free!"

"Oh no, Sir Henry," said Miss Marple. "Not scot-free. Neither you nor I believe that. Remember what you said not long ago. No. Greta Rosen will not escape punishment. To begin with, she must be in with a very queer set of people—blackmailers and terrorists—associates who will do her no good and will probably bring her to a miserable end. As you say, one mustn't waste thoughts on the guilty—it's the innocent who matter. Mr. Templeton, who I daresay will marry that German cousin, his tearing up her letter looks—

well, it looks suspicious—using the word in quite a different sense from the one we've been using all the evening. A little as though he were afraid of the other girl noticing or asking to see it? Yes, I think there must have been some little romance there. And then there's Dobbs—though, as you say, I daresay it won't much matter to him. His elevenses are probably all he thinks about. And then there's that poor old Gertrud—the one who reminded me of Annie Poultny. Poor Annie Poultny. Fifty years' faithful service and suspected of making away with Miss Lamb's will, though nothing could be proved. Almost broke the poor creature's faithful heart. And then after she was dead it came to light in the secret drawer of the tea caddy where old Miss Lamb had put it herself for safety. But too late then for poor Annie.

"That's what worries me so about that poor old German woman. When one is old, one becomes embittered very easily. I felt much more sorry for her than for Mr. Templeton, who is young and good-looking and evidently a favourite with the ladies. You will write to her, won't you, Sir Henry, and just tell her that her innocence is established beyond doubt? Her dear old master dead, and she no doubt brooding and feeling herself suspected of . . . Oh! It won't bear thinking about!"

"I will write, Miss Marple," said Sir Henry. He looked at her curiously. "You know, I shall never quite understand you. Your outlook is always a different one from what I expect."

"My outlook, I'm afraid, is a very petty one," said Miss Marple humbly. "I hardly ever go out of St. Mary Mead."

"And yet you have solved what may be called an international mystery," said Sir Henry. "For you have solved it. I am convinced of that."

Miss Marple blushed, then bridled a little.

"I was, I think, well educated for the standard of my day.

My sister and I had a German governess—a Fräulein. A very sentimental creature. She taught us the language of flowers—a forgotten study nowadays, but most charming. A yellow tulip, for instance, means 'Hopeless Love,' while a China aster means 'I Die of Jealousy at Your Feet.' That letter was signed Georgina, which I seem to remember as dahlia in German, and that of course made the whole thing perfectly clear. I wish I could remember the meaning of dahlia, but alas, that eludes me. My memory is not what it was."

"At any rate, it didn't mean 'Death.' "

"No, indeed. Horrible, is it not? There are very sad things in the world."

"There are," said Mrs. Bantry with a sigh. "It's lucky one has flowers and one's friends."

"She puts us last, you observe," said Dr. Lloyd.

"A man used to send me purple orchids every night to the theater," said Jane dreamily.

" 'I Await Your Favours'—that's what that means," said Miss Marple brightly.

Sir Henry gave a peculiar sort of cough and turned his head away.

Miss Marple gave a sudden exclamation.

"I've remembered. Dahlias mean 'Treachery and Misrepresentation.' "

"Wonderful," said Sir Henry. "Absolutely wonderful."

And he sighed.

A Christmas Tragedy

I have a complaint to make," said Sir Henry Clithering. His eyes twinkled gently as he looked round at the assembled company. Colonel Bantry, his legs stretched out, was frowning at the mantelpiece as though it were a delinquent soldier on parade, his wife was surreptitiously glancing at a catalogue of bulbs which had come by the late post, Dr. Lloyd was gazing with frank admiration at Jane Helier, and that beautiful young actress herself was thoughtfully regarding her pink polished nails. Only that elderly, spinster lady, Miss Marple, was sitting bolt upright, and her faded blue eyes met Sir Henry's with an answering twinkle.

"A complaint?" she murmured.

"A very serious complaint. We are a company of six, three representatives of each sex, and I protest on behalf of the down-trodden males. We have had three stories told to-night—and told by the three men! I protest that the ladies have not done their fare share."

"Oh!" said Mrs. Bantry with indignation. "I'm sure we have. We've listened with the most intelligent appreciation. We've displayed the true womanly attitude—not wishing to thrust ourselves into the limelight!"

"It's an excellent excuse," said Sir Henry; "but it won't do. And there's a very good precedent in the Arabian Nights! So, forward, Scheherazade!"

"Meaning me?" said Mrs. Bantry. "But I don't know anything to tell. I've never been surrounded by blood or mystery."

"I don't absolutely insist upon blood," said Sir Henry. "But I'm sure one of you three ladies has got a pet mystery. Come now, Miss Marple—the 'Curious Coincidence of the Charwoman' or the 'Mystery of the Mothers' Meeting.' Don't disappoint me in St. Mary Mead."

Miss Marple shook her head.

"Nothing that would interest you, Sir Henry. We have our little mysteries, of course—there was that gill of picked shrimps that disappeared so incomprehensibly; but that wouldn't interest you because it all turned out to be so trivial, though throwing a considerable light on human nature."

"You have taught me to dote on human nature," said Sir Henry solemnly.

"What about you, Miss Helier?" asked Colonel Bantry. "You must have had some interesting experiences."

"Yes, indeed," said Dr. Lloyd.

"Me?" said Jane. "You mean—you want me to tell you something that happened to me?"

"Or to one of your friends," amended Sir Henry.

"Oh!" said Jane vaguely. "I don't think anything has ever happened to me—I mean not that kind of thing. Flowers, of course, and queer messages—but that's just men, isn't it? I don't think"—she paused and appeared lost in thought.

"I see we shall have to have that epic of the shrimps," said Sir Henry. "Now then, Miss Marple."

"You're so fond of your joke, Sir Henry. The shrimps are only nonsense; but now I come to think of it, I *do* remember one incident—at least not exactly an incident, something very much more serious—a tragedy. And I was, in a way, mixed up in it; and for what I did, I have never had any regrets—no, no regrets at all. But it didn't happen in St. Mary Mead."

"That disappoints me," said Sir Henry. "But I will endeavour to bear up. I knew we should not rely upon you in vain."

He settled himself in the attitude of a listener. Miss Marple grew slightly pink.

"I hope I shall be able to tell it properly," she said anxiously. "I fear I am very inclined to become *rambling*. One wanders from the point—altogether without knowing that one is doing so. And it is so hard to remember each fact in its proper order. You must all bear with me if I tell my story badly. It happened a very long time ago now.

"As I say it was not connected with St. Mary Mead. As a matter of fact, it had to do with a Hydro—"

"Do you mean a seaplane?" asked Jane with wide eyes.

"You wouldn't know, dear," said Mrs. Bantry, and explained. Her husband added his quota:

"Beastly places—absolutely beastly! Got to get up early and drink filthy-tasting water. Lot of old women sitting about. Ill-natured tittle tattle. God, when I think—"

"Now, Arthur," said Mrs. Bantry placidly. "You know it did you all the good in the world."

"Lot of old women sitting round talking scandal," grunted Colonel Bantry.

"That, I am afraid, is true," said Miss Marple. "I myself—"

"My dear Miss Marple," cried the colonel, horrified. "I didn't mean for one moment—"

With pink cheeks and a little gesture of the hand, Miss Marple stopped him.

"But it is *true,* Colonel Bantry. Only I should just like to say this. Let me recollect my thoughts. Yes. Talking scandal, as you say—well, it *is* done a good deal. And people are very down on it—especially young people. My nephew, who writes books—and very clever ones, I believe—has said some most *scathing* things about taking people's characters away without any kind of proof—and how wicked it is, and all that. But what I say is that none of these young people ever stop to *think*. They really don't examine the facts. Surely the whole crux of the matter is this: *How often is tittle tattle,* as you call it, *true*! And I think if, as I say, they really examined the facts they would find that it was true nine times out of ten. That's really just what makes people so annoyed about it."

"The inspired guess," said Sir Henry.

"No, not that, not that at all! It's really a matter of practice and experience. An Egyptologist, so I've heard, if you show him one of those curious little beetles, can tell you by the look and the feel of the thing what date B.C. it is, or if it's a Birmingham imitation. And he can't always give a definite rule for doing so. He just *knows*. His life has been spent handling such things.

"And that's what I'm trying to say (very badly, I know). What my nephew calls 'superfluous women' have a lot of time on their hands, and their chief interest is usually *people*. And so, you see, they get to be what one might call *experts*. Now young people nowadays—they talk very freely about things that weren't mentioned in my young days, but on the other hand their minds are terribly innocent. They believe in everyone and everything. And if one tries to warn them, ever so gently, they tell one that one has a Victorian mind—and that, they say, is like a *sink*."

"After all," said Sir Henry, "what is wrong with a *sink*?"

"Exactly," said Miss Marple eagerly. "It's the most necessary thing in any house; but, of course, not romantic. Now

I must confess that I have my *feelings,* like everyone else, and I have sometimes been cruelly hurt by unthinking remarks. I know gentlemen are not interested in domestic matters, but I must just mention my maid Ethel—a very good-looking girl and obliging in every way. Now I realized as soon as I saw her that she was the same type as Annie Webb and poor Mrs. Bruitt's girl. If the opportunity arose *mine and thine* would mean nothing to her. So I let her go at the month and I gave her a written reference saying she was honest and sober, but privately I warned old Mrs. Edwards against taking her; and my nephew, Raymond, was exceedingly angry and said he had never heard of anything so wicked—yes, *wicked.* Well, she went to Lady Ashton, whom I felt no obligation to warn—and what happened? All the lace cut off her underclothes and two diamond brooches taken—and the girl departed in the middle of the night and never heard of since!"

Miss Marple paused, drew a long breath, and then went on.

"You'll be saying this has nothing to do with what went on at Keston Spa Hydro—but it has in a way. It explains why I felt no doubt in my mind the first moment I saw the Sanders together that he meant to do away with her."

"Eh?" said Sir Henry, leaning forward.

Miss Marple turned a placid face to him.

"As I say, Sir Henry, I felt no doubt in my own mind. Mr. Sanders was a big, good-looking, florid-faced man, very hearty in his manner and popular with all. And nobody could have been pleasanter to his wife than he was. But I knew! He meant to make away with her."

"My dear Miss Marple—"

"Yes, I know. That's what my nephew Raymond West, would say. He'd tell me I hadn't a shadow of proof. But I remember Walter Hones, who kept the Green Man. Walking home with his wife one night she fell into the river—and *he* collected the insurance money! And one or two other people that are walking about scot-free to this day—one indeed in our own class of life. Went to Switzerland for a summer holiday climbing with his wife. I warned her not to go—the poor dear didn't get angry with me as she might have done—she only laughed. It seemed to her funny that a queer old thing like me should say such things about her Harry. Well, well, there was an accident—and Harry is married to another woman now. But what could I *do*? I *knew,* but there was no proof."

"Oh! Miss Marple," cried Mrs. Bantry. "You don't really mean—"

"My dear, these things are very common—very common indeed. And gentlemen are especially tempted, being so much the stronger. So easy if a thing looks like an accident. As I say, I knew at once with the Sanders. It was on a tram. It was full inside and I had had to go on top. We all three got up to get off and Mr. Sanders lost his balance and fell right against his wife, sending her head first down the stairs. Fortunately the conductor was a very strong young man and caught her."

"But surely that must have been an accident."

"Of course it was an accident—nothing could have looked more accidental. But Mr. Sanders had been in the Merchant Service, so he told me, and a man who can keep his balance on a nasty tilting boat doesn't lose it on top of a tram if an old woman like me doesn't. Don't tell me!"

"At any rate we can take it that you made up your mind, Miss Marple," said Sir Henry. "Made it up then and there."

The old lady nodded.

"I was sure enough, and another incident in crossing the street not long afterwards made me surer still. Now I ask you, what could I do, Sir Henry? Here was a nice contented happy little married woman shortly going to be murdered."

"My dear lady, you take my breath away."

"That's because, like most people nowadays, you won't face facts. You prefer to think such a thing couldn't be. But it was so, and I knew it. But one is so sadly handicapped! I couldn't, for instance, go to the police. And to warn the young woman would, I could see, be useless. She was devoted to the man. I just made it my business to find out as much as I could about them. One has a lot of opportunities, doing one's needlework round the fire. Mrs. Sanders (Gladys, her name was) was only too willing to talk. It seems they had not been married very long. Her husband had some property that was coming to him, but for the moment they were very badly off. In fact, they were living on her little income. One has heard that tale before. She bemoaned the fact that she could not touch the capital. It seems that somebody had had some sense somewhere! But the money was hers to will away—I found that out. And she and her husband had made wills in favour of each other directly after their marriage. Very touching. Of course, when Jack's affairs came right—that was the burden all day long, and in the meantime they were very hard up indeed—actually had a room on the top floor, all among the servants—and so dangerous in case of fire, though, as it happened, there was a fire escape just outside their window. I inquired carefully if there was a balcony—dangerous things, balconies. One push—you know!

"I made her promise not to go out on the balcony; I said I'd had a dream. That impressed her—one can do a lot with superstition sometimes. She was a fair girl, rather washed-out complexion, and an untidy roll of hair on her neck. Very credulous. She repeated what I had said to her husband, and I noticed him looking at me in a curious way once or twice.

He wasn't credulous; and he knew I'd been on that tram.

"But I was very worried—terribly worried—because I couldn't see how to circumvent him. I could prevent anything happening at the Hydro, just by saying a few words to show him I suspected. But that only meant his putting off his plan till later. No. I began to believe that the only policy was a bold one—somehow or other to lay a trap for him. If I could induce him to attempt her life in a way of my own choosing—well, then he would be unmasked, and she would be forced to face the truth however much of a shock it was to her."

"You take my breath away," said Dr. Lloyd. "What conceivable plan could you adopt?"

"I'd have found one—never fear," said Miss Marple. "But the man was too clever for me. He didn't wait. He thought I might suspect, and so he struck before I could be sure. He knew I would suspect an accident. So he made it murder."

A little gasp went round the circle. Miss Marple nodded and set her lips grimly together.

"I'm afraid I've put that rather abruptly. I must try and tell you exactly what occurred. I've always felt very bitterly about it—it seems to me that I ought, somehow, to have prevented it. But doubtless Providence knew best. I did what I could at all events.

"There was what I can only describe as a curiously eerie feeling in the air. There seemed to be something weighing on us all. A feeling of misfortune. To begin with, there was George, the hall porter. Had been there for years and knew everybody. Bronchitis and pneumonia, and passed away on the fourth day. Terribly sad. A real blow to everybody. And four days before Christmas too. And then one of the housemaids—such a nice girl—a septic finger, actually died in twenty-four hours.

"I was in the drawing-room with Miss Trollope and old

Mrs. Carpenter, and Mrs. Carpenter was being positively ghoulish—relishing it all, you know.

" 'Mark my words,' she said. '*This isn't the end.* You know the saying? *Never two without three.* I've proved it true time and again. There'll be another death. Not a doubt of it. And we shan't have long to wait. *Never two without three.*'

"As she said the last words, nodding her head and clicking her knitting needles, I just chanced to look up and there was Mr. Sanders standing in the doorway. Just for a minute he was off guard, and I saw the look in his face as plain as plain. I shall believe till my dying day that it was that ghoulish Mrs. Carpenter's words that put the whole thing into his head. I saw his mind working.

"He came forward into the room smiling in his genial way.

" 'Any Christmas shopping I can do for you ladies?' he asked. 'I'm going down to Keston presently.'

"He stayed a minute or two, laughing and talking, and then went out. As I tell you I was troubled, and I said straight away:

" 'Where's Mrs. Sanders? Does anyone know?'

"Miss Trollope said she'd gone out to some friends of hers, the Mortimers, to play bridge, and that eased my mind for the moment. But I was still very worried and most uncertain as to what to do. About half an hour later I went up to my room. I met Dr. Coles, my doctor, there, coming down the stairs as I was going up, and as I happened to want to consult him about my rheumatism, I took him into my room with me then and there. He mentioned to me then (in confidence, he said) about the death of the poor girl Mary. The manager didn't want the news to get about, he said, so would I keep it to myself. Of course, I didn't tell him that we'd all been discussing nothing else for the last hour—ever since the poor girl breathed her last. These things are always known at once, and a man of his experience should know that well enough; but Dr. Coles always was a simple unsuspicious fellow who believed what he wanted to believe and that's just what alarmed me a minute later. He said as he was leaving that Sanders had asked him to have a look at his wife. It seemed she'd been seedy of late—indigestion, etc.

"*Now that very selfsame day Gladys Sanders had said to me that she'd got a wonderful digestion and was thankful for it.*

"You see? All my suspicions of that man came back a hundredfold. He was preparing the way—for what? Dr. Coles left before I could make up my mind whether to speak to him or not—though really if I had spoken I shouldn't have known what to say. As I came out of my room, the man himself—Sanders—came down the stairs from the floor above. He was dressed to go out and he asked me again if he could do anything for me in town. It was all I could do to be civil to the man! I went straight into the lounge and ordered tea. It was just on half-past five, I remember.

"Now I'm very anxious to put clearly what happened next. I was still in the lounge at a quarter to seven when Mr. Sanders came in. There were two gentlemen with him and all three of them were inclined to be a little on the lively side. Mr. Sanders left his two friends and came right over to where I was sitting with Miss Trollope. He explained that he wanted our advice about a Christmas present he was giving his wife. It was an evening bag.

"'And you see, ladies,' he said. 'I'm only a rough sailorman. What do I know about such things? I've had three sent to me on approval and I want an expert opinion on them.'

"We said, of course, that we would be delighted to help him, and he asked if we'd mind coming upstairs, as his wife might come in any minute if he brought the things down.

So we went up with him. I shall never forget what happened next—I can feel my little fingers tingling now."

"Mr. Sanders opened the door of the bedroom and switched on the light. I don't know which of us saw it first . . .

"*Mrs. Sanders was lying on the floor, face downwards—dead.*

"I got to her first. I knelt down and took her hand and felt for the pulse, but it was useless, the arm itself was cold and stiff. Just by her head was a stocking filled with sand—the weapon she had been struck down with. Miss Trollope, silly creature, was moaning and moaning by the door and holding her head. Sanders gave a great cry of 'My wife, my wife,' and rushed to her. I stopped him touching her. You see, I was sure at the moment that he had done it, and there might have been something that he wanted to take away or hide.

"'Nothing must be touched,' I said. 'Pull yourself together, Mr. Sanders. Miss Trollope, please go down and fetch the manager.'

"I stayed there, kneeling by the body. I wasn't going to leave Sanders alone with it. And yet I was forced to admit that if the man was acting, he was acting marvellously. He looked dazed and bewildered and scared out of his wits.

"The manager was with us in no time. He made a quick inspection of the room then turned us all out and locked the door, the key of which he took. Then he went off and telephoned to the police. It seemed a positive age before they came (we learned afterwards that the line was out of order). The manager had to send a messenger to the police station, and the Hydro is right out of the town, up on the edge of the moor; and Mrs. Carpenter tried us all very severely. She was so pleased at her prophecy of 'Never two without three' coming true so quickly. Sanders, I hear, wandered out into the grounds, clutching his head and groaning and displaying every sign of grief.

"However, the police came at last. They went upstairs with the manager and Mr. Sanders. Later they sent down for me. I went up. The inspector was there, sitting at a table writing. He was an intelligent-looking man and I liked him.

" 'Miss Jane Marple?' he said.

" 'Yes.'

" 'I understand, Madam, that you were present when the body of the deceased was found?'

"I said I was and I described exactly what had occurred. I think it was a relief to the poor man to find someone who could answer his questions coherently, having previously had to deal with Sanders and Emily Trollope, who, I gather, was completely demoralized—she would be, the silly creature! I remember my dear mother teaching me that a gentlewoman should always be able to control herself in public, however much she may give way in private."

"An admirable maxim," said Sir Henry gravely.

"When I had finished the inspector said:

" 'Thank you, Madam. Now I'm afraid I must ask you just to look at the body once more. Is that exactly the position in which it was lying when you entered the room? It hasn't been moved in any way?'

"I explained that I had prevented Mr. Sanders from doing so, and the inspector nodded approval.

" 'The gentleman seems terribly upset,' he remarked.

" 'He seems so—yes,' I replied.

"I don't think I put any special emphasis on the 'seems,' but the inspector look at me rather keenly.

" 'So we can take it that the body is exactly as it was when found?' he said.

" 'Except for the hat, yes,' I replied.

"The inspector looked up sharply.

" 'What do you mean—the hat?'

"I explained that the hat had been on poor Gladys's head, whereas now it was lying beside her. I thought, of course, that the police had done this. The inspector, however, denied it emphatically. Nothing had, as yet, been moved or touched. He stood looking down at that poor prone figure with a puzzled frown. Gladys was dressed in her outdoor clothes—a big dark-red tweed coat with a grey fur collar. The hat, a cheap affair of red felt, lay just by her head.

"The inspector stood for some minutes in silence, frowning to himself. Then an idea struck him.

" 'Can you, by any chance, remember, Madam, whether there were ear-rings in the ears, or whether the deceased habitually wore ear-rings?'

"Now fortunately I am in the habit of observing closely. I remembered that there had been a glint of pearls just below the hat brim, though I had paid no particular notice to it at the time. I was able to answer his first question in the affirmative.

" 'Then that settles it. The lady's jewel case was rifled—not that she had anything much of value, I understand—and the rings were taken from her fingers. The murderer must have forgotten the ear-rings, and come back for them after the murder was discovered. A cool customer! Or perhaps'—He stared around the room and said slowly, 'He may have been concealed here in this room—all the time.'

"But I negatived that idea. I myself, I explained, had looked under the bed. And the manager had opened the doors of the wardrobe. There was nowhere else where a man could hide. It is true the hat cupboard was locked in the middle of the wardrobe, but as that was only a shallow affair with shelves, no one could have been concealed there.

"The inspector nodded his head slowly whilst I explained all this.

" 'I'll take your word for it, Madam,' he said. 'In that case, as I said before, he must have come back. A very cool customer.'

" 'But the manager locked the door and took the key!'

" 'That's nothing. The balcony and the fire escape—that's the way the thief came. Why, as likely as not, you actually disturbed him at work. He slips out of the window, and when you've all gone, back he comes and goes on with his business.'

" 'You are sure,' I said, 'that there *was* a thief?'

"He said dryly:

" 'Well, it looks like it, doesn't it?'

"But something in his tone satisfied me. I felt that he wouldn't take Mr. Sanders in the role of the bereaved widower too seriously.

"You see, I admit it frankly. I was absolutely under the opinion of what I believe our neighbours, the French, call the *idée fixe*. I knew that that man, Sanders, intended his wife to die. What I didn't allow for was that strange and fantastic thing, coincidence. My views about Mr. Sanders were—I was sure of it—absolutely right and *true*. The man was a scoundrel. But although his hypocritical assumptions of grief didn't deceive me for a minute, I do remember feeling at the time that his *surprise* and *bewilderment* were marvellously well done. They seemed absolutely *natural*—if you know what I mean. I must admit that after my conversation with the inspector, a curious feeling of doubt crept over me. Because if Sanders had done this dreadful thing, I couldn't imagine any conceivable reason why he should creep back by means of the fire escape and take the ear-rings from his wife's ears. It wouldn't have been a *sensible* thing to do, and Sanders was such a very sensible man—that's just why I always felt he was so dangerous."

Miss Marple looked round at her audience.

"You see, perhaps, what I am coming to? It is, so often, the unexpected that happens in this world. I was so *sure*, and that, I think, was what blinded me. The result came as a shock to me. *For it was proved, beyond any possible doubt, that Mr. Sanders could not possibly have committed the crime . . ."*

A surprised gasp came from Mrs. Bantry. Miss Marple turned to her.

"I know, my dear, that isn't what you expected when I began this story. It wasn't what I expected. But facts are facts, and if one is proved to be wrong, one must just be humble about it and start again. That Mr. Sanders was a murderer at heart I knew—and nothing ever occurred to upset that firm conviction of mine.

"And now, I expect you would like to hear the actual facts themselves. Mrs. Sanders, as you know, spent the afternoon playing bridge with some friends, the Mortimers. She left them at about a quarter past six. From her friends' house to the Hydro was about a quarter of an hour's walk—less if one hurried. She must have come in then, about six-thirty. No one saw her come in, so she must have entered by the side door and hurried straight up to her room. There she changed (the fawn coat and skirt she wore to the bridge party were hanging up in the cupboard) and was evidently preparing to go out again, when the blow fell. Quite possibly, they say, she never even knew who struck her. The sandbag, I understand, is a very efficient weapon. That looks as though the attackers were concealed in the room, possibly in one of the big wardrobe cupboards—the one she didn't open.

"Now as to the movements of Mr. Sanders. He went out, as I have said, at about five-thirty—or a little after. He did some shopping at a couple of shops and at about six o'clock he entered the Grand Spa Hotel where he encountered two friends—the same with whom he returned to the Hydro later. They played billiards and, I gather, had a good many whiskies and sodas together. These two men (Hitchcock and Spender, their names were) were actually with him the whole time from six o'clock onwards. They walked back to the Hydro with him and he only left them to come across to me and Miss Trollope. That, as I told you, was about a quarter to seven—at which time his wife must have been already dead.

"I must tell you that I talked myself to these two friends of his. I did not like them. They were neither pleasant nor gentlemanly men, but I was quite certain of one thing, that they were speaking the absolute truth when they said that Sanders had been the whole time in their company.

"There was just one other little point that came up. It seems that while bridge was going on Mrs. Sanders was called to the telephone. A Mr. Littleworth wanted to speak to her. She seemed both excited and pleased about something—and incidentally made one or two bad mistakes. She left rather earlier than they had expected her to do.

"Mr. Sanders was asked whether he knew the name of Littleworth as being one of his wife's friends, but he declared he had never heard of anyone of that name. And to me that seems borne out by his wife's attitude—she too, did not seem to know the name of Littleworth. Nevertheless she came back from the telephone smiling and blushing, so it looks as though whoever it was did not give his real name, and that in itself has a suspicious aspect, does it not?

"Anyway, that is the problem that was left. The burglar story, which seems unlikely—or the alternative theory that Mrs. Sanders was preparing to go out and meet somebody. Did that somebody come to her room by means of the fire escape? Was there a quarrel? Or did he treacherously attack her?"

Miss Marple stopped.

"Well?" said Sir Henry. "What is the answer?"

"I wondered if any of you could guess."

"I'm never good at guessing," said Mrs. Bantry. "It seems

a pity that Sanders had such a wonderful alibi; but if it satisfied you it must have been all right."

Jane Helier moved her beautiful head and asked a question.

"Why," she said, "was the hat cupboard locked?"

"How very clever of you, my dear," said Miss Marple, beaming. "That's just what I wondered myself, though the explanation was quite simple. In it were a pair of embroidered slippers and some pocket handkerchiefs that the poor girl was embroidering for her husband for Christmas. That's why she locked the cupboard. The key was found in her handbag."

"Oh!" said Jane. "Then it isn't very interesting after all."

"Oh, but it is," said Miss Marple. "It's just the one really interesting thing—the thing that made all the murderer's plans go wrong."

Everyone stared at the old lady.

"I didn't see it myself for two days," said Miss Marple. "I puzzled and puzzled—and then suddenly there it was, all clear. I went to the inspector and asked him to try something and he did."

"What did you ask him to try?"

"*I asked him to fit that hat on the poor girl's head*—and of course he couldn't. It wouldn't go on. *It wasn't her hat, you see.*"

Mrs. Bantry stared.

"But it was on her head to begin with?"

"Not on *her* head—"

Miss Marple stopped a moment to let her words sink in, and then went on.

"We took it for granted that it was poor Gladys's body there; but we never looked at the face. She was face downwards, remember, and the hat hid everything."

"But she *was* killed?"

"Yes, later. At the moment that we were telephoning to the police, Gladys Sanders was alive and well."

"You mean it was someone pretending to be her? But surely when you touched her—"

"It was a dead body, right enough," said Miss Marple gravely.

"But dash it all," said Colonel Bantry, "you can't get hold of dead bodies right and left. What did they do with the—the first corpse afterwards?"

"He put it back," said Miss Marple. "It was a wicked idea—but a very clever one. It was our talk in the drawing-room that put it into his head. The body of poor Mary, the housemaid—why not use it? Remember, the Sanders' room was up amongst the servants' quarters. Mary's room was two doors off. The undertakers wouldn't come till after dark—he counted on that. He carried the body along the balcony (it was dark at five), dressed it in one of his wife's dresses and her big red coat. And then he found the hat cupboard locked! There was only one thing to be done, he fetched one of the poor girl's own hats. No one would notice. He put the sandbag down beside her. Then he went off to establish his alibi.

"He telephoned to his wife—calling himself Mr. Little-worth. I don't know what he said to her—she was a credulous girl, as I said just now. But he got her to leave the bridge party early and not to go back to the Hydro, and arranged with her to meet him in the grounds of the Hydro near the fire escape at seven o'clock. He probably told her he had some surprise for her.

"He returns to the Hydro with his friends and arranges that Miss Trollope and I shall discover the crime with him. He even pretends to turn the body over—and I stop him! Then the police are sent for, and he staggers out into the grounds.

"Nobody asked him for an alibi *after* the crime. He meets his wife, takes her up the fire escape, they enter their room. Perhaps he has already told her some story about the body. She stoops over it, and he picks up his sandbag and strikes. . . . Oh, dear! it makes me sick to think of, even now! Then quickly he strips off her coat and skirt, hangs them up, and dresses her in the clothes from the other body.

"*But the hat won't go on.* Mary's head is shingled. Gladys Sanders, as I say, had a great bun of hair. He is forced to leave it beside the body and hope no one will notice. Then he carries poor Mary's body back to her own room and arranges it decorously once more."

"It seems incredible," said Dr. Lloyd. "The risks he took. The police might have arrived too soon."

"You remember the line was out of order," said Miss Marple. "That was a piece of *his* work. He couldn't afford to have the police on the spot too soon. When they did come, they spent some time in the manager's office before going up to the bedroom. That was the weakest point—the chance that someone might notice the difference between a body that had been dead two hours and one that had been dead just over half an hour; but he counted on the fact that the people who first discovered the crime would have no expert knowledge."

Dr. Lloyd nodded.

"The crime would be supposed to have been committed about a quarter to seven or thereabouts, I suppose," he said. "It was actually committed at seven or a few minutes after. When the police surgeon examined the body it would be about half-past seven at earliest. He couldn't possibly tell."

"I am the person who should have known," said Miss Marple. "I felt the poor girl's hand and it was icy cold. Yet a short time later the inspector spoke as though the murder must have been committed just before we arrived—and I saw nothing!"

"I think you saw a good deal, Miss Marple," said Sir Henry. "The case was before my time. I don't even remember hearing of it. What happened?"

"Sanders was hanged," said Miss Marple crisply. "And a good job too. I have never regretted my part in bringing that man to justice. I've no patience with modern humanitarian scruples about capital punishments."

Her stern face softened.

"But I have often reproached myself bitterly with failing to save the life of that poor girl. But who would have listened to an old woman jumping to conclusions? Well, well—who knows? Perhaps it was better for her to die while life was still happy than it would have been for her to live on, unhappy and disillusioned, in a world that would have seemed suddenly horrible. She loved that scoundrel and trusted him. She never found him out."

"Well, then," said Jane Helier, "she was all right. Quite all right. I wish—" she stopped.

Miss Marple looked at the famous, the beautiful, the successful Jane Helier and nodded her head gently.

"I see, my dear," she said very gently. "I see."

The Herb
of Death

N ow then, Mrs. B," said Sir Henry Clithering encouragingly.

Mrs. Bantry, his hostess, looked at him in cold reproof.

"I've told you before that I will not be called Mrs. B. It's not dignified."

"Scheherazade, then."

"And even less am I Sche— What's her name? I never can tell a story properly; ask Arthur if you don't believe me."

"You're quite good at the facts, Dolly," said Colonel Bantry, "but poor at the embroidery."

"That's just it," said Mrs. Bantry. She flapped the bulb catalogue she was holding on the table in front of her. "I've been listening to you all and I don't know how you do it. 'He said, she said, you wondered, they thought, everyone implied'—well, I just couldn't, and here it is! And besides, I don't know anything to tell a story about."

"We can't believe that, Mrs. Bantry," said Dr. Lloyd. He shook his grey head in mocking disbelief.

Old Miss Marple said in her gentle voice, "Surely, dear—"

Mrs. Bantry continued obstinately to shake her head.

"You don't know how banal my life is. What with the

servants and the difficulties of getting scullery maids, and just going to town for clothes, and dentists, and Ascot, which Arthur hates, and then the garden—"

"Ah!" said Dr. Lloyd. "The garden. We all know where your heart lies, Mrs. Bantry."

"It must be nice to have a garden," said Jane Helier, the beautiful young actress. "That is, if you hadn't got to dig or to get your hands messed up. I'm ever so fond of flowers."

"The garden," said Sir Henry. "Can't we take that as a starting point? Come, Mrs. B. The poisoned bulb, the deadly daffodils, the herb of death!"

"Now it's odd your saying that," said Mrs. Bantry. "You've just reminded me. Arthur, do you remember that business at Clodderham Court? You know, old Sir Ambrose Bercy. Do you remember what a courtly charming old man we thought him?"

"Why, of course. Yes, that was a strange business. Go ahead, Dolly."

"You'd better tell it, dear."

"Nonsense. Go ahead. Must paddle your own canoe. I did my bit just now."

Mrs. Bantry drew a deep breath. She clasped her hands and her face registered complete mental anguish. She spoke rapidly and fluently.

"Well, there's really not much to tell. The Herb of Death—that's what put it into my head, though in my own mind I call it sage and onions."

"Sage and onions?" asked Dr. Lloyd.

Mrs. Bantry nodded.

"That was how it happened, you see," she explained. "We were staying, Arthur and I, with Sir Ambrose Bercy at Clodderham Court, and one day, by mistake (though very stupidly, I've always thought), a lot of foxglove leaves were picked with the sage. The ducks for dinner that night were stuffed with it and everyone was very ill, and one poor girl—Sir Ambrose's ward—died of it."

She stopped.

"Dear, dear," said Miss Marple, "how very tragic."

"Wasn't it?"

"Well," said Sir Henry, "what next?"

"There isn't any next," said Mrs. Bantry. "That's all."

Everyone gasped. Though warned beforehand, they had not expected quite such brevity as this.

"But, my dear lady," remonstrated Sir Henry, "it can't be all. What you have related is a tragic occurrence but not in any sense of the word a problem."

"Well, of course there's some more," said Mrs. Bantry. "But if I were to tell you, you'd know what it was."

She looked defiantly round the assembly and said plaintively:

"I told you I couldn't dress things up and make it sound properly like a story ought to do."

"Ah ha!" said Sir Henry. He sat up in his chair and adjusted an eyeglass. "Really, you know, Scheherazade, this is most refreshing. Our ingenuity is challenged. I'm not so sure you haven't done it on purpose—to stimulate our curiosity. A few brisk rounds of 'Twenty Questions' is indicated, I think. Miss Marple, will you begin?"

"I'd like to know something about the cook," said Miss Marple. "She must have been a very stupid woman, or else very inexperienced."

"She was just very stupid," said Mrs. Bantry. "She cried a great deal afterward and said the leaves had been picked and brought into her as sage, and how was she to know?"

"Not one who thought for herself," said Miss Marple. "Probably an elderly woman and, I daresay, a very good cook?"

"Oh, excellent," said Mrs. Bantry.

"Your turn, Miss Helier," said Sir Henry.

"Oh! You mean—to ask a question?" There was a pause while Jane pondered. Finally she said helplessly, "Really—I don't know what to ask."

Her beautiful eyes looked appealingly at Sir Henry.

"Why not dramatis personae, Miss Helier?" he suggested, smiling.

Jane still looked puzzled.

"Characters in order of their appearance," said Sir Henry gently.

"Oh, yes," said Jane. "That's a good idea."

Mrs. Bantry began briskly to tick people off on her fingers.

"Sir Ambrose—Sylvia Keene (that's the girl who died)—a friend of hers who was staying there, Maud Wye, one of those dark ugly girls who manage to make an effect somehow—I never know how they do it. Then there was a Mr. Curle who had come down to discuss books with Sir Ambrose—you know, rare books—queer old things in Latin—all musty parchment. There was Jerry Lorimer—he was a kind of next-door neighbour. His place, Fairlies, joined Sir Ambrose's estate. And there was Mrs. Carpenter, one of those middle-aged pussies who always seem to manage to dig themselves in comfortably somewhere. She was by way of being *dame de compagnie* to Sylvia, I suppose."

"If it is my turn," said Sir Henry, "and I suppose it is, as I'm sitting next to Miss Helier, I want a good deal. I want a short verbal portrait, please, Mrs. Bantry, of all the foregoing."

"Oh!" Mrs. Bantry hesitated.

"Sir Ambrose now," continued Sir Henry. "Start with him. What was he like?"

"Oh, he was a very distinguished-looking old man—and not so very old really—not more than sixty, I suppose. But he was very delicate—he had a weak heart, could never go upstairs—had had to have a lift put in, and so that made him seem older than he was. Very charming manners—courtly—that's the word that describes him best. You never saw him ruffled or upset. He had beautiful white hair and a particularly charming voice."

"Good," said Sir Henry. "I see Sir Ambrose. Now the girl Sylvia—what did you say her name was?"

"Sylvia Keene. She was pretty—really very pretty. Fair-haired, you know, and a lovely skin. Not, perhaps, very clever. In fact, rather stupid."

"Oh, come, Dolly," protested her husband.

"Arthur, of course, wouldn't think so," said Mrs. Bantry dryly. "But she was stupid—she really never said anything worth listening to."

"One of the most graceful creatures I ever saw," said Colonel Bantry warmly. "See her playing tennis—charming, simply charming. And she was full of fun—most amusing little thing. And such a pretty way with her. I bet the young fellows all thought so."

"That's just where you're wrong," said Mrs. Bantry. "Youth, as such, has no charms for young men nowadays. It's only old duffers like you, Arthur, who sit maundering on about young girls."

"Being young's no good," said Jane. "You've got to have S.A."

"What," said Miss Marple, "is S.A.?"

"Sex appeal," said Jane.

"Ah yes," said Miss Marple. "What in my day they used to call 'having the come hither in your eye.'"

"Not a bad description," said Sir Henry. "The *dame de compagnie* you described, I think, as a pussy, Mrs. Bantry?"

"I didn't mean a cat, you know," said Mrs. Bantry. "It's quite different. Just a big soft white purry person. Always very sweet. That's what Adelaide Carpenter was like."

"What sort of aged woman?"

"Oh! I should say fortyish. She'd been there some time—ever since Sylvia was eleven, I believe. A very tactful person. One of those widows left in unfortunate circumstances, with plenty of aristocratic relations, but no ready cash. I didn't like her myself—but then I never do like people with very white long hands. And I don't like pussies."

"Mr. Curle?"

"Oh, one of those elderly stooping men. There are so many of them about, you'd hardly know one from the other. He showed enthusiasm when talking about his musty books, but not at any other time. I don't think Sir Ambrose knew him very well."

"And Jerry next door?"

"A really charming boy. He was engaged to Sylvia. That's what made it so sad."

"Now I wonder—" began Miss Marple, and then stopped.

"What?"

"Nothing, dear."

Sir Henry looked at the old lady curiously. Then he said thoughtfully:

"So this young couple were engaged. Had they been engaged long?"

"About a year. Sir Ambrose had opposed the engagement on the plea that Sylvia was too young. But after a year's engagement he had given in and the marriage was to have taken place quite soon."

"Ah! Had the young lady any property?"

"Next to nothing—a bare hundred or two a year."

"No rat in that hole, Clithering," said Colonel Bantry, and laughed.

"It's the doctor's turn to ask a question," said Sir Henry. "I stand down."

"My curiosity is mainly professional," said Dr. Lloyd. "I

should like to know what medical evidence was given at the inquest—that is, if our hostess remembers, or, indeed, if she knows."

"I know roughly," said Mrs. Bantry. "It was poisoning by digitalin—is that right?"

Dr. Lloyd nodded.

"The active principle of the foxglove—digitalis—acts on the heart. Indeed, it is a very valuable drug in some forms of heart trouble. A very curious case altogether. I would never have believed that eating a preparation of foxglove leaves could possibly result fatally. These ideas of eating poisonous leaves and berries are very much exaggerated. Very few people realize that the vital principle, or alkaloid, has to be extracted with much care and preparation."

"Mrs. MacArthur sent some special bulbs round to Mrs. Toomie the other day," said Miss Marple. "And Mrs. Toomie's cook mistook them for onions, and all the Toomies were very ill indeed."

"But they didn't die of it," said Dr. Lloyd.

"No, they didn't die of it," admitted Miss Marple.

"A girl I knew died of ptomaine poisoning," said Jane Helier.

"We must get on with investigating the crime," said Sir Henry.

"Crime?" said Jane, startled. "I thought it was an accident."

"If it were an accident," said Sir Henry gently, "I do not think Mrs. Bantry would have told us this story. No, as I read it, this was an accident only in appearance—behind it is something more sinister. I remember a case—various guests in a house party were chatting after dinner. The walls were adorned with all kinds of old-fashioned weapons. Entirely as a joke, one of the party seized an ancient horse pistol and pointed it at another man, pretending to fire it. The pistol was loaded and went off, killing the man. We had to ascertain in that case, first who had secretly prepared and loaded that pistol, and secondly, who had so led and directed the conversation that that final bit of horseplay resulted—for the man who had fired the pistol was entirely innocent!

"It seems to me we have much the same problem here. Those digitalin leaves were deliberately mixed with the sage, knowing what the result would be. Since we exonerate the cook—we do exonerate the cook, don't we?—the question arises: Who picked the leaves and delivered them to the kitchen?"

"That's easily answered," said Mrs. Bantry. "At least the last part of it is. It was Sylvia herself who took the leaves to the kitchen. It was part of her daily job to gather things like salad or herbs, bunches of young carrots—all the sort of things that gardeners never pick right. They hate giving you anything young and tender—they wait for them to be fine specimens. Sylvia and Mrs. Carpenter used to see a lot of these things themselves. And there was foxglove actually growing all among the sage in one corner, so the mistake was quite natural."

"But did Sylvia actually pick them herself?"

"That nobody ever knew. It was assumed so."

"Assumptions," said Sir Henry, "are dangerous things."

"But I do know that Mrs. Carpenter didn't pick them," said Mrs. Bantry. "Because, as it happened, she was walking with me on the terrace that morning. We went out there after breakfast. It was unusually nice and warm for early spring. Sylvia went alone down into the garden, but later I saw her walking arm in arm with Maud Wye."

"So they were great friends, were they?" asked Miss Marple.

"Yes," said Mrs. Bantry. She seemed as though about to say something but did not do so.

"Had she been staying there long?" asked Miss Marple.

"About a fortnight," said Mrs. Bantry.

There was a note of trouble in her voice.

"You didn't like Miss Wye?" suggested Sir Henry.

"I did. That's just it. I did."

The trouble in her voice had grown to distress.

"You're keeping something back, Mrs. Bantry," said Sir Henry accusingly.

"I wondered just now," said Miss Marple, "but I didn't like to go on."

"When did you wonder?"

"When you said that the young people were engaged. You said that that was what made it so sad. But, if you know what I mean, your voice didn't sound right when you said it—not convincing, you know."

"What a dreadful person you are," said Mrs. Bantry. "You always seem to know. Yes, I was thinking of something. But I don't really know whether I ought to say it or not."

"You must say it," said Sir Henry. "Whatever your scruples, it mustn't be kept back."

"Well, it was just this," said Mrs. Bantry. "One evening—in fact the very evening before the tragedy—I happened to go out on the terrace before dinner. The window in the drawing-room was open. And as it chanced I saw Jerry Lorimer and Maud Wye. He was—well—kissing her. Of course I didn't know whether it was just a sort of chance affair, or whether—well, I mean, one can't tell. I knew Sir Ambrose never had really liked Jerry Lorimer—so perhaps he knew he was that kind of young man. But one thing I am sure of: that girl, Maud Wye, was really fond of him. You'd only to see her looking at him when she was off guard. And I think, too, they were really better suited than he and Sylvia were."

"I am going to ask a question quickly, before Miss Marple

can," said Sir Henry. "I want to know whether, after the tragedy, Jerry Lorimer married Maud Wye?"

"Yes," said Mrs. Bantry. "He did. Six months afterward."

"Oh! Scheherazade, Scheherazade," said Sir Henry. "To think of the way you told us this story at first! Bare bones indeed—and to think of the amount of flesh we're finding on them now."

"Don't speak so ghoulishly," said Mrs. Bantry. "And don't use the word flesh. Vegetarians always do. They say, 'I never eat flesh,' in a way that puts you right off your nice little beefsteak. Mr. Curle was a vegetarian. He used to eat some peculiar stuff that looked like bran for breakfast. Those elderly stooping men with beards are often faddy. They have patent kinds of underwear too."

"What on earth, Dolly," said her husband, "do you know about Mr. Curle's underwear?"

"Nothing," said Mrs. Bantry with dignity. "I was just making a guess."

"I'll amend my former statement," said Sir Henry. "I'll say instead that the dramatis personae in your problem are very interesting. I'm beginning to see them all—eh, Miss Marple?"

"Human nature is always interesting, Sir Henry. And it's curious to see how certain types always tend to act in exactly the same way."

"Two women and a man," said Sir Henry. "The old eternal human triangle. Is that the base of our problem here? I rather fancy it is."

Dr. Lloyd cleared his throat.

"I've been thinking," he said rather diffidently. "Do you say, Mrs. Bantry, that you yourself were ill?"

"Was I not! So was Arthur! So was everyone!"

"That's just it—everyone," said the doctor. "You see what I mean? I'm saying that whoever planned this thing went about it very curiously, either with a blind belief in chance, or else with an absolutely reckless disregard for human life. I can hardly believe there is a man capable of deliberately poisoning eight people with the object of removing one among them."

"I see your point," said Sir Henry thoughtfully. "I confess I ought to have thought of that."

"And mightn't he have poisoned himself too?" asked Jane.

"Was anyone absent from dinner that night?" asked Miss Marple.

Mrs. Bantry shook her head.

"Everyone was there."

"Except Mr. Lorimer, I suppose, my dear. He wasn't staying in the house, was he?"

"No, but he was dining there that evening," said Mrs. Bantry.

"Oh!" said Miss Marple in a changed voice. "That makes all the difference in the world."

She frowned vexedly to herself.

"I've been very stupid," she murmured. "Very stupid indeed."

"I confess your point worries me, Lloyd," said Sir Henry. "How ensure that the girl, and the girl only, should get a fatal dose?"

"You can't," said the doctor. "That brings me to the point I'm going to make. Supposing the girl was not the intended victim, after all?"

"What?"

"In all cases of food poisoning the result is very uncertain. Several people share a dish. What happens? One or two are slightly ill; two more, say, are seriously indisposed; one dies. That's the way of it—there's no certainty anywhere. But there are cases where another factor might enter in. Digitalin is a drug that acts directly on the heart—as I've told you, it's prescribed in certain cases. Now, there was one person in this house who suffered from a heart complaint. Suppose he was the victim selected? What would not be fatal to the rest would be fatal to him—or so the murderer might reasonably suppose. That the thing turned out differently is only proof of what I was saying just now—the uncertainty and unreliability of the effect of drugs on human beings."

"Sir Ambrose," said Sir Henry, "you think he was the person aimed at? Yes, yes—and the girl's death was a mistake."

"Who got his money after he was dead?" asked Jane.

"A very sound question, Miss Helier. One of the first we always ask in my late profession," said Sir Henry.

"Sir Ambrose had a son," said Mrs. Bantry slowly. "He had quarrelled with him many years previously. The boy was wild, I believe. Still, it was not in Sir Ambrose's power to disinherit him—Clodderham Court was entailed. Martin Bercy succeeded to the title and estate. There was, however, a good deal of other property that Sir Ambrose could leave as he chose, and that he left to his ward Sylvia. I know this because Sir Ambrose died less than a year after the events I am telling you of, and he had not troubled to make a new will after Sylvia's death. I think the money went to the Crown—or perhaps it was to his son as next of kin—I don't really remember."

"So it was only to the interest of a son who wasn't there and the girl who died herself to make away with him," said Sir Henry thoughtfully. "That doesn't seem very promising."

"Didn't the other woman get anything?" asked Jane. "The one Mrs. Bantry calls the Pussy woman."

"She wasn't mentioned in the will," said Mrs. Bantry.

"Miss Marple, you're not listening," said Sir Henry. "You're somewhere far away."

"I was thinking of old Mr. Badger, the chemist," said Miss Marple. "He had a very young housekeeper—young enough to be not only his daughter but his granddaughter. Not a word to anyone, and his family, a lot of nephews and nieces, full of expectations. And when he died, would you believe it, he'd been secretly married to her for two years? Of course, Mr. Badger was a chemist, and a very rude, common old man as well, and Sir Ambrose Bercy was a very courtly gentleman, so Mrs. Bantry says, but for all that human nature is much the same everywhere."

There was a pause, Sir Henry looked very hard at Miss Marple who looked back at him with gently quizzical blue eyes. Jane Helier broke the silence.

"Was this Mrs. Carpenter good-looking?" she asked.

"Yes, in a very quiet way. Nothing startling."

"She had a very sympathetic voice," said Colonel Bantry.

"Purring—that's what I call it," said Mrs. Bantry. "Purring!"

"You'll be called a cat yourself one of these days, Dolly."

"I like being a cat in my home circle," said Mrs. Bantry. "I don't much like women anyway, and you know it. I like men and flowers."

"Excellent taste," said Sir Henry. "Especially in putting men first."

"That was tact," said Mrs. Bantry. "Well, now, what about my little problem? I've been quite fair, I think. Arthur, don't you think I've been fair?"

"Yes, my dear. I don't think there'll be any inquiry into the running by the stewards of the Jockey Club."

"First boy," said Mrs. Bantry, pointing a finger at Sir Henry.

"I'm going to be long-winded. Because, you see, I haven't really got any feeling of certainty about the matter. First, Sir Ambrose. Well, he wouldn't take such an original method of committing suicide—and on the other hand, he certainly had nothing to gain by the death of his ward. Exit Sir Ambrose. Mr. Curle. No motive for death of girl. If Sir Ambrose was intended victim, he might possibly have purloined a rare manuscript or two that no one else would miss. Very thin, and most unlikely. So I think that, in spite of Mrs. Bantry's suspicions, Mr. Curle is cleared. Miss Wye. Motive for death of Sir Ambrose—none. Motive for death of Sylvia pretty strong. She wanted Sylvia's young man, and wanted him rather badly—from Mrs. Bantry's account. She was with Sylvia that morning in the garden so had opportunity to pick leaves. No, we can't dismiss Miss Wye so easily. Young Lorimer. He's got a motive in either case. If he gets rid of his sweetheart, he can marry the other girl. Still it seems a bit drastic to kill her—what's a broken engagement these days? If Sir Ambrose dies, he will marry a rich girl instead of a poor one. That might be important or not—depends on his financial position. If I find that his estate was heavily mortgaged and that Mrs. Bantry has deliberately withheld that fact from us, I shall claim a foul. Now Mrs. Carpenter. You know, I have suspicions of Mrs. Carpenter. Those white hands, for one thing, and her excellent alibi at the time the herbs were picked—I always distrust alibis. And I've got another reason for suspecting her which I shall keep to myself. Still, on the whole, if I've got to plump, I shall plump for Miss Maud Wye, because there's more evidence against her than anyone else."

"Next boy," said Mrs. Bantry, and pointed at Dr. Lloyd.

"I think you're wrong, Clithering, in sticking to the theory that the girl's death was meant. I am convinced that the murderer intended to do away with Sir Ambrose. I don't think that young Lorimer had the necessary knowledge. I am inclined to believe that Mrs. Carpenter was the guilty party. She had been a long time with the family, knew all about the state of Sir Ambrose's health, and could easily arrange for this girl Sylvia (who, you said yourself, was rather stupid) to pick the right leaves. Motive, I confess, I don't see; but I hazard the guess that Sir Ambrose had at one time made a will in which she was mentioned. That's the best I can do."

Mrs. Bantry's pointing finger went on to Jane Helier.

"I don't know what to say," said Jane, "except this: Why shouldn't the girl herself have done it? She took the leaves into the kitchen after all. And you say Sir Ambrose had been sticking out against her marriage. If he died, she'd get the money and be able to marry at once. She'd know just as much about Sir Ambrose's health as Mrs. Carpenter would."

Mrs. Bantry's finger came slowly round to Miss Marple.

"Now then, school marm," she said.

"Sir Henry has put it all very clearly—very clearly indeed," said Miss Marple. "And Dr. Lloyd was so right in what he said. Between them they seem to have made things so very clear. Only I don't think Dr. Lloyd quite realized one aspect of what he said. You see, not being Sir Ambrose's medical adviser, he couldn't know just what kind of heart trouble Sir Ambrose had, could he?"

"I don't quite see what you mean, Miss Marple," said Dr. Lloyd.

"You're assuming—aren't you?—that Sir Ambrose had the kind of heart that digitalin would affect adversely? But there's nothing to prove that that's so. It might be just the other way about."

"The other way about?"

"Yes, you did say that it was often prescribed for heart trouble?"

"Even then, Miss Marple, I don't see what that leads to?"

"Well, it would mean that he would have digitalin in his possession quite naturally—without having to account for it. What I am trying to say (I always express myself so badly) is this: Supposing you wanted to poison anyone with a fatal dose of digitalin. Wouldn't the simplest and the easiest way be to arrange for everyone to be poisoned—actually by digitalin leaves? It wouldn't be fatal in anyone else's case, of course, but no one would be surprised at one victim because, as Dr. Lloyd said, these things are so uncertain. No one would be likely to ask whether the girl had actually had a fatal dose of infusion of digitalis or something of that kind. He might have put it in a cocktail or in her coffee or even made her drink it quite simply as a tonic."

"You mean Sir Ambrose poisoned his ward, the charming girl whom he loved?"

"That's just it," said Miss Marple. "Like Mr. Badger and his young housekeeper. Don't tell me it's absurd for a man of sixty to fall in love with a girl of twenty. It happens every day—and I daresay with an old autocrat like Sir Ambrose, it might take him queerly. These things become a madness sometimes. He couldn't bear the thought of her getting married—did his best to oppose it—and failed. His mad jealousy became so great that he preferred killing her to letting her go to young Lorimer. He must have thought of it some time beforehand, because that foxglove seed would have to be sown among the sage. He'd pick it himself when the time came and send her into the kitchen with it. It's horrible to think of, but I suppose we must take as merciful a view of it as we can. Gentlemen of that age are sometimes very peculiar indeed where young girls are concerned. Our last organist—but there, I mustn't talk scandal."

"Mrs. Bantry," said Sir Henry, "is this so?"

Mrs. Bantry nodded.

"Yes. I'd no idea of it—never dreamed of the thing being anything but an accident. Then, after Sir Ambrose's death, I got a letter. He had left directions to send it to me. He told me the truth in it. I don't know why—but he and I always got on very well together."

In the momentary silence she seemed to feel an unspoken criticism and went on hastily:

"You think I'm betraying a confidence—but that isn't so. I've changed all the names. He wasn't really called Sir Ambrose Bercy. Didn't you see how Arthur stared stupidly when I said that name to him? He didn't understand at first. I've changed everything. It's like they say in magazines and in the beginning of books: 'All the characters in this story are purely fictitious.' You'll never know who they really are."

The Affair at
the Bungalow

I've thought of something," said Jane Helier.

Her beautiful face was lit up with the confident smile of a child expecting approbation. It was a smile such as moved audiences nightly in London, and which had made the fortunes of photographers.

"It happened," she went on carefully, "to a friend of mine."

Everyone made encouraging but slightly hypocritical noises. Colonel Bantry, Mrs. Bantry, Sir Henry Clithering, Dr. Lloyd and old Miss Marple were one and all convinced that Jane's "friend" was Jane herself. She would have been quite incapable of remembering or taking an interest in anything affecting anyone else.

"My friend," went on Jane, "(I won't mention her name) was an actress—a very well-known actress."

No one expressed surprise. Sir Henry Clithering thought to himself: "Now I wonder how many sentences it will be before she forgets to keep up the fiction, and says 'I' instead of 'She'?"

"My friend was on tour in the provinces—this was a year or two ago. I suppose I'd better not give the name of the place. It was a riverside town not very far from London. I'll call it—"

She paused, her brows perplexed in thought. The invention of even a simple name appeared to be too much for her. Sir Henry came to the rescue.

"Shall we call it Riverbury?" he suggested gravely.

"Oh, yes, that would do splendidly. Riverbury, I'll remember that. Well, as I say, this—my friend—was at Riverbury with her company, and a very curious thing happened."

She puckered her brows again.

"It's very difficult," she said plaintively, "to say just what you want. One gets things mixed up and tells the wrong thing first."

"You're doing it beautifully," said Dr. Lloyd encouragingly. "Go on."

"Well, this curious thing happened. My friend was sent for to the police station. And she went. It seemed there had been a burglary at a riverside bungalow and they'd arrested a young man, and he told a very odd story. And so they sent for her.

"She'd never been to a police station before, but they were very nice to her—very nice indeed."

"They would be, I'm sure," said Sir Henry.

"The sergeant—I think it was a sergeant—or it may have been an inspector—gave her a chair and explained things, and of course I saw at once that it was some mistake—"

"Aha," thought Sir Henry. "I! Here we are. I thought as much."

"My friend said so," continued Jane, serenely unconscious of her self-betrayal. "She explained she had been rehearsing with her understudy at the hotel and that she'd never even heard of this Mr. Faulkener. And the sergeant said, 'Miss Hel—' "

She stopped and flushed.

"Miss Helman," suggested Sir Henry with a twinkle.

"Yes—yes, that would do. Thank you. He said, 'Well,

Miss Helman, I felt it must be some mistake, knowing that you were stopping at the Bridge Hotel,' and he said would I have any objection to confronting—or was it being confronted? I can't remember."

"It doesn't really matter," said Sir Henry reassuringly.

"Anyway, with the young man. So I said, 'Of course not.' And they brought him and said, 'This is Miss Helier,' and—Oh!" Jane broke off open-mouthed.

"Never mind, my dear," said Miss Marple consolingly. "We were bound to guess, you know. And you haven't given us the name of the place or anything that really matters."

"Well," said Jane, "I did mean to tell it as though it happened to someone else. But it *is* difficult, isn't it? I mean one forgets so."

Everyone assured her that it was very difficult, and, soothed and reassured, she went on with her slightly involved narrative.

"He was a nice-looking man—quite a nice-looking man. Young, with reddish hair. His mouth just opened when he saw me. And the sergeant said, 'Is this the lady?' And he said, 'No, indeed it isn't. What an ass I have been.' And I smiled at him and said it didn't matter."

"I can picture the scene," said Sir Henry.

Jane Helier frowned.

"Let me see—how had I better go on?"

"Supposing you tell us what it was all about, dear?" said Miss Marple, so mildly that no one could suspect her of irony. "I mean what the young man's mistake was, and about the burglary."

"Oh, yes," said Jane. "Well, you see, this young man—Leslie Faulkener, his name was—had written a play. He'd written several plays, as a matter of fact, though none of them had ever been taken. And he had sent this particular play to me to read. I didn't know about it, because of course I have hundreds of plays sent to me and I read very few of them myself—only the ones I know something about. Anyway, there it was, and it seems that Mr. Faulkener got a letter from me—only it turned out not to be really from me—you understand—"

She paused anxiously, and they assured her that they understood.

"Saying that I'd read the play, and liked it very much and would he come down and talk it over with me. And it gave the address—The Bungalow, Riverbury. So Mr. Faulkener was frightfully pleased and he came down and arrived at this place—The Bungalow. A parlourmaid opened the door, and he asked for Miss Helier, and she said Miss Helier was in and expected him and showed him into the drawing-room, and there a woman came to him. And he accepted her as me as a matter of course—which seems queer because after all he had seen me act and my photographs are very well known, aren't they?"

"Over the length and breadth of England," said Mrs. Bantry promptly. "But there's often a lot of difference between a photograph and its original, my dear Jane. And there's a great deal of difference between behind the footlights and off the stage. It's not every actress who stands the test as well as you do, remember."

"Well," said Jane, slightly mollified, "that may be so. Anyway, he described this woman as tall and fair with big blue eyes and very good-looking, so I suppose it must have been near enough. He certainly had no suspicions. She sat down and began talking about his play and said she was anxious to do it. Whilst they were talking, cocktails were brought in and Mr. Faulkener had one as a matter of course. Well—that's all he remembers—having this cocktail. When he woke up, or came to himself, or whatever you call it—he was lying out in the road, by the hedge, of course, so that there would be no danger of his being run over. He felt very queer and shaky—so much so that he just got up and staggered along the road not quite knowing where he was going. He said if he'd had his senses about him he'd have gone back to the Bungalow and tried to find out what had happened. But he felt just stupid and mazed and walked along without quite knowing what he was doing. He was just more or less coming to himself when the police arrested him."

"Why did the police arrest him?" asked Dr. Lloyd.

"Oh! didn't I tell you?" said Jane opening her eyes very wide. "How very stupid I am. The burglary."

"You mentioned a burglary—but you didn't say where or what or why," said Mrs. Bantry.

"Well, this bungalow—the one he went to, of course—it wasn't mine at all. It belonged to a man whose name was—"

Again Jane furrowed her brows.

"Do you want me to be godfather again?" asked Sir Henry. "Pseudonyms supplied free of charge. Describe the tenant and I'll do the naming."

"It was taken by a rich city man—a knight."

"Sir Herman Cohen," suggested Sir Henry.

"That will do beautifully. He took it for a lady—she was the wife of an actor, and she was also an actress herself."

"We'll call the actor Claud Leason," said Sir Henry, "and the lady would be known by her stage name, I suppose, so we'll call her Miss Mary Kerr."

"I think you're awfully clever," said Jane. "I don't know how you think of these things so easily. Well, you see this was sort of a weekend cottage for Sir Herman—did you say Herman?—and the lady. And, of course, his wife knew nothing about it."

"Which is so often the case," said Sir Henry.

"And he'd given this actress woman a good deal of jewellery including some very fine emeralds."

"Ah!" said Dr. Lloyd. "Now we're getting at it."

"This jewellery was at the bungalow, just locked up in a jewel case. The police said it was very careless—anyone might have taken it."

"You see, Dolly," said Colonel Bantry. "What do I always tell you?"

"Well, in my experience," said Mrs. Bantry, "it's always the people who are so dreadfully careful who lose things. I don't lock mine up in a jewel case—I keep it in a drawer loose, under my stockings. I dare say if—what's her name?—Mary Kerr had done the same, it would never have been stolen."

"It would," said Jane, "because all the drawers were burst open, and the contents strewn about."

"Then they weren't really looking for jewels," said Mrs. Bantry. "They were looking for secret papers. That's what always happens in books."

"I don't know about secret papers," said Jane doubtfully. "I never heard of any."

"Don't be distracted, Miss Helier," said Colonel Bantry. "Dolly's wild red-herrings are not to be taken seriously."

"About the burglary," said Sir Henry.

"Yes. Well the police were rung up by someone who said she was Miss Mary Kerr. She said the bungalow had been burgled and described a young man with red hair who had called there that morning. Her maid had thought there was something odd about him and had refused him admittance, but later they had seen him getting out through a window. She described the man so accurately that the police arrested him only an hour later and then he told his story and showed them the letter from me. And as I told you, they fetched me and when he saw me he said what I told you—that it hadn't been me at all!"

"A very curious story," said Dr. Lloyd. "Did Mr. Faulkener know this Miss Kerr?"

"No, he didn't—or he said he didn't. But I haven't told you the most curious part yet. The police went to the bungalow of course, and they found everything as described— drawers pulled out and jewels gone, but the whole place was empty. It wasn't till some hours later that Mary Kerr came back, and when she did she said she'd never rung them up at all and this was the first she'd heard of it. It seemed that she had had a wire that morning from a manager offering her a most important part and making an appointment, so she had naturally rushed up to town to keep it. When she got there, she found that the whole thing was a hoax. No telegram had ever been sent."

"A common enough ruse to get her out of the way," commented Sir Henry. "What about the servants?"

"The same sort of thing happened there. There was only one, and she was rung up on the telephone—apparently by Mary Kerr, who said she had left a most important thing behind. She directed the maid to bring up a certain handbag which was in the drawer of her bedroom. She was to catch the first train. The maid did so, of course locking up the house; but when she arrived at Miss Kerr's club, where she had been told to meet her mistress, she waited there in vain."

"H'm," said Sir Henry. "I begin to see. The house was left empty, and to make an entry by one of the windows would present few difficulties, I should imagine. But I don't quite see where Mr. Faulkener comes in. Who did ring up the police, if it wasn't Miss Kerr?"

"That's what nobody knew or ever found out."

"Curious," said Sir Henry. "Did the young man turn out to be genuinely the person he said he was?"

"Oh, yes, that part of it was all right. He'd even got the letter which was supposed to be written by me. It wasn't the least bit like my handwriting—but then, of course, he couldn't be supposed to know that."

"Well, let's state the position clearly," said Sir Henry. "Correct me if I go wrong. The lady and the maid are decoyed from the house. This young man is decoyed down there by means of a bogus letter—colour being lent to this last by the fact that you actually are performing at Riverbury that week. The young man is doped, and the police are rung up and have their suspicions directed against him. A burglary actually has taken place. I presume the jewels were taken?"

"Oh, yes."

"Were they ever recovered?"

"No, never. I think, as a matter of fact, Sir Herman tried to hush things up all he knew how. But he couldn't manage it, and I rather fancy his wife started divorce proceedings in consequence. Still, I don't really know about that."

"What happened to Mr. Leslie Faulkener?"

"He was released in the end. The police said they hadn't really got enough against him. Don't you think the whole thing was rather odd?"

"Distinctly odd. The first question is whose story to believe? In telling it, Miss Helier, I noticed that you incline towards believing Mr. Faulkener. Have you any reason for doing so beyond your own instinct in the matter?"

"N-no," said Jane unwillingly. "I suppose I haven't. But he was so very nice, and so apologetic for having mistaken anyone else for me, that I feel sure he *must* have been telling the truth."

"I see," said Sir Henry smiling. "But you must admit that he could have invented the story quite easily. He could write the letter purporting to be from you himself. He could also dope himself after successfully committing the burglary. But I confess I don't see where the *point* of all that would be. Easier to enter the house, help himself, and disappear quietly—unless just possibly he was observed by someone in the neighbourhood and knew himself to have been observed. Then he might hastily concoct this plan for diverting suspicion from himself and accounting for his presence in the neighbourhood."

"Was he well off?" asked Miss Marple.

"I don't think so," said Jane. "No, I believe he was rather hard up."

"The whole thing seems curious," said Dr. Lloyd. "I must confess that if we accept the young man's story as true, it seems to make the case much more difficult. Why should the unknown woman who pretended to be Miss Helier drag this unknown man into the affair? Why should she stage such an elaborate comedy?"

"Tell me, Jane," said Mrs. Bantry. "Did young Faulkener ever come face to face with Mary Kerr at any stage of the proceedings?"

"I don't quite know," said Jane slowly, as she puzzled her brows in remembrance.

"Because if he didn't the case is solved!" said Mrs. Bantry. "I'm sure I'm right. What is easier than to pretend you're called up to town? You telephone to your maid from Paddington or whatever station you arrive at, and as she comes up to town, you go down again. The young man calls by appointment, he's doped, you set the stage for the burglary, overdoing it as much as possible. You telephone the police, give a description of your scapegoat, and off you go to town again. Then you arrive home by a later train and do the surprised innocent."

"But why should she steal her own jewels, Dolly?"

"They always do," said Mrs. Bantry. "And anyway, I can think of hundreds of reasons. She may have wanted money at once—old Sir Herman wouldn't give her cash, perhaps, so she pretends the jewels are stolen and then sells them secretly. Or she may have been being blackmailed by someone who threatened to tell her husband or Sir Herman's wife. Or she may have already sold the jewels and Sir Herman was getting ratty and asking to see them, so she had to do something about it. That's done a good deal in books. Or perhaps he was going to have them reset and she'd got paste replicas. Or—here's a very good idea—and not so much done in books—she pretends they are stolen, gets in an awful state and he gives her a fresh lot. So she gets two lots instead of one. That kind of woman, I am sure, is most frightfully artful."

"You are clever, Dolly," said Jane admiringly. "I never thought of that."

"You may be clever, but she doesn't say you're right," said Colonel Bantry. "I incline to suspicion of the city gentleman. He'd know the sort of telegram to get the lady out of the way, and he could manage the rest easily enough with the help of a new ladyfriend. Nobody seems to have thought of asking *him* for an alibi."

"What do you think, Miss Marple?" asked Jane, turning towards the old lady who had sat silent, a puzzled frown on her face.

"My dear, I really don't know what to say. Sir Henry will laugh, but I recall no village parallel to help me this time. Of course there are several questions that suggest themselves. For instance, the servant question. In—ahem—an irregular ménage of the kind you describe, the servant employed would doubtless be perfectly aware of the state of things, and a really nice girl would not take such a place—her mother wouldn't let her for a minute. So I think we can assume that the maid was *not* a really trustworthy character. She may have been in league with the thieves. She would leave the house open for them and actually go to London as though sure of the pretence telephone message so as to divert suspicion from herself. I must confess that that seems the most probable solution. Only if ordinary thieves were concerned it seems very odd. It seems to argue more knowledge than a maidservant was likely to have."

Miss Marple paused and then went on dreamily:

"I can't help feeling that there was some—well, what I must describe as personal feeling about the whole thing. Supposing somebody had a spite, for instance? Don't you think that that would explain things better? A deliberate attempt to get him into trouble. That's what it looks like. And yet—that's not entirely satisfactory. . . ."

"Why, Doctor, you haven't said anything," said Jane. "I'd forgotten you."

"I'm always getting forgotten," said the grizzled doctor sadly. "I must have a very inconspicuous personality."

"Oh, no!" said Jane. "Do tell us what you think?"

"I'm rather in the position of agreeing with everyone's solution—and yet with none of them. I myself have a far-fetched and probably totally erroneous theory that the wife may have had something to do with it. Sir Herman's wife, I mean. I've no grounds for thinking so—only you would be surprised if you knew the extraordinary things that a wronged wife will take it into her head to do."

"Oh! Dr. Lloyd," cried Miss Marple excitedly. "How clever of you. And I never thought of poor Mrs. Pebmarsh."

Jane stared at her.

"Mrs. Pebmarsh? Who is Mrs. Pebmarsh?"

"Well—" Miss Marple hesitated. "I don't know that she really comes in. She's a laundress. And she stole an opal pin that was pinned into a blouse and put it in another woman's house."

Jane looked more fogged than ever.

"And that makes it all perfectly clear to you, Miss Marple?" said Sir Henry, with his twinkle.

But to his surprise Miss Marple shook her head.

"No, I'm afraid it doesn't. I must confess myself completely at a loss. What I do realize is that women must stick together—one should, in an emergency, stand by one's own sex. I think that's the moral of the story Miss Helier has told us."

"I must confess that that particular ethical significance of the mystery has escaped me," said Sir Henry gravely. "Perhaps I shall see the significance of your point more clearly when Miss Helier has revealed the solution."

"Eh?" said Jane looking rather bewildered.

"I was observing that, in childish language, we 'give it up.' You and you alone, Miss Helier, have had the high honour of presenting such an absolutely baffling mystery that even Miss Marple has to confess herself defeated."

"You all give it up?" asked Jane.

"Yes." After a minute's silence during which he waited for the others to speak, Sir Henry constituted himself spokesman once more. "That is to say we stand or fall by the sketchy solutions we have tentatively advanced. One each for the mere men, two for Miss Marple, and a round dozen by Mrs. B."

"It was not a dozen," said Mrs. Bantry. "They were variations on a main theme. And how often am I to tell you that I will *not* be called Mrs. B?"

"So you all give it up," said Jane thoughtfully. "That's very interesting."

She leant back in her chair and began to polish her nails rather absent-mindedly.

"Well," said Mrs. Bantry. "Come on, Jane. What is the solution?"

"The solution?"

"Yes. What really happened?"

Jane stared at her.

"I haven't the least idea."

"*What?*"

"I've always wondered. I thought you were all so clever one of you would be able to tell *me*."

Everybody harboured feelings of annoyance. It was all very well for Jane to be so beautiful—but at this moment everyone felt that stupidity could be carried too far. Even the most transcendent loveliness could not excuse it.

"You mean the truth was never discovered?" said Sir Henry.

"No. That's why, as I say, I did think you would be able to tell *me*."

Jane sounded injured. It was plain that she felt she had a grievance.

"Well—I'm—I'm—" said Colonel Bantry, words failing him.

"You are the most aggravating girl, Jane," said his wife. "Anyway, I'm sure and always shall be that I was right. If you just tell us the proper names of all the people, I shall be *quite* sure."

"I don't think I could do that," said Jane slowly.

"No, dear," said Miss Marple. "Miss Helier couldn't do that."

"Of course she could," said Mrs. Bantry. "Don't be so highminded, Jane. We older folks must have a bit of scandal. At any rate tell us who the city magnate was."

But Jane shook her head, and Miss Marple, in her old-fashioned way, continued to support the girl.

"It must have been a very distressing business," she said.

"No," said Jane truthfully. "I think—I think I rather enjoyed it."

"Well, perhaps you did," said Miss Marple. "I suppose it was a break in the monotony. What play were you acting in?"

"*Smith.*"

"Oh, yes. That's one of Mr. Somerset Maugham's, isn't it? All his are very clever, I think. I've seen them nearly all."

"You're reviving it to go on tour next Autumn, aren't you?" asked Mrs. Bantry.

Jane nodded.

"Well," said Miss Marple rising, "I must go home. Such late hours! But we've had a very entertaining evening. Most unusually so. I think Miss Helier's story wins the prize. Don't you agree?"

"I'm sorry you're angry with me," said Jane. "About not knowing the end, I mean. I suppose I should have said so sooner."

Her tone sounded wistful. Dr. Lloyd rose gallantly to the occasion.

"My dear young lady, why should you? You gave us a very pretty problem to sharpen our wits upon. I am only sorry we could none of us solve it convincingly."

"Speak for yourself," said Mrs. Bantry. "I *did* solve it. I'm convinced I am right."

"Do you know, I really believe you are," said Jane. "What you said sounded so probable."

"Which of her seven solutions do you refer to?" asked Sir Henry teasingly.

Dr. Lloyd gallantly assisted Miss Marple to put on her go-loshes. "Just in case," as the old lady explained. The doctor was to be her escort to her old-world cottage. Wrapped in several woollen shawls, Miss Marple wished everyone good night once more. She came to Jane Helier last and leaning forward, she murmured something in the actress's ear. A startled "Oh!" burst from Jane—so loud as to cause the others to turn their heads.

Smiling and nodding, Miss Marple made her exit, Jane Helier staring after her.

"Are you coming to bed, Jane?" asked Mrs. Bantry.

"What's the matter with you? You're staring as though you'd seen a ghost."

With a deep sigh Jane came to herself, shed a beautiful and bewildering smile on the two men and followed her hostess up the staircase. Mrs. Bantry came into the girl's room with her.

"Your fire's nearly out," said Mrs. Bantry, giving it a vicious and ineffectual poke. "They can't have made it up properly. How stupid housemaids are. Still, I suppose we are rather late tonight. Why, it's actually past one o'clock!"

"Do you think there are many people like her?" asked Jane Helier.

She was sitting on the side of the bed apparently wrapped in thought.

"Like the housemaid?"

"No. Like that funny old woman—what's her name—Marple?"

"Oh! I don't know. I suppose she's a fairly common type in a small village."

"Oh, dear," said Jane. "I don't know what to do."

She sighed deeply.

"I'm worried."

"What about?"

"Dolly," Jane Helier was portentously solemn. "Do you know what that queer old lady whispered to me before she went out of the door tonight?"

"No. What?"

"She said: *'I shouldn't do it if I were you, my dear. Never put yourself too much in another woman's power, even if you think she's your friend at the moment.'* You know, Dolly, that's awfully true."

"The maxim? Yes, perhaps it is. But I don't see the application."

"I suppose you can't ever really trust a woman. And I

should be in her power. I never thought of that."

"What woman are you talking about?"

"Netta Greene, my understudy."

"What on earth does Miss Marple know about your understudy?"

"I suppose she guessed—but I can't see how."

"Jane, will you kindly tell me at once what you are talking about?"

"The story. The one I told. Oh, Dolly, that woman, you know—the one that took Claud from me?"

Mrs. Bantry nodded, casting her mind back rapidly to the first of Jane's unfortunate marriages—to Claud Averbury, the actor.

"He married her; and I could have told him how it would be. Claud doesn't know, but she's carrying on with Sir Joseph Salmon—weekends with him at the bungalow I told you about. I wanted her shown up—I would like everyone to know the sort of woman she was. And you see, with a burglary everything would be bound to come out."

"Jane!" gasped Mrs. Bantry. "Did *you* engineer this story you've been telling us?"

Jane nodded.

"That's why I chose *Smith*. I wear parlourmaid's kit in it, you know. So I should have it handy. And when they sent for me to the police station it's the easiest thing in the world to say I was rehearsing my part with my understudy at the hotel. Really, of course, we would be at the bungalow. I just to open the door and bring in the cocktails, and Netta to pretend to be me. He'd never see *her* again, of course, so there would be no fear of his recognizing her. And I can make myself look quite different as a parlourmaid; and besides, one doesn't look at parlourmaids as though they were people. We planned to drag him out into the road afterwards, bag the jewel case, telephone the police and get back to the hotel. I shouldn't like the poor young man to suffer, but Sir Henry didn't seem to think he would, did he? And she'd be in the papers and everything—and Claud would see what she was really like."

Mrs. Bantry sat down and groaned.

"Oh! my poor head. And all the time—Jane Helier, you deceitful girl! Telling us that story the way you did!"

"I *am* a good actress," said Jane complacently. "I always have been, whatever people choose to say. I didn't give myself away once, did I?"

"Miss Marple was right," murmured Mrs. Bantry. "The personal element. Oh, yes, the personal element. Jane, my good child, do you realize that theft is theft, and you might have been sent to prison?"

"Well, none of you guessed," said Jane. "Except Miss Marple." The worried expression returned to her face. "Dolly, do you *really* think there are many like her?"

"Frankly, I don't," said Mrs. Bantry.

Jane sighed again.

"Still, one had better not risk it. And of course I should be in Netta's power—that's true enough. She might turn against me or blackmail me or anything. She helped me think out the details and she professed to be devoted to me, but one never *does* know with women. No, I think Miss Marple was right. I had better not risk it."

"But, my dear, you have risked it."

"Oh, no." Jane opened her blue eyes very wide. "Don't you understand? *None of this has happened yet!* I was—well, trying it on the dog, so to speak."

"I don't profess to understand your theatrical slang," said Mrs. Bantry with dignity. "Do you mean this is a future project—not a past deed?"

"I was going to do it this Autumn—in September. I don't know what to do now."

"And Jane Marple guessed—actually guessed the truth and never told us," said Mrs. Bantry wrathfully.

"I think that was why she said that—about women sticking together. She wouldn't give me away before the men. That was nice of her. I don't mind *your* knowing, Dolly."

"Well, give the idea up, Jane. I beg of you."

"I think I shall," murmured Miss Helier. "There might be other Miss Marples. . . ."

Death by Drowning

ir Henry Clithering, ex-Commissioner of Scotland
Yard, was staying with his friends the Bantrys at their
place near the little village of St. Mary Mead.

On Saturday morning, coming down to breakfast at the
pleasant guestly hour of ten-fifteen, he almost collided with
his hostess, Mrs. Bantry, in the doorway of the breakfast
room. She was rushing from the room, evidently in a condition of some excitement and distress.

Colonel Bantry was sitting at the table, his face rather red-
der than usual.

" 'Morning, Clithering," he said. "Nice day. Help yourself."

Sir Henry obeyed. As he took his seat, a plate of kidneys
and bacon in front of him, his host went on:

"Dolly's a bit uspet this morning."

"Yes—er—I rather thought so," said Sir Henry, mildly.

He wondered a little. His hostess was of a placid disposition, little given to moods or excitements. As far as Sir
Henry knew, she felt keenly on one subject only—gardening.

"Yes," said Colonel Bantry. "Bit of news we got this
morning upset her. Girl in the village—Emmott's daughter—Emmott who keeps the Blue Boar."

"Oh, yes, of course."

"Ye-es," said Colonel Bantry ruminatively. "Pretty girl. Got herself into trouble. Usual story. I've been arguing with Dolly about that. Foolish of me. Women never see sense. Dolly was all up in arms for the girl—you know what women are—men are brutes—all the rest of it, et cetera. But it's not so simple as all that—not in these days. Girls know what they're about. Fellow who seduces a girl's not necessarily a villain. Fifty-fifty as often as not. I rather liked young Sandford myself. A young ass rather than a Don Juan, I should have said."

"It is this man Sandford who got the girl into trouble?"

"So it seems. Of course I don't know anything personally," said the colonel cautiously. "It's all gossip and chat. You know what this place is! As I say, I *know* nothing. And I'm not like Dolly—leaping to conclusions, flinging accusations all over the place. Damn it all, one ought to be careful in what one says. You know—inquest and all that."

"Inquest?"

Colonel Bantry stared.

"Yes. Didn't I tell you? Girl drowned herself. That's what all the pother's about."

"That's a nasty business," said Sir Henry.

"Of course it is. Don't like to think of it myself. Poor pretty little devil. Her father's a hard man by all accounts. I suppose she just felt she couldn't face the music."

He paused.

"That's what's upset Dolly so."

"Where did she drown herself?"

"In the river. Just below the mill it runs pretty fast. There's a footpath and a bridge across. They think she threw herself off that. Well, well, it doesn't bear thinking about."

And with a portentous rustle, Colonel Bantry opened his newspaper and proceeded to distract his mind from painful matters by an absorption in the newest iniquities of the government.

Sir Henry was only mildly interested by the village tragedy. After breakfast, he established himself on a comfortable chair on the lawn, tilted his hat over his eyes and contemplated life from a peaceful angle.

It was about half-past eleven when a neat parlourmaid tripped across the lawn.

"If you please, sir, Miss Marple has called, and would like to see you."

"Miss Marple?"

Sir Henry sat up and straightened his hat. The name surprised him. He remembered Miss Marple very well—her gentle, quiet, old-maidish ways, her amusing penetration. He remembered a dozen unsolved and hypothetical cases—and how in each case this typical 'old maid of the village' had leaped unerringly to the right solution of the mystery. Sir Henry had a very deep respect for Miss Marple. He wondered what had brought her to see him.

Miss Marple was sitting in the drawing-room—very upright as always, a gaily coloured marketing basket of foreign extraction beside her. Her cheeks were rather pink, and she seemed flustered.

"Sir Henry—I am so glad. So fortunate to find you. I just happened to hear that you were staying down here. . . . I do hope you will forgive me. . . ."

"This is a great pleasure," said Sir Henry, taking her hand. "I'm afraid Mrs. Bantry's out."

"Yes," said Miss Marple. "I saw her talking to Footit, the butcher, as I passed. Henry Footit was run over yesterday—that was his dog. One of those smooth-haired fox terriers, rather stout and quarrelsome, that butchers always seem to have."

"Yes," said Sir Henry helpfully.

"I was glad to get here when she wasn't at home," continued Miss Marple. "Because it was you I wanted to see. About this sad affair."

"Henry Footit?" asked Sir Henry, slightly bewildered.

Miss Marple threw him a reproachful glance.

"No, no. Rose Emmott, of course. You've heard?"

Sir Henry nodded.

"Bantry was telling me. Very sad."

He was a little puzzled. He could not conceive why Miss Marple should want to see him about Rose Emmott.

Miss Marple sat down again, Sir Henry also sat. When the old lady spoke her manner had changed. It was grave, and had a certain dignity.

"You may remember, Sir Henry, that on one or two occasions we played what was really a pleasant kind of game. Propounding mysteries and giving solutions. You were kind enough to say that I—that I did not do too badly."

"You beat us all," said Sir Henry warmly. "You displayed an absolute genius for getting to the truth. And you always instanced, I remember, some village parallel which had supplied you with the clue."

He smiled as he spoke, but Miss Marple did not smile. She remained very grave.

"What you said has emboldened me to come to you now. I feel that if I say something to you—at least you will not laugh at me."

He realized suddenly that she was in deadly earnest.

"Certainly, I will not laugh," he said gently.

"Sir Henry—this girl—Rose Emmott. She did not drown herself—*she was murdered.* . . . And I know who murdered her."

Sir Henry was silent with sheer astonishment for quite three seconds. Miss Marple's voice had been perfectly quiet and unexcited. She might have been making the most ordinary statement in the world for all the emotion she showed.

"That is a very serious statement to make, Miss Marple," said Sir Henry when he had recovered his breath.

She nodded her head gently several times.

"I know—I know—that is why I have come to you."

"But, my dear lady, I am not the person to come to. I am merely a private individual nowadays. If you have knowledge of the kind you claim, you must go to the police."

"I don't think I can do that," said Miss Marple.

"But why not?"

"Because, you see, I haven't got any—what you call *knowledge*."

"You mean it's only a guess on your part?"

"You can call it that, if you like, but it's not really that at all. I *know*. I'm in a position to know; but if I gave my reasons for knowing to Inspector Drewitt—well, he'd simply laugh. And really, I don't know that I'd blame him. It's very difficult to understand what you might call specialized knowledge."

"Such as?" suggested Sir Henry.

. Miss Marple smiled a little.

"If I were to tell you that I know because of a man called Peasegood leaving turnips instead of carrots when he came round with a cart and sold vegetables to my niece several years ago—"

She stopped eloquently.

"A very appropriate name for the trade," murmured Sir Henry. "You mean that you are simply judging from the facts in a parallel case."

"I know human nature," said Miss Marple. "It's impossible not to know human nature living in a village all these years. The question is, do you believe me, or don't you?"

She looked at him very straight. The pink flush had heightened on her cheeks. Her eyes met his steadily without wavering.

Sir Henry was a man with a very vast experience of life. He

made his decisions quickly without beating about the bush. Unlikely and fantastic as Miss Marple's statement might seem, he was instantly aware that he accepted it.

"I *do* believe you, Miss Marple. But I do not see what you want me to do in the matter, or why you have come to me."

"I have thought and thought about it," said Miss Marple. "As I said, it would be useless going to the police without any facts. I have no facts. What I would ask you to do is to interest yourself in the matter—Inspector Drewitt would be most flattered, I am sure. And, of course, if the matter went further, Colonel Melchett, the Chief Constable, I am sure, would be wax in your hands."

She looked at him appealingly.

"And what data are you going to give me to work upon?"

"I thought," said Miss Marple, "of writing a name—*the* name—on a piece of paper and giving it to you. Then if, on investigation, you decide that the—the *person*—is not involved in any way—well, I shall have been quite wrong."

She paused and then added with a slight shiver. "It would be so dreadful—so very dreadful—if an innocent person were to be hanged."

"What on earth—" cried Sir Henry, startled.

She turned a distressed face upon him.

"I may be wrong about that—though I don't think so. Inspector Drewitt, you see, is really an intelligent man. But a mediocre amount of intelligence is sometimes most dangerous. It does not take one far enough."

Sir Henry looked at her curiously.

Fumbling a little, Miss Marple opened a small reticule, took out a little notebook, tore out a leaf, carefully wrote a name on it and folding it in two, handed it to Sir Henry.

He opened it and read the name. It conveyed nothing to him, but his eyebrows lifted a little. He looked across at Miss Marple and tucked the piece of paper in his pocket.

"Well, well," he said. "Rather an extraordinary business,

this. I've never done anything like it before. But I'm going to back my judgment—of *you*, Miss Marple."

Sir Henry was sitting in a room with Colonel Melchett, the Chief Constable of the county, and Inspector Drewitt.

The Chief Constable was a little man of aggressively military demeanour. The Inspector was big and broad and eminently sensible.

"I really do feel I'm butting in," said Sir Henry, with a pleasant smile. "I can't really tell you why I'm doing it." (Strict truth, this!)

"My dear fellow, we're charmed. It's a great compliment."

"Honoured, Sir Henry," said the inspector.

The Chief Constable was thinking: "Bored to death, poor fellow, at the Bantrys. The old man abusing the government and the old woman babbling on about bulbs."

The Inspector was thinking: "Pity we're not up against a real teaser. One of the best brains in England, I've heard it said. Pity it's all such plain sailing."

Aloud, the Chief Constable said:

"I'm afraid it's all very sordid and straightforward. First idea was that the girl had pitched herself in. She was in the family way, you understand. However, our doctor, Haydock, is a careful fellow. He noticed the bruises on each arm—upper arm. Caused before death. Just where a fellow would have taken her by the arms and flung her in."

"Would that require much strength?"

"I think not. There would be no struggle—the girl would be taken unawares. It's a footbridge of slippery wood. Easiest thing in the world to pitch her over—there's no handrail that side."

"You know for a fact that the tragedy occurred there?"

"Yes. We've got a boy—Jimmy Brown—aged twelve. He was in the woods on the other side. He heard a kind of scream from the bridge and a splash. It was dusk, you know—difficult to see anything. Presently he saw something white floating down in the water and he ran and got help. They got her out, but it was too late to revive her."

Sir Henry nodded.

"The boy saw no one on the bridge?"

"No. But, as I tell you, it was dusk, and there's mist always hanging about there. I'm going to question him as to whether he saw anyone about just afterwards or just before. You see he naturally assumed that the girl had thrown herself over. Everybody did to start with."

"Still, we've got the note," said Inspector Drewitt. He turned to Sir Henry.

"Note in the dead girl's pocket, sir. Written with a kind of artist's pencil it was, and all of a sop though the paper was we managed to read it."

"And what did it say?"

"It was from young Sandford, 'All right,' that's how it ran. 'I'll meet you at the bridge at eight-thirty—R.S.' Well, it was as near as might be to eight-thirty—a few minutes after—when Jimmy Brown heard the cry and the splash."

"I don't know whether you've met Sandford at all?" went on Colonel Melchett. "He's been down here about a month. One of those modern-day young architects who build peculiar houses. He's doing a house for Allington. God knows what it's going to be like—full of new-fangled stuff, I suppose. Glass dinner table and surgical chairs made of steel and webbing. Well, that's neither here nor there, but it shows the kind of chap Sandford is. Bolshie, you know—no morals."

"Seduction," said Sir Henry mildly, "is quite an old-established crime though it does not, of course, date back so far as murder."

Colonel Melchett stared.

"Oh! yes," he said. "Quite. Quite."

"Well, Sir Henry," said Drewitt, "there it is—an ugly

business, but plain. This young Sandford gets the girl into trouble. Then he's all for clearing off back to London. He's got a girl there—nice young lady—he's engaged to be married to her. Well, naturally this business, if she gets to hear of it, may cook his goose good and proper. He meets Rose at the bridge—it's a misty evening, no one about—he catches her by the shoulders and pitches her in. A proper young swine—and deserves what's coming to him. That's my opinion."

Sir Henry was silent for a minute or two. He perceived a strong undercurrent of local prejudice. A new-fangled architect was not likely to be popular in the conservative village of St. Mary Mead.

"There is no doubt, I suppose, that this man, Sandford, was actually the father of the coming child?" he asked.

"He's the father all right," said Drewitt. "Rose Emmott let out as much to her father. She thought he'd marry her. Marry her! Not he!"

"Dear me," thought Sir Henry, "I seem to be back in mid-Victorian melodrama. Unsuspecting girl, the villain from London, the stern father, the betrayal—we only need the faithful village lover. Yes, I think it's time I asked about him."

And aloud he said:

"Hadn't the girl a young man of her own down here?"

"You mean Joe Ellis?" said the inspector. "Good fellow, Joe. Carpentering's his trade. Ah! If she'd stuck to Joe—"

Colonel Melchett nodded approval.

"Stick to your own class," he snapped.

"How did Joe Ellis take this affair?" asked Sir Henry.

"Nobody knew how he was taking it," said the inspector. "He's a quiet fellow, is Joe. Close. Anything Rose did was right in his eyes. She had him on a string all right. Just hoped she'd come back to him some day—that was his attitude, I reckon."

"I'd like to see him," said Sir Henry.

"Oh! We're going to look him up," said Colonel Melchett. "We're not neglecting any line. I thought myself we'd see Emmott first, then Sandford, and then we can go on and see Ellis. That suit you, Clithering?"

Sir Henry said it would suit him admirably.

They found Tom Emmott at the Blue Boar. He was a big burly man of middle age with a shifty eye and a truculent jaw.

"Glad to see you, gentlemen—good morning, Colonel. Come in here and we can be private. Can I offer you anything, gentlemen? No? It's as you please. You've come about this business of my poor girl. Ah! She was a good girl, Rose was. Always was a good girl—till this bloody swine—beg pardon, but that's what he is—till he came along. Promised her marriage, he did. But I'll have the law of him. Drove her to it, he did. Murdering swine. Bringing disgrace on all of us. My poor girl."

"Your daughter distinctly told you that Mr. Sandford was responsible for her condition?" asked Melchett crisply.

"She did. In this very room she did."

"And what did you say to her?" asked Sir Henry.

"Say to her?" The man seemed momentarily taken aback.

"Yes. You didn't, for example, threaten to turn her out of the house."

"I was a bit upset—that's only natural. I'm sure you'll agree that's only natural. But, of course, I didn't turn her out of the house. I wouldn't do such a thing." He assumed virtuous indignation. "No. What's the law for—that's what I say. What's the law for? He'd got to do the right thing by her. And if he didn't, by God, he'd got to pay."

He brought down his fist on the table.

"What time did you last see your daughter?" asked Melchett.

"Yesterday—tea time."

"What was her manner then?"

"Well—much as usual. I didn't notice anything. If I'd known—"

"But you didn't know," said the inspector dryly.

They took their leave.

"Emmott hardly creates a favourable impression," said Sir Henry thoughtfully.

"Bit of a blackguard," said Melchett. "He'd have bled Sandford all right if he'd had the chance."

Their next call was on the architect. Rex Sandford was very unlike the picture Sir Henry had unconsciously formed of him. He was a tall young man, very fair and very thin. His eyes were blue and dreamy, his hair was untidy and rather too long. His speech was a little too ladylike.

Colonel Melchett introduced himself and his companions. Then passing straight to the object of his visit, he invited the architect to make a statement as to his movements on the previous evening.

"You understand," he said warningly. "I have no power to compel a statement from you and any statement you make may be used in evidence against you. I want the position to be quite clear to you."

"I—I don't understand," said Sandford.

"You understand that the girl Rose Emmott was drowned last night?"

"I know. Oh! it's too, too distressing. Really, I haven't slept a wink. I've been incapable of any work today. I feel responsible—terribly responsible."

He ran his hands through his hair, making it untidier still. "I never meant any harm," he said piteously. "I never thought. I never dreamt—she'd take it that way."

He sat down at a table and buried his face in his hands.

"Do I understand you to say, Mr. Sandford, that you refuse to make a statement as to where you were last night at eight-thirty?"

"No, no—certainly not. I was out. I went for a walk."

"You went to meet Miss Emmott?"

"No. I went by myself. Through the woods. A long way."

"Then how do you account for this note, sir, which was found in the dead girl's pocket?"

And Inspector Drewitt read it unemotionally aloud.

"Now, sir," he finished. "Do you deny that you wrote that?"

"No-no. You're right. I did write it. Rose asked me to meet her. She insisted. I didn't know what to do. So I wrote that note."

"Ah, that's better," said the inspector.

"But I didn't go!" Sandford's voice rose high and excited. "I didn't go! I felt it would be much better not. I was returning to town tomorrow. I felt it would be better not—not to meet. I intended to write from London and—and make—some arrangement."

"You are aware, sir, that this girl was going to have a child, and that she had named you as its father?"

Sandford groaned, but did not answer.

"Was that statement true, sir?"

Sandford buried his face deeper.

"I suppose so," he said in a muffled voice.

"Ah!" Inspector Drewitt could not disguise his satisfaction. "Now about this 'walk' of yours. Is there anyone who saw you last night?"

"I don't know. I don't think so. As far as I can remember, I didn't meet anybody."

"That's a pity."

"What do you mean?" Sandford stared wildly at him. "What does it matter whether I was out for a walk or not? What difference does that make to Rose drowning herself?"

"Ah!" said the inspector. "But you see, *she didn't*. She was thrown in deliberately, Mr. Sandford."

"She was—" It took him a minute or two to take in all the horror of it. "My God! Then—"

He dropped into a chair.

Colonel Melchett made a move to depart.

"You understand, Sandford," he said, "You are on no account to leave this house."

The three men left together. The inspector and the Chief Constable exchanged glances.

"That's enough, I think, sir," said the inspector.

"Yes. Get a warrant made out and arrest him."

"Excuse me," said Sir Henry, "I've forgotten my gloves."

He re-entered the house rapidly. Sandford was sitting just as they had left him, staring dazedly in front of him.

"I have come back," said Sir Henry, "to tell you that I, personally, am anxious to do all I can to assist you. The motive of my interest in you I am not at liberty to reveal. But I am going to ask you, if you will, to tell me as briefly as possible exactly what passed between you and this girl Rose."

"She was very pretty," said Sandford. "Very pretty and very alluring. And—and she made a dead set for me. Before God, that's true. She wouldn't let me alone. And it was lonely down here, and nobody liked me much, and—and, as I say she was amazingly pretty and she seemed to know her way about and all that—" His voice died away. He looked up. "And then this happened. She wanted me to marry her. I didn't know what to do. I'm engaged to a girl in London. If she ever gets to hear of this—and she will, of course—well, it's all up. She won't understand. How could she? And I'm a rotter, of course. As I say, I didn't know what to do. I avoided seeing Rose again. I thought I'd get back to town—see my lawyer—make arrangements about money and so forth, for her. God, what a fool I've been! And it's all so clear—the case against me. But they've made a mistake. She *must* have done it herself."

"Did she ever threaten to take her life?"

Sandford shook his head.

"Never. I shouldn't have said she was that sort."

"What about a man called Joe Ellis?"

"The carpenter fellow? Good old village stock. Dull fellow—but crazy about Rose."

"He might have been jealous?" suggested Sir Henry.

"I suppose he was a bit—but he's the bovine kind. He'd suffer in silence."

"Well," said Sir Henry. "I must be going."

He rejoined the others.

"You know, Melchett," he said. "I feel we ought to have a look at this other fellow—Ellis—before we do anything drastic. Pity if you made an arrest that turned out to be a mistake. After all, jealousy is a pretty good motive for murder—and a pretty common one, too."

"That's true enough," said the inspector. "But Joe Ellis isn't that kind. He wouldn't hurt a fly. Why, nobody's ever seen him out of temper. Still, I agree we'd better just ask him where he was last night. He'll be at home now. He lodges with Mrs. Bartlett—very decent soul—a widow, she takes in a bit of washing."

The little cottage to which they bent their footsteps was spotlessly clean and neat. A big stout woman of middle age opened the door to them. She had a pleasant face and blue eyes.

"Good morning, Mrs. Bartlett," said the inspector. "Is Joe Ellis here?"

"Came back not ten minutes ago," said Mrs. Bartlett. "Step inside, will you, please, sirs."

Wiping her hands on her apron she led them into a tiny front parlour with stuffed birds, china dogs, a sofa and several useless pieces of furniture.

She hurriedly arranged seats for them, picked up a what-not bodily to make further room and went out calling:

"Joe, there's three gentlemen want to see you."

A voice from the back kitchen replied:

"I'll be there when I've cleaned myself."

Mrs. Bartlett smiled.

"Come in, Mrs. Bartlett," said Colonel Melchett. "Sit down."

"Oh no, sir, I couldn't think of it."

Mrs. Bartlett was shocked at the idea.

"You find Joe Ellis a good lodger?" inquired Melchett in a seemingly careless tone.

"Couldn't have a better, sir. A ready steady young fellow. Never touched a drop of drink. Takes a pride in his work. And always kind and helpful about the house. He put up those shelves for me, and he's fixed a new dresser in the kitchen. And any little thing that wants doing in the house—why, Joe does it as a matter of course, and won't hardly take thanks for it. Ah! there aren't many young fellows like Joe, sir."

"Some girl will be lucky some day," said Melchett carelessly. "He was rather sweet on that poor girl, Rose Emmott, wasn't he?"

Mrs. Bartlett sighed.

"It made me tired, it did. Him worshipping the ground she trod on and her not caring a snap of the fingers for him."

"Where does Joe spend his evenings, Mrs. Bartlett?"

"Here, sir, usually. He does some odd piece work in the evenings, sometimes, and he's trying to learn bookkeeping by correspondence."

"Ah! really. Was he in yesterday evening?"

"Yes, sir."

"You're sure, Mrs. Bartlett?" said Sir Henry sharply.

She turned to him.

"Quite sure, sir."

"He didn't go out, for instance, somewhere about eight to eight-thirty?"

"Oh no." Mrs. Bartlett laughed. "He was fixing the kitchen dresser for me nearly all the evening, and I was helping him."

Sir Henry looked at her smiling assured face and felt his first pang of doubt.

A moment later Ellis himself entered the room.

He was a tall broad-shouldered young man, very good-looking in a rustic way. He had shy blue eyes and a good-tempered smile. Altogether an amiable young giant.

Melchett opened the conversation. Mrs. Bartlett withdrew to the kitchen.

"We are investigating the death of Rose Emmott. You knew her, Ellis."

"Yes." He hesitated, then muttered, "Hoped to marry her one day. Poor lass."

"You have heard what her condition was?"

"Yes." A spark of anger showed in his eye. "Let her down, he did. But 'twere for the best. She wouldn't have been happy married to him. I reckoned she'd come to me when this happened. I'd have looked after her."

"In spite of—"

"'Tweren't her fault. He led her astray with fine promises and all. Oh! she told me about it. She'd no call to drown herself. He weren't worth it."

"Where were you, Ellis, last night at eight-thirty?"

Was it Sir Henry's fancy, or was there really a shade of constraint in the ready—almost too ready—reply.

"I was here. Fixing up a contraption in the kitchen for Mrs. B. You ask her. She'll tell you."

"He was too quick with that," thought Sir Henry. "He's a slow-thinking man. That popped out so pat that I suspect he'd got it ready beforehand."

Then he told himself that it was imagination. He was imagining things—yes, even imagining an apprehensive glint in those blue eyes.

A few more questions and answers and they left. Sir Henry made an excuse to go to the kitchen. Mrs. Bartlett was busy at the stove. She looked up with a pleasant smile. A new dresser was fixed against the wall. It was not quite finished. Some tools lay about and some pieces of wood.

"That's what Ellis was at work on last night?" said Sir Henry.

"Yes, sir, it's a nice bit of work, isn't it? He's a very clever carpenter, Joe is."

No apprehensive gleam in her eye—no embarrassment.

But Ellis—had he imagined it? No, there *had* been something.

"I must tackle him," thought Sir Henry.

Turning to leave the kitchen, he collided with a perambulator.

"Not woken the baby up, I hope," he said.

Mrs. Bartlett's laugh rang out.

"Oh, no, sir. I've no children—more's the pity. That's what I take the laundry on, sir."

"Oh! I see—"

He paused, then said on an impulse:

"Mrs. Bartlett. You knew Rose Emmott. Tell me what you really thought of her."

She looked at him curiously.

"Well, sir, I thought she was flighty. But she's dead—and I don't like to speak ill of the dead."

"But I have a reason—a very good reason for asking."

He spoke persuasively.

She seemed to consider, studying him attentively. Finally she made up her mind.

"She was a bad lot, sir," she said quietly. "I wouldn't say

so before Joe. She took *him* in good and proper. That kind can—more's the pity. You know how it is, sir."

Yes, Sir Henry knew. The Joe Ellises of the world were peculiarly vulnerable. They trusted blindly. But for that very cause the shock of discovery might be greater.

He left the cottage baffled and perplexed. He was up against a blank wall. Joe Ellis had been working indoors all yesterday evening. Mrs. Bartlett had actually been there watching him. Could one possibly get round that? There was nothing to set against it—except possibly that suspicious readiness in replying on Joe Ellis's part—that suggestion of having a story pat.

"Well," said Melchett. "That seems to make the matter quite clear, eh?"

"It does, sir," agreed the inspector. "Sandford's our man. Not a leg to stand up on. The thing's as plain as daylight. It's my opinion as the girl and her father were out to—well—practically blackmail him. He's no money to speak of—he didn't want the matter to get to his young lady's ears. He was desperate and he acted accordingly. What do you say, sir?" he added, addressing Sir Henry deferentially.

"It seems so," admitted Sir Henry. "And yet—I can hardly picture Sandford committing any violent action."

But he knew as he spoke that that objection was hardly valid. The meekest animal, when cornered, is capable of amazing actions.

"I should like to see the boy, though," he said suddenly. "The one who heard the cry."

Jimmy Brown proved to be an intelligent lad, rather small for his age, with a sharp, rather cunning face. He was eager to be questioned and was rather disappointed when checked in his dramatic tale of what he had heard on the fatal night.

"You were on the other side of the bridge, I understand,"

said Sir Henry. "Across the river from the village. Did you see anyone on that side as you came over the bridge?"

"There was someone walking up in the woods. Mr. Sandford, I think it was, the architect gentleman who's building the queer house."

The three men exchanged glances.

"That was about ten minutes or so before you heard the cry?"

The boy nodded.

"Did you see anyone else—on the village side of the river?"

"A man came along the path that side. Going slow and whistling he was. Might have been Joe Ellis."

"You couldn't possibly have seen who it was," said the inspector sharply. "What with the mist and its being dusk."

"It's on account of the whistle," said the boy. "Joe Ellis always whistles the same tune—'I wanner be happy'—it's the only tune he knows."

He spoke with the scorn of the modernist for the old-fashioned.

"Anyone might whistle a tune," said Melchett. "Was he going towards the bridge?"

"No. Other way—to village."

"I don't think we need concern ourselves with this unknown man," said Melchett. "You heard the cry and the splash and a few minutes later you saw the body floating downstream and you ran for help, going back to the bridge, crossing it, and making straight for the village. You didn't see anyone near the bridge as you ran for help?"

"I think as there were two men with a wheelbarrow on the river path; but they were some way away and I couldn't tell if they were going or coming and Mr. Giles's place was nearest—so I ran there."

"You did well, my boy," said Melchett. "You acted very

creditably and with presence of mind. You're a scout, aren't you?"

"Yes, sir."

"Very good. Very good indeed."

Sir Henry was silent—thinking. He took a slip of paper from his pocket, looked at it, shook his head. It didn't seem possible—and yet—

He decided to pay a call on Miss Marple.

She received him in her pretty, slightly over-crowded old-style drawing-room.

"I've come to report progress," said Sir Henry. "I'm afraid that from our point of view things aren't going well. They are going to arrest Sandford. And I must say I think they are justified."

"You have found nothing in—what shall I say—support of my theory, then?" She looked perplexed—anxious. "Perhaps I have been wrong—quite wrong. You have such wide experience—you would surely detect it if it were so."

"For one thing," said Sir Henry, "I can hardly believe it. And for another we are up against an unbreakable *alibi*. Joe Ellis was fixing shelves in the kitchen all the evening and Mrs. Bartlett was watching him do it."

Miss Marple leaned forward, taking in a quick breath.

"But that can't be so," she said. "It was Friday night."

"Friday night?"

"Yes—Friday night. On Friday evenings Mrs. Bartlett takes the laundry she has done round to the different people."

Sir Henry leaned back in his chair. He remembered the boy Jimmy's story of the whistling man and—yes—it would all fit in.

He rose, taking Miss Marple warmly by the hand.

"I think I see my way," he said. "At least I can try. . . ."

Five minutes later he was back at Mrs. Bartlett's cottage

and facing Joe Ellis in the little parlour among the china dogs.

"You lied to us, Ellis, about last night," he said crisply. "You were not in the kitchen here fixing the dresser between eight and eight-thirty. You were seen walking along the path by the river towards the bridge a few minutes before Rose Emmott was murdered."

The man gasped.

"She weren't murdered—she weren't. I had naught to do with it. She threw herself in, she did. She was desperate like. I wouldn't have harmed a hair on her head, I wouldn't."

"Then why did you lie as to where you were?" asked Sir Henry keenly.

The man's eyes shifted and lowered uncomfortably.

"I was scared. Mrs. B. saw me around there and when we heard just afterwards what had happened—well, she thought it might look bad for me. I fixed I'd say I was working here, and she agreed to back me up. She's a rare one, she is. She's always been good to me."

Without a word Sir Henry left the room and walked into the kitchen. Mrs. Bartlett was washing up at the sink.

"Mrs. Bartlett," he said, "I know everything. I think you'd better confess—that is, unless you want Joe Ellis hanged for something he didn't do . . . No. I see you don't want that. I'll tell you what happened. You were out taking the laundry home. You came across Rose Emmott. You thought she'd given Joe the chuck and was taking up with this stranger. Now she was in trouble—Joe was prepared to come to the rescue—marry her if need be, and if she'd have him. He's lived in your house for four years. You've fallen in love with him. You want him for yourself. You hated this girl—you couldn't bear that this worthless little slut should take your man from you. You're a strong woman, Mrs. Bartlett. You caught the girl by the shoulders and shoved

her over into the stream. A few minutes later you met Joe
Ellis. The boy Jimmy saw you together in the distance—but
in the darkness and the mist he assumed the perambulator
was a wheelbarrow and two men wheeling it. You persuaded
Joe that he might be suspected and you concocted what was
supposed to be an alibi for him, but which was really an alibi
for *you*. Now then, I'm right, am I not?"

He held his breath. He had staked all on this throw.

She stood before him rubbing her hands on her apron,
slowly making up her mind.

"It's just as you say, sir," she said at last, in her quiet subdued voice (a dangerous voice, Sir Henry suddenly felt it to
be). "I don't know what came over me. Shameless—that's
what she was. It just came over me—she shan't take Joe
from me. I haven't had a happy life, sir. My husband, he was
a poor lot—an invalid and cross-grained. I nursed and looked
after him true. And then Joe came here to lodge. I'm not
such an old woman, sir, in spite of my grey hair. I'm just
forty, sir. Joe's one in a thousand. I'd have done anything for
him—anything at all. He was like a little child, sir, so gentle
and so believing. He was mine, sir, to look after and see to.
And this—this—" She swallowed—checked her emotion.
Even at this moment she was a strong woman. She stood up
straight and looked at Sir Henry curiously. "I'm ready to
come, sir. I never thought anyone would find out. I don't
know how you knew, sir—I don't, I'm sure."

Sir Henry shook his head gently.

"It was not I who knew," he said—and he thought of the
piece of paper still reposing in his pocket with the words on
it written in neat old-fashioned handwriting.

*Mrs. Bartlett, with whom Joe Ellis lodges at 2 Mill Cot-
tages.*

Miss Marple had been right again.

THE
REGATTA
MYSTERY

Miss Marple
Tells a Story

I don't think I've ever told you, my dears—you, Raymond, and you, Joyce, about a rather curious little business that happened some years ago now. I don't want to seem *vain* in any way—of course I know that in comparison with you young people I'm not clever at all—Raymond writes those very modern books all about rather unpleasant young men and women—and Joyce paints those very remarkable pictures of square people with curious bulges on them—very clever of you, my dear, but as Raymond always says (only quite kindly, because he is the kindest of nephews) I am hopelessly Victorian. I admire Mr. Alma-Tadema and Mr. Frederic Leighton and I suppose to you they seem hopelessly *vieux jeu*. Now let me see, what was I saying? Oh, yes—that I didn't want to appear vain—but I couldn't help being just a teeny weeny bit pleased with myself, because, just by applying a little common sense, I believe I really did solve a problem that had baffled cleverer heads than mine. Though really I should have thought the whole thing was *obvious* from the beginning. . . .

Well, I'll tell you my little story, and if you think I'm inclined to be conceited about it, you must remember that I did at least help a fellow creature who was in very grave distress.

The first I knew of this business was one evening about nine o'clock when Gwen—(you remember Gwen? My little maid with red hair) well—Gwen came in and told me that Mr. Petherick and a gentleman had called to see me. Gwen had showed them into the drawing-room—quite rightly. I was sitting in the dining-room because in early spring I think it is so wasteful to have two fires going.

I directed Gwen to bring in the cherry brandy and some glasses and I hurried into the drawing-room. I don't know whether you remember Mr. Petherick? He died two years ago, but he had been a friend of mine for many years as well as attending to all my legal business. A very shrewd man and a really clever solicitor. His son does my business for me now—a very nice lad and very up to date—but somehow I don't feel quite the *confidence* I had in Mr. Petherick.

I explained to Mr. Petherick about the fires and he said at once that he and his friend would come into the dining-room—and then he introduced his friend—a Mr. Rhodes. He was a youngish man—not much over forty—and I saw at once that there was something very wrong. His manner was most *peculiar*. One might have called it *rude* if one hadn't realized that the poor fellow was suffering from *strain*.

When we were settled in the dining-room and Gwen had brought the cherry brandy, Mr. Petherick explained the reason for his visit.

"Miss Marple," he said, "you must forgive an old friend for taking a liberty. What I have come here for is a consultation."

I couldn't understand at all what he meant, and he went on:

"In a case of illness one likes two points of view—that of the specialist and that of the family physician. It is the fashion to regard the former as of more value, but I am not sure that I agree. The specialist has experience only in his own

subject—the family doctor has, perhaps, less knowledge—
but a wider experience."

I knew just what he meant, because a young niece of mine
not long before had hurried her child off to a very well-
known specialist in skin diseases without consulting her
own doctor whom she considered an old dodderer, and the
specialist had ordered some very expensive treatment, and
later they found that all the child was suffering from was
rather an unusual form of measles.

I just mention this—though I have a horror of *di-
gressing*—to show that I appreciated Mr. Petherick's point—
but I still hadn't any idea of what he was driving at.

"If Mr. Rhodes is ill—" I said, and stopped—because the
poor man gave the most dreadful laugh.

He said: "I expect to die of a broken neck in a few
months' time."

And then it all came out. There had been a case of murder
lately in Barnchester—a town about twenty miles away. I'm
afraid I hadn't paid much attention to it at the time, because
we had been having a lot of excitement in the village about
our district nurse, and outside occurrences like an earth-
quake in India and a murder in Barnchester, although of
course far more important really—had given way to our own
little local excitements. I'm afraid villages are like that. Still,
I *did* remember having read about a woman having been
stabbed in a hotel, though I hadn't remembered her name.
But now it seemed that this woman had been Mr. Rhodes's
wife—and as if that wasn't bad enough—he was actually
under suspicion of having murdered her himself.

All this Mr. Petherick explained to me very clearly, saying
that, although the Coroner's jury had brought in a verdict of
murder by a person or persons unknown, Mr. Rhodes had
reason to believe that he would probably be arrested within a
day or two, and that he had come to Mr. Petherick and

placed himself in his hands. Mr. Petherick went on to say that they had that afternoon consulted Sir Malcolm Olde, K.C., and that in the event of the case coming to trial Sir Malcolm had been briefed to defend Mr. Rhodes.

Sir Malcolm was a young man, Mr. Petherick said, very up to date in his methods, and he had indicated a certain line of defense. But with that line of defense Mr. Petherick was not entirely satisfied.

"You see, my dear lady," he said, "it is tainted with what I call the specialist's point of view. Give Sir Malcolm a case and he sees only one point—the most likely line of defense. But even the best line of defense may ignore completely what is, to my mind, the vital point. It takes no account of what actually happened."

Then he went on to say some very kind and flattering things about my acumen and judgment and my knowledge of human nature, and asked permission to tell me the story of the case in the hopes that I might be able to suggest some explanation.

I could see that Mr. Rhodes was highly skeptical of my being of any use and that he was annoyed at being brought here. But Mr. Petherick took no notice and proceeded to give me the facts of what occurred on the night of March 8th.

Mr. and Mrs. Rhodes had been staying at the Crown Hotel in Barnchester. Mrs. Rhodes who (so I gathered from Mr. Petherick's careful language) was perhaps just a shade of a hypochondriac, had retired to bed immediately after dinner. She and her husband occupied adjoining rooms with a connecting door. Mr. Rhodes, who is writing a book on prehistoric flints, settled down to work in the adjoining room. At eleven o'clock he tidied up his papers and prepared to go to bed. Before doing do, he just glanced into his wife's room to make sure that there was nothing she wanted. He discov-

ered the electric light on and his wife lying in bed stabbed
through the heart. She had been dead at least an hour—probably longer. The following were the points made. There was
another door in Mrs. Rhodes's room leading to the corridor.
This door was locked and bolted on the inside. The only
window in the room was closed and latched. According to
Mr. Rhodes nobody had passed through the room in which
he was sitting except a chambermaid bringing hot water
bottles. The weapon found in the wound was a stiletto dagger which had been lying on Mrs. Rhodes's dressing-table.
She was in the habit of using it as a paper knife. There were
no fingerprints on it.

The situation boiled down to this—no one but Mr.
Rhodes and the chambermaid had entered the victim's
room.

I inquired about the chambermaid.

"That was our first line of inquiry," said Mr. Petherick.
"Mary Hill is a local woman. She has been chambermaid at
the Crown for ten years. There seems absolutely no reason
why she should commit a sudden assault on a guest. She is,
in any case, extraordinarily stupid, almost half-witted. Her
story has never varied. She brought Mrs. Rhodes her hot
water bottle and says the lady was drowsy—just dropping off
to sleep. Frankly, I cannot believe, and I am sure no jury
would believe, that she committed the crime."

Mr. Petherick went on to mention a few additional details. At the head of the staircase in the Crown Hotel is a
kind of miniature lounge where people sometimes sit and
have coffee. A passage goes off to the right and the last door
in it is the door into the room occupied by Mr. Rhodes. The
passage then turns sharply to the right again and the first
door around the corner is the door into Mrs. Rhodes's room.
As it happened, both these doors could be seen by witnesses.
The first door—that into Mr. Rhodes's room, which I will

call A, could be seen by four people, two commercial travelers and an elderly married couple who were having coffee. According to them nobody went in or out of door A except Mr. Rhodes and the chambermaid. As to the other door in passage B, there was an electrician at work there and he also swears that nobody entered or left door B except the chambermaid.

It was certainly a very curious and interesting case. On the face of it, it looked as though Mr. Rhodes *must* have murdered his wife. But I could see that Mr. Petherick was quite convinced of his client's innocence and Mr. Petherick was a very shrewd man.

At the inquest Mr. Rhodes had told a hesitating and rambling story about some woman who had written threatening letters to his wife. His story, I gathered, had been unconvincing in the extreme. Appealed to by Mr. Petherick, he explained himself.

"Frankly," he said, "I never believed it. I thought Amy had made most of it up."

Mrs. Rhodes, I gathered, was one of those romantic liars who go through life embroidering everything that happens to them. The amount of adventures that, according to her own account, happened to her in a year was simply incredible. If she slipped on a bit of banana peel it was a case of near escape from death. If a lamp-shade caught fire, she was rescued from a burning building at the hazard of her life. Her husband got into the habit of discounting her statements. Her tale as to some woman whose child she had injured in a motor accident and who had vowed vengeance on her— well—Mr. Rhodes had simply not taken any notice of it. The incident had happened before he married his wife and although she had read him letters couched in crazy language, he had suspected her of composing them herself. She had actually done such a thing once or twice before. She was a woman of hysterical tendencies who craved ceaselessly for excitement.

Now, all that seemed to me very natural—indeed, we have a young woman in the village who does much the same thing. The danger with such people is that when anything at all extraordinary really does happen to them, nobody believes they are speaking the truth. It seemed to me that that was what had happened in this case. The police, I gathered, merely believed that Mr. Rhodes was making up this unconvincing tale in order to avert suspicion from himself.

I asked if there had been any women staying by themselves in the Hotel. It seems there were two—a Mrs. Granby, an Anglo-Indian widow, and a Miss Carruthers, rather a horsey spinster who dropped her g's. Mr. Petherick added that the most minute inquiries had failed to elicit anyone who had seen either of them near the scene of the crime and there was nothing to connect either of them with it in any way. I asked him to describe their personal appearance. He said that Mrs. Granby had reddish hair rather untidily done, was sallow-faced and about fifty years of age. Her clothes were rather picturesque, being made mostly of native silks, etc. Miss Carruthers was about forty, wore pince-nez, had close-cropped hair like a man and wore mannish coats and skirts.

"Dear me," I said, "that makes it very difficult."

Mr. Petherick looked inquiringly at me, but I didn't want to say any more just then, so I asked what Sir Malcolm Olde had said.

Sir Malcolm Olde, it seemed, was going all out for suicide. Mr. Petherick said the medical evidence was dead against this, and there was the absence of fingerprints, but Sir Malcolm was confident of being able to call conflicting medical testimony and to suggest some way of getting over the fingerprint difficulty. I asked Mr. Rhodes what he thought and he said all doctors were fools but he himself couldn't really believe his wife had killed herself. "She wasn't that kind of woman," he said simply—and I believed him. Hysterical people don't usually commit suicide.

I thought a minute and then I asked if the door from Mrs. Rhodes's room led straight to the corridor. Mr. Rhodes said no—there was a little hallway with bathroom and lavatory. It was the door from the bedroom to the hallway that was locked and bolted on the inside.

"In that case," I said, "the whole thing seems to me remarkably simple."

And really, you know, it *did*. . . . The simplest thing in the world. And yet no one seemed to have seen it that way.

Both Mr. Petherick and Mr. Rhodes were staring at me so that I felt quite embarrassed.

"Perhaps," said Mr. Rhodes, "Miss Marple hasn't quite appreciated the difficulties."

"Yes," I said, "I think I have. There are four possibilities. Either Mrs. Rhodes was killed by her husband, or by the chambermaid, or she committed suicide, or she was killed by an outsider whom nobody saw enter or leave."

"And that's impossible," Mr. Rhodes broke in. "Nobody could come in or go out through my room without my seeing them, and even if anyone did manage to come in through my wife's room without the electrician seeing them, how the devil could they get out again leaving the door locked and bolted on the inside?"

Mr. Petherick looked at me and said: "Well, Miss Marple?" in an encouraging manner.

"I should like," I said, "to ask a question. Mr. Rhodes, what did the chambermaid look like?"

He said he wasn't sure—she was tallish, he thought—he didn't remember if she was fair or dark. I turned to Mr. Petherick and asked him the same question.

He said she was of medium height, had fairish hair and blue eyes and rather a high color.

Mr. Rhodes said: "You are a better observer than I am, Petherick."

I ventured to disagree. I then asked Mr. Rhodes if he could describe the maid in my house. Neither he nor Mr. Petherick could do so.

"Don't you see what that means?" I said. "You both came here full of your own affairs and the person who let you in was only a *parlourmaid*. The same applies to Mr. Rhodes at the Hotel. He saw only a *chambermaid*. He saw her uniform and her apron. He was engrossed by his work. But Mr. Petherick has interviewed the same woman in a different capacity. He has looked at her as a *person*.

"That's what the woman who did the murder counted upon."

As they still didn't see, I had to explain.

"I think," I said, "that this is how it went. The chambermaid came in by door A, passed through Mr. Rhodes' room into Mrs. Rhodes' room with the hot water bottle and went out through the hallway into passage B. X—as I will call our murderess—came in by door B into the little hallway, concealed herself in—well, in a certain apartment, ahem—and waited until the chambermaid had passed out. Then she entered Mrs. Rhodes' room, took the stiletto from the dressing-table—(she had doubtless explored the room earlier in the day) went up to the bed, stabbed the dozing woman, wiped the handle of the stiletto, locked and bolted the door by which she had entered, and then passed out through the room where Mr. Rhodes was working."

Mr. Rhodes cried out: "But I should have *seen* her. The electrician would have seen her go in."

"No," I said. "That's where you're wrong. You wouldn't see her—*not if she were dressed as a chambermaid*." I let it sink in, then I went on, "You were engrossed in your work—out of the tail of your eye you saw a chambermaid come in, go into your wife's room, come back and go out. It was the same *dress*—but not the same woman. That's what the people having coffee saw—a chambermaid go in and a chambermaid come out. The electrician did the same. I daresay if a chambermaid were very pretty a gentleman might notice her face—human nature being what it is—but if she were just an ordinary middle-aged woman—well—it would be the chambermaid's *dress* you would see—not the woman herself."

Mr. Rhodes cried: "Who was she?"

"Well," I said, "that is going to be a little difficult. It must be either Mrs. Granby or Miss Carruthers. Mrs. Granby sounds as though she might wear a wig normally—so she could wear her own hair as a chambermaid. On the other hand, Miss Carruthers with her close-cropped mannish head might easily put on a wig to play her part. I daresay you will find out easily enough which of them it is. Personally, I incline myself to think it will be Miss Carruthers."

And really, my dears, that is the end of the story. Carruthers was a false name, but she was the woman all right. There was insanity in her family. Mrs. Rhodes, who was a most reckless and dangerous driver, had run over her little girl, and it had driven the poor woman off her head. She concealed her madness very cunningly except for writing distinctly insane letters to her intended victim. She had been following her about for some time, and she laid her plans very cleverly. The false hair and maid's dress she posted in a parcel first thing the next morning. When taxed with the truth she broke down and confessed at once. The poor thing is in Broadmoor now. Completely unbalanced, of course, but a very cleverly planned crime.

Mr. Petherick came to me afterwards and brought me a very nice letter from Mr. Rhodes—really, it made me blush.

Then my old friend said to me: "Just one thing—why did you think it was more likely to be Carruthers than Granby? You'd never seen either of them."

"Well," I said. "It was the g's. You said she dropped her g's. Now, that's done a lot by hunting people in books, but I don't know many people who do it in reality—and certainly no one under sixty. You said this woman was forty. Those dropped g's sounded to me like a woman who was playing a part and overdoing it."

I shan't tell you what Mr. Petherick said to that—but he was very complimentary—and I really couldn't help feeling just a teeny weeny bit pleased with myself.

And it's extraordinary how things turn out for the best in this world. Mr. Rhodes has married again—such a nice, sensible girl—and they've got a dear little baby and—what do you think?—they asked me to be godmother. Wasn't it nice of them?

Now I do hope you don't think I've been running on too long. . . .

THREE
BLIND
MICE

Strange Jest

And this," said Jane Helier, completing her introductions, "is Miss Marple!"

Being an actress, she was able to make her point. It was clearly the climax, the triumphant finale! Her tone was equally compounded of reverent awe and triumph.

The odd part of it was that the object thus proudly proclaimed was merely a gentle elderly spinster. In the eyes of the two young people who had just, by Jane's good offices, made her acquaintance, there showed incredulity and a tinge of dismay. They were nice-looking people—the girl, Charmian Stroud, slim and dark; the man, Edward Rossiter, a fair-haired, amiable young giant.

Charmian said, a little breathlessly, "Oh, we're awfully pleased to meet you." But there was doubt in her eyes. She flung a quick, questioning glance at Jane Helier.

"Darling," said Jane, answering the glance, "she's absolutely marvellous. Leave it to her. I told you I'd get her here and I have." She added to Miss Marple: "You'll fix it for them, I know. It will be easy for you."

Miss Marple turned her placid, china-blue eyes toward Mr. Rossiter. "Won't you tell me," she said, "what all this is about?"

"Jane's a friend of ours," Charmian broke in impatiently. "Edward and I are in rather a fix. Jane said if we would come to her party, she'd introduce us to someone who was—who would—who could—"

Edward came to the rescue. "Jane tells us you're the last word in sleuths, Miss Marple!"

The old lady's eyes twinkled, but she protested modestly: "Oh no, no! Nothing of the kind. It's just that living in a village as I do, one gets to know so much about human nature. But really you have made me quite curious. Do tell me your problem."

"I'm afraid it's terribly hackneyed—just buried treasure," said Edward.

"Indeed? But that sounds most exciting!"

"I know. Like Treasure Island. But our problem lacks the usual romantic touches. No point on a chart indicated by a skull and crossbones, no directions like 'four paces to the left, west by north.' It's horribly prosaic—just where we ought to dig."

"Have you tried at all?"

"I should say we'd dug about two solid acres! The whole place is ready to be turned into a market garden. We're just discussing whether to grow vegetable marrows or potatoes."

Charmian said, rather abruptly, "May we really tell you all about it?"

"But, of course, my dear."

"Then let's find a peaceful spot. Come on, Edward." She led the way out of the overcrowded and smoke-laden room, and they went up the stairs, to a small sitting-room on the second floor.

When they were seated, Charmian began abruptly: "Well, here goes! The story starts with Uncle Mathew, uncle—or rather, great-great-uncle—to both of us. He was incredibly ancient. Edward and I were his only relations. He was fond of us and always declared that when he died he would leave his money between us. Well, he died last March and left everything he had to be divided equally between Edward and myself. What I've just said sounds rather callous—I don't mean that it was right that he died—actually we were very fond of him. But he'd been ill for some time.

"The point is that the 'everything' he left turned out to be practically nothing at all. And that, frankly, was a bit of a blow to us both, wasn't it, Edward?"

The amiable Edward agreed. "You see," he said, "we'd counted on it a bit. I mean, when you know a good bit of money is coming to you, you don't—well—buckle down and try to make it yourself. I'm in the Army—not got anything to speak of outside my pay—and Charmian herself hasn't got a bean. She works as a stage manager in a repertory theater—quite interesting and she enjoys it—but no money in it. We'd counted on getting married but weren't worried about the money side of it because we both knew we'd be jolly well off some day."

"And now, you see, we're not!" said Charmian. "What's more, Ansteys—that's the family place, and Edward and I both love it—will probably have to be sold. And Edward and I feel we just can't bear that! But if we don't find Uncle Mathew's money, we shall have to sell."

Edward said, "You know, Charmian, we still haven't come to the vital point."

"Well, you talk then."

Edward turned to Miss Marple. "It's like this, you see. As Uncle Mathew grew older, he got more and more suspicious. He didn't trust anybody."

"Very wise of him," said Miss Marple. "The depravity of human nature is unbelievable."

"Well, you may be right. Anyway, Uncle Mathew thought so. He had a friend who lost his money in a bank and another friend who was ruined by an absconding solicitor, and he lost some money himself in a fraudulent company. He got so that he used to hold forth at great length that the only safe and sane thing to do was to convert your money into solid bullion and bury it."

"Ah," said Miss Marple. "I begin to see."

"Yes. Friends argued with him, pointed out that he'd get no interest that way, but he held that that didn't really matter. The bulk of your money, he said, should be 'kept in a box under the bed or buried in the garden.' Those were his words."

Charmian went on: "And when he died, he left hardly anything at all in securities, though he was very rich. So we think that that's what he must have done."

Edward explained: "We found that he had sold securities and drawn out large sums of money from time to time, and nobody knows what he did with them. But it seems probable that he lived up to his principles and that he did buy gold and bury it."

"He didn't say anything before he died? Leave any paper? No letter?"

"That's the maddening part of it. He didn't. He'd been unconscious for some days, but he rallied before he died. He looked at us both and chuckled—a faint, weak little chuckle. He said, 'You'll be all right, my pretty pair of doves.' And then he tapped his eye—his right eye—and winked at us. And then—he died. . . . Poor old Uncle Mathew."

"He tapped his eye," said Miss Marple thoughtfully.

Edward said eagerly, "Does that convey anything to you? It made me think of an Arsène Lupin story where there was something hidden in a man's glass eye. But Uncle Mathew didn't have a glass eye."

Miss Marple shook her head. "No—I can't think of anything at the moment."

Charmian said, disappointedly, "Jane told us you'd say at once where to dig!"

Miss Marple smiled. "I'm not quite a conjurer, you know. I didn't know your uncle, or what sort of man he was, and I don't know the house or the grounds."

Charmian said, "If you did know them?"

"Well, it must be quite simple really, mustn't it?" said Miss Marple.

"Simple!" said Charmian. "You come down to Ansteys and see if it's simple!"

It is possible that she did not mean the invitation to be taken seriously, but Miss Marple said briskly, "Well, really, my dear, that's very kind of you. I've always wanted to have the chance of looking for buried treasure. And," she added, looking at them with a beaming, late-Victorian smile, "with a love interest too!"

"You see!" said Charmian, gesturing dramatically.

They had just completed a grand tour of Ansteys. They had been round the kitchen garden—heavily trenched. They had been through the little woods, where every important tree had been dug round, and had gazed sadly on the pitted surface of the once smooth lawn. They had been up to the attic, where old trunks and chests had been rifled of their contents. They had been down to the cellars, where flagstones had been heaved unwillingly from their sockets. They had measured and tapped walls, and Miss Marple had been shown every antique piece of furniture that contained or could be suspected of containing a secret drawer.

On a table in the morning room there was a heap of papers—all the papers that the late Mathew Stroud had left. Not one had been destroyed, and Charmian and Edward were wont to return to them again and again, earnestly perusing bills, invitations, and business correspondence in the hope of spotting a hitherto unnoticed clue.

"Can you think of anywhere we haven't looked?" demanded Charmian hopefully.

Miss Marple shook her head. "You seem to have been very thorough, my dear. Perhaps, if I may say so, just a little too thorough. I always think, you know, that one should have a plan. It's like my friend, Mrs. Eldritch; she had such a nice little maid, polished linoleum beautifully, but she was so thorough that she polished the bathroom floors too much, and as Mrs. Eldritch was stepping out of the bath the cork mat slipped from under her and she had a very nasty fall and actually broke her leg! Most awkward, because the bathroom door was locked, of course, and the gardener had to get a ladder and come in through the window—terribly distressing to Mrs. Eldritch, who had always been a very modest woman."

Edward moved restlessly.

Miss Marple said quickly, "Please forgive me. So apt, I know, to fly off at a tangent. But one thing does remind one of another. And sometimes that is helpful. All I was trying to say was that perhaps if we tried to sharpen our wits and think of a likely place—"

Edward said crossly, "You think of one, Miss Marple. Charmian's brains and mine are now only beautiful blanks!"

"Dear, dear. Of course—most tiring for you. If you don't mind I'll just look through all this." She indicated the papers on the table. "That is, if there's nothing private—I don't want to appear to pry."

"Oh, that's all right. But I'm afraid you won't find anything."

She sat down by the table and methodically worked through the sheaf of documents. As she replaced each one, she sorted them automatically into tidy little heaps. When she had finished she sat staring in front of her for some minutes.

Edward asked, not without a touch of malice, "Well, Miss Marple?"

She came to herself with a little start. "I beg your pardon. Most helpful."

"You've found something relevant?"

"Oh no, nothing like that, but I do believe I know what sort of man your Uncle Mathew was. Rather like my own Uncle Henry, I think. Fond of rather obvious jokes. A bachelor, evidently—I wonder why—perhaps an early disappointment? Methodical up to a point, but not very fond of being tied up—so few bachelors are!"

Behind Miss Marple's back Charmian made a sign to Edward. It said, "She's ga-ga."

Miss Marple was continuing happily to talk of her deceased Uncle Henry. "Very fond of puns, he was. And to some people puns are most annoying. A mere play upon words may be very irritating. He was a suspicious man too. Always was convinced the servants were robbing him. And sometimes, of course, they were, but not always. It grew upon him, poor man. Toward the end he suspected them of tampering with his food and finally refused to eat anything but boiled eggs! Dear Uncle Henry, he used to be such a merry soul at one time—very fond of his coffee after dinner. He always used to say, 'This coffee is very Moorish,' meaning, you know, that he'd like a little more."

Edward felt that if he heard any more about Uncle Henry he'd go mad.

"Fond of young people, too," went on Miss Marple, "but inclined to tease them a little, if you know what I mean. Used to put bags of sweets where a child just couldn't reach them."

Casting politeness aside, Charmian said, "I think he sounds horrible!"

"Oh no, dear, just an old bachelor, you know, and not used to children. And he wasn't at all stupid, really. He used to keep a good deal of money in the house, and he had a safe put in. Made a great fuss about it—and how very secure it was. As a result of his talking so much, burglars broke in one night and actually cut a hole in the safe with a chemical device."

"Served him right," said Edward.

"Oh, but there was nothing in the safe," said Miss Marple. "You see, he really kept the money somewhere else—behind some volumes of sermons in the library, as a matter of fact. He said people never took a book of that kind out of the shelf!"

Edward interrupted excitedly, "I say, that's an idea. What about the library?"

But Charmian shook a scornful head. "Do you think I hadn't thought of that? I went through all the books Tuesday of last week, when you went off to Portsmouth. Took them all out, shook them. Nothing there."

Edward sighed. Then, rousing himself, he endeavoured to rid himself tactfully of their disappointing guest. "It's been awfully good of you to come down as you have and try to help us. Sorry it's been all a washout. Feel we trespassed a lot on your time. However, I'll get the car out and you'll be able to catch the three-thirty—"

"Oh," said Miss Marple, "but we've got to find the money, haven't we? You mustn't give up, Mr. Rossiter. 'If at first you don't succeed, try, try, try again.' "

"You mean you're going to go—on trying?"

"Strictly speaking," said Miss Marple, "I haven't begun yet. 'First catch your hare,' as Mrs. Beeton says in her cookery book—a wonderful book but terribly expensive; most of the recipes begin, 'Take a quart of cream and a dozen eggs.' Let me see, where was I? Oh yes. Well, we have, so to speak, caught our hare—the hare being, of course, your Uncle Mathew, and we've only got to decide now where he would have hidden the money. It ought to be quite simple."

"Simple?" demanded Charmian.

"Oh yes, dear. I'm sure he would have done the obvious thing. A secret drawer—that's my solution."

Edward said dryly, "You couldn't put bars of gold in a secret drawer."

"No, no, of course not. But there's no reason to believe the money is in gold."

"He always used to say—"

"So did my Uncle Henry about his safe! So I should strongly suspect that that was just a simple blind. Diamonds, now they could be in a secret drawer quite easily."

"But we've looked in all the secret drawers. We had a cabinetmaker over to examine the furniture."

"Did you, dear? That was clever of you. I should suggest your uncle's own desk would be the most likely. Was it the tall escritoire against the wall there?"

"Yes. And I'll show you." Charmian went over to it. She took down the flap. Inside were pigeonholes and little drawers. She opened a small door in the center and touched a spring inside the left-hand drawer. The bottom of the center recess clicked and slid forward. Charmian drew it out, revealing a shallow well beneath. It was empty.

"Now isn't that a coincidence," exclaimed Miss Marple. "Uncle Henry had a desk just like this one, only his was burr walnut and this is mahogany."

"At any rate," said Charmian, "there's nothing there, as you can see."

"I expect," said Miss Marple, "your cabinetmaker was a young man. He didn't know everything. People were very artful when they made hiding places in those days. There's such a thing as a secret inside a secret."

She extracted a hairpin from her neat bun of grey hair. Straightening it out, she stuck the point into what appeared to be a tiny wormhole in one side of the secret recess. With a little difficulty she pulled out a small drawer. In it was a bundle of faded letters and a folded paper.

Edward and Charmian pounced on the find together. With trembling fingers Edward unfolded the paper. He dropped it with an exclamation of disgust.

"A cookery recipe. Baked ham!"

Charmian was untying a ribbon that held the letters together. She drew one out and glanced at it. "Love letters!"

Miss Marple reacted with Victorian gusto. "How interesting! Perhaps the reason your uncle never married."

Charmian read aloud:

"My ever dear Mathew, I must confess that the time seems long indeed since I received your last letter. I try to occupy myself with the various tasks allotted to me, and often say to myself that I am indeed fortunate to see so much of the globe, though little did I think when I went to America that I should voyage off to these far islands!"

Charmian broke off. "Where is it from? Oh, Hawaii!" She went on:

"Alas, these natives are still far from seeing the light. They are in an unclothed and savage state and spend most of their time swimming and dancing, adorning themselves with garlands of flowers. Mr. Gray has made some converts but it is up-hill work and he and Mrs. Gray get sadly discouraged. I try to do all I can to cheer and encourage him, but I, too, am often sad for a reason you can guess, dear Mathew. Alas, absence is a severe trial to a loving heart. Your renewed vows and protestations of affection cheered me greatly. Now and always you have my faithful and devoted heart, dear Mathew, and I remain—

Your true love,
Betty Martin

"P.S.—I address my letter under cover to our mutual friend, Matilda Graves, as usual. I hope Heaven will pardon this little subterfuge."

Edward whistled. "A female missionary! So that was Uncle Mathew's romance. I wonder why they never married?"

"She seems to have gone all over the world," said Charmian, looking through the letters. "Mauritius—all sorts of places. Probably died of yellow fever or something."

A gentle chuckle made them start. Miss Marple was apparently much amused. "Well, well," she said. "Fancy that, now!"

She was reading the recipe for baked ham. Seeing their inquiring glances, she read out: " 'Baked Ham with Spinach. Take a nice piece of gammon, stuff with cloves and cover with brown sugar. Bake in a slow oven. Serve with a border of puréed spinach.'

"What do you think of that now?"

"I think it sounds filthy," said Edward.

"No, no, actually it would be very good—but what do you think of the whole thing?"

A sudden ray of light illuminated Edward's face. "Do you think it's a code—cryptogram of some kind?" He seized it.

"Look here, Charmian, it might be, you know! No reason to put a cooking recipe in a secret drawer otherwise."

"Exactly," said Miss Marple. "Very, very significant."

Charmian said, "I know what it might be—invisible ink! Let's heat it. Turn on the electric fire."

Edward did so. But no signs of writing appeared under the treatment.

Miss Marple coughed. "I really think, you know, that you're making it rather too difficult. The recipe is only an indication, so to speak. It is, I think, the letters that are significant."

"The letters?"

"Especially," said Miss Marple, "the signature."

But Edward hardly heard her. He called excitedly, "Charmian! Come here! She's right. See—the envelopes are old right enough, but the letters themselves were written much later."

"Exactly," said Miss Marple.

"They're only fake old. I bet anything old Uncle Mat faked them himself—"

"Precisely," said Miss Marple.

"The whole thing's a sell. There never was a female missionary. It must be a code."

"My dear, dear children—there's really no need to make it all so difficult. Your uncle was really a very simple man. He had to have his little joke, that was all."

For the first time they gave her their full attention. "Just exactly what do you mean, Miss Marple?" asked Charmian.

"I mean, dear, that you're actually holding the money in your hand this minute."

Charmian stared down.

"The signature, dear. That gives the whole thing away. The recipe is just an indication. Shorn of all the cloves and brown sugar and the rest of it, what is it actually? Why, gammon and spinach to be sure! Gammon and spinach! Meaning—nonsense! So it's clear that it's the letters that are important. And then, if you take into consideration what your uncle did just before he died. He tapped his eye, you said. Well, there you are—that gives you the clue, you see."

Charmian said, "Are we mad, or are you?"

"Surely, my dear, you must have heard the expression meaning that something is not a true picture, or has it quite died out nowadays: *'All my eye and Betty Martin.'*"

Edward gasped, his eyes falling to the letter in his hand. "Betty Martin—"

"Of course, Mr. Rossiter. As you have just said, there isn't—there wasn't any such person. The letters were written by your uncle, and I dare say he got a lot of fun out of writing them! As you say, the writing on the envelopes is much older—in fact, the envelopes couldn't belong to the letters anyway, because the postmark of the one you are holding is eighteen fifty-one."

She paused. She made it very emphatic: "Eighteen fifty-one. And that explains everything, doesn't it?"

"Not to me," said Edward.

"Well, of course," said Miss Marple. "I dare say it wouldn't to me if it weren't for my great-nephew Lionel. Such a dear little boy and a passionate stamp collector. Knows all about stamps. It was he who told me about rare and expensive stamps and that a wonderful new find had come up for auction. And I actually remember his mentioning one stamp —an 1851 blue 2 cent. It realized something like $25,000, I believe. Fancy! I should imagine that the other stamps are something also rare and expensive. No doubt your uncle bought through dealers and was careful to 'cover his tracks,' as they say in detective stories."

Edward groaned. He sat down and buried his face in his hands.

"What's the matter?" demanded Charmian.

"Nothing. It's only the awful thought that, but for Miss Marple, we might have burned these letters in a decent, gentlemanly way!"

"Ah," said Miss Marple, "that's just what these old gentlemen who are fond of their joke never realize. My Uncle Henry, I remember, sent a favourite niece a five-pound note for a Christmas present. He put it inside a Christmas card, gummed the card together, and wrote on it: 'Love and best wishes. Afraid this is all I can manage this year.'

"She, poor girl, was annoyed at what she thought was his meanness and threw it all straight into the fire. So then, of course, he had to give her another."

Edward's feelings toward Uncle Henry had suffered an abrupt and complete change.

"Miss Marple," he said, "I'm going to get a bottle of champagne. We'll all drink the health of your Uncle Henry."

The Case of
the Perfect Maid

O
h, if you please, madam, could I speak to you a moment?"

It might be thought that this request was in the
nature of an absurdity, since Edna, Miss Marple's little maid,
was actually speaking to her mistress at the moment.

Recognizing the idiom, however, Miss Marple said
promptly, "Certainly, Edna. Come in and shut the door.
What is it?"

Obediently shutting the door, Edna advanced into the
room, pleated the corner of her apron between her fingers,
and swallowed once or twice.

"Yes, Edna?" said Miss Marple encouragingly.

"Oh, please, ma'am, it's my cousin Gladdie. You see, she's
lost her place."

"Dear me, I am sorry to hear that. She was at Old Hall,
wasn't she, with the Miss—Misses—Skinner?"

"Yes, ma'am, that's right, ma'am. And Gladdie's very
upset about it—very upset indeed."

"Gladys has changed places rather often before, though,
hasn't she?"

Note: This story has also been published under the title "The Perfect
Maid."

249

"Oh yes, ma'am. She's always one for a change, Gladdie is. She never seems to get really settled, if you know what I mean. But she's always been the one to give the notice, you see!"

"And this time it's the other way round?" asked Miss Marple dryly.

"Yes, ma'am, and it's upset Gladdie something awful."

Miss Marple looked slightly surprised. Her recollection of Gladys, who had occasionally come to drink tea in the kitchen on her "days out," was a stout, giggling girl of unshakably equable temperament.

Edna went on: "You see, ma'am, it's the way it happened—the way Miss Skinner looked."

"How," inquired Miss Marple patiently, "did Miss Skinner look?"

This time Edna got well away with her news bulletin.

"Oh, ma'am, it was ever such a shock to Gladdie. You see, one of Miss Emily's brooches was missing, and such a hue and cry for it as never was, and of course, nobody likes a thing like that to happen; it's upsetting, ma'am. If you know what I mean. And Gladdie's helped search everywhere, and there was Miss Lavinia saying she was going to the police about it, and then it turned up again, pushed right to the back of a drawer in the dressing-table, and very thankful Gladdie was.

"And the very next day as ever was a plate got broken, and Miss Lavinia, she bounced out right away and told Gladdie to take a month's notice. And what Gladdie feels is it couldn't have been the plate and that Miss Lavinia was just making an excuse of that, and that it must be because of the brooch and they think as she took it and put it back when the police was mentioned, and Gladdie wouldn't do such a thing, not never she wouldn't, and what she feels is as it will get round and tell against her, and it's a very serious thing for a girl as you know, ma'am."

Miss Marple nodded. Though having no particular liking for the bouncing, self-opinioned Gladys, she was quite sure of the girl's intrinsic honesty and could well imagine that the affair must have upset her.

Edna said wistfully, "I suppose, ma'am, there isn't anything you could do about it?"

"Tell her not to be silly," said Miss Marple crisply. "If she didn't take the brooch—which I'm sure she didn't—then she has no cause to be upset."

"It'll get about," said Edna dismally.

Miss Marple said, "I—er—am going up that way this afternoon. I'll have word with the Misses Skinner."

"Oh, thank you, madam," said Edna.

Old Hall was a big Victorian house surrounded by woods and park land. Since it had been proved unlettable and unsalable as it was, an enterprising speculator had divided it into four flats with a central hot-water system, and the use of "the grounds" to be held in common by the tenants. The experiment had been satisfactory. A rich and eccentric old lady and her maid occupied one flat. The old lady had a passion for birds and entertained a feathered gathering to meals every day. A retired Indian judge and his wife rented a second. A very young couple, recently married, occupied the third, and the fourth had been taken only two months ago by two maiden ladies of the name of Skinner. The four sets of tenants were only on the most distant terms with each other, since none of them had anything in common. The landlord had been heard to say that this was an excellent thing. What he dreaded were friendships followed by estrangements and subsequent complaints to him.

Miss Marple was acquainted with all the tenants, though she knew none of them well. The elder Miss Skinner, Miss Lavinia, was what might be termed the working member of the firm. Miss Emily, the younger, spent most of her time in bed, suffering from various complaints which, in the opinion of St. Mary Mead, were largely imaginary. Only Miss Lavinia believed devoutly in her sister's martyrdom and patience under affliction and willingly ran errands and trotted up and down to the village for things that "my sister had suddenly fancied."

It was the view of St. Mary Mead that if Miss Emily suffered half as much as she said she did, she would have sent for Dr. Haydock long ago. But Miss Emily, when this was hinted to her, shut her eyes in a superior way and murmured that her case was not a simple one—the best specialists in London had been baffled by it—and that a wonderful new man had put her on a most revolutionary course of treatment and that she really hoped her health would improve under it. No humdrum G.P. could possibly understand her case.

"And it's my opinion," said the outspoken Miss Hartnell, "that she's very wise not to send for him. Dear Dr. Haydock, in that breezy manner of his, would tell her that there was nothing the matter with her and to get up and not make a fuss! Do her a lot of good!"

Failing such arbitrary treatment, however, Miss Emily continued to lie on sofas, to surround herself with strange little pillboxes, and to reject nearly everything that had been cooked for her and ask for something else—usually something difficult and inconvenient to get.

The door was opened to Miss Marple by "Gladdie," looking more depressed than Miss Marple had ever thought possible. In the sitting-room (a quarter of the late drawing-room, which had been partitioned into a dining-room, drawing-room, bathroom, and housemaid's cupboard), Miss Lavinia rose to greet Miss Marple.

Lavinia Skinner was a tall, gaunt, bony female of fifty. She had a gruff voice and an abrupt manner.

"Nice to see you," she said. "Emily's lying down—feeling low today, poor dear. Hope she'll see you—it would cheer her up—but there are times when she doesn't feel up to seeing anybody. Poor dear, she's wonderfully patient."

Miss Marple responded politely. Servants were the main topic of conversation in St. Mary Mead, so it was not difficult to lead the conversation in that direction. Miss Marple said she had heard that that nice girl, Gladys Holmes, was leaving.

Miss Lavinia nodded.

"Wednesday week. Broke things, you know. Can't have that."

Miss Marple sighed and said we all had to put up with things nowadays. It was so difficult to get girls to come to the country. Did Miss Skinner really think it was wise to part with Gladys?

"Know it's difficult to get servants," admitted Miss Lavinia. "The Devereuxs haven't got anybody—but then I don't wonder—always quarrelling, jazz on all night—meals any time—that girl knows nothing of housekeeping. I pity her husband! Then the Larkins have just lost their maid. Of course, what with the judge's temper and his wanting Chota Hazri, as he calls it, at six in the morning, and Mrs. Larkin always fussing, I don't wonder at that, either. Mrs. Carmichael's Janet is a fixture, of course—though in my opinion she's the most disagreeable woman and absolutely bullies the old lady."

"Then don't you think you might reconsider your decision about Gladys. She really is a nice girl. I know all her family; very honest and superior."

Miss Lavinia shook her head.

"I've got my reasons," she said importantly.

Miss Marple murmured: "You missed a brooch, I understand—"

"Now who has been talking? I suppose the girl has. Quite

frankly, I'm almost certain she took it. And then got frightened and put it back—but of course one can't say anything unless one is sure." She changed the subject. "Do come and see Miss Emily, Miss Marple. I'm sure it would do her good."

Miss Marple followed meekly to where Miss Lavinia knocked on a door, was bidden enter, and ushered her guest into the best room in the flat, most of the light of which was excluded by half-drawn blinds. Miss Emily was lying in bed, apparently enjoying the half gloom and her own indefinite sufferings.

The dim light showed her to be a thin, indecisive-looking creature, with a good deal of greyish yellow hair untidily wound around her head and erupting into curls, the whole thing looking like a bird's nest of which no self-respecting bird could be proud. There was a smell in the room of eau de cologne, stale biscuits, and camphor.

With half-closed eyes and in a thin, weak voice, Emily Skinner explained that this was "one of her bad days."

"The worst of ill-health is," said Miss Emily in a melancholy tone, "that one knows what a burden one is to everyone around one.

"Lavinia is very good to me. Lavvie dear, I do so hate giving trouble, but if my hot water bottle could only be filled in the way I like it—too full it weighs on me so; on the other hand, if it is not sufficiently filled, it gets cold immediately!"

"I'm sorry, dear. Give it to me. I will empty a little out."

"Perhaps, if you're doing that, it might be refilled. There are no rusks in the house, I suppose—no, no, it doesn't matter. I can do without. Some weak tea and a slice of lemon—no lemons? No, really, I couldn't drink tea without lemon. I think the milk was slightly turned this morning. It has put me right against milk in my tea. It doesn't matter. I can do without my tea. Only I do feel so weak. Oysters, they say, are nourishing. I wonder if I could fancy a few. No, no, too much bother to get hold of them so late in the day. I can fast until tomorrow."

Lavinia left the room murmuring something incoherent about bicycling down to the village.

Miss Emily smiled feebly at her guest and remarked that she did hate giving anyone any trouble.

Miss Marple told Edna that evening that she was afraid her mission had met with no success.

She was rather troubled to find that rumours as to Gladys's dishonesty were already going around the village.

In the post office Miss Wetherby tackled her: "My dear Jane, they gave her a written reference saying she was willing and sober and respectable, but saying nothing about honesty. That seems to me most significant! I hear there was some trouble about a brooch. I think there must be something in it, you know, because one doesn't let a servant go nowadays unless it's something rather grave. They'll find it most difficult to get anyone else. Girls simply will not go to Old Hall. They're nervous coming home on their days out. You'll see, the Skinners won't find anyone else, and then perhaps that dreadful hypochondriac sister will have to get up and do something!"

Great was the chagrin of the village when it was made known that the Misses Skinner had engaged, from an agency, a new maid who, by all accounts, was a perfect paragon.

"A three years' reference recommending her most warmly, she prefers the country and actually asks less wages than Gladys. I really feel we have been most fortunate."

"Well, really," said Miss Marple, to whom these details were imparted by Miss Lavinia in the fishmonger's shop. "It does seem too good to be true."

It then became the opinion of St. Mary Mead that the paragon would cry off at the last minute and fail to arrive.

None of the prognostications came true, however, and the village was able to observe the domestic treasure, by name, Mary Higgins, driving through the village in Reed's taxi to Old Hall. It had to be admitted that her appearance was good. A most respectable-looking woman, very neatly dressed.

When Miss Marple next visited Old Hall, on the occasion of recruiting stall holders for the Vicarage Fete, Mary Higgins opened the door. She was certainly a most superior-looking maid, at a guess forty years of age, with neat black hair, rosy cheeks, a plump figure discreetly arrayed in black with a white apron and cap—"quite the good, old-fashioned type of servant," as Miss Marple explained afterward, and with the proper, inaudible, respectful voice, so different from the loud but adenoidal accents of Gladys.

Miss Lavinia was looking far less harassed than usual and, although she regretted that she could not take a stall, owing to her preoccupation with her sister, she nevertheless tendered a handsome monetary contribution and promised to produce a consignment of penwipers and babies' socks.

Miss Marple commented on her air of well-being.

"I really feel I owe a great deal to Mary. I am so thankful I had the resolution to get rid of that other girl. Mary is really invaluable. Cooks nicely and waits beautifully and keeps our little flat scrupulously clean—mattresses turned over every day. And she is really wonderful with Emily!"

Miss Marple hastily inquired after Emily.

"Oh, poor dear, she has been very much under the weather lately. She can't help it, of course, but it really makes things a little difficult sometimes. Wanting certain things cooked and then, when they come, saying she can't eat now—and then wanting them again half an hour later and everything spoiled and having to be done again. It makes, of course, a lot of work—but fortunately Mary does not seem to mind at all. She's used to waiting on invalids, she says, and understands them. It is such a comfort."

"Dear me," said Miss Marple. "You are fortunate."

"Yes, indeed. I really feel Mary has been sent to us as an answer to prayer."

"She sounds to me," said Miss Marple, "almost too good to be true. I should—well, I should be a little careful if I were you."

Lavinia Skinner failed to perceive the point of this remark. She said, "Oh, I assure you I do all I can to make her comfortable. I don't know what I should do if she left."

"I don't expect she'll leave until she's ready to leave," said Miss Marple and stared very hard at her hostess.

Miss Lavinia said, "If one has no domestic worries, it takes such a load off one's mind, doesn't it? How is your little Edna shaping?"

"She's doing quite nicely. Not like your Mary. Still I do know all about Edna, because she's a village girl."

As she went out into the hall she heard the invalid's voice fretfully raised: "This compress has been allowed to get quite dry—Dr. Allerton particularly said moisture continually renewed. There, there, leave it. I want a cup of tea and a boiled egg—boiled only three minutes and a half, remember, and send Miss Lavinia to me."

The efficient Mary emerged from the bedroom and, saying to Lavinia, "Miss Emily is asking for you, madam," proceeded to open the door for Miss Marple, helping her into her coat and handing her her umbrella in the most irreproachable fashion.

Miss Marple took the umbrella, dropped it, tried to pick it up, and dropped her bag which flew open. Mary politely retrieved various odds and ends—a handkerchief, an engagement book, an old-fashioned leather purse, two shillings, three pennies, and a striped piece of peppermint rock.

Miss Marple received the last with some signs of confusion.

"Oh dear, that must have been Mrs. Clement's little boy. He was sucking it, I remember, and he took my bag to play with. He must have put it inside. It's terribly sticky, isn't it?"

"Shall I take it, madam?"

"Oh, would you? Thank you so much."

Mary stooped to retrieve the last item, a small mirror, upon recovering which Miss Marple exclaimed fervently, "How lucky now that that isn't broken."

She thereupon departed, Mary standing politely by the door holding a piece of striped rock with a completely expressionless face.

For ten days longer St. Mary Mead had to endure hearing of the excellencies of Miss Lavinia's and Miss Emily's treasure.

On the eleventh day the village awoke to its big thrill.

Mary, the paragon, was missing! Her bed had not been slept in and the front door was found ajar. She had slipped out quietly during the night.

And not Mary alone was missing! Two brooches and five rings of Miss Lavinia's, three rings, a pendant, a bracelet, and four brooches of Miss Emily's were missing also!

It was the beginning of a chapter of catastrophe.

Young Mrs. Devereux had lost her diamonds which she kept in an unlocked drawer and also some valuable furs given to her as a wedding present. The judge and his wife also had had jewelry taken and a certain amount of money. Mrs. Carmichael was the greatest sufferer. Not only had she some very valuable jewels, but she also kept a large sum of money in the flat which had gone. It had been Janet's evening out and her mistress was in the habit of walking round the gardens at dusk, calling to the birds and scattering crumbs. It seemed clear that Mary, the perfect maid, had had keys to fit all the flats!

There was, it must be confessed, a certain amount of ill-natured pleasure in St. Mary Mead. Miss Lavinia had boasted so much of her marvellous Mary.

"And all the time, my dear, just a common thief!"

Interesting revelation followed. Not only had Mary disappeared into the blue, but the agency which had provided her and vouched for her credentials was alarmed to find that the Mary Higgins who had applied to them and whose references they had taken up had, to all intents and purposes, never existed. It was the name of a bona fide servant who had lived with the bona fide sister of a dean, but the real Mary Higgins was existing peacefully in a place in Cornwall.

"Clever, the whole thing," Inspector Slack was forced to admit. "And, if you ask me, that woman works in with a gang. There was a case of much the same kind in Northumberland a year ago. Stuff was never traced and they never caught her. However, we'll do better than that in Much Benham!"

Inspector Slack was always a confident man.

Nevertheless, weeks passed and Mary Higgins remained triumphantly at large. In vain Inspector Slack redoubled that energy that so belied his name.

Miss Lavinia remained tearful. Miss Emily was so upset and felt so alarmed by her condition that she actually sent for Dr. Haydock.

The whole of the village was terribly anxious to know what he thought of Miss Emily's claims to ill-health but naturally could not ask him. Satisfactory data came to hand on the subject, however, through Mr. Meek, the chemist's assistant, who was walking out with Clara, Mrs. Price-Ridley's maid. It was then known that Dr. Haydock had prescribed a mixture of asafoetida and valerian which, according to Mr. Meek, was the stock remedy for malingerers in the army!

Soon afterward it was learned that Miss Emily, not relishing the medical attention she had had, was declaring that in the state of her health she felt it her duty to be near the specialist in London who understood her case. It was, she said, only fair to Lavinia.

The flat was put up for subletting.

It was a few days after that that Miss Marple, rather pink and flustered, called at the police station in Much Benham and asked for Inspector Slack.

Inspector Slack did not like Miss Marple. But he was aware that the chief constable, Colonel Melchett, did not share that opinion. Rather grudgingly, therefore, he received her.

"Good afternoon, Miss Marple. What can I do for you?"

"Oh, dear," said Miss Marple, "I'm afraid you're in a hurry."

"Lot of work on," said Inspector Slack, "but I can spare a few moments."

"Oh, dear," said Miss Marple. "I hope I shall be able to put what I say properly. So difficult, you know, to explain oneself, don't you think? No, perhaps you don't. But you see, not having been educated in the modern style—just a governess, you know, who taught one the dates of the Kings of England and General Knowledge—and how needles are made and all that. Discursive, you know, but not teaching one to keep to the point. Which is what I want to do. It's about Miss Skinner's maid, Gladys, you know."

"Mary Higgins," said Inspector Slack.

"Oh yes, the second maid. But it's Gladys Holmes I

mean—rather an impertinent girl and far too pleased with herself, but really strictly honest, and it's so important that that should be recognized."

"No charge against her so far as I know," said the inspector.

"No, I know there isn't a charge—but that makes it worse. Because, you see, people go on thinking things. Oh, dear—I knew I should explain badly. What I really mean is that the important thing is to find Mary Higgins."

"Certainly," said Inspector Slack. "Have you any ideas on the subject?"

"Well, as a matter of fact, I have," said Miss Marple. "May I ask you a question? Are fingerprints of no use to you?"

"Ah," said Inspector Slack, "that's where she was a bit too artful for us. Did most of her work in rubber gloves or housemaid's gloves, it seems. And she'd been careful—wiped off everything in her bedroom and on the sink. Couldn't find a single fingerprint in the place!"

"If you did have her fingerprints, would it help?"

"It might, madam. They may be known at the Yard. This isn't her first job, I'd say!"

Miss Marple nodded brightly. She opened her bag and extracted a small cardboard box. Inside it, wedged in cotton wool, was a small mirror.

"From my handbag," said Miss Marple. "The maid's prints are on it. I think they should be satisfactory—she touched an extremely sticky substance a moment previously."

Inspector Slack stared.

"Did you get her fingerprints on purpose?"

"Of course."

"You suspected her then?"

"Well, you know it did strike me that she was a little too good to be true. I practically told Miss Lavinia so. But she simply wouldn't take the hint! I'm afraid, you know, Inspector, that I don't believe in paragons. Most of us have our faults—and domestic service shows them up very quickly!"

"Well," said Inspector Slack, recovering his balance, "I'm obliged to you, I'm sure. We'll send these up to the Yard and see what they have to say."

He stopped. Miss Marple had put her head a little on one side and was regarding him with a good deal of meaning.

"You wouldn't consider, I suppose, Inspector, looking a little nearer home?"

"What do you mean, Miss Marple?"

"It's very difficult to explain, but when you come across a peculiar thing you notice it. Although, often, peculiar things may be the merest trifles. I've felt that all along, you know; I mean about Gladys and the brooch. She's an honest girl; she didn't take that brooch. Then why did Miss Skinner think she did? Miss Skinner's not a fool, far from it! Why was she so anxious to let a girl go who was a good servant when servants are hard to get? It was peculiar, you know. So I wondered. I wondered a good deal. And I noticed another peculiar thing! Miss Emily's a hypochondriac, but she's the first hypochondriac who hasn't sent for some doctor or other at once. Hypochondriacs love doctors. Miss Emily didn't!"

"What are you suggesting, Miss Marple?"

"Well, I'm suggesting, you know, that Miss Lavinia and Miss Emily are peculiar people. Miss Emily spends nearly all her time in a dark room. And if that hair of hers isn't a wig, I—I'll eat my own back switch! And what I say is this—it's perfectly possible for a thin, pale, grey-haired, whining woman to be the same as a black-haired, rosy-cheeked, plump woman. And nobody that I can find ever saw Miss Emily and Mary Higgins at one and the same time.

"Plenty of time to get impressions of all the keys, plenty of time to find out all about the other tenants, and then— get rid of the local girl. Miss Emily takes a brisk walk across country one night and arrives at the station as Mary Higgins next day. And then, at the right moment, Mary Higgins disappears, and off goes the hue and cry after her. I'll tell you where you'll find her, Inspector. On Miss Emily Skinner's sofa! Get her fingerprints if you don't believe me, but you'll find I'm right! A couple of clever thieves, that's what the Skinners are—and no doubt in league with a clever post and rails or fence or whatever you call it. But they won't get away with it this time! I'm not going to have one of our village girl's character for honesty taken away like that! Gladys Holmes is as honest as the day and everybody's going to know it! Good afternoon!"

Miss Marple had stalked out before Inspector Slack had recovered.

"Whew!" he muttered. "I wonder if she's right."

He soon found out that Miss Marple was right again.

Colonel Melchett congratulated Slack on his efficiency, and Miss Marple had Gladys come to tea with Edna and spoke to her seriously on settling down in a good situation when she got one.

The Case of
the Caretaker

"Well," demanded Dr. Haydock of his patient, "and how goes it today?"

Miss Marple smiled at him wanly from pillows.

"I suppose, really, that I'm better," she admitted, "but I feel so terribly depressed. I can't help feeling how much better it would have been if I had died. After all, I'm an old woman. Nobody wants me or cares about me."

Dr. Haydock interrupted with his usual brusqueness: "Yes, yes, typical after-reaction to this type of 'flu.' What you need is something to take you out of yourself. A mental tonic."

Miss Marple sighed and shook her head.

"And what's more," continued Dr. Haydock, "I've brought my medicine with me!"

He tossed a long envelope onto the bed.

"Just the thing for you. The kind of puzzle that is right up your street."

"A puzzle?" Miss Marple looked interested.

"Literary effort of mine," said the doctor, blushing a little. "Tried to make a regular story of it. 'He said, she said, the girl thought, et cetera.' Facts of the story are true."

"But why a puzzle?" asked Miss Marple.

Dr. Haydock grinned. "Because the interpretation is up to you. I want to see if you're as clever as you always make out."

With that Parthian shot he departed.

Miss Marple picked up the manuscript and began to read.

"And where is the bride?" asked Miss Harmon genially.

The village was all agog to see the rich and beautiful young wife that Harry Laxton had brought back from abroad. There was a general indulgent feeling that Harry—wicked young scapegrace—had had all the luck. Everyone had always felt indulgent toward Harry. Even the owners of windows that had suffered from his indiscriminate use of a catapult had found their indignation dissipated by young Harry's abject expression of regret. He had broken windows, robbed orchards, poached rabbits, and later had run into debt—been disentangled and sent off to Africa—and the village, as represented by various aging spinsters, had murmured indulgently, "Ah well! Wild oats! He'll settle down!"

And now, sure enough, the prodigal had returned—not in affliction, but in triumph. Harry Laxton had "made good," as the saying goes. He had pulled himself together, worked hard, and had finally met and successfully wooed a young Anglo-French girl who was the possessor of a considerable fortune.

Harry might have lived in London, or purchased an estate in some fashionable hunting county, but he preferred to come back to the part of the world that was home to him. And there, in the most romantic way, he purchased the derelict estate in the Dower House of which he had passed his childhood.

Kingsdean House had been unoccupied for nearly seventy years. It had gradually fallen into decay and abandon. An elderly caretaker and his wife lived in the one habitable corner of it. It was a vast, unprepossessing, grandiose mansion, the gardens overgrown with rank vegetation and the trees hemming it in like some gloomy enchanter's den.

The Dower House was a pleasant, unpretentious house and had been let for a long term of years to Major Laxton, Harry's father. As a boy, Harry had roamed over the Kingsdean estate and knew every inch of the tangled woods, and the old house itself had always fascinated him.

Major Laxton had died some years ago, so it might have been thought that Harry would have had no ties to bring him back; nevertheless, it was to the home of his boyhood that Harry brought his bride. The ruined old Kingsdean House was pulled down. An army of builders and contractors swooped down upon the place and in almost a miraculously short space of time—so marvellously does wealth tell—the new house rose, white and gleaming among the trees.

Next came the posse of gardeners and after them a procession of furniture vans.

The house was ready. Servants arrived. Lastly a costly limousine deposited Harry and Mrs. Harry at the front door.

The village rushed to call, and Mrs. Price, who owned the largest house, and who considered herself to lead society in the place, sent out cards of invitation for a party "to meet the bride."

It was a great event. Several ladies had new frocks for the occasion. Everyone was excited, curious, anxious to see this fabulous creature. They said it was all so like a fairy story!

Miss Harmon, weather-beaten, hearty spinster, threw out her question as she squeezed her way through the crowded drawing-room door. Little Miss Brent, a thin, acidulated spinster, fluttered out information.

"Oh, my dear, quite charming. Such pretty manners. And

quite young. Really, you know, it makes one feel quite envious to see someone who has everything like that. Good looks and money and breeding—most distinguished, nothing in the least common about her—and dear Harry so devoted!"

"Ah," said Miss Harmon, "it's early days yet!"

Miss Brent's thin nose quivered appreciatively.

"Oh, my dear, do you really think—"

"We all know what Harry is," said Miss Harmon.

"We know what he was! But I expect now—"

"Ah," said Miss Harmon, "men are always the same. I know them."

"Dear, dear. Poor young thing." Miss Brent looked much happier. "Yes, I expect she'll have trouble with him. Someone ought really to warn her."

"Beasts!" said Clarice Vane indignantly to her uncle, Dr. Haydock. "Absolute beasts some people are."

He looked at her curiously.

She was a tall, dark girl, handsome, warmhearted and impulsive. Her big brown eyes were alight now with indignation as she said, "All these cats—saying things—hinting things."

"About Harry Laxton?"

"Yes. It's like ghouls feasting on dead bodies."

"I daresay, my dear, it does seem like that to you. But you see, they have very little to talk about down here, and so I'm afraid they do tend to dwell upon past scandals. But I'm curious to know why it upsets you so much."

Clarice Vane bit her lip and flushed. She said, in a curiously muffled voice, "They—they look so happy. The Laxtons, I mean. They're young and in love and it's all so lovely for them. I hate to think of it being spoiled by whispers and hints and innuendoes and general beastliness."

"H'm. I see."

Clarice went on: "He was talking to me just now. He's so happy and eager and excited and—yes, thrilled—at having got his heart's desire and rebuilt Kingsdean. He's like a child about it all. And she—well, I don't suppose anything has ever gone wrong in her whole life. She's always had everything. You've seen her. What did you think of her?"

The doctor did not answer at once. For other people, Louise Laxton might be an object of envy. A spoiled darling of fortune. To him she had brought only the refrain of a popular song heard so many years ago: "Poor Little Rich Girl . . ."

A small, delicate figure, with flaxen hair curled rather stiffly round her face and big, wistful blue eyes.

Louise was drooping a little. The long stream of congratulations had tired her. She was hoping it might soon be time to go. Perhaps, even now, Harry might say so. She looked at him sideways. So tall and broad-shouldered with his eager pleasure in this horrible dull party.

"Poor little rich girl . . ."

"Ooph!" It was a sigh of relief.

Harry turned to look at his wife amusedly. They were driving away from the party. She said, "Darling, what a frightful party!"

Harry laughed.

"Yes, pretty terrible. Never mind, my sweet. It had to be done, you know. All those old pussies knew me when I lived here as a boy. They'd have been terribly disappointed not to have got a good look at you close up."

Louise made a grimace. She said, "Shall we have to see a lot of them?"

"What? On no. They'll come and make ceremonious calls with card cases, and you'll return the calls and then you needn't bother any more. You can have your own friends down or whatever you like."

Louise said, after a minute or two, "Isn't there anyone amusing living down here?"

"Oh yes. There's the County, you know. Though you may find them a bit dull too. Mostly interested in bulbs and dogs and horses. You'll ride, of course. You'll enjoy that. There's a horse over at Eglinton I'd like you to see. A beautiful animal, perfectly trained, no vice in him, but plenty of spirit."

The car slowed down to take the turn into the gates of Kingsdean. Harry wrenched the wheel and swore as a grotesque figure sprang up in the middle of the road and he only just managed to avoid it. It stood there, shaking a fist and shouting after them.

Louise clutched his arm. "Who's that—that horrible old woman?"

Harry's brow was black.

"That's old Murgatroyd. She and her husband were caretakers in the old house. They were there for nearly thirty years."

"Why does she shake her fist at you?"

Harry's face got red.

"She—well, she resented the house being pulled down. And she got the sack, of course. Her husband's been dead two years. They say she got a bit queer after he died."

"Is she—she isn't—starving?"

Louise's ideas were vague and somewhat melodramatic. Riches prevented you from coming into contact with reality.

Harry was outraged.

"Good Lord, Louise, what an idea. I pensioned her off, of course—and handsomely too! Found her a new cottage and everything."

Louise asked, bewildered, "Then why does she mind?"

Harry was frowning, his brows drawn together. "Oh, how should I know? Craziness! She loved the house."

"But it was a ruin, wasn't it?"

"Of course it was—crumbling to pieces—roof leaking—more or less unsafe. All the same, I suppose it meant something to her. She'd been there a long time. Oh, I don't know! The old devil's cracked, I think."

Louise said uneasily, "She—I think she cursed us. Oh, Harry, I wish she hadn't."

It seemed to Louise that her new home was tainted and poisoned by the malevolent figure of one crazy old woman. When she went out in the car, when she rode, when she walked out with the dogs, there was always the same figure waiting. Crouched down on herself, a battered hat over wisps of iron-grey hair, and the slow muttering of imprecations.

Louise came to believe that Harry was right—the old woman was mad. Nevertheless, that did not make things easier. Mrs. Murgatroyd never actually came to the house, nor did she use definite threats, nor offer violence. Her squatting figure remained always just outside the gates. To appeal to the police would have been useless and, in any case, Harry Laxton was averse to that course of action. It would, he said, arouse local sympathy for the old brute. He took the matter more easily than Louise did.

"Don't worry about it, darling. She'll get tired of this silly cursing business. Probably she's only trying it on."

"She isn't, Harry. She—she hates us! I can feel it. She—she's ill-wishing us!"

"She's not a witch, darling, although she may look like one! Don't be morbid about it all."

Louise was silent. Now that the first excitement of settling in was over, she felt curiously lonely and at a loose end.

She had been used to life in London and the Riviera. She had no knowledge of or taste for English country life. She was ignorant of gardening, except for the final act of "doing the flowers." She did not really care for dogs. She was bored by such neighbours as she met. She enjoyed riding best, sometimes with Harry, sometimes, when he was busy about the estate, by herself. She hacked through the woods and lanes, enjoying the easy paces of the beautiful horse that Harry had bought for her. Yet even Prince Hal, most sensitive of chestnut steeds, was wont to shy and snort as he carried his mistress past that huddled figure of a malevolent old woman.

One day Louise took her courage in both hands. She was out walking. She had passed Mrs. Murgatroyd, pretending not to notice her, but suddenly she swerved back and went right up to her. She said, a little breathlessly, "What is it? What's the matter? What do you want?"

The old woman blinked at her. She had a cunning, dark gypsy face, with wisps of iron-grey hair, and bleared, suspicious eyes. Louise wondered if she drank.

She spoke in a whining and yet threatening voice: "What do I want, you ask? What, indeed! That which has been took away from me. Who turned me out of Kingsdean House? I'd lived there, girl and woman, for near on forty years. It was a black deed to turn me out, and it's black bad luck it'll bring to you and him!"

Louise said, "You've got a very nice cottage and—"

She broke off. The old woman's arms flew up. She screamed. "What's the good of that to me? It's my own place I want and my own fire as I sat beside all them years. And as for you and him, I'm telling you there will be no happiness for you in your new fine house. It's the black sorrow will be upon you! Sorrow and death and my curse. May your fair face rot."

Louise turned away and broke into a little stumbling run. She thought, "I must get away from here! We must sell the house! We must go away."

At the moment such a solution seemed easy to her. But Harry's utter incomprehension took her aback. He exclaimed, "Leave here? Sell the house? Because of a crazy old woman's threats? You must be mad."

"No, I'm not. But she—she frightens me. I know something will happen."

Harry Laxton said grimly, "Leave Mrs. Murgatroyd to me. I'll settle her!"

A friendship had sprung up between Clarice Vane and young Mrs. Laxton. The two girls were much of an age, though dissimilar both in character and in tastes. In Clarice's company Louise found reassurance. Clarice was so self-reliant, so sure of herself. Louise mentioned the matter of Mrs. Murgatroyd and her threats, but Clarice seemed to regard the matter as more annoying than frightening.

"It's so stupid, that sort of thing," she said. "And really very annoying for you."

"You know, Clarice, I—I feel quite frightened sometimes. My heart gives the most awful jumps."

"Nonsense, you mustn't let a silly thing like that get you down. She'll soon tire of it."

Louise was silent for a minute or two. Clarice said, "What's the matter?"

Louise paused for a minute, then her answer came with a rush: "I hate this place! I hate being here. The woods and this house, and the awful silence at night, and the queer noise owls make. Oh, and the people and everything."

"The people. What people?"

"The people in the village. Those prying, gossiping old maids."

Clarice said sharply, "What have they been saying?"

"I don't know. Nothing particular. But they've got nasty minds. When you've talked to them you feel you wouldn't trust anybody—not anybody at all."

Clarice said harshly, "Forget them. They've nothing to do but gossip. And most of the muck they talk they just invent."

Louise said, "I wish we'd never come here. But Harry adores it so." Her voice softened. Clarice thought, "How she adores him."

She said abruptly, "I must go now."

"I'll send you back in the car. Come again soon."

Clarice nodded. Louise felt comforted by her new friend's visit. Harry was pleased to find her more cheerful and from then on urged her to have Clarice often to the house.

Then one day he said, "Good news for you, darling."

"Oh, what?"

"I've fixed the Murgatroyd. She's got a son in America, you know. Well, I've arranged for her to go out and join him. I'll pay her passage."

"Oh, Harry, how wonderful. I believe I might get to like Kingsdean after all."

"Get to like it? Why, it's the most wonderful place in the world!"

Louise gave a little shiver. She could not rid herself of her superstitious fear so easily.

If the ladies of St. Mary Mead had hoped for the pleasure of imparting information about her husband's past to the bride, this pleasure was denied them by Harry Laxton's own prompt action.

Miss Harmon and Clarice Vane were both in Mr. Edge's shop, the one buying moth balls and the other a packet of boracic, when Harry Laxton and his wife came in.

After greeting the two ladies, Harry turned to the counter and was just demanding a toothbrush when he stopped in mid-speech and exclaimed heartily, "Well, well, just see who's here! Bella, I do declare."

Mrs. Edge, who had hurried out from the back parlour to attend to the congestion of business, beamed back cheerfully at him, showing her big white teeth. She had been a dark, handsome girl and was still a reasonably handsome woman, though she had put on weight and the lines of her face had coarsened, but her large brown eyes were full of warmth as she answered, "Bella it is, Mr. Harry, and pleased to see you after all these years."

Harry turned to his wife.

"Bella's an old flame of mine, Louise," he said. "Head-over-ears in love with her, wasn't I, Bella?"

"That's what you say," said Mrs. Edge.

Louise laughed. She said, "My husband's very happy seeing all his old friends again."

"Ah," said Mrs. Edge, "we haven't forgotten you, Mr. Harry. Seems like a fairy tale to think of you married and building up a new house instead of that ruined old Kingsdean House."

"You look very well and blooming," said Harry, and Mrs. Edge laughed and said there was nothing wrong with her and what about that toothbrush?

Clarice, watching the baffled look on Miss Harmon's face, said to herself exultantly, "Oh, well done, Harry. You've spiked their guns."

Dr. Haydock said abruptly to his niece Clarice, "What's all this nonsense about old Mrs. Murgatroyd hanging about Kingsdean and shaking her fist and cursing the new regime?"

"It isn't nonsense. It's quite true. It's upset Louise a good deal."

"Tell her she needn't worry—when the Murgatroyds were caretakers they never stopped grumbling about the place—they only stayed because Murgatroyd drank and couldn't get another job."

"I'll tell her," said Clarice doubtfully, "but I don't think she'll believe you. The old woman fairly screams with rage."

"Always used to be fond of Harry as a boy. I can't understand it."

Clarice said, "Oh well—they'll be rid of her soon. Harry's paying her passage to America."

Three days later Louise was thrown from her horse and killed.

Two men in a baker's van were witnesses of the accident. They saw Louise ride out of the gates, saw the old woman spring up and stand in the road, waving her arms and shouting, saw the horse start, swerve, and then bolt madly down the road, flinging Louise Laxton over his head.

One of them stood over the unconscious figure, not knowing what to do, while the other rushed to the house to get help.

Harry Laxton came running out, his face ghastly. They took off a door of the van and carried her on it to the house. She died without regaining consciousness and before the doctor arrived.

(End of Dr. Haydock's manuscript.)

When Dr. Haydock arrived the following day, he was pleased to note that there was a pink flush in Miss Marple's cheek and decidedly more animation in her manner.

"Well," he said, "what's the verdict?"

"What's the problem?" countered Miss Marple.

"Oh, my dear lady, do I have to tell you that?"

"I suppose," said Miss Marple, "that it's the curious conduct of the caretaker. Why did she behave in that very odd way? People do mind being turned out of their old homes.

But it wasn't her home. In fact, she used to complain and grumble while she was there. Yes, it certainly looks very fishy. What became of her, by the way?"

"Took flight to Liverpool. The accident scared her. Thought she'd wait there for her boat."

"All very convenient for somebody," said Miss Marple. "Yes, I think the 'Problem of the Caretaker's Conduct' can be solved easily enough. Bribery, was it not?"

"That's your solution?"

"Well, if it wasn't natural for her to behave in that way, she must have been 'putting on an act,' as people say, and that means that somebody paid her to do what she did."

"And you know who that somebody was?"

"Oh, I think so. Money again, I'm afraid. And I've always noticed that gentlemen always tend to admire the same type."

"Now I'm out of my depth."

"No, no, it all hangs together. Harry Laxton admired Bella Edge, a dark, vivacious type. Your niece Clarice was the same. But the poor little wife was quite a different type—fair-haired and clinging—not his type at all. So he must have married her for her money. And murdered her for her money too!"

"You use the word murder?"

"Well, he sounds the right type. Attractive to women and quite unscrupulous. I suppose he wanted to keep his wife's money and marry your niece. He may have been seen talking to Mrs. Edge. But I don't fancy he was attached to her any more. Though I daresay he made the poor woman think he was, for ends of his own. He soon had her well under his thumb, I fancy."

"How exactly did he murder her, do you think?"

Miss Marple stared ahead of her for some minutes with dreamy blue eyes.

"It was well timed—with the baker's van as witness. They could see the old woman and, of course, they'd put down the horse's fright to that. But I should imagine, myself, that an air gun, or perhaps a catapult—he used to be good with a catapult. Yes, just as the horse came through the gate. The horse bolted, of course, and Mrs. Laxton was thrown."

She paused, frowning.

"The fall might have killed her. But he couldn't be sure of that. And he seems the sort of man who would lay his plans carefully and leave nothing to chance. After all, Mrs. Edge could get him something suitable without her husband knowing. Otherwise why would Harry bother with her? Yes, I think he had some powerful drug handy, that could be administered before you arrived. After all, if a woman is thrown from her horse and has serious injuries and dies without recovering consciousness, well—a doctor wouldn't normally be suspicious, would he? He'd put it down to shock or something."

Dr. Haydock nodded.

"Why did you suspect?" asked Miss Marple.

"It wasn't any particular cleverness on my part," said Dr. Haydock. "It was just the trite, well-known fact that a murderer is so pleased with his cleverness that he doesn't take proper precautions. I was just saying a few consolatory words to the bereaved husband—and feeling sorry for the fellow, too—when he flung himself down on the settee to do a bit of play-acting and a hypodermic syringe fell out of his pocket.

"He snatched it up and looked so scared that I began to think. Harry Laxton didn't drug; he was in perfect health. What was he doing with a hypodermic syringe? I did the autopsy with a view to certain possibilities. I found strophanthin. The rest was easy. There was strophanthin in Laxton's possession, and Bella Edge, questioned by the police, broke down and admitted to having got it for him. And finally old Mrs. Murgatroyd confessed that it was Harry Laxton who had put her up to the cursing stunt."

"And your niece got over it?"

"Yes, she was attracted by the fellow, but it hadn't gone far."

The doctor picked up his manuscript.

"Full marks to you, Miss Marple—and full marks to me for my prescription. You're looking almost yourself again."

Tape-Measure Murder

Miss Politt took hold of the knocker and rapped politely on the cottage door. After a discreet interval she knocked again. The parcel under her left arm shifted a little as she did so, and she readjusted it. Inside the parcel was Mrs. Spenlow's new green winter dress, ready for fitting. From Miss Politt's left hand dangled a bag of black silk, containing a tape measure, a pincushion, and a large, practical pair of scissors.

Miss Politt was tall and gaunt, with a sharp nose, pursed lips, and meager iron-grey hair. She hesitated before using the knocker for the third time. Glancing down the street, she saw a figure rapidly approaching. Miss Hartnell, jolly, weather-beaten, fifty-five, shouted out in her usual loud bass voice, "Good afternoon, Miss Politt!"

The dressmaker answered, "Good afternoon, Miss Hartnell." Her voice was excessively thin and genteel in its accents. She had started life as a lady's maid. "Excuse me," she went on, "but do you happen to know if by any chance Mrs. Spenlow isn't at home?"

"Not the least idea," said Miss Hartnell.

Note: This story has also been published under the title "The Case of the Retired Jeweler."

"It's rather awkward, you see. I was to fit on Mrs. Spenlow's new dress this afternoon. Three-thirty, she said."

Miss Hartnell consulted her wrist watch. "It's a little past the half-hour now."

"Yes. I have knocked three times, but there doesn't seem to be any answer, so I was wondering if perhaps Mrs. Spenlow might have gone out and forgotten. She doesn't forget appointments as a rule, and she wants the dress to wear the day after tomorrow."

Miss Hartnell entered the gate and walked up the path to join Miss Politt outside the door of Laburnam Cottage.

"Why doesn't Gladys answer the door?" she demanded. "Oh, no, of course, it's Thursday—Gladys's day out. I expect Mrs. Spenlow has fallen asleep. I don't expect you've made enough noise with this thing."

Seizing the knocker, she executed a deafening *rat-a-tat-tat* and, in addition, thumped upon the panels of the door. She also called out in a stentorian voice: "What ho, within there!"

There was no response.

Miss Politt murmured, "Oh, I think Mrs. Spenlow must have forgotten and gone out. I'll call around some other time." She began edging away and down the path.

"Nonsense," said Miss Hartnell firmly. "She can't have gone out. I'd have met her. I'll just take a look through the window and see if I can find any signs of life."

She laughed in her usual hearty manner, to indicate that it was a joke, and applied a perfunctory glance to the nearest windowpane—perfunctory because she knew quite well that the front room was seldom used. Mr. and Mrs. Spenlow preferred the small back sitting-room.

Perfunctory as it was, though, it succeeded in its object. Miss Hartnell, it is true, saw no signs of life. On the contrary, she saw, through the window, Mrs. Spenlow lying on the hearthrug—dead.

"Of course," said Miss Hartnell, telling the story afterward, "I managed to keep my head. That Politt creature wouldn't have had the least idea of what to do. 'Got to keep our heads,' I said to her. 'You stay here and I'll go for Constable Palk.' She said something about not wanting to be left, but I paid no attention at all. One has to be firm with that sort of person. I've always found they enjoy making a fuss. So I was just going off when, at that very moment, Mr. Spenlow came round the corner of the house."

Here Miss Hartnell made a significant pause. It enabled her audience to ask breathlessly, "Tell me, how did he look?" Miss Hartnell would then go on: "Frankly, I suspected something at once! He was far too calm. He didn't seem surprised in the least. And you may say what you like, it isn't natural for a man to hear that his wife is dead and display no emotion whatever."

Everybody agreed with this statement.

The police agreed with it too. So suspicious did they consider Mr. Spenlow's detachment that they lost no time in ascertaining how that gentleman was situated as a result of his wife's death. When they discovered that Mrs. Spenlow had been the moneyed partner, and that her money went to her husband under a will made soon after their marriage, they were more suspicious than ever.

Miss Marple, that sweet-faced (and some said vinegar-tongued) elderly spinster who lived in the house next to the rectory, was interviewed very early—within half an hour of the discovery of the crime. She was approached by Police Constable Palk, importantly thumbing a notebook. "If you don't mind, ma'am, I've a few questions to ask you."

Miss Marple said, "In connection with the murder of Mrs. Spenlow?"

Palk was startled. "May I ask, madam, how you got to know of it?"

"The fish," said Miss Marple.

The reply was perfectly intelligible to Constable Palk. He assumed correctly that the fishmonger's boy had brought it, together with Miss Marple's evening meal.

Miss Marple continued gently, "Lying on the floor in the sitting room, strangled—possibly by a very narrow belt. But whatever it was, it was taken away."

Palk's face was wrathful. "How that young Fred gets to know everything—"

Miss Marple cut him short adroitly. She said, "There's a pin in your tunic."

Constable Palk looked down, startled. He said, "They do say: 'See a pin and pick it up, all the day you'll have good luck.'"

"I hope that will come true. Now what is it you want me to tell you?"

Constable Palk cleared his throat, looked important, and consulted his notebook. "Statement was made to me by Mr. Arthur Spenlow, husband of the deceased. Mr. Spenlow says that at two-thirty, as far as he can say, he was rung up by Miss Marple and asked if he would come over at a quarter past three, as she was anxious to consult him about something. Now, ma'am, is that true?"

"Certainly not," said Miss Marple.

"You did not ring up Mr. Spenlow at two-thirty?"

"Neither at two-thirty nor any other time."

"Ah," said Constable Palk, and sucked his moustache with a good deal of satisfaction.

"What else did Mr. Spenlow say?"

"Mr. Spenlow's statement was that he came over here as requested, leaving his own house at ten minutes past three; that on arrival here he was informed by the maidservant that Miss Marple was 'not at 'ome.'"

"That part of it is true," said Miss Marple. "He did come

here, but I was at a meeting at the Women's Institute."

"Ah," said Constable Palk again.

Miss Marple exclaimed, "Do tell me, Constable, do you suspect Mr. Spenlow?"

"It's not for me to say at this stage, but it looks to me as though somebody, naming no names, had been trying to be artful."

Miss Marple said thoughtfully, "Mr. Spenlow?"

She liked Mr. Spenlow. He was a small, spare man, stiff and conventional in speech, the acme of respectability. It seemed odd that he should have come to live in the country; he had so clearly lived in towns all his life. To Miss Marple he confided the reason. He said, "I have always intended, ever since I was a small boy, to live in the country someday and have a garden of my own. I have always been very much attached to flowers. My wife, you know, kept a flower shop. That's where I saw her first."

A dry statement, but it opened up a vista of romance. A young, prettier Mrs. Spenlow, seen against a background of flowers.

Mr. Spenlow, however, really knew nothing about flowers. He had no idea of seeds, of cuttings, of bedding out, of annuals or perennials. He had only a vision—a vision of a small cottage garden thickly planted with sweet-smelling, brightly coloured blossoms. He had asked, almost pathetically, for instruction and had noted down Miss Marple's replies to questions in a little book.

He was a man of quiet method. It was, perhaps, because of this trait that the police were interested in him when his wife was found murdered. With patience and perseverance they learned a good deal about the late Mrs. Spenlow—and soon all St. Mary Mead knew it too.

The late Mrs. Spenlow had begun life as a betweenmaid in a large house. She had left that position to marry the second gardener and with him had started a flower shop in London. The shop had prospered. Not so the gardener, who before long had sickened and died.

His widow had carried on the shop and enlarged it in an ambitious way. She had continued to prosper. Then she had sold the business at a handsome price and embarked upon matrimony for the second time—with Mr. Spenlow, a middle-aged jeweler who had inherited a small and struggling business. Not long afterward they had sold the business and come down to St. Mary Mead.

Mrs. Spenlow was a well-to-do woman. The profits from her florist's establishment she had invested—"under spirit guidance," as she explained to all and sundry. The spirits had advised her with unexpected acumen.

All her investments had prospered, some in quite a sensational fashion. Instead, however, of this increasing her belief in spiritualism, Mrs. Spenlow basely deserted mediums and sittings and made a brief but wholehearted plunge into an obscure religion with Indian affinities which was based on various forms of deep breathing. When, however, she arrived at St. Mary Mead, she had relapsed into a period of orthodox Church-of-England beliefs. She was a good deal at the Vicarage and attended church services with assiduity. She patronized the village shops, took an interest in the local happenings, and played village bridge.

A humdrum, everyday life. And—suddenly—murder.

Colonel Melchett, the chief constable, had summoned Inspector Slack.

Slack was a positive type of man. When he made up his mind, he was sure. He was quite sure now. "Husband did it, sir," he said.

"You think so?"

"Quite sure of it. You've only got to look at him. Never

showed a sign of grief or emotion. He came back to the
house knowing she was dead."

"Wouldn't he at least have tried to act the part of the distracted husband?"

"Not him, sir. Too pleased with himself. Some gentlemen
can't act. Too stiff. As I see it, he was just fed up with his
wife. She'd got the money and, I should say, was a trying
woman to live with—always taking up some 'ism' or other.
He cold-bloodedly decided to do away with her and live
comfortably on his own."

"Yes, that could be the case, I suppose."

"Depend upon it, that was it. Made his plans careful. Pretended to get a phone call—"

Melchett interrupted him: "No call been traced?"

"No, sir. That means either that he lied or that the call
was put through from a public telephone booth. The only
two public phones in the village are at the station and the
post office. Post office it certainly wasn't. Mrs. Blade sees everyone who comes in. Station it might be. Train arrives at
two twenty-seven and there's a bit of bustle then. But the
main thing is he says it was Miss Marple who called him up,
and that certainly isn't true. The call didn't come from her
house, and she herself was away at the Institute."

"You're not overlooking the possibility that the husband
was deliberately got out of the way—by someone who
wanted to murder Mrs. Spenlow?"

"You're thinking of young Ted Gerard, aren't you, sir?
I've been working on him—what we're up against there is
lack of motive. He doesn't stand to gain anything."

"He's an undesirable character, though. Quite a pretty little spot of embezzlement to his credit."

"I'm not saying he isn't a wrong 'un. Still, he did go to his
boss and own up to that embezzlement. And his employers
weren't wise to it."

"An Oxford Grouper," said Melchett.

"Yes, sir. Became a convert and went off to do the straight thing and own up to having pinched money. I'm not saying, mind you, that it mayn't have been astuteness—he may have thought he was suspected and decided to gamble on honest repentance."

"You have a skeptical mind, Slack," said Colonel Melchett. "By the way, have you talked to Miss Marple at all?"

"What's she got to do with it, sir?"

"Oh, nothing. But she hears things, you know. Why don't you go and have a chat with her? She's a very sharp old lady."

Slack changed the subject. "One thing I've been meaning to ask you, sir: That domestic-service job where the deceased started her career—Sir Robert Abercrombie's place. That's where the jewel robbery was—emeralds—worth a packet. Never got them. I've been looking it up—must have happened when the Spenlow woman was there, though she'd have been quite a girl at the time. Don't think she was mixed up in it, do you, sir? Spenlow, you know, was one of those little tuppenny-ha'penny jewelers—just the chap for a fence."

Melchett shook his head. "Don't think there's anything in that. She didn't even know Spenlow at the time. I remember the case. Opinion in police circles was that a son of the house was mixed up in it—Jim Abercrombie—awful young waster. Had a pile of debts, and just after the robbery they were all paid off—some rich woman, so they said, but I don't know—old Abercrombie hedged a bit about the case—tried to call the police off."

"It was just an idea, sir," said Slack.

Miss Marple received Inspector Slack with gratification, especially when she heard that he had been sent by Colonel Melchett.

"Now, really, that is very kind of Colonel Melchett. I didn't know he remembered me."

"He remembers you, all right. Told me that what you didn't know of what goes on in St. Mary Mead isn't worth knowing."

"Too kind of him, but really I don't know anything at all. About this murder, I mean."

"You know what the talk about it is."

"Of course—but it wouldn't do, would it, to repeat just idle talk?"

Slack said, with an attempt at geniality. "This isn't an official conversation, you know. It's in confidence, so to speak."

"You mean you really want to know what people are saying? Whether there's any truth in it or not?"

"That's the idea."

"Well, of course, there's been a great deal of talk and speculation. And there are really two distinct camps, if you understand me. To begin with, there are the people who think that the husband did it. A husband or a wife is, in a way, the natural person to suspect, don't you think so?"

"Maybe," said the inspector cautiously.

"Such close quarters, you know. Then, so often, the money angle. I heard that it was Mrs. Spenlow who had the money and therefore Mr. Spenlow does benefit by her death. In this wicked world I'm afraid the most uncharitable assumptions are often justified."

"He comes into a tidy sum, all right."

"Just so. It would seem quite plausible, wouldn't it, for him to strangle her, leave the house by the back, come across the fields to my house, ask for me and pretend he'd had a telephone call from me, then go back and find his wife murdered in his absence—hoping, of course, that the crime would be put down to some tramp or burglar."

The inspector nodded. "What with the money angle— and if they'd been on bad terms lately?"

But Miss Marple interrupted him: "Oh, but they hadn't."

"You know that for a fact?"

"Everyone would have known if they'd quarrelled! The maid, Gladys Brent—she'd have soon spread it round the village."

The inspector said feebly, "She mightn't have known," and received a pitying smile in reply.

Miss Marple went on: "And then there's the other school of thought. Ted Gerard. A good-looking young man. I'm afraid, you know, that good looks are inclined to influence one more than they should. Our last curate but one—quite a magical effect! All the girls came to church—evening service as well as morning. And many older women became un- usually active in parish work—and the slippers and scarves that were made for him! Quite embarrassing for the poor young man.

"But let me see, where was I? Oh yes, this young man, Ted Gerard. Of course, there has been talk about him. He's come down to see her so often. Though Mrs. Spenlow told me herself that he was a member of what I think they call the Oxford Group. A religious movement. They are quite sincere and very earnest, I believe, and Mrs. Spenlow was impressed by it all."

Miss Marple took a breath and went on: "And I'm sure there was no reason to believe that there was anything more in it than that, but you know what people are. Quite a lot of people are convinced that Mrs. Spenlow was infatuated with the young man and that she'd lent him quite a lot of money. And it's perfectly true that he was actually seen at the station that day. In the train—the two twenty-seven down train. But of course it would be quite easy, wouldn't it, to slip out of the other side of the train and go through the cutting and over the fence and round by the hedge and never come out of the station entrance at all? So that he need not have been seen going to the cottage. And of course people do think that what Mrs. Spenlow was wearing was rather peculiar."

"Peculiar."

"A kimono. Not a dress." Miss Marple blushed. "That sort of thing, you know, is, perhaps, rather suggestive to some people."

"You think it was suggestive?"

"Oh no, I don't think so. I think it was perfectly natural."

"You think it was natural?"

"Under the circumstances, yes." Miss Marple's glance was cool and reflective.

Inspector Slack said, "It might give us another motive for the husband. Jealousy."

"Oh no, Mr. Spenlow would never be jealous. He's not the sort of man who notices things. If his wife had gone away and left a note on the pincushion, it would be the first he'd know of anything of that kind."

Inspector Slack was puzzled by the intent way she was looking at him. He had an idea that all her conversation was intended to hint at something he didn't understand. She said now, with some emphasis, "Didn't you find any clues, Inspector—on the spot?"

"People don't leave fingerprints and cigarette ash nowadays, Miss Marple."

"But this, I think," she suggested, "was an old-fashioned crime—"

Slack said sharply. "Now what do you mean by that?"

Miss Marple remarked slowly, "I think, you know, that Constable Palk could help you. He was the first person on the—on the 'scene of the crime,' as they say."

Mr. Spenlow was sitting in a deck chair. He looked bewildered. He said, in his thin, precise voice, "I may, of course, be imagining what occurred. My hearing is not as good as it was. But I distinctly think I heard a small boy call after me, 'Yah, who's a Crippen?' It—it conveyed the impression to me that he was of the opinion that I had—had killed my dear wife."

Miss Marple, gently snipping off a dead rose head, said, "That was the impression he meant to convey, no doubt."

"But what could possibly have put such an idea into a child's head?"

Miss Marple coughed. "Listening, no doubt, to the opinions of his elders."

"You—you really mean that other people think that also?"

"Quite half the people in St. Mary Mead."

"But, my dear lady, what can possibly have given rise to such an idea? I was sincerely attached to my wife. She did not, alas, take to living in the country as much as I had hoped she would do, but perfect agreement on every subject is an impossible ideal. I assure you I feel her loss very keenly."

"Probably. But if you will excuse my saying so, you don't sound as though you do."

Mr. Spenlow drew his meager frame up to its full height. "My dear lady, many years ago I read of a certain Chinese philosopher who, when his dearly loved wife was taken from him, continued calmly to beat a gong in the street—a customary Chinese pastime, I presume—exactly as usual. The people in the city were much impressed by his fortitude."

"But," said Miss Marple, "the people of St. Mary Mead react rather differently. Chinese philosophy does not appeal to them."

"But you understand?"

Miss Marple nodded. "My Uncle Henry," she explained, "was a man of unusual self-control. His motto was 'Never display emotion.' He, too, was very fond of flowers."

"I was thinking," said Mr. Spenlow with something like eagerness, "that I might, perhaps, have a pergola on the west side of the cottage. Pink roses and, perhaps, wisteria. And there is a white starry flower, whose name for the moment escapes me—"

In the tone in which she spoke to her grandnephew, aged three, Miss Marple said, "I have a very nice catalogue here, with pictures. Perhaps you would like to look through it—I have to go up to the village."

Leaving Mr. Spenlow sitting happily in the garden with his catalogue, Miss Marple went up to her room, hastily rolled up a dress in a piece of brown paper, and, leaving the house, walked briskly up to the post office. Miss Politt, the dressmaker, lived in rooms over the post office.

But Miss Marple did not at once go through the door and up the stairs. It was just two-thirty, and, a minute later, the Much Benham bus drew up outside the post-office door. It was one of the events of the day in St. Mary Mead. The post-mistress hurried out with parcels, parcels connected with the shop side of her business, for the post office also dealt in sweets, cheap books, and children's toys.

For some four minutes Miss Marple was alone in the post office.

Not till the postmistress returned to her post did Miss Marple go upstairs and explain to Miss Politt that she wanted her own grey crepe altered and made more fashionable if that were possible. Miss Politt promised to see what she could do.

The chief constable was rather astonished when Miss Marple's name was brought to him. She came in with many apologies. "So sorry—so very sorry to disturb you. You are so busy, I know, but then you have always been so very kind, Colonel Melchett, and I felt I would rather come to you instead of to Inspector Slack. For one thing, you know, I should hate Constable Palk to get into any trouble. Strictly speaking, I suppose he shouldn't have touched anything at all."

Colonel Melchett was slightly bewildered. He said, "Palk? That's the St. Mary Mead constable, isn't it? What has he been doing?"

"He picked up a pin, you know. It was in his tunic. And it occurred to me at the time that it was quite probable he had actually picked it up in Mrs. Spenlow's house."

"Quite, quite. But, after all, you know, what's a pin? Matter of fact, he did pick the pin up just by Mrs. Spenlow's body. Came and told Slack about it yesterday—you put him up to that, I gather? Oughtn't to have touched anything, of course, but, as I said, what's a pin? It was only a common pin. Sort of thing any woman might use."

"Oh no, Colonel Melchett, that's where you're wrong. To a man's eye, perhaps, it looked like an ordinary pin, but it wasn't. It was a special pin, a very thin pin, the kind you buy by the box, the kind used mostly by dressmakers."

Melchett stared at her, a faint light of comprehension breaking in on him. Miss Marple nodded her head several times eagerly.

"Yes, of course. It seems to me so obvious. She was in her kimono because she was going to try on her new dress, and she went into the front room, and Miss Politt just said something about measurements and put the tape measure round her neck—and then all she'd have to do was to cross it and pull—quite easy, so I've heard. And then of course she'd go outside and pull the door to and stand there knocking as though she'd just arrived. But the pin shows she'd already been in the house."

"And it was Miss Politt who telephoned to Spenlow?"

"Yes. From the post office at two-thirty—just when the bus comes and the post office would be empty."

Colonel Melchett said, "But, my dear Miss Marple, why? In heaven's name, why? You can't have a murder without a motive."

"Well, I think, you know, Colonel Melchett, from all I've heard, that the crime dates from a long time back. It reminds me, you know, of my two cousins. Antony and Gordon. Whatever Antony did always went right for him, and with poor Gordon it was just the other way about: race horses went lame, and stocks went down, and property depreciated. . . . As I see it, the two women were in it together."

"In what?"

"The robbery. Long ago. Very valuable emeralds, so I've heard. The lady's maid and the tweeny. Because one thing hasn't been explained—how, when the tweeny married the gardener, did they have enough money to set up a flower shop?

"The answer is, it was her share of the—the swag, I think is the right expression. Everything she did turned out well. Money made money. But the other one, the lady's maid, must have been unlucky. She came down to being just a village dressmaker. Then they met again. Quite all right at first, I expect, until Mr. Ted Gerard came on the scene.

"Mrs. Spenlow, you see, was already suffering from conscience and was inclined to be emotionally religious. This young man no doubt urged her to 'face up' and to 'come clean,' and I daresay she was strung up to do so. But Miss Politt didn't see it that way. All she saw was that she might go to prison for a robbery she had committed years ago. So she made up her mind to put a stop to it all. I'm afraid, you know, that she was always rather a wicked woman. I don't believe she'd have turned a hair if that nice, stupid Mr. Spenlow had been hanged."

Colonel Melchett said slowly, "We can—er—verify your theory—up to a point. The identity of the Politt woman with the lady's maid at the Abercrombies', but—"

Miss Marple reassured him.

"It will all be quite easy. She's the kind of woman who will break down at once when she's taxed with the truth. And then, you see, I've got her tape measure. I—er—abstracted it yesterday when I was trying on. When she misses it and thinks the police have got it—well, she's quite an ignorant woman and she'll think it will prove the case against her in some way."

She smiled at him encouragingly. "You'll have no trouble, I can assure you." It was the tone in which his favourite aunt had once assured him that he could not fail to pass his entrance examination into Sandhurst.

And he had passed.

DOUBLE
SIN

Greenshaw's Folly

The two men rounded the corner of the shrubbery.
"Well, there you are," said Raymond West.
"That's It."

Horace Bindler took a deep, appreciative breath.

"How wonderful," he cried. His voice rose in a high screech of esthetic delight, then deepened in reverent awe. "It's unbelievable. Out of this world! A period piece of the best."

"I thought you'd like it," said Raymond West complacently.

"Like it?" Words failed Horace. He unbuckled the strap of his camera and got busy. "This will be one of the gems of my collection," he said happily. "I do think, don't you, that it's rather amusing to have a collection of monstrosities? The idea came to me one night seven years ago in my bath. My last real gem was in the Campo Santo at Genoa, but I really think this beats it. What's it called?"

"I haven't the least idea," said Raymond.

"I suppose it's got a name?"

"It must have. But the fact is that it's never referred to round here as anything but Greenshaw's Folly."

"Greenshaw being the man who built it?"

"Yes. In eighteen sixty or seventy or thereabouts. The local success story of the time. Barefoot boy who had risen to immense prosperity. Local opinion is divided as to why he built this house, whether it was sheer exuberance of wealth or whether it was done to impress his creditors. If the latter, it didn't impress them. He either went bankrupt or the next thing to it. Hence the name, Greenshaw's Folly."

Horace's camera clicked. "There," he said in a satisfied voice. "Remind me to show you Number Three-ten in my collection. A really incredible marble mantelpiece in the Italian manner." He added, looking at the house, "I can't conceive of how Mr. Greenshaw thought of it all."

"Rather obvious in some ways," said Raymond. "He had visited the châteaux of the Loire, don't you think? Those turrets. And then, rather unfortunately, he seems to have travelled in the Orient. The influence of the Taj Mahal is unmistakable. I rather like the Moorish wing," he added, "and the traces of a Venetian palace."

"One wonders how he ever got hold of an architect to carry out these ideas."

Raymond shrugged his shoulders.

"No difficulty about that, I expect," he said. "Probably the architect retired with a good income for life while poor old Greenshaw went bankrupt."

"Could we look at it from the other side?" asked Horace, "or are we trespassing?"

"We're trespassing all right," said Raymond, "but I don't think it will matter."

He turned toward the corner of the house and Horace skipped after him.

"But who lives here? Orphans or holiday visitors? It can't be a school. No playing fields or brisk efficiency."

"Oh, a Greenshaw lives here still," said Raymond over his shoulder. "The house itself didn't go in the crash. Old Greenshaw's son inherited it. He was a bit of a miser and lived here in a corner of it. Never spent a penny. Probably never had a penny to spend. His daughter lives here now. Old lady—very eccentric."

As he spoke Raymond was congratulating himself on having thought of Greenshaw's Folly as a means of entertaining his guest. These literary critics always professed themselves as longing for a weekend in the country and were wont to find the country extremely boring when they got there. Tomorrow there would be the Sunday papers, and for today Raymond West congratulated himself on suggesting a visit to Greenshaw's Folly to enrich Horace Bindler's well-known collection of monstrosities.

They turned the corner of the house and came out on a neglected lawn. In one corner of it was a large artificial rockery, and bending over it was a figure at the sight of which Horace clutched Raymond delightedly by the arm.

"Do you see what she's got on?" he exclaimed. "A sprigged print dress. Just like a housemaid—when there were housemaids. One of my most cherished memories is staying at a house in the country when I was quite a boy where a real housemaid called you in the morning, all crackling in a print dress and a cap. Yes, my boy, really—a cap. Muslin with streamers. No, perhaps it was the parlourmaid who had the streamers. But anyway, she was a real housemaid and she brought in an enormous brass can of hot water. What an exciting day we're having."

The figure in the print dress had straightened up and turned toward them, trowel in hand. She was a sufficiently startling figure. Unkempt locks of iron-grey fell wispily on her shoulders, and a straw hat, rather like the hats that horses wear in Italy, was crammed down on her head. The coloured print dress she wore fell nearly to her ankles. Out of a weather-beaten, not too clean face, shrewd eyes surveyed them appraisingly.

"I must apologize for trespassing, Miss Greenshaw," said

Raymond West, as he advanced toward her, "but Mr. Horace Bindler who is staying with me—"

Horace bowed and removed his hat.

"—is most interested in—er—ancient history and—er—fine buildings."

Raymond West spoke with the ease of a famous author who knows that he is a celebrity, that he can venture where other people may not.

Miss Greenshaw looked up at the sprawling exuberance behind her.

"It *is* a fine house," she said appreciatively. "My grandfather built it—before my time, of course. He is reported as having said that he wished to astonish the natives."

"I'll say he did that, ma'am," said Horace Bindler.

"Mr. Bindler is the well-known literary critic," said Raymond West.

Miss Greenshaw had clearly no reverence for literary critics. She remained unimpressed.

"I consider it," said Miss Greenshaw, referring to the house, "as a monument to my grandfather's genius. Silly fools come here and ask me why I don't sell it and go and live in a flat. What would I do in a flat? It's my home and I live in it," said Miss Greenshaw. "Always have lived here." She considered, brooding over the past. "There were three of us. Laura married the curate. Papa wouldn't give her any money, said clergymen ought to be unworldly. She died, having a baby. Baby died too. Nettie ran away with the riding master. Papa cut her out of his will, of course. Handsome fellow, Harry Fletcher, but no good. Don't think Nettie was happy with him. Anyway, she didn't live long. They had a son. He writes to me sometimes, but of course he isn't a Greenshaw. I'm the last of the Greenshaws." She drew up her bent shoulders with a certain pride and readjusted the rakish angle of the straw hat. Then, turning, she said sharply:

"Yes, Mrs. Cresswell, what is it?"

Approaching them from the house was a figure that, seen side by side with Miss Greenshaw, seemed ludicrously dissimilar. Mrs. Cresswell had a marvellously dressed head of well-blued hair towering upward in meticulously arranged curls and rolls. It was as though she had dressed her head to go as a French marquise to a fancy dress party. The rest of her middle-aged person was dressed in what ought to have been rustling black silk but was actually one of the shinier varieties of black rayon. Although she was not a large woman, she had a well-developed and sumptuous bosom. Her voice was unexpectedly deep. She spoke with exquisite diction—only a slight hesitation over words beginning with h, and the final pronunciation of them with an exaggerated aspirate gave rise to a suspicion that at some remote period in her youth she might have had trouble over dropping her h's.

"The fish, madam," said Mrs. Cresswell, "the slice of cod. It has not arrived. I have asked Alfred to go down for it and he refuses."

Rather unexpectedly, Miss Greenshaw gave a cackle of laughter.

"Refuses, does he?"

"Alfred, madam, has been most disobliging."

Miss Greenshaw raised two earth-stained fingers to her lips, suddenly produced an earsplitting whistle, and at the same time yelled, "Alfred, Alfred, come here."

Round the corner of the house a young man appeared in answer to the summons, carrying a spade in his hand. He had a bold, handsome face, and as he drew near he cast an unmistakably malevolent glance toward Mrs. Cresswell.

"You wanted me, miss?" he said.

"Yes, Alfred. I hear you've refused to go down for the fish. What about it, eh?"

Alfred spoke in a surly voice.

"I'll go down for it if you wants it, miss. You've only got to say."

"I do want it. I want it for my supper."

"Right you are, miss. I'll go right away."

He threw an insolent glance at Mrs. Cresswell, who flushed and murmured below her breath.

"Now that I think of it," said Miss Greenshaw, "a couple of strange visitors are just what we need, aren't they, Mrs. Cresswell?"

Mrs. Cresswell looked puzzled.

"I'm sorry, madam—"

"For you-know-what," said Miss Greenshaw, nodding her head. "Beneficiary to a will mustn't witness it. That's right, isn't it?" She appealed to Raymond West.

"Quite correct," said Raymond.

"I know enough law to know that," said Miss Greenshaw, "and you two are men of standing."

She flung down the trowel on her weeding basket.

"Would you mind coming up to the library with me?"

"Delighted," said Horace eagerly.

She led the way through French windows and through a vast yellow-and-gold drawing-room with faded brocade on the walls and dust covers arranged over the funiture, then through a large dim hall, up a staircase, and into a room on the second floor.

"My grandfather's library," she announced.

Horace looked round with acute pleasure. It was a room from his point of view quite full of monstrosities. The heads of sphinxes appeared on the most unlikely pieces of furniture; there was a colossal bronze representing, he thought, Paul and Virginia, and a vast bronze clock with classical motifs of which he longed to take a photograph.

"A fine lot of books," said Miss Greenshaw.

Raymond was already looking at the books. From what he could see from a cursory glance there was no book here of any real interest or, indeed, any book which appeared to have been read. They were all superbly bound sets of the classics as supplied ninety years ago for furnishing a gentleman's library. Some novels of a bygone period were included. But they too showed little signs of having been read.

Miss Greenshaw was fumbling in the drawers of a vast desk. Finally she pulled out a parchment document.

"My will," she explained. "Got to leave your money to someone—or so they say. If I died without a will, I suppose that son of a horse trader would get it. Handsome fellow, Harry Fletcher, but a rogue if ever there was one. Don't see why his son should inherit this place. No," she went on, as though answering some unspoken objection, "I've made up my mind. I'm leaving it to Cresswell."

"Your housekeeper?"

"Yes. I've explained it to her. I make a will leaving her all I've got and then I don't need to pay her any wages. Saves me a lot in current expenses, and it keeps her up to the mark. No giving me notice and walking off at any minute. Very la-di-dah and all that, isn't she? But her father was a working plumber in a very small way. She's nothing to give herself airs about."

By now Miss Greenshaw had unfolded the parchment. Picking up a pen, she dipped it in the inkstand and wrote her signature, *Katherine Dorothy Greenshaw.*

"That's right," she said. "You've seen me sign it, and then you two sign it, and that makes it legal."

She handed the pen to Raymond West. He hesitated a moment, feeling an unexpected repulsion to what he was asked to do. Then he quickly scrawled his well-known autograph, for which his morning's mail usually brought at least six requests.

Horace took the pen from him and added his own minute signature.

"That's done," said Miss Greenshaw.

She moved across the bookcases and stood looking at them uncertainly, then she opened a glass door, took out a book, and slipped the folded parchment inside.

"I've my own places for keeping things," she said.

"*Lady Audley's Secret*," Raymond West remarked, catching sight of the title as she replaced the book.

Miss Greenshaw gave another cackle of laughter.

"Best-seller in its day," she remarked. "But not like your books, eh?"

She gave Raymond a sudden friendly nudge in the ribs. Raymond was rather surprised that she even knew he wrote books. Although Raymond West was a "big name" in literature, he could hardly be described as a best-seller. Though softening a little with the advent of middle age, his books dealt bleakly with the sordid side of life.

"I wonder," Horace demanded breathlessly, "if I might just take a photograph of the clock."

"By all means," said Miss Greenshaw. "It came, I believe, from the Paris Exhibition."

"Very probably," said Horace. He took his picture.

"This room's not been used much since my grandfather's time," said Miss Greenshaw. "This desk's full of old diaries of his. Interesting, I should think. I haven't the eyesight to read them myself. I'd like to get them published, but I suppose one would have to work on them a good deal."

"You could engage someone to do that," said Raymond West.

"Could I really? It's an idea, you know. I'll think about it."

Raymond West glanced at his watch.

"We mustn't trespass on your kindness any longer," he said.

"Pleased to have seen you," said Miss Greenshaw graciously. "Thought you were the policeman when I heard you coming round the corner of the house."

"Why a policeman?" demanded Horace, who never minded asking questions.

Miss Greenshaw responded unexpectedly.

"If you want to know the time, ask a policeman," she carolled, and with this example of Victorian wit she nudged Horace in the ribs and roared with laughter.

"It's been a wonderful afternoon." Horace sighed as he and Raymond walked home. "Really, that place has everything. The only thing the library needs is a body. Those old-fashioned detective stories about murder in the library—that's just the kind of library I'm sure the authors had in mind."

"If you want to discuss murder," said Raymond, "you must talk to my Aunt Jane."

"Your Aunt Jane? Do you mean Miss Marple?" Horace felt a little at a loss.

The charming old-world lady to whom he had been introduced the night before seemed the last person to be mentioned in connection with murder.

"Oh yes," said Raymond. "Murder is a specialty of hers."

"How intriguing! What do you really mean?"

"I mean just that," said Raymond. He paraphrased: "Some commit murder, some get mixed up in murders, others have murder thrust upon them. My Aunt Jane comes into the third category."

"You are joking."

"Not in the least. I can refer you to the former Commissioner of Scotland Yard, several chief constables, and one or two hard-working inspectors of the C.I.D."

Horace said happily that wonders would never cease. Over the tea table they gave Joan West, Raymond's wife, Louise Oxley, her niece, and old Miss Marple a résumé of the afternoon's happenings, recounting in detail everything that Miss Greenshaw had said to them.

"But I do think," said Horace, "that there is something a little sinister about the whole setup. That duchess-like creature, the housekeeper—arsenic, perhaps, in the teapot, now that she knows her mistress has made the will in her favour?"

"Tell us, Aunt Jane," said Raymond, "will there be murder or won't there? What do you think?"

"I think," said Miss Marple, winding up her wool with a rather severe air, "that you shouldn't joke about these things as much as you do, Raymond. Arsenic is, of course, quite a possibility. So easy to obtain. Probably present in the tool shed already in the form of weed killer."

"Oh, really, darling," said Joan West affectionately. "Wouldn't that be rather too obvious?"

"It's all very well to make a will," said Raymond. "I don't suppose the poor old thing has anything to leave except that awful white elephant of a house, and who would want that?"

"A film company possibly," said Horace, "or a hotel or an institution?"

"They'd expect to buy it for a song," said Raymond, but Miss Marple was shaking her head.

"You know, dear Raymond, I cannot agree with you there. About the money, I mean. The grandfather was evidently one of those lavish spenders who make money easily but can't keep it. He may have gone broke, as you say, but hardly bankrupt, or else his son would not have had the house. Now the son, as is so often the case, was of an entirely different character from his father. A miser. A man who saved every penny. I should say that in the course of his lifetime he probably put by a very good sum. This Miss Greenshaw appears to have taken after him—to dislike spending money, that is. Yes, I should think it quite likely that she has quite a substantial sum tucked away."

"In that case," said Joan West, "I wonder now—what about Louise?"

They looked at Louise as she sat, silent, by the fire.

Louise was Joan West's niece. Her marriage had recently, as she herself put it, come unstuck, leaving her with two young children and a bare sufficiency of money to keep them on.

"I mean," said Joan, "if this Miss Greenshaw really wants someone to go through diaries and get a book ready for publication . . ."

"It's an idea," said Raymond.

Louise said in a low voice. "It's work I could do—and I think I'd enjoy it."

"I'll write to her," said Raymond.

"I wonder," said Miss Marple thoughtfully, "what the old lady meant by that remark about a policeman?"

"Oh, it was just a joke."

"It reminded me," said Miss Marple, nodding her head vigorously, "yes, it reminded me very much of Mr. Naysmith."

"Who was Mr. Naysmith?" asked Raymond curiously.

"He kept bees," said Miss Marple, "and was very good at doing the acrostics in the Sunday papers. And he liked giving people false impressions just for fun. But sometimes it led to trouble."

Everybody was silent for a moment, considering Mr. Naysmith, but as there did not seem to be any points of resemblance between him and Miss Greenshaw, they decided that dear Aunt Jane was perhaps getting a little bit disconnected in her old age.

Horace Bindler went back to London without having collected any more monstrosities, and Raymond West wrote a letter to Miss Greenshaw telling her that he knew of a Mrs.

Louise Oxley who would be competent to undertake work on the diaries. After a lapse of some days a letter arrived, written in spidery old-fashioned handwriting, in which Miss Greenshaw declared herself anxious to avail herself of the services of Mrs. Oxley, and making an appointment for Mrs. Oxley to come and see her.

Louise duly kept the appointment, generous terms were arranged, and she started work the following day.

"I'm awfully grateful to you," she said to Raymond. "It will fit in beautifully. I can take the children to school, go on to Greenshaw's Folly, and pick them up on my way back. How fantastic the whole setup is! That old woman has to be seen to be believed."

On the evening of her first day at work she returned and described her day.

"I've hardly seen the housekeeper," she said. "She came in with coffee and biscuits at half-past eleven, with her mouth pursed up very prunes and prisms, and would hardly speak to me. I think she disapproves deeply of my having been engaged." She went on, "It seems there's quite a feud between her and the gardener, Alfred. He's a local boy and fairly lazy, I should imagine, and he and the housekeeper won't speak to each other. Miss Greenshaw said in her rather grand way, 'There have always been feuds as far as I can remember between the garden and the house staff. It was so in my grandfather's time. There were three men and a boy in the garden then, and eight maids in the house, but there was always friction.' "

On the next day Louise returned with another piece of news.

"Just fancy," she said, "I was asked to ring up the nephew today."

"Miss Greenshaw's nephew?"

"Yes. It seems he's an actor playing in the stock company that's doing a summer season at Boreham-on-Sea. I rang up the theater and left a message asking him to lunch tomorrow. Rather fun, really. The old girl didn't want the housekeeper to know. I think Mrs. Cresswell has done something that's annoyed her."

"Tomorrow another installment of this thrilling serial," murmured Raymond.

"It's exactly like a serial, isn't it? Reconciliation with the nephew, blood is thicker than water—another will to be made and the old will destroyed.

"Aunt Jane, you're looking very serious."

"Was I, my dear? Have you heard any more about the policeman?"

Louise looked bewildered. "I don't know anything about a policeman."

"That remark of hers, my dear," said Miss Marple, "must have meant something."

Louise arrived at her work the following day in a cheerful mood. She passed through the open front door—the doors and windows of the house were always open. Miss Greenshaw appeared to have no fear of burglars, and was probably justified, as most things in the house weighed several tons and were of no marketable value.

Louise had passed Alfred in the drive. When she first noticed him he had been leaning against a tree smoking a cigarette, but as soon as he had caught sight of her he had seized a broom and begun diligently to sweep leaves. An idle young man, she thought, but good-looking. His features reminded her of someone. As she passed through the hall on the way upstairs to the library, she glanced at the large picture of Nathaniel Greenshaw which presided over the mantelpiece, showing him in the acme of Victorian prosperity, leaning back in a large armchair, his hands resting on the gold Albert chain across his capacious stomach. As her glance swept up from the stomach to the face with its heavy jowls, its bushy eyebrows and its flourishing black moustache, the thought occurred to her that Nathaniel Greenshaw must have been handsome as a young man. He had looked, perhaps, a little like Alfred. . . .

She went into the library on the second floor, shut the door behind her, opened her typewriter, and got out the diaries from the drawer at the side of her desk. Through the open window she caught a glimpse of Miss Greenshaw below, in a puce-coloured sprigged print, bending over the rockery, weeding assiduously. They had had two wet days, of which the weeds had taken full advantage.

Louise, a town-bred girl, decided that if she ever had a garden, it would never contain a rockery which needed weeding by hand. Then she settled down to her work.

When Mrs. Cresswell entered the library with the coffee tray at half-past eleven, she was clearly in a very bad temper. She banged the tray down on the table and observed to the universe:

"Company for lunch—and nothing in the house! What am I supposed to do, I should like to know? And no sign of Alfred."

"He was sweeping the drive when I got here," Louise offered.

"I daresay. A nice soft job."

Mrs. Cresswell swept out of the room, slamming the door behind her. Louise grinned to herself. She wondered what "the nephew" would be like.

She finished her coffee and settled down to her work again. It was so absorbing that time passed quickly. Nathaniel Greenshaw, when he started to keep a diary, had succumbed to the pleasures of frankness. Typing out a passage relating to the personal charms of a barmaid in the neighbouring town, Louise reflected that a good deal of editing would be necessary.

As she was thinking this, she was startled by the scream from the garden. Jumping up, she ran to the open window.

Below her Miss Greenshaw was staggering away from the rockery toward the house. Her hands were clasped to her breast, and between her hands there protruded a feathered shaft that Louise recognized with stupefaction to be the shaft of an arrow.

Miss Greenshaw's head, in its battered straw hat, fell forward on her breast. She called up to Louise in a failing voice: ". . . shot . . . he shot me . . . with an arrow . . . get help . . ."

Louise rushed to the door. She turned the handle, but the door would not open. It took her a moment or two of futile endeavor to realize that she was locked in. She ran back to the window and called down.

"I'm locked in!"

Miss Greenshaw, her back toward Louise and swaying a little on her feet, was calling up to the housekeeper at a window farther along.

"Ring police . . . telephone . . ."

Then, lurching from side to side like a drunkard, Miss Greenshaw disappeared from Louise's view through the window and staggered into the drawing-room on the ground floor. A moment later Louise heard a crash of broken china, a heavy fall, and then silence. Her imagination reconstructed the scene. Miss Greenshaw must have stumbled blindly into a small table with a Sèvres tea set on it.

Desperately Louise pounded on the library door, calling and shouting. There was no creeper or drainpipe outside the window that could help her to get out that way.

Tired at last of beating on the door, Louise returned to the window. From the window of her sitting-room farther along the housekeeper's head appeared.

"Come and let me out, Mrs. Oxley. I'm locked in."

"So am I," said Louise.

"Oh, dear, isn't it awful? I've telephoned the police. There's an extension in this room, but what I can't understand, Mrs. Oxley, is our being locked in. I never heard a key turn, did you?"

"No, I didn't hear anything at all. Oh, dear, what shall we do? Perhaps Alfred might hear us." Louise shouted at the top of her voice, "Alfred, Alfred."

"Gone to his dinner as likely as not. What time is it?"

Louise glanced at her watch.

"Twenty-five past twelve."

"He's not supposed to go until half-past, but he sneaks off earlier whenever he can."

"Do you think—do you think—"

Louise meant to ask, "Do you think she's dead?"—but the words stuck in her throat.

There was nothing to do but wait. She sat down on the window sill. It seemed an eternity before the stolid helmeted figure of a police constable came round the corner of the house. She leaned out of the window and he looked up at her, shading his eyes with his hand.

"What's going on here?" he demanded.

From their respective windows Louise and Mrs. Cresswell poured a flood of excited information down on him.

The constable produced a notebook and pencil. "You ladies ran upstairs and locked yourselves in? Can I have your names, please?"

"Somebody locked us in. Come and let us out."

The constable said reprovingly, "All in good time," and disappeared through the French window below.

Once again time seemed infinite. Louise heard the sound of a car arriving, and after what seemed an hour, but was actually only three minutes, first Mrs. Cresswell and then Louise were released by a police sergeant more alert than the original constable.

"Miss Greenshaw?" Louise's voice faltered. "What— what's happened?"

The sergeant cleared his throat.

"I'm sorry to have to tell you, madam," he said, "what I've already told Mrs. Cresswell here. Miss Greenshaw is dead."

"Murdered," said Mrs. Cresswell. "That's what it is—murder."

The sergeant said dubiously, "Could have been an accident—some country lads shooting arrows."

Again there was the sound of a car arriving.

The sergeant said, "That'll be the M.O.," and he started downstairs.

But it was not the M.O. As Louise and Mrs. Cresswell came down the stairs, a young man stepped hesitatingly through the front door and paused, looking around him with a somewhat bewildered air.

Then, speaking in a pleasant voice that in some way seemed familiar to Louise—perhaps it reminded her of Miss Greenshaw's—he asked, "Excuse me, does—er—does Miss Greenshaw live here?"

"May I have your name if you please?" said the sergeant, advancing upon him.

"Fletcher," said the young man. "Nat Fletcher. I'm Miss Greenshaw's nephew, as a matter of fact."

"Indeed, sir, well—I'm sorry—"

"Has anything happened?" asked Nat Fletcher.

"There's been an—accident. Your aunt was shot with an arrow—penetrated the jugular vein—"

Mrs. Cresswell spoke hysterically and without her usual refinement: "Your h'aunt's been murdered, that's what's 'appened. Your h'aunt's been murdered."

Inspector Welch drew his chair a little nearer to the table and let his gaze wander from one to the other of the four people in the room. It was evening of the same day. He had called at the Wests' house to take Louise Oxley once more over her statement.

"You are sure of the exact words? *Shot—he shot me—with an arrow—get help?*"

Louise nodded.

"And the time?"

"I looked at my watch a minute or two later—it was then twelve twenty-five—"

"Your watch keeps good time?"

"I looked at the clock as well." Louise left no doubt of her accuracy.

The inspector turned to Raymond West.

"It appears, sir, that about a week ago you and a Mr. Horace Bindler were witnesses to Miss Greenshaw's will?"

Briefly Raymond recounted the events of the afternoon visit he and Horace Bindler had paid to Greenshaw's Folly.

"This testimony of yours may be important," said Welch. "Miss Greenshaw distinctly told you, did she, that her will was being made in favour of Mrs. Cresswell, the housekeeper, and that she was not paying Mrs. Cresswell any wages in view of the expectations Mrs. Cresswell had of profiting by her death?"

"That is what she told me—yes."

"Would you say that Mrs. Cresswell was definitely aware of these facts?"

"I should say undoubtedly. Miss Greenshaw made a reference in my presence to beneficiaries not being able to witness a will, and Mrs. Cresswell clearly understood what she meant by it. Moreover, Miss Greenshaw herself told me that she had come to this arrangement with Mrs. Cresswell."

"So Mrs. Cresswell had reason to believe she was an interested party. Motive clear enough in her case, and I daresay she'd be our chief suspect now if it wasn't for the fact that she was securely locked in her room like Mrs. Oxley here, and also that Miss Greenshaw definitely said a man shot her—"

"She definitely was locked in her room?"

"Oh yes. Sergeant Cayley let her out. It's a big old-fashioned lock with a big old-fashioned key. The key was in the lock and there's not a chance that it could have been turned from inside or any hanky-panky of that kind. No, you can take it definitely that Mrs. Cresswell was locked inside that room and couldn't get out. And there were no bows and arrows in the room and Miss Greenshaw couldn't in any case have been shot from her window—the angle forbids it. No, Mrs. Cresswell's out."

He paused, then went on: "Would you say that Miss Greenshaw, in your opinion, was a practical joker?"

Miss Marple looked up sharply from her corner.

"So the will wasn't in Mrs. Cresswell's favour after all?" she said.

Inspector Welch looked over at her in a rather surprised fashion.

"That's a very clever guess of yours, madam," he said. "No, Mrs. Cresswell isn't named as beneficiary."

"Just like Mr. Naysmith," said Miss Marple, nodding her head. "Miss Greenshaw told Mrs. Cresswell she was going to leave her everything and so got out of paying her wages, and then she left her money to somebody else. No doubt she was vastly pleased with herself. No wonder she chortled when she put the will away in *Lady Audley's Secret.*"

"It was lucky Mrs. Oxley was able to tell us about the will and where it was put," said the inspector. "We might have had a long hunt for it otherwise."

"A Victorian sense of humour," murmured Raymond West.

"So she left her money to her nephew after all," said Louise.

The inspector shook his head.

"No," he said, "she didn't leave it to Nat Fletcher. The story goes around here—of course, I'm new to the place and I only get the gossip that's secondhand—but it seems that

in the old days both Miss Greenshaw and her sister were set
on the handsome young riding master, and the sister got
him. No, she didn't leave the money to her nephew—" Inspector Welch paused, rubbing his chin. "She left it to
Alfred," he said.

"Alfred—the gardener?" Joan spoke in a surprised voice.

"Yes, Mrs. West. Alfred Pollock."

"But why?" cried Louise.

"I daresay," said Miss Marple, "that she thought Alfred
Pollock might have a pride in the house, might even want to
live in it, whereas her nephew would almost certainly have
no use for it whatever and would sell it as soon as he could
possibly do so. He's an actor, isn't he? What play exactly is
he acting in at present?"

Trust an old lady to wander from the point, thought Inspector Welch; but he replied civilly, "I believe, madam,
they are doing a season of Sir James M. Barrie's plays."

"Barrie," said Miss Marple thoughtfully.

"*What Every Woman Knows*," said Inspector Welch, and
then blushed. "Name of a play," he said quickly. "I'm not
much of a theater-goer myself," he added, "but the wife
went along and saw it last week. Quite well done, she said it
was."

"Barrie, wrote some very charming plays," said Miss Marple, "though I must say that when I went with an old friend
of mine, General Easterly, to see Barrie's *Little Mary*"—she
shook her head sadly—"neither of us knew where to look."

The inspector, unacquainted with the play *Little Mary*,
seemed completely fogged.

Miss Marple explained: "When I was a girl, Inspector, nobody ever mentioned the word stomach."

The inspector looked even more at sea. Miss Marple was
murmuring titles under her breath.

"*The Admirable Crichton*. Very clever. *Mary Rose*—a
charming play. I cried, I remember. *Quality Street* I didn't

care for so much. Then there was *A Kiss for Cinderella*. Oh, of course!"

Inspector Welch had no time to waste on theatrical discussion. He returned to the matter at hand.

"The question is," he said, "did Alfred Pollock know the old lady had made a will in his favour? Did she tell him?" He added, "You see—there's an archery club over at Boreham—and Alfred Pollock's a member. He's a very good shot indeed with a bow and arrow."

"Then isn't your case quite clear?" asked Raymond West. "It would fit in with the doors being locked on the two women—he'd know just where they were in the house."

The inspector looked at him. He spoke with deep melancholy.

"He's got an alibi," said the inspector.

"I always think alibis are definitely suspicious," Raymond remarked.

"Maybe, sir," said Inspector Welch. "You're talking as a writer."

"I don't write detective stories," said Raymond West, horrified at the mere idea.

"Easy enough to say that alibis are suspicious," went on Inspector Welch, "but unfortunately we've got to deal with facts." He sighed. "We've got three good suspects," he went on. "Three people who, as it happened, were very close upon the scene at the time. Yet the odd thing is that it looks as though none of the three could have done it. The housekeeper I've already dealt with; the nephew, Nat Fletcher, at the moment Miss Greenshaw was shot, was a couple of miles away, filling up his car at a garage and asking his way; as for Alfred Pollock, six people will swear that he entered the Dog and Duck at twenty past twelve and was there for an hour, having his usual bread and cheese and beer."

"Deliberately establishing an alibi," said Raymond West hopefully.

"Maybe," said Inspector Welch, "but if so, he did establish it."

There was a long silence. Then Raymond turned his head to where Miss Marple sat upright and thoughtful.

"It's up to you, Aunt Jane," he said. "The inspector's baffled, the sergeant's baffled, Joan's baffled, Louise is baffled. But to you, Aunt Jane, it is crystal clear. Am I right?"

"I wouldn't say that," said Miss Marple, "not crystal clear. And murder, dear Raymond, isn't a game. I don't suppose poor Miss Greenshaw wanted to die, and it was a particularly brutal murder. Very well-planned and quite cold-blooded. It's not a thing to make jokes about."

"I'm sorry," said Raymond. "I'm not really as callous as I sound. One treats a thing lightly to take away from the—well, the horror of it."

"That is, I believe, the modern tendency," said Miss Marple. "All these wars, and having to joke about funerals. Yes, perhaps I was thoughtless when I implied that you were callous."

"It isn't," said Joan, "as though we'd known her at all well."

"That is very true," said Miss Marple. "You, dear Joan, did not know her at all. I did not know her at all. Raymond gathered an impression of her from one afternoon's conversation. Louise knew her for only two days."

"Come now, Aunt Jane," said Raymond, "tell us your views. You don't mind, Inspector?"

"Not at all," said the inspector politely.

"Well, my dear, it would seem that we have three people who had—or might have thought they had—a motive to kill the old lady. And three quite simple reasons why none of the three could have done so. The housekeeper could not have killed Miss Greenshaw because she was locked in her room and because her mistress definitely stated that a man shot her. The gardener was inside the Dog and Duck at the time, the nephew at the garage."

"Very clearly put, madam," said the inspector.

"And since it seems most unlikely that any outsider should have done it, where, then, are we?"

"That's what the inspector wants to know," said Raymond West.

"One so often looks at a thing the wrong way round," said Miss Marple apologetically. "If we can't alter the movements or the positions of those three people, then couldn't we perhaps alter the time of the murder?"

"You mean that both my watch and the clock were wrong?" asked Louise.

"No, dear," said Miss Marple, "I didn't mean that at all. I mean that the murder didn't occur when you thought it occurred."

"But I saw it," cried Louise.

"Well, what I have been wondering, my dear, was whether you weren't meant to see it. I've been asking myself, you know, whether that wasn't the real reason why you were engaged for this job."

"What do you mean, Aunt Jane?"

"Well, dear, it seems odd. Miss Greenshaw did not like spending money—yet she engaged you and agreed quite willingly to the terms you asked. It seems to me that perhaps you were meant to be there in that library on the second floor, looking out of the window so that you could be the key witness—someone from outside of irreproachably good character—to fix a definite time and place for the murder."

"But you can't mean," said Louise incredulously, "that Miss Greenshaw intended to be murdered."

"What I mean, dear," said Miss Marple, "is that you didn't really know Miss Greenshaw. There's no real reason, is there, why the Miss Greenshaw you saw when you went up to the house should be the same Miss Greenshaw that Raymond saw a few days earlier? Oh yes, I know," she went on, to prevent Louise's reply, "she was wearing the peculiar old-fashioned print dress and the strange straw hat and had unkempt hair. She corresponded exactly to the description Raymond gave us last weekend. But those two women, you know, were much the same age, height, and size. The housekeeper, I mean, and Miss Greenshaw."

"But the housekeeper is fat!" Louise exclaimed. "She's got an enormous bosom."

Miss Marple coughed.

"But, my dear, surely, nowadays I have seen—er—them myself in shops most indelicately displayed. It is very easy for anyone to have a—a bosom—of any size and dimension."

"What are you trying to say?" demanded Raymond.

"I was just thinking that during the two days Louise was working there, one woman could have played both parts. You said yourself, Louise, that you hardly saw the housekeeper, except for the one minute in the morning when she brought you the tray with coffee. One sees those clever artists on the stage coming in as different characters with only a moment or two to spare, and I am sure the change could have been effected quite easily. That marquise headdress could be just a wig slipped on and off."

"Aunt Jane! Do you mean that Miss Greenshaw was dead before I started work there?"

"Not dead. Kept under drugs, I should say. A very easy job for an unscrupulous woman like the housekeeper to do. Then she made the arrangements with you and got you to telephone to the nephew to ask him to lunch at a definite time. The only person who would have known that this Miss Greenshaw was not Miss Greenshaw would have been Alfred. And if you remember, the first two days you were working there it was wet, and Miss Greenshaw stayed in the house. Alfred never came into the house because of his feud with the housekeeper. And on the last morning Alfred was in the drive, while Miss Greenshaw was working on the rockery—I'd like to have a look at that rockery."

"Do you mean it was Mrs. Cresswell who killed Miss Greenshaw?"

"I think that after bringing you your coffee, the house-keeper locked the door on you as she went out, then carried the unconscious Miss Greenshaw down to the drawing room, then assumed her 'Miss Greenshaw' disguise and went out to work on the rockery where you could see her from the upstairs window. In due course she screamed and came staggering to the house clutching an arrow as though it had penetrated her throat. She called for help and was careful to say 'he shot me' so as to remove suspicion from the house-keeper—from herself. She also called up to the housekeeper's window as though she saw her there. Then, once inside the drawing-room, she threw over a table with porcelain on it, ran quickly upstairs, put on her marquise wig, and was able a few moments later to lean her head out of the window and tell you that she, too, was locked in."

"But she was locked in," said Louise.

"I know. That is where the policeman comes in."

"What policeman?"

"Exactly—what policeman? I wonder, Inspector, if you would mind telling me how and when you arrived on the scene?"

The inspector looked a little puzzled.

"At twelve twenty-nine we received a telephone call from Mrs. Cresswell, housekeeper to Miss Greenshaw, stating that her mistress had been shot. Sergeant Cayley and myself went out there at once in a car and arrived at the house at twelve thirty-five. We found Miss Greenshaw dead and the two ladies locked in their rooms."

"So, you see, my dear," said Miss Marple to Louise, "the

police constable you saw wasn't a real police constable at all. You never thought of him again—one doesn't—one just accepts one more uniform as part of the law."

"But who—why?"

"As to who—well, if they are playing *A Kiss for Cinderella*, a policeman is the principal character. Nat Fletcher would only have to help himself to the costume he wears on the stage. He'd ask his way at a garage, being careful to call attention to the time—twelve twenty-five; then he would drive on quickly, leave his car round a corner, slip on his police uniform, and do his 'act.' "

"But why—why?"

"Someone had to lock the housekeeper's door on the outside, and someone had to drive the arrow through Miss Greenshaw's throat. You can stab anyone with an arrow just as well as by shooting it—but it needs force."

"You mean they were both in it?"

"Oh yes, I think so. Mother and son as likely as not."

"But Miss Greenshaw's sister died long ago."

"Yes, but I've no doubt Mr. Fletcher married again—he sounds like the sort of man who would. I think it possible that the child died, too, and that this so-called nephew was the second wife's child and not really a relation at all. The woman got the post as housekeeper and spied out the land. Then he wrote to Miss Greenshaw as her nephew and proposed to call on her—he may have even made some joking reference to coming in his policeman's uniform—remember, she said she was expecting a policeman. But I think Miss Greenshaw suspected the truth and refused to see him. He would have been her heir if she had died without making a will—but of course once she had made a will in the housekeeper's favour, as they thought, then it was clear sailing."

"But why use an arrow?" objected Joan. "So very far-fetched."

"Not far-fetched at all, dear. Alfred belonged to an archery club—Alfred was meant to take the blame. The fact that he was in the pub as early as twelve-twenty was most unfortunate from their point of view. He always left a little before his proper time and that would have been just right." She shook her head. "It really seems all wrong—morally, I mean, that Alfred's laziness should have saved his life."

The inspector cleared his throat.

"Well, madam, these suggestions of yours are very interesting. I shall, of course, have to investigate—"

Miss Marple and Raymond West stood by the rockery and looked down at a gardening basket full of dying vegetation.

Miss Marple murmured:

"Alyssum, saxifrage, cystis, thimble campanula . . . Yes, that's all the proof I need. Whoever was weeding here yesterday morning was no gardener—she pulled up plants as well as weeds. So now I know I'm right. Thank you, dear Raymond, for bringing me here. I wanted to see the place for myself."

She and Raymond both looked up at the outrageous pile of Greenshaw's Folly.

A cough made them turn. A handsome young man was also looking at the monstrous house.

"Plaguey big place," he said. "Too big for nowadays—or so they say. I dunno about that. If I won a football pool and made a lot of money, that's the kind of house I'd like to build."

He smiled bashfully at them, then rumpled his hair.

"Reckon I can say so now," said Alfred Pollock. "And a fine house it is, for all they call it Greenshaw's Folly!"

Sanctuary

The vicar's wife came round the corner of the vicarage with her arms full of chrysanthemums. A good deal of rich garden soil was attached to her strong brogue shoes and a few fragments of earth were adhering to her nose, but of that fact she was perfectly unconscious.

She had a slight struggle in opening the vicarage gate which hung, rustily, half off its hinges. A puff of wind caught at her battered felt hat, causing it to sit even more rakishly than it had done before. "Bother!" said Bunch.

Christened by her optimistic parents Diana, Mrs. Harmon had become Bunch at an early age for somewhat obvious reasons and the name had stuck to her ever since. Clutching the chrysanthemums, she made her way through the gate to the churchyard and so to the church door.

The November air was mild and damp. Clouds scudded across the sky with patches of blue here and there. Inside, the church was dark and cold; it was unheated except at service times.

"Brrrrrh!" said Bunch expressively. "I'd better get on with this quickly. I don't want to die of cold."

With the quickness born of practice she collected the necessary paraphernalia: vases, water, flower holders. "I wish we had lilies," thought Bunch to herself. "I get so tired of these scraggy chrysanthemums." Her nimble fingers arranged the blooms in their holders.

There was nothing particularly original or artistic about the decorations, for Bunch Harmon herself was neither original nor artistic, but it was a homely and pleasant arrangement. Carrying the vases carefully, Bunch stepped up the aisle and made her way toward the altar. As she did so the sun came out.

It shone through the east window of somewhat crude coloured glass, mostly blue and red—the gift of a wealthy Victorian churchgoer. The effect was almost startling in its sudden opulence. "Like jewels," thought Bunch. Suddenly she stopped, staring ahead of her. On the chancel steps was a huddled dark form.

Putting down the flowers carefully, Bunch went up to it and bent over it. It was a man lying there, huddled over on himself. Bunch knelt down by him and slowly, carefully, she turned him over. Her fingers went to his pulse—a pulse so feeble and fluttering that it told its own story, as did the almost greenish pallor of his face. There was no doubt, Bunch thought, that the man was dying.

He was a man of about forty-five, dressed in a dark, shabby suit. She laid down the limp hand she had picked up and looked at his other hand. This seemed clenched like a fist on his breast. Looking more closely, she saw that the fingers were closed over what seemed to be a large wad or handkerchief which he was holding tightly to his chest. All round the clenched hand there were splashes of a dry brown fluid which, Bunch guessed, was dry blood. Bunch sat back on her heels, frowning.

Up till now the man's eyes had been closed, but at this point they suddenly opened and fixed themselves on Bunch's face. They were neither dazed nor wandering. They seemed fully alive and intelligent. His lips moved, and Bunch bent forward to catch the words, or rather the word. It was only one word that he said:

"Sanctuary."

There was, she thought, just a very faint smile as he breathed out this word. There was no mistaking it, for after a moment he said it again, "Sanctuary . . ."

Then, with a faint, long-drawn-out sigh, his eyes closed again. Once more Bunch's fingers went to his pulse. It was still there, but fainter now and more intermittent. She got up with decision.

"Don't move," she said, "or try to move. I'm going for help."

The man's eyes opened again, but he seemed now to be fixing his attention on the coloured light that came through the east window. He murmured something that Bunch could not quite catch. She thought, startled, that it might have been her husband's name.

"Julian?" she said. "Did you come here to find Julian?" But there was no answer. The man lay with eyes closed, his breathing coming in slow, shallow fashion.

Bunch turned and left the church rapidly. She glanced at her watch and nodded with some satisfaction. Dr. Griffiths would still be in his surgery. It was only a couple of minutes' walk from the church. She went in, without waiting to knock or ring, passing through the waiting-room and into the doctor's surgery.

"You must come at once," said Bunch. "There's a man dying in the church."

Some minutes later Dr. Griffiths rose from his knees after a brief examination.

"Can we move him from here into the vicarage? I can attend to him better there—not that it's any use."

"Of course," said Bunch. "I'll go along and get things ready. I'll get Harper and Jones, shall I? To help you carry him."

"Thanks." I can telephone from the vicarage for an ambulance, but I'm afraid—by the time it comes . . ." He left the remark unfinished.

Bunch said, "Internal bleeding?"

Dr. Griffiths nodded. He said, "How on earth did he come here?"

"I think he must have been here all night," said Bunch, considering. "Harper unlocks the church in the morning as he goes to work, but he doesn't usually come in."

It was about five minutes later when Dr. Griffiths put down the telephone receiver and came back into the morning-room where the injured man was lying on quickly arranged blankets on the sofa. Bunch was moving a basin of water and clearing up after the doctor's examination.

"Well, that's that," said Griffiths. "I've sent for an ambulance and I've notified the police." He stood, frowning, looking down on the patient who lay with closed eyes. His left hand was plucking in a nervous, spasmodic way at his side.

"He was shot," said Griffiths. "Shot at fairly close quarters. He rolled his handkerchief up into a ball and plugged the wound with it so as to stop the bleeding."

"Could he have gone far after that happened?" Bunch asked.

"Oh yes, it's quite possible. A mortally wounded man has been known to pick himself up and walk along a street as though nothing had happened and then suddenly collapse five or ten minutes later. So he needn't have been shot in the church. Oh no. He may have been shot some distance away. Of course, he may have shot himself and then dropped the revolver and staggered blindly toward the church. I don't quite know why he made for the church and not for the vicarage."

"Oh, I know that," said Bunch. "He said it: 'Sanctuary.' "

The doctor stared at her. "Sanctuary?"

"Here's Julian," said Bunch, turning her head as she heard her husband's steps in the hall. "Julian! Come here."

The Reverend Julian Harmon entered the room. His vague, scholarly manner always made him appear much older than he really was. "Dear me!" said Julian Harmon, staring in a mild, puzzled manner at the surgical appliances and the prone figure on the sofa.

Bunch explained with her usual economy of words. "He was in the church, dying. He'd been shot. Do you know him, Julian? I thought he said your name."

The vicar came up to the sofa and looked down at the dying man. "Poor fellow," he said, and shook his head. "No, I don't know him. I'm almost sure I've never seen him before."

At the moment the dying man's eyes opened once more. They went from the doctor to Julian Harmon and from him to his wife. The eyes stayed there, staring into Bunch's face. Griffiths stepped forward.

"If you could tell us," he said urgently.

But with his eyes fixed on Bunch, the man said in a weak voice, "Please—please—" And then, with a slight tremor, he died. . . .

Sergeant Hayes licked his pencil and turned the page of his notebook.

"So that's all you can tell me, Mrs. Harmon?"

"That's all," said Bunch. "These are the things out of his coat pockets."

On a table at Sergeant Hayes's elbow was a wallet, a rather battered old watch with the initials W.S., and the return half of a ticket to London. Nothing more.

"You've found out who he is?" asked Bunch.

"A Mr. and Mrs. Eccles phoned up the station. He's her brother, it seems. Name of Sandbourne. Been in a low state of health and nerves for some time. He's been getting worse lately. The day before yesterday he walked out and didn't come back. He took a revolver with him."

"And he came out here and shot himself with it?" said Bunch. "Why?"

"Well, you see, he'd been depressed . . ."

Bunch interrupted him. "I don't mean that. I mean, why here?"

Since Sergeant Hayes obviously did not know the answer to that one he replied in an oblique fashion, "Come out here, he did, on the five-ten bus."

"Yes," said Bunch again. "But why?"

"I don't know, Mrs. Harmon," said Sergeant Hayes. "There's no accounting. If the balance of the mind is disturbed—"

Bunch finished for him. "They may do it anywhere. But it still seems to me unnecessary to take a bus out to a small country place like this. He didn't know anyone here, did he?"

"Not so far as can be ascertained," said Sergeant Hayes. He coughed in an apologetic manner and said, as he rose to his feet, "It may be as Mr. and Mrs. Eccles will come out and see you, ma'am—if you don't mind, that is."

"Of course I don't mind," said Bunch. "It's very natural. I only wish I had something to tell them."

"I'll be getting along," said Sergeant Hayes.

"I'm only so thankful," said Bunch, going with him to the front door, "that it wasn't murder."

A car had drawn up at the vicarage gate. Sergeant Hayes, glancing at it, remarked, "Looks as though that's Mr. and Mrs. Eccles come here now, ma'am, to talk with you."

Bunch braced herself to endure what, she felt, might be rather a difficult ordeal. "However," she thought, "I can always call Julian to help me. A clergyman's a great help when people are bereaved."

Exactly what she had expected Mr. and Mrs. Eccles to be

like, Bunch could not have said, but she was conscious, as she greeted them, of a feeling of surprise. Mr. Eccles was a stout and florid man whose natural manner would have been cheerful and facetious. Mrs. Eccles had a vaguely flashy look about her. She had a small, mean, pursed-up mouth. Her voice was thin and reedy.

"It's been a terrible shock, Mrs. Harmon, as you can imagine," she said.

"Oh, I know," said Bunch. "It must have been. Do sit down. Can I offer you—well, perhaps it's a little early for tea—"

Mr. Eccles waved a pudgy hand. "No, no, nothing for us," he said. "It's very kind of you, I'm sure. Just wanted to . . . well . . . what poor William said and all that, you know?"

"He's been abroad a long time," said Mrs. Eccles, "and I think he must have had some very nasty experiences. Very quiet and depressed he's been, ever since he came home. Said the world wasn't fit to live in and there was nothing to look forward to. Poor Bill, he was always moody."

Bunch stared at them both for a moment or two without speaking.

"Pinched my husband's revolver, he did," went on Mrs. Eccles. "Without our knowing. Then it seems he come out here by bus. I suppose that was nice feeling on his part. He wouldn't have liked to do it in our house."

"Poor fellow, poor fellow," said Mr. Eccles, with a sigh. "It doesn't do to judge."

There was another short pause, and Mr. Eccles said, "Did he leave a message? Any last words, nothing like that?"

His bright, rather piglike eyes watched Bunch closely. Mrs. Eccles, too, leaned forward as though anxious for the reply.

"No," said Bunch quietly. "He came into the church when he was dying, for sanctuary."

Mrs. Eccles said in a puzzled voice, "Sanctuary? I don't think I quite . . ."

Mr. Eccles interrupted. "Holy place, my dear," he said impatiently. "That's what the vicar's wife means. It's a sin—suicide, you know. I expect he wanted to make amends."

"He tried to say something just before he died," said Bunch. "He began, 'Please,' but that's as far as he got." Mrs. Eccles put her handkerchief to her eyes and sniffed.

"Oh, dear," she said. "It's terribly upsetting, isn't it?"

"There, there, Pam," said her husband. "Don't take on. These things can't be helped. Poor Willie. Still, he's at peace now. Well, thank you very much, Mrs. Harmon. I hope we haven't interrupted you. A vicar's wife is a busy lady, we know that."

They shook hands with her. Then Eccles turned back suddenly to say, "Oh, yes, there's just one other thing. I think you've got his coat here, haven't you?"

"His coat?" Bunch frowned.

Mrs. Eccles said, "We'd like all his things, you know. Sentimental like."

"He had a watch and a wallet and a railway ticket in the pockets," said Bunch. "I gave them to Sergeant Hayes."

"That's all right, then," said Mr. Eccles. "He'll hand them over to us, I expect. His private papers would be in the wallet."

"There was a pound note in the wallet," said Bunch. "Nothing else."

"No letters? Nothing like that?"

Bunch shook her head.

"Well, thank you again, Mrs. Harmon. The coat he was wearing—perhaps the sergeant's got that, too, has he?"

Bunch frowned in an effort of remembrance.

"No," she said. "I don't think . . . let me see. The doctor and I took his coat off to examine the wound." She looked around the room vaguely. "I must have taken it upstairs with the towels and basin."

"I wonder now, Mrs. Harmon, if you don't mind . . . We'd like his coat, you know, the last thing he wore. Well, the wife feels rather sentimental about it."

"Of course," said Bunch. "Would you like me to have it cleaned first? I'm afraid it's rather—well—stained."

"Oh no, no, no, that doesn't matter."

Bunch frowned. "Now I wonder where . . . Excuse me a moment." She went upstairs and it was some few minutes before she returned.

"I'm so sorry," she said breathlessly. "My daily woman must have put it aside with other clothes that were going to the cleaners. It's taken me quite a long time to find it. Here it is. I'll do it up for you in brown paper."

Disclaiming their protests, she did so; then once more effusively bidding her farewell, the Eccleses departed.

Bunch went slowly back across the hall and entered the study. The Reverend Julian Harmon looked up and his brow cleared. He was composing a sermon and was fearing that he'd been led astray by the interest of the political relations between Judaea and Persia, in the reign of Cyrus.

"Yes, dear?" he said hopefully.

"Julian," said Bunch, "what's *sanctuary* exactly?"

Julian Harmon gratefully put aside his sermon paper.

"Well," he said, "sanctuary in Roman and Greek temples applied to the *cella* in which stood the statue of a god. The Latin word for altar, *ara,* also means protection." He continued learnedly: "In A.D. 399 the right of sanctuary in Christian churches was finally and definitely recognized. The earliest mention of the right of sanctuary in England is in the Code of Laws by Ethelbert in A.D. 600 . . ."

He continued for some time with his exposition but was, as often, disconcerted by his wife's reception of his erudite pronouncement.

"Darling," she said, "you are sweet."

Bending over, she kissed him on the tip of his nose. Julian felt rather like a dog who had been congratulated for performing a clever trick.

"The Eccles have been here," said Bunch.

The vicar frowned. "The Eccles? I don't seem to remember . . ."

"You don't know them. They're the sister and her husband of the man in the church."

"My dear, you ought to have called me."

"There wasn't any need," said Bunch. "They were not in need of consolation. I wonder now." She frowned. "If I put a casserole in the oven tomorrow, can you manage, Julian? I think I shall have to go up to London for the sales."

"The sails?" Her husband looked at her blankly. "Do you mean a yacht or a boat or something?"

Bunch laughed.

"No, darling. There's a special white sale at Burrows and Portman's. You know, sheets, tablecloths, and towels and glass cloths. I don't know what we do with our glass cloths, the way they wear through. Besides," she added thoughtfully, "I think I ought to go and see Aunt Jane."

That sweet old lady, Miss Jane Marple, was enjoying the delights of the metropolis for a fortnight, comfortably installed in her nephew's studio flat.

"So kind of dear Raymond," she murmured. "He and Joan have gone to America for a fortnight and they insisted I should come up here and enjoy myself. And now, dear Bunch, do tell me what it is that's worrying you."

Bunch was Miss Marple's favourite godchild, and the old lady looked at her with great affection as Bunch, thrusting her best felt hat further on the back of her head, started on her story.

Bunch's recital was concise and clear. Miss Marple nodded

her head as Bunch finished. "I see," she said. "Yes, I see."

"That's why I felt I had to see you," said Bunch. "You see, not being clever—"

"But you are clever, my dear."

"No, I'm not. Not clever like Julian."

"Julian, of course, has a very solid intellect," said Miss Marple.

"That's it," said Bunch. "Julian's got the intellect, but on the other hand, I've got the sense."

"You have a lot of common sense, Bunch, and you're very intelligent."

"You see, I don't really know what I ought to do. I can't ask Julian because—well, I mean, Julian's so full of rectitude . . ."

This statement appeared to be perfectly understood by Miss Marple, who said, "I know what you mean, dear. We women—well, it's different." She went on, "You told me what happened, Bunch, but I'd like to know first exactly what you think."

"It's all wrong," said Bunch. "The man who was there in the church, dying, knew all about sanctuary. He said it just the way Julian would have said it. I mean he was a well-read, educated man. And if he'd shot himself, he wouldn't drag himself into a church afterward and say 'sanctuary.' Sanctuary means that you're pursued, and when you get into a church you're safe. Your pursuers can't touch you. At one time even the law couldn't get at you."

She looked questioningly at Miss Marple. The latter nodded. Bunch went on, "Those people, the Eccles, were quite different. That watch—the dead man's watch. It had the initials W.S. on the back of it. But inside—I opened it—in very small lettering there was 'To Walter from his father' and a date. *Walter*. But the Eccles kept talking of him as William or Bill."

Miss Marple seemed about to speak, but Bunch rushed on,

"Oh, I know you're not always called the name you're baptized by. I mean, I can understand that you might be christened William and called 'Porky' or 'Carrots' or something. But your sister wouldn't call you William or Bill if your name was Walter."

"You mean that she wasn't his sister?"

"I'm quite sure she wasn't his sister. They were horrid—both of them. They came to the vicarage to get his things and to find out if he'd said anything before he died. When I said he hadn't I saw it in their faces—relief. I think, myself," finished Bunch, "it was Eccles who shot him."

"Murder?" said Miss Marple.

"Yes," said Bunch, "murder. That's why I came to you, darling."

Bunch's remark might have seemed incongruous to an ignorant listener, but in certain spheres Miss Marple had a reputation for dealing with murder.

"He said 'please' to me before he died," said Bunch. "He wanted me to do something for him. The awful thing is I've no idea what."

Miss Marple considered for a moment or two and then pounced on the point that had already occurred to Bunch. "But why was he there at all?" she asked.

"You mean," said Bunch, "if you wanted sanctuary, you might pop into a church anywhere. There's no need to take a bus that only goes four times a day and come out to a lonely spot like ours for it."

"He must have come there for a purpose," Miss Marple thought. "He must have come to see someone. Chipping Cleghorn's not a big place, Bunch. Surely you must have some idea of who it was he came to see?"

Bunch reviewed the inhabitants of her village in her mind before rather doubtfully shaking her head. "In a way, " she said, "it could be anybody."

"He never mentioned a name?"

"He said Julian, or I thought he said Julian. It might have been Julia, I suppose. As far as I know, there isn't any Julia living in Chipping Cleghorn."

She screwed up her eyes as she thought back to the scene. The man lying there on the chancel steps, the light coming through the window with its jewels of red and blue light.

"Jewels," said Bunch suddenly. "Perhaps that's what he said. The light coming through the east window looked like jewels."

"Jewels," said Miss Marple thoughtfully.

"I'm coming now," said Bunch, "to the most important thing of all. The reason why I've really come here today. You see, the Eccles made a great fuss about having his coat. We took it off when the doctor was seeing to him. It was an old, shabby sort of coat—there was no reason they should have wanted it. They pretended it was sentimental, but that was nonsense.

"Anyway, I went up to find it, and as I was going up the stairs I remembered how he'd made a kind of picking gesture with his hand, as though he was fumbling with the coat. So when I got hold of the coat I looked at it very carefully and I saw that in one place the lining had been sewn up again with a different thread. So I unpicked it and found a little piece of paper inside. I took it out and sewed it up again properly with thread that matched. I was careful and I don't really think that the Eccles would know I've done it. I don't think so, but I can't be sure. And I took the coat down to them and made some excuse for the delay."

"The piece of paper?" asked Miss Marple.

Bunch opened her handbag. "I didn't show it to Julian," she said, "because he would have said that I ought to have given it to the Eccles. But I thought I'd rather bring it to you instead."

"A cloakroom ticket," said Miss Marple, looking at it. "Paddington Station."

"He had a return ticket to Paddington in his pocket," said Bunch.

The eyes of the two women met.

"This calls for action," said Miss Marple briskly. "But it would be advisable, I think, to be careful. Would you have noticed at all, Bunch dear, whether you were followed when you came to London today?"

"Followed!" exclaimed Bunch. "You don't think—"

"Well, I think it's possible," said Miss Marple. "When anything is possible, I think we ought to take precautions." She rose with a brisk movement. "You came up here ostensibly, my dear, to go to the sales. I think the right thing to do, therefore, would be for us to go to the sales. But before we set out, we might put one or two little arrangements in hand. I don't suppose," Miss Marple added obscurely, "that I shall need the old speckled tweed with the beaver collar just at present. . . ."

It was about an hour and a half later that the two ladies, rather the worse for wear and battered in appearance, and both clasping parcels of hard-won household linen, sat down at a small and sequestered hostelry called the Apple Bough to restore their forces with steak-and-kidney pudding followed by apple tart and custard.

"Really a prewar-quality face towel," gasped Miss Marple, slightly out of breath. "With a J on it too. So fortunate that Raymond's wife's name is Joan. I shall put them aside until I really need them and then they will do for her if I pass on sooner than I expect."

"I really did need the glass cloths," said Bunch. "And they were very cheap, though not as cheap as the ones that woman with the ginger hair managed to snatch from me."

A smart young woman with a lavish application of rouge

and lipstick entered the Apple Bough at that moment. After looking round vaguely for a moment or two, she hurried to their table. She laid down an envelope by Miss Marple's elbow.

"There you are, miss," she said briskly.

"Oh, thank you, Gladys," said Miss Marple. "Thank you very much. So kind of you."

"Always pleased to oblige, I'm sure," said Gladys. "Ernie always says to me, 'Everything what's good you learned from that Miss Marple of yours that you were in service with,' and I'm sure I'm always glad to oblige you, miss."

"Such a dear girl," said Miss Marple as Gladys departed again. "Always so willing and so kind."

She looked inside the envelope and then passed it on to Bunch. "Now be very careful, dear," she said. "By the way, is there still that nice young inspector at Melchester that I remember?"

"I don't know," said Bunch. "I expect so."

"Well, if not," said Miss Marple thoughtfully, "I can always ring up the chief constable. I think he would remember me."

"Of course he'd remember you," said Bunch. "Everybody would remember you. You're quite unique." She rose.

Arrived at Paddington, Bunch went to the Parcels Office and produced the cloakroom ticket. A moment or two later a rather shabby old suitcase was passed across to her, and carrying this, she made her way to the platform.

The journey home was uneventful. Bunch rose as the train approached Chipping Cleghorn and picked up the old suitcase. She had just left her carriage when a man, sprinting along the platform, suddenly seized the suitcase from her hand and rushed off with it.

"Stop!" Bunch yelled. "Stop him, stop him. He's taken my suitcase."

The ticket collector who, at this rural station, was a man of somewhat slow processes had just begun to say, "Now, look here, you can't do that—" when a smart blow in the chest pushed him aside, and the man with the suitcase rushed out from the station. He made his way toward a waiting car. Tossing the suitcase in, he was about to climb after it, but before he could move a hand fell on his shoulder, and the voice of Police Constable Abel said, "Now then, what's all this?"

Bunch arrived, panting, from the station. "He snatched my suitcase," she said.

"Nonsense," said the man. "I don't know what this lady means. It's my suitcase. I just got out of the train with it."

"Now, let's get this clear," said Police Constable Abel.

He looked at Bunch with a bovine and impartial stare. Nobody would have guessed that Police Constable Abel and Mrs. Harmon spent long half hours in Police Constable Abel's off time discussing the respective merits of manure and bone meal for rose bushes.

"You say, madam, that this is your suitcase?" said Police Constable Abel.

"Yes," said Bunch. "Definitely."

"And you, sir?"

"I say this suitcase is mine."

The man was tall, dark, and well dressed, with a drawling voice and a superior manner. A feminine voice from inside the car said, "Of course it's your suitcase, Edwin. I don't know what this woman means."

"We'll have to get this clear," said Police Constable Abel. "If it's your suitcase, madam, what do you say is inside it?"

"Clothes," said Bunch. "A long speckled coat with a beaver collar, two wool jumpers, and a pair of shoes."

"Well, that's clear enough," said Police Constable Abel. He turned to the other.

"I am a theatrical costumer," said the dark man importantly. "This suitcase contains theatrical properties which I brought down here for an amateur performance."

"Right, sir," said Police Constable Abel. "Well, we'll just look inside, shall we, and see? We can go along to the police station, or if you're in a hurry, we'll take the suitcase back to the station and open it there."

"It'll suit me," said the dark man. "My name is Moss, by the way. Edwin Moss."

The police constable, holding the suitcase, went back into the station. "Just taking this into the Parcels Office, George," he said to the ticket collector.

Police Constable Abel laid the suitcase on the counter of the Parcels Office and pushed back the clasp. The case was not locked. Bunch and Mr. Edwin Moss stood on either side of him, their eyes regarding each other vengefully.

"Ah!" said Police Constable Abel, as he pushed up the lid.

Inside, neatly folded, was a long, rather shabby tweed coat with a beaver fur collar. There were also two wool jumpers and a pair of country shoes.

"Exactly as you say, madam," said Police Constable Abel, turning to Bunch.

Nobody could have said that Mr. Edwin Moss underdid things. His dismay and compunction were magnificent.

"I do apologize," he said. "I really do apologize. Please believe me, dear lady, when I tell you how very, very sorry I am. Unpardonable—quite unpardonable—my behavior has been." He looked at his watch. "I must rush now. Probably my suitcase has gone on the train." Raising his hat once more, he said meltingly to Bunch, "Do, do forgive me," and rushed hurriedly out of the Parcels Office.

"Are you going to let him get away?" asked Bunch in a conspiratorial whisper to Police Constable Abel.

The latter slowly closed a bovine eye in a wink.

"He won't get too far, ma'am," he said. "That's to say, he won't get far unobserved, if you take my meaning."

"Oh," said Bunch, relieved.

"That old lady's been on the phone," said Police Constable Abel, "the one as was down here a few years ago. Bright she is, isn't she? But there's been a lot cooking up all today. Shouldn't wonder if the inspector or sergeant was out to see you about it tomorrow morning."

It was the inspector who came, the Inspector Craddock whom Miss Marple remembered. He greeted Bunch with a smile as an old friend.

"Crime in Chipping Cleghorn again," he said cheerfully. "You don't lack for sensation here, do you, Mrs. Harmon?"

"I could do with rather less," said Bunch. "Have you come to ask me questions or are you going to tell me things for a change?"

"I'll tell you some things first," said the inspector. "To begin with, Mr. and Mrs. Eccles have been having an eye kept on them for some time. There's reason to believe they've been connected with several robberies in this part of the world. For another thing, although Mrs. Eccles has a brother called Sandbourne who has recently come back from abroad, the man you found dying in the church yesterday was definitely not Sandbourne."

"I knew that he wasn't," said Bunch. "His name was Walter, to begin with, not William."

The inspector nodded. "His name was Walter St. John, and he escaped forty-eight hours ago from Charrington Prison."

"Of course," said Bunch softly to herself, "he was being hunted down by the law, and he took sanctuary." Then she asked, "What had he done?"

"I'll have to go back rather a long way. It's a complicated

story. Several years ago there was a certain dancer doing turns at the music halls. I don't expect you'll have ever heard of her, but she specialized in an Arabian Night's turn. 'Aladdin in the Cave of Jewels,' it was called.

"She wasn't much of a dancer, I believe, but she was—well—attractive. Anyway, a certain Asiatic royalty fell for her in a big way. Among other things he gave her a very magnificent emerald necklace."

"The historic jewels of a rajah?" murmured Bunch ecstatically.

Inspector Craddock coughed. "Well, a rather more modern version, Mrs. Harmon. The affair didn't last very long, broke up when our potentate's attention was captured by a certain film star whose demands were not quite so modest.

"Zobeida, to give the dancer her stage name, hung on to the necklace, and in due course it was stolen. It disappeared from her dressing-room at the theater, and there was a lingering suspicion in the minds of the authorities that she herself might have engineered its disappearance. Such things have been known as a publicity stunt, or indeed from more dishonest motives.

"The necklace was never recovered, but during the course of the investigation the attention of the police was drawn to this man, Walter St. John. He was a man of education and breeding who had come down in the world and who was employed as a working jeweler with a rather obscure firm which was suspected as acting as a fence for jewel robberies.

"There was evidence that this necklace had passed through his hands. It was, however, in connection with the theft of some other jewelry that he was finally brought to trial and convicted and sent to prison. He had not very much longer to serve, so his escape was rather a surprise."

"But why did he come here?" asked Bunch.

"We'd like to know that very much, Mrs. Harmon. Following up his trail, it seems that he went first to London. He didn't visit any of his old associates, but he visited an elderly woman, a Mrs. Jacobs who had formerly been a theatrical dresser. She won't say a word of what he came for, but according to other lodgers in the house, he left carrying a suitcase."

"I see," said Bunch. "He left it in the cloakroom at Paddington and then he came down here."

"By that time," said Inspector Craddock, "Eccles and the man who calls himself Edwin Moss were on his trail. They wanted that suitcase. They saw him get on the bus. They must have driven out in a car ahead of him and been waiting for him when he left the bus."

"And he was murdered?" said Bunch.

"Yes," said Craddock. "He was shot. It was Eccles's revolver, but I rather fancy it was Moss who did the shooting. Now, Mrs. Harmon, what we want to know is, where is the suitcase that Walter St. John actually deposited at Paddington Station?"

Bunch grinned. "I expect Aunt Jane's got it by now," she said. "Miss Marple, I mean. That was her plan. She sent a former maid of hers with a suitcase packed with her things to the cloakroom at Paddington and we exchanged tickets. I collected her suitcase and brought it down by train. She seemed to expect that an attempt would be made to get it from me."

It was Inspector Craddock's turn to grin. "So she said when she rang up. I'm driving up to London to see her. Do you want to come, too, Mrs. Harmon?"

"Wel-l," said Bunch, considering, "Wel-l, as a matter of fact, it's very fortunate. I had a toothache last night, so I really ought to go to London to see the dentist, oughtn't I?"

"Definitely," said Inspector Craddock.

*   *   *

Miss Marple looked from Inspector Craddock's face to the eager face of Bunch Harmon. The suitcase lay on the table. "Of course, I haven't opened it," the old lady said. "I wouldn't dream of doing such a thing till somebody official arrived. Besides," she added, with a demurely mischievous Victorian smile, "it's locked."

"Like to make a guess at what's inside, Miss Marple?" asked the inspector.

"I should imagine, you know," said Miss Marple, "that it would be Zobeida's theatrical costumes. Would you like a chisel, Inspector?"

The chisel soon did its work. Both women gave a slight gasp as the lid flew up. The sunlight coming through the window lit up what seemed like an inexhaustible treasure of sparkling jewels, red, blue, green, orange.

"Aladdin's Cave," said Miss Marple. "The flashing jewels the girl wore to dance."

"Ah," said Inspector Craddock. "Now, what's so precious about it, do you think, that a man was murdered to get hold of it?"

"She was a shrewd girl, I expect," said Miss Marple thoughtfully. "She's dead, isn't she, Inspector?"

"Yes, died three years ago."

"She had this valuable emerald necklace," said Miss Marple musingly. "Had the stones taken out of their setting and fastened here and there on her theatrical costume, where everyone would take them for merely coloured rhinestones. Then she had a replica made of the real necklace, and that, of course, was what was stolen. No wonder it never came on the market. The thief soon discovered the stones were false."

"Here is an envelope," said Bunch, pulling aside some of the glittering stones.

Inspector Craddock took it from her and extracted two official-looking papers from it. He read aloud, " 'Marriage certificate between Walter Edmund St. John and Mary Moss.' That was Zobeida's real name."

"So they were married," said Miss Marple. "I see."

"What's the other?" asked Bunch.

"A birth certificate of a daughter, Jewel."

"Jewel?" cried Bunch. "Why, of course. Jewel! Jill! That's it. I see now why he came to Chipping Cleghorn. That's what he was trying to say to me. Jewel. The Mundys, you know. Laburnam Cottage. They look after a little girl for someone. They're devoted to her. She's been like their own granddaughter. Yes, I remember now, her name is Jewel, only, of course, they call her Jill.

"Mrs. Mundy had a stroke about a week ago, and the old man's been very ill with pneumonia. They were both going to go to the infirmary. I've been trying hard to find a good home for Jill somewhere. I didn't want her taken away to an institution.

"I suppose her father heard about it in prison and he managed to break way and get hold of this suitcase from the old dresser he or his wife left it with. I suppose if the jewels really belonged to her mother, they can be used for the child now."

"I should imagine so, Mrs. Harmon. If they're here."

"Oh, they'll be here all right," said Miss Marple cheerfully. . . .

"Thank goodness you're back, dear," said the Reverend Julian Harmon, greeting his wife with affection and a sigh of content. "Mrs. Burt always tries to do her best when you're away, but she really gave me some very peculiar fish cakes for lunch. I didn't want to hurt her feelings so I gave them to Tiglash Pileser, but even he wouldn't eat them, so I had to throw them out of the window."

"Tiglash Pileser," said Bunch, stroking the vicarage cat,

who was purring against her knee, "is very particular about what fish he eats. I often tell him he's got a proud stomach!"

"And your tooth, dear? Did you have it seen to?"

"Yes," said Bunch. "It didn't hurt much, and I went to see Aunt Jane again, too . . ."

"Dear old thing," said Julian. "I hope she's not failing at all."

"Not in the least," said Bunch, with a grin.

The following morning Bunch took a fresh supply of chrysanthemums to the church. The sun was once more pouring through the east window, and Bunch stood in the jeweled light on the chancel steps. She said very softly under her breath, "Your little girl will be all right. I'll see that she is. I promise."

Then she tidied up the church, slipped into a pew, and knelt for a few moments to say her prayers before returning to the vicarage to attack the piled-up chores of two neglected days.

What do a soldier, a rancher and a millionaire
have in common?
They all meet their match in a woman,
and they all end up in

HOT PURSUIT

Relive the romance...

Three complete novels
by three sizzling hot authors!

Joan Johnston is the celebrated author of nearly forty books and novellas, which have appeared on national bestseller lists more than fifty times and have been translated into nineteen languages in twenty-five countries. Ms. Johnston writes historical, contemporary mainstream and category romance, and has won numerous awards for her work.

Anne Stuart has, in her twenty-five years as a published author, won every major award in the business, appeared on various bestseller lists, been quoted by *People, USA Today* and *Vogue,* appeared on *Entertainment Tonight* and warmed the hearts of readers worldwide. She has written more than thirty novels for Harlequin and Silhouette, plus another thirty or more suspense and historical titles for other publishers.

Mallory Rush is an award-winning, bestselling author of seventeen novels, whose favorite claim to fame is having "Harlequin's Sexiest Book Ever," *Love Game,* appear in a "Ziggy" cartoon. Her sizzling, innovative stories have made her a reader favorite the world over.

HOT PURSUIT

JOAN JOHNSTON
ANNE STUART
MALLORY RUSH

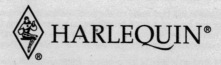

HARLEQUIN®

TORONTO • NEW YORK • LONDON
AMSTERDAM • PARIS • SYDNEY • HAMBURG
STOCKHOLM • ATHENS • TOKYO • MILAN • MADRID
PRAGUE • WARSAW • BUDAPEST • AUCKLAND

HARLEQUIN BOOKS

by Request—HOT PURSUIT

CONTENTS

Harriet Alistair was a city slicker out of her element;
Nathan Hazard was a lone wolf in Stetson and blue jeans.
The only thing they had in common was a burning
passion that defied nature itself....

A WOLF IN SHEEP'S CLOTHING
Joan Johnston

One

___

What do newcomers find abounding in Woolly West towns?
Answer: Quaintness and charm.

Nathan Hazard was mad enough to chew barbed wire. Cyrus Alistair was dead, but even in death the old curmudgeon had managed to thwart Nathan's attempts to buy his land. Cyrus had bequeathed his tiny Montana sheep ranch to a distant relative from Virginia, someone named Harry Alistair. For years that piece of property had been an itch Nathan couldn't scratch—a tiny scrap of Alistair land sitting square in the middle of the Hazard ranch—the last vestige of a hundred-year-old feud between the Hazards and the Alistairs.

Nathan had just learned from John Wilkinson, the

executor of the Alistair estate, that Cyrus's heir hadn't
let any grass grow under his feet. Harry Alistair had
already arrived in the Boulder River Valley to take
possession of Cyrus's ranch. Nathan only hoped the
newest hard-nosed, ornery Alistair hadn't gotten too
settled in. Because he wasn't staying. Not if Nathan
had anything to say about it. Oh, he planned to offer
a fair price. He was even willing to be generous if it
came to that. But he was going to have that land.

Nathan gunned the engine on his pickup, disdain-
ing the cavernous ruts in the dirt road that led to Cyrus's tiny, weather-beaten log cabin. It was a pretty
good bet that once Harry Alistair got a look at the
run-down condition of Cyrus's property, the Easterner
would see the wisdom of selling. Cyrus's ranch—
what there was of it—was falling down. There
weren't more than five hundred sheep on the whole
place.

Besides, what could a man from Williamsburg,
Virginia, know about raising sheep? The greenhorn
would probably take one look at the work, and risk,
involved in trying to make a go of such a small, dilapidated spread and be glad to have Nathan take it
off his hands. Nathan didn't contemplate what he
would do if Harry Alistair refused to sell, because he
simply wasn't going to take no for an answer.

As he drove up to the cabin, Nathan saw someone
bounce up from one of the broken-down sheep pens
that surrounded the barn. That had to be Harry Alistair. Nathan couldn't tell what the greenhorn was doing, but from the man's agitated movements it was
plain something was wrong. A second later the fellow
was racing for the barn. He came out another second

later carrying a handful of supplies. Once again he ducked out of sight in the sheep pen.

Nathan sighed in disgust. The newcomer sure hadn't wasted any time getting himself into a pickle. For a moment Nathan considered turning his truck around and driving away. But despite the Hazard-Alistair feud, he couldn't leave without offering a helping hand. There were rules in the West that governed such conduct. A man in trouble wasn't friend or foe; he was merely a man in trouble. As such, he was entitled to whatever assistance Nathan could offer. Once the trouble was past and they were on equal footing again, Nathan could feel free to treat this Alistair as the mortal enemy the century-old feud made him.

Nathan slammed on the brakes and left his truck door hanging open as he raced across the snowy ground toward the sheep pen on foot. The closer Nathan got, the more his brow furrowed. The man had stood up again and put a hand behind his neck to rub the tension there. He was tall, but the body Nathan saw was gangly, the shoulders narrow. The man's face was smooth, unlined. Nathan hadn't been expecting someone so young and…the only word that came to mind was *delicate,* but he shied from thinking it. He watched the greenhorn drop out of sight again. With that graceful downward movement Nathan realized what had caused his confusion. That was no man in Cyrus Alistair's sheep pen—it was a woman!

When Nathan arrived at her side, he saw the problem right away. A sheep was birthing, but the lamb wasn't presenting correctly. The ewe was baaing in distress. The woman had dropped to her knees and was crooning to the animal in a low, raspy voice that sent shivers up Nathan's spine.

The woman was concentrating so hard on what she was doing that she wasn't even aware of Nathan until he asked, "Need some help?"

"What? Oh!" She looked up at him with stricken brown eyes. Her teeth were clenched on her lower lip and her cheeks were pale. He noticed her hand was trembling as she brushed her brown bangs out of her eyes with a slender forearm. "Yes. Please. I don't know what to do."

Nathan felt a constriction in his chest at the desperate note in her voice. He had an uncontrollable urge to protect her from the tragic reality she faced. The feeling was unfamiliar, and therefore uncomfortable. He ignored it as best he could, and quickly rolled up his sleeves. "Do you have some disinfectant handy?"

"Yes. Here." She poured disinfectant over his hands and arms.

Nathan shook off the excess and knelt beside the ewe. After a quick examination, he said flatly, "This lamb is dead."

"Oh, no! It's all my fault."

"Maybe not," Nathan contradicted. "Can't always save a case of dystocia."

"What?"

"The lamb is out of position. Its head is bent back, not forward along its legs like it ought to be."

"I read in a book what to do for a problem delivery. I just didn't realize..." She reached out a hand to briefly touch the lamb's foot that extended from the ewe. "Will the mother die, too?"

"Not if I can help it," Nathan said grimly. There was a long silence while he used soapy water to help the dead lamb slip free of the womb. Almost immediately contractions began again. "There's another lamb."

"Is it alive?" the woman asked, her voice full of hope.

"Don't know yet." Nathan wanted the lamb to be born alive more than he had wanted anything in a long time. Which made no sense at all. This was an Alistair sheep.

"Here it comes!" she exclaimed. "Is it all right?"

Nathan waited to see whether the lamb would suck air. When it didn't, he grabbed a nearby gunnysack and rubbed vigorously. The lamb responded by bleating pitifully. And Nathan let out the breath he hadn't known he'd been holding.

"It's alive!" she shouted.

"That it is," Nathan said with satisfaction. He cut the umbilical cord about an inch and a half from the lamb's navel and asked, "Where's the iodine?"

Nathan helped the ewe to her feet while the woman ran to fetch a wide-mouth jar full of iodine. When she returned he held the lamb up by its front legs and sloshed the jar over the navel cord until it was covered with iodine. He set the lamb back down beside its mother where, after some bumping and searching with its nose, it found a teat and began to nurse.

Nathan glanced at the woman to share the moment, which he found profoundly moving no matter how many times he'd seen it. Once he did, he couldn't take his eyes off her.

She was watching the nursing lamb, and her whole

face reflected a kind of joy he had seldom seen and wasn't sure he had ever felt. When the lamb made a loud, slurping sound, a laugh of relief bubbled up from her throat. And she looked up into his eyes and smiled.

He was stunned. Poleaxed. Smitten. In a long-ago time he would have thrown her on his horse and ridden off into the sunset. But this was now, and he was a civilized man. So he simply swallowed hard, gritted his teeth and smiled back.

Her smile revealed a slight space between her front teeth that made her look almost winsome. A dimple appeared in her left cheek when the smile became a grin. Her bangs had fallen back over her brows, and it took all his willpower to leave it alone. Her nose was small and tilted up at the end, and he noticed her cheeks, now that they weren't so pale, were covered with a scattering of freckles. Her lips were full, despite the wide smile, and her chin, tilted up toward him, seemed to ask for his touch. He had actually lifted a hand toward her when he realized what he was about to do.

Nathan was confused by the strength of his attraction to the woman. He didn't need—refused to take on—any more obligations in his lifetime. This was a woman who looked in great need of a lot of care and attention. This kind of woman spelled RESPONSIBILITY in capital letters. He shrugged inwardly. He had done his share of taking care of the helpless. He hadn't begrudged the sacrifice, because it had been necessary, but he was definitely gun-shy. When he chose a woman to share his life, it would be someone who could stand on her own two feet, someone who could be a helpmate and an equal partner. He would never choose someone like the winsome woman kneeling before him, whose glowing brown eyes beseeched him to take her into his arms and comfort her there.

Not by a long shot!

Nathan bolted to his feet, abruptly ending the intense feeling of closeness he felt with the woman. ''Where the hell is Harry Alistair?'' he demanded in a curt voice. ''And what the hell are you doing out here trying to handle a complicated lambing all alone?''

His stomach knotted when he saw the hurt look in her eyes at his abrupt tone of voice, but he didn't have a chance even to think about apologizing before a spark of defiance lit up her beautiful brown eyes, and she rose to her feet. Her hands balled into fists and found her hipbones. She was tall. Really tall. He stood six foot three and she was staring him practically in the eye.

''You're looking for Harry Alistair?'' she asked in a deceptively calm voice.

''I am.''

''What for?''

''That's between him and me. Look, do you know where he is or not?''

''I do.''

But that was all she said. Nathan was damned if he was going to play games with her. He yanked the worn Stetson off his head, forked an agitated hand through his blond hair and settled the cowboy hat back in place over his brow. He placed his fists on his hips in a powerful masculine version of her pose and grated out, "Well, where the hell is he?"

"*He's* standing right here."

There was a long pause while Nathan registered what she'd said. "*You're* Harry Alistair?"

"Actually, my name is Harriet." She forgave him for his rudeness with one of those engaging smiles and said, "But my friends all call me Harry."

She stuck out her hand for him to shake, and before he could curb his automatic reaction he had her hand clasped in his. It was soft. Too damn soft for a woman who hoped to survive the hard life of a Montana sheep rancher. He held on to her hand as he examined her—the Harry Alistair he had come to see—more closely.

He was looking for reasons to find fault with her, to prove he couldn't possibly be physically attracted to her, and he found them. She was dressed in a really god-awful outfit: brand-new bibbed overalls, a red-and-black plaid wool shirt, a down vest, galoshes for heaven's sake, and a Harley's Feed Store baseball cap, which meant she'd already been to Slim Harley's Feed Store in Big Timber. Nathan hadn't realized her hair was so long, but two childish braids fell over each shoulder practically to her breasts.

Nothing wrong with them, a voice inside taunted.

Nathan forced his eyes back up to her face, which now bore an expression of amusement. A slow red flush crept up his neck. There was no way he could hide it or stop it. His Swedish ancestors had bequeathed him blue eyes and blond hair and skin that got ruddy in the sun, but never tanned. Unfortunately his Nordic complexion also displayed his feelings when he most wanted them hidden. He suddenly dropped her hand as though it had caught fire.

"We have to talk," he said flatly.

"I'd like that," Harry replied. "After everything we've just been through together, I feel like we're old friends, Mr.— Oh, my," she said with a self-deprecating laugh. "I don't even know your name."

"Nathan Hazard."

"Come on inside, Nathan Hazard, and have a cup of coffee, and we'll talk."

Nathan was pretty sure he could conduct his business right here. After all, how many words did it take to say "I want to buy this place"? Only six. But he was curious to see the inside of Cyrus Alistair's place. He had heard the tiny log cabin called "rustic" by those who had actually been inside, though they were few and far between.

Against his better judgment Nathan said, "Sure. A cup of coffee sounds good."

"I don't have things very organized," Harry apologized.

Nathan soon realized that was an understatement. Harry took him in through the back door, which led to the kitchen. What he saw was *chaos*. What he felt was *disappointment*. Because despite everything he had already seen of her, he had been holding out hope that he was wrong about Harry Alistair. The shambles he beheld in the kitchen of the tiny cabin—dishes piled high in the sink, half-empty bottles of formula on the counters, uneaten meals side by side with stacks of brochures on the table, several bags of garbage in one corner, and a lamb sleeping on a wadded-up blanket in the other—confirmed his worst fears.

Harry Alistair needed a caretaker. This wasn't a woman who was ever going to be anyone's equal partner.

Harry had kicked off her galoshes when she came in the door, and let them lie where they fell. Her down vest warmed the back of the kitchen chair, and she hooked her Harley's Feed Store cap on a deer antler that graced the dingy, wooden-planked wall.

Poor woman, he thought. She must have given up trying to deal with all the mess and clutter. He hardened himself against feeling sympathy for her. He was more convinced than ever that he would be doing her a favor by buying Cyrus's place from her.

While he stood staring, Harry grabbed some pottery mugs for the coffee from kitchen cupboards that appeared to be all but bare. He was able to notice that because all the cupboards hung open on dragging hinges. As quickly as she shoved the painted yellow kitchen cupboards closed, they sprang open again. And stayed that way. She turned to him, shrugged and let go with another one of her smiles. He stuck his hands deep into his pockets to keep from reaching out to enfold her in his arms.

Not the woman for me, he said to himself.

The walls and floor of the room consisted of unfinished wooden planks. A step down from "rustic," he thought. More like "primitive." The refrigerator was so old that the top was rounded instead of square. The gas stove was equally ancient, and she had to light the burner with a match.

"Darned thing doesn't work from the pilot," Harry explained as she set a dented metal coffeepot on the burner. "Make yourself at home," she urged, seating herself at the kitchen table.

Nathan set his Stetson on the table and draped his sheepskin coat over the back of one of the three chrome-legged chairs at the Formica table. Then he flattened the torn plastic seat and sat down. The table was cluttered with brochures. One title leaped out at him—"Sheep Raising for Beginners." He didn't have a chance to comment on it before she started talking.

"I'm from Williamsburg, Virginia," she volunteered. "I didn't even know my Great-Uncle Cyrus. It was really a surprise when Mr. Wilkinson from the bank contacted me. At first I couldn't believe it. Me, inheriting a sheep ranch! I suppose the sensible thing would have been to let Mr. Wilkinson sell the place for me. He said there was a buyer anxious to have it. Then I thought about what it would be like to have a place of my very own, far away from—" She jumped up and crossed to the stove to check the coffeepot.

Nathan wanted her to finish that sentence. What, or whom, had she wanted to escape? What, or who, had made her unhappy enough that she had to run all the way to Montana? He fought down the possessive, protective feelings that arose. She didn't belong to him. Never would.

She was talking in breathless, jerky sentences, which was how he knew she was nervous. It was as though she wasn't used to entertaining a man in her kitchen. Maybe she wasn't. He wished he knew for sure.

Not your kind of woman, he repeated to himself.

"Do you have a place around here?" Harry asked. Nathan cleared his throat and said with a rueful smile, "You could say I have a place that goes all around here."

He watched her brows lower in confusion at his comment. She filled the two coffee mugs to the very brim and brought them carefully to the table.

"Am I supposed to know what that means?" she asked as she seated herself across from him again.

"My sheep ranch surrounds yours." When she still looked confused he continued, "Your property sits square in the center of mine. Your access road to the highway runs straight across my land."

A brilliant smile lit her face, and she cocked her head like a brown sparrow on a budding limb and quipped, "Then we most certainly *are* neighbors, aren't we? I'm so glad you came to see me, Nathan— is it all right if I call you Nathan?—so we can get to know each other. I could really use some advice. You see—"

"Wait a minute," he interrupted.

In the first place it wasn't all right with him if she called him Nathan. It would be much more difficult to be firm with her if they were on a first-name basis. In the second place he hadn't come here to be neighborly; he had come to make an offer on her land. And in the third, and most important, place, he had *absolutely no intention of offering her any advice.* And he was going to tell her all those things...just as soon as she stopped smiling so trustingly at him.

"Look, Harry-et," he said, pausing a second between the two syllables, unable to make himself address her by the male nickname. "You probably should have taken the banker's advice. If the rest of this cabin looks as bad as the kitchen, it can't be very comfortable. The buildings and sheds are a disgrace. Your hay fields are fallow. Your access road is a mass of ruts. You'll be lucky to make ends meet let alone earn enough from this sheep ranch you inherited to enjoy any kind of pleasant life. The best advice I can give you is to sell this place to me and go back to Virginia where you belong.''

He watched her full lips firm into a flat line and her jaw tauten. Her chin came up pugnaciously. ''I'm not selling out.''

''Why the hell not?'' he retorted in exasperation.

''Because.''

He waited for her to explain. But she was keeping her secrets to herself. He was convinced now that she must be running from something...or someone.

''I'm going to make a go of this place. I can do it. I may not be experienced, but I'm intelligent and hardworking and I have all the literature on raising sheep that I could find.''

Nathan stuck the brochure called ''Sheep Raising for Beginners'' under her nose and said, ''None of these brochures will compensate for practical experience. Look what happened this afternoon. What would you have done if I hadn't come along?'' He had the unpleasant experience of watching her chin drop to her chest and her cheeks flush while her thumb brushed anxiously against the plain pottery mug.

''I would probably have lost both lambs, and the ewe, as well,'' she admitted in a low voice. She looked up at him, her brown eyes liquid with tears she was trying to blink away. ''I owe you my thanks. I don't know how I can ever repay you. I know I have a lot to learn. But—'' she leaned forward, and her voice became urgent ''—I intend to work as hard as I have to, night and day if necessary, until I succeed!''

Nathan was angry and irritated. She wasn't going to succeed; she was going to fail miserably. And unless he could somehow talk her into selling this place to him, he was going to have to stand by and watch it happen. Because he *absolutely, positively,* was *not* going to offer to help. There were no ifs, ands or buts about it. He had been through this before. A small commitment had a way of mushrooming out of control. Start cutting pines and pretty soon you had a whole mountain meadow.

''Look, Harry-et,'' he said, ''the reason I came here today is to offer to buy this place from you.''

''It's not for sale.''

Nathan sighed. She'd said it as if she'd meant it. He had no choice except to try to convince her to change her mind. ''Sheep ranching involves a whole lot more than lambing and shearing, Harry-et.'' He was distracted from his train of thought by the way the flush on her cheeks made her freckles show up. He forced his attention back where it belonged and continued. ''For instance, do you have any idea what wool pool you're in?''

She raised a blank face and stared at him.

''Do you even know what a wool pool is?''

She shook her head.

''A wool pool enables small sheepmen like yourself to concentrate small clips of wool into carload lots so that they can get a better price on—'' He cut himself off. He was supposed to be proving her ignorance to her, not educating it away. He ignored her increasingly distressed look and asked, "Do you have any idea what's involved with docking and castrating lambs?"

This time she nodded, but the flush on her face deepened.

"What about keeping records? Do you have any accounting experience?"

"A little," she admitted in a quiet voice.

He felt like a desperado in a black hat threatening the schoolmarm, but he told himself it was for her own good in the long run and continued, "Can you figure adjusted weaning weight ratios? Measure ram performance? Calculate shearing dates? Compute feed gain ratios?"

By now she was violently shaking her head. A shiny tear streaked one cheek.

He pushed himself up out of his chair. He braced one callused palm on the table and leaned across to cup her jaw in his other hand and lift her chin. He looked into her eyes, and it took every bit of determination he had not to succumb to the plea he saw there. "I can't teach you to run this ranch. I have a business of my own that needs tending. You can't make it on your own, Harry-et. Sell your land to me."

"No."

"I'll give you a fair—a generous—price. Then you can go home where you belong."

She was out of his grasp and gone before he had time to stop her. She didn't go far, just to the sink, where she stood in front of the stack of dirty dishes and stared out the dirt-clouded window at the ramshackle sheep pens and the derelict barn. "I will succeed. With or without your help."

She sounded so sure of herself, despite the fact that she was doomed to fail. Nathan refused to admire her. He chose to be furious with her instead. In three angry strides he was beside her. "You're as stubborn as every other hard-nosed, ornery Alistair who ever lived on this land!" He snorted in disgust. "I can sure as hell see now why Hazards have been feuding with Alistairs for a hundred years."

She whirled to confront him. "And I can see why Alistairs chose to feud with Hazards," she retorted. "How dare you pretend to be a friend!" She poked him in the chest with a stiff finger. "How dare you sneak in under my guard and pretend to help—"

"I wasn't pretending," he said heatedly, grabbing her wrist to keep her from poking him again. "I *did* help. Admit it!"

"Sure! So I'd be grateful. All the time you only wanted to buy my land right out from under me. You are the lowest, meanest—"

He wasn't about to listen to any insults from a greenhorn female! A moment later her arm was twisted up behind her and he had pulled her flush against him. She opened her mouth to lambaste him again and he shut her up the quickest, easiest way he knew. He covered her mouth with his.

Nathan was angry, and he wasn't gentle. That is, until he felt her lips soften under his. It felt like he had been wanting her for a long time. His mouth moved slowly over hers while his hand cupped her head and kept her still so he could take what he needed. She struggled against his hold, her breasts brushing against his chest, her hips hard against his. That only made him want her more. It was when he felt her trembling that he came to his senses, mortified at the uncivilized way he had treated her.

He abruptly released the hand he had twisted behind her back. But instead of coming up to slap him, as he had expected, her palm reached up to caress his cheek. Her fingertips followed the shape of his cheekbone upward to his temple, where she threaded her fingers into his hair and slowly pulled his head back down. And then she kissed him back.

That was when he realized she was trembling with desire. Not fear. Desire. With both hands free he cupped her buttocks and pulled her hard against him. For every thrust he made, she countered. He was as full and hard as he had ever been in his life. His tongue ravaged her mouth, and she responded with an ardor that made him hungry for her. He spread urgent kisses across her face and neck, but they didn't satisfy as much as the taste of her, so he sought her mouth again. His tongue found the space between her teeth. And the inside of her lip. And the roof of her mouth. When he mimicked the thrust and parry of lovers, she held his tongue and sucked it until he thought his head was going to explode.

When he slipped his hand over her buttocks and between her legs, she moaned, a sound that came from deep in her throat and spoke of an agony of unappeased passion.

And the lamb in the corner bleated.

Nathan lifted his head and stared at the woman in his arms. Her brown eyes were half-veiled by her lids, and her pupils were dilated. She was breathing as heavily as he was, her lips parted to gasp air. Her knees had already buckled, and his grasp on her was all that kept them both from the floor.

Are you out of your mind?

He tried to step away, but her hand still clutched his hair. He reached up and drew her hand away. She suddenly seemed to realize he had changed his mind and backed up abruptly. Nathan refused to look at her face. He already felt bad enough. He had come within a lamb's tail of making love to Harry-et Alistair. He had made a narrow escape, for which he knew he would later, when his body wasn't so painfully objecting, be glad for.

"I think it's time you left, Mr. Hazard," Harry said in a rigidly controlled voice.

He couldn't leave without trying once more to accomplish what he'd come to do. "Are you sure you won't—"

The change in her demeanor was so sudden that it took him by surprise. Her expression was fierce, determined. "I will not sell this land," she said through clenched teeth. "Now get out of here before—"

"Goodbye, Harry-et. If you have a change of heart, John Wilkinson at the bank knows how to get in touch with me."

He settled his hat on his head and pulled it down with a tug. Then he shrugged broad shoulders into his sheepskin-lined coat. Before he was even out the kitchen door Harry Alistair had already started heating a bottle of formula for the lamb she had snuggled in her arms. It was the first time he'd ever envied one of the fleecy orphans.

The last thing Nathan Hazard wanted to do was

leave that room. But he turned resolutely and marched out the door. As he gunned the engine of his truck, he admitted his encounter with Harry-et Alistair had been a very close call.

Not the woman for you, he reminded himself. *Definitely not the woman for you.*

Two

Are there bachelors in them thar hills?
Answer: Yep.

Once the lamb had been fed and settled back on its pallet, Harry sank into a kitchen chair, put her elbows on the table and let her head drop into her hands. What on earth had she been thinking to let Nathan Hazard kiss her like that! And worse, why had she kissed him back in such a wanton manner? It was perfectly clear now that she hadn't been *thinking* at all; she had been feeling, and the feelings had been so overwhelming that they hadn't allowed for any kind of rational consideration.

Harry had felt an affinity to the rancher from the instant she'd laid eyes on him. His broad shoulders, his narrow hips, the dusting of fine blond hair on his powerful forearms all appealed to her. His eyes were framed by crow's-feet that gave character to a sharp-boned, perfectly chiseled face. That pair of sapphire-blue eyes, alternately curious and concerned, had stolen her heart.

Harry wasn't surprised that she was attracted to someone more handsome than any man had a right to be. What amazed her was that having known Nathan Hazard for only a matter of hours she would readily have trusted him with her life. That simply wasn't logical. Although, Harry supposed in retrospect, she had probably seen in Nathan Hazard exactly what she wanted to see. She had needed a legendary, bigger-than-life western hero, someone tall, rugged and handsome to come along and rescue her. And he had obligingly arrived.

And he had been stunning in his splendor, though that had consisted merely of a pair of butter-soft jeans molded to his long legs, western boots, a dark blue wool shirt topped by a sheepskin-lined denim jacket, and a Stetson he had pulled down so that it left his features shadowed. The shaggy, silver-blond hair that fell a full inch over his collar had made him look untamed, perhaps untamable. Harry remembered wondering what such fine blond hair might feel like to touch. His lower lip was full, and he had a wide, easy smile that pulled one side of his mouth up a little higher than the other. She had also wondered, she realized with chagrin, what it would be like to kiss that mouth. Unbelievably she had actually indulged her fantasies.

Harry wasn't promiscuous. She wasn't even sexually experienced when it came right down to it. So she had absolutely no explanation for what had just happened between her and the Montana sheepman. She only knew she had felt an urgent, uncontrollable need to touch Nathan Hazard, to kiss him and to have him kiss her back. And she hadn't wanted him to stop there. She had wanted him inside her, mated to her.

Her mother and father, not to mention her brother, Charlie, and her eight uncles and their dignified, decorous wives, would have been appalled to think that any Williamsburg Alistair could have behaved in such a provocative manner with a man she had only just met. Harry was a little appalled herself.

But then nothing in Montana was going the way she had planned.

It had seemed like such a good idea, when she had gotten the letter from John Wilkinson, to come to the Boulder River Valley and learn how to run Great-Uncle Cyrus's sheep ranch. She loved animals and she loved being out-of-doors and she loved the mountains—she had heard that southwestern Montana had a lot of beautiful mountains. She had expected opposition to such a move from her family, so she had carefully chosen the moment to let them know about her decision.

No Alistair ever argued at the dinner table. So, sitting at the elegant antique table that had been handed down from Alistair to Alistair for generations, she had waited patiently for a break in the dinner conversation and calmly announced, "I've decided to take advantage of my inheritance from Great-Uncle Cyrus. I'll be leaving for Montana at the end of the week."

"But you can't possibly manage a sheep ranch on your own, Harriet," her mother admonished in a cultured voice. "And since you're bound to fail, darling, I can't understand why you would even want to give it a try. Besides," she added, "think of the smell!"

Harry—her mother cringed every time she heard the masculine nickname—had turned her compelling brown eyes to her father, looking for an encouraging word.

"Your mother is right, sweetheart," Terence Waverly Alistair said. "My daughter, a sheep farmer?" His thick white brows lowered until they nearly met at the bridge of his nose. "I'm afraid I can't lend my support to such a move. You haven't succeeded at a single job I've found for you, sweetheart. Not the one as a teller in my bank, not the one as a secretary, nor the the one as a medical receptionist. You've gotten yourself fired for ineptness at every single one. It's foolhardy to go so far—Montana is a long way from Virginia, my dear—merely to fail yet again. Besides," he added, "think of the cold!"

Harry turned her solemn gaze toward her older brother, Charles. He had been her champion in the past. He had even unbent so far as to call her Harry when their parents weren't around. Now she needed his support. Wanted his support. Begged with her eyes for his support.

"I'm afraid I have to agree with Mom and Dad, Harriet."

"But, Charles—"

"Let me finish," he said in a determined voice. Harry met her brother's sympathetic gaze as he continued. "You're only setting yourself up for disappointment. You'll be a lot happier if you learn to accept your limitations.''

''Meaning?'' Harry managed to whisper past the ache in her throat.

''Meaning you just aren't clever enough to pull it off, Harriet. Besides,'' he added, ''think of all that manual labor!''

Harry felt the weight of a lifetime of previous failures in every concerned but discouraging word her family had offered. They didn't believe she could do it. She took a deep breath and let it out. She could hardly blame them for their opinion of her. To be perfectly honest, she had never given them any reason to think otherwise. So why was she so certain that this time things would be different? Why was she so certain that this time she would succeed? Because she knew something they didn't: *she had done all that failing in the past on purpose!*

Harry was paying now for years of deception. It had started innocently enough when she was a child and her mother had wanted her to take ballet lessons. At six Harry had already towered over her friends. Gawky and gangly, she knew she was never going to make a graceful prima ballerina. One look at her mother's face, however, and Harry had known she couldn't say, ''No, thank you. I'd rather be playing basketball.''

Instead, she had simply acquired two left feet. It had worked. Her ballet instructor had quickly labeled her irretrievably clumsy and advised Isabella Alistair that she would only be throwing her money away if Harriet continued in the class. Isabella was forced to admit defeat. Thus, unbeknownst to her parents,

Harry had discovered at a very early age a passive way of resisting them.

Over the years Harry had never said no to her parents. It had been easier simply to go along with whatever they had planned. Piano lessons were thwarted with a deaf ear; embroidery had been abandoned as too bloody; and her brief attempt at tennis had resulted in a broken leg.

As she had gotten older, the stakes had gotten higher. She had only barely avoided a plan to send her away to college at Radcliffe by getting entrance exam scores so low that they had astonished the teachers who had watched her get straight A's through high school. She had been elated when her distraught parents had allowed her to enroll at the same local university her friends from high school were attending.

Harry knew she should have made some overt effort to resist each time her father had gotten her one of those awful jobs after graduation, simply stood up to him and said, "No, I'd rather be pursuing a career that I've chosen for myself." But old habits were hard to break. It had been easier to prove inept at each and every one.

When her parents chose a husband for her, she had resorted to even more drastic measures. She had concealed what looks she had, made a point of reciting her flaws to her suitor and resisted his amorous advances like a starched-up prude. She had led the young man to contemplate life with a plain, clumsy, cold-natured, brown-eyed, brown-haired, freckle-faced failure. He had beat a hasty retreat.

Now a lifetime of purposeful failure had come

home to roost. She couldn't very well convince her
parents she was ready to let go of the apron strings
when she had so carefully convinced them of her inability to succeed at a single thing they had set for
her to do. She might have tried to explain to them her
failure had only been a childish game that had been
carried on too long, but that would mean admitting
she had spent her entire life deceiving them. She
couldn't bear to hurt them like that. Anyway, she
didn't think they would believe her if she told them
her whole inept life had been a sham.

Now Harry could see, with the clarity of twenty-
twenty hindsight, that she had hurt herself even more
than her parents by the choices she had made. But
the method of dealing with her parents' manipulation,
which she had started as a child and continued as a
teenager, she had found impossible to reverse as an
adult. Until now. At twenty-six she finally had the
perfect opportunity to break the pattern of failure she
had pursued for a lifetime. She only hoped she hadn't
waited too long.

Harry was certain she could manage her Great-
Uncle Cyrus's sheep ranch. She was certain she could
do anything she set her brilliant mind to do. After all,
it had taken brilliance to fail as magnificently, and
selectively, as she had all these years. So now, when
she was determined to succeed at last, she had wanted
her family's support. It was clear she wasn't going to
get it. And she could hardly blame them for it. She
was merely reaping what she had so carefully sowed.

Harry had a momentary qualm when she wondered
whether they might be right. Maybe she was biting
off more than she could chew. After all, what did she

know about sheep or sheep ranching? Then her chin tilted up and she clenched her hands in her lap under the table. They were wrong. She wouldn't fail. She could learn what she didn't know. And she would succeed.

Harriet Elizabeth Alistair was convinced in her heart that she wasn't a failure. Surely, once she made up her mind to stop failing, she could. Once she was doing something she had chosen for herself, she was bound to succeed. She would show them all. She wasn't what they thought her—someone who had to be watched and protected from herself and the cold, cruel world around her. Rather, she was a woman with hopes and dreams, none of which she had been allowed—or rather, allowed herself—to pursue.

Like a pioneer of old, Harry wanted to go west to build a new life. She was prepared for hard work, for frigid winter mornings and searing summer days. She welcomed the opportunity to build her fortune with the sweat of her brow and the labor of her back. Harry couldn't expect her family to understand why she wanted to try to make it on her own in a cold, smelly, faraway place where she would have to indulge in manual labor. She had something to prove to herself. This venture was the Boston Tea Party and the Alamo and Custer's Last Stand all rolled into one. In the short run she might lose a few battles, but she was determined to win the war.

At last Harry broke the awesome silence that had descended on the dinner table. "Nothing you've said has changed my mind," she told her family. "I'll be leaving at the end of the week."

Nothing her family said the following week, and

they had said quite a lot, had dissuaded Harry from
the course she had set for herself. She had been delighted to find, when she arrived a week later in Big
Timber, the town closest to Great-Uncle Cyrus's
ranch, that at least she hadn't been deceived about the
beauty of the mountains in southwestern Montana.
The Crazy Mountains provided a striking vista to the
north, while the majestic, snow-capped Absarokas
greeted her to the south each morning. But they were
the only redeeming feature in an otherwise daunting
locale.

The Boulder River Valley was a desolate place in
late February. The cottonwoods that lined the Boulder
River, which meandered the length of the valley, were
stripped bare of leaves. And the grass, what wasn't
covered by patches of drifted snow, was a ghastly
straw-yellow. All that might have been bearable if
only she hadn't found such utter decay when she arrived at Great-Uncle Cyrus's ranch.

Her first look at the property she had inherited had
been quite a shock. Harry had been tempted to turn
tail and run back to Williamsburg. But something—
perhaps the beauty of the mountains, but more likely
the thought of facing her family if she gave up without even trying—had kept her from giving John Wilkinson the word to sell. She would never go home
until she could do so with her head held high, the
owner and manager of a prosperous sheep ranch.

Harry had discovered dozens of reasons to question
her decision ever since she had moved to Montana,
not the least of which was the meeting today with her
nearest neighbor. Nathan Hazard hadn't exactly fulfilled her expectations of the typical western hero. A

more provoking, irritating, exasperating man she had never known! Whether he admitted it or not, it had been a pretty sneaky thing to do, helping her so generously with the difficult lambing when he knew all along he was only softening her up so that he could make an offer on her land.

Thoughts of the difficult birthing reminded her that she still had to dispose of the dead lamb. Harry knew she ought to bury it, but the ground was frozen. She couldn't imagine burning it. And she couldn't bear the thought of taking the poor dead lamb somewhere up into the foothills and leaving it among the juniper and jack pine for nature's scavengers to find. None of the brochures she had read discussed this particular problem. Harry knew there must be some procedures the local ranchers followed. Surely they also had deaths at lambing time. But she would dig a hole in the frozen ground with her fingernails before she asked Nathan Hazard what to do.

For now Harry decided to move the dead lamb behind the barn and cover it with a tarp. As long as the weather stayed cold, the body wouldn't decay. When she could spare the time, she would take a trip into Big Timber and strike up a conversation with Slim Harley at the feed store. Somehow she would casually bring up the subject of dead lambs in the conversation and get the answers she needed. Harry's lips twisted wryly. Western conversations certainly tended to have a grittier tone than those in the East.

Harry couldn't put off what had to be done. She slipped her vest back on, pulled her cap down on her head and stepped back into her galoshes. A quick search turned up some leather work gloves in the drawer beside the sink. A minute later she was headed back out to the sheep pens.

Harry actually shuddered when she picked up the dead lamb. It had stiffened in death. It was also heavier than she had expected, so she had to hold it close to her chest in order to carry it. Despite everything Harry had read about not getting emotionally involved, she was unable to keep from mourning the animal's death. It seemed like such a waste. Although, if the lamb had lived it would have gone to market, where it would eventually have become lamb chops on some eastern dinner table.

Maybe she ought to call Nathan Hazard and take him up on his offer, after all.

Before Harry had a chance to indulge her bout of maudlin conjecture she heard another sheep baaing in distress.

Not again!

Harry raced for the sheep pens where she had separated the ewes that were ready to deliver. Instead she discovered a sheep had already given birth to one lamb; while she watched it birthed a twin. Harry had learned from her extensive reading that her sheep had been genetically bred so that they bore twins, thus doubling the lamb crop. But to her it was a unique happening. She stopped and leaned against the pen and smiled with joy at having witnessed such a miraculous event.

Then she realized she had work to do. The cords had to be cut and dipped in iodine. And the ewe and her lambs had to be moved into a jug, a small pen separate from the other sheep, for two or three days until the lambs had bonded with their mothers and gotten a little stronger.

Harry had read that lambing required constant attention from a rancher, but she hadn't understood that to mean she would get no sleep, no respite. For the rest of the night she never had a chance to leave the sheep barn, as the ewes dropped twin lambs that lived and died depending on the whims of fate. The stack under the tarp beside her barn got higher. If Harry had found a spare second, she would have swallowed her pride and called Nathan Hazard for help. But by the time she got a break near dawn, the worst seemed to be over. Harry had stood midwife to the delivery of forty-seven lambs. Forty-three were still alive.

She dragged herself into the house, and only then realized she had forgotten about the orphan lamb in her kitchen. He was bleating pitifully from hunger. Despite her fatigue, Harry took the time to fix the lamb a bottle. She fell asleep sitting on the wooden-plank floor with her back against the wooden-plank wall, with the hungry lamb in her lap sucking at a nippled Coke bottle full of milk replacer.

That was how Nathan Hazard found her the following morning at dawn.

Nathan had lambing of his own going on, but unlike Harriet Alistair, he had several hired hands to help with the work. When suppertime arrived, he left the sheep barn and came inside to a hot meal that Katoya, the old Blackfoot Indian woman who was his housekeeper, had ready and waiting for him.

Katoya had mysteriously arrived on the Hazard doorstep on the day Nathan's mother had died, as though by some prearranged promise, to take her place in the household. Nathan had been sixteen at the time. No explanation had ever been forthcoming as to why the Blackfoot woman had come. And despite Nathan's efforts in later years to ease the older woman's chores, Katoya still worked every day from dawn to dusk with apparent tirelessness, making Nathan's house a home.

As Nathan sat down at the kitchen table, he wondered whether Harriet Alistair had found anything worth eating in her bare cupboards. The fact he should find himself worrying about an Alistair, even if it was a woman, made him frown.

"Were you able to buy the land?" Katoya asked as she poured coffee into his cup.

Nathan had learned better than to try to keep secrets from the old Indian woman. "Harry Alistair wouldn't sell," he admitted brusquely.

The diminutive Blackfoot woman merely nodded. "And so the feud will go on." She seated herself in a rocker in the kitchen that was positioned to get the most heat from the old-fashioned wood stove.

Nathan grimaced. "Yeah."

"Is it so important to own the land?"

Nathan turned to face her and saw skin stretched tight with age over high, wide cheekbones, and black hair threaded with silver in two braids over her shoulders. He suddenly wondered how old she was. Certainly she had clung to the old Blackfoot ways. "It must be the Indian in you," he said at last, "that doesn't feel the same need as I do to possess land."

Katoya looked back at him with eyes that were a deep black well of wisdom. "The Indian knows what the white man has never learned. You cannot own the land. You can only use it for so long as you walk the earth.''

Katoya started the rocker moving, and its creak made a familiar, comforting sound as Nathan ate the hot lamb stew she had prepared for him.

Nathan had to admit there was a lot to be said for the old woman's argument. Why was he so determined to own that piece of Alistair land? After all, when he was gone, who would know or care? Maybe he could have accepted Katoya's point of view if he hadn't met Harry Alistair first. Now he couldn't leave things the way they stood. That piece of land smack in the middle of his spread had always been a burr under the saddle. He didn't intend to stop bucking until the situation was remedied.

Nathan refilled his own coffee cup to keep the old woman from having to get up again, then settled down into the kitchen chair with his legs stretched out toward the stove. Because he respected Katoya's advice, Nathan found himself explaining the situation. ''The Harry Alistair who inherited the land from Cyrus turned out to be a woman, Harry-et Alistair. She's greener than buffalo grass in spring and doesn't know a thing about sheep that hasn't come out of an extension service bulletin. Harry-et Alistair hasn't got a snowball's chance in hell of making a go of Cyrus's place. But I never saw a woman so determined, so stubborn...''

''You admire her,'' Katoya said.

''I don't... Yes, I do,'' he admitted with a disbelieving shake of his head. Nathan kept his face averted from the Indian woman as he continued, ''But

I can't imagine why. She's setting herself up for a fall. I just hate to see her have to take it.''

"We always have choices. Is there truly nothing that can be done?''

"Are you suggesting I offer to help her out?'' Nathan demanded incredulously. "Because I won't. I'm not going to volunteer a shoulder to cry on, let alone one to carry a yoke. I've learned my lessons well,'' he said bitterly. "I'm not going to let that woman get under my skin.''

"Perhaps it is too late. Perhaps you already care for her. Perhaps you will have no choice in the matter.''

Nathan's jaw flexed as he ground his teeth. The Indian woman was more perceptive than was comfortable. How could he explain to her the feeling of possessiveness, of protectiveness that had arisen the moment he'd seen Harry-et Alistair. He didn't understand it himself. Hell, yes, he already cared about Harry-et Alistair. And that worried the dickens out of him. What if he succumbed to her allure? What if he ended up getting involved with her, deeply, emotionally involved with her, and it turned out she needed more than he could give? He knew what it meant to have someone solely dependent upon him, to have someone rely upon him for everything, and to know that no matter how much he did it wouldn't be enough. Nathan couldn't stand the pain of that kind of relationship again.

"You must face the truth,'' Katoya said. "What will be must be.''

The old woman's philosophy was simple but irrefutable. "All right,'' Nathan said. "I'll go see her again tomorrow morning. But that doesn't mean I'm going to get involved in her life.''

Nathan repeated that litany until he fell asleep, where he dreamed of a woman with freckles and braids and bibbed overalls who kissed with a passion that had made his pulse race and his body throb. He woke up hard and hungry. He didn't shave, didn't eat, simply pulled on jeans, boots, shirt, hat and coat and slammed out the door.

When he arrived at the Alistair place, it was deathly quiet. There was no smoke coming from the stone chimney, no sounds from the barn, or from the tiny, dilapidated cabin.

Something's wrong!

Nathan thrust the pickup truck door open and hit the ground running for the cabin. His heart was in his throat, his breath hard to catch because his chest was constricted.

Let her be all right, he prayed. *I promise I'll help if only she's all right!*

The kitchen door not only wasn't locked, it wasn't even closed. Nathan shoved it open and roared at the top of his voice, "Harry-et! Are you in here? Harry-et!''

That was when he saw her. She was sitting on the floor, in the corner, with a lamb clutched to her chest, her eyes wide with terror at the sight of him. He was so relieved, and so angry that she had frightened him for nothing, that he raced over, grabbed her by the shoulders and hauled her to her feet.

"What the hell do you think you're doing, leaving the back door standing wide open? You'll catch your death of cold," he yelled, giving her shoulders a shake to make his point. "Of all the stupid, idiotic, greenhorn—"

And then it dawned on him what he was doing, and he let her go as abruptly as he'd grabbed her. She backed up to the wall and stood there, staring at him.

Harry Alistair had a death grip on the lamb in her arms. There were dark circles under her eyes, which were wide and liquid with tears that hadn't yet spilled. Her whole body was trembling with fatigue and the aftereffects of the shaking Nathan had given her. Her mouth was working but the words weren't coming out in much more than a whisper.

Nathan leaned closer to hear what she was trying to say.

"Get out," she rasped. And then, stronger, "Get out of my house."

Nathan felt his heart miss a thump. "I'm sorry. Look, I only came over—"

Her chin came up. "I don't care why you came. I want you to leave. And don't come back."

Nathan's lips pressed flat. *What will be must be.* It was just as well things had turned out this way. It would have been a mistake to try to help her, anyway. But there was a part of him that died inside at the thought of not seeing her again. He wanted her. More than he had ever wanted another woman in his life. But she was all wrong for him. She needed the kind of caretaking he had sworn he was through with forever.

It took every bit of grit he had to turn on his booted heel and walk out of the room. And out of her life.

Three

What is accepted dress-for-success garb for country women?

Answer: Coveralls, scabby work shoes, holey hat and shredded gloves.

I am not a failure. I can do anything I set my mind to do. I will succeed.

Over the next two months there were many times when Harry wanted to give up. Often, it was only the repetition of those three sentences that kept her going. For, no matter how hard she tried, things always went awry. She had been forced to learn some hard lessons, and learn them fast.

About a week after the majority of the lambs had been born most of them got sick. Harry called in the vet, who diagnosed lamb scours and prescribed antibiotics. Despite her efforts a dozen more lambs died. She stacked them under the tarp beside the barn.

Early on the lambs had to have their tails docked, and the ram lambs, except those valuable enough to be sires, had to be castrated. Several of the older brochures described cutting off the lamb tails with a knife and searing the stump with a hot iron. Castration was described even more graphically. Faced with such onerous chores, Harry had known she would never make it as a sheepman.

At her lowest moment a brochure, describing a more modern technique for docking and castration, mysteriously arrived in her mailbox. An "elastrator" and rubber bands were placed on the appropriate extremities, which wasted away and dropped off on their own within two to three weeks. She found the process unpleasant, time-consuming work. But with the information provided in the timely brochure, she had succeeded when she might have given up.

Unfortunately Harry also lost several ewes during delivery and found herself with more orphan lambs, which she had learned were called bums, that had to be fed with milk replacer. Bottle-feeding lambs turned out to be surprisingly expensive. She had to dip into the meager financial reserves Cyrus had left in the bank. She would have run out of money except that Harley's Feed Store had been having a sale on milk replacer. That had seemed a little odd to Harry, but a blushing Slim had assured her that he'd ordered too much replacer, and if he didn't sell it cheap, it was just going to sit on the shelf for another year. Cyrus's money had gone farther than she had dared to hope.

It was a month of exhausting days and nights before Harry could wean the lambs to a solid feed of pellet rations. But she had made it. She still had money in the bank, and the lambs had all gotten fed. In fact, Harry was still bottle-feeding some that had been born late in the season. She had forgotten what it was like to get more than four hours of sleep in a row. When there was work to be done, she would repeat those three pithy sentences. They kept her awake and functioning despite what felt very much like battle fatigue. But then, wasn't she engaged in the greatest battle of her life?

By now even a novice like Harry had figured out that in its best days, Cyrus's sheep ranch had been a marginal proposition. With all the neglect over the years, it took every bit of time and attention she had to give simply to keep her head above water. But she was still afloat. And paddling for all she was worth. She hadn't failed. Yet. With a lot of hard work, and more than a little luck, she just might surprise everyone and make a go of Cyrus's ranch.

In the brief moments when Harry wasn't taking care of livestock—she had six laying hens, a rooster, a sow with eight piglets and a milk cow, as well as the sheep to attend—she had thought over her last meeting with Nathan Hazard.

Perhaps if she hadn't been quite so tired the morning he had come to see her, or if he hadn't woken her quite so abruptly, or been quite so upset, she might have been able to listen to what he had to say. If he had offered help, she might have accepted. She would never know for sure. Harry hadn't seen hide nor hair of him since.

Nor had anyone else come to visit. She had made

a number of phone calls to John Wilkinson at the
bank for advice, and had managed to get a few more
tidbits of information from Slim every time she made
a trip to Harley's Feed Store. But, quite frankly, Harry
was beginning to feel the effects of the extreme iso-
lation in which she had been living for the past two
months.

Which was probably why she hadn't argued more
when her mother, father and brother had said they
were coming out to Montana to visit her. Unfortunately, with the time it had taken her to finish her
chores this morning, she only had about fifteen
minutes left to put herself together before she had to
meet them at The Grand, the bed-and-breakfast in Big
Timber where they were staying.

The varnished wooden booths that lined one wall
of the luncheon dining room at The Grand had backs
high enough to conceal the occupants and give them
privacy. Thus, it wasn't until Nathan heard her exu-
berant greeting that he realized who was soon to occupy the next booth.

"Mom, Dad, Charlie, it's so good to see you!"
Harry said.

"I'm sorry I can't say the same, darling," an uppi-
ty-sounding woman replied in a dismayed voice.
"You look simply awful. What have you done to
yourself? And what on earth is that you have on your
head?"

Nathan smiled at the thought of Harry-et in her
Harley's Feed Store cap.

A young man joined in with, "For Pete's sake,
Harriet! Are you really wearing bibbed overalls?"

Nathan grinned. Very likely she was.

Before Harry had a chance to respond, an older man's bass voice contributed, "I knew I should have put my foot down. I didn't think you could manage on your own in this godforsaken place. And from the look of you, I wasn't wrong. When are you coming home?"

Nathan listened for Harriet's answer to that last question with bated breath.

There was a long pause before she answered, "I am home. And I have no intention of going back to Williamsburg, if that's what you're asking, Dad."

Nathan took advantage of the stunned silence that followed her pronouncement to take a quick swallow of coffee. He knew he ought not to eavesdrop on the Alistairs, but it wasn't as though he had come here with that thought in mind. He'd been minding his own business when *they'd* interrupted *him*. He signaled Dora Mae for a refill of his coffee and settled back to relax for a few minutes after lunch as was his custom. He didn't listen, exactly, but he couldn't help but hear what was being said.

"I've been to see John Wilkinson at the bank," her father began. "And he—"

"Dad! You had no right—"

"I have every right," he interrupted. "I'm your father. I—"

"In case you haven't noticed, I'm not a child anymore," Harry interrupted right back. "I can take of myself."

"Darling," her mother said soothingly, "take a good, close look at yourself. There are dark circles under your eyes, your fingernails are chipped and broken and those awful clothes you're wearing are filthy. All I can conclude is that you're not taking good care of yourself. Your father and I only want the best for you. It hurts us to think of you suffering like this for nothing when in the end you'll only fail.''

"I'm *not* suffering!" Harry protested. "And I will *not* fail. In fact, I'm doing just fine." That might have been an overstatement, but it was in a good cause.

"Fine?" her father questioned. "You can't possibly know enough about sheep ranching to succeed on your own. Why, even ranchers who know what they're doing sometimes fail."

"Dad..."

Nathan heard the fatigue and frustration in Harryet's voice. Her father shouldn't be allowed to browbeat her like that. Nathan ignored the Western code that admonished him not to interfere, in favor of the one that said a woman must always be protected. A moment later he was standing beside the next booth.

Harry was explaining, "I know what I'm doing, Dad. I've been reading all the brochures I can find about sheep ranching—"

"And she's had help from her neighbors whenever she ran into trouble," Nathan finished. A charming smile lit his face as he tipped his hat to Mrs. Alistair and said, "Howdy, ma'am. I'm Nathan Hazard, a neighbor of your daughter's."

Nathan bypassed Harry's stunned expression and turned an assessing gaze to her father and brother. "I couldn't help overhearing you, sir," he said to Harry's father. "And I just want to say that we've all been keeping an eye on Harry-et to make sure—"

"You've been what?"

Nathan turned to Harry, who had risen from her seat and was staring at him with her eyes wide and her mouth hanging open in horror.

"I was just saying that we've been keeping a neighborly eye on you." Before Harry could respond he had turned back to her father and continued, "You see, sir, we have a great deal of respect for women out here, and there isn't a soul in the valley who would stand by if he thought Harry-et was in any real trouble.

"Of course, you're right that she probably won't be able to make a go of Cyrus Alistair's place. But then it's doubtful whether anyone could. That's why I've offered to buy the place from her. And I have every hope that once she's gotten over the silly notion that—"

"Don't say another word!" Harry was so hot she could have melted icicles in January. She hung on to her temper long enough to say, "Mom, Dad, Charles, I hope you'll excuse us. I have a few words to say to Mr. Hazard. Alone."

Harry turned and stalked out to the front lobby of The Grand without waiting to see whether Nathan followed her. After tipping his hat once more to Mrs. Alistair, he did.

Just as Harry turned and opened her mouth to speak, Nathan took her by the elbow and started upstairs with her.

"Where do you think you're going?" Harry snapped, tugging frantically against his hold.

"Upstairs."

"There are *bedrooms* upstairs!"

"Yep. Sarah keeps all the doors open to show off

her fancy antiques. We can use one of the rooms for a little privacy." He pulled her into the first open bedroom and shut the door behind them. "Now what's on your mind?"

"What's on my—?" Harry was so furious that she was gasping for air. "How dare you drag me up here—"

"We can go back downstairs and argue. That way everyone in the valley will know your business," he said, reaching for the doorknob.

"Wait!" Harry made the mistake of touching his hand and felt an arc of heat run up her arm. She jerked her hand away and took two steps back from him, only to come up against the edge of the ornate brass bed. She stepped forward again, only to find herself toe-to-toe with Nathan.

"Hold on a minute," she said, trying desperately to regain the upper hand. "How dare you insinuate to my family that I haven't been making it on my own! I most certainly have!"

Nathan shook his head.

"Don't try to deny it!" she retorted. "I haven't seen a soul except Slim Harley for the past two months. Just who, may I ask, has been helping me?"

"Me."

Harry was so stunned that she took a step back. When the backs of her legs hit the bed, she sat down. Her eyes never left Nathan's face, so she saw the flash of guilt in his blue eyes and the tinge of red growing on his cheeks. "You helped me? How?"

Nathan lifted his hat and shoved his fingers through his hair in agitation, then pulled his hat down over his brow again. "Little ways."

"How?"

He cleared his throat and admitted, "Dropped off a brochure once. Broke the ice on your ponds."

That explained some things she had wondered about. She had needed the knowledge the farm brochure had provided, but it wasn't as though he'd come over and helped with the docking and castration of the lambs. And while she had appreciated having the ice broken on her ponds, she could have done that herself. His interference didn't amount to as much as she had feared.

"And I talked Slim into putting his milk replacer on sale," he finished.

That was another matter entirely. Without the sale on milk replacer she'd have run out of money for sure. "You're responsible for that?"

"Wasn't a big deal. He really did order too much."

"Did anybody else get their milk replacer on sale?" she asked in a strained voice.

"No."

Harry's chest hurt. She couldn't breathe. "Why did you bother if you were so certain I'd fail in the end?"

"Thought you'd come to your senses sooner than this," he said gruffly. "Figured there was no sense letting all those lambs starve."

Harry turned to stare out a window draped with antique lace curtains. Her hand gripped the brass bedstead so hard that her knuckles were white. "Did it ever occur to you that I'd rather not have your help? Did it ever occur to you that whether I was going to fail or succeed I would rather do it all by myself?"

Nathan didn't know how to answer her. He willed her to look up at him, but he could tell how she felt even without seeing her face. Her pulse pounded in her throat and her jaw worked as she ground her teeth.

To tell the honest truth, he didn't know why he'd interfered in her life. If he had just left well enough alone, she would probably have quit and gone home a long time ago. Maybe that had something to do with it. Maybe he didn't want her to go away. He still felt the same attraction every time he got anywhere near her. And it was impossible to control his protective instincts whenever she was around. Just look what had happened today.

He reached out to touch her on the shoulder, and she jumped like a scalded cat. Only, when she came up off the bed she ran right flat into him. Instinctively his arms surrounded her.

The only sound in the room was the two of them breathing. Panting, actually, as though they had just run a footrace. Nathan didn't dare move, for fear she would bolt. It felt good holding her. He wanted more. Slowly, ever so slowly, he raised a hand and brushed his knuckles across her cheek. It was so smooth!

She looked up at him then, and he saw her pupils were wide, her eyes dark. Her mouth was slightly open, her lips full. Her eyelids closed as he lowered his mouth to touch hers. He felt the tremor run through her as their lips made contact. Soft. So incredibly soft, and moist.

When he ran his tongue along the edge of her mouth, she groaned. And her mouth opened wider to let him in.

He took his time kissing her, letting his lips learn the touch and taste of her. He felt the tension in her body, felt her resistance even as she succumbed to the desire that flared between them.

Nathan felt the same war within himself that he knew she was fighting. Lord, how he wanted her! And knew he shouldn't! But there was something about her, something about the touch and taste of her, that drew him despite his resolve not to become involved.

When he broke the kiss at last, she leaned her forehead against his chest. All the starch seemed to come out of her. "Why did you do that?" she asked in a whisper.

"I can't explain it myself. I don't want...I don't think we're very well suited to each other." He felt her tense again in his arms. "I don't mean to hurt your feelings. I'm only telling you the truth as I see it."

Harry dropped her hands, which she discovered were clutching either side of Nathan's waist, and stepped away from him. She raised her eyes to meet his steady gaze. "I can't disagree with you. I don't think we're well suited, either. I can't explain..." A rueful smile tilted her mouth up on one side. "You're quite good at kissing. You must have had a lot of practice."

Harry didn't realize she was fishing for information until the words were out of her mouth. She wanted to know if she was only one of many.

"I...uh...don't have much time for this sort of thing," he admitted. "Kissing women. A relationship with a woman, I mean."

"Oh?"

"Haven't had time for years," he blurted.

Harry was fascinated by the red patches that began

at Nathan's throat and worked their way up. But his admission, however much it embarrassed him, gave Harry a reason for their tremendous attraction to each other. "I think I know why this...thing...is so strong between us," Harry said, as though speaking about it could diffuse its power.

This time Nathan said, "Oh?"

"Yes, you see, I haven't had much time for a relationship with a man. That has to be it, don't you agree? We have these normal, primitive urges, and we just naturally—"

"Naturally kiss each other every time we meet?" Nathan said with disbelief.

"Have you got a better explanation?" Harry demanded. Her fists found her hips in a stance that Nathan recognized all too well.

He shrugged. "I can't explain it at all. All I can say is I don't plan to let this happen again."

"Well, that's good to hear," Harry said. "Now that we have that settled, I'm going back downstairs to inform my family that I am managing fine *on my own*. And you will not contradict me. Is that clear?"

"Perfectly."

"Let's go, Mr. Hazard." She opened the door, waited for him to leave, then followed him toward the stairs.

"Wait!" He turned and she collided with his chest. His arms folded around her. The desire flared between them faster than they could stop it. Nathan swore under his breath as he steadied Harry and stepped back away from her.

"I only wanted to say," he said harshly, "that if you plan to stay in the valley, you'd better get your fallow fields planted with some kind of winter forage.''

Harry wrapped her arms around herself as though that would protect her from the feeling roiling inside. ''I'll do that. Is that all?''

He opened his mouth to say something about the stack of dead lambs beside her barn and shut it again. She had already asked Slim Harley what to do about them. He didn't understand why she hadn't buried them yet, but the closed expression on her face didn't encourage any more advice, let alone the offer of help he'd been about to make. ''That's all,'' he said.

Nathan made his way back downstairs to the bar without once looking at Harry again. As he passed her family, he merely tipped his hat, grim-faced, and resumed his seat in the high-backed booth next to theirs.

Harry made quick work of reassuring her family that she was fine, and that she wouldn't be leaving Montana. There was no sound from the next booth. But Harry knew Nathan was there. And that he was listening.

''We'd like to see where you're living,'' her brother said. ''What's it like?''

''Rustic,'' Harry said, her smile reappearing for the first time since she had entered The Grand.

''It sounds charming,'' her mother said.

''That it is,'' Harry said, her sense of humor making her smile broaden. ''I'm afraid I can't invite you out to visit. It's a little small. And it doesn't have much in the way of amenities.''

She heard Nathan snort in the next booth.

''Well, I feel better knowing your neighbors are

keeping an eye on you," her father said. "That Hazard fellow seems a nice enough man."

Harry didn't think that deserved further comment, so she remained silent.

"Are you sure you can handle the financial end of things?" her father asked. "Mr. Wilkinson said you've got a big bill due next month for—"

"I can handle things, Dad," Harry said. "Don't worry."

She watched her father gnaw on his lower lip, then pull at the bushy white mustache that covered his upper lip. "All right, Harriet. If you insist on playing this game out to the bitter end, I suppose we have no choice except to go along—for now. But I think I should warn you, that if you aren't showing some kind of profit by the fall, I'll have to insist that you forget this foolishness and come home before winter sets in."

Harry was mortified to think that Nathan was hearing her father's ultimatum. She was tempted to let his words go without contesting them. That was the sort of passive resistance she had resorted to in the past. But the Harry who had come to Montana had turned over a new leaf. She felt compelled to say, "You're welcome to come and visit in the fall, Dad. I expect you'll be pleasantly surprised at how well I'm doing by then. But don't expect me to leave if I'm not."

Harry allowed her mother to admonish her to take better care of herself before she finally said, "I have to be getting back to the ranch. I've got stock that needs tending."

She rose and hugged her mother, father and brother, wishing things could be different, that she hadn't lived her life by pretending to fail. She would prove she could make it on her own if it was the last thing she did. Harry wished her family a pleasant drive from Big Timber to the airport in Billings, and a safe flight home. "I'll be in touch," she promised.

They would never know the effort it took to summon the confident smile with which she left them. "Things should be less hectic for me later in the summer," she said. "I'll look forward to seeing you then."

She could tell from their anxious faces that they didn't want to leave her in Montana alone. She reassured them the best she could with, "I'm all right, really. A little tired from all the hard work. But I love what I'm doing. It's challenging. And rewarding."

Harry smiled and waved as she left the restaurant. She was out the door before she realized Nathan Hazard had been standing behind her left shoulder the whole time she'd been waving goodbye.

"I'll follow you home," he said.

"Why on earth would you want to do that?"

Nathan looked up at a sky that was dark with storm clouds. "Looks like rain. All those potholes in your road, you could get stuck."

"If I do, Mr. Hazard, I'll dig myself out." Harry indignantly stalked away, but had to yank three or four times on the door to Cyrus's battered pickup before she finally got inside. She spent the entire trip home glaring at Nathan Hazard's pickup in her rearview mirror. He followed her all the way up to the tiny cabin door.

Harry hopped out of the pickup and marched back

to Nathan's truck. He had the window down and his elbow stuck out.

"Rain, huh?" Harry said, looking up as the sun peered through the clouds, creating a glare on his windshield.

"Could have."

"Sheep dip," Harry said succinctly. "I've had it with helpful neighbors. From now on I want you to stay off my property. Stay away from me, and don't do me any more favors!"

"All right, Harry-et," he said with a long-suffering sigh. "We'll do it your way. For a while."

"For good!" Harry snapped back.

It was doubtful Nathan heard her, because he had already turned his pickup around and was headed back down the jouncy dirt road.

Harry kicked at a stone and sent it flying across the barren yard. Yes, the work was hard, and yes, she was tired. But she had loved every minute of the challenge she had set for herself. Before her talk with Nathan Hazard today she had indulged fully in the satisfaction of knowing she had done it all by herself. Darn him! Darn his interference! Darn the man for being such a darn good kisser!

If Nathan Hazard knew what was good for him, he wouldn't show his face around here anytime soon.

Four

What do you do when people drop by to visit and they haven't been invited?
Answer: Serve them coffee.

Harry was standing in the pigpen, slopping the hogs and thinking about Nathan, when she spied a pickup bumping down the dirt road that led to her place. At first she feared it was her nemesis and began tensing for another battle with Nathan. But the battered truck wasn't rusted in the right places to be Nathan's. After two months of being left so completely alone, Harry was surprised to have visitors. She couldn't help wondering who had come to see her, and why.

The man who stepped out of the driver's side of the beat-up vehicle was a stranger. Harry stood staring as a beautiful woman dressed in form-fitting jeans and a fleece-lined denim jacket shoved open the passenger door of the truck. The couple exchanged a glance that led Harry to believe they must be married, probably some of her neighbors, finally come to call.

The slight blond woman approached her and said, "Hello, I'm Abigail Dayton. Fish and Wildlife Service."

Harry was dumbfounded. *The woman was a government official!* What on earth was someone from the Fish and Wildlife Service doing here? Her heart caught in her throat, keeping her from responding. Her mind searched furiously for the reason for such a visit. Had she done something wrong? Broken some law? Forgotten to fill out some form? Had she let too many lambs die? Was there a penalty for that?

Harry recognized the instinct to flee and fought it. She had come west to start over, to confront her problems and deal with them. She would have to face this woman and find out what she wanted. Only first she had to get out of the pigpen, which wasn't as easy as it sounded.

Harry finally resorted to climbing over the top of the pen instead of going through the gate, which was wired shut. She heard a rip when her overalls caught on a stray barb, but ignored it as she extended her hand to the Fish and Wildlife agent. When the woman didn't take her hand immediately, Harry realized she was still wearing her work gloves, tore them off and tried again. "I'm Harriet Alistair. People mostly call me Harry."

"It's nice to meet you, Harry," Abigail said. She shook Harry's hand once, then let it go.

Harry turned and looked steadily at the tall, dark-haired, gray-eyed man standing beside Abigail Dayton, until he finally held out a callused hand and said, "I'm Luke Granger, your neighbor to the south. Sorry I haven't been over to see you sooner."

Harry was so glad Luke Granger was just a neighbor and not another government official that she smiled, exposing the tiny space between her teeth, and said, "I've been pretty busy myself. It's good to meet you."

So, one agent, one neighbor. Not related. But still no explanation as to why they had come.

Harry felt a growing discomfort as she watched Luke and Abigail survey her property. It wasn't that they openly displayed disgust or disbelief at what they saw; in fact, they were both careful to keep their expressions neutral. But a tightening of Luke's jaw, and a clenching of Abigail's hand, made their feelings plain. Harry wasn't exactly ashamed of her place. After all, she was hardly responsible for the sad state of repairs. But her stomach turned over when Abigail narrowed her green-eyed gaze on the stack of dead lambs beside the barn that were only partially covered by a black plastic tarp. Harry waited for the official condemnation that was sure to come.

"Have you seen any wolves around here?" Abigail asked.

"Wolves?" That wasn't at all what Harry had been expecting the Fish and Wildlife agent to say. The thought of wolves somewhere on her property was terrifying. "Wolves?" she repeated.

"A renegade timber wolf killed two of Luke's sheep," Abigail continued. "I wondered if you've suffered any wolf depredation on your spread."

"Not that I know of," Harry said. "I didn't even know there were any wolves around here."

"There aren't many," Abigail reassured her. "And there's going to be one less as soon as I can find and capture the renegade that killed Luke's sheep."

Harry watched a strange tension flare between her two visitors at Abigail's pronouncement. Before Harry had time to analyze it further, Abigail asked, "Have you seen any wolf sign at all?"

Harry grimaced and shook her head. "I wouldn't know it if I saw it. But you're welcome to take a look around."

"I think I will if you really don't mind."

Abigail carefully looked the grounds over, with Luke by her side. Harry did her best to keep them headed away from the tiny log cabin. She had already tasted their disapproval once and was reluctant to have them observe the primitive conditions under which she lived. However, before Harry knew it, they were all three standing at her kitchen door; there wasn't much she could do except invite them inside.

Harry felt a flush of embarrassment stain her cheeks when both Luke and Abigail stopped dead just inside the door. The scene that greeted them in the kitchen was pretty much the same one that had greeted Nathan the first time he'd come to visit. Only now there were six lambs sleeping on a blanket wadded in the corner instead of just one. The shambles in Harry's kitchen gave painful evidence of how hard she was struggling to cope with the responsibilities she had assumed on Cyrus Alistair's death. Harry didn't know what to say. What could she say?

Abigail finally broke the looming silence. "I'd love some coffee. Wouldn't you, Luke?"

Grateful for the simple suggestion, Harry urged her company to seat themselves at the kitchen table. While she made coffee, Harry lectured herself about how it didn't really matter what these people thought. The important thing was that she had survived the past two months.

Harry poured three cups of coffee and brought them to the table, then seated herself across from Abigail, who was saying something about how wolves weren't really as bad as people thought, and how their reputation had been exaggerated by all those fairy tales featuring a Big Bad Wolf.

Harry wasn't convinced. She took a sip of the hot, bitter coffee and said, "I've been meaning to learn how to use a rifle in case I had trouble with predators, but—"

Abigail leaped up out of her chair in alarm. "You can't *shoot* a timber wolf! They're an endangered species. They're protected!"

"I'm sorry!" Harry said. "I didn't know." She shook her head in disgust. "There's just so much I don't know!"

Abigail sat back down a little sheepishly. "I'm afraid I tend to get on my high horse whenever the discussion turns to wolves."

Harry ran her fingers aimlessly across the pamphlets and brochures that littered the table, shouting her ignorance of sheep ranching to anyone who cared to notice.

"You really shouldn't leave those dead lambs lying

around, though," Abigail said. "They're liable to attract predators."

Harry chewed on her lower lip. "I know I'm supposed to bury them, but I just can't face the thought of doing it."

"I've got some time right now," Luke said. "Why don't you let me help?"

Harry leaned forward to protest. "But I can't pay—"

"Neighbors don't have to pay each other for lending a helping hand," he said brusquely. A moment later he was out the door.

"You know, I bet there's a really nice man behind that stony face he wears," Harry said as she stared after him.

"I wouldn't know," Abigail said. "I only met him this morning."

"Oh, I thought…" Harry didn't finish her thought, discouraged by the shuttered look on Abigail's face. There was something going on between Luke and Abigail, all right. But if they'd just met, the sparks must have been pretty instantaneous. Just like the desire that had flared between her and Nathan. Harry felt an immediate affinity to the other woman. After all, they had both been attracted to rough-hewn Montana sheepmen.

Abigail rose and took her coffee cup to the sink, and without Harry quite being aware how it happened, Abigail was soon washing the mound of dirty dishes, while Harry dried then and put them away. While they worked, they talked, and Harry found herself confiding to Abigail, "Sometimes I wake up in the morning and I wonder how long it'll take me to get this place into shape, or if I ever will.''

"Why would you want to?" Abigail blurted. "I mean... To be perfectly frank this place needs a lot of work."

Harry's sense of humor got the better of her, and she grinned. "That's an understatement if I ever heard one. This place is a *wreck*."

"So tell me why you're staying," Abigail urged.

"It's a long story."

"I'd like to hear it."

Harry took a deep breath and let it out. "All right."

It was a tremendous relief to Harry to be able to tell someone—someone who had no reason to be judgmental—how she had lived her life. Abigail's interested green eyes and sympathetic oohs and ahs helped Harry relate the various fiascos that littered her past. It wasn't until she started talking about Nathan Hazard that words became really difficult to find.

"At first I was so grateful he was there," Harry said as she explained how Nathan had helped in the birthing of the dead lamb and its twin. "I think that was why I was so angry when it turned out he had only come because he wanted to buy this place from me. I'm determined to manage on my own, but the man keeps popping up when I least expect him. And somehow, every time we've crossed paths, we end up—"

"End up what?"

"Kissing," Harry admitted. "I know that sounds absurd—"

"Not so absurd as you think," Abigail muttered.

"Must be more to these Montana sheepmen then meets the eye," she said with a rueful smile.

"Nathan Hazard is driving me crazy," Harry said. What she didn't add, couldn't find words to explain, was how every time she inevitably ended up in his arms, the fire that rose between them seemed unquenchable. "I wish he would just leave me alone."

That wasn't precisely true. What she wanted was a different kind of attention from Nathan Hazard than she was getting. Something more personal and less professional. But that was too confusing, and much too complicated, to contemplate.

Harry looked around her and was amazed to discover that while she had been talking Abigail had continued doing chores around the kitchen. The dishes were washed, the floor was swept, the counters were clear and the brochures on the table had been separated into neat stacks. Several lambs had woken, and Abigail had matter-of-factly joined Harry on the floor to help her bottle-feed the noisy bums.

"Have you thought about getting a hired hand to help with the heavy work?" Abigail asked.

"Can't afford one," Harry admitted. "Although Mr. Wilkinson at the bank said there's a shepherd who'll keep an eye on my flock once I get it moved onto my federal lease in the mountains for the summer. Anyway, I'm determined to make it on my own."

"That's a laudable goal," Abigail said, "but is it realistic?"

"I thought so," Harry mused. "Since I didn't know a thing about sheep ranching when I arrived in

Montana, I've made my share of mistakes. But I'm learning fast.''

"You don't have to answer if you don't want to," Abigail said, "but why on earth don't you just sell this place—''

"To Nathan Hazard? Don't get me started again. I'll never sell to that man. Nathan Hazard is the meanest, ugliest son of a—''

Harry never got a chance to finish her sentence because Luke arrived at the door and announced, "I've buried those lambs. Anything else you'd like me to do while I'm here?''

"No thanks," Harry said, scrambling to her feet. "We're about finished here." She put the empty nippled Coke bottle on the kitchen counter and said, "I really appreciate your help, Luke.''

"You're welcome, anytime.''

It took a moment for Harry to realize that although Luke was speaking to her, his attention was totally absorbed by the woman still sitting on the floor feeding the last ounce of milk replacer to a hungry lamb. From the look on Luke's face it appeared he would gladly take the lamb's place. Harry had wondered why Luke had come visiting with the Fish and Wildlife agent. Now she had her answer.

Harry was envious of what she saw in Luke Granger's eyes. No man had ever looked at her with such raw hunger, such need.

Unless you counted Nathan Hazard.

Harry watched as Abigail raised her eyes to Luke, a beatific smile on her face, watched as the smile faded, watched as Abigail's eyes assumed the wary look of an animal at bay.

Luke's gray eyes took on a feral gleam; his muscles tensed and coiled in readiness.

The hunter. And the hunted. Harry recognized the relationship because she had felt it herself. With Nathan Hazard.

An instant later Luke reached out a hand and pulled Abigail to her feet. Harry was uncomfortably aware of the frisson of sexual attraction that arced between them as they touched. She observed their cautious movements as Abigail inched past Luke in the tiny kitchen and joined Harry at the sink.

"I suppose Luke and I should get going," Abigail said. "We've got a few more ranchers to ask about wolf sightings before the day's done. I've enjoyed getting to know you, Harry. I wish you luck with your ranch."

"Thanks," Harry said with a smile as she escorted Abigail and Luke back outside. "I need all the luck I can get." She turned to Luke and said, "I hope you'll come back and visit again soon, neighbor."

"Count on it," he replied, tipping his Stetson.

"And I hope you capture that renegade wolf," Harry said to Abigail.

Harry watched as Abigail gave Luke a determined, almost defiant, look and said, "Count on it."

Abigail had trouble getting the passenger door of the pickup open, and Harry was just about to lend a hand when Luke stepped up and yanked it free. Abigail frowned at him and said, "I could have done that."

He shrugged. "Never said you couldn't." But he waited for her to get inside and closed the door snugly behind her before heading around to the driver's side of the truck.

"So long," Harry shouted after them as they drove away. "Careful on that road. It's a little bumpy!" A perfect farewell, Harry thought with an ironic twist of her mouth, seeing as how this had been a day for understatement.

Harry felt sorry to see them leave. She was probably being unnecessarily stubborn about trying to manage all by herself. Nathan Hazard was convinced she couldn't manage on her own. She could take advantage of Luke's offer of help and avoid making any more costly mistakes. But the whole purpose of coming to Montana, of putting herself in this isolated position, was to prove that she could do anything she set her mind to do *on her own*. She wasn't the person she had led her parents to believe she was. Harry had realized over the past two months that she wanted to prove that fact to herself even more than she wanted to prove it to them.

It would be too easy to stop resisting Nathan Hazard's interference in her business. Harry reminded herself that Nathan didn't really want her to succeed; he wanted Cyrus's land. And he wanted to take care of her, as one would care for someone incapable of taking care of herself. Letting Nathan Hazard into her life right now would be disastrous. Because Harry didn't want any more people taking care of her; she wanted to prove she could take care of herself.

Harry had another motive for wanting to keep Nathan at a distance. Whenever he was around she succumbed to the attraction she felt for him. At a time when she was trying to take control of her life, the feelings she had for Nathan Hazard were uncontrollable. She wanted to touch him, and have him touch her, to kiss him and be kissed back with all the passion she felt whenever he held her in his arms, to share with him and to have him share the feelings she was hard put to name, but couldn't deny. Those powerful emotions left her feeling threatened in a way she couldn't explain. It was far better, Harry decided, to keep the man at a distance.

The next time Nathan Hazard came calling, if there was a next time, he wouldn't be welcome.

Harry woke the next day to the clang of metal on metal. She bolted upright in bed, then sat unmoving while she tried to place the sound. She couldn't, and quickly pulled on a heavy flannel robe and stepped into ice-cold slippers as she headed for the window to look outside. Her jaw dropped at what she saw. Nathan Hazard stood bare-chested, wrench in hand, working on the engine of Cyrus's farm tractor.

Her first thought was, he must be freezing to death! Then she looked at the angle of the sun and realized it had to be nearly midday and would be much warmer outside than in the cabin, which held the cold. How had she slept so long? The lambs usually woke her at dawn to be fed. She hurried to the kitchen, and they were all there—sleeping peacefully. A quick glance at the kitchen counter revealed several empty nippled Coke bottles. Nathan Hazard had been inside her house this morning! He had fed her lambs!

Harry felt outraged at Nathan's presumption. And then she had another, even more disturbing thought. Had he come into her bedroom? Had he seen her sleeping? She blushed at the thought of what she must have looked like. She had worn only a plain white torn T-shirt to sleep in Cyrus's sleigh bed. Harry was disgusted with herself when she realized that what upset her most was the thought that she couldn't have looked very attractive.

It took three shakes of a lamb's tail for Harry to dress in jeans, blue work shirt and boots. She stomped all the way from her kitchen door to the barn, where the tractor stood. Nathan had to hear her coming, but he never moved from his stance bent over concentrating on some part of the tractor's innards.

"Good morning!" she snarled.

Slowly, as though it were the most ordinary thing in the world for him to be working on her tractor, he straightened. "Good afternoon," he corrected.

Harry caught her breath at the sight of him. She didn't see the whole man, just perceptions of him. A bead of sweat slid slowly down the crease in his muscular chest to dampen the waist of his jeans. Only the waist wasn't at his waist. His jeans had slid down over his hips to reveal a navel and a line of downy blond hair that disappeared from sight under the denim; she didn't see any sign of underwear. The placket over the zipper was worn white with age. When she realized where she was staring, Harry jerked her head up to look at his face and noticed that a stubble of beard shadowed his jaws and chin. Hanks of white-blond hair were tousled over his forehead. And his shockingly bright blue eyes were focused on her as though she were a lamb chop and he were a starving man.

Harry's mouth went dry. She slicked her tongue

over her lips and saw the resulting spark of heat in
Nathan's gaze. His nostrils flared, and she felt her
body tighten with anticipation. The hunter. Its prey.
The scene was set.

Only Harry had no intention of becoming a sacri-
ficial lamb to this particular wolf.

"Don't you know how to knock?" she demanded.

It might have seemed an odd question, but Nathan
knew what she was asking. "I did knock. You didn't
answer. I was worried, so I came inside."

"And fed my lambs!" Harry said indignantly.

"Yes. I fed them."

"Why didn't you come wake me up?"

Nathan had learned enough about Harry-et Alistair's pride to know he couldn't tell her the truth. She
had looked tired. More than tired, exhausted. He had
figured she could use the sleep. So he had fed her
lambs. Was that so bad? Obviously Harry-et thought
so.

But her need for sleep wasn't the only reason he
hadn't woken her. When Nathan had entered Harry-
et's bedroom, she was lying on her side, with one
long, bare, elegantly slender leg curled up outside the
blankets. The tiny bikini panties she'd been wearing
had revealed a great expanse of hip, as well. Her long
brown hair was spread across the pillow in abandon.
One breast was pushed up by the arm she was lying
on, and he had seen a dark nipple through the thin
cotton T-shirt she was wearing. Not that he'd looked
on purpose. Or very long. In fact, once he'd realized
the full extent of her dishevelment, he had backed out
of the room so fast he'd almost tripped over her work

boots that lay where they'd fallen when she had taken them off the previous night.

He had wanted to wake her more than she would ever know. He had wanted to take her in his arms and feel her nipples against his bare chest. He had wanted to wrap those long, luscious legs around himself and... No, she was damn lucky he hadn't woken her. But he could never tell her that. Instead he said, "Anybody offered me another hour or two of sleep, I'd be grateful."

Harry sputtered, unable to think of an appropriate retort. She *was* grateful for the sleep. She just didn't like the way she'd gotten it. "What are you doing to this tractor?"

"Fixing it."

"I didn't know it was broken."

"Neither did I until I tried starting it up."

"Why would you want to start it up?"

Nathan leaned back over and began tinkering again, so he wouldn't have to look her in the eye when he said, "So I could plow your fallow fields."

"So you could..." Harry was flabbergasted. "I thought you were too busy doing your own work to lend me a hand."

Nathan stood and leaned a hip against the tractor while he wiped his hands on his chambray work shirt. "I had a visit yesterday from a good friend of mine, Luke Granger. He was with an agent of the Fish and Wildlife Service, Abigail—"

"They were here yesterday. So?"

"Luke pointed out to me that I haven't been a very good neighbor."

Harry felt her stomach churn. "What else did he have to say?"

"That was enough, don't you think?"

Harry met Nathan's solemn gaze and found it even more unsettling than the heat that had so recently been there.

Nathan never took his eyes off her when he added, "I think maybe I've been a little pigheaded about helping you out. On the other hand, Harry-et, I can't help thinking—"

The blaring honk of a truck horn interrupted Nathan. A battered pickup was wending its way up the rutted dirt road.

Harry recognized Luke Granger and Abigail Dayton. "I wonder what they're doing back here today?"

"I invited them."

Harry whirled to face Nathan. "You what?"

"I called Luke this morning to see if he could spare a little time to do some repairs around here." He took a look around the dilapidated buildings and added, "There's plenty here for both of us to do."

"You all got together and figured I needed help, so here you are riding to the rescue like cowboys in white hats," Harry said bitterly. "Darn. Oh, darn, darn, darn." Harry fisted her hands and placed them on her hips to keep from hauling off and hitting Nathan. She clamped her teeth tight to keep her chin from quivering. She wanted to scream and rant and rave. And she was more than a little afraid she was going to cry.

Nathan couldn't understand what all the fuss was about. In all the years he had been offering help to others, the usual response had been a quick and ready acceptance of his assistance. This woman was totally different. She seemed to resent his support. He found her reaction bewildering. And not a little frustrating. He should have been glad she didn't need his help. He should have been glad she didn't need any caretaking. But he found himself wanting to help, needing to help. Her rejection hurt in ways he wasn't willing to acknowledge. He turned and began working on the tractor again, keeping his hands busy to keep from grabbing Harry and kissing some sense into her.

"Hello, there," Luke said as he and Abigail approached the other couple.

"Hello," Harry muttered through clenched teeth. Her angry eyes remained on Nathan.

Nathan never looked up. "I ran into a little problem, Luke. The tractor needs some work before I can do anything about those fallow fields."

"Anything I can do?" Luke asked Nathan.

Harry whirled on him and said, "You can turn that truck around and drive right back out of here."

"We just want to help," Abigail said quietly.

"I don't need your charity," Harry cried in an anguished voice. "I don't need—"

Nathan suddenly dropped his wrench on the engine with a clatter and grabbed Harry by the arms, forcing her to face him. "That'll be enough of that!"

"Just who do you think you are?" Harry rasped. "I didn't ask you to come here. I didn't ask you to—"

"I'm doing what a good neighbor should do."

"Right! Where was all this neighborliness when I had lambs dying because I didn't know how to deliver them? Where was all this friendly help when I really needed it?''

"You need it right now," Nathan retorted, his grip tightening. "And I intend to give it to you."

"Over my dead body!" Harry shouted.

"Be reasonable," Nathan said in a voice that was losing its calm. "You need help."

"I don't need it from you," Harry replied stubbornly.

"Maybe you'd let us help," Abigail said, stepping forward to place a comforting hand on Harry's arm.

Harry's shoulders suddenly slumped, all the fight gone out of her. Maybe she should just take their help. Maybe her parents had been right all along. She bit her quivering lower lip and closed her eyes to hold back the threatening tears.

But some spark inside Harry refused to be quenched by the dose of reality she'd just suffered. She could give up, and give in, as she had in the past. Or she could fight. Her shoulders came up again, and when her eyes opened, they focused on Nathan Hazard, flashing with defiance. "I want you off my property, Nathan Hazard. Now. I..." Her voice caught in an angry sob, but her jaw stiffened. "I have things to do inside. I expect you can see yourself off my land."

Harry turned and marched toward the tiny log house without a single look back to see if he had obeyed her command.

Five

What do you say when asked, "How's it going?"
Answer: "Oh, could be worse. Could be better."

Nathan spent the rest of the afternoon working outside with Luke, while Abigail worked in and around
the barn with a still-seething Harry. Luke and Abigail
left just before sundown, knowing Harry's fallow
fields were plowed and planted and that the pigpen
gate, among other things, had been repaired. Nathan
worked another quarter hour before admitting there
wasn't enough light to continue. He pulled on the
chambray shirt he'd been using for an oil rag and
headed toward the only light on in Cyrus's log cabin.

He knocked at Harry's kitchen door, but didn't wait
for an answer before he pushed the screen door open
and stepped inside. Harry was standing at the sink

rinsing out Coke bottles. She turned when she saw him, grabbed a towel from the counter and wiped her hands dry. She stood backed up against the sink, waiting, wary.

"I'm sorry." Nathan hadn't said those two words very often in his lifetime, and they stuck in his craw.

It didn't help when Harry retorted, "You should be!"

"Now look here, Harry-et—"

"No, *you* look here, Nathan," she interrupted. "I thought I'd made it plain to you that I didn't want your help. At least not the way you're offering it. I wouldn't mind so much if you wanted to teach me how to run this place. But you seem bound and determined to treat me like the worst sort of tenderfoot, which I am—a tenderfoot, I mean. But not the worst sort. Oh, this isn't making any sense!"

Harry was so upset that she gulped air, and she trembled as though she had the ague. Nathan took a step toward her, wanting to comfort her, but stopped when she stuck out a flat palm.

"Wait. I'm not finished talking. I don't know how to make it any plainer. I don't want the sort of help you're offering, Nathan."

Nathan opened his mouth to offer her the kind of help she was asking for and snapped it shut. Even if he taught her what she wanted to know, she would be hard-pressed to make a go of this place by herself. And if, by some miracle, she did succeed, he would only be stuck with another Alistair planted square in the middle of Hazard land.

"All right, Harry-et," he said, "I'll stop trying to help."

Her shoulders sagged, and he wasn't sure if she was relieved or disappointed. Neither reaction pleased him. So he said, "I think maybe what we ought to do is call a truce."

"A truce?"

"Yeah. You know, raise the white flag. Stop fighting. Call a halt to hostilities." He tried a smile of encouragement. It wasn't his best, but apparently it was good enough, because she smiled back.

"All right," she agreed. "Shall we shake on it?"

She stuck her hand out and, like a fool, he took it. And suffered the consequences. Touching her was like shooting off fireworks on the Fourth of July. He liked what he felt. Too much. So he dropped her hand and turned to leave. Before he even got to the door he had turned back—he didn't have the faintest idea why—and caught her looking bereft. The words were out of his mouth before he could stop them. "What would you say to a dinner to celebrate our truce?" She looked doubtfully around her kitchen, and he quickly added, "I meant dinner out."

"A date?"

"Not a date," he quickly reassured her. "Just a dinner between two neighbors who've agreed to make peace."

"All right."

It was the most reluctant acceptance he'd ever heard. Nathan figured he'd better get the plans finalized and get out of here before she changed her mind. "I'll pick you up at eight. Dress up fancy."

"Fancy?"

"Sure. Something soft and ladylike. You have a dress like that, don't you?" He hadn't realized how much he wanted to see her in a dress, so he could admire those long legs of hers again.

"Where is this dinner going to be?" she asked suspiciously.

"Have you ever been to the hot springs at Chico?"

"No. Where is that?"

"About an hour south. Best lamb chops in two counties." He saw her moue of distress and added, "Or you can have beef prime ribs if you'd rather."

She smiled, and he felt his heart beat faster at the shy pleasure revealed in the slight curl of her lips.

"All right. I'll be ready," she said.

Nathan left in a hurry before he did something really stupid, like take her in his arms and kiss that wide, soft mouth of hers and run his hands all over her body. He had it bad, all right. The worst. The woman was under his skin and there was no denying it.

Nathan drove home so fast that his head hit the top of the pickup twice on his way down Harry-et's road. He showered and shaved and daubed some manly-smelling, female-alluring scent on himself in record time. He donned a sandy-colored, tailored western suit that hugged him across the shoulders like a second skin and added snakeskin boots and a buff felt cowboy hat.

Nathan wasn't conscious of how carefully he had dressed until Katoya stopped him at the bottom of the stairs and said, "You are going hunting."

"I'm not exactly dressed for bear."

"Not for bear. For dear. One dear," the old woman clarified with a cackle of glee.

Nathan grimaced. "Is it that obvious?"

"Noticeable, yes. As a wolf among sheep."

He started back up the stairs again. "I'll change."

"It will do no good."

Nathan walked back down to her. "Why not?"

"Even if you change the outer trappings, she will know what you feel."

"How?" he demanded.

"She will see it in your eyes. They shine with excitement. And with hunger."

Nathan looked down at his fisted hands so that his lids would veil what the old woman had seen. "I want her," he said. He looked up, and there was a plea in his eyes he didn't know was there. "I know I'm asking for trouble. She's all wrong for me. But I can't seem to stop myself."

"Maybe you shouldn't try," Katoya said softly. "Maybe it is time you let go of the past."

"Wish I could," he said. "It isn't easy."

"We do the best we can," the Blackfoot woman said. "Go. Enjoy yourself. What must be will be."

He grabbed the tiny woman and hugged her hard. "You're a wise old woman. I'll do my best to take your advice."

He let her go and hurried out the door, anxious to be on his way. He didn't see the sadness in her eyes as he left or the pain in her step as she headed for the window to watch him drive away in a classic black sports car that spent most of its time in his garage.

For the entire trip to Cyrus's ranch Nathan imagined how wonderful Harry-et would look dressed up. But the reality still exceeded his expectation.

"I can't believe it's you," he said in an awestruck

voice when Harry opened the front door to the cabin. She stepped out, rather than inviting him in, and having seen the broken-down couch and chairs from the 1950s that served as living room furniture, Nathan understood why. But he wouldn't let Harry into his car until he'd taken a good look at her.

"Wait. Turn around."

"Do you like it?" she asked anxiously.

How could he describe how beautiful she looked to him? He didn't think he could find the words. "I love it," he managed.

The dress was a vibrant red and made of material that looked soft to the touch. The skirt was full, so it floated around her. The bodice was fitted, crisscrossing in a V over her breasts, so for the first time he could see just how lovely she was. The chiffonlike material fell off her shoulders, leaving them completely bare, but enticed with a hint of cleavage. She'd taken her hair out of the tomboyish braids, and a mass of rich brown curls draped her bare shoulders, begging to be taken up in his hands. She was wearing high heels that lengthened her already-long legs and brought her eyes almost even with his.

He could see how easy it would be to push the material down from her shoulders, leaving her breasts free to touch and taste. How easy it would be to slip his hands under the full skirt and capture her thighs, pulling her close. That thought pushed him over the edge. He felt himself responding to the wanton images that besieged him while she stood there looking lovely and desirable.

"Get in the car," he said in a voice harsh with the need he was struggling to control.

He hates the dress, Harry thought as she obeyed Nathan's curt order. She'd known the red dress was all wrong for her when she'd bought it two years ago. Too bright. Too sexy. Too sensual. Not at all like the Harriet Alistair of Williamsburg, Virginia. But tonight, when she'd looked into her closet, there it was. And it had seemed exactly right for the bold and daring woman who'd moved to Big Timber, Montana. The one who was attracted to Nathan Hazard.

Apparently Nathan didn't agree.

On the other hand, Harry thought Nathan looked wonderful. His western suit fit him to perfection. The tailoring showed off his broad shoulders and narrow hips, his flat stomach and long legs. Of course, she had never found any fault with the way Nathan looked. Indeed, she had wanted to touch the rippled chest and belly she'd seen this morning. Would Nathan's skin be soft? Or as hard as the muscles that corded his flesh? Harry had even fantasized what Nathan would look like without a stitch on. But she had never seen a naked man, and the only images she could conjure were the marble statues of Greek gods she had seen. And a leaf had always covered the pertinent parts.

Tonight there was a barely leashed power in the way Nathan moved that made Harry want to test the limits of his control. She wanted to touch. She wanted to taste. And she wanted to tempt Nathan to do the same.

Their personal relationship had nothing to do with the land, Harry told herself. It was separate and apart from that. She could desire Nathan without compromising her stand, because they were in the midst of a truce. So when she sat down in Nathan's sports car, she let her skirt slip halfway up her thighs before pulling it back down, and leaned toward Nathan so that her breast brushed against his arm.

He inhaled sharply.

Harry looked at him, stunned by the flood of desire in his eyes. And began to reevaluate Nathan's reaction to her red dress.

Nathan didn't leave her in doubt another moment. He leaned over slowly but surely until their mouths were nearly touching and said, "Don't do that again unless you mean it."

Harry shivered and made a little noise in her throat.

Nathan groaned as his lips covered hers and sipped the nectar there. Her mouth was soft and oh, so sweet, and his body tightened like a bowstring with need. His tongue found the edge of her lips and followed it until she opened her mouth and his tongue slipped inside. He mimed the stroke of their two bodies joined and heard her moan. He reached up a hand to cup her breast and felt the weight of it in his hand. His thumb stroked across the tip, and he realized it had already tightened into a tiny nub. His hand followed the shape of her, from her ribs to her waist and down her thigh to the hem of her skirt, where Harry caught his wrist and stopped him.

Abruptly Nathan lifted his mouth from hers. Damn if she didn't have him as hot and bothered as a high school kid! And she'd stopped him as if she were some teenage virgin who'd never done it before. On the other hand, though he felt like a kid, he wasn't one. The small car was damn close for comfort. He could wait. Before the night was through he'd know what it was like to hold her in his arms, and feel himself inside her. She wanted it. And so did he.

"All right, Ms. Alistair," he said through gritted teeth. "We'll do this your way."

Nathan started the car, made a spinning turn and, in deference to his delicate suspension, headed at a slow crawl back down the bumpy dirt road toward the main highway and Chico.

Harry was stunned. How had one kiss turned into so much so fast? She hadn't wanted to stop Nathan. But things were moving too quickly. She didn't want the first time to be in the front seat of a car. They both deserved more than that.

Nathan was on the verge of suggesting they forget dinner and go back to his place. But from the nervous fidgeting Harry was doing, that probably wasn't a good idea. He figured he'd better say something quick before he said what was really on his mind. So he cleared his throat of the last remnants of passion and asked, "What was your life like before you came to Montana?"

"Overprotected."

Nathan glanced briefly at Harry-et to see if she was kidding. She wasn't. "I guess I saw a little of that when your parents were here. They sure don't think you can make a go of Cyrus's ranch, do they?"

"That isn't their fault," Harry said, coming to their defense. "I wasn't exactly what you'd call a roaring success when I lived in Williamsburg."

"What were you, exactly?"

Harry paused for a moment before she admitted, "I had several occupations, but I wasn't interested in any of them. I managed to do poorly at them, so I could get fired.''

''Why did you take the jobs in the first place if you weren't interested in them?''

''Because I couldn't say no to my father.''

Nathan snorted. ''You haven't had any trouble saying no to me.''

''I turned over a new leaf when I came to Montana,'' Harry said with an impish smile. ''I made up my mind to do what I wanted to do, my way.'' Her expression became earnest. ''That's why I was so upset by your interference. Don't you see? I wanted to prove to my family, and to myself, that I could succeed at something on my own.''

''I'm sorry I butted in,'' Nathan said curtly.

Harry put a hand on Nathan's arm and felt him tense beneath her fingertips. ''How could you know? Now that we've called this truce, things will be better, I'm sure. What about you? Did you always want to be a sheep rancher?''

''No. Actually, I had plans to be an architect once upon a time.''

''What happened?''

Nathan glanced at Harry and was surprised by the concerned look on her face. He hardened himself against the growing emotional attachment he felt to her. ''Things got in the way.''

''What kind of things?''

''Parents.''

''You weren't overprotected, too, were you?''

''Not hardly. I was the one who did the protecting in my household.''

Harry was stunned by the bitterness in his voice.

"I don't understand. Are you saying you took care of your parents? Were they hurt or something?"

"Yes, and yes."

But he didn't say any more. Harry wasn't sure whether to press him for details. His lips had flattened into a grim line, and the memories obviously weren't happy ones. But her curiosity got the better of her and she asked, "Will you tell me about it?"

At first she thought he wasn't going to speak. Then the words started coming, and the bitterness and anger and regret and sadness poured out along with them.

"My mother was an alcoholic," he said. "I didn't know her very well. But I took care of her the best I could. Dumped the bottles when I found them. Cleaned up when I could. Made meals for me and my dad. She didn't eat much. The alcohol finally killed her when I was sixteen.

"It was a relief," he said in a voice that grated with pain. "I was glad she was gone. She was an embarrassment. She was a lush. I hated her." Harry watched him swallow hard and add in a soft voice, "And I loved her so much I would have died in her place."

Harry felt a lump in her own throat and tears burning her eyes. What a heavy burden for a child!

"My father and I missed her when she was gone. Dad wanted me to stay on the ranch—Hazards had been sheep ranchers for a hundred years—but I wanted to be an architect. So I went away to college despite his wishes and learned to design buildings to celebrate the spirit of life.

"The month I graduated my father had an accident. A tractor turned over on him and crippled him. I came home to take over for him. And to take care of him. That was fifteen years ago. He died two years ago an old man. He was fifty-eight.''

"Did you ever have the opportunity to design anything?''

"I designed and built the house I live in now. I haven't had time to do more than that.''

She could hear the pride in his voice. And the disappointment. "I'm sorry.''

"Don't pity me. I've had a good life. Better than most.''

"But it wasn't the life you had planned for yourself. What about a wife? Didn't you ever want to marry and have children?''

"I was too busy until two years ago to think about anything but making ends meet,'' Nathan said. "Since then I've been looking. But I haven't found the right woman yet.''

Harry heard Nathan's "yet'' loud and clear. Nathan knew her, therefore he must have excluded her from consideration. Which hurt more than she had expected. "What kind of woman are you looking for?''

Nathan didn't pull any punches. "One who can stand on her own. One who can carry her half of the burden. Ranching's a hard life. I can't afford to marry a woman who can't contribute her share to making things work.''

Harry threaded her hands together in her lap. Well, that settled that. She obviously wasn't the kind of woman who could stand on her own two feet. In fact, Nathan had been holding her up for the past two months.

How he must have hated that! Harry thought. He

had taken care of her with concern and consideration, but he had done it because she was someone who was helpless to help herself. Not as though she was an equal. Not as though she was someone who could one day be his partner. How Harry wanted the chance to show Nathan she could manage on her own! Maybe with this truce it would happen. She would continue to learn and grow. As success followed success, he would see her with new eyes. Maybe then…

Harry suddenly realized the implications of what she was thinking. She was thinking of a future that included Nathan Hazard. She pictured little Nathans and Harrys—blue-eyed blondes and brown-eyed brunettes with freckles. Oh, what a lovely picture it was!

However, a look at Nathan's stern visage wasn't encouraging. He was obviously not picturing the same idyllic scene.

In fact, Nathan was picturing something very similar. And calling himself ten times a fool for doing so. How could he even consider a life with Harry-et Alistair. The woman was a disaster waiting for a place to happen. She didn't know the first thing about ranching. She was a tenderfoot. A city girl. She would never be the kind of partner who could pull her own weight.

Fortunately they had reached the turnoff to the restaurant at Chico. The lag in the conversation wasn't as noticeable because Nathan took the opportunity to fill Harry-et in on the history of Chico. The hotel and restaurant were located at the site of a natural hot spring that now fed into a swimming pool that could be seen from the bar. It had become a hangout for all the movie stars who regularly escaped the bright lights and big city for what was still Montana wilderness. The pool was warm enough that it could be used even when the night was cool, as it was this evening.

Nathan and Harry were a little early for their dinner reservations, so Nathan escorted her into the bar where they could watch the swimmers.

"Would you like to take a dip in the pool?" Nathan asked. "They have suits—"

"Not this time," Harry said. "I don't think—" Harry stopped in midsentence, staring, unable to believe her eyes. She pointed toward the sliding glass doors. "Doesn't that man in the pool look a lot like—"

"Luke," Nathan finished for her. "I think you're right. He seems to be with someone. Maybe they'd like to join us for a drink. I'll go see."

Nathan had grasped at the presence of his friend as though it were a lifeline. He had realized, suddenly and certainly, that it wasn't a good idea to be alone with Harry-et Alistair. The more time he spent with her, the lower his resistance to her. If he wasn't careful, he'd end up letting his heart tell his head what to do. He could use his friend's presence to help him keep his sense of perspective. Of course, knowing Luke, and seeing how cozy he was with the lady, he knew his friend wasn't going to appreciate the interruption. But, hell, what were friends for?

Thus, a moment later he was standing next to Luke and the woman who had her face hidden against his chest. "Hey, Luke, I thought it was you. Who's that with you?"

After a brief pause, Luke answered, "It's Abby."

Nathan searched his memory for any woman he knew by that name. "Abby?"

"Abigail Dayton," Luke bit out.

"From Fish and Wildlife?" Nathan asked, astonished.

Abigail turned at last to face him. "Luke and I are just relaxing a few tired muscles."

Nathan grinned. "Yeah. Sure."

A female voice from the doorway called, "Nathan?"

The light behind Harry made her face nearly invisible in the shadows. At the same time it silhouetted a fantastic figure and a dynamite pair of legs. It irked Nathan that Luke couldn't seem to take his eyes off the woman in the doorway.

"Who's that with you?" Luke asked Nathan.

"Uh…"

"Nathan, is it Luke?" Harry asked. "Oh, hello. It is you. Nathan thought he recognized you."

This time it was Luke who stared, astonished. "Harry? That's Harry?"

Harry grinned. "Sure is. Nathan tried to convince me to take a swim, but I was too chicken. How's the water?" she asked Abigail.

"Marvelous."

"What are you two doing here together?" Luke asked his friend sardonically. "I thought you hated each other's guts."

Nathan stuck a hand in the trouser pocket of his western suit pants to keep from clapping it over his friend's mouth. "We called a truce. Why don't you two dry off and join us for a drink?" he invited.

Nathan could see Luke wasn't too hot on the idea.

But he gave his friend his most beseeching look, and at last Luke said, "Fine."

Luke gave Nathan a penetrating stare, but made no move to leave the pool. Obviously Luke wanted a few more minutes alone with the Fish and Wildlife agent. Nathan turned to Harry-et and suggested, "Why don't we go inside and wait for Luke and Abby."

He took Harry's arm and led her back inside. "You really look beautiful tonight, Harry-et," he said as he seated her at their table.

"Thank you, Nathan." Ever since she'd come outside Nathan had been looking at her a little differently. She'd seen the admiration in Luke's eyes, and watched Nathan stiffen. Really, men could be so funny sometimes. There was no reason for Nathan to be jealous. She didn't find Luke's dark, forbidding looks nearly so attractive as she found Nathan's sharp-boned Nordic features.

She was almost amused when Nathan took her hand possessively once he was seated across from her. He held it palm up in his while his fingertips traced her work-roughened palm and the callused pads of her fingertips.

Harry felt goose bumps rise on her arm. She was all set for a romantic pronouncement when Nathan said, "It's a shame you have to work so hard. A lady like you shouldn't have calluses on her hands."

Harry jerked her hand from his grasp. "I have to work hard."

"No, you don't. Look at you, Harry-et. You spend so much time in the sun your face is as freckled as a six-year-old's."

"Are you finished insulting me?" Harry asked, confused and annoyed by Nathan's behavior.

"I think you ought to sell your place to me and get back to being the beautiful woman—"

Harry's hand came up without her really being aware it had. She slapped Nathan with the full force of the anger and betrayal she was feeling. The noise was lost in the celebration of the busy bar, but it was the only sound Harry heard above the pounding of her heart. "You never wanted a truce at all, did you, Nathan? You just wanted a chance to soften me up and make another plea to buy my land. I can't think of anything lower in this life than a lying, sneaky snake-in-the-grass Hazard!"

"Now just a minute, Harry-et. I—"

She grabbed his keys from the table where he'd set them and stood up. "I'm taking your car. You can pick it up at my place tomorrow. But I don't want to see your sorry face when you do it."

"Be reasonable, Harry-et. How am I supposed to get home?"

"You can ask your friend, Luke, to give you a ride, but I'd be pleased as punch if you have to walk."

"Harry-et—"

"Shut up and listen! You're going to have an Alistair ranching smack in the middle of your land for the rest of your life, Nathan. And you can like or lump it. I don't really care!"

Harry marched out of the bar with her head held high, but she couldn't see a blamed thing through the haze of tears in her eyes. How could she have believed that handsome devil's lies? And worse, oh, far worse, how could she still want a man who only wanted her land?

Nathan stood up to follow her, and then sat back down. That woman was so prickly, so short-tempered, and so stubborn—how on earth could he want her the way he did? It was his own fault for provoking her. But he had been frightened by his possessive feelings when Luke had admired Harry-et. So, perversely, he'd enumerated to her all the reasons why he couldn't possibly be attracted to her, and managed to drive her away in the bargain.

He had to find a way to make peace with the woman. This Hazard-Alistair feud had gone on long enough. There had to be a happy medium somewhere, some middle ground, neither his nor hers, on which they could meet.

Nathan made up his mind to find it.

Six

How should you behave in a Woolly West bar?
Answer: You don't have to behave in a Woolly West
bar.

Over the next three weeks Nathan thought about all
the ways he could end the Hazard-Alistair feud. And
kept coming back to the same one: *He could marry
Harry-et Alistair.* Of course, that solution raised its
own set of problems. Not the least of which was how
he was going to convince Harry-et Alistair to marry
him.

The way Nathan had it figured, marrying Harry-et
would have all kinds of benefits. First of all, once
they were married, there wouldn't be any more Alistair land; it would all be Hazard land. Second, the
feud would necessarily come to an end, since all fu-

ture Hazards would also be Alistairs. And third—and Nathan found this argument for marriage both the most and the least compelling—he would have Harry-et Alistair for his wife.

Although Nathan was undeniably attracted to Harry-et, he wasn't convinced she was the right woman for him. Except every time he thought of a lifetime spent without her, it seemed a bleak existence, indeed. So maybe he was going to have to take care of her more than he would have liked. It wasn't something he hadn't done in the past. He could handle it. He had finally admitted to himself that he was willing to pull ten times the normal load in order to spend his life with Harry-et Alistair.

Only the last time he'd driven onto her place she had met him at the end of her road with a Winchester. He'd had no choice except to leave. He hadn't figured out a way yet to get past that rifle.

Nathan was sitting at his regular booth at The Grand, aimlessly stirring his chicken noodle soup, when Slim Harley came running in looking for him.

"She's done it now!" Slim said, skidding to a stop at Nathan's booth.

"Done what?"

"Lost Cyrus's ranch for sure," Slim said.

Nathan grabbed Slim by his shirt at the throat. "Lost it how? You didn't call in her bill, did you? I told you I was good for it if you needed the cash."

"Weren't me," Slim said, trying to free Nathan's hold without success. "It's John Wilkinson at the bank. Says he can't loan her any money to pay the lease on her government land. Says she ain't a good credit risk."

"Where is she now?"

"At the bank. I just—" Slim found himself talking to thin air as Nathan shoved past him and took off out the door of The Grand, heading for the bank across the street.

When Nathan entered the bank, he saw Harry sitting in front of John Wilkinson's desk. He casually walked over to one of the tellers nearby and started filling out a deposit slip.

"But I've told you I have a trust I can access when I'm thirty," Harry was saying.

"That's still four years off."

Nathan folded the deposit slip in half and stuck it in his back pocket. He meandered over toward John's desk and said, "I couldn't help overhearing. Is there anything I can do to help, Harry-et?"

She glared at him and stared down at her hands, which were threaded tightly together in the lap of her overalls.

"So, John, what's the problem?" Nathan asked, setting a hip on the corner of the banker's oversize desk.

"Don't expect it's any secret," John said. "Mizz Alistair here doesn't have the cash to renew her government lease. And I don't think I can risk the bank's money making her a loan."

"What if I cosign the note?" Nathan asked.

"No!" Harry said, shooting to her feet to confront Nathan. "I don't want to get the money that way. I'd rather lose the ranch first!"

The banker stroked his whiskered chin with a bony hand. "Well, now, sounds like maybe we could work something out here, Mizz Alistair."

"I meant what I said," Harry declared, her chin tilting up mulishly. "I don't want your money if Nathan Hazard has to cosign the note. I'll go to a bank in Billings or Bozeman. I'll—"

"Now hold on a minute. There's no call to take your business elsewhere." John Wilkinson hadn't become president of the Big Timber First National Bank without being a good judge of human nature. What he had here was a man-woman problem, sure as wolves ate sheep. Only both the man and the woman were powerful prideful. The man wanted to help; the woman wanted to do it on her own.

"I might be willing to make that loan to you, Mizz Alistair, if Nathan here would agree to advise you on ranch management till your lamb crop got sold in the fall."

Nathan frowned. Teaching ranch management to Harry-et Alistair was a whole other can of worms from cosigning her note.

"Done," Harry said. She ignored Nathan and stuck out her hand to the banker, who shook it vigorously.

"Now wait a minute," Nathan objected. "I never said—"

"Some problem, Nathan?" the banker asked.

Nathan saw the glow of hope in Harry's eyes, and didn't have the heart to put it out. "Aw, hell, I'll do it."

"I'll expect you over later today," Harry said, throwing a quick grin in Nathan's direction. "I have a problem that needs solving right away." She turned to the banker and added, "I'll pick up that check on Monday, John."

Nathan stood with his mouth hanging open as Harry marched by him and out the door.

"That's quite a woman," the banker said as he stared after her.

"You can say that again," Nathan muttered. "She's Trouble with a capital T."

"Never saw trouble you couldn't handle," the banker said with a confident smile. "Anything else you need, Nathan?"

"No thanks, John. I think you've done quite enough for me today."

"We aim to please, Nathan. We aim to please."

Nathan was still half stunned as he walked out of the bank door and headed back to The Grand. He found Slim sitting at his booth, finishing off his chicken noodle soup.

"Didn't know you was coming back, Nathan," Slim said. "I'll have Dora Mae ladle you up another bowl."

"I'm not hungry."

"What happened?" Slim asked. "Mizz Alistair get her loan?"

"She got it," Nathan snapped. "But it's going to cost me plenty."

"You loan her the money?" Slim asked, confused.

"I loaned her *me*." Nathan sat down and dropped his head into his hands. "I'm the new manager for Cyrus's ranch."

Word spread fast in the Boulder River Valley, and by suppertime it was generally believed that Nathan Hazard must have lost his mind...or his heart. Nathan was sure it was both.

Of course, on the good side, he had Harry-et Alistair exactly where he wanted her. She would have to see him, whether she wanted to or not. He would have a chance to woo her, to convince her they ought to become man and wife. Unfortunately, he still had a job to do—making her ranch profitable—which he took seriously. And Harry-et didn't strike him as the sort of woman who was going to take well to the kind of orders he would necessarily have to give.

Meanwhile, Harry was in hog heaven. She had what she had always wanted—not someone to do it for her, but someone to teach her how to do it herself. Of course, having Nathan Hazard for her ranch manager wasn't a perfect solution. She still had to put up with the man. But once she had learned what she needed to know, she wouldn't let him set foot on her place again.

Harry was especially glad that she had secured Nathan's expertise today, because now that she had the funds to pay the lease on her mountain grazing land, she had another problem that needed to be resolved. So when Nathan arrived shortly after dark, Harry greeted him at her kitchen door with a smile of genuine welcome.

"Come in," she said, gesturing Nathan to a seat at the kitchen table. "I've got some coffee and I just baked a batch of cookies for you."

"They smell great," Nathan said, finding himself suddenly sitting at the table with a cup of coffee and a plateful of chocolate chip cookies in front of him.

Harry fussed over him like a mother hen with one chick until he had no choice except to take a sip of coffee. He had just taken his first bite of cookie, and was feeling pretty good about the way this was turning out, when Harry said, "Now, to get down to business."

With a mouthful of cookie it was difficult to protest.

"The way I see it," Harry began, "I haven't been doing all that badly on my own. All I really need, what I expect from you, is someone I can turn to when I hit a snag."

"Wait a minute," Nathan said through a mouthful of cookie he was trying desperately to swallow. "I think you're underestimating what it takes to run a marginal spread like this in the black."

"I don't think I am," Harry countered. "I'll admit I've made some mistakes, like the one I wanted to see you about tonight." Harry paused and caught her lower lip in her teeth. "I just never thought he'd do such a thing."

"*Who* would do *what* thing?" Nathan demanded.

"My shepherd. I never thought he'd take his wages and go get drunk."

"You paid your shepherd his wages? Before the summer's even begun? Whatever possessed you to do such a thing?"

"He said he needed money for food and supplies," Harry said. "How was I supposed to know—"

"Any idiot could figure out—"

"Maybe an idiot could, but I'm quite intelligent myself. So it never occurred to me!" Harry finished.

"Aw, hell." Nathan slumped back into the chair he hadn't been aware he'd jumped out of.

Harry remained standing across from him, not relaxing an inch.

"So what do you want me to do?" Nathan asked when he thought he could speak without shouting.

"I want you to go down to Whitey's Bar in Big Timber and get him out, then sober him up so he can go to work for me."

"I don't think this is what John Wilkinson had in mind when he suggested I manage your ranch," Nathan said, rubbing a hand across his forehead.

"I would have gone and done it myself if I'd known you were going to make such a big deal out of it," Harry muttered.

Suddenly Nathan was on his feet again. "You stay out of Whitey's. That's no place for a woman."

"I'm not just a woman. I'm a rancher. And I'll go where I have to go."

"Not to Whitey's, you won't."

"Oh, yeah?" she goaded. "Who's going to stop me?"

"I am."

Harry found herself in Nathan's grasp so quickly that she didn't have a chance to escape. She stared up into his blue eyes and saw he'd made up his mind she wasn't going anywhere. She hadn't intended to force a confrontation, yet that was exactly what she'd done. She didn't want Nathan doing things *for* her; she wanted him doing things *with* her. So she made herself relax in his hold, and even put her hands on his upper arms and let them rest there.

"All right," she said. "I won't go there alone. But I ought to be perfectly safe if I go there with you."

"Harry-et—"

"Please, Nathan." Nathan's hands had relaxed their hold on her shoulders, and when Harry stepped closer, they curved around her into an embrace. Her hands slid up to his shoulders and behind his neck. He seemed a little unsure of what she intended. Which was understandable, since Harry wasn't sure what she intended herself—other than persuading Nathan to make her a partner rather than a mere petitioner. "I really want to help," she said, her big brown eyes locked on Nathan's.

"But you—"

She put her fingertips on his lips to quiet him, then rested one hand against his chest, so she could feel the heavy beat of his heart, while she let the other drift up to play with the hair at his nape. "This is important to me, Nathan. Let me help."

Harry felt Nathan's body tense beneath her touch, and thought for sure he was going to say no. A second later she was sure he was going to kiss her.

She was wrong on both counts.

Nathan determinedly put his hands back on her shoulders and separated them by a good foot. Then he looked her right in the eye. "Just stay behind me and let me do the talking."

"You've got a deal! When are we going?"

A long-suffering sigh slipped through Nathan's lips. "I suppose there's no time like the present. If we can get your shepherd dried out, we can move those sheep up into the mountains over the weekend."

Whitey's Bar in Big Timber was about what you would expect a Western bar to be: rough, tough and no holds barred. It was a relic from the past, with everything from bat-wing doors to a twenty-foot-long bar with brass rail at the foot, sawdust on the floor and a well-used spittoon in the corner. The room was thick with cigarette smoke—no filter tips to be found here—and raucous with the wail of fiddles from a country tune playing on the old jukebox in the corner.

Some serious whiskey-drinking hombres sat at the small wooden tables scattered around the room. Harry was amazed that both cowboys and sheepmen caroused in the same bar, but Nathan explained that they relished the opportunity to argue the merits of their particular calling, with the inevitable brawl allowing them all an opportunity to vent the violence that civilization forced them to keep under control the rest of the time.

"Is there a fight every night?" Harry asked as they edged along the wall of the bar, hunting for her shepherd.

"Every night I've been here," he answered.

Harry gave him a sideways look, wondering how often that was. But her attention was distracted by what was happening on the stairs. Two men were arguing over a woman. Nathan hadn't exactly been honest when he'd said no women ever went to Whitey's. There were women here, all right, but they were working in an age-old profession. Twice in the few minutes they'd been in the bar, Harry had seen a woman head upstairs with a man.

The argument over the female at the foot of the stairs was escalating, and Harry noticed for the first time that one man appeared to be a cowboy, the other a sheepman.

Then she spotted her shepherd. "There he is!" she said to Nathan, pointing at a white-bearded old man slumped at a table not too far from the stairs.

Nathan swore under his breath. In order to get to the shepherd, he had to get past the two men at the foot of the stairs. He turned to Harry-et. "Wait for me outside."

Harry started to object, but the fierce look in Nathan's eyes brooked no refusal. Reluctantly she turned and edged back along the wall toward the door. She never made it.

"Why, hello there, little lady. What brings you here tonight?"

The cowboy had put one hand, which held a beer bottle, up along the wall to stop her. When she turned to face him, he braced his palm on the other side of her, effectively trapping her.

"I was just leaving," Harry said, trying to duck under his arm.

He grabbed her sleeve, and she heard a seam rip as he pushed her back against the wall. "Not so fast, darlin'."

Harry's eyes darted toward Nathan. He had just slipped his hands under the drunken shepherd's arms and was lifting him out of his chair. She couldn't bear the thought of shouting for help, drawing the attention of everyone in the bar. So she tried again to handle the cowboy by herself. "Look," she said, "I just came here to find someone—"

"Hell, little lady, you found me. Here I am."

Before Harry realized what he was going to do, the cowboy had pressed the full length of his body against her to hold her to the wall and sought her mouth with his.

She jerked her face from side to side to avoid his slobbering kisses. "Stop! Don't! I—"

An instant later the cowboy was decorating the floor and Nathan was standing beside her, eyes dark, nostrils flared, a vision of outrage. "The lady doesn't care for your attentions," he said to the burly cowboy. "I suggest you find someone who does."

The cowboy dragged himself up off the ground, still holding the neck of the beer bottle, which had broken off when he'd fallen. He recognized Nathan for a sheepman, which magnified the insult to his dignity. With all eyes on him there was no way he could back down. "Find your own woman," he blustered. "I saw her first."

"Nathan, please, don't start anything," Harry begged.

Nathan took his eyes off the other man for a second to glance at Harry, and the cowboy charged.

"Nathan!" Harry screamed.

Nathan's hand came up to stop the downward arc of the hand holding the broken bottle, while his fist found the cowboy's gut. The cowboy bent over double, and Nathan straightened him with a fist to the chin. The man crumpled to the floor, out cold.

Nathan looked up to find that pandemonium had broken out in the bar. He grabbed Harry's wrist. "Let's get out of here."

"Not without my shepherd!"

"Are you crazy, woman? There's a fight going on."

"I'm not leaving without my shepherd!"

Nathan dodged a flying chair to reach the drunken man he'd left sitting against the wall. He picked the man up, threw him over his shoulder fireman-style and marched back through the melee to Harry. "Are you satisfied?"

Harry grinned. "Now I am."

Nathan grabbed her wrist with his free hand, and glaring at anyone foolish enough to get in his way, was soon standing outside in front of Whitey's. He dumped the shepherd none too gently into the back of his pickup and ordered Harry to get in.

She hurried to obey him.

Nathan took out his fury at Harry-et on the truck, gunning the engine, only to have to slam on the brakes when he caught the red light at the corner. He raced the engine several times and made the tires squeal when he took off as the light turned green.

"Did that bastard hurt you?" he demanded through tight lips.

"I'm all right," Harry said soothingly. "I'm fine, Nathan. Nothing happened."

"You had no business being there in the first place. You should have stayed home where you belong."

"I had as much right to be there as you. More right," she argued. "It was my shepherd we went after."

"You and your damned shepherd. The greenest greenhorn would know not to pay the man in advance. This whole business tonight was your fault."

"I didn't do anything!" Harry protested.

"You were there. That was enough. If I hadn't been there—"

"But you were," Harry said. "And you were wonderful."

That shut him up. How could you complain when

a woman was calling you wonderful? But if anything had happened to her... Nathan had known his feelings toward Harry-et were possessive, but he hadn't known until tonight that she was *his woman*. Woe be unto the man who harmed the tiniest hair on her head.

Nathan shook his head in disbelief. He hadn't been involved in one of Whitey's barroom brawls since he'd been a very brash young man. If this evening was any indication of what he had in store as the manager of Cyrus's ranch, he had a long, long summer ahead of him.

As they pulled up in front of Cyrus's cabin, Harry said, "If you'll leave my shepherd in the sheep barn, I'll do what I can to sober him up."

"I'll take him home with me," Nathan countered. "I'm sure my housekeeper has some Blackfoot remedy that'll do the trick. We'll be back here bright and early tomorrow morning. Think you can stay in a western saddle long enough to help us drive your sheep into the mountains?"

"I rode hunters and jumpers in Virginia."

Nathan shook his head in disgust. "I should have known. All right. I'll be here at dawn. Be ready."

Harry stepped down out of the truck and started toward the house. An instant later she ran back around the truck and gestured for Nathan to open his window.

"I just wanted to thank you again." She leaned over and kissed him flush on the mouth. "You were really wonderful." Then she turned and ran into the cabin.

Nathan waited until he saw the lights go on before he gunned the engine and took off down the rutted road. Before he'd gone very far he reached up to touch his lips where she'd kissed him. There was still a bit of dampness there, and he touched it with his tongue. And tasted her. His lips turned up in a smile.

He felt as if he could move mountains.

He felt as if he could soar in the sky.

He felt like a damn fool in love.

He felt really wonderful.

Seven

When Wade or Clyde or Harley comes a-courtin',
how will you, the greenhorn female person, recognize
a compliment?
Answer: He'll compare your hair to the mane on his
sorrel horse.

Harry had aches where she'd forgotten she had muscles. She knew how to ride, but that didn't mean she'd
done much riding lately. Her back, thighs and buttocks could attest to that. But she had accomplished
what she'd set out that morning to do. Her flock of
sheep had been moved up into the leased mountain
pastures, and the wiry old shepherd had been settled
in his gypsy wagon with a stern warning to keep a
sharp eye out for wolves.

Harry was doing the same thing herself. Actually,

she was keeping a sharp eye out for one particular wolf. Nathan Hazard had been acting strangely all day. Silent. Predatory. He hadn't done anything overtly aggressive. In fact, he seemed to be playing some sort of game, stalking her, waiting for the moment when he could make his move. Her nerves were beginning to fray.

After the fracas of the previous evening, Harry hadn't expected Nathan to be enthusiastic about joining her on this mountain pilgrimage. Nor was he. But at least he hadn't said a word about what had happened in Whitey's Bar. Of course, he hadn't said much of anything. Harry had been determined not to provoke him in any way, so she had kept her aches and pains to herself. Was it any wonder she had leaped at Nathan's suggestion that they halt their trek halfway down the mountain and take a rest? She had to bite her lip to keep from groaning aloud when she dismounted, but she was so stiff and sore that her knees nearly buckled when she put her weight on them.

Nathan heard Harry's gasp and turned to watch her grab the horn of the saddle and hang on for a few moments until her legs were firmly under her. He had to hand it to the woman. She was determined. He couldn't help admiring her gumption. Nathan had suspected for some time that Harry was feeling the effects of the long ride. That had suited him just fine. He'd had plans of his own that depended on getting her off that horse while they were still in the mountains. They had reached Nyla's Meadow. The time had come.

He spread a family heirloom quilt in the cool shade

of some jack pines and straightened the edges over the layer of rich grass that graced the mountain meadow. At the last moment he rescued a handful of flowers that were about to be crushed, bringing them to Harry.

"Here. Thought you might like these."

Harry smiled and reached out a hand for the delicate blossoms. She brought them to her nose and was surprised at the pungent sweetness of the colorful bouquet. "They smell wonderful."

"Thought you also might like to lie down for a while here on Nyla's Meadow," Nathan said nonchalantly, gesturing toward the inviting square of material.

Harry wasted no time sagging down onto the quilt. She groaned again, but it was a sound of satisfaction as she stretched out flat on her back. "You have no idea how good this feels."

He settled himself Indian-style on a corner of the quilt near her head. "Don't guess I do. But if you moan any louder some moose is going to come courting."

Harry laughed. "I'll try to keep it down." She turned on her side and braced her head on her elbow, surveying the grassy, flower-laden clearing among the pines and junipers. "Nyla's Meadow. That sounds so beautiful. Almost poetical. How did this place get its name?"

Nathan's lips twisted wryly. "It's a pretty far-fetched story, but if you'd like to hear it—"

"Yes, I would!" Harry tried sitting up, but groaned and lay back down. "Guess I've stiffened up a little."

She massaged the nape of her neck. "Make that a lot."

"I'd be glad to give your shoulders a rubdown."

That sounded awfully good to Harry. "Would you?"

"Sure. Turn over on your stomach."

A moment later Nathan was straddling her at the waist and his powerful hands had found the knots in her shoulders and were working magic. "You have no idea how good that feels," she said with another groan of pleasure.

Nathan's lips curled into a satisfied smile. Oh, yes, he did. He longed for the time when there would be nothing between his fingertips and her skin. And it seemed like he'd been waiting his whole life for this woman. He didn't plan to wait much longer.

Harry felt the strength in Nathan's hands, yet his touch was a caress. A frisson of excitement ran the length of her spine. She imagined her naked body molded to Nathan's. Joined to Nathan's. Harry closed her eyes against the vivid picture she'd painted. She had no business thinking such thoughts. The sheepman only wanted her land. He'd as much as told her she wasn't the woman for him. And last night certainly couldn't have convinced him she would be the kind of wife he had in mind. No, the minute she had learned all she could from him, she intended to bid him a fast farewell.

So why was her body coming alive to his touch? Why did she yearn for his hands to slip around and cup her breasts, to mold her waist and stroke the taut and achy places that had nothing to do with the long ride of the morning? Harry tensed against the unwelcome, uncontrollable sensations deep inside.

"Relax," Nathan murmured as his hands slipped down from her shoulders to the small of her back and began to massage the soreness away.

"Tell me about Nyla's Meadow," Harry said breathlessly.

Nathan's thumbs slowly worked their way up her spine, easing, soothing, relaxing. "Nyla was an Egyptian princess."

Harry lifted herself on her hands and turned to eye Nathan over her shoulder. "What?"

Nathan shoved her back down. "Actually, the princess's name was N-I-L-A, after the Nile River, but somewhere over the years the spelling got changed."

"How did a Montana meadow get named after an Egyptian princess?" Harry asked suspiciously.

"Be quiet and listen and I'll tell you. Long before the first settlers came to the Boulder River Valley, a mountain man named Joshua Simmons arrived here. He had traveled the world over just for the pleasure of seeing a new horizon, or so the story goes. He'd been to Egypt and to China and to the South Sea islands. But when he reached Montana, he knew he'd found God's country—limitless blue skies, snow-capped mountains and grassy prairies as far as the eye could see."

"You're making this up, aren't you?" Harry demanded.

"Shut up and listen," Nathan insisted. His hands moved down Harry's back to her waist and around to her ribs, where they skimmed the fullness of her breasts at the sides before moving back to her spine.

Harry shivered. She would have asked Nathan to stop what he was doing, but his hands were there and gone before she could speak. The sensations remained. And the ache grew.

"When Joshua reached this meadow, he encountered an Indian maiden," Nathan continued. "She appeared as exotic to him, as foreign and mystical, as an Egyptian princess."

"The Princess Nila," Harry murmured sardonically.

"Right. They fell in love at first sight. And made love that same day here on the meadow. When he awoke, the Indian maiden—though she was a maiden no more—was gone. Joshua never learned her name, and he never saw her again. But he never forgot her. He named this place Nyla's Meadow after the Egyptian princess she had reminded him of."

Harry shifted abruptly so that her buttocks rocked against Nathan. He felt his loins tighten and rose slightly to put some space between the heat of their two bodies.

Oblivious to Nathan's difficulties, Harry rolled over between his legs and scooted far enough away to sit up facing him. He was still straddling her at thigh level. "So Nyla's Meadow is a place for falling in love? A place where lovers meet?" she teased. She pulled the band off one braid and began to unravel it, seemingly unconscious of the effect her action would have on Nathan.

Nathan swallowed hard. "Yes. A place for lovers." He couldn't take his eyes off Harry-et. Her gaze was lambent, her pupils dilated, her lids lowered. She was clearly aroused, yet her mood seemed almost playful, as though she didn't realize the powerful need she had unleashed within him.

When Harry started to free her other braid, Nathan reached out a hand. "I'll do that."

Her hands dropped onto his thighs. And slid upward.

Nathan hissed in a breath and put his hands over hers to keep them from moving any farther. There was no need for her to actually touch him. The mere thought of her hands on him excited him. He slid her hands back down his thighs, away from the part of him that desperately wanted her touch. When he was relatively sure he'd made his position clear, he let her hands go and reached for the other braid.

Her hair was soft, and rippled where the tight braids had left their mark. When both braids were unraveled, he thrust his hands into her rich brown hair and spread the silky mass around her head and shoulders like a nimbus. "You are so beautiful, Harry-et."

Harry hadn't meant to let the game go so far. She hadn't realized just how aroused Nathan was. She hadn't realized how the sight of his desire would increase her own. Now she wanted to see what would happen next. Now she wanted to feel what she had always imagined she would feel in a lover's embrace. Her hands once again followed the corded muscles along Nathan's thighs until she reached the part of him that strained against the worn denim. She molded the shape of him with her hands, awed by the heat and hardness of him.

Nathan closed his eyes and bit the inside of his mouth to keep from groaning aloud. The sweetness of it. The agony and the ecstasy of it. "Harry-et," he gasped. "Do you know what you're doing?"

"No," she replied. "But I'm learning fast."

Choked laughter erupted from Nathan's throat. At the same time he grabbed her by her wrists and lowered her to the ground, pinning her hands above either side of her head. He stretched out over the length of her, placing his hips in the cradle of her thighs. "That's what you're doing, lady," he said in a guttural voice, thrusting once with his hips. "I want you, Harry-et."

Harry heard the slight hesitation between the two syllables as he spoke her name that made the word an endearment. He wanted her, but he hadn't spoken of needing, or caring. Maybe that was as it should be. Alistairs and Hazards were never meant to love. History was against it. She wanted him, too. Wasn't that enough?

The decision was made for her when Nathan captured both her wrists in one hand and reached down between the two of them to caress the heart of her with the other. She felt herself arching toward him, toward the new and unbelievable sensations of pleasure.

Nathan caught her cries of ecstasy with his mouth. His kisses were urgent, needful. He let go of her wrists because he needed his hand to touch her, to caress her. When he did, Harry's fingers thrust into Nathan's hair and tugged to keep him close, so she could kiss him back. Her hands slipped down to caress his chest through his shirt, but the cotton was in her way. She yanked on his shirt and the snaps came free. She quickly helped him peel the shirt down off his shoulders. Just as quickly he freed the buttons of her shirt and stripped it off, along with her bra.

An instant later they paused and stared at each other.

Harry had seen Nathan's muscular chest once before and wanted to touch. Now she indulged that need. Her fingertips traced the crease down the center of his chest to his washboard belly.

He had imagined her naked a dozen, dozen times, but still had failed to see her as beautiful as she was. Her breasts were full and the nipples a rose color that drew his eye, his callused fingers and finally his mouth.

Harry's fingernails drew crescents on Nathan's shoulders as his mouth and tongue suckled her breast. She arched toward him, urging him to take more of her into his mouth. He cupped her breast with his hand and let his mouth surround her, while his teeth and tongue turned her nipple into a hard bud.

Harry moaned. Her body arched into his, her softness seeking his hardness.

"Please." She didn't know what came next. She'd always stopped in the past before she got this far. Only this time she didn't want to stop. She wanted to know how it ended.

"It's all right, sweetheart," he murmured in her ear. "Soon. Soon."

"Now, Nathan. Now."

He sat up and pulled off her boots, and then began pulling his own off. They both rid themselves of their jeans in record time. Nathan threw his jeans aside, then went searching for them a moment later. He ransacked the pockets, cursing as he went.

"Did you forget something?" Harry asked.

Nathan grinned as his fisted hand withdrew from his jeans pocket. "Nope."

Suddenly Harry was aware of her nakedness. And Nathan's. He looked awfully big. Not that she had anything to compare him with, but surely that thing was too large to fit...

"What's the matter, Harry-et?" Nathan said as he lay down beside her and pulled her into his embrace.

"Nothing," she mumbled against his chest.

"Having second thoughts?" Nathan held his breath, wondering why he was giving her a chance to back away when he wanted her so much that he was hurting.

Harry had opened her mouth to suggest maybe this wasn't such a good idea when Nathan's lips closed over hers. His tongue traced the edges of her mouth and then slipped inside, warm and wet. Seducing. Entrancing. Changing her mind all over again.

"Hold this for me," he said. "I need both hands free."

"What is it?" she asked through a haze of euphoria.

He quickly removed the foil packet and dropped a condom into her palm.

"Oh. Dear. Oh." Harry giggled with embarrassment. In her nervousness Harry was unable to keep from blurting something she'd read in a magazine article. "It's Mr. Prophylactic. The guy with the cute little button nose."

Nathan burst out laughing.

Harry blushed a fiery red. Thank goodness Nathan still had his sense of humor. Maybe this wasn't going to be so impossible, after all. Her relief was premature.

"Would you like to put it on me?" he asked.

"I've never done it before," she admitted. "I wouldn't know how. I might do it wrong."

A frown arose between Nathan's brows. He couldn't believe she'd be so irresponsible as not to use some kind of protection in this day and age. As Harry's eyes fell, the truth dawned on Nathan. *She hadn't used protection because she hadn't needed it.*

"How long?" he demanded, grasping her hair and angling her face up toward him.

"What?"

"How long since you've been with a man."

"I haven't ever…that is…this is the first time."

Nathan watched as she lowered her eyes to avoid his gaze, as if she'd committed some kind of crime. Didn't she know what a precious gift she was giving him? Didn't she know how special she had made him feel? He pulled her into his arms and held her tightly. He had never felt so protective of a woman in his life. He was awed to be the man she had chosen. And terrified by the responsibility she had placed in his hands.

"The first time for a woman…sometimes there's pain," he said, his mouth close to her temple. "I don't want to hurt you, sweetheart."

"You won't," Harry reassured him.

"Darling, sweetheart, I wouldn't mean to, but I'm afraid—"

Harry pushed him far enough away that she could see his face. "You? Afraid? Of what?"

He looked her in the eye. "That it won't be everything you expect. That it won't be perfect."

Harry smiled a beatific smile. "If I'm with you, Nathan, it will be perfect. Trust me."

He eased her back down on the quilt and lowered himself beside her, giving her a quick, hard hug.

Harry noticed something different about the embrace. Something missing. She chanced a brief glance down at him. "Oh, no," she said, dismayed.

"What's the matter Harry-et?"

"You're not...well, you're not...anymore," she said, pointing at a no-longer-aroused Nathan.

Nathan chuckled. "You're precious, Harry-et," he said with a quick grin. "One of a kind."

Harry took a swipe at his shoulder with her fist—the same fist that was still holding the condom he'd handed to her. "I don't like being laughed at, Nathan."

He laughed. "I'm not laughing at you." He rolled over onto his back and let his arms flop free, a silly grin on his face.

Harry tackled him.

An instant later she was under him, his body mantling hers. His mouth found hers, and he kissed her with all the passion he felt for her. His hands found her breasts and teased the nipples to a peak. He felt the blood thrumming through the veins in her throat with his mouth. By the time his hand finally slipped between their bodies, she was wet.

And he was hard.

"Oh. It's back," she said in an awed voice.

Nathan grinned. "So it is. Where is Mr. Prophylactic?"

Harry grinned and opened her hand to reveal a slightly squashed condom. "Will it still work?"

"Not unless you put it on."

Her chin slipped down to her chest. She glanced up at him shyly. "Will you help me?"

Nathan helped her place the condom and roll it on until he was fully covered. The way she handled him so carefully, as though he would break, made him feel treasured and very, very special.

"Is that all there is to it?" she asked.

"Pretty simple, huh?"

She caressed him through the sheath. "Can you still feel that?"

Nathan jerked. "Uh-huh."

"Really?" She let her fingers trace the shape of him, encircle him, run down the length of him from base to tip. "You can feel that?"

Nathan inhaled sharply. Slowly he inserted a finger inside her. "Can you feel that?"

Harry gasped. "Uh-huh."

He inserted another finger. "And that?"

Harry tightened her thighs around his hand, reminding Nathan this was new to her. He slowly worked his fingers inside her, stretching her, feeling the tightness and the wetness. He had to be patient. And gentle. And exercise rigid control over a body that ached with wanting her.

"Harry-et," he breathed against her throat. "Touch me."

Harry had been too caught up in her own sensations to think about Nathan's. Until he'd spoken she hadn't been aware that her hands each grasped a handful of quilt. She brought her hands up to grasp his waist instead. Slowly her fingers slipped around to his belly and down to the crease where hip met thigh.

Nathan grunted. The feel of her fingertips on his skin, on his belly, in those other places he hadn't known were so sensitive, was exquisite.

Harry relaxed her thighs, allowing Nathan greater freedom of movement. His mouth found a breast and teased it, then moved down her ribs to her belly, and then lower, where it replaced his hands at the portal she had guarded against invasion for so many years.

Her hands clutched his hair as she arched up toward the sensations of his mouth on her flesh. "Nathan, please," she cried. She had no idea what it was she needed, but she was desperate.

Nathan's eyes glittered with passion as he rose over her. She expected one quick thrust, and was prepared for the pain. Instead she felt the tip of him pushing against her. Just when she started to feel the pain, he distracted her by nipping her breast. Then his mouth found hers and his tongue mimed the action below. Thrusting and withdrawing. Pushing farther each time. Teasing and tempting. A guttural sound rose in her throat as she surged toward him, urging him inside.

Nathan thrust once more with tongue and hips, and filled her full.

Harry tensed with the extraordinary feeling of being joined to Nathan. Her legs captured his hips and held him in thrall. As he withdrew and thrust again, she met his rhythm, feeling the tension build within. His hand came between them to touch her and intensify the need for relief. For release. For something.

Harry was gasping for air, her heart pounding, her

pulse racing. "Nathan," she cried. "Please. I ache. Make it stop."

God, he loved her! He wanted to say the words. Here. Now. But once said, they couldn't be taken back. He had no idea how she felt about him. She trusted him; that much was clear. But did her feelings for him run as deep as his for her? She hadn't offered those three words; there was no way he could ask for them. He could only show her how he felt, and trust that it would be enough.

"Come with me, sweetheart. Let yourself fly. It's all right. I'll take care of you."

Harry took him at his word and let herself soar. Nathan joined her in her aerie, two souls surpassing the physical, seeking a world somewhere beyond Nyla's Meadow.

It was long moments later before either of them touched ground again. Their bodies were slick with sweat, despite the shade in which they lay. Nathan was stretched out beside her with an arm and a leg thrown possessively over her. He couldn't see Harry's face, so he wasn't able to judge what she was thinking. But there was a tension in her body that was at odds with the release he'd felt within her just moments before.

"Harry-et? What's wrong?" He must have hurt her. He hadn't meant to, but he had.

She sighed. A huge, deafening sound. Those last few words Nathan had spoken before she had found ecstasy resounded in her ears: "I'll take care of you." Those words reminded her of why it would be foolish to give her heart to Nathan Hazard. She wanted to stand on her own two feet. He was liable to sweep her off them. She freed herself from his embrace and sat up, pulling her knees to her chest and hugging them with her arms. "This can't happen again, Nathan."

"I'm sorry if I hurt you. I—"

"You didn't hurt me, Nathan. I just don't want to do it...this...with you again."

"It sounds to me like you're sorry it happened the first time," he said angrily, sitting up to face her. "You were willing. You can't deny it."

"I'm not denying it. I wanted this as much as you," she admitted. "I'm only saying it can't happen again."

"Give me one good reason why not," he demanded.

Because I'm in danger of falling in love with you.

Because I'm in danger of losing myself to you.

Because I find you irresistible, even though I know we have no business being together like this.

That was three reasons. None of which she had any intention of mentioning to him. Harry turned away from him and slipped on her bra and panties. She could hear the rustle of clothing behind her as he dressed. The metal rasp of the zipper on his jeans was loud in the silence. She stood and pulled up the zipper on her own jeans before reaching for her boots.

He grabbed the boot out of her hand and shook it, then handed it back to her. "Snakes," he said curtly. "And spiders."

Harry shivered and made sure she dumped the other boot as well before she slipped it on. His warning had been an abrupt reminder that she was a very sore tenderfoot. Harry couldn't very well avoid Nathan until she learned everything from him that she needed to know. She would just have to learn to control the need to touch, and be touched, that arose every time she got near him.

Nathan had no idea what he'd done that was so wrong, but after the most profound lovemaking he'd ever experienced, Harry-et was avoiding him as if he had the measles. She wasn't going to get away with it.

"Harry-et."

"Yes, Nathan?"

"Come here."

"No." Harry turned and marched over to the tree where her horse was tied. She tried to mount, but couldn't raise her leg high enough to reach the stirrup. She laid her face against the saddle and let her shoulders slump.

An instant later Nathan grabbed her by the waist and hoisted her into the saddle. "Move your leg out of the way, tenderfoot," he ordered.

Harry gritted her teeth and did as he ordered, painfully sliding her leg up out of his way as he worked on the saddle.

"Damned good thing you couldn't reach the stirrup," he snarled. "Damn cinch wasn't tightened. Saddle would have slid around and dumped you flat."

"Stop treating me like I'm helpless!" she snapped. "I can take care of myself."

"I'll believe it when I see it," he retorted.

"I pulled my own weight today. Don't tell me I didn't."

Nathan neither confirmed nor denied her assertion. He tightened the cinch on his own saddle and 'mounted, then reined his horse to face her. "That story I told you about Nyla's Meadow?"

"Yes?"

"I made it all up."

Harry struggled to keep the disappointment out of her voice. "All of it?"

"Every last word. No one knows how the meadow got its name."

He had invented a place for falling in love. A place where lovers meet. Then brought her here. And made love to her. Now he wanted her to believe it had all been a lie.

"We made love in Nyla's Meadow, Nathan. That was real."

Nathan met her imploring gaze with stony eyes. "We had sex. Damn good sex. But that's all it was." And if she believed that, he had a bog he'd like to sell her for grazing land.

He was waiting for the retort he was sure was on her lips. But she didn't argue, just kicked her horse and loped away from him toward the trail back down the mountain.

"Damn you, Harry-et!" he muttered. "Damn you for stealing my heart and leaving *me* feeling helpless."

He kicked his horse and loped down the mountain after her. As he followed her down the mountain, he thought back on the day he'd spent working with Harry-et. Not once had she asked for his help. Not once had she complained. In fact, she had done extraordinarily well for a tenderfoot. Was it possible that someday Harry-et Alistair could actually stand on her own two feet? He found the idea fascinating if far-fetched. He stared at the way she rode stiff-backed in the saddle. She had grit, that woman. It sure couldn't hurt to hang around long enough to find out!

Harry's thoughts weren't nearly so sanguine. All day she had been careful not to let Nathan do too much. If she was going to feel like a success, she had to make it on her own. She had left her family to get away from people ordering her around. But somehow Nathan had never ordered her to do anything. He had made suggestions and left the decisions up to her. So maybe she could endure his company a little longer. Maybe she could forget what had happened between them today in Nyla's Meadow and simply take advantage of his expertise.

But it was clear she was going to have to be careful. Give Nathan an inch and he might take an acre. And the man had made no secret of the fact that he wanted the whole darn spread.

Eight

In a small town out West what do you do if you become ill?
Answer: Put on a big pot of coffee, because an hour after you get your prescription from the drugstore, five people will phone with sympathy and two will fetch you a hot dish.

Harry didn't see Nathan for a week, but he called her every day with instructions for some job or other that she had to complete: repairing the henhouse, planting a vegetable garden, spreading manure, harrowing the fields and cleaning the sheep shed. She took great pride in the fact that she managed to accomplish every task alone. Successfully. She knew Nathan had expected her to cave in and ask for help long before now. So when he phoned one evening and told her to clean out all the clogged irrigation channels on her property in preparation for starting the irrigation water through the main ditch, she headed out bright and early the next morning, expecting to get the job done. And failed abysmally.

All Harry could figure was that Nathan had left something out of his instructions. She tried calling him for more directions, but he was out working in his fields and couldn't be reached until noon. She left a message with Nathan's housekeeper for him to call her as soon as he got in.

Nathan did better than that. Shortly after noon he arrived on her kitchen doorstep. "Harry-et, are you in there? Are you all right?"

He didn't wait for her to answer, just shoved the screen door open and stepped inside. When Nathan saw her sitting at the table with a sandwich in her hand, his relief was palpable. His heart had been in his throat ever since he'd read the message Katoya had left him. He'd had visions of Harry wounded and bleeding from some farm accident. He was irritated that he cared enough about her to feel so relieved that she wasn't hurt. He forced the emotion he was feeling from his voice and asked, "What was the big emergency?"

"No emergency," Harry answered through a mouthful of peanut butter and jelly. "I just couldn't get the irrigation system to work with the directions you gave me."

"What was wrong with my directions?"

"If I knew that, I wouldn't have called you."

"I'll go take a look."

"I'll come with you." She threw her sandwich down and headed toward him.

Nathan felt his groin tighten at the sight of Harry sucking a drop of grape jelly off her finger. "Don't bother. I can do it quicker on my own."

Harry hurried to block his exit from the kitchen. "But if I don't come along, I won't know what I did wrong the next time I have to do it by myself," she pointed out in a deceptively calm voice.

Nathan stared at the jutting chin of the woman standing before him. Stubborn. As a mule. And sexy. Even in bibbed overalls. "All right," he muttered. "But don't get in my way."

When Nathan crossed behind the barn, he saw the backhoe sitting in the middle of her field by the main irrigation ditch. "I didn't know you could manage a backhoe." Handling the heavy farm machinery was how he'd feared she'd hurt herself.

"It wasn't so hard to figure out. I used it to widen the main ditch and clear the larger debris from the irrigation channels. But I still didn't get any water."

She was a remarkable woman, all right. It wasn't the first time he'd had that thought, but Nathan didn't understand why it irritated him so much to admit it now. Could it be that he *wanted* her to need him? *Needed* her to need him? What if she turned out to be really self-sufficient? Where did that leave him? *With an Alistair smack in the middle of his property.* Nathan pursed his lips. The thought didn't irk him near as much as it ought to.

When they arrived at the main ditch, Nathan examined her work. He could find no fault with it. "Did you follow the main ditch all the way across your property?''

''As far as that stand of cottonwoods over there along the river.'' She didn't add that the thought of snakes hiding in the thick vegetation around the cottonwoods had scared her off.

''Let's go take a look.''

Harry was happy to follow him. The way Nathan was stomping around it wasn't likely any snake was going to hang around long enough to take him on.

Harry stayed close behind Nathan and actually bumped into him when he stopped dead and said, ''There's your problem.''

She leaned around him to see where he was pointing. ''That bunch of sticks?''

''Beaver dam. Has to come out of there. It's blocking the flow of water along the main ditch.''

''How do I get rid of it?''

Nathan grinned ruefully. ''Stick by stick. You'd better head back to the house and get your thigh-high rubber boots.''

''Rubber boots? Thigh-high?''

''I take it you don't have any rubber boots,'' Nathan said flatly.

''Just my galoshes.''

He sighed. ''They're better than nothing. Go put them on. Get a pair of gloves, too.''

''All right. But don't start without me,'' she warned.

''Wouldn't think of it.''

Harry ran all the way to the cabin, stepped into her galoshes and galomphed all the way back to the beaver dam. True to his word, Nathan was sitting on a log that stuck out from the dam, doing nothing more strenuous than chewing on a blade of sweet grass. But he hadn't been idle in her absence. He was leaning on two shovels, wore thigh-high rubber boots and had a pair of leather gloves stuck in his belt.

"All ready?" he asked.

"Ready."

The beaver dam was several feet long and equally wide and thick, and Harry felt as if she were playing a game of Pick-up Sticks. She never knew whether the twig she pulled would release another twig or tumble a log. Leaves and moss also had to be shoveled away from the elaborate dam. The work was tedious and backbreaking. Toward the end of the afternoon it looked as if they might be able to clear the ditch before the sun went down, if they kept working without a break.

Harry was determined not to quit before Nathan. Sweat soaked her shirt and dripped from her nose and chin. Her face was daubed with mud. Her hands were raw beneath the soaked leather gloves. There were blisters on her heels where the galoshes rubbed as she mucked her way through the mud and slime. It was little consolation to her that Nathan didn't look much better.

He had taken off his shirt, and his skin glistened with sweat. He kept a red scarf in the back pocket of his jeans, and every so often he pulled it out and swiped at his face and neck and chest. Sometimes he missed a spot, and she had the urge to take the kerchief from his hand and do the job for him. But it was as plain as peach pie cooling on a windowsill that Nathan was a heap better at dishing out help than he was at taking it. And though they worked side by side all day, he kept his distance.

Touching might be off-limits, but that didn't mean she couldn't look. Harry was mesmerized by the play of corded muscles under Nathan's skin as he hefted logs and shoveled mud. She turned abruptly when he caught her watching, and was thankful for the mud that hid her flush of chagrin.

Nathan hadn't been as unaware of Harry as he'd wanted her to think. The outline of her hips appeared in those baggy overalls every time she stretched to reach another part of the dam. He had even caught a glimpse of her breasts once when she'd bent over to help him free a log. There was nothing the least bit attractive about what she had on. He didn't understand why he couldn't seem to take his eyes off her.

Suddenly, as though they'd opened a lever, the water began to rush past them into the main irrigation ditch and outward along each of the ragged channels that crisscrossed Harry's fields.

"It's clear! We did it!" Harry shouted, exuberantly throwing her arms into the air and leaping up and down.

Nathan saw the moment she started to fall. One of her galoshes was stuck in the mud, and when Harry started to jump, one foot was held firmly to the ground while the other left it.

Nathan was never quite sure later how it all happened. He made a leap over some debris in an attempt to catch Harry-et before she fell, but tripped as he took off. Thus, when he caught her, they were both on their way down. He twisted his body to take the brunt of the fall, only his boot was caught on something and his ankle twisted instead of coming free. They both hit the ground with a resounding "Ooomph!"

Neither moved for several seconds.

Then Harry untangled herself from the pile of arms and legs and came up on her knees beside Nathan, who still hadn't moved. "Nathan? Are you all right? Say something."

Nathan said a four-letter word.

"Are you hurt?"

Nathan said another four-letter word.

"You *are* hurt," Harry deduced. "Don't move. Let me see if anything's broken."

"My shoulder landed on a rock," he said between clenched teeth as he tried to rise. "Probably just bruised. And my ankle got twisted."

"Don't move!" Harry ordered. "Let me check."

"Harry-et, I—" He sucked in a breath of air as he sat up. His right shoulder was more than bruised. Something was broken. "Help me up."

"I don't think—"

"Help...me...up," he said through gritted teeth.

Harry reached an arm around him and tried lifting his right arm to her shoulder. He grunted.

"Try the other side," he told her.

She slipped his other arm over her shoulder and used the strength in her legs to maneuver them both upright.

Nathan tried putting weight on his left leg. It crumpled under him. "Help me get to that boulder over there."

Harry supported Nathan as best she could, and with a sort of hopping, hobbling movement that left him gasping, they made it. She settled Nathan on the knee-high stone and stood back, facing him with her hands on her hips. "I'll go get the pickup. You need a doctor."

"I'll be fine. Just give me a minute to rest." A moment later he tried to stand on his own. The pain forced him back down.

"Are you going to admit you need some help? Or do I have to leave you sitting here for the next few weeks until somebody notices you're missing?"

"Go get the pickup," he snarled.

"Why thank you, Mr. Hazard, for that most brilliant suggestion. I wish I'd thought of it myself." She sashayed away, hips swaying. Her attempt at nonchalance was a sham. As soon as she was out of sight, she started running, and sprinted all the way to her cabin. She tore through the kitchen, hunting for the truck keys, then remembered she'd left them in the ignition. She headed the pickup straight back across the fields, skidding the last ten feet to a stop in front of Nathan.

"You just took out half a field of hay," Nathan said.

"I'm afraid I was in too much of a hurry to notice," she retorted. She forced herself to slow down and be gentle with Nathan as she helped him into the truck, but even so, the tightness of his jaw, and his silence, attested to his pain.

"Where's the closest hospital?" she demanded as she scooted behind the wheel.

"Take me home."

"Nathan, you need—"

"Take me home. Or let me out and I'll walk there myself."

"You need a doctor."

"I'll call Doc Witley when I get home."

It didn't occur to her to ask whether Doc Witley practiced on humans. It shouldn't have surprised her that he turned out to be the local vet.

Several hired hands came running when Harry drove into Nathan's yard, honking her horn like crazy. They helped her get Nathan upstairs to the loft bedroom of his A-frame home. Harry's mouth kept dropping open as she took in her surroundings. She had never suspected Nathan's home would be so beautiful.

The pine logs of which the house was constructed had been left as natural as the day they were cut. The spacious living room was decorated in pale earth tones, accented with navy. A tan corduroy couch and chair faced a central copper-hooded fireplace. Nearby stood an ancient wooden rocker. The living room had a cathedral ceiling, with large windows all around, so that no matter where you looked there was a breathtaking view: the sparkling Boulder River bounded by cottonwoods to the east; the Crazy Mountains to the north; the snowcapped Absarokas to the south; and to the east, pasture land dotted with ewes and their twin lambs.

If this was an example of how Nathan Hazard designed homes, the world had truly lost someone special when he had given up his dream.

If she'd had any doubt at all about his eye for beauty, the art and artifacts on display in his home laid them fully to rest. Bronze sculptures and oil and watercolor paintings by famous western artists graced his living room. Harry indulged her curiosity by carefully examining each and every one during the time Doc Witley spent with Nathan.

When the vet finally came downstairs, he found Harry waiting for him.

"How is he?"

"Nothing's broke."

"Thank God."

"Dislocated his shoulder, though. Put that to rights. Couldn't do much with his ankle. Bad sprain. May have cracked the bone. Can't tell without an X ray and don't think he'll hold still for one. Best medicine for that boy is rest. Keep him off his feet and don't let him use that shoulder for a few weeks. I'll be going now. Have a prize heifer calving over at the Truman place. You mind my words now. Keep that boy down." He gave her a bottle of pills. "Give him a couple of these every four hours if he's in pain."

Harry looked down to find the vet had handed her a bottle of aspirin. She showed him out the door and turned to stare up toward the loft bedroom that could be seen from the living room. Nathan must have heard what the doctor had said. It shouldn't be too hard to get him to cooperate. For the first time since she'd arrived, Harry realized Nathan's housekeeper hadn't made an appearance. Maybe Katoya was out shopping. If so, Harry would have to stick around until she got back. Nathan was in no shape to be left alone.

Nathan's bedroom was done in darker colors: rust, burnt sienna and black. The four-poster bed was huge, and flanked by a tall, equally old-fashioned piece of furniture that Harry assumed must hold his clothes.

The other side of the room was taken up by a rolltop desk. The oak floor was mantled with a bearskin rug. Of course there were windows, wide, clear windows that brought the sky and the mountains inside.

Nathan had pillows piled behind his shoulders and an equally large number under his left foot.

She took a step into his bedroom. "Is there anything I can do for you?"

"Just leave me alone. I'll manage fine."

"Your home is lovely. You show a lot of promise as an architect," she said with a halting smile.

"It turned out all right," he said. "As soon as it was built, I thought of a dozen things I could have done better."

She didn't feel comfortable encroaching farther into his bedroom, so she leaned back against the doorway. "You'll make all those improvements next time."

"A sheepman doesn't have the leisure time to be designing houses," he said brusquely.

"Actually, you're going to have quite a bit of free time over the next couple of weeks," she replied. "The vet gave orders for you to stay in bed. By the way, I haven't seen your housekeeper. Do you expect her back soon?"

"In about a month," Nathan said. "She left early this afternoon to visit her granddaughter, Sage Little-wolf, on the Blackfoot reservation up near Great Falls."

"Do you suppose she'd come back if she knew—"

"Yes, she would. Which is why I have no intention of contacting her. There's some problem with her granddaughter that needs settling. She's gone there to settle it. I'll manage.''

Harry marched over to stand at Nathan's bedside. ''How do you intend to get along without any help?''

''It's not your problem.''

''I'm making it my problem.''

''Look, Harry-et, I don't need your help—''

''You need help,'' she interrupted. ''You can't walk.''

''I'll use crutches.''

''With your right arm in a sling?''

''I'll hop.''

''What if you fall?''

''I won't.''

''But if you do—''

''I'll get back up. I don't need you here, Harry-et. I don't want you here. I don't think I can say it any plainer than that.''

''I'm staying. Put that in your pipe and smoke it, Mr. Hazard.'' Harry turned and headed for the door.

''Harry-et, come back here! Harry-et!''

She kept on marching all the way downstairs until she stood in his immaculate, perfectly antiquated kitchen, trying to decide what she should make for his supper.

Nathan spent the first few minutes after Harry left the room, proving he could get to the bathroom on his own. With his father's cane in his left hand he was able to hobble a little. But it was an awkward and painful trip, to say the least. He couldn't imagine trying to get up and down the stairs to feed himself. Of course, he could sleep downstairs on the couch, but that would put the closest bathroom too far away for comfort.

By the time Harry showed up with a bowl of chicken noodle soup on a wicker lap tray, Nathan was willing to concede that he needed someone to bring his meals. But only for a day or so until he could get up and and down stairs more easily.

"All right, Harry-et," he said, "you win. I'll send a man to take care of your place for the next couple of days so you can play nursemaid."

"Thank you for admitting you need help. I, on the other hand, can manage just fine on my own."

"Look, Harry-et, be reasonable. There's no sense exhausting yourself trying to handle two things at once."

"I *like* exhausting myself," Harry said contrarily. "I feel like I've accomplished something. And I'm quite good at managing three or four things at once, if you want to know the truth."

"Stop being stubborn and let me help."

"That's the pot calling the kettle black," she retorted.

"Have it your way, then," he said sullenly.

"Thank you. I will. I'll be back in a little while to collect your soup bowl. Be sure it's empty." She stopped on her way out the door and added, "I'll be sleeping on the couch downstairs. That way you can call if you need me during the night."

Nathan was lying back with his eyes closed when Harry returned for the dinner tray he had set aside. She sat down carefully beside him on the bed, so as not to wake him. He was breathing evenly, and since she believed him to be asleep, she risked checking his forehead to see if he had a fever. Just as she was brushing a lock of blond hair out of the way, his eyes blinked open. She saw the pain before he thought to hide it from her.

She finished her motion, letting it be the caress it had started out as when she'd thought he was asleep. "I was checking to see if you have a fever."

"I don't."

"You do."

He didn't argue. Which was all the proof she needed that he wasn't a hundred percent. "Doc Witley left some aspirin. He said you might need it for the pain. Do you?"

"No."

She sighed. "I'll leave two on the bedside table with a glass of water, just in case."

He grabbed her wrist as she was rising from the bed to keep her from leaving. "Harry-et."

"What is it, Nathan?"

The words stuck in his throat, but at last he got them out. "Thank you."

"You're welcome, Nathan. I—"

Harry was interrupted by a commotion downstairs. "What on earth—" Someone was coming up, taking the stairs two at a time.

"Hey, Nathan," a masculine voice shouted, "heard you slipped and landed flat on your ass—" Luke stopped abruptly when he saw Harry Alistair standing beside Nathan. "Sorry about the language, ma'am." He tipped his hat in apology. "Didn't know there were ladies present."

"How on earth did you find out what happened?"

Harry asked. "I swear I haven't been near a phone—"

"No phone is as fast as gossip in the West," Luke said with a grin. "I'm here to see if there's anything I can do to help out."

Nathan opened his mouth to respond and then closed it again, staring pointedly at Harry.

"I was just taking this downstairs," she said, grabbing Nathan's dinner tray. "I'll leave you two alone." She hurried from Nathan's bedroom, closing the door behind her.

Luke turned back to Nathan and waggled his eyebrows. "Should have known you wouldn't spend your time in bed all alone."

"Watch what you say, Luke," Nathan warned. "You're talking about a lady."

"So that's the way the wind blows."

"Harry-et is only here as a nurse."

"One of the hired hands could nurse you," Luke pointed out.

"She refuses to leave, so she might as well do some good while she's here," Nathan said defensively.

"Who's going to take care of her place while she's taking care of you?"

Nathan grimaced. "I offered to have one of my hands help her out. She insists on doing everything herself. Look, Luke, I'd appreciate it if you'd look in on her over the next couple of days. Make sure she doesn't overdo it."

"Sure, Nathan. I'd be glad to."

"I'd really appreciate it. You see, Harry-et just doesn't know when to quit."

"Sounds a lot like my Abby."

"Your Abby?"

"Abigail Dayton and I got engaged yesterday."

"I thought you hadn't seen her since she caught that renegade wolf and headed back home to Helena."

"Well, I hadn't. Until yesterday. I figured life is too short to live it without the woman you love. I was already headed over here to give you the big news when I heard about your accident."

Nathan reached out and grasped Luke's hand. "I really envy you. When's the wedding?"

Luke grinned wryly. "As soon as my best man is back on his feet again. You'd better make it quick, because Abby's pregnant."

Harry heard Nathan's whoop at the same time she heard the front door knocker. She didn't know which one to check out first. Since the door was closer, she hurried to open it.

"Hi! I'm Hattie Mumford. You must be Harry Alistair. I'm pleased to meet you. I brought one of my apple spice cakes for Nathan. Thought it might cheer him up. Can I see him?"

The door knocker rattled again.

"Oh, you get the door, dear," Hattie said. "I know the way upstairs."

Harry just barely resisted the urge to race up ahead of Hattie to warn Nathan what was coming. The knocker rapped again. She waited to answer it because Luke was skipping down the stairs.

"Is he all right?" Harry asked anxiously. "I heard him holler."

Luke grinned. "Nathan was just celebrating the

news of my engagement and forthcoming marriage to Abigail Dayton.''

"You and Abigail?" Harry smiled. "How wonderful! Congratulations!"

"You'd better get that door," Luke said. "I'll just let myself out the back way."

Harry opened the door to a middle-aged couple.

"I'm Babs Sinclair and this is my husband, Harve. We just heard the bad news about Nathan. Thought he might enjoy my macaroni-and-cheese casserole. I'll just take this into the kitchen. Harve, why don't you go up and check on Nathan."

For want of something better to do, Harry followed Babs Sinclair into the kitchen. The woman slipped the casserole into the oven and turned on the heat. Harry didn't have the heart to tell her Nathan had already eaten his supper.

"You better get some coffee on the stove, young'un," Babs said. "If I know my Harve, he'll—"

"Babs," a voice shouted down from the loft, "send some coffee up here, will you?"

The door knocker rapped.

"You better get that, young'un. I'll take care of making the coffee."

For the next three hours neighbors dropped by to leave tokens of their concern for Nathan Hazard. Besides the apple spice cake and the macaroni-and-cheese casserole, Nathan had been gifted with a loaf of homemade bread and a crock of newly made butter, magazines, and a deck of cards. The game of checkers was only on loan and had to be returned once Nathan was well. Harry met more people that evening than in the nearly four months since she'd moved to the Boulder River Valley.

What she hadn't realized until Hattie Mumford mentioned it was that her neighbors had been waiting for her to indicate that she was ready for company. They would never have thought to intrude on her solitude without an invitation. Now that Harry was acquainted with her neighbors, Hattie assured her they would all make it a point to come calling.

Over the next few weeks as she nursed Nathan, Harry was blessed with innumerable visits from the sheepmen of Sweet Grass County and their wives. They always turned up when she was busy with chores and managed to stay long enough to see them finished. She found herself the recipient of one of Hattie's apple spice cakes. And she thoroughly enjoyed Babs Sinclair's macaroni-and-cheese casserole.

It never occurred to her, not once in all the propitious visits when she'd been exhausted and a neighbor had arrived to provide succor, that while she had been acting as Nathan's hostess in the kitchen, he had been upstairs entreating, encouraging and exhorting his friends and neighbors to keep an eye out for her while he was confined to his bed.

So when Harry overheard Hattie and Babs talking about how she was a lucky woman to have Nathan Hazard *taking care of her,* she began asking a few questions.

When Nathan woke up the next morning and stretched with the sunrise, he yelped in surprise at the sight that greeted him at the foot of his bed.

Nine

How do you know when a handsome Woolly Western-
erner is really becoming dead serious about you?
Answer: He invites you to his ranch and shows you
a basket overflowing with three hundred unmated
socks. You realize your own heart is lost when you
begin pairing them.

Nathan wasn't a good patient. He simply had no experience in the role. He was used to being the caretaker. He didn't know how to let somebody take care
of him. Harry bore the brunt of his irascibility. Well,
that wasn't exactly true. Nathan had more than once
provoked an argument and found himself shouting at
thin air. Over the three weeks he'd spent recuperating,
he'd learned that Harry picked her fights.

So when he woke up to find her standing at the

foot of his bed, fists on hips, brown eyes flashing, jaw
clamped tight to still a quivering chin, he knew he
was in trouble.

"I have tried to be understanding," she said
hoarsely. "But this time you've gone too far."

"I haven't left this bed for three weeks!" he protested.

"You know what I mean! I found out what you
did, Nathan. There's no sense trying to pretend you
didn't do it."

Nathan stared at her, completely nonplussed. "If I
had the vaguest idea what you're talking about,
Harry-et—"

"I'm talking about what you said to Hattie Mumford and Babs and Harve Sinclair and Luke Granger
and all the other neighbors who've been showing up
at my place over the past three weeks to *help* me.
How could you?" she cried. "How could you?"

Harry turned her back to him and walked over to
the window to look out at the mountains. "I thought
you understood how important it was to me to manage on my own," she said in an agonized voice.

She swiped the tears away, then turned back to face
him. "Do you know how many times over the past
three weeks I've let you do something for yourself,
knowing it was more than you could handle? Sometimes you surprised me and managed on your own.
More often you needed my help. But I never offered
it until you asked, Nathan. I respected your right to
decide for yourself just how much you could handle.

"That's all I ever wanted, Nathan. The same respect I was willing to give to you." Her lips curled
as she spit out, "Equal partners. You have no concept

what that means. Until you do, you're going to have a hard time finding a woman to *share* your life.''

As she whirled and fled the room, Nathan shouted, ''Harry-et! Wait!'' He shoved the covers out of the way and hit the floor with both feet.

Harry was halfway down the stairs when she heard him fall. She paused, waiting for the muttered curse that would mean he was all right. When it didn't come, she turned and ran back up the stairs as fast as she could. He was lying facedown on the bearskin rug, his right arm hugged tightly to his body. She fell onto her knees beside him, her hands racing over him, checking the pulse at his throat. ''Nathan. Oh, God. Please be all right. I—''

An instant later he grasped her wrist and pulled her down beside him. A moment after that he had her under him and was using the weight of his body to hold her down. ''Stop bucking like that,'' he rasped. ''You're liable to throw my shoulder out again.''

''You'll be lucky if that's all the damage I do,'' she snapped back at him. She shoved at his chest with both hands, and knew she'd hurt him when his lips drew back over his teeth.

''That's it.'' He caught both of her hands in one of his and clamped them to the floor above her head. With his other hand he captured her chin and made her look at him. ''Are you going to listen to me, or not?''

''I don't know anything you could say—''

''Shut up and let me talk!''

She pressed her lips into a flat, uncompromising line and glared at him.

''I want another chance,'' he began. She opened

her mouth, and he silenced her with a hard kiss. "Uh-uh," he said, wagging a finger at her. "Don't interrupt, or I'll have to kiss you again."

She narrowed her eyes, but said nothing.

"I've listened to every word you've ever said to me since I met you, but I never really heard what you were saying. Until just now. I'm sorry, Harry-et. You'll never know how sorry. I guess the truth is, I didn't want you to be able to manage on your own."

"Why not?" she cried.

He swallowed hard. "I wanted you to need me." He paused. "I wanted you to love me."

"Oh, Nathan. I do. I—"

He kissed her hard to shut her up so that he could finish, but somehow her lips softened under his. Her tongue found the seam of his lips and slipped inside and searched so gently, so sweetly, that he groaned and returned the favor. It was a long time before he came to his senses.

"So, will you give me another chance?" he asked.

She smiled. "Will you call off your neighbors?"

"Done. I have one more question to ask."

"I'm listening."

"Will you marry me?"

The smile faded from her lips and worry lines furrowed her brow. "I do love you, Nathan, but..."

"But you won't marry me," he finished tersely.

"Not right now. Not yet."

"When?"

"When I've proved I can manage on my own," she said simply. "And when I'm sure you've learned what it means to be an equal partner."

"But—"

She put her fingertips on his lips to silence him. "Let's not talk any more right now, Nathan. There are other things I'd rather be doing with you." She suited deed to word and let her fingers wander over his face in wonder. To the tiny crow's-feet at the corners of his eyes. To the deep slashes on either side of his mouth. To the bristled cheeks that needed shaving.

"Smile for me, Harry-et."

It was harder than she'd thought it would be. She had just turned down a proposal of marriage from a man she loved. Harry told herself she'd done the right thing. If she'd said yes, she would never have known for sure how much she could accomplish by herself. When she sold her lambs in the fall and paid off the bank, then she'd know for sure. Then, if Nathan held to his promise to treat her as an equal, she could marry him. That was certainly something she could smile about.

Nathan watched the smile begin at the corners of her mouth. Then her lower lip rounded and her upper lip curled, revealing the space between her two front teeth that he found so enchanting. He captured her mouth and searched for that enticing space with his tongue, tracing it, and then the roof of her mouth, and the soft underskin of her upper lip. Then his teeth closed gently over her lower lip and nibbled before his tongue sought the honeyed recesses of her mouth once more.

Harry groaned with pleasure. She wasn't an anxious virgin now. She knew what was coming. Her body responded to the memories of Nathan's lovemaking that had never been far from her mind over

the past month since they had made love. But she saw
the flash of pain when Nathan tried to raise himself
on his arms. And that took away all the pleasure for
her.

"Nathan. Stop. I think we should wait until your
shoulder's better before—"

He rolled over onto his back and positioned her on
his belly, with her legs on either side of him. "There.
Now my shoulder will be fine."

"But how…"

His hands cupped her breasts through her shirt, his
thumbs teasing the nipples into hard buds. "Use your
imagination, sweetheart. Do whatever feels right to
you."

Harry smiled. Nathan wasn't wearing a shirt. She
took both of his hands and laid them beside him on
the bearskin rug. "Don't move. Until I say you can."

Then she leaned over and circled his nipple with
her tongue. His gasp widened her grin of delight. Her
fingertips traced the faint traces of bruise that were
the only remaining signs that he'd dislocated his
shoulder. Her lips soothed where her fingers had been.
She traced the length of his neck with kisses and
nipped the lobe of his ear. Then her tongue traced the
rim of his ear, and she whispered two words she'd
never thought she'd say out loud to a man. She saw
his pulse jump, felt his breath halt. The guttural sound
in his throat was raw, filled with need.

His hands clutched her waist and pulled her hard
against him, but she sat up abruptly. "You're not
playing by the rules, Nathan," she chastised, placing
his hands palm down on the floor. "No touching."

She smiled a wanton, delicious smile and added, "Yet."

She felt his hardness growing beneath her and rubbed herself against him through his jeans.

"Harry-et," he groaned. "You're killing me. Whatever you do, just don't stop," he rasped.

Harry laughed at his nonsensical request. She reached down and cupped him with her hand, and felt his whole body tighten like a bowstring. Her exploration was gentle but thorough. By the time she was done, Nathan was arched off the floor, his lower lip clenched in his teeth.

"Have I ever told you what a gorgeous man you are, Nathan?"

"No," he gasped.

"You are. These high cheekbones." She kissed each one tenderly. "This stubborn chin." She nipped it with her teeth. "Those blue, blue eyes of yours." She closed them with her fingertips and anointed them with kisses. She moved down his body, her fingertips tracing the ridges and curves of his masculine form, her mouth following to praise without words.

With every caress Harry gave Nathan she felt herself blossom as a woman. She wanted a chance to return the pleasure he'd given her on Nyla's Meadow. She unsnapped his jeans and slowly pulled the zipper down. She started to pull his jeans off, then paused. Her hand slipped into his pockets one by one. Right front. Left front. Right rear. In the left rear pocket she found what she was looking for. "My, my," she said, holding out what she'd found. "Mr. Prophylactic."

"I don't know how that got there," Nathan protested.

"Just thank goodness it was, and shut up," Harry said with a laugh. She dropped the condom onto the bearskin nearby and finished dragging Nathan's jeans down, pulling off his briefs along with them, leaving him naked. And aroused.

She couldn't take her eyes off him. She certainly couldn't keep her hands off him. She opened the condom and sheathed him with it, taking her time, arousing him, teasing him, taunting him.

Nathan had reached his limit. He grasped Harryet's shirt and ripped the buttons free. Her jeans didn't fare much better. He had her naked in under nine seconds and impaled her in ten. She was slick and wet and tight. "You feel so good, Harry-et. Let me love you, sweetheart."

Harry felt languorous. Her body surged against Nathan's. He put a hand between them, increasing the tension she felt as he sought out the source of her desire. When she leaned over, he captured her breast in his mouth and suckled her. Sensations assaulted her: pleasure, desire, and her body's pulsing demand for release.

"Nathan," she gasped.

His mouth found hers as his hands captured her hips. They moved together, man and woman, part and counterpart, equal to equal.

Harry clutched Nathan's waist, arching toward the precipice, reaching for the satisfaction that was just beyond her reach.

Nathan felt her tensing, felt her fight against release. "Let go, sweetheart. It's all right. Soar. Back to Nyla's Meadow, darling. We can go there together."

Then it was too late for words. She was rushing toward satisfaction. Nathan stayed with her, his face taut with the passion raging within him. She cried out, and he thrust again. A harsh sound rose from deep in his throat as he released his seed.

Harry felt the tears coming and was helpless to stop them. They stung her cheeks, hot and wet. Nathan felt them against his face and raised his head in disbelief.

"Harry-et?"

She reached a hand up to brush the golden locks from his brow. "It's all right, Nathan. I just felt so...overwhelmed for a moment."

He pulled her into his arms and held her tightly. "You have to marry me Harry-et. I love you. I want to keep you safe."

Harry buried her face in his shoulder. "I love you, Nathan, but it scares me."

"How so?"

"It's taken me a long time to get the courage to strike out on my own. I've hardly had a chance to try my wings."

"We'll learn to fly together, Harry-et."

What she couldn't explain, what she hardly understood herself, was her fear of surrendering her new-found control over her life. Nathan needed to be needed. She loved him enough to do anything she could to make him happy. That gave him a great deal of power. She simply had to find a way to accept his gestures of loving concern...and still keep the independence she was fighting so hard to achieve.

A knock on the door sent them both scrambling for their clothes.

"That'll be Luke," Nathan said as he yanked on

his jeans. "I told him I wanted to talk over the plans for his bachelor party."

"Abigail's likely to be with him," Harry said as she tied her buttonless shirt in a knot. "I wanted to make sure it's all right with her to plan a combination bridal/baby shower."

They finished dressing at almost the same time, then stood grinning at each other.

"Shall we go greet our guests?" Nathan asked.

"I'm ready."

Harry fitted herself against Nathan as he slipped his arm around her shoulder for support. It took them a while to get downstairs, but Nathan had already shouted at Luke to let himself in and make himself at home. Sure enough, when they reached the living room, they found that Abigail was with him. After exchanging greetings, Nathan and Luke settled down in the living room while Harry and Abigail headed for the kitchen.

Luke waited only long enough for the two women to disappear before he asked, "Did you ask her?"

"Yep."

"So?"

"She said she'd think about it."

"For how long?"

Nathan thrust a hand through his hair in frustration. "She didn't give me a definite timetable. But at least until she sells her lambs in the fall."

"Guess that shoots the double wedding," Luke muttered.

"There's no reason why we can't go ahead and plan your wedding to Abby," Nathan said.

"We've got a few months yet before the baby

comes. I'm willing to wait a while." He grinned. "I've gotten sort of attached to the idea of having a double wedding with my best friend."

Nathan smiled. "What's Abigail going to say about the delay?"

"You won't believe this, but I'm the one in a rush to get married. Abby says she won't love me any less if we never have a ceremony and get a legal piece of paper that proclaims us man and wife."

At that moment Harry was hearing approximately the same speech from Abigail's lips.

"I'm willing to wait to have a ceremony until you and Nathan can stand at the altar with us," Abigail said. "Really, Harry, I can't believe you turned him down!"

"I had no idea you and Luke were thinking about a double wedding with the two of us," Harry said as she measured the coffee into the pot.

"Well, now that you know, why not change your mind and say yes to Nathan?" Abigail said with an impish grin.

Harry pursed her lips. "I'm sorry to throw a screw in the works, but I have some very good reasons for wanting to wait."

"Fear. Fear. And fear," Abigail said.

"Do I hear the voice of experience talking?"

Abigail bowed in recognition of the dubious honor. "But of course. You're speaking to a woman who was afraid to fall in love again. Everyone I had ever cared about had died. I didn't want to face the pain of losing someone else I loved."

"But Luke is perfectly healthy!" Harry exclaimed.

"Reason has very little to do with fear. What is it you're afraid of, Harry?"

Harry poured a cup of coffee and stared into the blackness. "That I'll be swallowed up by marriage to Nathan." She turned and searched out Abigail's green eyes, looking for understanding. "I'm just learning to make demands. With Nathan it's too tempting to simply acquiesce. Does that make any sense?"

"Like I said, there's nothing rational about our fears. I know mine was very real. You just have to figure out a way to overcome it."

"I thought I was taking a big step just coming to Montana," Harry said. "Nathan's proposal strikes me as a pretty big leap into a pretty big pond."

"Come on in," Abigail said with a smile. "The water's fine."

Harry couldn't help smiling back at Abigail. She had come to Montana knowing there were battles to be fought and won. At stake now was a lifetime of happiness with Nathan. All she had to do was find the courage to deal with whatever the future brought.

There was yet another war to be fought, but on an entirely different field. Harry wanted to convince Nathan it wasn't too late to pursue the dreams he'd given up so long ago. She had already put her battle plan in motion.

While searching for some extra sheets in a linen closet, Harry had discovered Nathan's drafting table. It was in pieces, and she had spent the past few weeks finding the right place to locate it. She had finally set it up in front of the window that overlooked the majestic, snowcapped Absarokas. Surely such a view would provide the inspiration an aspiring architect needed.

She had seen Nathan eye the table when they'd come downstairs to greet Luke and Abigail. She knew that as soon as the couple left, she would have some fast talking to do. As Nathan waved a final goodbye to Luke and Abigail, Harry walked into the living room and settled herself in the rocker that Nathan usually claimed.

The instant he closed the front door, Nathan turned to Harry and demanded, "What's that doing in here?"

"I would think that's obvious. It's there so you can use it."

"I've already told you I don't have time for drawing," he said harshly.

"Not drawing, designing," she corrected. Harry watched him limp over to the table. Watched as his hand smoothed lovingly over the wooden surface. *He misses it.* That revelation was enough to convince Harry she should keep pushing. "I couldn't help thinking that all those movie stars moving into Montana are going to be needing spacious, beautiful homes. Someone has to design their mountain sanctuaries. Why not you?"

"I'm a sheep rancher, that's why." He settled into the ladder-back stool she had found in the tack room in the barn, and shifted the T square up and down along the edge of the drafting table. "Besides, when would I have time to draw?"

"Montana is blessed with a lot of long winter nights," she quipped.

He rose from the table and limped over to stand in

front of her. "There are other things I'd rather be doing on a long winter night." He took her hands and pulled her out of the rocker and into his embrace. "Like holding my woman," he murmured in her ear. "Loving her good and hard."

"Sounds marvelous," she said. "Designing beautiful houses. Designing beautiful babies."

"You make it sound simple."

"It can be. Won't you give it a try?"

He hugged her hard. "Don't start me dreaming again, Harry-et. I've spent a long time learning to accept the hand fate has dealt me."

"Maybe it's time to ask for some new cards."

Nathan shook his head. "You never give up, do you? All right, Harry-et. I'll give it a try."

She gave him a quick kiss. "I'm glad."

Nathan had no explanation for why he felt so good. He'd given up all hope of designing significant buildings a long time ago. But mountain sanctuaries for movie stars? It was just whimsical enough to work. He would make sure that the structures fitted in with the environment, that they utilized the shapes and materials appropriate to the wide open Montana spaces. Maybe it wasn't such a crazy idea, after all.

He looked down into Harry-et's glowing brown eyes. He had never loved anyone as much as he loved her. "Come back upstairs with me," he urged.

"I can't. It's time for me to go home."

"Stay."

"I can't. I'll be in touch, Nathan. Goodbye."

Harry kept her chin up and her shoulders back as she walked out the door. It made no sense to be walking away from the man she loved. Maybe over the next few weeks she could get everything straightened out in her mind. Maybe she could convince herself that nothing mattered as much as loving Nathan. Not even the independence she had come to Montana to find.

Ten

Where is a western small-town wedding reception held?

Answer: The church basement if large enough, otherwise the Moose Hall.

Harry found it hard living in her dilapidated cabin again. Of course, her place was tiny and primitive and utterly unlivable in comparison to Nathan's. But she had coped with those things for months and had never minded. Now she couldn't wait to leave Cyrus's cabin each morning. Because it felt empty without Nathan in it.

Harry had spent a lot of time lately thinking about what was important to her. Nathan headed the list. Independence wasn't even running a close second. Harry was having trouble justifying her continued refusal of the sheepman's wedding proposal. These days Harry was so self-sufficient that it was hard to remember a time when she hadn't taken care of herself. She was starting to feel foolish for insisting that Nathan wait for an answer until she sold her lambs and paid off her loan at the bank.

Everything was clarified rather quickly when she received a call from her father.

"Your mother and I will be coming for a visit in two weeks, Harriet, to check on your progress. While we're there we'd really like to see where you're living."

"My place is too small for company, Dad. I'll meet you at The Grand in Big Timber," Harry countered.

"By the way, how are you, darling?" her mother asked.

"Just fine, Mom. I've had a proposal of marriage," Harry mentioned casually. "From a rancher here."

"Oh, dear. Don't rush into anything, darling," her mother said. "Promise me you won't do anything rash before we get there."

"What did you have in mind, Mom?"

"Just don't get married, dear. Not until your father and I have a chance to look the young man over."

"Your mother is right, Harriet. Marriage is much too important a step to take without careful consideration."

"I'll keep that in mind, Dad. I've got to go now." She couldn't help adding, "I've got to feed the chickens and slop the hogs."

Harry felt a twinge of conscience when she heard her mother's gasp of dismay. But her father's snort of disgust stiffened her resolve. She was proud of what she'd accomplished since coming to the valley. If her parents couldn't appreciate all she had done, that was their loss. She wasn't going to apologize for what she'd become. And she sure wasn't going to apologize for the man she had just decided to marry.

As soon as her parents clicked off, she dialed Nathan's ranch. She heard his phone ring once and quickly hung up. This was too important an announcement to make over the phone. Besides, she hadn't seen Nathan for ten long, lonely days. She wanted to be there, to see Nathan's face, and share her excitement with him. The pigs and the chickens would have to wait.

Halfway to Nathan's house, Harry realized he would probably be working somewhere on the ranch, out of communication with the house. To her surprise, when she knocked on the door, he answered it.

"What are you doing home?" she asked as he ushered her inside. "You're supposed to be out somewhere counting sheep."

"I'm drawing," he said with a smug smile. "I've been hired to design a house for a celebrity who's moving to Big Timber. Very high-muckety-muck. Cost is no object."

She heard the eagerness in his voice. And the pride and satisfaction. "Then I guess I'd better say yes before you get too famous to have anything to do with us small-time sheep ranchers. So, Nathan, the answer is yes."

"What did you say?"

"Yes, I'll marry you."

"Don't play games with me, Harry-et."

"I'm not playing games, Nathan. I said I'll marry you, and I meant it."

A moment later Harry knew why she'd come in person. Nathan dragged her into his arms and hugged her so tightly that she had to beg for air. Then his mouth found hers and they headed for Nyla's Meadow. When she came to her senses, she was lying under Nathan on the couch and her shirt was unbuttoned all the way to her waist. That didn't do him as much good as it might have, since she was wearing bibbed overalls that got in his way.

Nathan's mouth was nuzzling its way up her neck to her ear when he stopped abruptly. "I don't mean to look a gift horse in the mouth, Harry-et, but what changed your mind?"

"I had a call from my parents. They're coming to visit again."

"And?"

"They wanted to look you over. Like a side of beef. To make sure you were Grade A Prime. I thought that sort of behavior particularly inappropriate for a sheepman. So I've decided to make this decision without them."

"And in spite of them?" Nathan asked somberly. He sat up, pushing Harry-et off him, putting the distance of the couch between them. "I don't want you to marry me to prove a point to your parents. Or to yourself."

"My parents have nothing to do with my decision," Harry protested. "I thought you'd be happy."

"I was. I am. I just don't want you to have regrets later. Once we tie the knot, I expect it to be forever. No backing out. No second thoughts. I want you to

be sure you're choosing to be a sheepman's wife—
my wife—of your own free will.''

Harry felt tears burning behind her eyes and a lump
growing in her throat at Nathan's sudden hesitance.
''Are you sure you haven't changed your mind?'' she
accused.

''I was never the one in doubt, Harry-et. I love you.
I want to spend my life with you. You're the one who
said you didn't want to give up your independence.
Do you wonder that I question your sudden about-
face?''

''What can I do to prove to you that I'm sincere?''

Nathan took a deep breath. ''Introduce me to your
parents as your fiancé. Let them get to know me without stuffing me down their throats. Give yourself a
chance to react to their reactions. See if you still feel
the same way after they've gone. If you want to marry
me then, Harry-et, I'll have you at the altar so fast
it'll make your head spin.''

''It's a deal.''

Harry-et held out her hand to seal the bargain and,
like a fool, he took it. His reaction was the same today
as it had been yesterday, as it would be tomorrow. A
bolt of electricity shot up his arm, his heart ham-
mered, his pulse quickened. But instead of letting her
go he pulled her into his embrace, holding her close,
breathing the scent of her—something stronger than
My Sin…more like…Her Sheep. It was the smell of
a sheepman's woman. And he loved her for it.

Harry suffered several bouts of ambivalence in the
days before her parents were due to arrive.

Maybe she should have pressed Nathan to get married.

Maybe she should have left well enough alone.

Maybe she should have sold her lambs early.

Maybe she should have sold out and gone home long ago.

Harry didn't know why confronting her parents with her decision to marry Nathan should be so difficult. She only knew it was.

She arrived at The Grand on the appointed day with Nathan in tow. "I'll make the introductions," Harry said. "Just let me do the talking."

"It's all right, Harry-et. Relax. Your parents love you."

"I'll try to remember that." And then they were there and she was hugging her mother and then her father and Nathan was shaking their hands. "Where's Charlie?" she asked.

"Your mother and I decided to come alone."

That sounded ominous. "Mom, Dad, this is Nathan Hazard. Nathan, my mother and father."

"It's nice to see you again Mr. and Mrs. Alistair. Why don't we all go find a booth inside?" Nathan suggested.

Harry let him lead her to a booth and shove her in on one side. He slid in after her while her parents arranged themselves on the other side.

"So, Mr. Hazard—"

"Nathan, please."

"So, Nathan, what's this we hear about your wanting to marry our girl?" Harry's father demanded.

Harry groaned. She felt Nathan's hand grasp her thigh beneath the table. She took heart from his reassurance. Only his hand didn't stay where he'd put it. It crept up her thigh under the skirt she'd worn in hopes of putting her best foot forward with her parents. She grabbed his hand to keep it where it was and tried to pay attention to what Nathan was saying to her father.

"And you'd be amazed at what Harry's done with the place."

"What about that federal lease for grazing land, Harriet? Your banker told me the last time I was here that there isn't much chance he could make you a loan to cover it."

"We worked it out, Dad," Harry said. "I'll be selling my lambs in a couple of weeks. Barring some sort of catastrophe, I'll make enough money to pay off the bank and have some working capital left over for next year."

"Well. That's a welcome relief, I imagine," Harry's mother said. "Now about this wedding—"

"My mind is made up, Mom. You can't change it. I'm marrying Nathan. I love him. I want to spend my life with him."

"I don't think I've ever heard you speak so forcefully, my dear," her mother said.

"It does appear you're determined to go through with this," her father said.

Harry's hand fisted around her fork. "I am," Harry said. "And I'm staying in Montana. I'm where I belong."

"Well, then, I guess there's nothing left to do except welcome you to the family, young man." Harry's father held out his hand to Nathan, who grinned and let go of Harry's thigh long enough to shake her father's hand.

Harry was stunned at her parents' acquiescence.

Was that all it took? Was that all she'd ever needed to do? Had she only needed to speak up for what she wanted all these years to live her life as she'd wanted and not as they'd planned? Maybe it was that simple. But until she'd come to Montana, until she had met and fallen in love with Nathan, Harry hadn't cared enough about anything to fight for it.

She sat up straighter in her seat and slipped her hand under the table to search out interesting parts of Nathan she could surreptitiously caress. His thigh was rock-hard under her hand. So were other parts of him. The smile never left her face during the entire dinner with her parents.

When the meal was over, Harry's mother and father rose to leave. Nathan stayed seated, excusing himself and Harry. "We have a few more things to discuss before we go our separate ways, if you don't mind."

"Not at all," Harry's father said.

Her mother leaned over and whispered in her ear, "Your young man has lovely manners, dear. You must bring him to Williamsburg for a visit sometime soon. And let me know as soon as you set a date for the wedding."

Harry stood and hugged her mother across the table. "To tell you the truth, we'd really like to get married while you're here, so you can come to the wedding. It isn't going to be a large gathering. Just a simple ceremony with me and Nathan...and another bride and groom."

"A double wedding! My goodness. Who's the other happy couple? Have we met them?"

"You will. They're friends of mine and Nathan's," Harry said.

"At least let me help with the reception," her mother said.

"I don't know, Mom. You don't know anyone in town. How can you possibly—"

"Trust me, dear. Just say you'd like my help."

Harry grinned. "All right, Mom. I'll leave the reception in your hands."

Nathan waited only long enough for Harry's parents to leave before he grabbed her by the hand and hauled her out of the booth. "You've got some nerve, young lady," he said as he dragged her up the stairs and closed one of The Grand's bedroom doors behind them.

"What do you mean, Nathan?"

He caught her by the shoulders and inserted his thigh between her legs, pulling her forward so that she was riding him.

Harry gasped.

His mouth came down on hers with all the passion she'd aroused in him when he'd been unable to take her in his arms. "That'll teach you to play games under the table."

"I've learned my lesson, Nathan," she said with a sigh of contentment. "Teach me more."

Nathan reached over and turned the lock on the door. "Your wish is my command."

"Nathan?"

"Yes, Harry-et."

"I love you."

"I love you, too."

They didn't say anything for long moments because their mouths were otherwise pleasantly occupied.

"Nathan?" Harry murmured.

"Yes, Harry-et."

"Where do you suppose my mother will end up having the reception?"

"The Moose Hall," he said as he nuzzled her throat.

Harry laughed. "You're kidding."

"Nope. It's the only place available except for the church basement, and that's too small."

"Too small? How many people are you inviting?"

Nathan smiled and kissed her nose. "You really are a tenderfoot, Harry-et. Everyone in Sweet Grass County, of course."

Harry's eyes widened. "Will they all show up?"

"Enough of them to make your mother's reception a success. Now, if you're through asking questions, I'd like to kiss that mouth of yours."

"Your wish is my command," Harry replied.

Nathan laughed. "Don't overdo it, Harry-et. A simple 'Yes, dear' will do."

"Yes, dear," she answered with an impudent grin.

"You're mine now, Harry-et. Forever and ever."

"Yes, dear."

"We'll live happily ever after. There'll be no more feuding Hazards and Alistairs. Your land is mine, and my land is yours. It's all *ours*."

"Yes, dear."

"And there'll be lots of little Hazard-Alistairs to carry on after us."

Harry's eyes softened and she surrendered to Nathan's encompassing embrace. "Oh, yes, dear."

* * * * * *

Escorting a novice nun and an orphaned baby through the jungle was tougher than any assignment Reilly had had in the army. He couldn't fight his own desires... or camouflage his hope that Sister Carlie would give in to temptations of the flesh....

THE SOLDIER & THE BABY
Anne Stuart

Chapter One

She moved through the empty hallways, her sandaled feet silent beneath the heavy swish of her long skirts. It was a quiet afternoon—the jungle surrounding the decaying remains of the Convent of Our Lady of Repose was thick and heavy with heat and somnolence. Even the birds and the monkeys had lapsed into a drowsy trance.

Every living creature with sense napped during the hottest part of the day in the tiny Central American country of San Pablo. Every living creature, that is, except for Carlie Forrest, better known as Sister Maria Carlos, novice of the order of the Sisters of Benevolence. She was the only member of the religious community still trapped in that revolution-torn place.

The others had left, swiftly, safely. Most of them would be in Spain by now, Mother Superior had said, though a few would head down to Brazil, where there was a large and thriving sister house. Only Carlie had remained behind. Carlie and her patients.

"I don't like leaving you behind in this situation," Reverend Mother Ignacia had said, her wrinkled face creased with worry. "I don't like leaving anyone behind, but Sister Mary Agnes is too old and sick to travel, and Caterina's baby is already a week overdue. I don't dare risk taking either of them, and you're the only one with midwifery skills as well as medical knowledge.''

''I'll be fine,'' Carlie had answered with deceptive serenity. ''I doubt you could make me leave.''

''I haven't forgotten what brought you here to us, my child,'' Mother Ignacia had said gently. ''I would give anything not to put you in the way of that kind of situation again.''

''I survived when I was seventeen,'' Carlie had replied, pleating the folds of her habit. ''I'm stronger now.''

''I know you are,'' Mother Ignacia had said. ''But I still would spare you if I could. I suppose I shouldn't worry—this might be just what you need. It might give you time to think a few things through. You'll be safe enough here—neither the soldiers nor the rebels would dare interfere with a convent. I'm afraid that Sister Mary Agnes hasn't long, poor old lady, but Caterina is young and strong. Once she delivers her baby her family will see to her, and you can follow us to Brazil if things haven't stabilized. And if it's still what you want. Matteo will arrange safe transport.''

''It's what I want,'' Carlie had said quietly. ''There's nothing I need to think through. I've been with the Sisters of Benevolence for nine years now, and all I've ever wanted was to take my final vows.''

It was an old argument, one Mother Ignacia was skilled at countering. ''When you join us in Brazil we will talk about it again.''

"I'm ready, Mother," Carlie had said, allowing the note of desperation to creep in.

"I'm sure you feel that way, my child. I just can't rid myself of the notion that you are running away from life, rather than running to us."

Even now, on that still and silent afternoon, Mother Ignacia's words rang in her head. Carlie prided herself on her self-knowledge, and the fear that Reverend Mother might be right terrified her more than any human or wild beast that might roam the jungle outside the abandoned convent.

It was blistering hot, even for one who was used to it. She didn't dare go swimming—there were newcomers in the area, soldiers, people who didn't want to be seen. She hadn't yet sent word to Matteo and for very good reason.

The baby wasn't ready to travel.

Mother Ignacia had been right about one thing. Sister Mary Agnes hadn't lasted long—within three days of the emptying of the convent the old nun had breathed her last. She'd received her last rites more than a week before, and she hadn't regained consciousness. It had been a good life, a long one, serving God, and Carlie hadn't even wept when she'd laid her out.

But the Reverend Mother had been wrong about something else. Caterina Rosaria Morrissey de Mendino had delivered her baby easily enough, a small, healthy little boy she'd named William Timothy. And then she'd quietly, swiftly died.

Matteo had come to bury them. Matteo had crossed himself, muttered something about seeing to her escape, then looked askance at the newborn. "The baby will never survive," he'd said. "And just as well."

"What do you mean?" Carlie had demanded, exhaustion and shock tearing away at her fundamental calm.

"This country has had enough of the Mendinos. They have ruled San Pablo, bled it dry for the past forty years. It is better than no trace of them remain. God has chosen to take the little one's mother—if God doesn't take the baby, then the soldiers will. They, or the rebels."

"Caterina had nothing to do with her father's crimes."

"She was the daughter of the *presidente*. Her son would be of the same line."

"Son?" Carlie had said instantly. "What makes you think the child is a boy?"

Matteo had looked confused for a moment. "I thought you said..."

"Caterina gave birth to a baby girl," Carlie had said firmly. "She named her after her mother."

Matteo had crossed himself. "Poor little thing. I promised Mother Ignacia I would find a way out for you, Sister Maria Carlos. I can't promise I can find a way for the baby."

"I won't leave without...her." The hesitation had been so brief Matteo hadn't noticed.

"I will see what I can manage."

It had been three weeks. The baby had grown stronger, the supply of powdered formula and clean water had been more than sufficient, and it seemed as if everyone, including Matteo and the baby's father, had forgotten their existence.

For that Carlie would only be grateful.

It was bad enough that she was alone in the midst of a revolution-torn country, with an infant, no weapons and no disposition to use any if she were to possess them. But that baby was the only grandchild of the notorious Hector Mendino, deposed and executed dictator of San Pablo.

Hector Mendino had fathered no children. His second wife already had a daughter from her previous marriage—Caterina—and Mendino had adopted her. Caterina had always disliked her brutal stepfather, but that hadn't stopped Mendino. And it wouldn't stop the rebels, who saw any connection to Mendino as something to be wiped out.

There was no way Carlie was going to let anyone wipe out the threat of one tiny little life. Timothy was a blond-haired angel, with nothing like Hector Mendino's heavy, brutal good looks. He probably looked like the American soldier who'd married Caterina. The American soldier who should arrive, sooner or later, to collect his son and wife, only to learn he was now a widower.

The fighting had been growing steadily closer to the mountain area surrounding the convent. At night Carlie would lie in bed and listen to the sound of gunfire in the distance. Timothy lay in the crib near her narrow cot, and the sound of his light, even breathing would calm her. Nothing, nothing would be allowed to hurt him.

She'd moved into Caterina's room in the infirmary, rather than drag all the baby paraphernalia back to her tiny cell. Caterina's clothes still hung in the closet, her jewelry sat in a small satin bag on a table. All except for her wedding ring. Billy Morrissey would want that, she knew, when she told him of Caterina's death. She'd slid it on her own hand, keeping it safe for him.

She was miserably hot and tired. Timothy hadn't slept well the night before, and consequently neither had she. The generator was out of fuel, there was no way to cool the place, and the current thick heat was worse than she could ever remember. The baby was napping peacefully now, his diaper changed, his tiny belly full, his miniature thumb tucked in his mouth. Without hesitation Carlie stripped off the heavy layers of clothing that comprised her old-fashioned habit, ruffled her fingers through her short-cropped hair and headed for the shower.

The water was blessedly cool as it sluiced over her body, and she stood beneath its fall, comfortable for the first time in days. In all these years she'd never grown accustomed to the heat. Sister Mary Agnes used to tease her, tell her she should go back to the States and join an order that advocated modern clothes and air-conditioning. And Carlie had managed to smile in return, secure in the knowledge that no one would ever make her go back.

She stepped from the shower, reluctant to leave its coolness, and pulled one of the threadbare towels around her body. Timothy would sleep for hours now, and Carlie couldn't afford to waste time daydreaming in the shower. There were diapers to fold and some sort of meal to forage. Beans and rice, her staple, would have to do, washed down with water. It had been all she'd had to eat for weeks now, and her bones were beginning to stick out. She glanced at

herself in the mirror as she continued to towel her
body dry.

It was just as well she'd chosen a religious life, she
thought wryly. She was hardly the epitome of any
man's dreams.

She was too short, barely topping five feet. Too
skinny, with small, immature breasts, narrow, bony
hips and small, delicate hands and feet. Her dark hair
was hacked off as short as it could go, since it was
usually tucked under a simple white wimple. She
looked into the mirror and saw her parents' faces staring back. Her mother's blue eyes, her father's dark
brown hair and high cheekbones. Her mother's stubborn, generous mouth and short nose. Her father's
pale skin and freckles.

Her face was all she had left of them. They were
long dead, their blood soaking into the jungle floor of
San Pablo, as was the blood of so many others. She
would be damned before she let them hurt Timothy,
as well.

There was no noise beyond the closed door of the
bathroom. Timothy still slept soundly. And yet Carlie
paused, her hand on the doorknob, the oversize towel
draped around her body, all her senses suddenly alert.

She heard it then. A sound so faint it was almost
indiscernible. A faint, scraping sound, as someone
moved about the bedroom.

She turned, looking around the bathroom, but she'd
left her long black habit tossed across the bed. There
was one window in the room, high up, but she could
reach it if she stood on the toilet. She could climb
through—she was small enough to fit—and she could
be away from there before the intruder even realized

she was gone. She could be gone, but she would have to leave Timothy behind.

There was no question in her mind. The towel was threadbare but the size of a small blanket. She wrapped it around her more securely, reached for the door and opened it, as silently as she could.

He was leaning over the crib. At first all she could see was his back, his long legs, dressed in camouflage and khaki, and she felt a sick knot of dread in the pit of her stomach. "Don't touch him," she said, wanting to sound dangerous, but the words came out in a breathless plea.

He turned slowly, and there was a gun in his hand. A very large, nasty-looking gun, pointed straight at her.

For a moment all she could see was the weapon. If he shot her, who would take care of Timothy? Panic clouded in around her, but she fought it, lifting her head to stare at his face.

That's where she got her second shock. This immense, dangerous-looking man pointing a gun at her was no member of Mendino's black-shirted brigade, and no ragtag revolutionary ready to kill for his beliefs. The man staring at her through eyes the color of amber was undoubtedly an American.

"Billy?" she managed to choke out, stepping toward him, out of the shadows, ignoring the threat of the gun.

It was no longer a threat. He tucked it in his belt, staring at her, an unreadable expression in his eyes. "Don't you know your own husband, Caterina?" he responded.

She blinked. "You're not Billy," she said. She'd

seen an old photograph among Caterina's belongings, and this man looked nothing like Billy Morrissey. The man in front of her was much taller, whipcord lean, with long dark hair that would be tolerated by no military. It was tied behind his head with a leather thong, and his face was cool, distant and severe. He was no kin to the tiny cherub still sleeping soundly. Therefore he was a danger.

"I'm Reilly," he said, as if that should explain everything.

It explained nothing. "Where's Billy?" she asked, fighting to keep her concentration. She glanced over at the bed. Her habit lay there, in an anonymous pile of black-and-white cotton, but there was no way she could casually stroll over and grab it.

"He asked me to come for you and the kid. What is it?" He turned back to stare down at Timothy.

"A girl," she said automatically. A girl stood a marginally better chance at surviving the male-dominated warfare of San Pablo.

He kept his back to her. "A girl?" he said. "Billy would've liked that."

"What do you mean by that?"

He turned back. "Billy's dead, Caterina. I'm sorry to be the one to tell you that, but the sooner you accept it the sooner we can get the hell out of here."

"I'm not Caterina," she said numbly.

He had a narrow, dark face. Not particularly handsome, but arresting. It twisted now, in a kind of gentle contempt. "Lady, I'm not in the mood for playing games. Billy told me where I'd find you. You're here, the baby's here and everyone else is long gone. Your clothes are in the closet, your jewelry's on the dresser and that looks like Billy's ring on your finger or I miss my guess. So don't try to tell me you aren't Caterina Morrissey because I'm not going to believe it.''

"All right," she said in a surprisingly steady voice. "I won't."

"I'll get you and the kid out of here and back to the States," he said. "I promised Billy and his parents I'd see to it."

"And how do you plan to do that, Mr….Reilly, did you say?"

"Just Reilly. I was in the service with Billy. I just had the sense to get out in time. But I've been trained, Mrs. Morrissey, by some of the best. I won't let anyone get to you."

"Don't call me that."

"Why? You rather be called Miss Mendino? That could bring trouble down on you real fast. Most people didn't like your father much, and they tend to hold grudges."

She stared at him for a moment. He must have realized she had just come from the shower and was wearing nothing but a towel, but he ignored it as unimportant. A good sign. He was a big man, with a sense of coiled strength about him. Not bulky, but very strong. He stared at her impassively, and that, too, was reassuring. He didn't care about her. He didn't care about the baby. He was simply doing his duty. A last favor for an old friend. And he didn't strike her as the kind of man who would fail in anything he set out to do.

"Call me Carlie," she said faintly.

"That's a hell of a nickname for Caterina," he said.

"It's what I'm used to."

He nodded. "How long will it take you to get ready?" His eyes drifted down over her body, impassive, incurious. Thank God, Carlie thought.

"A couple of days at the most. I have to pack enough for the baby, and I need to be in touch with Matteo—"

"Matteo's dead," Reilly said flatly. "He was killed a week ago by renegade soldiers. They were looking for you."

A wave of sickness and guilt washed over Carlie. "How do you know? How long have you been here?"

"Two days. I had to wait until it was safe enough to get in here. They're looking for you, you know. You and Mendino's grandchild. They're all around here."

"Who are? The rebels, or the soldiers?"

Reilly smiled then, a slow, cynical smile that still had an astonishing effect on his austere face. "Soldiers on the north side of the convent. Rebels on the south. Cliffs to the west. Jungles and swamp to the east. Choose your poison."

"It's up to me?"

"Hell, no. I just thought you might like being consulted. We're taking the jungle."

"There are pit vipers in the jungle."

"I'd rather face a pit viper than a political fanatic any day," Reilly said. "We'll leave at sunrise."

"I can't be ready—"

"We'll leave at sunrise, Caterina," he said. "Or I'll take the baby and go without you."

She stared at him. She had no doubt whatsoever he would do just that. No matter if he didn't know how to take care of a newborn, no matter if he had to strap him to his back amid grenades and rifles and machetes. He would do it, without a backward glance.

"I'll be ready," she said, allowing herself the sinful luxury of a glare.

There was no sign of triumph on his dark face. "I thought you would," he said. "Where do I find food in this place?"

"There isn't much. Beans and rice. And baby formula."

"It'll do," he said in a neutral voice. "I think I'll pass on the formula, though. Aren't you breast-feeding?" Those embarrassingly acute eyes dropped to the direction of her chest with all the interest of a farmer checking a breeding sow.

Carlie had already pulled the towel closely around her, and her arms were folded across her chest. "You wouldn't believe me if I told you I wasn't Caterina, would you?" She tried one more time. She wasn't used to lying, but fate seemed to have arranged this without consulting her.

"No, I wouldn't believe it. Why aren't you nursing the baby?"

"I'm too flat-chested."

She was hoping to embarrass him. Instead she felt a flush of color wash over her. She had been in the convent, surrounded only by women, since she was seventeen, and in that time she had never considered discussing her breasts with anyone, male or female.

His eyes dropped again, considering. "Size doesn't have anything to do with the ability to nurse."

Carlie blinked. In her capacity as local midwife she already knew that, but she'd doubted the overgrown ex-soldier would be as knowledgeable. However, her embarrassment had reached fever pitch by now. "I'm not going to discuss anatomy with you," she said stiffly.

"Good, because I'm more interested in food than your breasts right now," he said in a cool voice. "Where the hell's the kitchen?"

The mortification vanished abruptly, replaced by anger. "You'll find it if you look hard enough," she said. "In the meantime maybe you'd let me get dressed."

Again his gaze swept over her body, and she realized he had absurdly long lashes in such a dark, masculine face. "Suit yourself," he murmured. "I'll make enough for both of us. But I wouldn't bother with too much clothing if I were you. It's hotter 'n hell around here."

Carlie thought of the enveloping habit lying on the narrow bed. It would serve him right if she appeared in the kitchen fully garbed.

But she wasn't going to. It hadn't been her idea, but the choice had been taken out of her hands. Sister Maria Carlos had already left for Brazil with the twelve other Sisters of Benevolence. Caterina Rosaria Morrissey de Mendino would go with Reilly and take her child with her.

There was no way she was going to entrust the baby to a stranger. She would see him safely out of there, and then she would tell him the truth. And not a moment before.

Chapter Two

Reilly closed the door quietly behind him, shutting Caterina Morrissey and her towel-draped body away from him. She wasn't at all what he had expected. He'd known Billy for almost fifteen years, and during all that time he'd never seen him fall for anything other than a stacked, leggy blonde. He'd assumed Caterina would be cut from the same cloth—Billy had certainly never said anything to lead him to expect anything else.

She didn't look like the stepdaughter of a notorious Latin American dictator. She didn't look like the pampered socialite who'd abruptly married an American army officer, run back home to San Pablo and her life of privilege when the novelty had worn off and then tried to rejoin him once she'd found out she was pregnant. The woman in the bedroom didn't have the face of a woman used to getting her own way.

But then, who the hell was he to know what kind of face she had? He'd been far too distracted by her body, though he was pretty sure he'd managed to disguise that fact.

Like Billy, he'd never had a weakness for small,

strong women. He preferred the large, decorative sort. The woman clutching a threadbare towel around her wet body didn't seem like the kind who was used to having things handed to her. Maybe motherhood gave a spoiled brat character.

Interesting thought, but it was none of his damn business. He was there for one reason, and one reason only. To take Billy's baby home to the States, where it belonged. If Billy's widow wanted to come along, then fine. The Morrisseys would see to her, and unless motherhood had had a miraculous effect on Caterina Mendino she would be more than happy to hand the child over to her wealthy in-laws so that she could go back to enjoying life.

She hadn't realized just how thin the cloth of that enveloping towel was. He was hot, he was thirsty, and she'd stood there, glaring at him, fiercely determined to defend her child, and the water had beaded on her smooth, pale skin. He'd wanted to cross that room and lick the water from her throat.

Even now the notion made him grin wryly. She was deceptively appealing. It was no wonder Billy had married her, the man who always swore it wouldn't be fair to limit his attentions to just one woman. The woman in the other room had a subtle grace to her that was well-nigh irresistible.

It was a good thing he'd never been a slave to his powerful libido. It would take them a good four days to get back to the plane, and that was if they were extremely lucky, the weather cooperated and she wasn't the hothouse orchid he'd assumed she'd be.

She didn't look like a hothouse orchid. For all her

slender bones she looked tough and strong. They might even make it out to the plane in three days.

He hoped so. She was distracting as hell. He wasn't interested in spoiled rich girls, in new mothers, in heiresses or in the tangled politics of San Pablo. He just wanted to get the hell out, so that he could get back to his place in Colorado. And get on with his new life.

She was right—the kitchen wasn't hard to find. And the food supply was pretty damn pathetic. Red beans, rice, a hunk of hard cheese wrapped in a damp cloth and canisters of formula. He picked one up. It weighed a ton, and he cursed beneath his breath. Why the hell couldn't she have nursed her own baby? It would have made life a hell of a lot easier.

She probably didn't want to ruin her small, perfect breasts. The cotton terry of the huge towel had been thin, worn. He had seen the shape of her breasts quite clearly the moment she'd walked into the room, and he'd found himself envying the baby. Apparently there was no need. That baby wouldn't get to taste those breasts any more than he would.

Still, there was no harm in fantasy, as long as he remembered that was what it was. He could dream all he wanted about Caterina Morrissey's breasts. He just wasn't going to touch.

IF THERE WAS ONE THING Carlie was unused to, it was men. Tall, young men. Men with dark, arresting faces, bold eyes and a lethal, unconscious grace. Not to mention the gun he carried. It was no wonder she was unnerved.

She wasn't used to swearing. The words *hell* and

damn held a more literal meaning for her during the past nine years—they weren't used for punctuation.

And she certainly wasn't used to the clothes Caterina had brought with her to the Convent of Our Lady of Repose.

She stuffed the habit under the bed, squashing her instinctive guilt as she did so. Caterina's clothes still lay in the drawers, and Carlie searched through them in growing dismay.

Most of them, of course, were maternity clothes. Caterina had been a wealthy young woman, spoiled, self-absorbed, who possessed only the finest in clothing. Unfortunately most of that clothing was provocative, flimsy and huge on Carlie's smaller frame.

There was no bra that came even close to fitting her, so she had no choice but to dispense with one entirely. The silk shirts were fuchsia and turquoise, dangerously bright colors, and the pants were all miles too long. Fortunately her wardrobe came equipped with a number of fine cotton knit camisoles, and she could take a pair of scissors to the jeans and make herself cutoffs. When she finished she couldn't bring herself to look down at her body.

It had been so long since she'd worn jeans. So long since her arms and throat and head had been bare. She felt naked, exposed, vulnerable.

And cool.

She walked barefoot across the stone floor to look down at Timothy. He was sleeping still, worn-out from the night before, and she pulled the thin cotton coverlet over his little body, brushing her hand against his wispy blond hair. He had no father or mother, no one to love him and care for him.

No one but her. Caterina, her once-pretty face flushed with the fever that had ravaged her body, had clung to her hand during the last hours. "Take care of my baby," she'd whispered.

And Carlie had promised. She wasn't about to go back on that deathbed vow. Timothy was hers now, and she wouldn't relinquish him until she was certain she was doing the best thing for him.

She left the door open so that she could hear him as she made her way down the empty corridor to the kitchen. She could smell the food, and her empty stomach churned in sudden longing, her hunger overriding her nervousness.

Reilly was sitting at the table, eating slowly, steadily, his gun in front of him, close at hand. There was another place set across from him, a plate full of food and a mug of steaming liquid. She paused in the doorway, feeling faint.

"Coffee?" she whispered. "I used up the last of it two weeks ago."

"I brought some with me."

She moved slowly across the room, forgetting her exposed legs, forgetting her bare arms, forgetting everything but the food waiting for her. "What is it?"

"What you had. Beans and rice and cheese."

"Then why does it smell so good?"

"I can cook."

She paused by the side of the table, staring at him curiously, her self-consciousness evaporating beneath his impassive gaze. He was barely aware that she was female, a fact that brought her nothing but relief. It was hard enough being around a man like this. It would be even worse if he was aware of her as a woman.

"Not very many men can cook," she murmured.

"You just haven't met the right men, lady."

Lady, she thought. In her entire life no one had called her lady. Certainly no one had spoken to her in that drawling, cynical tone.

"I suppose not," she said, taking the seat opposite him. The coffee was hot, black and strong. She took a deep, scalding sip and felt courage race through her bones.

He'd already finished his meal, and he leaned back in the straight-backed chair that used to be reserved for Reverend Mother Ignacia and watched her. She was too hungry to be self-conscious at first, but gradually the coffee and the good food began to take effect.

"You're a cool one, aren't you?" he drawled.

She jerked her head up. "Why do you say that?"

"Oh, I wouldn't have expected any less. Given your jet-set life-style."

Treacherous ground, Carlie thought, reaching for her coffee. "Just how much do you know about me?"

"Not much. I never was one to read gossip columns, and you're a minor celebrity. Hell, I don't think you even get fifteen minutes of fame."

"I'd prefer it that way."

"Really?" He sounded disbelieving. "Don't you have any questions to ask me?"

"About what?"

His smile was far from pleasant. "Why, about the death of your husband? Don't you care what happened to Billy? Or do you believe there's no use crying over spilt milk?''

A wash of color flooded her face. "I care. I just… that is…I—''

"He died in a car accident," Reilly said in his cool, emotionless voice. "He was in D.C. visiting his parents. As a matter of fact, he'd gone to tell them they were about to become grandparents, and to prepare for a daughter-in-law. Unfortunately he always drove like a bat out of hell, and this time the roads were too icy. He slammed into a concrete wall and that was it.''

"Oh," she said.

"Oh," he echoed, his voice heavy with sarcasm. "I was lucky to be near enough to make it to the hospital before he died. He asked me to make sure his kid was safe. You know anything about deathbed promises?''

The memory of Caterina's dark, fevered eyes still burned a hole in Carlie's brain. "A bit," she said faintly.

"Then you'll know that I'm bringing the baby back. And if you behave yourself, do as I say, then you'll get to the States, as well. But if I have to choose between you and the kid, the kid wins.''

"As it should be," she said.

A flash of surprise lightened his eyes for a moment. "I imagine you'll find life in Washington to your liking," he said. "There are lots of parties, shopping, that sort of thing.''

"What makes you think I'd stay in Washington?''

"That's up to you. But that's where the baby stays. With his grandparents.''

"You think his grandparents have precedent over his mother?"

"I think you'll probably be ready to get on with your life. You're young enough, used to parties and having a good time. Why would you want a baby holding you back?"

"If you don't know, Mr. Reilly, I'm not about to explain it to you," she said in a furious voice.

"You might be marginally safer from your father's enemies in Washington, as well," he added in a noncommittal voice.

"I beg your pardon?"

"You know as well as I do that you're in danger, no matter where you go. People have long memories, and not very fond feelings for your stepfather."

"What makes you think Hector Mendino's enemies are interested in me? Wasn't killing him enough?"

"Not for a true fanatic. They'll be after you, and they'll be after your kid."

She stared at him, aghast. "And that's what you're taking me back to?"

"You think you're safer here?"

"No."

"As long as you're with me, no one will get to you."

For some odd reason she had no doubt of that, but she fought against such implicit, uncomfortable trust. "You're pretty sure of yourself, aren't you?"

"I know my job," he said, his voice noncommittal. "Once you're in the Capital District the professionals can take over. I'm not interested in playing hero anymore. I've done my time. This is just a last favor to an old friend. I'll see you and the kid safely to the

States, and then I'm gone. You'll never have to see me again. Understood?''

''Understood,'' she said, wondering why the notion of never seeing this man again should both relieve and disturb her. She'd met him less than an hour ago, she knew next to nothing about him, and he made her nervous.

She jerked her head up at the soft cry echoing down the corridor, a sound so faint most people wouldn't have heard it. He turned at the same time, caught by the same distant sound. ''The baby's awake,'' he said.

''I know,'' she said. ''You have good hearing.''

''It comes with being a soldier. So do you.''

''It comes with being a mother.'' It was amazing how easily the lie tripped off her tongue. A sin, one of many, and all so very easy.

He nodded. ''I'll find some place to bed down. We'll be out of here by first light.''

''I'll need to pack some supplies...''

''I'll take care of it.''

''But you don't know what the baby needs....''

''Lady, I've got a total of twelve nieces and nephews, ranging from two months to twenty-three years, and I helped raise my brothers and sisters. I know about babies.''

She believed him. At that moment she was ready to believe he knew about everything. Except who and what she was.

She nodded, rising. ''I trust you.'' The moment the words were out of her mouth she wanted to call them back.

She'd never thought she would trust a man, especially one who had been a soldier, again. But this time she had no choice. Not for her own sake. But for Timothy's.

He didn't seem surprised. He simply nodded, leaning back in his chair and looking at her, as the faint thread of sound grew louder as the baby decided he was tired of waiting. "Smart of you," he murmured.

It was no wonder women chose to live such peaceful lives, cloistered away from men, Carlie thought as she rushed back toward the baby's room. She'd forgotten, or perhaps never realized, how vastly irritating men could be.

To be sure, they had their uses. Reilly would have no trouble shooting that gun he carried, and he would see them safely out of San Pablo, she had no doubt. He could also cook, and he came equipped with coffee. Things could be worse.

He also came equipped with an attitude, and presumptions, and a condescending manner that made her want to use those very words, and worse, that he dropped so casually into his conversation. And the fact that he was huge and undeniably good-looking didn't help matters. Particularly since he was probably all too aware of how his size affected people.

No, she didn't like him. But she didn't have to like him to trust him. By the time she reached Timothy he was wailing with unrestrained fury, and she scooped him up, holding him against her breast and murmuring soft reassurances.

"You'll never grow up to be a pig, will you, sweetie?" she cooed.

And Timothy, settling down into a watery snuffle, socked her in the eye with his tiny fist.

REILLY DRAINED THE LAST of his coffee. He'd given up cigarettes more than ten years ago, and there wasn't a day that went by that he didn't miss them. But right now had to be the ultimate. He would have killed for a cigarette.

Fortunately he wasn't given that choice—a deserted convent in the middle of a jungle was not the best place to find cigarettes. He would simply have to do without.

At least it might distract him from the memory of Billy's widow. Caterina—the name didn't suit her one bit. Granted, she was only half Spanish, but she looked more Irish than anything else, with her pale skin and blue eyes. Carlie suited her. Though he was better off thinking of her simply as Mrs. Morrissey.

He pushed away from the table and began packing tins of formula in a backpack. He hoped that tiny little creature in the crib was tougher than she looked. The next few days would be rough on the adults, including a woman who'd given birth not that long ago.

It was just too damned bad he couldn't afford to wait a couple of weeks, till the baby got bigger, till Carlie got stronger. Though she certainly looked strong enough, despite the unexpected paleness of her arms and legs.

But the soldiers were moving down from the north. The rebels were moving up from the south. Reilly had learned to trust his instincts in these matters, and he knew the whole place was about to go up like a firecracker. He needed to get those two safely out of here before it happened.

Why the hell did Billy have to fall in love with the daughter of a political hot potato? It would be tough enough if this was just any woman, any baby. But Mendino's only grandchild made it impossible.

Reilly didn't pay much attention to the word *impossible*. Not when there were no other alternatives. He was going to get Carlie and her baby out of San Pablo, safely back to the States, and then he was going back to his mountaintop, alone.

But before he left, he might give in to temptation and see whether her wide, pale mouth tasted as innocent as it looked.

"What are you doing?"

"Hell!" He whirled, the gun already drawn, as her voice startled him out of his faintly erotic reflection. "Don't ever do that."

She stared at him, at the gun pointed directly at her, and her huge eyes were even wider as she shifted the baby against her shoulder. "Are you always this jumpy?"

He shoved the gun back in his belt. "Let's just say I've got good reason. We're in the middle of a war zone, and no one around here is particularly fond of your family. What's wrong with the kid?"

"He's hungry."

"He?"

"I mean she," Carlie corrected herself, shifting the squirming baby in her arms. "I keep forgetting."

"There's a fundamental difference between boys and girls, Carlie. Or haven't you been changing the baby's diapers?"

"You'd know if I hadn't," she snapped, heading for the row of freshly washed bottles. She grabbed one and tossed it to him. "Maybe you'd better get used to doing this. Two scoops of powder, then fill it with the filtered water and shake it.''

She must have expected him to refuse. Hell, he could rise to that challenge, and any other she wanted to throw at him. He caught the plastic bottle deftly, mixing up the formula. ''Sure would be easier if you were nursing,'' he murmured, handing it to her when he was finished.

The baby obviously thought so, too. She was rooting around at Carlie's breast, making loud sucking noises. She made do with the bottle, however, when her mother tucked it in her mouth.

''I would if I could,'' she snapped.

He leaned against the table. He liked making her mad, he decided. She had too much of an otherworldly calm that she kept trying to pull around her. He didn't believe in other worlds. He didn't believe much in serenity, given the circumstances.

He liked watching her feed the kid, too, even if it was with a bottle. She was a natural mother, and the look she had as she bent over the baby was a far cry from her uneasy glares in his direction.

Maybe she wouldn't leave the kid with Billy's parents. Maybe she'd learned there were other things more important than parties and fancy clothes.

But that was none of his business. He was a courier, delivering his package safely. He needed to remember that.

Before it was too late.

Chapter Three

Carlie was used to the silence. She'd been virtually alone in the old building for the past three weeks, with only the baby and the jungle noises outside to keep her company. For all that Reilly was a large man, he moved with just as much silence as the most discreet Sister of Benevolence.

But she knew he was there. Even if she couldn't hear him, she could feel his presence, permeating the very air she breathed. Man, the invader, in this house of women.

She lay on the narrow bed, sweltering in the humid night heat. There wasn't even the hint of a breeze to cool her, and the jungle birds kept up their ceaseless chattering, while Timothy slept on.

She would be leaving this place in the morning, the only home she had known for the past nine years. Sometimes it seemed like the only real home she'd ever had, but she knew that wasn't the truth. There'd been other places, other homes. The first ten years of her life had been spent in California, where her parents had ministered to migrant workers. The next seven had been in a variety of places, always in her parents' footsteps, waiting for them to remember her existence among all the needy who ruled their lives.

Reverend Mother Ignacia said they died in grace. It didn't seem like grace to Carlie, hidden down behind the trees outside the small mountain town in the north where they'd been living. They had died in blood and pain, in a hail of bullets as they tried to bring their own version of God's words to the villagers. And Carlie had watched, frozen in horror and denial, crouched down with her fist shoved in her mouth to still her screams.

It was the harried relief workers who'd found her, who'd taken her down to the jungle convent of Our Lady of Repose, where Mother Ignacia and the others had clucked over her and soothed her and brought her reluctantly back into the sheltered world they lived in. As the years passed, no one seemed to remember she was there, and Carlie had grown secure, even as the country grew more explosive.

But now her safe life had come to an end. She would be back among the living, among the soldiers and the violence. She would put her fate, and that of Timothy, in the hands of a soldier, someone who killed. She had no other choice.

She heard a scream in the distance, and she sat bolt upright for a moment, her heart pounding. Then she lay back, trying to still her breathing. It was simply a jungle cat, out stalking its prey. Nothing to worry about. Nothing that could hurt her. Besides, it was the two-legged beasts she needed to fear. She'd known that for years.

There were no clocks in the tiny convent—the nuns ran their lives on God's time, not man's. Carlie hadn't noticed the lack before, but right then, in the middle of a heat-soaked night, she would have given anything to know what time it was. Whether it was getting close to sunrise, or if it was still worth struggling with an elusive sleep.

Where was Reilly? Sleeping in Mother Ignacia's bed? Prowling the night corridors? He looked like a man who would snore, but the only sound through the empty corridors was the occasional scream of the jaguar. Maybe he didn't need to sleep at all.

She did, but that blessed reward seemed to be denied her. The longer she lay sweltering on the bed, the worse it got. Finally she rose, pushing the rough cotton sheet away from her, and pulled on Caterina's clothes. She didn't bother to light the oil lamp by her bed—she didn't want to run the risk of waking the baby. Tiptoeing to the door, she opened it into the inky darkness of the hallway.

Her foot connected with something solid, and before she could stop herself she went sprawling onto the hard tile floor, onto the hard-boned body of her protector.

The words he muttered beneath his breath as he caught her narrow shoulders were words she'd forgotten existed. She scrambled away from him, ending up against the far wall, and as her eyes grew accustomed to the darkness she realized he'd been sleeping in front of her doorway, his bedroll a mute testimony to the fact.

"Sorry," she whispered, still mindful of the sleeping baby. "I didn't know you'd be there."

"Where'd you think I'd be?" he countered irritably. "It's part of my job."

She stared at him. In the murky light she could barely see him, but she realized belatedly that she'd felt hot, bare skin beneath her when she went tumbling over him, and she wondered just how much he was wearing.

"You could have told me," she said in a deceptively reasonable tone of voice. "What time is it?"

"Quarter past four. We'll be leaving in a little more than an hour."

"Then I suppose I shouldn't bother trying to get any more sleep."

"I suppose you shouldn't," he said, and she felt more than saw him rise, heard the rustle of clothing. "I'm going to scout around the place, see if we've had any uninvited visitors. You stay put till I get back."

"But—"

"Let's get one thing clear," he said, overriding her objections. "There's only one person in charge of this little expedition, and that's me. You'll do what I tell you, no questions asked, or I'll leave you behind. Your life might depend on obeying me. The baby's certainly does."

"Yes, sir," she muttered, struggling to her feet.

A large, strong hand came down on one shoulder, and she found herself pushed back down, this time onto his sleeping bag. "Stay put," he growled. And then he vanished into the darkness.

She started to get up, then paused. It wasn't like her to be defiant. She'd learned the safety and comfort of unquestioning obedience—why was she choosing now to rebel?

She sat back down again, tucking her feet under

her and leaning her head back against the stucco wall.
There was no sound at all now, except for Timothy's
regular breathing in the other room and the steady
pulse of her own heartbeat. The sleeping bag beneath
her offered very little padding between her body and
the hard tile floor, and it still retained his body heat.
She considered lying down on the cool tiles, but she
couldn't bring herself to do it. The steady sound of
the baby mixed with the sultry stillness of the night,
and Carlie felt her eyes begin to drift shut as she
waited for Reilly to return.

It wouldn't be an easy hike out of there—she knew
it far too well. Even under the best of circumstances
they were at the treacherous edge of the rain forest,
and the roads were narrow, rutted and overgrown.

Having two warring armies on their trail wouldn't
help matters. Reilly would push, and push hard, and
right then Carlie felt too weary to even crawl back to
her own bed.

She stretched out on the sleeping bag, just for a
moment. It smelled like coffee, and gun oil, and warm
male flesh. She closed her eyes, oddly lulled by the
faint, seductive odors, and fell asleep before she could
stop herself.

THE FIRST RAYS OF DAWN were just beginning to penetrate the old convent when Reilly returned to the
hallway where he'd spent a restless night. For a moment he frowned, certain that Carlie had ignored him
and taken off. And then he saw her, curled up on his
old army-issue sleeping bag, one small, strong hand
tucked under her willful chin.

He stood over her, staring, but she didn't move,

deep in a dreamless sleep. She looked younger in sleep, innocent, with that pale, delicate skin, that soft, unkissed mouth.

Though why the hell he should think of her mouth as unkissed was beyond him. She'd done a hell of a lot more than kissing, and Billy hadn't been the sentimental sort to be enticed by amateur lovemaking. The jet-setting daughter of Hector Mendino would have had more than her share of lovers, no matter how innocent she looked.

This time he heard the faint, snuffling cry of the baby before she did. She slept on, in an exhausted daze, while he moved past her into the bedroom, conquering the urge to lean down and touch her.

The baby lay on its back, snorting and snuffling plaintively. The look it gave Reilly when he leaned over the crib was unpromising, but it made no more than a token squawk of protest when he scooped it up, grabbed a folded diaper and headed back out toward the kitchen, stepping carefully over Carlie's sleeping figure.

By the time Carlie roused herself and wandered into the kitchen the coffee was made, the backpacks were loaded and ready to go and the baby was fed and dozing peacefully against Reilly's shoulder. She paused in the doorway, her spiky black hair rumpled around her pale face, yawning.

"Why didn't you wake me?" she asked, heading for the coffeepot.

"You looked like you needed some sleep. An hour or two isn't going to make that much of a difference in when we leave, and I'm used to babies."

She froze, the coffee halfway to her mouth, then

turned to stare at him. At the infant resting comfortably against his shoulder. "I need to change her..." she began hurriedly.

"I already did."

She blushed. Odd, he wouldn't have thought someone like Caterina Morrissey de Mendino would be capable of blushing, particularly over something as innocuous as a baby's sex. "You want to revise your story just a little bit?"

She lifted her gaze to his, and the defiance in her soft mouth was more expected. "This is a Latin country, Mr. Reilly. The rebels wouldn't consider Hector Mendino's granddaughter to be much of a threat. His grandson, however, is a different matter."

She obviously expected him to object. Instead he simply nodded. "Find yourself something to eat, and then we'll get out of here."

"Where are we going?"

"Through the swamp to begin with. On foot, at least for the first day. I left a jeep about twenty miles down the track—if no one found it we'll be able to reach it by dark."

"And if someone found it?"

"We'd better hope they didn't," he said blandly. "We'll take turns carrying the baby. The damned formula weighs a ton."

"Would you stop picking on me about the formula?" she shot back. "I didn't have any choice in the matter."

He let his eyes drop. She was wearing just what she had worn the night before—a sleeveless white cotton T-shirt and cutoffs. No bra; he'd noticed that right off. Her breasts were small and perfect. Well, not perfect, if they couldn't feed a baby, he amended. But close to it.

"You'll be carrying the formula as often as I will," he said evenly. "We'll take turns with the baby."

"No. I can manage him."

"I never would have pegged you for a protective mother," he drawled, shifting the sleeping infant.

She looked more surprised than offended. "What do you know about me? We just met."

"More than you imagine. I know Billy's taste in women, and they run to thoroughbreds with expensive habits. Before I came down here I asked a few questions, and I didn't like the answers. You're a spoiled young woman, you married Billy on a whim, left him on a whim, and if you hadn't happened to get knocked up you probably would never have planned to go back to him. For all Billy's parents know, this might not even be their grandson."

"What do Billy's parents have to do with anything?"

"I told you, that's where I'm taking you. That's definitely where the baby's going. They have the money, the connections, to see to his well-being. If you want to hang around that's fine. It'll be up to you."

"A child needs family. Grandparents," she said slowly, as if she were just considering the notion. "Are they good people, these Morrisseys? Will they love Timothy, take care of him, teach him right from wrong?"

It sounded as if she'd already made up her mind to abandon him. "Trying to assuage your conscience?

They've got money. They'll hire the best people to take care of him if they think he's their grandchild.''

"I see." She reached out for the baby, and he put him in her arms. "And if they don't believe he's their grandchild?"

"I don't know if belief has much to do with it. They'll arrange for the proper blood tests."

"They don't sound like very nice people," she said in a quiet voice, cuddling the sleeping baby against her.

"What's nice got to do with it? The world hasn't got much use for nice. When it comes right down to it, money talks."

She lifted her eyes and looked straight at him. Innocent eyes, clear blue and honest. Why would someone like Caterina Mendino have innocent eyes? "Do you really believe that?"

"I've been around long enough. So have you."

She looked down at the child in her arms. "Maybe," she said. "But he hasn't. I don't want him to have to live by those rules."

"He *is* Billy's son, isn't he?"

"Go to hell, Reilly," she replied. And it must have been his imagination that her words shocked her.

IT WAS CRAZY, but for some reason Carlie was even hotter in Caterina's skimpy clothing than she was in her usual garb. The light cotton of her habit had flowed against her skin, letting air circulate around her. The knit shirt clung to Carlie's body like a blanket, making her itch. The weight of Timothy's tiny body in the sling-type holder added to the smothering sensation, and the backpack full of baby paraphernalia and the minimum of clothing must have been thirty pounds at least.

Reilly hadn't said a word as he loaded her down, other than to look askance at the shorts. "That won't be much protection against pit vipers," he said pleasantly.

"Then you'd better make sure none of them get to me," she'd retorted without hesitation. "Otherwise you'll end up carrying everything."

"Good point." He was already loaded down with at least twice the amount she was carrying, though it didn't seem to bother him in the slightest. He was looking dark and dangerous in the light of dawn, with a stubble of beard, his long hair tied in a ponytail, his rough camouflage clothes rumpled as if he'd slept in them. But he hadn't slept in them, she remembered. She'd felt warm bare skin beneath her hands. "Let's do it."

"Do what?"

He paused, staring at her in baffled frustration. "Leave," he said impatiently. "Vamoose. Split. We're out of here. We're history. ¿*Comprende?*"

"*Sí,*" she said in a cool voice. "Spanish and English I understand. I'm just not too sure of the other stuff."

"Yeah, right," he muttered under his breath. "Keep quiet and stay close. And do exactly as I say."

"Yes, my lord and master," she retorted.

He didn't deign to answer her. He simply swung off down the narrow trail that led through the swampy undergrowth, with her following behind. She had more than enough time to think about her uncharacteristic behavior.

In nine years she'd never spoken in such a snippy tone. As far as she knew, she'd never felt the annoyance, the defiance that her reluctant rescuer brought out in her with nothing more than one of those long, calculating looks. She'd cursed, too, the word slipping from her as if it were entirely natural.

She was coming back to life, and she didn't like it. It was no wonder the Sisters of Benevolence had founded their convent deep in the heart of the jungle, away from the annoyances and distractions of civilization. The sooner Carlie found her way to the sister house in Brazil, the happier she would be.

Timothy would be fine. He had grandparents with money and privilege to look after him. She had no qualms about any blood tests—Caterina had made a halting, stumbling last confession to Carlie at the end, since there was no priest around, and while there had been any number of men before she met Billy Morrissey, she insisted that the baby was her husband's.

It would be hard to give the baby up; Carlie was honest enough to admit it. In the past few weeks it had felt as if Timothy were her own, and the bond had grown so strong she'd almost forgotten Caterina's sad, short life.

But he wasn't hers. Her life was with the Sisters of Benevolence, and sooner or later she would be able to convince Reverend Mother Ignacia of that fact. Timothy's life was back in the States, with his father's family.

She kept her eyes trained on the man ahead of her as he led the way deeper into the jungle. The sooner she got away from him the better. She knew perfectly well why she was suddenly full of frustration and temper, why blasphemies and more were simmering in her brain.

Convents existed to keep men and their distractions out. Women were much better off alone, away from the annoyances of the male sex. And that was what Carlie wanted to be—safe, alone, away from Reilly.

Unbidden, Mother Ignacia's words returned to her. Was she running away from something, rather than running to the sisters? She didn't want to be a coward, or someone with a weak vocation.

"This might be for the best," Reverend Mother had said. And Carlie could only trust her wisdom.

She would put up with Reilly's overbearing, disturbing presence. She would get safely away from San Pablo, relinquish Timothy and follow her calling, secure in the knowledge that it was a strong and true one.

She would weather these temptations and triumph.

Though why she should think of someone like Reilly as a temptation was a mystery. He was an attractive man, even with that long hair and unshaven face, but she was immune to such things. He was a strong man, when she needed strength, but he was a man of violence. She had seen enough violence to last her a lifetime.

The nightmares had stopped only in the past few years. Peace had finally come, and now it was being ripped away from her. She didn't want to remember. Didn't want to relive the day in the mountaintop village of Puente del Norte, when she could hear the screams, smell the thick, coppery smell of her parents' spilled blood washing down the streets.

She wanted nothing more than to run away and

hide. Again, Reverend Mother's words rang in her head.

She would survive. She would accept Reilly's help, for her sake and the baby's. From now on she would be unfailingly polite, docile, obedient, as the sisters had taught her to be. Unquestioning, she would do exactly as Reilly ordered her, knowing that he would keep them both safe.

She would pull her serenity around her heavy-laden shoulders like a silken robe, and not a cross word would pass her lips. She managed a smile, thinking of the statue of the Madonna they'd left behind in the convent.

A branch thwapped her in the face as Reilly brushed ahead of her. "Watch what you're doing!" she snapped.

And somewhere, the Madonna laughed.

Chapter Four

The man wasn't human, Carlie decided three hours later. It was that simple. He was some sort of genetic mutation, produced by the American government to replace human soldiers in the field. No man could keep going, impervious to the heat, to the bugs, to the thick, sucking sludge at their feet, or to the weight of his pack, which probably had to be three times what she was carrying.

She was accustomed to the heat. Accustomed to pacing herself. Her pack was evenly balanced, and the baby slept snugly in his sling, content with the world and the no doubt thundering sound of Carlie's heartbeat beneath his tiny ear. Even so, the sweat was pouring down her face, her shoulders ached, her legs trembled and her feet were undoubtedly a royal mess.

There had been no shoes to fit her. The sandals that the sisters wore would provide little protection in the jungle, and she'd had to make do with Caterina's leather running shoes. Which would have been fine, if they hadn't been two and a half sizes larger than what Carlie would have normally worn.

She wouldn't have thought overlarge shoes would

cause blisters. She was discovering she was wrong. The huge shoes were rubbing her skin raw, and she'd gone beyond pain into a kind of numb misery, plodding onward, only the sight of Reilly's tall, straight back giving her something to focus on and despise with a kind of blind fury.

"We have to stop." She had no idea how long they'd been walking, deeper and deeper into the swampy muck to the east of the convent. It was dark in there, and the trees so tall overhead that sunlight could barely penetrate. It was a true rain forest—the air thick and liquid, and the bush an overgrown tangle that Reilly hacked their way through.

He stopped, so abruptly that she barreled into him. He absorbed the force of her body, casually, and she registered once more how very strong he was. And how she found that strength alarming.

"Can't handle it, princess?"

His drawling tone shouldn't have annoyed her. After all, he was mocking the person he thought she was. He didn't know he was accusing Sister Mary Charles, a woman dedicated to poverty, chastity and obedience, of being a spoiled brat.

Nevertheless, the mockery rankled. "I can handle anything you can," she snapped back. "But we happen to have a baby with us. Timothy needs to be fed, he needs to be changed and he needs to be unstrapped from this contraption for a few minutes."

"I don't hear *him* complaining."

"That's because he's little enough that the rhythm of my footsteps is keeping him asleep. Sooner or later he's going to wake up and make it very clear how fretful he can be. He'll also probably leak through all the layers of clothing, and I don't have that many changes of clothes. I don't want to spend the day reeking of baby pee in this temperature.''

He turned to look down at her. ''You sound pretty fretful yourself,'' he observed with a faint smile. ''Okay, we'll rest. Half an hour, and no longer. We already got a much later start than I planned. You were the one who overslept.''

''You were the one who didn't wake me,'' she retorted instantly, and then stopped, appalled. What would Reverend Mother Ignacia say if she heard her? How many times would she have to remind herself of the vows she wanted to take? Hadn't she learned docility, obedience, the simple shouldering of responsibility whether it was deserved or not?

But Reilly didn't make her feel docile, or obedient, and she wasn't about to take responsibility for his decisions. She was out in the world, among men, thrust there by the vagaries of fate. For as long as she remained she might as well give in to temptation and let her emotions run free. For the next few days she'd give herself permission to feel anger. Fear. Tenderness. For the next few days she would give herself permission to live.

''True enough,'' he said, unmoved by what she considered to be a show of astonishing bad temper. He unshouldered his backpack and dumped it on the thick jungle floor, then reached for hers.

She backed away, suddenly nervous, but his hands clasped down over her shoulders, holding her there. ''Easy,'' he said, his voice roughly reassuring. ''I was just trying to help.''

She forced herself to be still, cradling the baby

against her while he released the straps. The sudden relief as he lifted the pack from her shoulders was dizzying, and she swayed for a moment. Then he touched her again.

"Careful." This time his hands were on her bare arms. Rough hands, the skin callused. The hands of a man who worked hard.

She didn't stumble when he released her, but it took an enormous amount of effort not to. She sank down on the thick forest growth and released Timothy from the sling. He looked up at her out of sleepy blue eyes, opened his mouth in a yawn that swiftly turned into a mighty howl of fury.

"I know, precious, you're hungry, you're wet and you're hot," Carlie murmured. "Let me get these wet things off you and we'll get you something to eat." The soft clear sound of her voice stilled his rage for a moment, and he stared up at her as she deftly, efficiently stripped the tiny diaper from him, then fastened a new one. The convent had had a small supply of disposable diapers, and Carlie had crammed every last one of them in her backpack. She had no idea how long they'd last, but for the time being she had every intention of using them.

"How does that feel, little man?" she cooed, scooping him up. "Is it nice to have clean diapers and not be jiggled around all the time? Now just keep your temper for a few minutes while I make your bottle and…"

A bottle appeared in her line of vision—in Timothy's limited line of vision as well, and he immediately voiced his noisy demand. She took the bottle, settled back with Timothy sucking noisily, then allowed herself a glance at Reilly.

"Thanks for getting the bottle," she said.

"The sooner the kid gets fed the sooner we'll get back on the trail," he said, dismissing his actions.

Sweat was trickling down into Carlie's eyes, and she blinked it back as she looked down at the baby lying in her arms. He'd gotten bigger, stronger in the past few weeks. He was getting ready to smile, to hold his tiny, wobbly head up, to face the world. And she wouldn't be around to see those advances.

He made a squeaking sound of protest as her arms tightened around him involuntarily, and she immediately loosened her grip, feeling guilty. She couldn't give this child what he needed. And he couldn't give her what she needed. Even if it felt as if all she ever wanted lay wrapped up in his tiny body.

She glanced over at Reilly again. He'd thrown himself down on the mossy undergrowth, and he was busy searching through his pack. He had a kerchief tied around his forehead, his dark hair was pulled back and his khaki shirt was unbuttoned in deference to the wicked, soaking heat. She found herself staring at his chest, surreptitiously.

She hadn't had much experience in looking at men's chests, but she knew instinctively that this was a prime specimen.

His skin was smooth, muscled, dark with tan and sweat. He was lounging there, unconsciously graceful, as he tipped back a canteen of water, and she watched the rivulets escape the side of his mouth and drip down his strong, tanned neck. She licked her lips.

She should have known he wouldn't miss that action. He rose, effortlessly, as if he hadn't been trudging heavy-laden miles through the jungle, and held out the canteen for her.

She couldn't take it from him without letting go of the bottle, and she knew very well just what the baby's reaction would be to that. She considered refusing, but despite the liquid air her mouth and throat were parched.

He didn't move, just waited. It was a challenge, she knew that instinctively, though she wasn't quite sure what was behind it. Control? Or something even more unsettling?

He put the canteen against her mouth and she drank, deeply, tasting the metallic flavor of the canteen and the warm, chemically purified water. Tasting his mouth, one step removed from hers.

He took the canteen away from her when she'd finished, without a word. And then he squatted next to her, reached out and calmly fastened his spare bandanna around her forehead, brushing her hair back from her face.

Her eyes met his, reluctantly, and for a moment she sat there in the sultry heat as something strange and disturbing flashed between them. Something intimate, with his open shirt at eye level, the baby in her arms, the quiet all around them.

She needed to break that moment, and quickly. She didn't understand it, and it frightened her. Or perhaps it was the fact that deep down she did understand it that was so terrifying. "Thanks," she said, tossing her head in an arrogant manner she'd seen Caterina perfect.

He blinked. For a moment his dark eyes shuttered,

and then he rose, surging upward as if he were desperate to get away from her. "We need to keep moving," he said. "You want me to carry the baby for a while?"

"He's my child," she said instinctively. "I'll carry him."

Reilly shrugged. "Suit yourself. Let's go."

She started to protest, then glanced down to see that Timothy had fallen asleep in her arms, happily replete. She racked her brain for some way to delay, then gave up. The sooner they reached their destination, the sooner she could do something about her feet. Besides, hadn't she spent the past nine years of her life hearing stories of the blessed martyrs? Men and women who'd endured far worse than sore feet for the sake of their faith.

She wasn't doing this for her faith. But for the safety of a child, which was surely of equal value in God's eyes.

She waited until Reilly's back was turned before she rose, unsteadily. By the time he turned, instantly alert, she was composed, with Timothy settled back in the sling.

Reilly had her pack in one hand, holding the monstrously heavy thing as if it weighed no more than a feather. She braced herself for the added burden, forcing herself to give him a cool, unmoved look.

He was almost impossible to fool. He took in her defiant expression, her no doubt bedraggled appearance, and a faint smile skimmed across his mouth before vanishing once again.

"I'll carry your pack for a while," he said, shouldering it effortlessly.

"You don't need to baby me," she said instantly.

"I'm not. I'm trying to maximize our speed. We'll move faster if you aren't dragging your feet."

She could barely lift her feet, but by sheer force she kept her gaze on his face. "How much farther are we going?"

"Today? At least another ten miles. With this kind of brush that'll take us the rest of the day. Think you can handle it, princess?"

"Why don't you like me, Mr. Reilly?" she asked in a bewildered voice. "What have I ever done to you?"

"I don't dislike you, lady. I don't even have an opinion."

"Now that's a lie," she said flatly. "You've got plenty of opinions, and you formed them long before you showed up at the Convent of Our Lady of Repose."

"As I said, you've got a reputation."

"And you believe in reputations?"

He surveyed her for a moment. "Tell you what, lady. I'll forget about your reputation and judge you by your actions. Okay?"

"Judge me? What gives you any right to judge me?"

"It's human nature."

"That doesn't make it commendable. And my name's not lady. It's Carlie."

"Better than Mrs. Morrissey," he agreed, and there was no missing the faint barb in his voice. "Okay, Carlie. Let's get moving. I don't want to have to stop again."

"Tough," she said flatly, like the sound of the word. "Timothy will need to be changed and fed."

"And if we don't stop?"

"I'll let you carry him if he gets really soaking. And he's got an amazing set of lungs. Unless you think we're the only human beings in the jungle."

His mouth thinned in irritation, and she knew she had him. "We'll stop in two hours. No sooner."

Years ago, when she'd been brought down from that mountain village where her parents and all the villagers had been slaughtered, she'd found herself able to lock her mind away in a dark, safe place, so that nothing could touch her. She brought that place up again as she walked, mile after miserable mile, keeping pace with Reilly's fiendishly long legs. Timothy slept on, not even giving her the tiny respite another feeding would have afforded her, but she found she was grateful. If she stopped, and sat, she might never get up again.

It was growing steadily darker, some distant part of her brain told her, but she paid little heed. Until she was suddenly halted, and it took her a moment to realize that Reilly had turned and stopped her, his hands on her forearms.

She looked up at him, dazed, uncomprehending. "We're stopping for the night," he said harshly.

She blinked, then looked around her. There was no sign of a vehicle, no sign of civilization. Merely a sluggish stream winding its way through the undergrowth.

"Why?" she asked.

He'd already dumped both packs. His hands were gentle as they reached out and released the baby from the sling. Timothy was suddenly, furiously awake, but Carlie was beyond noticing. "Because you can't make it any farther."

From some place deep inside she managed to summon up a trace of indignation. "I can keep going...."

"Maybe. But you wouldn't be going anywhere tomorrow. Enough of the early-Christian-martyr bit, Carlie. Take your damned shoes off."

She would have thought she was too weary to react, but the reference stung. Could he read her mind as well? She was about to protest, but Reilly had already turned his back on her.

She walked straight into the shallow stream, shoes and all, then sat on the bank as pain made her dizzy. She could hear the baby's noisy protests, but she couldn't bring herself to move. Within a moment he'd stilled, and there was blessed silence, broken only by the quiet sound of the slow-moving water and the call of the jungle birds.

She lay back against the grass, groaning softly, staring up into the leafy canopy overhead. Every muscle in her body screamed in agony, and not even for Timothy's sake could she rouse herself. She was never going to move again. She was going to lie here in the jungle, her feet in the water, and die. Reilly was a responsible man who knew his way around babies. He could get Timothy out of there. For now she was just going to drift....

HE STARED AT HER. She had long legs for such a little thing, and sun had penetrated the rain forest just enough to give her a faint dusting of color. She lay beside the river in an exhausted stupor, probably asleep.

It was just as well. He found her distracting when she was awake. Hell, he found her distracting when she was asleep, as well, but at least she wouldn't be aware of it.

Timothy lay on his stomach on his discarded shirt, cooing happily enough, his diaper clean, his stomach full. They were going to need to get supplies before too long—their purified water wouldn't last forever, and Timothy seemed to be going through the stash of disposable diapers at an impressive rate. Reilly worked swiftly, efficiently, setting up a protective tarp, laying out their bedrolls. He didn't think Carlie was going to look with approval on the sleeping arrangements, but that was too damned bad. He had only one tarp, and the best way to keep the baby safe was to keep him surrounded by adults. Besides, Reilly was hardly going to jump her bones with a month-old infant as chaperon.

Besides which, she wouldn't be ready to have her bones jumped for another few weeks, even if she looked as if she was pretty well recovered from childbirth. She was off-limits, for every reason he could think of. Now why couldn't he remember that?

She wasn't what he'd expected. He hadn't had time to do his research before he took off for San Pablo. Things were in a crisis situation, as usual, and he couldn't afford to wait even an extra twenty-four hours so he could know what he was getting into. All he could go on was stuff he'd picked up, mainly by osmosis, and what he knew of Billy's taste in women.

None of it was to Carlie's credit. And he was too

old and too experienced to be suckered by an innocent face and a vulnerable air. She was about as vulnerable as one of Mendino's black-shirted enforcers.

Still, she was pretty. Not drop-dead gorgeous, as Billy had assured him. Not stunning, not glamorous, not sophisticated. Pretty. He couldn't remember when he'd last used the word.

It made him think of cottages in England. It made him think of spring flowers, and baby lambs, and all those stupid things that made up camera commercials.

But she was brave. She'd stood up to him, when he'd been doing his best to terrorize her. He figured his best chance was to make her so scared she'd do everything he told her to, without complaining. He could be extremely intimidating when he set his mind to it. But Carlie didn't seem to be easily intimidated.

She was strong, uncomplaining. He knew she'd been in pain, but she hadn't said a word. And she was a good mother. The way she looked at her little baby, cooed to him, forgave a lot of sins. She'd do what needed to be done, he felt it in his bones. Maybe he didn't need to come down so hard on her.

He walked over to the stream. She was asleep, as he'd guessed, and her eyelashes lay against her cheeks. There was a faint flush of color in her face, but apart from that she was white and still. He looked down at her feet. And then he saw the blood.

He started to curse, rich, colorful invectives that could have turned the air blue, as he reached down under her armpits and hauled her out of the water. She hit at him, dazed and disoriented by the rude awakening, but he didn't give a damn. He simply dumped her farther up on the riverbank, still cursing, and then knelt by her sodden, blood-stained feet.

"Don't you have more sense than that?" he demanded when his first string of curses had run out. "Piranhas are the least of your worries in this climate. You lie there, trolling your bloody feet like some god-damn fishing lure while you take a little nap...." His voice was savage as he gently, carefully pried off her sodden running shoes.

There was no way he could keep from hurting her, especially once he got a good look at how bad they were. But she didn't say a word, simply clamped her teeth down on her full lower lip as he pulled the wet canvas and leather away from swollen feet.

"Whose shoes are these?" he demanded. "Don't you know better than to take off into the jungle without the proper footgear?"

"Piranhas are greatly overestimated," she said faintly. "They're not nearly as dangerous—"

"They're not nearly as dangerous as I'm feeling right now," he interrupted ruthlessly.

"For your information, I don't happen to have decent shoes with me," she said. "I wasn't expecting to go running through the jungle, and I didn't have a chance to go shopping before I left La Mensa."

"There hasn't been anything to buy in La Mensa for the last year and a half, and you know it." He sat back and looked at her feet. They were swollen, bloody, a complete mess. God only knew what kind of tropical diseases she'd picked up from the muddy water. He reached behind him for the backpack and the first-aid kit. "I'm going to have to hurt you."

He expected a smart crack. She didn't make one.

She simply looked at him, out of those big innocent eyes that he couldn't believe in, and waited.

He was fast, deft and careful. He'd done more than his share of field triage, and Carlie's injuries, as nasty as they looked, weren't life threatening, once he got them properly taken care of.

When he was finished he sat back on his heels. "I don't know if you'll be able to walk tomorrow...."

"I can walk."

"Maybe we should wait a day."

"Is it safe?"

"No."

She looked at the baby, now sound asleep on the discarded shirt. Dusk had settled down around the jungle, and Reilly felt an odd chill run across his skin. "I can walk," she said again, and he had no doubt she would, if she had to do it barefoot on hot coals.

"All right," he said mildly enough, not interested in arguing with her. "Why don't you go lie down and I'll get you something to eat? Unless you need to use the woods?"

"Use the woods?"

"Go to the bathroom, lady. If you want I can carry you."

She blushed. A deep, embarrassed red. He stared in fascination. Why would she blush over something like that?

"I can manage," she said stiffly, starting to climb to her feet.

She didn't get far. She fell back with a muffled cry of pain, and he caught her. He didn't bother arguing with her—she was ridiculously small and light, and he simply scooped her up in his arms and carried her a little way into the brush, dumping her on her butt.

"Call me when you're done," he said.

"I don't need—"

"If you don't call me, I won't let you out of my sight again." His voice was implacable.

She glared at him, some of the dull apathy of pain fading. "You're a bully, aren't you?"

"Be glad of it, lady. It'll keep you and the kid alive."

It took her a moment. "I am glad of it," she said in a quiet voice. "Thank you, Reilly. For everything."

He didn't like her softness. He didn't want her gratitude. He wanted her smart-mouthed and fighting him.

He turned his back, walking away from her. Wishing he could put the memory of those deceptively innocent eyes out of his mind with as little effort.

Chapter Five

She didn't like being carried by Reilly. She didn't like being touched by him. His hands were big, strong, callused. His body was warm, sleek, muscled, and he hadn't worn a shirt. When he'd scooped her up and carried her through the woods he'd doubtless thought of her as nothing more than another burden, like the too-heavy pack.

But she couldn't dismiss the sensations so easily. The feel of that warm, smooth skin beneath hers was disturbing. Upsetting. It took her a full five minutes to get her senses back in order, to calm the emotions that roiled up inside her.

He was there to help her. The fact that he caused all sorts of strange, inexplicable reactions within her was simply the result of loneliness and stress. She needed to remind herself that while he was far from the friendliest soul in the universe, his motives were beyond noble and downright heroic. She needed to remember that, and not let her emotions and her un-likely irritation get in the way.

She didn't make the mistake of not calling him when she was finished. He wasn't a man who made empty threats, and she had little doubt he'd stand over her while she accomplished her calls of nature if she didn't do as he told her.

He picked her up again as if she weighed no more than the baby. He'd pulled on a dun-colored T-shirt, which made things marginally better, but it still took all of Carlie's concentration to ignore the bulge and play of his muscles when he lifted her.

The gathering dusk sent eerie shadows around the small clearing. It was then that she noticed the sleeping bags, side by side beneath the makeshift tent. The baby lay on his stomach, sound asleep in the middle of the conjoined beds.

"Are you sure we can't go any farther tonight?" she asked, suddenly nervous.

"You aren't in any shape." He dropped her down on one end of the bedroll. "Crawl in."

"What about snakes?" She glanced around, trying to appear cool. "Or jaguars?"

"Don't worry about it. I'll keep you safe from jungle beasts."

She peered up at him. He looked rather like a magnificent beast himself, looming over her in the darkness. "How?"

"I'll be keeping watch." He sat on the ground and began to crawl beneath the tarp. She watched him for a moment, disconcerted.

"How are you going to do that if you sleep?"

"I'm not going to sleep."

"Then why are you lying down?"

"Because I'm tired," he said, stretching out. And that was when she noticed the big, heavy handgun he'd placed by his head.

"But if you're tired and you lie down, then won't you…"

"Lady," he said wearily, "I was in the military for more than fifteen years. I was trained for combat, and I've spent the better part of those years in places where I couldn't afford to let up for a minute. I've never fallen asleep during guard duty and I'm not about to make a habit of it. Now get in the damned bed."

All her noble resolve vanished in a wave of pure annoyance. "What if I don't want to sleep with you?"

He closed his eyes in weary exasperation. "If I wanted to get in your pants you'd know it. For now all I want is for you to be quiet and climb in your sleeping bag. Preferably without waking the baby."

She didn't have any choice in the matter, and she knew it. Timothy lay sleeping peacefully enough, and Reilly looked as if he found her about as interesting as a day-old slug. She slid down, stretching full length on the sleeping bag and closed her eyes determinedly.

She listened to the silence, trying to will herself to sleep. Until she heard the unmistakable sound of chewing.

Her eyes flew open. He was stretched out beside her, and he was eating something brown and nasty looking that nevertheless had her stomach churning in hunger.

"Are you planning on sharing that?"

He glanced over at her, and there was just a hint of amusement in his dark eyes. "I didn't think you were interested in food."

"I'm interested. What is it?"

"Dried beef jerky. We also have an assortment of dried prunes, dried apples and trail mix."

"Yummy," she said wryly. "Where is it?"

"Ask me nicely."

She reached out and snatched the piece of meat from his hand, scuttling out of his way before he could grab it back. Between them the baby slept on, secure between the two battling adults.

"I don't suppose you have any coffee?" she asked after a moment.

"All out. If we manage to make it to the jeep tomorrow we should be able to get supplies. Maybe even a bed for the night, though I'm not certain I want to risk it. Are you going to be able to walk?"

She wiggled her feet carefully. They hurt, but the salve Reilly had rubbed into them seemed to have done wonders. "I think so."

The night was growing darker around them, so that she could barely see him in the small confines of the makeshift tent. She heard him move, and a small pack of trail mix landed in front of her. "Where's your canteen?" he asked.

"I don't know. Besides, I'm not particularly thirsty."

"Damn it, woman, you can't go losing your canteen," he snapped. "And I don't care whether you're thirsty or not. In this climate you can get dehydrated real fast, and then I'd have two helpless creatures on my hands."

"Reilly, my name isn't woman, it isn't lady, and it isn't princess. It's Carlie."

"It's Caterina Morrissey," he reminded her. "And I don't particularly like that fact."

"Why not?"

"Maybe it reminds me that a buddy is dead, and that before he died he got suckered by a spoiled jet-setter." He shoved his canteen at her.

She didn't make the mistake of not taking a long drink. She might not be able to see him clearly in the dark, but she wouldn't put excellent night vision past his extraordinary list of capabilities. What in the world had Caterina ever done? Her deathbed confession, a talk shared between two unlikely friends and far from a religious ritual, hadn't been specific. It had been the weary cry of a wasted life that had once been full of promise, and it had broken Carlie's heart.

"Maybe you should think instead that he left a son behind," she said in a relatively calm voice. "And the spoiled jet-setter who suckered him is responsible for something of him continuing in this world."

"Maybe," he said, not sounding particularly convinced. "Go to sleep. I'm willing to bet the baby won't be sleeping through the night, and I sure as hell don't want to be feeding him and changing his diapers."

"You have already," she said sleepily, stretching out on the sleeping bag. "I'm surprised I haven't heard you complain before. You're very good with babies."

"I'm good at what I need to do. And I don't complain if things can't be helped. You might work on that, princess."

"Have you heard me complain yet?"

"No."

"You won't."

There was silence for a long moment. She waited,

half expecting him to come up with another barbed
comment. But her eyes drifted closed, and she told
herself he wasn't about to give an inch.

And neither was she.

SHE WOKE DURING THE NIGHT. She lay still in the
darkness, listening to the light, peaceful sound of the
baby sleeping beside her. Listening to the steady,
even breathing of the man who lay just on the other
side.

She could feel his body heat in those close quarters.
She could smell the scent of coffee and gun oil and
sweat that clung to both of them. She lay there and
listened, wondering if he slept. Wondering if they'd
be safe from marauding beasts, wondering if a bushmaster was going to slither into her sleeping bag
and...

"Go back to sleep, Carlie." His voice was nothing
more than a deep whisper of sound. "I'm not going
to let anything happen to either of you."

She should have resented him. She had learned to
put her trust in nothing but God, and a hostile man
in camouflage with a gun wasn't the first likely person
she'd feel like cozying up with.

But fate, or God, wasn't taking her feelings into
consideration. And despite her fears, her doubts, her
misgivings, she knew perfectly well that the man lying beside her would be true to his word. Nothing
would get past him. Nothing would harm the baby.
Nothing would harm her.

Except, perhaps, for this unwanted excursion into
the real world, complete with men and guns and life.

But she would survive. And for the time being she

was perfectly safe, with Reilly watching over them. Closing her eyes, she sank back into a deep, dreamless sleep.

THEY WERE ON THE TRAIL by a little past dawn the next morning. Reilly wasn't in the mood to be impressed, but he had always considered himself a fair man, and Billy's little princess had done herself proud. She could walk, gingerly, but with the bandages she'd wrapped around her feet those oversize running shoes fit her. She fed and changed the baby, ate trail mix without a murmur and even managed to look gorgeous when she struggled to her feet and began to hitch the kid into that sling-type thing she wore.

"Think you can make it another seven miles?" he asked, shouldering both their packs.

He saw her blue eyes blink at the number seven, but apart from that she showed no distress. "Yes."

"Good." He started through the forest, leaving her to follow along behind him.

He moderated his pace, just enough to make it easier on her, not so much that it would endanger them. Not so much that she would notice. Carlie Morrissey was turning out to be a far cry from the woman he'd expected, but she did have her share of pride. She wouldn't like knowing he was going easy on her. Hell, he didn't like knowing it, either.

They walked in silence for the better part of an hour, listening as the jungle awakened around them. The screech of the macaws, the random scream of the jaguar floated on the thick, liquid air, and Reilly felt the sweat pool at the base of his spine.

Damn, he hated the jungle. Hated this smothering heat, where a man couldn't breathe without filling his lungs full of ooze. He knew that accounted for part of his bad attitude toward Carlie. He wanted to be back on his mountaintop in Colorado, not hacking his way through the undergrowth with a woman and a baby behind him. He'd had enough of jungles in his life. Enough of heat. He wasn't sure which he hated more—the steamy tropical forests of Latin America, or the dry, searing heat of the Middle Eastern deserts. He'd left the army because he was fed up with heat, fed up with stupid little wars and innocent people getting in the way. So where did he end up? Smack-dab in a stupid little war, in the heat, trying to save a couple of innocent people.

He owed Billy. He owed him his life, he owed him anything Billy would ask. It was too late for that. But bringing his kid and his playgirl wife back to the States would even out a lot of old debts, even if he paid them beyond the grave. He could put up with a little heat and discomfort for that, couldn't he?

What he was having a hard time putting up with was Caterina Morrissey. He was fine when he thought of her as Caterina, when he didn't look so closely at her, when he kept himself wound so tightly that nothing could sneak through.

But when he looked at her, really looked, at the absurdly innocent eyes and vulnerable mouth, at the small, coltish body and the instinctive, natural grace, at the love she poured on that red-faced little baby, he found himself thinking other, dangerous thoughts. Like how Billy must have misjudged her. Like what a lucky man he'd been. Like what would she taste like if he kissed her. Like how long did it take for a small woman like her to recover from the physical trauma of childbirth.

He hadn't thought much about having kids of his own. He'd been too busy, there'd been no special woman and his horde of nieces and nephews had provided him with more than enough kids to last him.

But if he did get married, did find a woman to share his mountaintop, he'd want her to be just a little like Carlie. Not Caterina, the spoiled bitch, who'd married Billy, left him when she grew bored, and only came back when she found out she was unexpectedly pregnant and her cozy little life in San Pablo was collapsing.

No, he'd want her to be like Carlie, who snapped at him, trudged along behind him uncomplaining, and who loved her baby.

The terrain that comprised most of San Pablo was like no other place in the world. Half rain forest, half jungle, it was home to pit vipers and jaguars and hundreds of varieties of flesh-eating fish and birds that had never been cataloged or identified by the scientists who'd braved the revolutions and the natural dangers of the land to document the wildlife. And among all those deadly species, none were quite so threatening as the fanatical armies of San Pablo, the black-shirted goon squads of Hector Mendino and Endor Morales, his notorious general, and the ragtag rebels who wouldn't think twice about slaughtering an innocent baby who might someday pose a threat.

He didn't like it here, Reilly thought sourly, trudging onward. Hell, he didn't like it anywhere nowadays, except for Colorado. He'd spent too much time in San Pablo in the past, but he'd forgotten how bad the climate could really be. He wanted out of here, and he wanted out, fast.

He glanced back at Carlie. Her face was pale beneath the hot pink flags of sunburn against her cheeks, and her eyes were dull with exhaustion. She walked slowly, without limping, the baby cradled against her, and he wondered how much longer she was going to manage to keep going. If worse came to worst he could always carry her. She was a tiny thing, hardly big enough to have given birth to even a baby as small as Timothy. He couldn't imagine her lying beneath someone like Billy Morrissey, who'd been built like a linebacker.

He quickly shut off that line of thought. It was none of his damned business whether she was beneath or on top. The sex life of Caterina Morrissey was none of his business at all.

He halted abruptly, then turned, putting a hand on her shoulder to stop her. She looked up at him, her clear blue eyes dull and shadowed by exhaustion, her soft mouth grim. "We just stopped an hour ago, Reilly," she said in that calm voice of hers. "You don't need to pamper me—I don't need another rest yet."

She needed a hell of a lot more than a rest, but he didn't bother pointing that out to her. "We aren't resting," he said. "We're here." He jerked his head toward the underbrush.

She peered around him. "Where? I don't see anything."

"I do. The jeep's still in there. Just give me a couple of minutes to check for sabotage and then we can

start out of here. With luck we might make Dos Libros by nightfall. There's a cantina there, run by an
old scoundrel named Dutchy. We could probably
commandeer a bed for the night.''

''One bed?''

His mouth curved in a wry smile. ''This time I'll
do the sleeping and you can keep watch.''

She had the most expressive blue eyes. He could
see every thought, every emotion as it flitted through.
She was looking up at him, judging him, measuring
him. ''You look tired,'' she said flatly. ''You had me
thinking you were invulnerable.''

''I get tired,'' he said. ''I get hungry, I get thirsty,
I get horny. I just don't do anything about it if it's
not convenient.''

She still didn't respond as he expected her to.
''You didn't say whether you ever got lonely.''

He thought for a moment, of the remote mountain
cabin, half a continent away, with only the animals
and his work for company. ''No,'' he said flatly. Lying.

She didn't call him on it, as he'd expected her to.
She simply nodded, sinking onto the thick grass and
holding the sleeping baby against her. He handed her
his canteen, and she took it without argument.

By the time he'd managed to clear the camouflag-
ing brush away from the jeep, check over the entire
thing and load up the packs, Carlie looked as if she
were half-asleep. She barely made a sound when he
loaded her into the front seat, not even protesting
when Reilly took the sleeping baby away from her
and strapped him in the infant seat he'd stashed with
the gear. He almost teased her, but she sat in the

cracked leather seat, and if the old army vehicle hadn't come equipped with webbed seat belts to hold her in place he expected she might very well have slipped right onto the floor.

She was asleep before he put the jeep in gear, and even the bouncing, rolling ride over the rutted path didn't wake her. He had less than a quarter of a tank of gas—enough to get them to the tiny village of Dos Libros and not much farther. He just had to hope that the tiny outpost there had a reasonable supply of fuel. Otherwise they'd be walking again, and he wasn't sure how his frail little jungle flower would hold up.

Except that she wasn't frail. She was little, but she was surprisingly strong, and he'd put her through a workout that would make an aerobics instructor collapse. And she wasn't his.

He needed to keep that firmly in mind. She was dependent on him right now, and she didn't like it. She also looked up at him with a kind of innocent wondering in her eyes that made him damnably uncomfortable. Though why someone with a reputation like Caterina Morrissey would be possessed of either wonder or innocence was beyond him.

He had to be careful. Billy's wife was the kind of woman who was used to having a man take care of her. Since he was the only one around, it would be only natural that she would turn to him. And he didn't want that.

He wasn't quite sure why. He had a healthy interest in sex, when it didn't interfere with other, more important matters, and he would be a fool to deny that he found Carlie…irresistible. There was no real reason he shouldn't have sex with her if she was willing and eager.

But he didn't want to. For the first time in his life he wanted the same woman Billy Morrissey had wanted. For the first time in his life he could feel the slow, strangling tendrils of longing for something more than the fast, hot release of sex. When he looked at the pale face of the woman sleeping beside him, he didn't see a manipulative socialite or a cheating wife. He didn't see a mother who would doubtless abandon her child the first chance she got, or a woman with a score of rich and powerful lovers.

When he looked at her he saw hope. And a dream. And it scared the bloody hell out of him.

Chapter Six

Carlie's eyes flew open in sudden, mind-shearing panic. She was alone, in the parked jeep, in the middle of a narrow jungle track. It was already growing dark, and the night insects were darting around her head. There was no sign of Reilly. No sign of the baby.

She tried to leap out of the car seat, but the seat belt held her back. She fumbled with it, taking forever to release the old clasp, telling herself not to panic. He wouldn't have abandoned her. Wouldn't have stolen the baby and left her alone in the heart of the jungle.

But then again, why wouldn't he? He'd proved he was more than capable of taking care of Timothy—he didn't need her around to feed or change him. She was just an inconvenience, something Billy Morrissey's family would have to deal with. Everyone would be a lot happier to know that Caterina Morrissey was really dead.

Maybe she should have insisted on telling Reilly the truth. She'd tried, but he hadn't believed her. What would he have done, once he'd known? Would he have taken the baby and left her behind? She'd promised Caterina she'd take care of her son, and she hadn't wanted to give him up. Perhaps this was God's punishment for her lies and her selfishness. Timothy would be better off with his grandparents, but she hadn't wanted to let him go.

Had Reilly been planning this all along? Why had he bothered taking her this far, only to abandon her to what was probably certain death in the night-shrouded jungle? Why hadn't she remembered what men with guns and uniforms were capable of?

She sat back in the car seat, pulling her legs up under her. The air had grown cool on her bare arms, and she shivered. If she were anyone else she would have had the luxury of tears. But it had been nine years since she'd cried, and she wasn't about to start now.

"Did you think I'd abandoned you?" The voice came from close behind her, drawing, laconic.

She whirled around in the seat, to see Reilly standing on the edge of the clearing, watching her out of wary eyes.

Relief and something more washed over her. She didn't even think, she simply moved, bolting out of the seat and racing across the clearing. She flung herself against him, babbling in relief and exhaustion.

"I thought you weren't coming back," she said against the soft cotton of his T-shirt. "I thought you'd left me her to die.…"

His hands had come up to catch her arms, holding her, and she was vaguely aware of his strength. His warmth. His surprising tenderness. He didn't push her away. He simply held her there as she ranted, cradling her against his body, and she breathed in the warmth and the scent of him, and the words ran down as she let out a long, shuddering sigh.

"That's better," he murmured. He'd moved his hand up to the nape of her neck, beneath her short-cropped hair, and he was kneading the tension away with his long fingertips. "I've found us a place for the night. You were dead to the world when we got here, so I decided to let you sleep."

She looked up at him, as the slow, sensual kneading erased the tension in her body. "I was frightened."

"You had reason to be."

His face was very close to hers. It came to her, belatedly, that she was standing in a man's arms, pressed against his body. She stepped back, suddenly nervous, and he released her.

"Where's the baby?"

"Dos Libros is just over the rise. The women are looking after him. I realize you probably aren't too happy about the fact that I turned your son over to strangers, but the women of the Shumi tribe are excellent mothers and nurturers, and I figured he would be much safer."

"It's all right," Carlie said. "I trust your judgment."

She'd managed to startle him. And then his mouth curved in a faint smile. "That's good. Because I decided we'd better share a bedroom."

"I..."

"Keep your mouth shut and your head down," he added, heading off the way he'd come, obviously assuming she'd follow. "I don't think the Shumi have had much traffic with the outside world, but Dutchy has some dangerous friends, and he might very well recognize you. I don't want to raise any suspicions if I can help it.''

''What did you tell the Shumi?''

''That you're my woman. That the baby is ours, and that I'm a very jealous man. The Shumi will leave us alone. I'm not so sure about Dutchy. He'd sell his own grandmother for a handful of pesos, and the reward on you and the kid is a lot higher than that.''

She strained to match his steady pace through the underbrush. ''Reward?'' she echoed, not certain if she had heard right.

''Enough to keep me in style for the next decade,'' he said lightly.

''Are you trying to frighten me, Reilly?'' she demanded, panting slightly as she struggled to keep up with him. ''If you are, I think I ought to mention that there's no need to try quite so hard. I'm officially terrified.''

He glanced over his shoulder, his eyes glittering in the darkness. ''I'd say you're about as frightened as the Terminator,'' he drawled.

''What's the Terminator?''

''Give me a break, Carlie. You know what I'm talking about.''

She didn't, but she obviously should have. If she'd lived anywhere near civilization for the past ten years she would have been conversant with the entity. ''You think I don't get scared?'' she demanded.

He stopped and looked at her. ''Well, I don't know. I've already admitted I get tired and hungry and scared and horny. You have all those human weaknesses?''

"Most of them," she said carefully.

He laughed, and it wasn't an unpleasant sound. "We'll get you some food and some rest tonight," he said. "We'll have to see about the other stuff. In the meantime, you stick to me like glue. There've been bands of Mendino's ex-soldiers roaming the area, and Morales himself has been seen not too far from here. Not to mention the rebels, who are just as bloodthirsty as your stepfather's goons. I didn't bring you this far just to lose you."

"I have no intention of letting you out of my sight if I can help it."

"Why, princess," he said with a slash of a smile. "I didn't know you cared."

She'd seen tiny villages like Dos Libros, though not in the nine years she'd been cloistered with the sisters. Her parents had died in a village very much like this one, and the memory sent a shudder of remembered pain through her, one that she was able to hide from Reilly. She'd seen places like Dutchy's— a combination store, post office, bar and hotel, but most of all a hovel. There was no sign of the Shumi women, or Timothy for that matter, and she quickly stilled her flash of possessive panic, resisting her need to go after him.

"Get behind me," Reilly muttered under his breath. She quickly did as she was told, and he put his arm around her, pushing her face against his shoulder. She couldn't see anything, could only trust in him to steer her safely toward the door.

"This your wife, Reilly?" The voice was jovial,

Germanic and not to be trusted for a moment. Even Carlie could tell that much.

"Close enough," Reilly drawled. "You got a bed and a shower for us, Dutchy?"

"Is the pope Catholic?" Dutchy responded. "I've also got a hot meal and the best whiskey in all of San Pablo. I make it myself."

"We'll take a bottle," Reilly said, pulling her toward the stairs. She could see her feet out of the corner of her eye, feel the other people watching her. Dutchy, and others, as well. "You can send it up to our room."

"Now, Reilly. You know how cut off we get around here. Starved for information, we are, aren't we, boys? You can't just hole up in your room with that pretty little thing. We want to know where you've been. What you've seen. These boys have to report back to their commander, and they need to hear about any trouble you may have run into. These are dangerous times, my boy, and we need to be prepared."

She didn't need to see Reilly's mocking smile to know his expression. "Information doesn't come free, Dutchy. And I'm more interested in having my woman in a bed for a change than gossiping. They'll have to go out and find their own information, instead of sitting around in a bar."

It was just as well her face was pressed against his body. The color flooded her pale skin, and her faint sound of protest was uncontrollable.

"You sure she wants that?" Another voice spoke, this time in Spanish. Slow, and menacing. "The lady seems uncertain. My men and I would be glad to provide her with an alternative."

They'd reached the foot of the stairs. She could feel the tension coiling through Reilly's body, the utter, deadly calm. He put his hand under her chin, drawing her face into the dim light of the building. The watching men were at a distance, the room was thick with smoke and the greasy light of oil lamps, and there was no way they could get a clear look at her. No way they could recognize the daughter of Hector Mendino in the face of a nun. "What do you say, woman? Are you interested in leaving my protection?"

She shook her head, staring at him in mute pleading. He turned, shielding her behind his strong back. "You see, gentlemen. The lady is not uncertain, merely tired and impatient."

"If she grows tired of you, hombre," the man said with a coarse laugh, "I'll be more than happy to step in. I have…" She didn't understand the rest of the sentence. She could guess what he was referring to, but she didn't want to. Color stained her cheeks once more as Reilly guided her up the rickety old staircase.

Dutchy was waiting for them, peering at her in the dim light. "Second door on the right, bathroom down the hall." He spat for emphasis. "You're our only guests right now, so it's a private bath. Fifty American dollars a night."

"You're the soul of generosity," Reilly said.

"A man must support himself the best he can. Just be glad the soldiers downstairs are moving on tonight."

"Why should it matter one way or the other?" Reilly said carefully.

Dutchy smiled, revealing chipped, stained teeth. "You tell me, amigo."

Carlie waited until they were in the tiny room. Waited until Reilly closed the door behind them and Dutchy's footsteps echoed down the hall. And then she looked around her.

It was far from reassuring. There was one bed in the room, a small, sagging iron one, with a faded chenille cover, two limp pillows and an oil lamp beside it. There was nothing else in the room.

"Where will the baby sleep?" she asked carefully, avoiding the more disturbing question.

"He'll stay with the Shumi. I figure he'll be safer there. Right now he's with the chief's wives, being treated like royalty."

"I wonder how they'd feel if they knew he was the grandson of the man who was responsible for the genocide of three-quarters of their population," Carlie said bitterly.

"It would make no difference. The Shumi revere children, even those of their enemies." He tilted his head, looking at her. "You don't sound too fond of old Hector yourself."

"He was a monster."

"That's right, he was your stepfather, wasn't he? Still, it was his money that provided you with your comfortable life-style. His death that took it away from you. I would have thought you'd be more grateful."

"His money was drained from the blood of the people."

"Are you certain you're not a revolutionary?" he asked in a lazy voice. "It's a little late to change sides—the rebels aren't going to welcome you and your son with open arms.''

''They're just as bad. They're willing to kill anyone who gets in their way, all for the sake of their noble cause,'' she said bitterly. ''And it's the children, the innocents, who get caught in the middle.''

''Lord, what a bleeding heart,'' he said mockingly. ''You ought to be a missionary.''

It took her unawares, the sharp stab of pain. Suddenly she was seventeen years old again, on a hot afternoon in a mountain village, and her parents were being gunned down, they were screaming, she was screaming, there was blood....

''Stop it!'' His voice was rough, hurried, as he yanked her against him. The room was hot, he was hot, and yet she shivered, unbearably cold and alone.

His hands were hard and painful on her arms, forcing her out of the miasma of horror. Back into reality, the here and now, which wasn't much better. ''Stop what?'' she managed to say faintly.

''You looked as if you were about to faint. Or scream. I'm not sure which would be worse.'' He didn't release her, though his grip had loosened slightly so that she felt the warmth, the strength, the imprint of each long finger as it wrapped around her arms. ''Then again, I don't suppose either would be much of a problem. If you fainted I could simply dump you on the bed and not have to worry.''

''And if I screamed?''

His smile was slow and dangerous. ''There's a logical explanation for that, as well.''

''What?'' She was genuinely perplexed.

His smile faded, the stormy color of his eyes growing darker still as he watched her. "Lady," he said bluntly, "your love affairs have been the scandal of three continents. Don't tell me in all that time that no one ever made you scream when you made love."

She blinked. Her practical knowledge of sex was nonexistent, her theoretical knowledge so vague and so outdated that it was almost useless. She had only the faintest notion of what he was talking about, but she certainly wasn't going to ask him to explain. She tried to pull away, but he wasn't about to let her go.

"If they haven't," he continued, his voice low, disturbing, "then maybe I'll expand your horizons."

She held very still. He was going to kiss her. She knew it. She wasn't quite sure why—he hadn't shown much fondness for her up to now. But then, fondness didn't seem to have much to do with desire. She'd gathered that much over the years, from scraps of conversations she'd heard. It had never made much sense to her.

He gave her plenty of time to escape, to turn her head. But she couldn't. She felt mesmerized, curious, as his head dipped down, blocking out the light, and his mouth touched hers.

It was pleasant, she thought with surprise. The roughness of his beard, the firm contours of his mouth, the warmth of his body so close to hers were all quite…nice.

He lifted his head, and she took a startled breath. "That's very pleasant," she said ingenuously. "I think I—"

He didn't let her finish the sentence. His mouth came down over hers again, but this time it was open, against hers, and he was putting his tongue in her mouth. She tried to jerk away, but he'd threaded one large, strong hand through her hair to hold her in place, and there was no escape, nothing to do but stand still and let him kiss her with devastating thoroughness.

Her eyelids fluttered closed, blotting out the faint light, blotting out everything but the feel and taste of him. It was terrifying, it was smothering, it was dangerously splendid. She wanted to kiss him back, but she hadn't the faintest idea how to go about it. She wanted to lift her arms and touch him, but she was afraid to. He had his mouth on hers, his hand behind her head, but otherwise he wasn't touching her. And yet she felt captured, possessed, yearning, and she started to sway toward him, wanting that heat and strength tight around her.

He pulled away abruptly, taking a step back. She wrapped her arms around her body, suddenly cold, and lifted her eyes to look at him.

His breathing was slightly rapid, his mouth was damp, but apart from that he appeared completely unmoved. "You kiss like a virgin," he said flatly.

It was probably meant to be an insult. Instead it simply frightened her. Now wasn't the time for Reilly to discover she wasn't who he thought she was. Not with Timothy out of reach and the place crawling with soldiers.

"I don't like kissing," she said. A complete lie. As devastating as it was, she'd found her first kiss to be downright wonderful. She wanted him to kiss her again.

"That's a shame," he drawled. "It's a lost art."

I'm Caterina, she reminded herself, trying to hold on to her fast-fading self-control. "Perhaps," she said coolly, trying to sound suitably sophisticated. "I've never learned to appreciate it." True enough, she congratulated herself.

"Perhaps I could give you lessons."

She backed away from him, unable to hide her instant panic. Reilly didn't miss it—he wasn't a man who missed much—but he said nothing.

"I don't think so," she finally managed to say, pushing her short-cropped hair away from her face. "And I don't see why we have to share a room. Didn't the owner say this place was empty right now? Surely I could have my own room?"

Reilly's smile was cool and fleeting. "Sorry, princess. You're staying with me. Those weren't just any ex-soldiers lounging around downstairs, propositioning you. I made sure you couldn't see them and they couldn't see you, but I imagine you recognized their leader's voice."

"I don't know what you're talking about," she said, no longer caring if he guessed the truth.

"Well, maybe you wouldn't be that likely to run into your stepfather's chief executioner. He didn't run in the same social circles. That was Endor Morales, sweetheart. Quite possibly the most dangerous man in all of San Pablo, and it was just our dumb luck to run smack into him."

She fought back the panic that threatened to overwhelm her. "Do you think he suspected anything?"

"Morales didn't get as far as he did by being a trusting soul. He suspects everything and everybody. But as far as Dutchy knows, I'm just a low-life expatriate, probably a drug runner, with no interest in San Pablo politics. Morales won't be able to get anything else out of him, though I imagine he'll try. At lest the baby's out of the way, and we can probably manage to keep him a secret for a few hours. Long enough for a decent night's sleep and then get the hell out of here.''

''Can't we leave now?''

''No way. Morales and his men will be watching us like hawks. Any change in our plans would set off alarm bells. We said we were going to spend the night, so we'll spend the night.''

''But the baby...''

''The baby will be safe enough. The Shumi will keep him out of everybody's sight, and we'll be out of here first thing in the morning. For the time being all we can do is sit tight.''

She looked up at him. ''I'm afraid.''

''Don't be. Morales didn't seem any more than casually interested. As long as you stay close you'll be safe enough.''

''I'm not sleeping with you, Reilly!''

''Stop sounding like an outraged virgin,'' he said wearily. ''Your honor, such as it is, is safe with me.''

That was the second time in as many minutes that he'd called her a virgin. If she pushed it, he might begin to realize there was an unexpected truth to his accusation. He'd already turned his back on her, moving to the front of the room to stare out into the streets, dismissing her, and she told herself he wasn't interested. His kiss had been nothing more than another intimidation tactic.

"Am I allowed to take a shower alone?" she demanded frostily.

"Unless you want me to wash your back?"

She couldn't tell from his voice whether he was being facetious or not, but she decided not to push it. "When can I see the baby?"

He turned. "Keep away from the kid. He's as safe as he can be, and having you come waltzing around will just put him in danger. Dutchy's out of gas, and so is the damned jeep. He's supposed to get a shipment in the next day or two, so if Morales and his men have gone, it would be worth our while to wait. Otherwise we'll have to head out on the river. Or by foot."

"I think I'd prefer to ride," she said faintly.

"I imagine you would. Don't hog all the hot water. Assuming there is any," he added. "I wanted a shave, as well." He rubbed a hand over his bristly jaw.

"Don't do it on my account."

"Honey," he said wearily, "this is all on your account. If you hadn't run off from Billy and then decided to come back when things got a little hairy, neither of us would be in this mess. You'd be safe and sound in the States, the baby would have a nanny and you wouldn't have to be bothered with worrying about the little kid. You'd be out partying."

"I doubt he'd find a better nanny than the Shumi women," Carlie said. "And I don't like parties."

"Since when?"

She shut her mouth. She wasn't made for deception. She wasn't made for hostility, she wasn't made for men, or kisses. And yet here she was, trapped smack-dab in the middle of it all. Unable, and unwilling, to escape.

"Take your shower, Carlie," he said, turning back to the window, dismissing her. "I'll be here when you come out."

"Is that supposed to be reassuring?"

"You'd better believe it. Unless you'd rather take your chances with the soldiers downstairs?"

"What's the difference?"

He turned to look at her. "If you don't know, then I'm not going to bother explaining."

For a moment she didn't move. He was a big man, tall, lean and strong. The stubble of beard on his chin, the dark amber eyes, the rough contours of his face suggested power and danger. And yet she trusted him. More than she ever thought possible.

The gun was tucked in the waistband of his khakis. It was a big gun that fit his big hands. It would keep her safe. It would keep Timothy safe.

"I know the difference, Reilly," she said, her soft voice an apology. She grabbed her knapsack and shut the door behind her, heading in search of the bathroom.

But behind her she heard the slow, savage curse of a man pushed to his limits. And she wondered why.

Chapter Seven

There was no question about it—she was making him crazy. There was no escape, either—with Dutchy prowling around, his piggy eyes suspicious, alert for ways to make an easy buck, he had to keep up pretenses. Not to mention that small band of Mendino's Black Shirts downstairs, complete with Butcher Morales watching over them. It wouldn't take much for them to come after Carlie, even without knowing who she was. She was female, she was pretty and he was the only thing that was stopping them. If they decided they could take him, it would be her death warrant. And it wouldn't be a pleasant way to die.

He glanced over at the bed. It barely qualified as a double, and that concave middle would roll their bodies together despite their best efforts. Maybe he should just say the hell with it, give in to temptation and have her.

Despite her maidenly airs, he knew perfectly well he could. Hector Mendino's daughter was notoriously easy, and she needed him. Add to that the look in the back of her eyes when she glanced his way, when she thought he wouldn't notice. She wanted him, all right.

It was neither conceit nor imagination that told him so. It was his instinct, honed over time, that hadn't failed him yet.

He sank onto the bed, the springs screaming in protest beneath his big frame. At least the place looked relatively clean, and the sheets smelled like sunlight. He wondered what it would be like to sleep beside Carlie's shower-fresh body, on sheets that smelled of sunlight.

The notion was dangerous. He could always spread his bedroll on the floor, though the scarred wood promised to be a lot harder than the packed jungle earth. He'd found Billy's wife in a convent—it would be suitably penitential for him to sleep on the floor.

The very notion of Our Lady of Repose still unnerved him. He'd always made an effort not to fall into that mind trap so many men, particularly those who'd been raised Catholic as he had, were prey to. Some thought women fell into two groups, whores or Madonnas. But in reality, life was never that orderly or convenient.

He liked women, he truly did. He liked their looks and their bodies, the foreign way their minds worked, the crazy way their emotions worked. He liked their laughter and their tears, their husky little cries, their feel and their scent and their taste.

But for so long there'd been no room in his life for anything more than the briefest of relationships that he'd almost forgotten how much he did like them.

And now was a hell of a time to be remembering. Trapped with a small, slight yet tough young woman who'd made his best friend's life a living hell. A woman who couldn't be further from what he wanted or needed. A woman he seemed to want and need anyway.

He heard a noise out on the street, and he wandered over to the window. Morales and his men were making a great show of leaving, something that failed to reassure him. He expected they wouldn't be going far.

There was no sign of Dutchy sending them on their way, another oddity. A man like the old innkeeper would be more likely to send his powerful customers off with admonitions to stop in again. If Dutchy wasn't downstairs, then he was somewhere else.

Reilly could move very fast, very quietly, even in heavy boots. He could hear the sound of the shower from the end of the darkened hall, hear Carlie humming beneath her breath. He paused for a moment, alone in the darkness, picturing her. What would she look like beneath the shower? The water sluicing down over those small, firm breasts of hers, breasts that had never nursed a baby. Her belly would still be soft from the pregnancy, her waist still thickened. The kid was less than a month old—it was amazing she'd had so much stamina. His sisters had been in a state of exhaustion when his nieces and nephews had been a month old, and they'd had all the benefits of modern life. Besides not having to trek through a jungle.

For a moment the thought of his older sister Mary, she of the placid disposition and the taste for sloth, being on a forced march through the rain forests of San Pablo brought a rare smile to his face. One that vanished when he heard a tiny knocking noise from the bedroom next to the shower.

The door was ajar. He pushed it open silently, and

his night-trained eyes focused on Dutchy, his fat face pressed up against the wall, staring avidly through a narrow crack that let in a shaft of light.

The rage that filled him was immediate and over-powering. Dutchy never knew what hit him. One moment he was pressed up against the wall, drooling over the inhabitant of the shower room, in the next he was flat on his back on the floor, with Reilly kneeling over him, his big hand wrapped around Dutchy's wattled throat.

"Get a good eyeful, Dutchy?" he demanded in a harsh whisper. "I could make you very sorry you decided to play Peeping Tom with my woman."

"Hey," Dutchy gasped, "I didn't mean no harm. I was just looking, is all. Do you know how long it's been since I've seen a white woman around here? A look doesn't do any harm, and I didn't figure you for a possessive guy."

"You figured wrong. I'm very possessive," he said, increasing the pressure just slightly. Enough so that Dutchy's tiny eyes began to bug out even more, and he clawed at Reilly's arms uselessly. "Mess with me or my woman again, and you'll get more than a warning."

He released him and rose. Dutchy immediately curled up into a fetal ball, gasping and choking, cursing as he fought to regain his breath. A moment later he managed to stagger to his feet, stumbling out of the room, falling against the doorframe as he went.

The sound of the shower was still going. Carlie probably hadn't heard a thing. For that matter, Dutchy probably hadn't seen a thing. He'd been waiting for

Carlie to finish, so he could watch her as she dried off.

He stood very still for a moment, in the darkened room. He could still feel Dutchy's neck beneath his hands, still feel the burning contempt that had washed over him, combined with an irrational, possessive rage. There was no reason for him to feel possessive. She wasn't his, and she never would be.

He needed to walk out of that room and slam the door behind him. But the crack in the wall let a narrow sliver of light into the room, and it called to him, with a siren lure.

He could think of any number of reasonable excuses. He needed to know just how much Dutchy had seen, so he could decide whether to poke his eyes out or not. He needed to look and see how strong she really appeared to be, whether she could withstand the rigors of the remainder of the journey. He needed to look and make sure she hadn't collapsed in the shower, oblivious to the scuffle in the other room.

He needed to look and remind himself that she wasn't the kind of woman he desired, that he didn't like small, trim bodies. He liked statuesque blondes, built along generous lines. He and Billy had been alike in that, though Reilly had always preferred his women to come equipped with brains, as well.

He needed to look and see what Billy had fallen in love with.

Damn it, he just needed to look.

There was no shower curtain. The shower was a rusted-out metal stall with a drain at the bottom, and Carlie stood beneath the stream of water, face upturned, oblivious to everything but the pleasure of the water sluicing down over her.

She was small, just as Reilly had suspected. Small, firm breasts, narrow waist, flat tummy. Smooth, creamy skin, beaded with water.

He backed away, furious with himself. Furious with the adolescent surge of desire that threatened to knock him to his knees. He was no better than Dutchy, a horny old man drooling over a naked woman.

He'd seen enough naked women in his thirty-six years to take one in stride. She wasn't the skinniest, the curviest, the shortest, the tallest, the ugliest, the prettiest. So why was he having this inexplicable reaction to her?

Jungle fever. Not enough food, not enough sleep. Hell, he needed a drink. Pushing away from the wall, he headed into the hallway in search of that very thing. Only to run smack-dab into Carlie, wrapped in an enveloping towel, hair and eyelashes spiky damp with water.

He looked down at her, keeping his expression cool and distant while he took into account that this towel was much thicker than the one he'd first seen her in. He couldn't see the shape of her breasts beneath it. But then, he didn't need to. He could remember quite vividly how they'd looked, taut with water streaming down around them.

"I take it you like prancing around in towels," he drawled. "Billy never told me that about you."

Even in the dimly lit hallway he could see her flush. "I didn't bring any clean clothes with me," she said. "What were you doing in that room?" She glanced over at the empty bedroom.

"Catching a Peeping Tom. Our friend Dutchy was watching you take a shower."

She clutched the towel even tighter around her slender body. It would be easy enough to take her hands, move them away and pull the towel off her. He could pull her into his arms, wrap her legs around his waist and carry her back to the room. And he had no doubt that Caterina Morrissey would let him.

"What did you do to him?"

"Let's say he won't be making that mistake again for a long time," Reilly drawled.

"What about you? Did you look?"

He gave her his best, most cynical smile. "What do you think, princess?"

"I think you're a pig," she said fiercely.

"Now that sounds more like the Caterina Mendino I've heard about," he drawled. "Did you save me any hot water like I asked?"

"No."

"Just as well. I think I'm needing a cold shower about now." And he sauntered past her, with just the right amount of swagger.

CARLIE WANTED TO KILL HIM. A white-hot surge of anger whipped through her veins, and she shook with the effort to control it. She didn't like anger. She wasn't used to strong emotions, love or hatred, desire or spite. She'd been in his company for less than forty-eight hours, and already she'd been through a lifetime of emotions. And each time she felt something fierce and implacable, it was harder to draw her hard-won serenity back around her.

She slammed the bedroom door behind her and

pulled on clean clothes. It was marginally cooler that night, and the oversize white T-shirt disguised her lack of a bra. The loose cotton skirt hung low on her hips, brushing her ankles, but she took comfort in the feel of cloth against her legs. She wanted to be back in the safety of her cell, in the safety of her habit. This world was strange and unsettling.

Reilly was strange and unsettling. But he was the only safety she had left in her life, at least for now. She could make it through the next few days, long enough for him to get the baby safely out of the country, on his way to his grandparents. And then she would tell him the truth, make her way down to Rio de Janeiro with the sure knowledge that she'd been tested, most thoroughly, and risen above temptation. Surely Reverend Mother Ignacia could no longer deny that she had a calling, that she was ready to take her vows.

She moved to the window, running a hand through her short, damp hair. It was dark and quiet out there, only the occasional bark of a stray dog, the call of a jungle bird, piercing the humid night. She leaned her head against the wall, staring.

She missed Timothy. His quiet little sounds, the warmth of his small body against her. She knew with complete conviction that he was well taken care of. Yet she couldn't ignore the small, empty ache in her heart.

It would be worse, of course, when they got out of the country. Reilly would take him away, up north, to the big, soulless cities of the United States, and she would most likely never see him again. He would have grandparents to love him, and he would never even know about Sister Mary Charles, so important a part of his life for such a short, sweet time.

She heard the door open behind her. ''You ready for dinner?'' Reilly asked casually.

She made the mistake of turning to look at him. In the dim light of the oil lamp she could see him far too clearly. He was wearing a towel, and nothing more, and she had no illusions he'd done it purposely. Though there was no reason that he'd think a woman like Caterina Morrissey de Mendino would be discomfited by the sight of a man dressed in nothing but a towel.

But Sister Mary Charles was. She stood there, momentarily transfixed, staring at him.

His long black hair was wet, pushed away from his angular face, and he'd cut himself shaving. She'd known he was a big man, but without clothes he seemed even more massive. Not that his shoulders were immense, or his muscles bulky. He was lean and wiry and powerful looking, like no other man she'd ever seen. Dangerous and beautiful, he was like a jaguar she'd once glimpsed beyond the walls of the convent. Sleek and hard and mesmerizing. And she wanted to touch him.

''Close your mouth, Carlie,'' he murmured. ''You'll catch flies.''

She closed her mouth, still staring. He had a very tempting mouth himself. Wide, mocking, narrow lipped and sensual, it curved into a mocking smile at her trancelike state. ''Better close those beautiful blue eyes of yours, as well,'' he added. ''I'm about to get dressed.''

She whirled back to the window just as he began

to reach for the towel at his waist. She could feel the color flood her body, and she could only thank God the room was dark enough that he wouldn't see her embarrassment.

She stood there, staring mindlessly out the window, listening to the sound of clothes rustling. The snap of elastic, the rustle of cotton, the unnerving rasp of a zipper being pulled. That zipper told her she was now safe from future embarrassment, and she started to turn back.

He was directly behind her, dressed, thank God, though he hadn't bothered to snap the faded jeans he wore, and he'd left the khaki shirt loose and unbuttoned, bringing his smooth, bare chest unnervingly close. "Even your ears are blushing," he said, reaching out and pushing a damp strand away from her face.

There was a shattering tenderness in the gesture. She didn't want tenderness from this man, from any man. "Why would I blush?" she said in what she hoped was a suitably offhand voice. "I've seen hundreds of naked men."

"Besides which, if you're going to prance around in nothing but a towel, you're going to have to expect me to follow suit," he murmured. He was no longer touching her, but he was dangerously close. She could smell the soap on his skin. Toothpaste on his mouth. Danger in the air.

"I wasn't prancing," she said in a strangled voice. "And I wasn't blushing."

"You've spent too long at that convent," he said, closer to the truth than he'd ever know. "Some of the sisters' modesty must have worn off on you."

She stiffened. If she had any sense she'd ignore him. But she wasn't feeling very sensible. "Are you accusing me of trying to entice you?" she snapped.

"Not likely. You've been giving off that touch-me-not look for days now. I would have thought Caterina Mendino would have been more interested in cementing her right to protection, but you seem to take my nobility for granted."

"You'll protect me for Billy's sake," she said, certain at least of that.

"Wrong." He touched her again, with both hands this time, pushing her damp hair away from her face.

"You won't protect me?" Her voice wavered slightly. It wasn't the fear of his withdrawing his protection. It was the feel of his long, hard fingers on her skin.

"Yeah," he said. "I'll protect you. But not for Billy, and not for the baby. Not for the sake of those beautiful, lying blue eyes of yours." He ran his fingers across her cheekbones, and her eyes fluttered closed for a brief, dangerous moment.

"Then why?"

"Because I don't like to see the bad guys win. I don't like bullies, I don't like it when weaker people get hurt."

Her eyes shot open. "Who says I'm weak?" she demanded.

"Oh, you're not. Not in spirit. But a strong man could snap your neck in an instant. If you pushed him far enough. And you're a pushy broad."

The notion was so bizarre she had to smile. Meek, gentle Sister Mary Charles was a far cry from a pushy broad, but as long as he believed it, so be it. But one more thing was troubling her.

"Why do you say I have lying eyes?" she asked, wishing he'd take his hands from her face. Afraid of where else he might put them.

That cynical smile broadened. "They look so innocent. So sweet, and honest, and shy. But I know damned well Caterina Morrissey de Mendino doesn't have a shy, innocent bone in her body. You're a barracuda, lady. You may not look the way Billy described you, but I imagine your soul is just as twisted."

This was dangerous ground. About the only thing she had in common with Caterina was dark hair. Caterina had been tall and shapely, even in the advanced stages of pregnancy. Her eyes had been brown, Carlie's were blue. Her feet were big, her manner imperious, her tastes extravagant.

She raised her eyes and looked at him, for a moment hiding nothing. "Maybe you should believe my eyes," she whispered, "and not what you've heard."

He stared for a moment, unmoving, his hands cupping her upturned face, and she wondered if he'd kiss her again. Instead he backed away, suddenly, as if he'd looked into the face of a bushmaster. For a moment he looked dazed, and her sense of disquiet grew.

She lifted a hand to call him back, but he'd already turned from her. "I'll find some food for us," he said brusquely. "If I were you I'd stay put. I put the fear of God into Dutchy, and Morales and his men have left, but I don't trust them to have gone that far."

"What about the baby?"

"I'm going to check on him right now. In the

meantime, sit tight. It's not safe around here, and I'm not in the mood to play hero.''

"You don't really have the right qualifications," she said sharply.

He paused by the door, buttoning his shirt. "Oh, yeah? I would have thought I'd be perfect hero material. I'm big, a number of women have told me I'm handsome, and I fight on the side of law and order."

"You're a conceited oaf," she said, shocked at herself.

"Now you, on the other hand, don't quite qualify as a damsel in distress. You're too strong, and you lie too much."

There it was again, that trickling of unease. One she quickly squashed, as she realized he was about to abandon her in this Spartan hotel room. "Can't I come with you? I want to make sure the baby's all right."

"You can stay put. I'm going to check out a few other things while I'm at it, and I don't want you trailing around behind me, getting in my way."

"I can be very quiet...."

"No," he said, his voice sharp. And he closed the door behind him before she could utter another protest.

She stared at that door, remembering. She'd promised to do as she was told, no questions asked. She needed to keep that promise, to sit on the bed and wait until he deigned to return. She needed to ignore her empty stomach, her anxiety, her curiosity. She needed to remember the vows she wanted to take. Vows of obedience. Poverty. Chastity.

But she hadn't made those vows yet—Mother Ig-

nacia hadn't let her. And she certainly had made no
vows of obedience to Reilly.

Nor vows of chastity, either. She wasn't going to
sit alone in that room, in the middle of the bed she'd
be sharing with him, waiting for him to return. She
was hungry, she was edgy, she was out in the world,
for a short, dangerous time.

She wasn't going to spend that time cloistered in a
hotel room as if it were her cell.

She opened the door and went after him.

Chapter Eight

Blue eyes, Reilly thought. Innocent, lying blue eyes, staring up at him. With a soft, tremulous mouth that needed to be kissed. Blue eyes, and a firm, slender body, with small, high breasts.

Billy Morrissey had had blue eyes, as well. Two blue-eyed parents, and the tiny baby Carlie carried strapped to her slender body had eyes that were already turning brown.

His knowledge of genetics wasn't that exact, but he somehow doubted that two blue-eyed parents would have a brown-eyed child. So who was the real parent? Carlie? Or Billy?

It made sense that Caterina Morrissey de Mendino had lied about the father of her child. After all, the Morrisseys were wealthy Americans who could provide a decent home for a baby. The real father could be anyone—a decadent member of the jet set Caterina used to pal around with, or one of her stepfather's bodyguards. Or anyone in between. No, her estranged husband was the most convenient choice, and whether he was anywhere near San Pablo ten months ago probably didn't matter.

He could hardly blame her. She was doing what was best for the baby, and if that included lying to everyone, so be it. He could find a certain grudging respect for a mother willing to risk it all for her child.

There was only one problem with that scenario. She didn't have the body of a woman who'd given birth less than a month ago. She might love that baby with a fierce, maternal passion, but she certainly hadn't given birth to him.

Of course, there could be any number of reasons for her masquerade. She could enter the United States as the widow of a citizen, but as the mother of a U.S. citizen, as well, her residency would be assured. She'd also have claim to the Morrissey money, which would be hard for anyone to resist. Chances were she was some friend of the real Caterina's, with the same expensive tastes.

Odd, he thought, moving silently through the shadowed street toward the Shumi encampment. She looked a lot younger than Caterina should have been. A lot more innocent. It must be part of her stock-in-trade. Along with an indefinable ability to make people want to believe in her. And he, the cynic of all time, was finding it far too easy to believe in her, as well.

Which all went to prove he'd been right in getting out. Not re-upping when his last tour of duty came to an end, heading out for his mountaintop in Colorado, away from danger and distractions. Whether he wanted to admit it or not, he was marginally more vulnerable than he liked. He had to be, falling for a lying little tease.

Except she hadn't kissed like a tease. One thing

was for sure—she was lying to him, lying through her teeth, and he intended to find out the truth. In that small, concave bed tonight, he had every intention of finding out exactly who and what she was.

He'd be gone a couple of hours. He'd check on the kid, though he had no doubt Timothy was in the lap of baby luxury among the Shumi women, then he'd scout out the village, quietly, assessing the danger. That should give Carlie just long enough to start worrying whether he was coming back or not. Just long enough to panic and be ready for the slightest bit of extra pressure.

Oddly enough, he didn't find the notion appealing. He didn't want to scare her. Didn't want to terrorize her into telling him the truth. He wanted her to offer it, freely.

Another sign of dangerous weakness, he thought with disgust. If he wasn't careful he'd end up as dead as Billy Morrissey. And he wasn't quite ready to die.

The night was still and marginally cooler than the heart of the jungle they'd just traversed. The slow-moving river that ran through the village was deep and brown, the currents sluggish, but he thought he felt his first hesitant breeze since he'd landed in this miserable country. The heat, the rebels, the murderous black-shirted soldiers, the presence of Morales himself, the jungle, all added up to dangers that were scaring the hell out of him. The sooner he got those two out of here and safely back to the States, the sooner he could retire to his mountain and pull himself together.

Oddly enough, he had no hesitation about taking them both back. One of them didn't belong, maybe both of them. It didn't matter. He wasn't going to leave a helpless baby in this war-torn country, not when he had the means to get him out. And whether Carlie had given birth to him or not, she truly loved him. He was sentimental enough to figure that counted for something.

In the distance he heard the faint scream of a jaguar, deep in the jungle. And like a great jungle cat himself, he slipped into the shadows, on the prowl.

IT DIDN'T TAKE CARLIE long to regret her decision to follow Reilly. Even though the old building seemed deserted as she tiptoed downstairs, she could feel eyes, watching her. Male eyes, hungry eyes. She'd felt those eyes on her ever since she'd arrived at this place, she admitted to herself.

The bar downstairs was deserted, thank God, the soldiers gone. She took a good look around through the murky lamplight. Cigarette smoke still hung in the air like a noxious cloud, and she could smell whiskey and chiles. The latter made her stomach growl in longing.

Surely someone like Dutchy would employ a cook. The Shumi were noted for their cooking as well as their family values—with any luck there'd be someone in the kitchen, eager to feed her.

Luck, however, was not with her. The kitchen was nothing more than a back shed, the stove was cold, the stores almost negligible. There was a bowl of eggs of doubtful vintage, a hunk of hard cheese, some plantains. And three cans of Campbell's soup.

She stared in disbelief. She had forgotten the existence of canned soup. Centuries ago, when she'd lived in the States, it had been a major part of her sustenance. Looking at those red cans, she could suddenly remember her mother—vague, preoccupied, opening a can with the assurance that this would provide a decent meal for a growing girl. She could always taste the toast and butter.

It seared through her with a sharp pain. Memory. Grief. Shock. She thought she'd put that all behind her, found a safe new life with the sisters, protected from harsh, unbearable time. And just as easily it came rushing back, simply by looking at a can of soup.

She was shaking all over. She could smell the blood once more, pooling beneath the beating sun. The screams were gone, but the shouts of the soldiers still echoed. They were searching for her—they knew she was somewhere in that mountain village, and they weren't about to leave a witness behind. And she'd backed down, curled into a fetal ball, and waited for them to come and finish her.

But they'd never found her. She'd been brought out safely, that time of horror locked safely away in the back of her brain. It had been so long since she'd even thought about it.

Until Reilly had dragged her back into life. And the memories came flooding back as well, crushing her.

She couldn't let it crush her. With sheer force of will she thrust the panic, the despair away from her. This time she couldn't curl up in a weeping, helpless ball on the floor, waiting for someone to rescue her. She had a vow, to Caterina, to the baby, to herself, even if Mother Ignacia wouldn't let her make a formal

vow. She would see Timothy safely into his grandparents' arms, and she would return to the sisters.
There the past would safely recede, and she would
find peace once more.

She reached for the can of soup, ignoring the
tremor in her hands. It took her a while to find the
can opener, longer still to use the rude contraption.
And then she sat on one of the stools, took a spoon
and began to eat out of the can, the cold salty stuff a
far cry from the warm comfort her mother had provided her so long ago.

The stale corn bread didn't taste anything at all like
buttered toast, either. And yet she knew the flavors.
It felt oddly like a kind of communion. Bread and
wine. Cold soup and corn bread. In remembrance of
her mother.

Would Mother Ignacia call it blasphemy? Perhaps.
But to Carlie it felt like a sacrament. Remembering.
And letting go, just a tiny bit.

"You eat my soup?" The heavily accented voice
was deep with outrage.

Carlie looked up to see Dutchy standing in the
doorway. He was a large, untidy man, with bloodshot
eyes, several days' growth of beard that didn't look
the slightest bit raffish, a pot belly and a stained, rumpled white suit. His gray hair stood up around his bald
spot, and he glared at her for a moment, his small
dark eyes cunning.

"I'm sorry," she stammered. "I was hungry, and
I couldn't find anything else. We'll pay for it...."
Belatedly she wondered if Reilly had any money with
him. Of course he did—he was infuriatingly efficient.

Dutchy pushed into the room, an expression of

false affability crossing his lined face as he pulled out a cigar. "No, no," he said grandly. "You should have let me know. I could have had one of the Shumi cook you something. A pretty girl like you shouldn't have to eat cold soup out of a can." He cast a sorrowful look at the empty container, the spoon still sticking out of it.

"It reminded me of my childhood." She said it on purpose, testing herself. There was no pain. Not at the moment.

"That's why I keep it around. To remind me of civilization while I'm in this godforsaken place. It's very hard to come by."

"And I took one. I'm sorry."

Dutchy moved closer, the cigar smoke wreathing around him like an anaconda. "For a pretty little girl like you," he said, breathing heavily, "I don't mind. Where's your friend?"

"He just went out for a walk. He'll be back at any moment." Alarm coursed through her, immediate, justified. There was no other exit to the kitchen shed. Just the door Dutchy was blocking. She slid off the stool, trying to summon up a cool smile. A Caterina, to-hell-with-you smile.

"That's right," Dutchy cooed, coming closer. "A nice, friendly smile. You be nice to Dutchy, and he'll be nice to you. Morales and his men haven't gone far, and they're coming back. They wondered about you, and your friend. They'll wonder even more about the baby you left with the Shumi women. You shouldn't expect to keep secrets in a place like this. The Shumi won't talk, but others will. And I've promised to report anything unusual to Morales. He wouldn't like it one bit if I held out on him.''

"What baby?" she demanded, unable to hide her panic.

"Don't be foolish. I found out, and so will Morales. But if you're nice to me, and you play your cards right, I can keep them away from you."

She backed away from him, surreptitiously, but he followed, until she was up against a wall, nowhere to run to, and he was far too close, his big belly pushing up against her, his cigar smoke wreathing them both. "You be friendly to me, little one, and I can be very helpful. People around here know that Dutchy is a good friend to have." He reached out a hand to touch her face. His fingers were short, stubby, stained with dirt and nicotine, and as he brushed them against her cheekbone she couldn't control her horrified shudder.

Dutchy's grin widened, exposing dark, broken teeth. "You like that, do you?" he murmured, completely misinterpreting her reaction. "You're a woman of discernment. Broad shoulders and a handsome face are all well and good, but there's a lot to be said for age and experience." His hand slid down the column of her neck, and her skin crawled. "Give me a little kiss, sweetheart, to show your good intentions."

He leaned forward, his belly pressing against her, his hand groping at her breast, and there was no escape. She stood motionless, terrified, defenseless, ready to suffer and endure, when a cool, mocking voice interrupted them.

"Messing with my woman, Dutchy?" Reilly stood

in the doorway, a silhouette in the shadowy light. "I thought you were smarter than that."

Dutchy backed away from her so quickly it would have been comical. But Carlie was in no mood to laugh. She realized she'd been holding her breath, and she let it out, wondering if she was going to throw up all over Dutchy's filthy white suit.

The old man was already across the kitchen, hands raised in the air in a defensive gesture. The fact that Reilly was pointing a gun at him probably encouraged his attitude. "I meant no harm, Reilly. I'm just a harmless old flirt, you know that. I can't let a pretty girl go by without making a pass at her. No need to point that gun at me—it was all in fun."

"Was it?"

His voice was grim, deadly. Carlie stood there, mesmerized. The sight of the gun in his strong hand brought back other memories, other hands holding guns, and the nausea rose farther in her throat. "He didn't hurt me, Reilly," she said, silently pleading with him to put the gun away.

Oddly enough, he did, tucking it back into the waistband of his jeans. "Lucky for him," Reilly murmured. "Get out of here, old man."

Dutchy left, almost tripping in his haste to escape, and they were alone in the tiny shack. She'd thought it was crowded with Dutchy bearing down on her. It was nothing compared to Reilly towering over her, looking dark and disapproving.

"I thought I told you to stay in your room," he said.

"I was starving," she said, squaring her shoulders and trying to pull some of her self-control back around her. She still felt shaken, frightened, helpless. She didn't like that feeling. Any more than she liked realizing that Reilly's presence was rapidly banishing that fear, replacing it with another, more disturbing kind of tension. "I didn't know when you were coming back."

"So you decided to come exploring. Were you looking for a meal, or a better offer? Morales may have been *el presidente*'s chief enforcer, but all that ended when your stepfather was assassinated. Those soldiers are renegades. Your stepfather's dead, Caterina, and those loyal to him have gone their own way. You're nothing more than a pawn now."

"I wasn't—"

"As for Dutchy, I think you already discovered exactly what he's interested in. He's a bigger danger than an anaconda, and if you think you can trust him—"

"I don't trust him!" she snapped. "I was hungry, I told you."

He looked at the empty can of soup. "You must have been desperate," he said calmly. "You want anything else, or are you ready to go up to bed?"

His even tone of voice was deceptive. She looked up at the big dark man, and fear was back. "I want my own room," she said. "My own bed."

"I'm sure you do. But you wouldn't get it. You can share with me, you can trust me, damn it," he said, suddenly angry. "Or you can start out the night alone. You wouldn't end up that way. Either Dutchy or one of Morales's men would be joining you."

"I can take care of myself."

"Sure you can. I just had a perfect example of just

how good you are at protecting yourself,'' he
drawled.

"I could have handled him," she said, knowing
just how unlikely that was.

"Maybe you could have. But I'm not going to risk
Billy's kid's life on that slim chance. You do as I say,
no questions asked, and we'll be out of here before
they even know we're gone."

"Are you really that confident?" she asked faintly.

"I'm really that good."

There was nothing she could say to that. It wasn't
a boast, it was a simple statement of fact. And she
believed him.

"All right," she said. "I won't argue with you."

"That'll be the day," he drawled, half to himself.

"I don't argue!" she said, shocked.

"Lady, you have a very cantankerous streak when
you forget you're trying to convince me you're a Madonna."

He probably thought he was being funny. The
words cut her to the quick, though, bringing into
doubt almost anything she'd ever believed about herself. "What do you mean by that?" she demanded.

"I mean there seem to be at least two people inside
that small, luscious body of yours. There's the saintly
mother of the year, trudging along behind me, following orders, biting her tongue, peaceful and serene and
not really of this world. Then there's the strong, angry
young woman who gives as good as she takes, who
questions authority and who's driving me crazy. And
somewhere in all that mess is Caterina Morrissey, a
spoiled, self-absorbed tramp. I'm just trying to figure
out which one is the real you."

"Who told you Caterina Morrissey is a tramp?"

"Honey, I read the letter you wrote Billy. Where you told him you were having a better time sleeping around the continent and you didn't feel like being the wife of an American soldier, even a rich one. Kind of put me off a bit, I do admit."

There was nothing she could say. She could remember Caterina's weak, hesitant last confession. A confession that was neither sanctioned by the church nor forgiven by the holy rites, but a confession free and honest and true nonetheless, between two unlikely friends.

"I'm not going to argue ancient history with you," she said instead, primly. "I'm ready to go up, but first I'm dying of thirst. That condensed soup was pure salt. Is there anything to drink around here?"

"This is a bar, Carlie. There's plenty."

"I was thinking of water."

"We'll save any decent water for the baby. You can make do with beer."

"I don't drink—"

"You'll drink beer and like it. Your other choices are so potent I'd end up carrying you and the kid for the next three days. I could do with a couple of beers myself."

By the time she followed him back into the bar he'd already pulled the caps off two tall dark beers. She took one from him, looking at it askance, but he was ignoring her, tipping the bottle back and pouring it down his throat with obvious enjoyment.

She had no choice in the matter—she was so thirsty she could go out and suck a cactus. She took a big gulp of the lukewarm stuff.

It tasted strong, dark and yeasty. She drank half of it, then wiped her mouth. "It's good," she said, half in surprise.

"The princess doesn't usually deign to drink beer?" he drawled.

"Not this kind." It was an easy enough lie.

"Funny, I would have thought Dos Equis would be just your style."

She drained the bottle. "Is there another one around?"

His mouth curved in a smile. She liked his mouth, she decided. It was one of the reasons she trusted him. "Here you go, princess."

"Don't call me princess," she snapped.

"Ah, the bitch is back."

She choked on the first gulp of beer. "I beg your pardon?" she said, glaring.

His smile was positively beatific. "I think I like you best this way," he said, taking her arm and herding her toward the stairs. "I suspect it's the real you."

"I want another beer," she said, hanging back.

"You haven't finished that one."

She pulled away, stumbling slightly when he let her go, and drained the second bottle. "There," she said triumphantly.

He just looked at her. "I thought you were used to drinking."

"I am."

"Not from the looks of it, kid. Two beers is the cheapest drunk I've ever seen in my life. I heard you used to be able to pack it away like a professional."

Dangerous ground, she thought hazily. "Maybe my metabolism changed since I gave birth."

"Maybe," he said. "Think you can walk upstairs?"

"Don't be ridiculous," she snapped, full of dignity, staring past him. The floor was slightly unsteady, and she reached out a hand to balance herself. Unfortunately he was the one she reached for.

If she'd felt dizzy before, it was nothing compared to being swooped up in Reilly's strong arms. Ascending the steep staircase didn't help the woozy state of her brain, either.

"Could you take it a little slower?" she murmured, sinking back against him, totally incapable of fighting him at that particular moment. "I'm dizzy."

"Don't worry, princess," he drawled. "The night is young. I'm not about to let you go to sleep."

"You're not?" She tried to summon up a latent wariness, then gave it up.

"Not until you answer a few questions."

They were in the upstairs hall by now, and it was very dark. She wondered hazily where Dutchy was now. If he'd gone after the soldiers. "I answered all your questions, Reilly."

"Oh. I just had a couple more." He kicked open the door to the bedroom, his voice deceptively affable. The oil lamp had burned down low, sending out only a small pool of yellow light.

"Such as?"

He carried her over to the bed, and she found herself strangely loath to let go of him. There was a strange glitter in his eyes, one she couldn't read, and his mouth was dangerously close. She wondered what he'd do if she kissed that mouth. She wanted to try it again. She'd liked her first attempt, liked it very much indeed. She imagined she'd improve with practice, and the amount of beer she'd drunk made her feel pleasantly warm and eager to try again.

"Such as who the hell you really are," he said softly. "And whose baby you're trying to pass off as your own."

Chapter Nine

Reilly wondered, quite calmly, whether the young woman in his arms was about to throw up on him. She looked green, her huge blue eyes were stricken and her body, even in this humid night air, felt tense and cold.

"You're crazy, Reilly," she said, but her voice shook.

He considered dropping her on the bed. He didn't want to—a dangerous reluctance he was willing to acknowledge, even as he deplored it. He didn't want to let go of her at all, but he knew the longer he cradled her against his body, the harder it would be. In more ways than one.

He put her down, gently enough, and took a step back, away from her. She made the very grave mistake of not staying put. She scrambled off the bed in a panic, the beer she'd drunk making her awkward. It was child's play to catch her by the door, pulling her back around, against him. Child's play to look down into her frightened, upturned face, and exert the last little bit of pressure.

"Crazy?" he replied in a low, menacing drawl. "I

don't think so. I don't know whose baby that is that you've been playing devoted mother to, but it's not yours. You didn't give birth a month ago. I don't think you've ever been pregnant in your life.''

"What would you know about it?" she demanded furiously. Another mistake on her part.

It was a simple enough matter to push his hand up under the loose white T-shirt she wore, to cover her small, perfect breast. She tried to jerk away in shock, but he held her tightly, allowing no escape. And then she held very still, looking up at him in mute despair, as his hand cupped her breast and the peak hardened against his palm. "I watched you in the shower, remember?" he taunted her in a low voice. "Babies wreak havoc on a body, especially one as small and slight as yours. Your breasts would sag, whether you were nursing him or not. The skin on your stomach would be loose, your waist would be thick, your stamina would be shot to hell. I don't know whose baby you've been cooing over, but it's not yours."

"You're crazy," she said again, trying to disguise the panic in her voice, and failing. "Timothy is mine and Billy Morrissey's, and you can't prove otherwise."

"Oh, yeah? What color were Billy's eyes?"

Her hesitation was so imperceptible he found he was impressed. "Hazel."

"Wrong. It was a pretty safe guess, though. I'll grant you that. Billy's eyes were a bright, bright blue. You have blue eyes yourself, princess. The baby's eyes are already turning brown."

He pulled her a little closer against him. He knew he ought to release her breast, but the feel of its small, mounded warmth against his palm, the hard nub of her nipple, the way she shivered in his arms, were all too delicious to resist. He was very hard, and he didn't mind her knowing that as well, as she stood plastered up against him. There was no way she could miss it, and yet she still seemed slightly disoriented, confused by him and her own body. Maybe those two beers had had an even greater effect on her than he'd originally thought.

"Whose baby?" he said again, softer now, arching her back slightly. "Does Caterina Morrissey have brown eyes?"

Her body slumped in defeat. Against his. "She had brown eyes," she said in a low voice. "She's dead."

"I thought so. But Timothy was hers?"

The woman nodded. "She died soon after he was born. It was a massive infection—there was nothing I could do. I could only promise that I would make sure Timothy got safely out of this wretched country."

Release her, he told himself. He loosened his grip marginally, but she made no effort to escape. He considered whether he could flatter himself into thinking she was starting to like it, but he didn't think so. She was simply too dazed to realize her compromising position.

If he had a speck of decency he'd let her go. She was ready to spill—he didn't need to use any sort of physical intimidation on her anymore to pry the truth from her. But the feel of her warm, smooth skin beneath his hand was irresistible. He wanted to cup the other breast, as well. He wanted to lean down and taste it.

"So he really is Billy's baby. His grandparents will be pleased to hear that. Why didn't you tell me the truth?"

"I did. You didn't believe me."

He nodded, remembering. "So you did. I guess I'm a little too used to liars. So who are you, if you're not Caterina Morrissey? And how did you end up at that deserted convent?"

Sudden awareness darkened her eyes as she realized her position, plastered up against him, his hand on her small, perfect breast. She wrenched herself away and he let her go, disguising his unwillingness. She sat back on the bed, keeping her face averted, but he could see the unexpected color on her cheekbones. Just as he recognized her rushed breathing, and her nipples pressing against the thin cotton of the white T-shirt. Her ladyship was turned on, and she either didn't know it or didn't like it. Maybe a combination of the two.

"I told you, I was a friend of Caterina's. My name really is Carlie. Short for Caroline. Caroline Forrest."

"How did you and Caterina become friends? She tended to fly with a pretty rich crowd. And what were you doing at that convent?"

"I was taking care of Caterina."

"Why?"

She looked up at him, her blue eyes wide and slightly dazed. She was about to lie to him. He recognized that fact with a combination of irritation and triumph. If she continued to lie, then all bets were off. There was no reason he should play the little gentleman with a liar.

"Because no one else would," she said. "All the nuns had left. I...I've known Caterina for years. We were in school together, in France, and we used to have fun together. She wrote me a few months ago and asked me to come visit. I thought we were going to continue to party when I came to San Pablo."

"You picked a lousy time for a vacation. Don't you read the newspapers? Don't you have the faintest idea of the political upheaval around here?"

"There's political unrest everywhere," she said with a brave attempt at a shrug. He was impressed. If he didn't already have reason to distrust her he would have believed that shrug. She looked up at him defiantly, and she would have convinced most people she was simply a spoiled party girl, caught in the middle of a revolution.

It would be easier on him if he did believe it. He could take full advantage of that small, trim body that had such a surprisingly potent effect on his, and if she was who she said she was, she'd be more than agreeable.

Dutchy had been scared off. Morales and his men were well out of reach, at least for now, the baby was safe and the door was locked. He looked at her, taking in the brave defiance in her pale mouth, and pulled the gun out of his waistband.

Her eyes followed that gun, nervously. She'd had a bad experience with guns in her life, he could tell that much. If he were a real bastard he could use that gun to make her tell him the truth this time. Not that half-baked lie of French finishing schools and the like.

But he put the gun down on the table beside the

bed, close enough so he could reach it if someone decided to interrupt them, and then moved closer to her. Her eyes were at the level of his zipper.

"All right," he murmured. "I'll believe you. What do you want from me?"

"I want Timothy to be reunited with his grandparents."

"And you'll accept safe transportation to the States, as well," he drawled cynically.

"I'm not sure."

Another lie, though this didn't sound like one. She wanted to get the hell out of this country, back to the same cushy life Caterina would have had. "Oh, I imagine you'll decide soon enough, princess," he said. "Tell me, were you going to tell anyone the truth? Or were you going to keep passing yourself off as Caterina Morrissey?"

"Caterina Morrissey wasn't exactly a recluse," she snapped, some of her anger struggling back. "Plenty of people would know I'm not her."

"Good point. Besides, I imagine you have family somewhere, who wouldn't take kindly to your up and disappearing."

"I have no family left." She didn't look at the gun lying on the table. She didn't need to. In certain ways she was a mystery to him. In certain ways she was far too clear.

"All right. Let's get your story straight," he said, moving around to the other side of the narrow bed and dropping down, lightly. She jerked, but she had enough sense not to leave the lumpy mattress.

"I don't need to get my story straight," she said irritably. "It's the truth. My name is Caroline Forrest.

I'm twenty-six years old, American, an old school friend of Caterina Mendino's. My family's dead, and I came to visit Caterina at the wrong time, that's all. She asked me to keep her company during the latter part of her pregnancy, and I agreed. When her step-father was killed we arranged to go to the Sisters of Benevolence, and we stayed there for the last two months. Caterina gave birth, she died soon after, but she asked me to make sure her baby was taken care of. She said Billy would be coming for them. But instead you showed up.''

''And the rest is history,'' he said, stretching out on the bed and eyeing her. ''Of course, there's no way to check it. Caterina, and Billy, and almost everyone else who would know the truth are all dead. The good sisters have deserted San Pablo, and that just leaves you and me and the baby.''

''You'll have to trust me.''

''Why should I?''

''Because I trusted you. Enough to come with you.''

''But not enough to tell me the truth,'' he said. ''Okay, I'll believe you.''

She was gullible enough to take him at his word. More proof that she wasn't part of Caterina's deca-dent crowd. She gave him a hesitant smile. A dan-gerous one. For both of them.

It would be simple enough to find out the truth. And more temptation than he felt like resisting at that particular moment. ''That means we don't need to worry,'' he said in a deliberately low voice.

''Worry about what?''

''About whether you can do it or not.''

"Do what?"

There was no coquetry in the question. He almost hesitated, but he wasn't in the mood for hesitation. He slid his fingers along the back of her neck, threading them through her short-cropped hair, bringing her close to him. She didn't resist, but her eyes were wide and dark and frightened.

"Do what?" he echoed mockingly. And he told her, in precise, Anglo-Saxon words. In detail. Exactly what he wanted to do to her.

He was totally unprepared for her reaction. He expected coyness, or even enthusiastic participation. She moved so fast, jerking away from him, that another man might have let her go.

But Reilly was in fighting form, in the midst of a war-torn country with the enemy surrounding him, and two people dependent on him. His reflexes were automatic, hauling her back across the bed so that she lay across his body, trapped, panting, staring at him with terror and something else indefinable in her eyes.

"I didn't say I was going to rape you," he said irritably. Though he wasn't sure why he should be so mad at himself. He'd set out to test her, to scare her. He'd succeeded in what he'd wanted, hadn't he?

Except what he wanted was her mouth. Her panicked blue eyes closing as he kissed her. He wanted her small, perfect breasts against his bare chest, he wanted her strong, pale legs wrapped around his hips. He wanted her strong hands with their short, unmanicured nails digging into his shoulders. He wanted to make love to her.

"No," she said. Her voice wavered just slightly, her only sign of fear.

"Who are you saving it for, princess? It's a long night, and who knows where we'll be tomorrow? We're sharing a bed, we might as well share the rest of it, as well."

"No," she said. She was still half lying across his lap, his unmistakable erection.

He slid his hand behind her neck, pulling her closer. She didn't resist, and there was resignation in her eyes. Resignation, and anticipation.

He kissed her then. Her mouth opened beneath his, willingly enough, though she jerked in surprise when he pushed his tongue past her lips. He held her still, his large hand cupping her neck, and she quieted after a moment. Letting him kiss her. Making no effort to fight him. No effort to kiss him back.

He lifted his head and looked down at her. "Practicing passive resistance, Carlie?" he murmured. "I told you, I'm not going to rape you."

"Then what are you doing?"

"Just satisfying my curiosity." He released her, and she moved to her side of the bed as quickly as she could. She didn't try to run again. She already knew he could catch her.

He leaned back against the lumpy pillows, watching her. "I'll make a deal with you, Carlie," he said lazily. "Kiss me back, and then tell me no. And I'll believe you."

Her blue eyes were clouded, wary. "You think I won't be able to resist you? Your conceit is really extraordinary, Reilly."

"I didn't say that. Just kiss me as if you mean it. And then tell me no. And I promise I won't touch you again."

She moved very fast, as if she didn't dare stop to think about it, swiveling around and pressing her closed lips against his, hard. Slamming his lips against his teeth, jarring his head, banging his nose, before she pulled back, obviously shaken.

He sighed. "You can do better than that," he said. "Kiss me as you'd kiss a lover. Or I'll kiss you."

As a threat it was hardly that devastating, but she reacted with unflattering fear. He waited, patiently enough, stretched out on the bed, and this time she considered it.

"All right," she said, getting to her knees, the long skirt swirling around her on the bed. He wondered whether she was wearing anything underneath it. He didn't think so, and the thought made him ache.

Unfortunately he'd made a bargain with her. And he had every intention of keeping his side of it, as long as she kept hers.

She tilted her head to one side, as if considering how to go about it. Leaning forward, she put her small, strong hands on his shoulders, and brought her face up close to his. He watched her through lowered lids, but there was no mistaking the indecision and panic in her eyes.

"What are you afraid of, Carlie?" he murmured, his voice low and hypnotic. "It's just a kiss."

She closed the distance between them and put her mouth on his. Lips still closed tight over her teeth, her hands gripping his shoulders, she kissed him like an early Christian martyr going to the stake.

She pulled back, but he reached up and covered her hands with his, holding her there. "You can do better than that," he taunted her. "Use your tongue."

He half expected her to argue, but instead she put her mouth against his again. He reached up and cupped her face, stroking the sides of her mouth with his thumbs, and her lips softened, opened against his. He lured her tongue forward, carefully, masterfully, rewarded with her tentative touch against his, the quiet moan of pleasure that came from the back of her throat. Her mouth was sheer delight, hypnotizing, innocent, like nothing he had ever tasted before, and the desire that was raging through his body rose to new heights as he deepened the kiss. He teased her, taught her, and she responded with growing delight, moving closer, her breasts within reach, her hands clutching his shoulders now, her eyes tightly closed, her mouth open, seeking, seeking....

In the distance there was the sound of gunfire. She tore herself away from him, scrambling back across the bed, but this time he let her go.

She looked at him as if he were the devil incarnate. He simply leaned back and managed a cool, deceptive smile. She had to know what was going through his body, but he wasn't about to belabor it. "You were just beginning to get the hang of it, Carlie. It's hard to believe you were part of Caterina's crowd of high-living jet-setters."

"I told you, I don't like kissing," she said.

"You could have fooled me. You seemed to be developing a definite affinity for it." He stretched back and closed his eyes, waiting.

It didn't take long. "Is that it?" she demanded, sounding uncharacteristically exasperated.

He opened one eye. "Is that what? I presumed the answer was still no. If you changed your mind..."

"The answer is still no."

He smiled sweetly. "Then good night."

She stared at him, baffled. It was something of a consolation. He would have found a great deal of satisfaction burying himself in her small, gorgeous body, but without her cooperation he'd have to settle for second best. Driving her crazy.

She sank down beside him, turning her back in a furious huff. Unfortunately the nature of the bed didn't allow for temperamental snits. She slid up against him on the concave mattress.

She immediately tried to scramble away, clinging to the side of the bed. "You aren't going to have a very comfortable night like that," he observed, sitting up and watching her.

"I don't anticipate having a comfortable night as long as you're around," she snapped.

"You're forgetting, I'm the one who's keeping you alive," he said lazily, reaching forward and turning down the oil lamp until the room was a dark cocoon. "If I hadn't gotten back, you'd be in Dutchy's bed, whether you liked it or not. And he probably has fleas."

Silence. "Thank you for saving me," she muttered. Belated. Grudging.

"My pleasure," he replied, glad the inky darkness hid his grin.

She wasn't falling asleep. The bed practically vibrated with her tension, and he wondered whether she was going to be fool enough to try to sneak off when she thought he was asleep. He deliberately relaxed his body, changed his breathing, to see whether she'd go for the bait.

"Reilly?" she whispered after a long moment.

He said nothing, waiting to see whether she'd slide off the bed and try to make it to the door.

But apparently escape wasn't on her mind, not at that point. "Reilly," she whispered again. "What are you going to do with me?"

"Keep my hands off you."

"That's not what I meant. I meant—"

"I know what you meant," he drawled. "And the answer hasn't changed. I'll take you where you want to go. To the States, if you want, or the closest safe airport outside of San Pablo. I'm taking the baby to his grandparents, but I'll make sure you're safe, as well."

"Even though I lied to you?"

"Even though you lied to me."

"And what do you want in return?" She sounded her usual distrustful self, and he allowed himself a weary sigh.

"I thought I made that clear. Nothing that you aren't willing to give. Now go to sleep, Carlie."

"But—"

"Go to sleep, or I'll give you another lesson in kissing. And I might even manage to change your mind."

She didn't make another sound. The tension in her body gradually began to lessen, and in less than ten minutes she was sound asleep, her small, sweet butt pressed up against him.

He only wished he could find a similar oblivion.

Chapter Ten

Her dreams were shameful. Lascivious, shocking things, the likes of which hadn't bothered her for years. She'd worked so hard at banishing dreams from her life. The terrifying nightmares that brought back full force the bloody day when her parents had died. The lustful dreams that left her feeling hot and trembly. Even the peaceful dreams, where God seemed to be speaking to her, had been blocked from her life. She would wake up once they started, jarred into consciousness and safety.

But she must have been too tired to fight it. The big, strong body stretched out beside hers, touching hers, worked its own insidious effect on her, invading her defenses, her longings, her dreams.

Her skin was hot. Prickling with awareness. There was a strange gnawing sensation in the pit of her stomach, and her mouth ached. In her dreams she knew she'd been wrong. She'd kissed a man. She'd taken pleasure in it, she who'd eschewed men and this world. And she wanted him to kiss her again.

Concrete images faded, to be replaced by shifting patterns, sensations. Heat and dampness, flesh and muscle, bone and sinew, taste and desire. She was running then, down a long hillside, chasing something that she couldn't quite see. And he was behind her, waiting for her. She had only to stop, to hold out her hand, and he'd pull her back, away from the pit filled with noisy, cawing blackbirds, their wings flapping, their white veils fluttering in the jungle breeze....

Her eyes flew open in sudden awareness. She was lying pressed up against Reilly's body, the thick darkness all around them, with only the soft glow of moonlight sending a faint light in the room. Her arms were around him, tight, and it was more than clear that she'd crawled over to his side, crept up to him while she slept, looking for comfort, looking for something she was too big a coward to define.

His eyes were open, still, in the moonlight, but he made no move to touch her. She found she was clinging to him, and he let her. Beneath her hands, beneath the thin cotton T-shirt he wore, she could feel the beat of his heart. Steady, slightly fast.

"You were dreaming," he said.

"Yes."

"Nightmares. About guns and death."

"I do sometimes," she said, too weary, too vulnerable to protect herself by lying. She was too close, and the heat and strength of him were irresistible. She knew she should apologize, move away. She knew she couldn't.

"What happened?"

Another time she would have been more wary. She would have remembered the story she'd been telling him, about the privileged life of French finishing schools. But she was still half-asleep, still shaken from the vivid dream, and she wanted to tell him what she'd never told another living being.

"They killed them," she whispered, her head down. She could feel the wetness of tears on her cheeks, and she pressed her face against the soft T-shirt, the hard, warm skin beneath, letting the soft cotton soak up the dampness.

He was holding her, loosely, comfortingly, one hand smoothing back her short hair. "Who did, Carlie?"

She tried to resist. "I don't want to…"

"Who did?"

She couldn't fight him, and herself, and her need to tell him. "The soldiers," she said, her voice barely discernible. But she knew he heard every word. "They came to Puente del Norte and they killed them all. My parents. The people in the village. Even the children."

"Why didn't they kill you, Carlie?" His voice was a soothing rumble beneath her tear-streaked face, and the large, rough hand kept stroking, stroking.

"They couldn't find me. I was hiding, behind a clump of trees. I couldn't move. I couldn't even hide my head. I just had to stay there, and watch, and… and…listen.…"

His arms tightened around her then. For a brief moment she fought it, but he simply held her, his voice that same comforting rumble. "There's no one to hear you, baby," he murmured. "No one to see you. No one to know if you cry."

"I'd know," she said.

His hand slid beneath her hair, tilting her face toward his. "You already know."

He took her breath away. She wouldn't have expected him to have an idea of her torment, and yet he'd honed in on it immediately. And there was no way she could deny the truth of his words.

"I…" she began, one more token protest. But her voice failed her, and she began to cry. Noisily. Wetly. Burying her face against him once more, howling out her misery and rage, her loneliness and pain. She cried until her stomach ached with the force of her sobs, cried until her eyes stung and her chest ached and her nose was running with no tissue in sight. And all the while he held her.

He was an astonishing man. When her storm of tears began to fade, a bandanna appeared in front of her. She pulled away from him with no more than a quavery sigh, wiped her face, blew her nose and looked at him defiantly.

His T-shirt was damp from her tears. His face was hidden in the shadows, but she imagined she could see the gleam in his eyes, the faint grimness to his mouth.

"Reilly," she said, hardly recognizing her tear-roughened voice.

She wasn't sure what she expected from him. Questions, mockery, a pass. She wasn't sure which she'd hate the most.

She'd underestimated him. He simply lay back on the bed, looking at her out of steady eyes. "Are you ready to sleep?" he asked. "We've got a long day tomorrow."

She wasn't sure what she should do. She was embarrassed, self-conscious.

He solved the problem for her. He caught her arm

and pulled her back down beside him. Up close, pressed against him. He draped an arm over her, a possessive, protective arm. And then he closed his eyes, obviously prepared to go to sleep.

She held still, barely daring to breathe, overwhelmingly conscious of the heat of his body, the warmth of his breath against her hair, the steady thump of his heartbeat. It thumped at deliberate counterpoint to hers, and she tried to match his breathing, but hers was lighter, faster, as if she'd been running. Punctuated by the remnants of her bout of tears.

Odd, that she could feel so comfortable and so uneasy at the same time. She wasn't used to touching other people, and the feel of his body plastered against hers, the casual possession of his arm, made her feel threatened.

And yet, she felt safer than she ever had. This was a man who would protect her, no matter what. This was a man who'd watch out for her, for the baby, who'd do what he said he would do, and nothing or no one would stop him. He was stubborn as a mule, but she realized for the first time in almost ten years that she wasn't frightened of the future.

And she wasn't frightened of the past.

She should have told someone, anyone, the story of what she'd seen in that tiny mountaintop village. The horror had been so real that she'd wanted to shut it out, and she'd been afraid that by talking about it she'd somehow make it real, give it power over her.

Not realizing the power it had already claimed.

She could have told Reverend Mother Ignacia. She could have confessed to Father Ramon, not any real sin, but the miserable guilt of surviving when so many had died. But instead she'd buried it in her heart, where it ate its way into her soul like a worm, until it came pouring out, confessed to a man of violence not that far removed from the men who had committed those atrocities.

And yet he was. Just because he carried a gun, because he was willing and able to kill, didn't mean he was one of them. He looked out for the innocents of this world. For Timothy. And for her.

"Reilly," she said, her voice husky and still in the darkness. She half expected he'd be asleep already—he didn't strike her as the sort of man who let a little thing like sleep disobey his command.

But a moment later he answered. "Yeah?"

"Thank you."

"For what?"

"For scaring Dutchy off. For bringing us out of the jungle. For letting me cry all over you. For putting up with me...."

"Don't get maudlin on me, princess," he drawled as his long fingers gently stroked her bare shoulder where the loose top had slipped down. It was a simple gesture, meant no doubt to reassure. So why did it strike a hot spark deep within that dark, evil part of her? Why did it make her want to move closer still, to wrap her body around his and soak up his strength, his heat, his very being?

She froze, terrified at the rush of longings surging through her. She needed to get away from him. He was seducing her simply with the force of his presence, seducing her away from the safety she'd longed for and worked for. And he didn't even want her.

She needed to be strong. She needed to remember

her priorities. Get the baby safely out of the country, on his way to his grandparents. And then join Mother Ignacia and the others, older but wiser.

"If you don't relax," Reilly whispered in her ear, "I'm going to figure out a way to tire you enough to make you fall asleep. Right now I can only think of one way to accomplish that, and while it seems like a fine idea to me, you've already said no. So if you want me to respect your wishes, you'll stop wiggling around and sighing. Unless you want that wiggling and sighing put to good use."

Carlie froze. He breathed a loud sigh and began to rub the tight muscles in her back with his strong hand. She tried to will herself to go limp, but she simply couldn't. Not surrounded by the heat and the scent and the feel of him.

"All right," he said in sudden exasperation. And before she knew what was happening he'd spun her over, onto her back, and he was straddling her, his big, strong body covering hers. "We'll do it my way." And he covered her mouth with his.

She struggled, but it was useless. He was so much bigger, so much stronger, so much more determined. Mother Ignacia had counseled her about rape. When they had first brought her to the Sisters of Benevolence she had scarcely been able to speak, so deep was her shock, and for the first few months it had been assumed that she had been raped. Even when part of the truth came out—that she was from a village destroyed by war—Reverend Mother was very matter-of-fact about the dangers of living in a country where their faith and their habits sometimes couldn't

protect them. She had escaped, physically unscathed.
There was no guarantee her luck would continue.

It was no sin, Reverend Mother had said. When
faced with rape, don't put your life in danger, trying
to fight. If you can't escape, submit. God has already
had enough martyrs.

Submit, she reminded herself, lying stiff and
straight as a board beneath him, waiting for his hands
to paw at her. It would be over soon enough. Perhaps
this was the price she had to pay for her sins, to suffer
this base degradation....

Except it didn't feel like degradation. His mouth
danced across hers with the lightness of a butterfly,
brushing against her tightly closed lips. He held her
pinned with his body, but with one hand he began
pulling the loose cotton shirt from the waistband of
the skirt. His warm hand was on her waist, sliding up
to cover her breast, and she squirmed, trying to buck
him off.

She might just as well have tried to dislodge a boulder. He was slow, deliberate in his caress of her
breast, and she opened her mouth to cry out in protest.

He slid his tongue inside her mouth. She arched
again, but it seemed to push her breast against his
rough-skinned hand, and the sensation was...
disturbing.

Not nearly as disturbing as what he did next. He
rolled to his side, taking her with him, and her skirt
was bunched up around her thighs. And his hand was
between her knees, sliding up toward the center of
her being.

Submit. She heard the words in her head again, but
she couldn't make them echo in her heart. She didn't

want to lie back and let him do this, she didn't want him to break his promise. She had trusted him—if he took her by force he would prove himself no better than Morales's men, or Dutchy. He just happened to smell better. And taste better. And feel better.

As she realized the way her mind was going, she panicked. Submission was all well and good, but not if she was going to enjoy it. There was no way Reverend Mother would countenance that.

She hit him, catching him on the side of the head with her fist. He barely seemed to notice. He simply caught her flailing arms with one strong hand, pinning them to the sagging mattress beneath them. And he pushed his other hand up under her skirt, between her legs, where no one had ever touched her before.

It was shocking, it was sinful, it was disgusting, it was...Carlie's eyes fluttered closed for a moment as he touched her, intimately. A faint shimmer of pleasure danced along her nerves, and her eyes opened again in outrage.

"Relax, Carlie," he murmured. "It's better than a sleeping pill."

She tried to jerk her hands free, but he was too strong. She opened her mouth to protest, but he simply put his own mouth over hers, as she let him kiss her, knowing it was wrong, unable to help herself.

She was wet between her legs. His hand was making her wet. It astonished her, as the tremors and trills of reaction amazed her. She considered begging him to stop, but she knew that would be a waste of time. She considered praying for deliverance, but quickly ruled that out. She didn't want to be delivered. Besides, the sinful, wonderful feelings that were lashing through her body were entirely incompatible with the stern God she'd followed for the past nine years.

His mouth left hers, trailing across her cheekbone, but she could no longer fight him. It was too late—her will, her honor had been sapped. He had no right to do this, no right at all, holding her there, forcing her...

"Let it happen," he said in her ear, a deep growl. "Stop fighting it, Carlie. You want it, you need it and I can give it to you. Just let it come."

She had no idea what he was talking about. She was cold, and hot, her brain had ceased to function and her entire body was racked with tremors. She wanted to cry out but she couldn't, she wanted to hit him, she wanted to put her arms around him, but her hands were trapped, her mouth was silenced by his, her body was imprisoned, and there was nothing she could do beneath the sleek, devilish onslaught of his hand between her legs, his fingers pushing deep inside her innermost being, his thumb pushing, pressing, sending shards of shimmering delight through her.

And then it happened. One moment she was trembling in helpless reaction to the terrible things he was doing to her, in the next her entire body convulsed. Releasing her hands, he shoved her face against his shoulder, muffling her hoarse cry, but she was beyond noticing. Blackness closed in around her, a timeless, deathless eternity, shot with a pinprick of stars dancing in front of her eyes, as everything stopped, her heart, her breathing, the world on its axis.

It lasted forever. And then she was suddenly dropped back, into reality, into the small, stuffy room at the edge of the tropical jungle, lying in bed with a professional soldier, her skirt up to her waist, her blouse shoved up to her armpits, her entire body a shaking, quivering mass of exhaustion.

Now he was going to do it, she thought distantly. He was going to rape her, and she couldn't bring herself to argue, or to care. She felt as if she'd run twenty miles, and her entire body was so limp she let her eyes drift closed, content to just let it happen.

He pulled her skirts back down around her legs with gentle hands. He pulled the shirt back down, as well. He stretched out beside her, pulling her up close to him, and she was too weak to do anything but curl up next to him. Now he'd hurt her, she thought sleepily. Now he'd force her.

And within moments, she was sound asleep.

REILLY LISTENED to the sound of her deep breathing with a mixture of amusement and exasperation. He'd accomplished just what he'd set out to accomplish, by force, no less. If a small, selfish part of him had hoped she'd get into the spirit of things long enough to return the favor, he should have known he'd be squat out of luck. He'd been through a streak of purely miserable misfortune for the past year and a half, starting with his realization that he just couldn't hack the army anymore, his falling-out with Billy, followed by Billy's crazy marriage and then his death. All ending up in this stupid trek through the jungle with a newborn infant and a woman who had no connection to either the Morrisseys or Reilly. A woman who didn't know how to kiss, seemed as out of touch with her own body as a puritan, and made him so damned horny he thought his insides would fall out.

How could anyone so small, so unpracticed, turn him into the human equivalent of Jell-O? He'd spent his entire military life following orders and giving them, but the bottom line had always been the most good for the most people. His priorities were very clear here. He needed to get Timothy Morrissey home to his grandparents. Carlie Forrest was just an unnecessary complication.

Her breathing was deep, even, drugged with sleep and satisfaction. The sound made him smile sourly. Lord, he was turning into a regular knight, rescuing damsels in distress as well as babies, and even providing safe sex when they needed a little cooling off.

But what about him? He could do with cooling off, or safe sex, or the hot, slick feel of her around him. And instead she fell asleep in his arms with as much trust as the third member of their odd little party.

The smart thing to do would be to leave her behind. She was good with the kid, but he could handle the little guy, as well. Timothy slept most of the time, drank formula, and Reilly had no problem with diapers.

What he did have a problem with was Carlie. More exactly, he had a problem with himself. She distracted him, and when he was distracted, they were all vulnerable.

He'd come too far, the stakes were too high, to risk everything because suddenly he couldn't stop thinking with his zipper.

She made a sound in her sleep. A wet, shuddering sound, a stray remnant of her crying jag. She'd seen her parents killed, she said. By the black-shirted soldiers of the San Pablo army.

Which was in direct odds with her story about making her first visit to San Pablo to visit an old school chum.

She'd been lying to him again, which came as no surprise. He could shake her awake, demand the truth from her and maybe precipitate a confrontation that would slake the burning thirst he had for her. Any excuse to touch her, to push her, to have her.

But he wasn't going to do it. Any more than he'd leave her behind for Dutchy's tender mercies. He'd find out the truth from her, sooner or later.

In the meantime, he'd indulge himself in the painful delight of sleeping with her soft, slight body pressed up against his. And he'd think of the look in her eyes when she came.

Chapter Eleven

"Fifteen minutes."

The words, gruff and abrupt, ripped through Carlie's sleep-dazed brain. Her face was pressed up against the pillow, and she was alone in the bed. However, the man she'd shared the bed with stood directly over her, and she wasn't particularly ready to face him after last night. Any more than she was ready to face herself.

She lifted her head, keeping her gaze on the pillow. The room was still fairly dark—only the faint light of sunrise pierced the gloom, sending mauvy-pink shadows against the cracked walls. "Fifteen minutes?" she echoed.

"We're meeting the Shumi down the river a ways. They'll be bringing the baby. Dutchy's passed out on the barroom floor, but when he wakes up I imagine he'll be going after Morales. We need to be long gone by then."

She still couldn't meet his gaze. "Why would he go after Morales?"

"Because I knocked the crap out of him. Because he got a good look at you and knew you weren't a camp follower. Because if he's heard about the baby he'll probably want to tell Morales about it. Don't forget about the reward. So the sooner we get out of here the better.''

''I can make it in five.''

''You've got time for a fast shower. God knows when you'll get another chance.''

She couldn't avoid it any longer. She turned her head to look in his general direction, still determined not to meet his gaze. It was a mistake. He was wearing jeans and nothing else, and his hair was slicked back from the shower. He was big and wet and dangerous, and yet far too familiar. His mouth, his hands had touched her. Caressed her. Turned her wanton.

''Stop blushing,'' he said irritably.

Of course, her blush deepened. For a moment, endless, eternal, her eyes met his. They were dark, brooding, filled with some latent emotion she couldn't begin to understand. She'd seen lust in the faces of men, seen it on Dutchy last night, but this didn't look as simple as lust. Besides, if he lusted after her, he wouldn't have stopped last night. He wouldn't have...done that to her, and then simply gone to sleep.

Though she suspected that she'd been the first to fall asleep. She'd lain there, waiting, and the next thing she knew it was morning, and she awoke feeling embarrassed, energized and achingly aware of life and all its possibilities.

''It's getting closer to ten minutes,'' he warned her.

She pushed back the covers. Her clothes were tangled around her, but she was still relatively decent once she yanked the skirt down around her legs. It wasn't as if he wasn't more acquainted with her body than any human being, herself included. But he'd only touched her body, not seen it, and she'd just as soon he didn't.

The room was small and the bed took up most of it. She skirted around it, grabbing clothes from the open backpack and heading for the door. He was standing there, watching her, too close.

She wanted to run. She wanted to scurry away like a small, embarrassed rabbit, and he probably knew it all too well. She paused beside him, squaring her shoulders and meeting his cool gaze. "Don't ever do that again," she said fiercely, despite her blushes.

It was a mistake. His dark eyes lightened with real amusement, and his mouth curved. "Don't do what?"

Her color deepened. "Just don't," she said in a strangled voice, wishing she'd had the sense to escape and keep her big mouth shut.

But she hadn't. He put his hands on her shoulders and pushed her up against the wall, gently, inexorably, his fingers kneading her. "Don't what?" he taunted again, softly. "Don't make you come? I thought I was a perfect little gentleman," he murmured, his mouth brushing against her ear, his breath tickling, disturbing her. "Ready to provide pleasure without asking a thing for myself." His mouth traveled across her cheekbone, down to the corner of her lips. "I thought next time I'd use my mouth."

If she turned her head, just a fraction of an inch, she could have kissed him. And the devastating thing was, she wanted to. She wanted his mouth covering hers again, taking, giving pleasure. She wanted him to push her back on that bed and show her that soul-shattering delight once more.

She started to tilt her head, to give him better access, when he whispered against her lips, "You're down to five minutes now."

She drove her fist into his stomach. Hard. He didn't even flinch. He simply backed away, his expression enigmatic. "Better hurry," he said, turning away from her.

He had a beautiful back. Long, graceful, with smooth, darkly tanned skin. She'd never realized a man's back could be quite so lovely.

"I'll be ready," she said tersely.

REILLY DECIDED it might be wiser not to be in the room when Carlie came back. Just as he resisted the temptation to join her in the shower. The sooner they got away from this little outpost, the better.

There was no sign of Dutchy when he reached the bottom of the stairs, and Reilly cursed beneath his breath. Last time he'd reconnoitered, Dutchy had been passed out beneath a table, snoring loudly, and Reilly had hoped his drunken stupor would last well into midmorning. Time enough for them to be long gone.

Apparently fate wasn't about to be so kind.

He could hear noise in the back shed that passed for a kitchen—the clanging of pots, the loud, muffled curse. He could move out of there without Dutchy knowing—Reilly was good enough at what he did to ensure that. But he couldn't count on Carlie, small though she was, being similarly light on her feet. Besides, he could hear the shower going overhead, and if he could, Dutchy could.

He had no real choice in the matter. He set the packs down wearily. He pulled the gun from his waist, checked the clip and then headed for the kitchen.

CARLIE WAS JUST PULLING on her clothes when she heard the sound of the gun. For a moment she didn't know what it was—she was still concentrating on not envisioning what Reilly had meant when he'd said next time he'd use his mouth.

All sorts of disasters flashed through her head when she finally realized just what that muffled explosion was. The worst was Reilly, lying dead in his own blood, murdered by Morales's soldiers.

She didn't stop to consider the safety of her actions. She was out of the bathroom, still buttoning the loose cotton shirt, and halfway down the stairs when she saw him.

Reilly stood in the darkened bar, whole and unharmed. He looked grim, shaken, but he looked up at the sound of her footsteps, and she thought she could see the dark despair in his eyes.

"I thought someone shot you," she said in a husky voice.

"No such luck," he said after a moment. He sounded weary beyond belief. "You're stuck with me."

Something was wrong. Something was terribly, terribly wrong. Carlie descended the last few steps, fighting the temptation to go to him. Touch him. Hold him.

"Is Timothy all right?"

He nodded. "I trust the Shumi. They should be waiting for us downriver." He moved to shoulder the two packs. "Let's get out of here."

"Where's Dutchy?"

"He won't be bothering us."

"Why not?"

He stopped beside her. He looked bleak and very, very angry. "Don't ask."

She looked at his hands, expecting them to be stained with blood. They looked no different. She looked up at his face, searching for the mark of death, the emptiness of a lost soul in his eyes.

But there was no difference. And little wonder, she reminded herself. He was a soldier, a man of death. This wouldn't be the first time he had killed in cold blood. It wouldn't be the last.

She followed him through the outlying jungle as the dawn lightened the sky, heading toward the muddy, slow-moving river, grieving. It wasn't that Dutchy was a worthy soul, but he was one of God's creatures, and he didn't deserve to be shot down like an animal.

But even more, she grieved for Reilly. For his lost soul, and the choices he made.

The sight of the baby, safe and smiling in a Shumi woman's dark arms, brought a measure of relief to her. She pushed past Reilly, rushing to the baby, and the majestic woman handed him over with a smile and a voluble conversation about his wisdom, his appetite, his sturdy limbs and the magnificent future such a young prince had in store for him. Surely with a strong, brave father like the Anglo and a good woman like her, he would be blessed throughout his life, and would enjoy the blessings of many brothers and sisters springing forth from their fruitful loins.

Carlie kept her back to Reilly, mentally thanking God he wouldn't understand the Shumi dialect. In a quiet voice she thanked the woman for her good care of her son, hoping Reilly wouldn't notice her conversant ability.

She should have realized that Reilly noticed everything. The Shumi woman launched into a frank, well-meaning discussion of exactly what Reilly and Carlie should do if they desired another boy, or how best to achieve a female offspring next time, complete with appreciative remarks about Reilly's no doubt remarkable proportions and skill as a warrior and a lover.

It was sheer force of will that kept Carlie from blushing this time. That, and the knowledge that at least Reilly didn't know what they were saying. And that he wouldn't understand her polite reply, promising that she would do her best to let him come at her from the back, with her hands over her head and nothing but a belt of gigua grass around her waist if she were interested in having twins.

"Your carriage awaits, milady," Reilly drawled.

Carlie turned, having composed her expression into one of polite interest. The politeness faded when she caught sight of the canoe. "We'll die," she said flatly.

"I doubt it. The Shumi have been using these for over a thousand years. They're small, but they're well made."

"Yes, but they know how to steer them," Carlie

protested, holding Timothy so tightly he let out a soft little sound of protest.

"So do I. Get in." He'd dumped the packs in the center of the dugout, and there was another basket of fresh fruit and flat bread that was almost enough to entice Carlie into that barge of death. Almost.

"We're not going anywhere in that thing," she said flatly.

He looked at her, and she could feel the anger simmering in him, ready to snap. He was a man at the edge. She didn't know how she knew, she didn't know what had put him there, but with a sure instinct she knew she had to be very careful.

Perhaps it was killing Dutchy. Even a man as hard as Reilly might have difficulty murdering in cold blood. Maybe it was something else. She just knew when he spoke in a quiet, clipped voice that she'd better listen.

"You'll get in the damned boat," he said between gritted teeth, "or so help me God I'll tie you up and drag you behind us. There won't be much left of you by the time we get to our next stop, given the piranhas and the crocodiles that infest this river, but at least I wouldn't have to listen to your infernal yapping."

He took a menacing step closer, and it was all she could do to stand her ground, the baby clasped protectively against her.

"You'll do what I say." His voice was cold and dangerous. "If you think the baby's in danger on the river, let me tell you that the alternatives are far worse. And the longer you stand about griping and moaning, the greater the danger is. Get in the boat."

Carlie got in the boat. It tipped for a moment, then

righted itself as she sank to the floor, cross-legged, the baby resting between her legs. She bit her lip, keeping her gaze forward, as she felt the solid weight of Reilly land behind her.

The Shumi waved them off, singularly unmoved by the battle they'd just witnessed. "Gigua grass," one of the women called after them in the Shumi language. "Have your man wear some as well, around his—"

"Goodbye," Carlie called nervously, interrupting the cheerful graphic instructions.

Reilly was right, of course. He did know how to handle the wide, slightly tippy canoe, and they slid through the water with surprising speed. Within moments they had turned a bend in the slow-moving river, out of sight of the Shumi.

"They'll be all right, won't they?" Carlie asked after a moment. "Morales and his men won't hurt them?"

"Morales and his men won't find them. The Shumi have twice their brains and half their bulk. They've had to deal with conquistadors and fascists. They know how to survive, how to disappear into the forest."

Carlie looked down at the baby's peaceful little face. "You promise?" she demanded.

Reilly began to curse. Colorful obscenities floated through the air, then were cut off with such abruptness that she turned to stare at him, sending the boat rocking dangerously.

"Life isn't fair, princess," he said flatly. "And promises aren't worth…squat. It's about time you learned that."

"But—"

"But nothing. You can't watch out for everyone. You can't save the world. You can concentrate on saving your own ass, and that's the way things work."

"Then why are you here?"

"Beats the hell out of me," he said.

The river was noisy that early in the morning. The birds were having an early gossip, the howler monkeys screeched to each other across the treetops, the somnolent river made its own steady sound as the boat moved with the current. Timothy slept in her arms, serene and replete, and Carlie leaned back against the stack of supplies, gazing skyward. It looked so peaceful, so far removed from blood and death, and unable to help herself, Carlie shivered.

"Did you have to kill him?"

Utter silence from the back of the boat. Then, "What the hell are you talking about?"

"Dutchy. Did you have to kill him?"

Reilly cursed under his breath, not quite loud enough for Carlie to make out the words. Another surprise—he hadn't minded cursing in front of her before. "I didn't realize you'd developed a fondness for old Dutchy. Maybe I shouldn't have gotten in his way last night."

"He was a horrid, disgusting old man," Carlie said fiercely. "But he didn't deserve to die."

"Trust me, angel, he more than deserved it. Dutchy's done more things, caused more harm than your vivid imagination could even begin to guess at. However, I didn't kill him."

She turned, and the boat rocked perilously. "I heard the gun," she said.

"I shot at him. It scared the living…it scared him, which was what I wanted. After that it was a simple enough matter to tie him and leave him in a back bedroom."

"Did you leave the ropes loose enough so that he could eventually escape?"

"Hell, no," he said irritably. "But Morales and his men will be back sooner or later, and they'll find him. If the snakes don't first."

"Reilly!"

"Don't worry, angel. Snakes are too smart to touch an old bastard like Dutchy. They wouldn't want to get poisoned."

"You wouldn't lie to me, would you, Reilly?"

"Lie to you?" There was something in his voice, a combination of amusement and irritation. "Now why would I do that? I don't like liars. Besides, isn't lying a sin?"

Alarm bells began to go off in Carlie's brain, but she carefully kept her face forward. "I wouldn't know," she said. "I don't spend my time thinking about sin."

"What about last night?" he taunted. "Was that a sin? Exactly what kind of religion do you follow? I presume you're Catholic, since you spent that time with Caterina and with all those nuns. If I remember my childhood catechism properly, there's a whole set of categories for each sin, isn't there?"

"I wouldn't know."

"Were they venial sins or mortal sins, I wonder?" he said, half to himself. "There ought to be some sort of grade of venial sins. I imagine kissing you was only a second-class sin,'' he murmured. "Touching your breasts would have been third class, making you come would have been bordering on major venial sin. But I imagine it would be a mortal sin if and when I actually did you.''

"Reilly…''

"But we weren't talking about sex, were we? We were talking about death. I don't give a damn whether you believe me or not, angel. But the fact of the matter is, if I'd blown Dutchy away, as I was sorely tempted to do, you would have smelled him. Death is ugly, and death stinks to high heaven.''

"Don't.'' It was a quiet moan of protest, one she doubted he'd listen to.

"You're right,'' he said. "I'd rather talk about sex.''

Carlie clenched the sides of the boat. She heard the plop of water as a crocodile slid into the river, eyeing them out of beady little eyes. He started toward them, then seemed to think better of it, using his tail to swerve back, away from the small boat as it moved swiftly downriver.

"Too bad,'' Reilly murmured. "I was in the mood to shoot something.''

"Where are we going?'' Carlie asked somewhat desperately. "Do you have any sort of plan, or are we just wandering through the jungle, one step ahead of Morales and his men?''

"Don't forget the noble rebels. They aren't any too friendly, either. Fortunately they're to the south of us, and we'll be heading north, once we reach our next stop.''

"What's our next stop?"

He seemed to consider it for a moment. "I suppose I'll trust you," he allowed.

"Big of you." She couldn't resist snapping back.

"After all, there's no one you're likely to tell. Caterina Morrissey de Mendino would have been out for her own tail, but I'm not so sure about Carlie Forrest. Besides, I don't intend to let you out of my sight."

"Reassuring."

"Isn't it, though?" he said with false sweetness. "We're heading due east to a small settlement called Cali Nobles. There's a small trading post there, run by a man named Simeon. A much better sort than our friend Dutchy. I can count on Simeon to find us some sort of transportation north."

"North?" She hadn't been in the hills north of San Pablo since the rescue workers had first taken her down out of the mountains. She didn't want to go back.

"That's where my plane is. If we're going to get out of here in one piece we need to get to my Cessna. Look at it this way, angel, at least you won't have to walk. Or do you have a problem with flying?"

"I haven't flown in years."

"Oh, really. Then how did you get to San Pablo to visit your old school friend Caterina?"

Damn him, she thought, savoring the first curse she'd uttered, mentally, in years. "By yacht, of course," she said serenely.

"Ah, yes, Transatlantic yacht. Remind me, Carlie. How long ago was that?"

"Two months," she said determined to bluff it out.

"And one more question," he said, paddling smoothly through the water.

"Yes?"

"Where do we find some gigua grass?"

Chapter Twelve

Carlie almost wished the trip downriver could have lasted forever. It was peaceful and quiet in the bottom of that little boat, with only the occasional whine of insects to disturb her calm.

Reilly seemed to be suffering from a massive case of the sulks, though she couldn't quite figure out why. He wasn't talking to her, which was just as well. She hadn't been able to come up with an answer to the gigua-grass question. Obviously he understood the Shumi language far better than she had imagined. He'd understood every word of the woman's cheerful advice on procreation, as well as her agreeable responses.

Fortunately the baby was growing more alert, and she concentrated her attention on him, talking in a low voice that she hoped wouldn't reach back to the taciturn Reilly. "Did you miss me, little boy?" she murmured. "I missed you. I know you must have liked being taken care of, not being jostled around all the time. It won't be too much longer before we get you home. You'll have a grandma and a grandpa to love you and take care of you, you'll probably have cousins and—''

''No cousins,'' Reilly interrupted from the back of the dugout. ''Billy was their only child.''

''Then they'll love you all the more,'' she assured the baby determinedly. ''They're probably just waiting to dote on you, sweetie. Though I hope your grandma isn't too old....''

''Actually, the Morrisseys can afford the best of everything for their only grandchild. Including the best of household help. He'll be looked after by experts. And I doubt a high-powered Washington hostess like Grace Morrissey would care to be referred to as 'grandma.'''

She turned back to look at him, her concern for the baby overriding her determined avoidance of him. ''They'll love him, won't they?''

''They sent me down here to get him, didn't they?'' he countered irritably. ''They were willing to foot the bill.''

''They're paying your expenses?'' she questioned, oddly surprised.

''No.'' He gave the paddle a harder push, sending the canoe skimming through the water. ''I owed Billy that much, and more. It was the least I could do.''

She turned back to the baby lying across her lap, looking up at her trustingly out of those surprisingly brown eyes. ''They'll love you,'' she said firmly, loud enough for Reilly to hear. ''Or your Uncle Reilly will beat them up.''

Reilly's response was a muffled obscenity. ''I'm not the kid's uncle,'' he protested.

''You told me you and Billy were like brothers.''

"We grew apart. People change. We had a couple of arguments."

"Still, you came after his wife and baby. You must have forgiven him."

"There was nothing to be forgiven," Reilly said. "Just a parting of the ways. And don't try to make me out as some kind of good guy. I happened to owe him for any number of things. This gives me a chance to pay my debt."

"You don't owe me anything. Why are you taking me along if you're not a good guy?"

"You keep this up and I'll toss you to the crocodiles," he drawled.

"Sure you will, Reilly," she said, feeling suddenly, surprisingly cheerful. She looked down at the baby. "Your uncle's a liar, sweetie. Don't pay any attention to a word he says. He'll look out for you."

She could practically hear Reilly's temper simmer. It was a mildly entertaining diversion, to be able to annoy him so thoroughly, and these days she needed mild diversions. All this excitement was a bit too much for her placid heart to handle.

Though she was beginning to wonder whether her heart was that placid after all. She'd taken the danger and adventure with surprising equanimity, and she'd survived her first taste of passion without dying of shock.

Reverend Mother Ignacia had always been frank about the sins of the flesh. She had maintained that God had given them all bodies to enjoy, and there was nothing shameful about pleasure. To be sure, it was better sanctified by God and a priest, but a pragmatic woman had to accept that life didn't always work out so neatly.

She'd listened to Carlie's protestations that she had no interest in sensual matters, but she still refused to let Carlie take her final vows. Carlie was finally beginning to suspect why.

She'd never had any doubt about Mother Ignacia's wisdom and perception in other matters—why had she assumed that when it came to Carlie she'd suddenly lost her ability to see clearly?

Carlie leaned back against the supplies, gazing out over the slow-moving river. The baby dozed peacefully, and behind her she could feel Reilly's strong, steady movements as he propelled them through the water. It was a perfect time for reflection, to consider what she'd never dared consider before.

Perhaps, just perhaps, she'd misunderstood her calling. Perhaps she really had been hiding, from memories, from pain, from life.

She still wanted to hide. She wanted to be back in the safety and stillness of the convent, her body unawakened, her soul single-minded, her heart determined. There were too many choices out here. Too many distractions.

Including the innocent child lying in her lap, trusting in her to keep him safe, to love him. And including the not-so-innocent man behind her. What did he want from her? Anything at all? And what was she willing to give him?

The fear fluttered in her stomach once more, combined with a tightening lower down, a clenching of memory that came against her will, and she wanted to run.

But there was nowhere to run to. Not in this crazy, war-torn country, not while she needed his help to protect the baby. She just had to get through the next few days, till they got out of here. Then, away from his distracting presence, back in the shelter of the convent, she could decide what she really needed in life.

The thought should have soothed her. But somehow the idea of leaving this man, and this child, cut her to the heart, and she closed her eyes against the brightness of the tropical sun, and the sting of her own tears.

IT WAS A STRANGE and novel sensation for Reilly, this urge to wrap his hands around her throat and strangle her. He wasn't a man prone to violent fantasies; he simply did what needed to be done. If that need included violence, he would do it, without undue hesitation or recriminations.

He knew perfectly well why he wanted to strangle her. Dutchy was out of the way, but he'd been quite voluble once Reilly had fired that bullet close enough to crease his filthy suit. And he'd been mad and drunk enough not to consider the benefits of discretion.

"So how does it feel to pork a nun, Reilly?" he'd demanded blearily as Reilly had lashed him to the old iron bed with the filthy sheets.

"What the hell are you talking about?" he'd said, yanking the ropes unnecessarily tighter.

"Your little lady friend. I thought she looked familiar, but it took a while before it came to me. She came from the convent, didn't she? Our Lady of the Perpetual Virgin, or whatever it was, right? Bet she was real tight."

He slammed Dutchy back against the bed, his hand around his wattled neck, ready to press the life out of him. "You're crazy, old man."

Dutchy wheezed in laughter, too drunk to realize his life was hanging by a thread. "You mean she didn't tell you? I wouldn't have thought she could put anything over on you—you're getting soft, Reilly. It's no wonder you're getting out of the game."

"You must have gotten into some bad whiskey," Reilly said between gritted teeth. "That, or the jungle's finally gotten to you."

"I even know her name," Dutchy said. "She was the only young one there, and I make it my business to keep track of all the young white women in the area. Sister Maria Carlos. Her parents were those missionaries that were killed a number of years back. But what I can't figure out is where the baby came from."

He pressed against his throat, just a bit harder. Dutchy's eyes began to bulge, and he gasped for breath.

Reilly timed it perfectly. Just until Dutchy passed out. Then he stepped back, watching him, and he realized he was shaking.

He should kill him, of course. Sooner or later, most likely sooner, Morales would come back and put two and two together. With Dutchy's pickled brain but still-sharp eyes, they'd come to their conclusions even more quickly, and now that Dutchy had managed to find out about the baby, things were getting too damned dangerous. The best way to protect the baby and the woman as well, would be to kill him.

He looked at the old man. He was the scum of the earth, and he certainly had earned death many times over.

The problem was, Dutchy was right. He had grown soft. Ten years ago he wouldn't have hesitated, and Dutchy would have already breathed his last.

But he'd seen enough death, enough killing to last him the rest of his life. He was going to take his chances. If they moved fast, they'd be out of reach before Dutchy started blabbing, safely up in the deserted village of Puente del Norte, ready to fly out of the country.

Of all the places, why had he chosen Puente del Norte to land? Fate wasn't making things any easier for him, or for the woman sitting in the front of the canoe.

Reilly looked at the top of Carlie's head. The short dark hair was lightening in the sun, streaked with gold among the dark brown. He didn't know whether she'd fallen asleep, but at least she'd ceased that soft, loving murmur she directed at the baby.

The sound of her voice, her damned *nun's* voice, should have infuriated him. Indeed, it did, but it also crept under his skin and teased at him, making him horny and crazy and wanting to hit something.

He'd left the Catholic church years ago, but he still knew that a nun was off-limits. And much as he wanted to discount Dutchy, and believe the man's words were all lies, he knew he couldn't. There were too many things pointing straight at that unpalatable truth, including her total unfamiliarity with her body's sexual potential. The way she kissed. The way she looked at him. The way she walked and talked, totally without sexual guile.

At first he'd assumed it was some act of a well-bred tramp like Caterina Morrissey—a sham innocence meant to be alluring, and he'd had to admit that it was.

Knowing it was real innocence should have destroyed any random traces of lust left in him. Unfortunately, life didn't work like that.

He looked at her sun-streaked head, bowed low over the baby, and he thought about the taste of her mouth, the wetness he'd coaxed between her legs, the perfect fit of her breast against his hand. He looked at her, and he still wanted her. And nothing, not decency, not charity, not wisdom, could still the desire surging through his body

He told himself he wouldn't do it. From now on it was strictly hands off. No touching, no loaded comments, no cursing if he could help it. She'd made her choice, and he wasn't able to offer her any reasonable alternatives. They were two people, thrown together for a few days in a dangerous situation. It was no wonder his hormones were running high.

Once they made it out of here, once she was safely settled wherever the rest of her…sisters were, he'd get beyond it. He'd spend a little extra time in D.C., looking up a few old friends. His buddies were always trying to match him up, and this time he'd let them. He needed a woman, not a girl. Someone a little older, a little more experienced, should wipe away Carlie's memory in no time.

He knew when she'd fallen asleep. When her tense shoulders relaxed, her entire posture softened and a faint, watery sigh drifted back to him. She'd been crying, he realized belatedly, with a pang he quickly stifled. Why had she been crying, for God's sake? Over her imagined sins?

The sun was growing brighter overhead, and he steered the dugout closer to the riverbank and the protecting overhang of greenery. She'd already absorbed enough sun on her pale skin—he didn't want her burned. It would slow them down, he added to himself. Lying to himself.

Damn, damn, hell and damnation. And then he found he still maintained a sense of humor. For all that his cursing was uncharacteristically mild, it was all too accurate. Hell and damnation would be awaiting him, for messing with a nun.

Particularly since he still wanted to mess with her, quite badly. He wanted to finish what he had started, and he didn't want to think about white-and-black robes, and vows of chastity. He wanted to think about the look in her eyes, the scream she'd made, pressed up against his shoulder. He wanted to see whether he could make her scream again.

He reined in his imagination with steely control. She'd been trouble enough in her other incarnations. As Caterina Morrissey she was a selfish tramp who was looking for a meal ticket, as Carlie Forrest she wasn't much better. But Sister Maria Carlos was the worst of all. The sooner he was out of this mess, the better. He'd head straight to his mountaintop and stay put, and nothing, but nothing, would make him come down.

After he got thoroughly and satisfyingly laid, of course. He needed to get this particular woman out of his mind, out of his blood, out of his fantasies. And it would take another woman to do it.

Hell, he might not wait until he got to D.C. If Simeon could find someone for him, he'd take care of his little problem right then and there, and too damned bad if the holy sister didn't like it.

There was no way he was going to pretend that he was in anything else but a foul mood that day on the river. He pulled alongside the riverbank for a brief stop, made the bottle for the kid when needed and grudgingly partook of the bread and fruit the Shumi had packed for them. But he wasn't about to indulge in any social amenities, and she seemed perfectly willing to accept his disapproving silence.

Hell, she was probably used to silence, he thought bitterly. What kind of vows did they take? Chastity, he knew that one for sure, and it was a thorn in his side and his conscience. Poverty and obedience. Well, she'd flunked the last one, but if she was supposed to keep silent she was doing a good job of it.

They reached the tiny landing of Cali Nobles by late afternoon. It wasn't much larger than the small outpost where Dutchy lived, but Simeon was standing on the rickety wharf in the dying sunlight, his eyes shaded with one beefy hand, looking toward them.

"I damned well don't believe it," he bellowed heartily. "I thought you told me nothing in God's name would ever bring you back to San Pablo?"

Reilly controlled his instinctive wince. "I decided I missed your blue eyes, Simeon. Not to mention this lovely peaceful climate."

"Yeah, sure," said Simeon, grabbing the end of the boat as it drifted toward the dock and taking a good long look at the woman in the front. "And who's this? You decided to experience the joys of marriage and fatherhood after all?"

"Not me, Sim," he said, jumping from the boat

and tying up the back end. "I'm too smart for that kind of trap." Carlie was struggling to her knees, and he moved to loom over her. "Simeon McCandless, let me introduce you to Carlie Forrest and her young son, Timothy."

She glanced up at him, her blue eyes wary and doubting, but she had enough sense to keep silent. It wasn't that he didn't trust Simeon—hell, he'd stake his life on Simeon's worth, and had more than once— but the fewer people who knew the truth about the baby, the better.

"Pleased to meet you, ma'am. You picked an odd time to be traveling downriver."

"It wasn't exactly a matter of choice," Reilly said in his driest voice as he reached down to help Carlie out of the boat. He hadn't wanted to touch her, but there was no way she could clamber out of that small dugout without tipping everything into the water, including the baby.

She landed on the dock beside him, lightly, the baby clasped capably in one arm. She looked like a natural mother, he thought distantly, gazing down at her. And she was a woman who'd turned her back on motherhood, and sex.

"It's nice to meet you, Mr. McCandless," she said with studious courtesy.

Simeon's laugh traveled from the base of his huge belly. He was a British expatriate who lived life on the edge of civilization, and he was one of the few men Reilly really missed from San Pablo.

"You're too good for the likes of Reilly anyway, lass," he said. "Come along to my place and we'll get you and the baby settled. I have a native woman who cooks for me, and she'll fix you up something nice and hearty while Reilly and I catch up on old times.''

"It sounds lovely," she said faintly.

"Lovely it's not, but it'll do," Simeon said. "And I promise, I won't keep your man from you for too long."

"He's not my—" she started to say hotly, but Reilly interrupted her smoothly.

"She's learned to be patient, Sim. Besides, I need to hear about what sort of visitors you've been having in this area. Any of Morales's renegades been visiting? And what about the noble revolutionaries?"

"Those stupid bastards," Simeon said, spitting for emphasis. "Fortunately for them, they've kept to the west. They're too mad to keep from killing and too damned stupid to keep from killing the wrong people. Morales has been in the west as well, near Dutchy's place. You hear about Dutchy?"

"Hear what?" It was a sign of just how dangerous his companion was to his state of mind. If he hadn't been thinking about her bare feet on the dirt-packed path to Sim's house, he would have realized that probably wasn't the best question to be asking.

"Dead, old man," Sim announced. "Happened sometime last night or this morning. Single gunshot to the back of the head, I gather. Not that he's any great loss, but it does seem strange that his good buddy Morales would suddenly turn on him. Unless it wasn't Morales."

"Is that who they're saying did it?" Reilly asked in a neutral tone of voice. He could feel the tension

vibrating through Carlie's body. There was no doubt
that she thought he'd killed him and then lied to her.

He was only slightly tempted to shove her against
the nearest wall and confront her. If she thought he
was capable of cold-blooded murder, so be it. It might
make her walk a little more warily around him.

It would be unlikely to encourage her to confide
the truth in him, but since she didn't seem in the
slightest hurry to do so in the first place, who was he
to care?

"Come on, angel," he drawled, taking her arm in
one strong hand. "The sooner we get to Sim's place
the sooner I can have a beer." He looked down into
her eyes, expecting to see rage and disgust. What he
saw instead startled him. Grief, pure and simple, and
a numb kind of despair.

"I have Scotch as well, Reilly," Sim said cheerfully, missing the furious undercurrents. "I remember
you were always partial to a good Scotch."

"I'd like some Scotch, too," Carlie said after a
moment in a strained voice.

"Of course," Sim said with perfect courtesy.

"No, you don't." Reilly overrode her. "You're too
easy a drunk as it is. Two beers and you collapse. We
aren't wasting good whiskey on you. Particularly
when we might have to hightail it out of here without
a moment's notice."

"Someone after you?" Sim questioned knowingly.

"Who isn't? If you've got a bed for the night and
transportation north that's all I ask."

"Why do you want to go north? That's where most
of the fighting's been during the last ten years.

There's not much up there but a few burned-out villages.''

I left the plane up there.''

Sim nodded. They'd reached the small frame house he called home. He pounded up the steps, past the empty hammock that stretched across the sagging porch, and paused by the dim interior of the place. ''I'm sure I can arrange something. For the three of you?''

He looked down at Carlie's bowed head. ''Can't leave my lady behind,'' he said deliberately.

''I though you two weren't…''

''We're not married,'' Reilly said. ''But we're together.''

''I'm glad for you, old man,'' he said sincerely, heading into the house. ''Just let me find us some glasses, and we'll have a toast.''

Not if you know what I've landed myself with, Reilly thought ruefully. Sister Maria Carlos looked about ready to take a knife to him herself.

He was damned if he was about to start making excuses to her. He wasn't the one who lied. ''You'll be staying in the room at the top of the stairs,'' he said. ''Why don't you take the kid and make yourself scarce? I need to talk to Sim.''

''You lied.''

''Bull.''

''You killed him. You murdered him in cold blood and then you lied to me.…''

''Liars are the scum of the earth, aren't they?'' he drawled. ''I can't say I'm any too fond of them, either, but now isn't the time to argue about it. Just get your cute little butt upstairs and we'll talk about it when I finish with Sim.''

"Finish with him? Are you going to take his Scotch and his hospitality and then kill him, too?''

"The only person I'm interested in killing right now is you,'' he said flatly, glaring down at her. "Now get upstairs before I take you there and give you something you'd regret even more than you regret last night.''

"Bastard,'' she said, her voice a furious hiss. It was probably the first time she'd ever uttered that word out loud, and her eyes widened in telltale shock at her own temerity.

"Why, Sister Maria Carlos,'' he drawled. "Such language from a Roman Catholic nun.''

For a moment he thought she'd faint. She turned a dead white beneath the soft pink color of sunlight across her cheeks, and he was ready to catch her, and the baby, if she crumpled.

But she was made of sterner stuff than that.

She didn't say a word. She simply turned her back on him, that narrow, straight back that he found so delectable, and marched up the stairs.

And not once did she look back.

Chapter Thirteen

Carlie could hear them downstairs. Talking. Laughing. She hadn't thought a man like Reilly could laugh.

She lay in the center of the wide bed, awake, listening, waiting. The baby was sound asleep in a makeshift cradle, and Carlie was half tempted to wake him up, just for the distraction. There were too many things hurtling about in her mind, not the least of which was whether Reilly was going to come up and join her in that bed.

It was a small house, she knew that. Two bedrooms—Simeon's and the one she was in. There was no other place for him to sleep, and he was hardly likely to worry about her feelings in the matter.

She ought to be able to sleep. She was exhausted from the three days of travel, from the worry, from the heat of the sun. She'd eaten well tonight, thanks to the cheerful native woman who was most likely Simeon's mistress, and she'd managed a decent sponge bath.

Reilly hadn't said a word to her since they'd arrived. Ever since he'd called her by her religious name he'd all but ignored her, leaving it up to Simeon to get her settled and fed. And even now, in the sultry heat of the jungle night, she still had no answers to her questions.

Why had he killed Dutchy and then lied about it? And how did he know the truth about her? And had he known last night, when he'd…he'd…

She slammed down the memory as heat suffused her body. She didn't want to think about last night. About the restless, desperate feelings he'd engendered inside her. And what he'd done to resolve those feelings.

The peace she'd fought so hard for seemed to be slipping away, and no matter how much she struggled, she couldn't bring it back. She'd been away from the others for less than a month, she'd been out of the convent for no more than seventy-two hours. And already she knew there was no going back.

At some point the voices below fell silent. At some point she slept, dozing in and out of a troubled, dream-filled sleep. She dreamed of guns and blood and sex, and when she awoke in the pitch darkness, alone, panic filled her.

She climbed out of bed, pulling a pair of cutoff jeans under the oversize white T-shirt, and looked down at Timothy. He was sleeping soundly, and Carlie blessed the fates that had given her a peaceful, noncolicky baby.

Except that he wasn't her baby. She needed to remember that—she'd be giving him up soon enough. By tomorrow they'd reach the plane, and then they'd be out of San Pablo. Reilly would take Timothy to his rich grandparents, and Carlie would go back to

Mother Ignacia. But she already knew she wouldn't go back to stay.

The night was silent, warm, and yet Carlie's skin was chilled. The dream still haunted her. Dutchy, his eyes dark and empty, blood pouring from his wounds, had held out his hands to her, begging for help.

There was no way she was going to get back to sleep without confronting Reilly. He might decide to take a gun to her, as well—so be it. If he'd killed Dutchy, then some of that guilt rested on her head. She needed to know.

She had no idea where she'd find him. There were no clocks in Simeon's house, few clocks in San Pablo, but Carlie knew well enough that it had to be around three in the morning. She crept down the narrow stairs. An empty whiskey bottle lay on its side on the rough table, two glasses, one empty, one half-filled, beside it. There was no sign of Reilly in the rough-and-tumble room.

Maybe he'd decided to abandon them after all. Or maybe he'd simply gone off with Simeon's well-endowed lady friend. She couldn't second-guess where he'd gone, and she didn't want to go too far in search of him. She could still hear the baby if he happened to wake up, as long as she went no farther than the porch.

The porch was what she needed. She picked up the half-full glass of whiskey, knowing instinctively it had been Reilly's, and took a tentative sip. It was burning, foul tasting, sending tendrils of warmth through her chilled limbs. She took another sip, wandering out onto the front porch in the moonless night.

It took her a moment to realize she wasn't alone. Reilly lay in the hammock, seemingly asleep.

She almost turned and went back inside. The idea of confronting Reilly no longer seemed quite so smart. Not when he turned her insides into a roiling mass of confusion.

But she wasn't a coward. The past three days had taught her that much. And when she moved toward the hammock she saw that his eyes were open, and he was watching her.

"I should have known I couldn't sneak up on you." She was resigned.

"You're lucky you didn't try. I might have cut your throat before I realized who you were."

The words hung heavily on the night air, and Carlie shivered once more. "Why did you lie to me?"

"About what?"

"About Dutchy. You killed him, and then you told me—"

"I didn't kill him." His voice was flat. "When I left him he was unconscious, tied to his bed but very much alive."

"I heard the gunshot."

"I'm not going to try to convince you," he snapped. "You can believe me or not. I have no reason to lie to you. I've killed before in this life, and I'll probably have to do it again. But I didn't kill Dutchy."

The realization hit her then, astonishing as it was. Reilly was offended that she didn't believe him. Even hurt. As ridiculous as it seemed, Reilly was angry that she didn't trust him.

Carlie shook her head, wondering if the small sip

of whiskey she'd taken had rattled her brain. "I do trust you, Reilly," she said softly, carefully.

"I don't give a damn whether you do or not."

"Yes, you do," she said, suddenly sure of herself. "If you say you didn't kill Dutchy then I believe you."

"You didn't before."

"I do now."

"Why?"

For a moment she couldn't answer. He was lying stretched out in the old rope hammock, his feet bare, his shirt open to the night breeze, his eyes dark and derisive. He looked dangerous and very strong, and the longing that washed through her made her soul tremble.

She managed what she hoped was a cocky half smile. "Maybe because I know you wouldn't lie to a nun."

He was not amused. He stared at her for a moment, as if considering the possibilities. "Come here," he said.

She ought to go right back upstairs, she knew it. "The baby might—"

"You can hear the baby if he cries. Come here."

Her body didn't seem interested in listening to her mind. She found herself standing beside the hammock, dangerously close to him. There was a soft night breeze, and it ruffled her T-shirt, danced through her hair. "I suppose you want me to say I'm sorry I lied to you," she said nervously. "And you want to know why I entered the convent and why I didn't tell you the truth. And you probably want me to tell you that—"

"I don't want you to tell me a damned thing," he said. He reached out and took her wrist in his big hand, and pulled her into the hammock.

She was too astonished to do more than put up a token struggle. Before she realized what was happening he'd tucked her up against the warm length of his body, cradled in the comfort of the old hammock. He held her there, lightly, his arms around her, her face nestled up against his shoulder. "Now go to sleep," he said gruffly.

She lay there, frozen, astonished. She waited for his hands to move, to stroke her once more, but they remained decorously still, and his body was calm, relaxed against hers, his breathing even, his heartbeat steady against her racing one.

It was probably close to ten minutes before she accepted the fact that that was all he intended to do. Simply hold her. The realization brought a rush of relief. And a surge of shameful frustration.

She knew he wasn't asleep, despite the evenness of his breathing. He lay peacefully beside her, but his body and mind were tuned to the night, to the creatures of the darkness that were an unbidden threat to their safety. Just as his body was tuned to hers.

"You don't want to know why I joined the convent?" she said finally, in a very quiet little voice.

He didn't answer for a moment, and she wondered whether she misjudged him, and he slept. And then his hand moved, long fingers threading through her shaggy hair. "I imagine it had something to do with seeing your parents killed."

She took a sharp breath. The words were so simple, and so painful. "They were missionaries, you know.

Not Catholic, but when the relief workers brought me down out of the mountains and took me to the Sisters of Benevolence, it seemed as if it were God's will that I follow in my parents' footsteps. To take their place.''

"So that's what you did," he said, his voice a low rumble in his chest. His skin was warm, sleek against her cheek, and she resisted the urge to push against him like a kitten seeking pleasure. "You took their place. How long have you been there, Carlie?"

"Nine years. It's been so peaceful. I never wanted to leave. I wanted to stay with the sisters, take my final vows and never have to deal with the real world. But then the revolution came. And Caterina."

"And me," he added.

"And you." Her hand had slid under the open khaki shirt, crept up to his muscled shoulder. She could smell the tang of whiskey on his breath, mixing with the thick smell of the rain forest.

"So what are you going to do now?" he murmured. His mouth was close to her ear, and she could feel the warmth of his breath as they rocked together in the narrow hammock. She was safe enough, she thought. Despite her limited knowledge of procreation, she knew people couldn't make love in a hammock. Could they?

"I'll go back and join the others," she said, trying to ignore the fluttering in the base of her stomach, the faint, clenching feeling between her breasts. "They've gone to a convent in Brazil. When we arrive in the States I can get in touch with the nearest diocese and they'll help me. That is, if you're still willing to take me back."

"If I wasn't?" The words were even, suggesting nothing other than mild curiosity.

"Then I'd find my way there myself."

"I'll get you there," he said, his voice deep and unreadable. "Once we get the baby to his grandparents I'll make sure you end up where you should be."

That promise should have comforted her. For some reason it didn't. She let out her pent-up breath, trying to will herself to relax against him. It wasn't that she couldn't get comfortable. Reilly's body fit hers all too well.

"Just tell me one more thing, Carlie," he murmured against the side of her face. "You've been in the convent for nine years. You're how old—twenty-three? Twenty-four?"

"Twenty-six," she said.

"Then how come in all that time you haven't taken your final vows? That's what you said, isn't it? You're still an apprentice nun, right? How come you didn't graduate?" he drawled.

"I'm going to. As soon as I join up with the others," she said.

"How come you haven't already?"

She actually considered lying, astonishingly enough. The only lies she'd told so far had been to protect a helpless infant, not herself. If she were to lie now, to him, it would only be for her own selfish sake, and there was no way she could justify it.

"Reverend Mother Ignacia didn't think I was ready," she muttered, hoping he'd leave it at that.

Somehow his arm had gotten underneath her, and his hand curved around her waist, dangerously close to her breast. He wasn't touching her, but she could feel the heat and the weight of his hand on her rib cage, near her racing heart.

"Why weren't you ready?"

"She wasn't certain if I had a calling."

"Are you certain?" he murmured, his mouth against her earlobe.

She was having a little trouble breathing. "Absolutely," she said in a strangled voice, waiting for his mouth to move, to settle against hers. Waiting for the dangerously sweet oblivion he could bring her, so easily.

He didn't move. For a moment time seemed to stand still. And then his hand fell away, to rest on her hip, and his body relaxed against hers. "It's always nice to be sure about what you want in life," he said in a deliberately neutral tone of voice.

She felt his withdrawal, even as his hand claimed her hip. He was letting her go, she realized with surprise and relief. And some other strange emotion she couldn't begin to identify.

It shouldn't have surprised her. He'd slept with her, stripped her clothes halfway off her, kissed her, caressed her, and yet she still remained as virginal as the day she was born. He'd told her he simply wanted to relax her into sleep last night, and that's exactly what he'd done. He hadn't seemed the slightest bit interested in...in making love to her, any more than he did right now.

He probably simply didn't find her attractive. Or if he had, finding out she was a nun put an end to his roving lust, and for that she could thank God. Couldn't she?

"Reilly?"

"Yeah?"

"How'd you find out I was a nun?"

"Dutchy told me. He remembered where he'd seen you before. It didn't seem to bother him that he'd almost raped a nun, and I guess he thought I'd think it was pretty funny. I didn't."

"But you didn't kill him."

"Carlie…" His voice carried a very definite warning.

"I'm not asking," she said hastily.

"I wanted to kill him," he said. "I was tempted. But I decided I'd seen enough killing to last me."

"Why did you want to kill him? Why then?"

"It was a question of shooting the messenger. I didn't like what he had to tell me. I didn't want to hear you were a nun and I'd just done my level best to despoil you."

She couldn't help it—she smiled against his shoulder. "That couldn't have been your best effort," she said, nestling closer to him, her hips up against his. He seemed a mass of tight, hard bulges and muscles, and she tried to imagine the male anatomy with her limited knowledge. "I can't imagine you not succeeding at anything you set your mind to, and I'm only slightly despoiled."

"Carlie." His voice was low, warning. "Watch it."

She felt safe, secure. He didn't want her, he wouldn't hurt her, he'd take her back to the convent and this would all be a wild dream. "Watch what?" she murmured, rubbing her face against the smooth heat of his skin.

He moved so fast the hammock swung wildly as

he pulled her underneath him, pushing between her legs so that she cradled him against her hips. He was hard, pulsing, alive.

"There's a limit, Sister Maria Carlos," he said in a tight voice, a deliberate reminder to both of them. "I'm a man, with a man's body and a man's needs, and if you push me you'll find out just what that involves."

She stared up at him in surprise. "Don't be ridiculous, Reilly. You don't really want me. You could have had me at any time when you thought I was Caterina, and you didn't. You..."

Her voice trailed off as he began to curse. She didn't even understand half the things he was saying, but she knew enough to know they were vile and heartfelt.

"I don't want you?" he muttered, half to himself. He took her hand in his, dragging it down between their bodies, pushing it against the straining zipper of his jeans. He was rigid, pulsing beneath her hand, and he held her there, forcibly. "If I don't want you, what the hell do you think that is?"

She looked up at him. "I've been in a convent since I was seventeen," she said quite frankly. "I don't know."

He froze as the simple truth of her words penetrated. And then he cursed again, but this time the words were directed at himself, as he released her hand from his iron grip.

She didn't move it. He felt strange to her fingers, hard and mesmerizing beneath the thick denim and the heavy zipper, and she traced her fingertips against the length of him, curious.

He yanked her hand away, shoving it against the hammock, and the look in his face as he loomed over her was full of fury and something else she wasn't ready to comprehend. "That's an erection, Sister Maria Carlos. It means I want you, so badly that it's tearing me apart. It also means I'm not quite the bad guy I like to think I am, because I'm not going to take you. I'm going to send you back to the Reverend Mother in the exact same shape I got you. If you want to experiment with sex you'll have to find someone else to cooperate."

"I don't want to experiment with sex," she said in a muffled voice, aware of the deep color flooding her face. Aware that she wanted to reach down and touch him again through the thick material. She kept her hands to herself.

"Just as well. Virgins are a bore, and a hammock's for the more advanced," he drawled, his fury seemingly gone. A mask of cynicism had fallen over his face.

"What makes you think I'm a virgin?" she said hotly.

"It's a fairly simple deduction. If the soldiers who wiped out that village had found you, you wouldn't be alive. Since you've been in a convent since you were seventeen and you've never even heard of an erection, I imagine you're probably the oldest living virgin left in San Pablo. Am I right?"

"You're a bastard."

"We've already agreed on that. Are you a virgin?"

"Yes, damn it."

"I don't know, Sister Maria Carlos. If your language keeps going the way it has been, the Reverend

Mother might not let you back into your safe little hiding place.''

Safe little hiding place. That was exactly what Mother Ignacia had told her. She was hiding from life.

She tried to pull away, but he held her tight, his long fingers wrapped around her wrists. ''I'm going upstairs to bed,'' she said furiously.

''No, you're not. You're staying right here, with me. We'll sleep in peaceful, celibate bliss,'' he snapped.

''Why?''

''Let's just say I believe in suffering the torments of the damned,'' he replied, shoving her face against his shoulder.

She lay there fuming. She lay there plotting revenge, escape, anything she could think of. She lay there tucked against his big, strong body, his smooth skin, and she wanted to cry.

Somewhere in the distance she could hear the sound of gunfire. Far enough away not to be a danger. The sky was growing light—they'd been arguing for hours. She closed her eyes, unutterably weary and sick of the battle. She could feel the warmth of his breath against her hair. The soft brush of his lips against her temple, but she knew it had to be her imagination. Reilly wouldn't want to kiss her. He wanted to be rid of her, just as much as she wanted to get away from him. Didn't she?

She sighed, letting her lips drift against the warm column of his throat, feeling his pulse beneath her mouth. Heavy, strong, hypnotic. She wanted to stay like this forever, safe in his arms, listening to the steady beat of his heart. As long as he held her, she was safe.

HE'D BEEN TOO HARD ON HER, and he knew it, Reilly thought as he felt her relax into a dreamless sleep. She'd been through so much in the past few days— it was no wonder she was confused. It wasn't her fault that her infuriating combination of unawakened sexuality and courage ignited some impossible longing deep inside him.

It was sex, pure and simple, he tried to tell himself. He wanted to get between her legs, and knowing she was forbidden made him want her even more.

He wasn't going to have her, but it wasn't her fault. He could probably talk her into it—she was vulnerable, she was grateful when she wasn't fighting him, and she was attracted to him, whether she knew it or not.

He could have her, and he'd be damned if he did. Literally.

Chapter Fourteen

The sound of the noisy engine dragged Carlie from her sound sleep, and she awoke, startled, alone, swinging back and forth in the old hammock.

It was daylight, and Reilly had left her. It was only to be expected. By tonight they'd be out of the country, perhaps even out of each other's company. Ready to go their separate ways.

She scrambled out of the hammock, wincing as her bare feet landed on the rough pine flooring, and leaned over the railing to look at the vehicle that had just driven up. The old truck had seen better days. Better decades, Carlie thought as Simeon jumped down from the driver's seat. It took three attempts to get the driver's door shut, and the passenger side was held together with chicken wire.

"What do you think?" Simeon surveyed the decrepit old truck with a misplaced satisfaction.

"This will take us to the airfield?" she asked doubtfully. "There doesn't look like room for the three of us."

"There isn't," Reilly said, appearing in the doorway of the ramshackle house. He was shirtless, with a day's growth of beard on his jaw, and he held the baby against him with a natural grace. Timothy was awake, looking up at him out of those somber brown eyes, waving one tiny fist. "You and the kid are riding in back."

"Without a baby carrier and a seat belt? No," she protested, moving to take the baby from him.

Reilly made no move to relinquish him into her waiting arms. "Listen, angel, Morales and his men are between us and the deserted village where I left the plane. You're more likely to get a bullet in your brain if you sit up front with me, and then what the hell good would a seat belt do? You'll be hidden down behind some boxes, and I won't need to worry about anyone but me being a sitting target if we have to make a run for it."

"Are we going to run into them?"

"God knows. I don't. So far we've been fairly lucky, but sooner or later our luck is going to run out."

She reached out again. "I'll take the baby."

"No, you won't. He and I are getting acquainted."

She dropped her hands, tucking them around her body, feeling oddly bereft. They made a cozy picture, the big, strong man and the little baby, both shirtless, both male, both gorgeous. A family picture, and she was excluded, on the outside, looking in.

It was her choice, she reminded herself. Her destiny. She'd have to relinquish both of them soon enough—she may as well get used to it.

"Fine," she said with a bright, false smile. "I'll get the rest of our things from the room."

"I already brought them down while you were

sleeping,'' he said brusquely. ''The baby's fed and changed, and everything's set to go. As soon as you're ready we can take off.''

She squashed down the feeling of guilt that accompanied her odd sense of bereavement. ''All right,'' she said in a deceptively tranquil voice. ''Obviously you can manage perfectly well without me.''

''I don't see that we're going to have much choice in the matter.''

''Children, children,'' Simeon said smoothly. ''There's no need to squabble. Let me get you some of my best coffee, Carlie, while Reilly plays make-believe daddy. Maybe it'll convince him that marriage and children aren't such a dismal prospect.''

''They're not a dismal prospect,'' Reilly said, moving out onto the porch in the early-morning breeze and settling into the hammock with Timothy clasped safely against his chest. ''They're just not for me.''

Simeon's bearded face creased in a smile. ''So you say. We'll see whether it ends up that way.''

She followed Simeon into the marginally cooler interior of the house, determined not to look behind her. To notice that there would have been room for her on that hammock as well, to curl up next to Reilly and the baby.

''So how do you like your coffee, Carlie?'' Simeon asked, handing her a mug. ''Black as night, sweet as sin, strong as love?''

''I hadn't thought of it that way,'' she said faintly, taking a deep, grateful gulp of the brew.

''No, I imagine you haven't,'' Simeon agreed innocently.

Carlie glanced up at him. ''He told you.''

"That you were a nun? Yes. I think he wanted to make sure I behaved myself. Not that Reilly seems to be making much of an effort," he added easily, lowering his impressive bulk to a rickety-looking chair.

"He doesn't like me."

Simeon frowned. "You don't believe that any more than I do, child. He may not approve of your life choices, but the problem is he likes you far too much. I never thought I'd see Reilly succumb."

"Succumb to what?" she said, curiosity getting the better of her wariness.

"To the fair sex. To family values. To love, child."

"Don't be ridiculous!" she snapped.

"I've known Reilly for more than ten years. I've seen him with lovers and enemies, friends and acquaintances, and during all that time I've never seen him look at a woman the way he looks at you. For what it's worth, I think it scares the hell out of him."

Carlie drained her coffee, failing to savor it. "I think," she said carefully, politely, "that you've been out here a little too long."

"Denial is not just a river in Egypt."

"I beg your pardon?" she said, mystified.

"That's right, he said you've been immured in a convent for the last decade. It means, child, that you're lying to me, but more important, you're lying to yourself." He waved an airy hand. "Go ahead, though. I won't argue with you. It's between you and Reilly. When the time comes for you to go back to your sisterhood, will you go? Or will you stay with Reilly and the child?"

"You don't understand," she said miserably. "We'll all go our separate ways, alone. Timothy will

go to live with his grandparents, Reilly will go back
to wherever he comes from, and I'll join the sisters.''

"Colorado," Simeon said.

"I beg your pardon?"

"Reilly lives on a mountaintop in Colorado, in a
house he built himself. He lives alone."

"He probably prefers it that way."

"So he says."

"And I'll be very happy to be back with the sisters," she said firmly.

"And you're sure that's what you really want?"

There was amazing kindness in Simeon's eyes, and
she wanted to tell him the truth. She wanted to put
her head in his lap and weep out her confusion and
doubt. The frightening truth of her feelings for Reilly,
feelings she didn't want to have. The convent was no
longer home for her. But what home did she have?

Reilly had appeared in the door behind her, silent,
but his shadow blocked out the early-morning sunlight. "It's what I really want," she said firmly.

Adding another lie to her list of sins.

THE PROBLEM WAS, Reilly thought as he pulled away
from Simeon's place, that she didn't look like a nun.
Part of the problem was Caterina Morrissey's clothes.
Those skimpy shorts, exposing a surprising length of
leg for such a small creature, the lack of bra beneath
the T-shirts, the short-cropped hair and the defiant
eyes added up to a potent, tempting package of wom-
anhood. If she was dressed in veils, with her eyes
modestly downcast and her language demure, he
could keep himself in line. But every time he glanced

at her, at her pale mouth and wary eyes, her lean, luscious body, he wanted her.

At least he didn't need to glance at her now. She was comfortably settled in the back of the truck. Timothy lay strapped in a makeshift bassinet, and there were several layers of blankets protecting her from the rusted floor of the old vehicle. It wasn't the safest arrangement, but safety was a relative issue in San Pablo these days. He just needed to get them through enemy lines, back up into the mountain village where he'd left the plane, and they'd be home free.

He knew his way around the northern forests. He'd been stationed just over the border, in Costa Rica, for two years back in the eighties, and during that time his platoon had spent the majority of their days and nights roaming through San Pablo. Back then he had been busy trying to make the world free for democracy. That was before he'd learned that one man's democracy was another man's fascism, and that all governments were screwed up.

It was almost over. By tonight, or tomorrow morning at the latest, they'd be back in the U.S. Sister Mary Charles would be back to the bosom of her convent, the baby would be on his way to D.C., and he could put all this behind him. Just four days of tropical madness. Four days of falling for the one person he couldn't have.

She'd been tempted, though. She might not know the signs, but he certainly did. The way her bones softened when he touched her, and her eyes glazed over. She wanted him almost as much as he wanted her.

Of course, he was about to take care of that. Once

she found out where they were actually headed she wasn't going to feel the slightest bit lustful. She was more likely to be downright murderous.

Hell, it wasn't his fault where he'd decided to land the plane. Just simple bad luck. There were few enough places in the sparsely populated mountains of San Pablo, and the only logical place to land a small plane was the burned-out remains of an old village. One that had seen a massacre just nine years before.

She wasn't going to like returning to Puente del Norte. For the past two days, ever since she'd told him the truth, he'd been racking his brains for another way out.

There wasn't one. She was going to have to return to the place where she'd watched her parents being slaughtered. And she wasn't going to like it. And she wasn't going to like him for taking her there.

Problem solved. So why didn't he feel just a little bit more cheerful about the prospect?

CARLIE WAS surprisingly comfortable in the back of the pickup truck. The canvas covering flapped in the wind, cooling her as they rumbled along, the baby slept and she didn't have to look at Reilly.

Which was definitely a mixed blessing. She liked looking at Reilly—liked it too much. It was just her luck that after being shut away from the majority of the opposite sex, she got thrown together with what was undoubtedly a prime specimen. It didn't require a great deal of experience to know a handsome man when she saw one. And Reilly was most definitely a handsome man, in his own, unbending way.

She was going to have to get used to not looking at him. Today was simply good practice.

The road was narrow, rutted, climbing through the jungle, higher and higher through the sultry, green-canopied forest. The smells were different here—different, and yet oddly familiar. Carlie glanced out past the flapping canvas, but all she could see were the endless, dark depths of the forest as they climbed higher.

It started with nothing more than a simple gnawing in the pit of her stomach. She knew it wasn't hunger, or sickness. She'd eaten enough of the simple food Simeon had packed for them, and she should have been content to doze on the pile of blankets, next to the baby.

But something was wrong. Something was terribly wrong. It began to spread through her body, a miasma, a sense of disaster, of a horror so great, a terror so deep she would never climb out of that bottomless hole. She knew where they were going.

She knew it from the grim expression on Reilly's face when they'd stopped earlier, and the way he'd refused to meet her gaze. She knew it from the pounding of her heart, the cold sweat that covered her, the trembling that started slowly and then grew more and more overwhelming.

She lost track of time. Hours, days, years passed as the truck rattled up the steep incline, an incline she knew too well. She knew when it would level off, and it did.

She told herself she might be wrong. Why would fate, and Reilly, have brought her back to this place of death? She tried to lift her hand, to move the canvas away to reassure herself that she'd been mistaken, but her hand lay motionless in her lap, paralyzed.

Timothy began to whimper. Just quiet little sounds as he stirred from his sleep. Carlie wanted to murmur something soothing, but her voice was trapped behind her mouth. She heard the whimper turn into a cry of protest, and she knew he needed her. Needed to be changed, needed a bottle, needed her arms around him.

She couldn't move. She couldn't go to him, comfort him, see to him. She sat, huddled against the side of the truck as it bounced along, listening as the cries turned to angry wails as he lay there, trapped, abandoned, and she couldn't help him, all she could do was curl up in a little ball, shaking, terrified, panting so loudly they might hear her, they might find her, they might do to her what they'd done to her mother and the girls of the village, while their screams echoed in her ears as she hid, she hid, and the blood was everywhere, and it was death, and pain, and she couldn't help him, couldn't go to him, couldn't go to them, couldn't...

"Carlie!"

She heard him calling her, but she wasn't sure whose voice it was. Her father, calling for help, calling her to run away and hide. Or Reilly.

She curled up tighter, her hands over her ears, trying to shut out their cries, the baby, her parents, the people of the village, the laughter and shouts of the soldiers, the gunfire, the gunfire...

REILLY WORKED FAST, efficiently, despite the uncharacteristic panic that filled him. The moment he heard the baby's wails a chill washed over him, and he ditched the truck in a copse just outside the village.

He just had time to see Carlie, curled up in a fetal ball, before he dealt with Timothy, stripping the sodden diaper from him, propping the hastily made bottle of formula in his hungry mouth before he could turn to Carlie and pull her into his arms.

She probably had no idea who he was, but it didn't matter. She needed someone to hold her, to murmur soothing words, to hold her so tightly the monsters in her memory abandoned her. She was icy cold, sweating in the thick heat of the jungle, her breathing was rapid and shallow, and her eyes were unseeing. He cursed himself inwardly, all the while keeping up a soothing litany of comforting nonsense. He should have found some other way out of the country, despite the risk. For now, all he could do was cradle her rigid body in his arms and try to warm her.

"The baby..." she managed to gasp through deep, shuddering breaths, her fingers digging into his arms as she tried to drag herself back.

Reilly glanced over at him. "He's fine. I gave him a bottle, and he's asleep again."

"I couldn't...help him...." The words were coming in hiccups as she shivered helplessly. "I couldn't save him."

"He's fine," Reilly said again. "Just take deep breaths, Carlie. It's over. It's in the past. No matter how bad it was, it's gone."

"They're screaming..." she gasped.

"No. It's over, long ago. No one's hurting anymore. They're at peace now. Except for you."

It jarred her. She jerked her head up to look at him

out of bleak, desperate eyes. "Make it go away, Reilly," she whispered.

He knew what she wanted. Oblivion, life. She wanted the one thing from him he'd been determined not to give her.

"No," he said as gently as he could, ignoring the need that swept through his own body. He couldn't do it to her. She was lost, broken, hurting. She needed comfort. Not a further betrayal.

"Please," she said, begging, her hands gripping his shirt. "Please."

And he knew that he was going to take her. He was going to deflower a nun in the back of a pickup truck, with a sleeping infant beside them. And nothing, either in heaven or hell, could stop him, no matter what the consequences.

Putting his mouth against hers broke the last of the spell. She kissed him back, desperately, as she pulled his shirt away from him.

Stilling her restless hands with one of his, he slowed the kiss, using his tongue, kissing her with a leisurely thoroughness that stole her terrified breath. He could feel the warmth begin to seep back into her flesh, feel the restless stirring in her limbs.

"Please," she said one more time when he lifted his head to look down at her.

"All right," he said, hating himself. "But we'll do it my way. Slowly. So there won't be any mistakes. So you know what you're doing, and you won't change your mind."

She wasn't listening to him. She wasn't interested in noble motives, she wanted oblivion. As he did.

He skimmed the T-shirt over her head, baring her

breasts, half hoping to shock her into a latent sense of self-preservation. She made no effort to cover herself, and he realized it was he who needed preserving.

She simply stared up at him, mute, pleading, and with a muffled curse he gave up his last attempt at decency.

He'd tried. God only knew, he'd tried to resist her. But now it was too late, and things had escalated beyond his control. He needed her, and the sweet death her body and soul could provide him, almost more than she needed him.

CARLIE LAY BACK on the rough wool blankets, lost. His hard, deft hands pulled her shorts off, tossing them away, and she was naked, vulnerable, as he leaned over her, darkness and longing in his eyes.

She was beyond rational thought, of sin or redemption, past or future. All that mattered was now. All that mattered was that he touch her, kiss her, take her. Now.

His hands covered her breasts, gentle, rough-skinned, and she closed her eyes, arching against his touch. His mouth followed, catching the tiny nub and suckling like a baby, his long hair flowing down around her.

She reached up to touch him, to pull him closer, and felt the frustrating barrier of his khaki shirt. She pushed at it, and it was gone, and his skin was smooth and warm against hers.

She felt no fear, for the first time in years. Just an overwhelming sense of rightness, of need. His hands, his mouth were everywhere, seducing her when she had no need to be seduced, filling her with a sense of power and delight.

He kissed her breasts, her stomach, her hips. He put his mouth between her legs, as he'd promised and warned her, and she cried out, feeling her body convulse immediately, darkness prickling against her eyes.

And then he moved up, lying between her legs, cradled against her hips, and she could feel the rough denim of his jeans.

"We'll stop now," he whispered in a tight voice. "You can— "

"No!" She caught his narrow hips with desperate, angry hands, clawing at the denim. She bucked against him, stray tremors still flashing through her body, as she tried to edge closer, to crawl inside his skin, to take him, to make him take her.

"Carlie." His voice was almost desperate now, but she was beyond rational thought. "I can't do this to you."

"You can't stop," she said, reaching between them for the zipper of his jeans.

It was tight over his erection, and her hands were awkward, hasty. He stopped her desperate fumbling, unfastened his jeans and shoved them out of the way.

He was hot and hard and heavy against her, but she wasn't going to let him stop. "Now," she whispered. "Please."

He cupped her face with his hands, looking down at her, as he slowly began to fill her. His face was taut with tension and he was big, huge, pushing into her. She knew a moment's panic, that it wasn't going to work, that he was going to pull away and leave her like this.

"Relax," he whispered against her mouth. He started to withdraw, and she clutched at him, desperate.

"Don't leave," she cried in a broken voice.

"I can't," he said, his voice full of despair and triumph. "Take a deep breath."

She did so, automatically, but before she could release it he'd pushed against her, breaking through the frail barrier of her innocence, filling her.

She screamed, more in shock than actual pain, but his hand was already against her mouth, muffling the sound.

She closed her eyes. She could feel the dampness of tears seeping down her cheeks. "That's enough," she said in a strangled voice. "I'm satisfied."

"No," he said shortly. "You're not." And he began to move, pushing into her, his hands cupping her hips and pulling her up to meet his strong, steady thrusts.

She struggled, for one brief moment. And then she clung to him tightly, and it took her only a heartbeat to catch his rhythm.

It all began to fall away—the jungle, the stillness around them. Her body was sick with sweat, and his was, too. He put his mouth against hers, kissing her hard, and she kissed him back, her legs coming up to wrap around his hips, her breath sobbing in her lungs, as she reached for the darkness once more, the endless oblivion she craved.

It hit her, fast and furious, but it was no oblivion. He was with her all the way, his body rigid in her arms as he pushed in deep and filled her with the pulsing heat of life and death.

She wept then, clinging to him, pulling him tightly against her as the spasms racked her body. She could hear his breath rasping in her ear, the shudders rippling through his big, slick body. He collapsed on top of her, his heart banging against hers, and she trembled, holding tightly, as errant waves of reaction scattered through her.

It seemed as if everything she knew, everything she believed had been shattered by his hands, his mouth, his body. She felt adrift, helpless, floating on a dangerous sea with no land in sight, nothing to cling to but the strong, tough body covering hers.

But he would disappear, as well. At any moment she'd be alone again, as she had been for so very long.

His breathing slowed, and she wondered whether he'd fall asleep. The women who came to the mission, bringing their children for Carlie to teach, would joke about their husbands when they thought Sister Mary Charles wouldn't hear.

What would they think if they saw her now?

She waited for the shame and misery to wash over her. They didn't come. Despite everything, there was a tiny burst of joy bubbling inside of her. And she knew that no matter what happened, she could never regret what she'd done. What she'd shared. Who she loved.

Reilly, it seemed, was a different matter. He began to curse, low in his throat, a tapestry of foul language that would have made her blush a few short days ago.

He pulled away from her abruptly, and she let him go, knowing that she couldn't hold him.

He yanked his jeans up, still swearing, then bounded off the back of the truck without looking at her.

So much for romance, she thought. She was wet between her legs, and blood stained her thighs. She'd have to wash, but for now it took all her energy to pull the big T-shirt over her head and wrap it around her body.

Timothy slept. The bottle had fallen to one side, drained, and she squashed the vision of guilt that danced through her mind. He would survive. They all would.

She leaned her head against the truck, weariness fighting with her odd exhilaration. She couldn't hear any trace of Reilly, and for a moment she wondered if he'd abandoned them.

She quickly discarded that notion. He wouldn't have brought them so far, only to leave them.

He'd return, sooner or later. In the meantime, all she could do was wait.

And remember the feel of his body against hers, and the sure, undeniable knowledge that she loved him.

Chapter Fifteen

This day, thought Reilly, had definitely gone from bad to worse. He'd just deflowered a nun in the back of a pickup truck, then abandoned her, cursing a blue streak. By the time he'd walked to the edge of the burned-out village street and realized she might need...something, it was too late. He'd come face-to-face once more with none other than former general Endor Córdoba Morales. Better known as the Butcher of La Mensa.

Morales was alone this time, which was a small blessing. He was also armed to the teeth and pointing a particularly nasty Luger directly at Reilly's gut. "I thought you might turn up sooner or later," he said pleasantly. "Though I must admit I thought you'd be a little better prepared. Didn't you realize we'd catch up with you?"

It didn't help, Reilly thought grimly, that he was shirtless and unarmed. And that he was scared to death that Carlie might take it into her head to follow him.

"We passed your men about ten miles down the

mountain," he said with deceptive calm. "How come you're alone?"

"I wouldn't worry about it, Reilly," Morales said pleasantly. "I can handle an ex-soldier like you and the little nun without any help."

Hearing his name didn't help Reilly's pessimism; neither did the fact that Morales knew who Carlie was. "I assume Dutchy was the one who filled you in on those little details."

"Dutchy was a very useful man when his head wasn't clouded with liquor."

"Then why did you kill him?"

Morales shrugged. "My wretched temper," he said with a disarming smile. "When I heard he'd let you get away, I'm afraid I reacted…hastily. Where's your little friend, the good sister?"

He didn't bother denying Carlie's identity. "I left her downriver. She was heading for La Mensa—she wanted to rejoin her convent."

Morales's smile broadened, exposing blackened teeth. He was an ugly man, with a pitted face, a short, stocky body and dark, tiny eyes radiating malice. "No," he said. "You just came from her—I know the look. You have scratch marks on your chest. The good sister must be a real tigress. Where is she?"

"I told you—"

"Don't anger me," Morales said. "It's been a while since I've had a nun," he added in a musing voice. "I like being the first, but then, she's prettier than most of the nuns I've raped. Tell me, Reilly, was she willing?"

"She's on her way to La Mensa," he said again.

"And did she take *el presidente*'s grandson with her?"

He didn't even flinch. "I don't know what the hell you're talking about."

"I must say, you impress me," Morales murmured. "Cool as a cucumber, don't they say? I will admit, part of the reason I killed Dutchy was that I was angry with myself. I didn't realize you were attempting to ferry the last Mendino out of San Pablo when you arrived at Dos Libros. If I had, I could have saved myself some time and trouble. And my men would have enjoyed Sister Maria Carlos." He shrugged, and the gun never wavered. "They will get their chance, though. They're off looking for you. I don't know how you missed passing them when you made your way up here."

"I know how to keep a low profile."

Morales frowned. "My men are the best."

"They're not good enough."

Morales considered the notion, the light of cruel madness dancing in his eyes. "Apparently not. Get on your knees, Reilly."

"Why?"

"Because you're too damned tall, like most yanquis. If you want to die fast and painlessly you'll get on your knees so that I can reach the back of your neck."

Reilly just looked down at the little pip-squeak. "I'm not going to die on my knees," he said calmly.

"I can shoot you in the eye, then. It'll take longer, but you'll be just as dead." Morales cocked the pistol. "Where are the nun and the baby?"

"There's no baby, and I left the nun outside of Dos

Libros,'' he said stubbornly. There was a shadow moving behind the burned-out shell of the nearby building, and he hoped to God it was something bigger than a rat. A jaguar, perhaps, looking for a tasty military treat. Though if he got a sniff of Morales's pungent odor he might have the good sense to run in the opposite direction.

There was nothing Reilly could do. Morales was too far away; if he dived for him he'd have a bullet in his brain before his feet left the ground. It just went to prove what he'd always known—once he started thinking below the belt he was doomed.

Lust confused a man, at least temporarily. Love killed him. Facing his own imminent death, he considered the possibility of love, something he'd managed to avoid in all his sexual relationships. It seemed to have crept up on him when he wasn't looking.

"I'll have to kill the nun as well, of course," Morales continued. "Though chances are my men will see to that—they're not very civilized, and few whores have survived their combined attentions. But there's the question of the baby. I can't afford to let a member of the Mendino family survive. He could disrupt my own plans. Should I feed him to the crocodiles? Or perhaps just leave him here, alone, for the jungle cats to find?"

"There is no baby," Reilly said stubbornly.

Morales fired the gun.

It hit him in the shoulder, spinning him around and knocking him to the ground. Morales moved to stand over him, an ugly smile on his ugly face. "I'll go for the knees next," he said. "I can keep it up for quite a while, until you tell me what I want to know. I'm certain you know I'm enjoying this. It's up to you. You can deprive me of my fun and make it easier on yourself. Or we'll do it my way.''

''There is no baby.''

Morales cocked the pistol again and aimed it at Reilly's zipper. ''Then again, there are other places we can start.''

Reilly didn't flinch. ''There is no baby,'' he said again.

And in the distance, floating toward them from the hidden pickup truck, came the unmistakable sound of a baby crying.

Morales jerked his head around, momentarily startled, though the gun never wavered. Reilly coiled his muscles, ready to kick at him, when the figure emerged from the shadows. Carlie.

Morales whirled around, but he wasn't fast enough. She had a huge section of burnt timber in her hand, and she sent it crashing down against his head with all her might.

He went down like a felled tree, and the gun scattered in the dust of the deserted village. He lay there, dazed, panting, as Carlie stood over him.

He started to rise, reaching for one of the guns tucked into his waistband. Carlie crossed herself, muttering something and whacked him again. This time Morales stayed down.

She looked across his fallen body to Reilly. To the blood streaming down his arm, soaking into his shirt, and he half expected her to faint.

She didn't. ''Have you got a first-aid kit?'' she demanded. ''I can take care of that for you.''

He shook his head, wondering if he'd imagined the

past few minutes. "It's just a flesh wound," he said, struggling to his feet, the blood running hotly down his arm.

"I know that," she said calmly. "I've had medical training—I've dealt with far worse."

He believed her. He believed her capable of anything.

"In the plane," he said. "It's just beyond the end of the street."

Her eyes closed for just a moment of pain. "Near the graveyard," she said.

"Yes."

She nodded, and he could see the visible effort it cost her. She looked down at Morales's comatose figure. "Is he alone?"

"For now. His men will be here soon enough."

"Then we'd better get out of here, hadn't we?"

"I'll get the baby."

"You're wounded...."

"As you said, it's just a flesh wound," Reilly said. "You've seen worse, I've had worse. I'll get the kid. Keep an eye on Morales. If he moves, mash him again. Though I expect I don't need to tell you that."

"No," she said. "You don't."

SHE WATCHED HIM GO, steeling herself not to panic at the sight of his blood. She knew it was only a slight wound, but the sight of it still tore at her. This wasn't a stranger's blood, a stranger's gunshot wound. It was Reilly. The man she loved.

He disappeared into the greenery, and a moment later Timothy's howling stopped. He was a good man,

Carlie thought. A good father. He was just what the baby needed.

She looked down at the evil creature lying in the dust. She hadn't killed him, though she almost wished she had. It hadn't been him that day, nine years ago, but he was part of the whole evil society that lived on blood and killing.

She lifted her head and looked down the street. It looked so different, and yet the same. The houses were burned to the ground, and the jungle was encroaching. No one lived here, no one had come to take over the abandoned lands. The place was haunted.

She knew where the cemetery was. Where the plane would be waiting. Down at the end of that narrow road.

She was still barefoot, as she had been most of the two years that she'd lived there. The dust caked her feet, and she remembered the blood that had pooled there. She looked ahead, down toward the plane, and saw that she wasn't alone.

They were there, all of them. The ghosts of Puente del Norte, watching her.

For one brief moment she wanted to run away and hide. Back to that secluded spot where she'd huddled behind a tree and tried to blot out the screams. The place where they'd found her, days later, numb with shock and horror.

But she held her ground. There was nothing to be frightened of. There was her best friend, Maria, smiling at her, red ribbons in her thick black hair, a fiesta dress swirling around her bare ankles. And Maria's parents, Amana, who'd been a second mother to her, and Carlos, the patriarch of the village, the stern, strong man who'd been the first to die.

They looked happy to see her. Smiling at her, waving to her as she started down the empty road.

Her parents were there, as well. Slightly distracted, as they always had been, more concerned with the well-being of mankind than the well-being of one small child, they nevertheless looked at her with love and pride.

It's not your fault, they said with their eyes. *We're glad you survived. That you lived. You live for all of us. Forever.*

She walked. Past friends and family, the old medicine man, the babies, the children and the ancients. Past their smiles and nods and love. And when she reached the end of the village path, and there were no more ghosts, she turned to look at them.

They were fading now. Almost into nothingness, and she realized she was letting them go. At last.

"Goodbye," she whispered. Barely the breath of a sound.

Goodbye, they called to her. And they were gone.

REILLY'S SHOULDER HURT like bloody hell. He'd flown one-armed before, in shock, and he'd managed to land the plane safely. He had no doubt whatsoever he could do it again, particularly since Carlie had managed to bandage the flesh wound with surprising dexterity.

He couldn't take any pain pills, though, and for that he was grateful. The constant throbbing in his shoulder kept him alert through the long hours of night flight. And it helped keep his mind off Carlie, asleep beside him.

But nothing could keep him distracted forever. Not when she was so close, her newly tanned legs stretched out beside his in the small cockpit. She'd be covering up those legs soon enough, draping them in long robes. It was wrong, he thought. Wrong that those beautiful legs would be covered. Wrong that her maternal love would be stifled. Wrong that she'd never lie in a man's arms again.

And most wrong that she'd never lie in his arms again.

He was flying into Hobby Airport in Texas, the closest, safest place for them to land. Wait Morrissey would be seeing to the paperwork, getting them cleared through customs, arranging for a proper birth certificate for his grandson. Would he mind not having a daughter-in-law? Probably not—it made the balance of power simpler. And Wait Morrissey was definitely into power.

He glanced over at Carlie. She was dozing, the lights from the instrument panel reflecting on her pale face. She looked tired and infinitely sad. He probably looked like hell himself.

But the baby sleeping in her arms appeared peaceful and healthy. He looked as if he'd gained weight over the past few days, while they'd fought for their lives. Kids were resilient, he'd always been told. Well, Timothy Morrissey was proof of it.

He was going to miss him. It was an odd notion— he loved his nieces and nephews, but he'd never felt the particular lack in his own life. He did now. The past four days, with the three of them forced together into their own nuclear family, had had a disturbing effect on him. All his carefully formed ideas about who and what he was, and what he needed in this life, had been shot to hell.

He'd do the right thing, of course. He'd give Timothy to his wealthy, powerful grandparents, he'd send Carlie back to the safety of her convent and he'd go home to Colorado, back to his mountaintop, alone. At peace.

Like hell. Peace wasn't going to have anything to do with it. It was going to be utter hell for the next few weeks. Maybe even a month or two. But sooner or later he'd forget her. Forget the kid. Get on with his life.

It was a good thing he'd already gotten out of this game. He could have killed them all, thinking with his hormones instead of his brain. He hadn't expected Morales to have separated from his men, but survival depended on expecting the unexpected. If it hadn't been for Carlie he'd be lying in a pool of his own blood, his extremities shot away. And God knows what would have happened to Carlie and the baby.

He shuddered, unable to help himself. He was too damned vulnerable, and he hated it. He needed to get rid of them, as soon as he could. And maybe then he'd return to normal.

Wait Morrissey had already done his part. It was three in the morning when Reilly approached Hobby Airport, and all it required to get landing clearance was Morrissey's name. Everything was taken care of, Major Reilly. Even hotel rooms.

Carlie barely roused when they landed. She took her return to her native soil with an odd diffidence, following silently behind him, the baby clasped in her arms.

Morrissey had booked them into a two-bedroom suite with all the amenities. It was past five and already growing light when Carlie settled the baby down in the portable crib. And then she looked over at Reilly, standing in the bedroom door.

"You need to get that shoulder looked at," she said.

"Why? You did a good enough job. I'll have someone take a glance at it when I get back to Colorado."

"Is that where you live?"

"Yes."

The silence was taut, nervous. "Do you want anything to eat?" he asked suddenly. "I was going to call room service."

She shook her head. "I think I'll just take a shower and sleep. When are we taking Timothy to his grandparents?"

"Wait Morrissey is coming here to get him. I have no doubt that someone informed him the moment our plane landed. We'll see him late this afternoon, I believe."

Her face looked stricken. "What about his grandmother? I wanted to see where he'd be living, I wanted…"

"He'll be fine, Carlie."

She took a deep, steadying breath. "Of course he will."

He didn't move. "Are you all right?" he asked abruptly.

She jerked her head up, and there was a faint wash of color on her pale face. "Why wouldn't I be?"

It was a challenge, but cowardice was one crime he had yet to commit. "You lost your virginity a few hours ago," he said calmly. "I wondered if you were feeling all right."

"Just peachy."

There was nothing he could say. She'd pulled a wall around herself, a brittle defense he could probably smash if he cared to. He didn't. She needed all the protection she could get. Particularly since he was about to withdraw his own.

"All right," he said, backing out of the room. "I'll see you later."

"Yes," she said. But it sounded like goodbye.

IT HAD BEEN SO LONG, Carlie thought. She wasn't used to this place. To the cleanliness, the elegance, the sheer size of everything. The bathroom was larger than some houses in San Pablo, and it came equipped with enough towels for a family of four, and a basket full of little bottles of sweet-smelling soaps and unguents.

The shower had endless hot water. A good thing, because she stood in there letting the years, the pain, the sorrow wash away from her, she stood until she almost fell asleep, with the water sluicing over her, washing San Pablo, washing the blood, washing the sex away.

She had sinned. In so many, many ways. She had hit a man, twice, instead of turning the other cheek. For all she knew he might be dead, and even worse than committing that crime, she didn't regret it.

She was awash with covetousness. She didn't want this luxury surrounding her, but she wanted warm showers and shampoo. She wanted a comfortable bed and enough food.

She had lied, to Reilly, and to herself. She had lied about who she was, she had lied about what she wanted.

She had sinned. She had lain with a man, she had kissed him and she had made love with him, and she wasn't sorry. She wasn't shamed, or repentant. She was defiantly, gloriously glad she had done it, and she was half-crazy with the burning desire to do it again. And again. And again.

It would be a mistake, she reminded herself when she finally turned off the still-warm shower. He didn't care about her, and he was about to abandon her. Most likely he would make love to her if she demanded, but it would mean nothing to him. And it would only tie her heart more closely to him.

She was going to have to release them, both the baby and the man. The two creatures she loved far too much, and she had no claim to. It was time she started letting go.

The hotel room came equipped with thick terry-cloth robes. She pulled one around her, then went and lay down on the bed in the twilight gloom, listening to the deep, even breathing of the sleeping child.

There was no noise from the adjoining room. Reilly must be sound asleep. Superhuman he might seem, but the past few days of running, little sleep, topped off with being shot, had to have taken their toll on him. He was probably dead to the world.

Whereas she had slept too much—on the plane, in the back of the truck. She'd slept enough to last her for quite a while—she wasn't going to sleep away the last few hours she had with Reilly and the baby.

It took her a moment to realize the odd feelings shimmering beneath her breastbone. She was happy. For the first time in nine years she was free, of the guilt, the horror, the memory. She was free of the past, with its pain and despair. She was free of the present, with its rules and repressions.

She was free of the future. It would be lonely, empty, without Reilly and the baby. But she'd survive. She'd survived so much already.

But for this brief moment she was blissfully, gloriously free.

And even if it hurt her more, made it even harder to get on with life, she wasn't going to waste this moment.

She'd made love with Reilly in despair and pain and panic, rough and quick in the back of a truck with death all around them. She was going to make love to Reilly in a huge bed, with clean white sheets and all the time in the world. The sin was committed, and she didn't regret it. Now she needed something to help her through the long empty years.

There would be no other man for her, she knew it with absolute certainty. There would be no other babies for her.

What she would have would be a perfect memory. And it would have to be enough.

Chapter Sixteen

He lay stretched out on the huge bed, his strong, tanned arms outflung, the white sheet covering his hips. She had no doubt he was naked underneath it. She moved to the bed, silent, unsure of herself, knowing this was foolish and wrong and terribly, terribly right.

He was lying on his stomach, his face turned away from her, covered with a long fall of dark hair. But as she stood there his hand lifted and caught hers, and he turned to gaze at her, his eyes dark and gleaming in the murky light.

He looked absolutely beautiful lying there, tanned skin against the white sheets, staring up at her. He'd shaved the rough stubble of beard, and it made him look oddly civilized, elegant, despite the long hair and the scarred, wounded body. ''Are you sure, Carlie?'' he said, his voice a low promise of desire. ''There are no excuses this time.''

''No excuses,'' she said, turning her hand to catch his, palm to palm.

He rolled onto his back, reaching up to unfasten the loose belted tie of the robe, so that it fell open.

And then he tugged her, gently, down onto the bed, pushing the terry cloth off her shoulders, holding her against him, carefully, tenderly, as he kissed her mouth.

It was a wonder of a kiss, sweet and searing, a promise of long dark nights and lazy afternoons. A false promise, she knew that, but she didn't care. All that mattered was now.

He rolled her over onto her back, leaning above her. "We'll take it slow this time," he murmured against her mouth. "We need to find out what you like. What you don't like. What frightens you." He bit her earlobe, gently.

"I don't know much about men's bodies," she said, feeling awkward and shy.

He smiled a gentle smile, free from mockery. "You can learn," he said. "What do you want?"

"I want you," she said, breathless, honest.

"You have me," he replied, the solemn words a kind of vow. "You can do anything you want. Nothing is forbidden." He leaned back, watching her, waiting.

She came up on her knees beside him, wondering where to start. She put her hands on his chest, on the smooth, warm skin, tracing the line of his ribs, the old scars, the definition of his musculature. She leaned over and kissed his throat, her tongue flicking out to taste the clean, soapy taste of him. He made a quiet growl that sounded like approval, and she moved her mouth downward, across his chest, kissing, tasting, biting.

His hands were on her shoulders, gentle, encouraging but not forcing, his long fingers kneading her pliant flesh, as she reached his flat belly, and the barrier of the white sheet.

She hesitated for only a moment. And then she pulled the sheet away, tossing it toward the end of the bed.

He wanted her, though she'd had no real doubt of that. He wanted her very badly indeed. And yet he made no move to take her, to force her, to hurry and control her, simply giving her free access to his big, strong body that had protected her so well, loved her so well.

She touched him, letting her fingers curl gently around the silken length of him. Once more it astonished her that she could accommodate him, but he'd already proved that she could. She would again.

He seemed to swell and grow beneath her touch, even though she wouldn't have thought it possible. She skimmed her fingers down the shaft, and he made a strangled sound in the back of his throat, almost like the purr of a man-eating tiger.

She slid her fingers down, to cup him, and his muffled word was more a prayer than a curse.

She stroked him, gently, amazed at the pleasure it gave her, as well. She was growing hotter, shakier, as she touched him, learned him.

The purr turned to a growl as he reached up and caught her hand, pressing it down over him, increasing the pressure, showing her the rhythm and force he wanted, until he arched his head back with a groan.

Nothing is forbidden, he'd told her. And with pure instinct she leaned down and put her mouth where her hand had been.

He gasped her name and caught her head between

his hands. She could feel the tension thrumming through his body as he tried to control his reaction, the strength in his hands as he tried to gentle his touch.

It astonished her—his powerful response to her experimental caresses. But what amazed her even more were her own emotions. She was trembling with arousal, needing him, lost in a dark maze of delight and desire until she no longer knew what she was doing.

She was barely aware of him moving. He lifted her off him gently, turning her to lie on the bed. She was shivering with longing, and she tried to pull him over, onto her, but he resisted easily.

"Your turn now," he said in a rough voice, but his hands and mouth were gentle as they danced across her skin.

She heard her quiet whimper from a distance, and she reached for him blindly, frightened, needing him. It was so strange and distant, this fear and trust, entwined around her like a vine, capturing her, so that all she could do was lie back and revel in the terrifying wonder of his hands on her body as he brought her to the screaming edge of completion.

He came to her then, stretching over her, resting between her legs. She braced herself, but she was slick and damp, and his thrust filled her, deep and full and glorious.

She arched against him, lifting her hips to draw him deeper still. "Hold on," he whispered in her ear. And then he flipped over, taking her with him, so that she was on top of him, his body still tight within hers.

For a moment she panicked. But he simply arched

his hips, thrusting up into her, showing her the rhythm, his big hands holding her hips, moving her in delicious counterpoint.

"That's right," he murmured, his voice a tight whisper of sound. "Take me, angel. Any way you want me."

She learned it, so quickly. She arched, flinging her head back, as she sank down on him, and she felt powerful, splendid, magical. She moved with perfect, erotic grace, reveling in the tension of his body beneath hers, the sweat-slick skin, the fierce, glazed look in his eyes.

She felt it start, a shimmering tension that threatened to shake her apart, and suddenly she lost the smooth rhythm she'd mastered and began to weep. Not knowing why, awash in emotions and feelings and fear she couldn't begin to understand. "I can't," she cried, but he simply took over, turning her once more so that she lay back against the mattress, fingers clutching the sheets.

"You can," he said, low in her ear. And he reached between their bodies and touched her.

It hit her with the force of a hurricane. Blackness clamped down over her as her body convulsed. She heard him, felt him come with her, and she clung to him as tightly as she could, riding the storm.

It seemed an eternity before she opened her eyes. She knew he was watching her. He lay beside her, holding her close, but there was no hiding from his searching gaze. She opened her eyes and met it.

He looked somber, troubled. His long hair fell loose about his face, and his eyes were haunted.

"Don't look so guilty," she said with an attempt at lightness. "I'm the one who came to you."

"Carlie," he said, but she reached up and covered his mouth with her hand, her fingers stroking the firm contour of his lips.

"It's all right, Reilly," she said. "The sin is mine, if that's what you're worried about. Though I expect you don't even believe in sin. But it's my sin, not yours. I just wanted to…wanted to…" Words failed her, and she dropped her head.

"Wanted to what?"

"To see what it could be like," she said in an apologetic voice. "When it's done out of love."

"Carlie…" he began, his voice dangerous.

"Don't worry about it, Reilly. I know you don't love me. That's perfectly understandable. I'm someone you were saddled with while you were trying to repay an old debt. But you see, like it or not, I love you. And I really believe that anything done in love isn't a sin."

Timothy set off a distant wail, and she slid out of bed instantly. Reilly grabbed for her, but she was already out of reach. "We haven't finished talking," he said, his voice rich with anger and frustration.

"Yes, we have." She paused by the door. "There's nothing more to say. I love you and the baby, and you don't love me. Don't make it harder for me, Reilly. I know how you feel. Just let me deal with losing both of you in my own way."

And she ran from the room before he could stop her.

REILLY LAY BACK and began to curse. He knew curses in a dozen languages, though he usually preferred Anglo-Saxon words. His second favorite were Arabic curses, and he let go with a few choice ones, aimed directly at himself.

It was her damned fault as well, he thought furiously. She hadn't given him a chance to say a word, to even think about things. The past few days had been so crazy, it was no wonder he was absolutely out of his mind. The worst thing he could do was make some stupid, impulsive gesture that he'd wind up regretting for the rest of his life.

It wasn't as if she didn't have a place to go to. He could count on Wait Morrissey to see her safely back to wherever she wanted to be, and if Morrissey dropped the ball, then he'd damned well hand-deliver her to her precious Mother Superior.

Of course, she'd be in slightly shopworn condition. And the thought of facing some stern old nun scared him more than seeing Endor Morales on the empty streets of Puente del Norte.

But she'd made her decision, clearly. This was best for all of them. They'd all go their separate ways, and it would give him time to think. To consider. To plan.

Except that he wasn't that kind of man. He made snap judgments, spur-of-the-moment decisions, and he lived with the consequences. His instincts were almost infallible, and they'd kept him alive for more than fifteen years in some of the world's most dangerous places.

His instincts were telling him he'd be a fool to let her go.

He climbed out of bed, in a thoroughly bad mood that his satisfied body didn't seem to share. He wanted to go after her, to grab her and shake some sense into her. Why didn't she make demands, demands he could give in to? Why was she making this so damned difficult?

He needed breathing space, and so did she. He'd give her time to think things through. A couple of hours for her to consider the alternatives. And then he'd go in search of her and inquire very politely whether she might be interested in spending a little time in Colorado. To see whether the climate might suit her.

He was just coming out into the living room of the suite when he heard the knocking. Maybe Carlie had ordered room service. Then again, maybe she hadn't. The door to the other bedroom was still tightly shut, and there was no sign of her or the baby.

For a brief moment he wondered whether she'd run. Taking the kid with her. He wouldn't blame her, but he didn't think it was likely. Sister Maria Carlos had a bit too much honor to take that route. Even if her heart was breaking.

The pounding on the door continued, and he strode toward it, yanking it open. "Yeah?" he snarled.

"Reilly!" Wait Morrissey stood there, glowering at him, looking so damned much like Billy that Reilly wanted to punch him.

"Wait," Reilly said in his most noncommittal voice, blocking the door. "We weren't expecting you till later."

"We have an important cocktail party tonight, so Gracie insisted I charter a plane and get here early. She would have come with me but there were too many last-minute details she had to take care of. She's hired a lovely Mexican gal. Doesn't speak a word of English, but then, neither will my grandson at this point. Where is he, Reilly?''

"Here." Carlie's voice came from directly behind him, and Reilly had no choice but to move out of the way and let the old man in. He didn't want to. He wanted to tell Wait Morrissey to go to hell and take his wife with him, but he clamped his jaw down.

Wait was staring at Carlie with undisguised doubt. "You're not Caterina Morrissey," he said in an accusing voice. "What the hell's going on here, Reilly?"

"I'm Carlie Forrest," she said. "Caterina was my friend."

"Was?" Wait echoed. "She's dead?"

"I'm afraid so. She died in childbirth."

Morrissey bore down on Carlie. He was an impressive man, bulky, powerful, with the ability to intimidate most people despite the overbearing charm he wielded like a weapon. Billy had been scared spitless of him, and even Reilly watched his step.

Carlie didn't move. "So you got Reilly to give you a free ride out of the country at my expense," Wait said. "Well, forget it. You're responsible for any extra passengers you pick up along the way. I'll take care of any debts my grandson incurred."

"I told you, I don't need any money," Reilly snapped, but Wait ignored him, staring down at the baby.

"We can sort that out later," he said grandly. "I take care of my own. Assuming he even is my grandson."

Timothy didn't like the sound of the old man's

voice. Reilly didn't blame him. The baby let out a loud, furious wail, the likes of which Reilly hadn't heard in the past four days, his little face turning red with temper.

"What do you mean by that?" Carlie asked calmly over the noise of the screeching kid.

"I mean we're going to have tests done. Reilly should have made that clear. He's going straight into the hospital so that they can check him out, run some DNA samples, that kind of stuff. I want to make sure he's in good shape before we take him. And I want to make damned sure he really is my grandson."

"And if he's not?" Reilly said in a deceptively polite voice.

"If he's not? Well, there's no way in hell I'm raising some bastard as my grandson. And you can kiss your expenses goodbye." Wait Morrissey took a deep, calming breath. "No offense intended, Reilly. I know you wouldn't try to pawn off some brat as Billy's. But who's to say this girl's telling you the truth?"

Reilly tilted his head sideways, considering him. "No way I'd do that, Wait. Which is why I hate to tell you, but he's not your grandson."

Fortunately his simple words drew all of Wait's attention, and he didn't notice Carlie's shocked expression. She tried to say something, but Timothy's wails drowned out her attempt, and Wait wheeled around, storming away from them, already dismissing them.

"What the hell are you talking about, Reilly? What are you trying to pull?"

"Absolutely nothing. Caterina died in childbirth,

and so did the baby. By the time I got to the mission the only person there was Carlie. She'd given birth a couple of weeks before Caterina, but she hadn't been strong enough to be evacuated with the others. I was there, I had the baby supplies. I brought her out with me.''

"I'm not paying for it," Morrissey said instantly.

"I don't expect you to."

"Can't you shut that brat up?" The old man snarled back at Carlie. "I can't hear myself think."

"You don't need to think, Wait. I'm sorry it worked out this way, but there's nothing to be done. Just tell Gracie what happened. I think she'll manage to survive." He tried to keep the wryness out of his voice. Gracie Morrissey wouldn't have let an infant grandson interfere with her social life, and she certainly wasn't going to let the loss of one she'd never even seen affect her.

For a long moment Wait just looked at him. For all his bluster, he was an intelligent man. He looked at Reilly, then glanced back toward the baby and the woman holding him so protectively.

"All right," he said suddenly, nodding. "It's probably just as well. Gracie and I weren't very good parents the first time around, and we're too old to change our ways. It'll work out better this way."

Reilly simply nodded, unwilling to say anything. Wait turned and walked back to the howling child, staring down at him. "Gracie'll be relieved," he muttered underneath his breath. He reached out one stubby, perfectly manicured finger and touched the baby's red face. "Have a good life, kid."

THE DOOR CLOSED behind him, and suddenly Timothy was still, a hiccupy little breath at odds with his tremulous smile.

"Such a noisy baby," Carlie whispered at him, holding him tightly. "I don't think you liked that old man very much, did you?"

Reilly crossed the room and took the baby from her arms, and she had no choice but to let him go. "He's going back to bed. He needs to start getting on a normal schedule."

"Babies don't have normal schedules," she protested.

"Well, we can try."

She looked up at him, startled. *We,* she thought, shocked. She wanted to say something, but he'd already carried the baby into the bedroom, settling him back down in the crib.

Timothy set up a tired screech of protest. "Forget it, kid," Reilly said, rubbing his back with a rhythmic pattern. "You need to sleep, and your ma and I need to talk."

She shouldn't have told him she loved him. For all his bluster, Reilly was an honorable man. He probably thought he had to make some grand sacrifice for her sake. Well, she wasn't about to let him, and she would tell him so. As soon as she got her courage together.

He looked at her over the sleeping baby. "Showdown time," he said quietly.

She followed him into the living room of the suite. "You lied to that old man," she said.

He turned to look at her. They were standing just a foot apart. She was afraid he might touch her.

Afraid that if he did, she'd never want him to let her go. She couldn't do that to him.

"He's smarter than he looks. He guessed the truth," Reilly said.

"Don't be ridiculous. He wouldn't have gone off and left his grandson with you...."

"That's exactly what he'd do. I doubt they would have done any better a job with him than they would have with Billy, and Billy, God love him, was royally screwed up. No, it's better this way."

"Living a lie?"

"I thought you said something wasn't a sin if it was done in love."

"Don't!" she said, feeling mortification wash over her as she held up a hand in protest.

He caught her hand, drawing her closer to him. "He's your son, Carlie. He always has been. You know that, deep in your heart." She wanted to pull away, but she couldn't. "What do you think of Colorado?"

"Reilly," she said, "I can't let you do this. I can't make you change your life, take on a couple of lost souls because you're too decent a human being to—"

Reilly began to curse again, his usual litany of obscenity that she'd begun to find oddly comforting. "You can't make me do a damned thing I don't want to do," he growled, hauling her up against him with enough force for her to know he meant it. "I'm a reasonable man. I consider alternatives, I think about things and then I make up my mind. And you're coming with me to Colorado, we're getting married and Timothy will be ours."

"No, Reilly. I can't..."

He caught her face in his hands, glaring down at her. "Listen, I've spent the last fifteen years of my life with no home, no family, no life. Now I've got Billy's kid, and I can raise him a damned sight better than anyone else can. And I've got you. And I'm not going to let you go."

"Why not?" Her voice was low, shaky. She already knew the answer. She could see it in his eyes, in his face, hear it in his voice. But she had to have the words.

"Because I love you, goddamn it," he said irritably. "And don't you dare give me any more crap about going away. I don't care whether you believe me or not—"

"I do," she said.

"You do what?"

She smiled up at him, a glorious, sunny smile. "I believe you. And the only place I'm going is Colorado, with you and our son."

He stared down at her for a moment in disbelief. "I thought you were going to put up more of a fight," he said.

"I only fight the battles I want to win," she said simply.

He kissed her then. A long, slow, sweet kiss, of promises and forever. And then he threw back his head and laughed. "We're going to make a hell of a family," he said. "A soldier, a nun and a baby."

"Ex-soldier," she said, resting her head against his chest and listening to his steady, strong heartbeat. "A not-quite nun. And babies grow up awfully fast."

He looked down at her, and there was toughness and tenderness in his smile. "Then we'll have to make some more."

"Yes," she said, against his heart. "Yes."

Epilogue

Three Years Later

Carlie sat curled up in the window seat, staring through the frosty panes of glass to the swirling snow beyond. Winter in the Colorado mountains seemed to go on forever, and she never tired of it. Even trapped in the house with a total of five kids, and one more on the way, with her husband off on some mysterious errand, she managed to still her anxiety at the way the snow was piling up and pay attention to the child curled up beside her, her hand resting trustingly in hers.

"Ma-a-a-a." Timothy managed to put half a dozen syllables into her name as he stormed through the huge, untidy living room, his three-year-old face flushed with tears. "Trina bit me."

"Caterina!" Carlie called out in the stern voice she'd been forced to master. A moment later two-year-old Caterina Reilly toddled out of the kitchen, a deceptively angelic expression on her face.

"Took my G. I. Joe," Trina announced with an air of infinite reasonableness.

"It was my action figure," Timothy shouted back in a fury.

"Wouldn't you guys rather play something nice and passive?" Carlie inquired, knowing the question was more rhetorical than practical.

"No, Ma," six-year-old Luis replied from his spot on the braided rug in front of the fire. "You know they're hellions."

Elena stirred beside her, murmuring a protest in Spanish. She and her brother, Rafael, were the latest additions to their ménage, two preschool-age orphans from Brazil, sent northward with Mother Ignacia's blessing. Luis had been the second member of their family, arriving at their mountain cabin when Timothy had just turned one, a shy, defensive four-year-old who'd gradually accepted the love and safety they offered him. Caterina arrived next, on a snowy night like this, when Carlie had gone into labor and Reilly had barely had time to get her down to the hospital, with both kids riding along in the pickup truck, listening to Reilly's panicked cursing with awe and delight.

Then came Rafael and Elena, ten months ago. It had taken them a little longer to adjust—they'd seen too much in their short lives to trust easily. But Elena had learned to snuggle, and Rafael had discovered that Luis was a soul mate. Together they kept their young siblings in line, and they both worshiped their father.

And now there was the huge, uncomfortable, much-anticipated creature doing its best to reshape Carlie's liver. She had two months to go—the baby wasn't due till April—but she was becoming increasingly aware that this baby wasn't going to wait. This time they'd need the four-wheel-drive van to take the children along to the hospital. And this time she wasn't about to let Reilly videotape the delivery and then drag it out when friends made the trek up Paradise Mountain.

The tears that had become increasingly common as her pregnancy progressed burned in her eyes, and she fought them back with an effort. She needed Reilly, she needed his strong arms around her, she needed his deep voice soothing her.

"Where's Papa?" Elena removed her thumb from her mouth long enough to ask.

Carlie brushed her hair away from her dark, worried face. "I'm not sure, angel. But you know your father—he always gets back. We can count on him."

Elena nodded, sticking her thumb back in her mouth and curling up beside Carlie, her head resting against the bulge of her new sibling.

She could hear the noise of a four-wheel-drive vehicle in the darkness beyond the cabin, but she couldn't be sure whether it was Reilly or the snowplow. She forced herself to remain still. The children needed her calm, composed, and fear never helped anyone.

She just wished she knew where the hell Reilly had gone.

He'd just up and left, three days ago, putting down his tools in the midst of turning the loft into additional bedrooms, and he hadn't told her where he was going. He'd simply kissed her, hard, on the mouth, told her he'd be back as soon as he could, and then disappeared, before she could demand a few answers.

He'd gotten better about giving answers in the past three years. It had taken a while, but he'd learned to talk to her, to laugh with her. On the rare occasions when she let her temper disintegrate, he knew just how to charm her out of her fury. When his own temper shook the rafters, she was equally adept at soothing him.

He was going to have his work cut out for him when he got home this time. She told herself she didn't mind his going—he doubtless had a very good reason and he'd be back as soon as he could. She just didn't like not knowing those reasons. Not when her back hurt, the baby seemed more like an octopus than a baby and each wild limb seemed to be wearing tap shoes. And she couldn't stop crying.

She could see the headlights now, through the blinding snow, coming closer. Too close together for the town plow. It looked like Reilly's pickup truck, and she breathed a sigh of relief.

"Is it Papa?" Elena roused herself, her beautiful dark eyes lighting up with delight.

"I expect so." Carlie slid off the window seat, carefully, and was rewarded with a fresh kick from her burgeoning offspring. She started toward the door, but the children were ahead of her, flinging it open, letting the wind and snow swirl inside.

Carlie leaned against the wall, one hand bracing her back, not even bothering to suggest the children calm down and close the door. They were too excited.

Indeed, she had a hard time turning her own expression into a suitably disapproving one. Moments later Reilly filled the doorway, his long dark hair thick with snow, his long arms outstretched to catch all five bodies as they hurtled into his arms. Above the shrieks of delight he met her stern gaze with a rueful expression.

"Miss me?" he mouthed at her above the din.

She tried to summon up a suitable snarl, but she found herself grinning instead. "Where were you this time?" she demanded.

"I brought you something."

"Oh, God," she said in a resigned voice. "How many this time?"

"Three," he said, looking suitably sheepish. "Two cousins, Matteo and Carlos, but they're only temporary. They're on their way to their family in Washington State, but they need to stay with us for a couple of months until their parents get settled."

She looked past her husband to the three small figures in the doorway. She could see the two children, dark faced, wary, eyeing the melee with tentative interest. The person standing behind them wasn't much taller, but the parka obscured the face and body.

"Welcome, Matteo and Carlos," Carlie said, crossing over to them. They looked willing enough, so she gave them a hug, one they returned.

And then she looked at the snow-covered figure beyond them. "And who is this, Reilly?"

The third visitor pushed back the fur-lined hood, exposing a lined, wrinkled little face, dark, sassy eyes and beaklike nose beneath the plain black veil. "Motherhood suits you, Sister Maria Carlos," Reverend Mother Ignacia announced.

"Oh, my God," Carlie gasped, then clapped a restrictive hand over her mouth.

"Don't worry. After listening to your husband

drive through a blizzard I imagine I've heard most curses known to man," Reverend Mother said briskly, folding Carlie into her arms. "I've come for a visit. Being the mother of the year is all well and good, but you've got another baby coming, and I need a vacation. I'm here to make sure you're taking proper care of yourself until after the baby arrives."

"Reverend Mother..." she said brokenly.

"Reilly," the old lady said in her bossiest voice, "take your wife into the bedroom and give her a backrub. I'm going to teach these children how to make fajitas."

Before Carlie could protest she found herself swept away, Reilly's strong arm around her as he pulled her into their bedroom and shut the door firmly behind him.

A relative, peaceful silence ensued. Carlie looked up, way up at him. "How did you know?" she murmured.

"That you were going crazy?" he replied, pulling her into his arms and resting a big hand on her rounded belly. "You forget, I know you pretty well by this point. There's nothing wrong with being overwhelmed occasionally. You're not a saint, Carlie, even if you sometimes wish you were."

"But they need me," she cried, leaning her head against his shoulder. "And I need them."

"And you're wonderful with them. You just need a little breathing space before Megatron makes his appearance." He stroked her belly possessively.

"Her appearance," she said.

"Besides," he said, "there's someone else who needs you around here."

She smiled up at him, leaning into his tough, strong body. "You've got me," she whispered.

"Reverend Mother Ignacia's staying for two months," he whispered in her ear. "I don't suppose there's any chance we can get Gargantua to make an appearance in the next week or two so that you and I might have a night or two of raunchy sex before we have to be parents again?"

"Maybe," she said. She looked up at him with sudden worry. "Are there too many children for you?"

He shook his head. "Nope. I could handle a few more than we've got already. What about you? Did you plan on turning into the Waltons in such a short time?"

She smiled up at him. "We can handle it," she said. "You'll just need to keep adding to the house. And I'm afraid a little sooner than you think."

For a moment a look of blank horror crossed his face. "You don't mean...?"

"Yup," she said. "I figure we have maybe an hour to get down to the hospital. Think you can do it?"

He began to curse, and she put her hand over his mouth with a giggle that turned into a moan and then back into a giggle again.

"You've got a nun out there, soldier," she hissed with mock disapproval.

"I've got a knocked-up nun in labor in here and there's a g.d. blizzard out there," he roared in outrage. "Let's go!"

He scooped her ungainly figure up in his arms and kicked open the door. Mother Ignacia was presiding over the horde of children in the kitchen, and Reilly paused in the doorway as Carlie grabbed for her parka. "We're going to the hospital," he announced.

"You always were an efficient child," Mother Ignacia said approvingly. "Go with God."

"And drive like hell," Reilly muttered under his breath.

They made it to the hospital in time. By six o'clock the next morning, Forrest Reilly made his appearance, weighing five pounds three ounces, followed, most unexpectedly, by his sister Ignacia, who was a portly five pounds eight ounces. Once they managed to revive Reilly from his dead faint, he looked down at his wife's exhausted expression with a glazed one of his own.

"Did you know?"

She shook her head, looking down at the babies nestled in her arms. "Reilly," she said with a faint grin, "you'd better buy more diapers."

He leaned down and kissed her, hard and deep. She kissed him back, somewhere summoning the energy to arch her back to reach him. "I love you, Reilly," she murmured.

He cupped her face. "I love you, too, Sister Maria Carlos," he said. And the snow-swept Colorado night slipped away into a glorious, white-glazed dawn. And all was peaceful.

For another four and a half minutes.

Being auctioned off in the white slave market was no less
dangerous for Rachel Tinsdale than dealing with
Rand Slick—a stranger who had her aching to share his
secrets and show him the joys to be found in the arms of
a woman who was no man's slave.

LOVE SLAVE
Mallory Rush

Prologue

"TIME TO SAY GOODBYE to your sister, Joshua." Mr. Johns patted the twelve-year-old boy's dark head.

Joshua stared hard at the social worker until the man glanced away uneasily, his Adam's apple bobbing up and down, just like a turkey's when he gobbled. Josh shrugged the comforting hand away. Didn't want no pity. Didn't want nobody but Sarah to even touch him.

"I gotta do this right," Joshua said quietly, so his sister wouldn't hear. The man looked sad, even guilty. Josh played it for all it was worth. He stuck his thumb in the opposite direction, just like his daddy used to do when he sent him to his room. "Mr. Johns... please?"

Mr. Johns headed the other way, taking along with him the grown-ups who'd accepted Sarah into their home.

"C'mon, Sarah." Josh led the silent five-year-old into her new bedroom. She clutched her baby doll against her as Josh sat on the canopy bed and pulled her onto his lap. "Let's talk," he said, tugging on a long blond braid.

She didn't respond to his hair pulling. All she did was stare out the lace-curtained window and stroke her little hand through the doll's ratty curls.

"Remember the Christmas Santa brought you that?"

"There's no such thing as Santa Claus." She blinked her eyes, and out rolled two big tears. "He's dead, too."

"Now don't you start crying. If you do, you'll make me start, and big boys don't cry. That's what Daddy always said. And we don't want to let him down. You and me, Sarah, we're gonna get through this and make him proud."

A huge sob shuddered through her small chest. Josh rocked her back and forth, the way he thought Daddy would have. And then he remembered his father telling him he was the man of the house and to watch after his sister while he went out for groceries that night he never came back.

"Oh, J-Josh," she stuttered out. "Josh, I'm s-scared. I think I killed Daddy."

"That's crazy talk, Sarah."

"No, it's not! 'Member when we got in trouble for laughing in church?"

"Yeah. My butt's still stinging from the licking I got when we came home."

"'Cause you couldn't quit laughin' at the old lady singing in front. But I quit. Know how?"

"How?" Josh picked up a coverlet from the foot of the bed and tucked it around them. He was going to miss his sister stealing the blanket when he went to sleep in his own strange bed.

"I pretended Daddy died. It was the horriblest, saddest thing I could think, and it made me stop laughin'." She stared at him with big, frightened eyes, guilt and remorse contorting her impish face. "I did it other times, too, and now he's dead. I made him dead from thinkin' it. I'm a bad girl. A bad, bad girl. And preacher says the bad ones go down there.

You know, that place where the devil's at, with the brim and firestone? I don' wanna go there,'' she wailed. Sarah clutched the doll in her arms, twisting her fingers into the shaggy mop of hair.

''Shhh...shhh,'' he said, trying to soothe her. ''Now quit thinkin' like that, Sarah. You didn't make it happen, and you're not gonna see any hellfire and brimstone. Don't go forgettin', you were always Daddy's angel, and you'll always be mine. Angels go to heaven, not hell.''

''Josh, you know you're not s'posed to say the *H* word. That'll earn you a licking for sure.''

''And who's gonna give it to me? You?'' He tweaked her nose, and she giggled past her receding tears.

''You're sure I'm safe?'' she said hopefully.

''Absolutely, positively sure.'' Josh swallowed past the lump in his throat. They'd be coming for him soon, to take him away from Sarah. Then who would look at him as if he'd hung the moon? Mr. Johns? The warden at the orphanage? A vision of iron bars and prison beds made him hug her tight.

''You're squishin' me, Josh.''

He forced himself to loosen his hold and fake an encouraging smile.

''This is sure a pretty new room you've got, Sarah. Lots better than the one at home. They look real nice, your new folks do, and they were so excited when you got here, saying you were the little girl they'd always wanted.''

''But they're not you. They're strangers, and I want my daddy back.''

''Me too. But that won't change anything, angel. We've got to say goodbye for a little while, but when

I'm old enough I'm gonna take you away from here. That's a promise.''

''When, Josh?''

He could visit on holidays. Big deal. He wanted his sister back, and all he could think of now was years and years of goodbyes like this. It was tearing his guts out just thinking about it.

And so he didn't. He thought about how he was going to keep his promise to Sarah. He knew he'd need a place for them to live and enough money to take care of her.

How could he do it? Mowing lawns? But maybe the orphanage wouldn't even let him out to do that. Just like they'd lock him in tonight so he couldn't comfort Sarah while she cried herself to sleep.

Something hard knotted up inside him and settled protectively around his heart. His hands clenched the sheet, and he held her as close as he could without making her yelp.

''I'll come back when I've got lots of money. Then I'll buy you and me a brand-new house where we'll live together again. No grown-ups around, so we can eat all the candy and have all the pillow fights we want. Whenever you feel sad, just think about that.''

''You promise?''

''Cross my heart, hope to—''

She threw her arms around his neck and nearly hugged the stuffings out of him. Josh stared at the window, which was lifted a crack. The warm Mississippi breeze cut through his emotions and cleared his head.

Suddenly he had the beginnings of a plan.

''Can you keep a secret, Sarah? A real important secret? 'Cause if you tell, I can't come back to get you." She nodded her head, her braid bouncing up and down. "I'm running away."

"No, Josh! You could get in bad trouble."

"Only if they catch me." Realizing he didn't have any time to waste, he forced himself to put her down. His expression was stern. "This is what we've got to do. You lay down and pretend to be resting. If they ask you where I am, you say I went to get a drink of water. That way they'll look around the house before they go after me."

"But that's lyin'!"

"It's a good lie, Sarah. If I don't get away, I'll never be able to get you back, and you want me to, don't you?"

"More'n anything." She looked real scared as Josh tucked her in and kissed her cheek. He was suddenly torn between crawling under the covers with her and making a run for it.

"I love you, angel. Be sure to say your prayers every night. And when you get homesick, just think about me and the day I'll take you back home."

"I love you, big brother."

He untangled her arms from around his neck and gave her the baby doll to cling to instead. Josh turned before she saw the tears brimming his eyes.

Big boys don't cry.... Big boys don't cry....

He crawled through the window, then shut it back to a crack as soon as his feet touched grass. Blowing his sister a final kiss, he made sure the coast was clear, then ran as fast as his feet could fly.

Sure wished he had some of those Keds so he could take off like Superman outrunning that train.

Train! He hadn't known where he was headed, but now he did. They'd passed some tracks a mile or so down the road. He'd hop the first train that whizzed by.

Josh was winded by the time he got there. He kept looking over his shoulder, expecting the orphanage's guard dogs to hunt him down.

He'd followed the tracks a good mile when he heard a chugging that sounded like his own labored breathing. Then the train was passing, passing too fast, and no way could he be Superman and outrun it. Just barely, he made out the oncoming blur of an open side door.

He started to run, trying to remember how he'd seen it done in the movies. Lordy, he wished he was taller, as tall as Sarah thought he was, tall enough to hang the moon and swing her on a star.

Do it! He sprang high at a dead run and caught the side edge of the railway car. Wind sucked at him, pulling him toward the slicing wheels and onto the iron tracks. He screamed, his fingers sliding and clawing to pull the rest of him to safety. He looked down, his eyes wild. He felt the mean steel all but eating up his feet and knew if he let go he'd be mangled like a mouse chewed up by a tomcat.

And then he felt something grab his locked arm. He raised his head, the wind whipping it so hard he thought his neck would snap. His eyes were glued to a grizzled face, a mouth that was gnashing out some urgent command.

Josh nearly pulled the man out with him before he was safely inside. He fell into a trembling heap on the coarse floor. He heard the door being shoved nearly closed while the locomotive's deadly wheels sang a rusty lullaby against his raw cheek.

And then he was being nudged gently, and a brown paper sack filled his stinging vision.

"Drink some, young'n. Not too much, or you'll puke. Just a swig to make your innards quit shakin'."

It felt like liquid fire going down. Josh coughed and sputtered, trying to regain his breath. By the time he had, his new comrade was guzzling freely.

"Running away?"

"No, sir, I'm just on vacation."

"Sir?" The man cackled, revealing dingy teeth.

Then the liquor hit, and Josh felt warm and numb. His insides quit shaking, and he leaned back, exhausted.

"Thank you, sir. You saved my life."

"That depends. Just might've saved you for somethin' worse than you were running from." He coughed and spit on the floor, then wiped his mouth against the arm of his ragged shirt. "What's your name, boy?"

"Joshua Smith."

"Wrong. First thing you got to learn on the run is, don't leave no trail. Names are like Hansel with his bread crumbs, and no bird around to eat the tracks."

Josh nodded, feeling weariness overtaking him.

"What's your name?" he asked, covering a yawn with the back of his hand.

"Ain't got no name. Left it behind when I took off on my own vacation." He patted Josh's bruised arm, and Josh could smell body odor and the sweat he'd worked up saving him. It was a comforting touch, all the same. "You listen up good, boy. This train's headed for Chicago. Don't make a peep, and you might make it. Big city makes it hard to find runaways. Want to tell me why you're running now?"

"My dad died. They put my sister in a home, and they were going to tote me off to an orphan—"

"Don't know why you're running, don't care to know."

"Then why'd you ask?"

"I'm tryin' to teach you somethin', give you some schoolin' that's not in the books."

Josh considered that. Sounded like good advice. "Are you going to Chicago?" he asked hopefully.

"Me, I'm getting off at the next refuel stop."

"Can I come with you? I won't be any bother, I promise."

"Best you learn right now, the only way to travel is alone. Now get you some rest and don't say no more. Me and the bottle want to get cozy."

Josh shut his eyes, meaning to pretend sleep. If he was careful, he could sneak out and follow his new friend long enough to pick up more lessons before striking out on his own.

But the liquor, the ordeal, the lull of the train's constant movement, seduced him into sleep.

When Josh awoke, the train was still moving, but he was alone. He looked around the emptiness—dark now, since it was night. Rubbing his eyes, he tried to remember....

And then he wished he hadn't. He was glad his father wasn't there, glad no one could see the tears that big boys weren't supposed to cry.

Reaching into his pocket, he found a torn-up Kleenex. And a five-dollar bill. He knew it hadn't been there when he'd jumped the train. Remembering that protective hardness he'd summoned in Sarah's room, he drew on it again, replacing his tears with something gritty and determined.

When Josh Smith hit Chicago, he had five dollars, the clothes on his back, and a promise to keep. In less than a week, he had a room in a deserted building where he fought the rats for space, a box he'd painted black and stuffed with clean rags and a can of saddle soap, plus a rickety chair he'd salvaged from an alley.

Joe at the greasy spoon next door loaned him a spot on the corner and leftovers from the grill in exchange for running errands and free shines.

Spotting a potential client, Josh wiped off the cracked vinyl seat of his chair and blocked the man's path.

"Shine your shoes, mister? Fifty cents'll get you the full treatment. Spit polished and shiny as a new penny."

The man sat down, and Josh had his first customer. "You got a name, son?"

"Rand Slick," Josh said, quickening his buffing strokes.

As good a name as any for a man with no roots. A man in a boy's body. A man who'd learned two rules from a bum: Trust no one, but if you do, make damn sure they earned it. And when you take the dark, endless road back home, go alone.

1

"Mister?"

"What?"

"I said, shine your shoes, mister?"

Rand Slick blinked several times, willing the present to come into focus.

"Sorry, son, can't spare the time." He pulled out a wad of big ones and peeled off a fifty. "Grab a square meal, but put the rest in your college fund. Believe me, it's a wise investment."

Rand hurried on, skirting a bum hugging a brown paper sack. He hated this sleazy quarter of Vegas. The atmosphere made him feel dirty, as though his fine clothes and supple leather wing tips were melting away, leaving him in rags and battered shoes. Nothing but his ongoing quest to find his sister could induce him to relive the bad old days of his youth.

He entered a run-down building, his hopes lowering with each step on the threadbare carpet. His sources had said this PI was good, but these seedy surroundings made him wonder.

He scanned the faded lettering on the yellowed milk-glass office doors until he stood in front of one that smelled of Windex. The black ink scored into the clear beveled glass was carefully etched and looked new.

It read Rachel Tinsdale, Private Investigator. His

flagging spirits climbed a notch when he opened the door and a tinkling wind chime announced his entry. The scents of potpourri and lemon oil masked the mustiness of age. The office was neat, the furniture secondhand but warm, vintage. A vacant desk with several stacks of paper, a cup of coffee, and only a mild litter of files rounded out the scene.

"Have a seat and I'll be right with you."

The invitation came from under the desk. He frowned. Voices could be deceiving, but this one sounded, well, kittenish, too young. An ingenue from an old Elvis movie. Not a good sign. Reflexes and courage and quick thinking were important for the job he needed done. Maybe his sources were wrong. If so, better to find out now. He'd check Ms. Tinsdale's rep out for himself.

His steps were muffled by a big oriental rug. Once he was positioned by the side of the desk, he got a view of flowing red hair, a slender back covered in white cotton, and what appeared to be a cute little tush bobbing on the edge of a wicker chair. The backside package was nice, but it was a minor credential. What he needed were skills he could trust. Yes, a test on how she faced unexpected danger was imperative.

"Don't move," he ordered in a low, menacing tone. "Stop what you're doing and don't move a hair."

"Just let me polish this last toenail, okay?"

Just let me polish this last toenail? Her safety was supposedly at risk and she was worried about the color of her toes? It was a cool and ridiculous response, but it certainly wasn't one that suggested she could handle this case.

"Before you ransack the office, you might as well

know I've got ten bucks to my name. Why don't you save yourself the bother of tearing the place up, and me the mess? Here's my purse.'' A large, ugly hand-bag was shoved across the floor in his direction. The action made her rear bob a little higher, and Rand's seasoned eyes narrowed appreciatively.

''Go ahead,'' she said. ''Pick it up. The billfold's at the bottom, and the money's stashed in the change compartment. But you'd better hurry, because I've got an appointment in one minute, and you're liable to get caught.''

Rand had to give her credit for ingenuity—as well as bad taste in purses. She had his interest, though, so he decided to play along. He stooped down to pick up the bag.

How she did it, he had no idea, but Ms. Tinsdale was no longer under the desk. She was crouched on the floor and pointing the muzzle of a gun straight at his face. He was too stunned to look past the chamber, but he got the impression of fire bending delicate glass.

''Okay, you scumball, drop the goods and lie on the floor. Arms locked behind your head, legs spread, and don't *you* move a hair while I make a body search.''

He should start talking—and fast. Then again, having his body searched by Ms. Tinsdale had a certain appeal. To check out her skills—investigator-wise, of course.

''Did you hear me? I mean business, buster. Lie down and spread 'em.''

He'd never been one to argue with a gun, especially when a lady was fingering the trigger. He followed her orders.

Her free hand efficiently frisked his arms. Then, when she glided it over his ribs and back, he had the keenest sensation of stimulation. What was he, some kind of pervert? He was actually enjoying this! Rand frowned in self-disapproval.

"I think you'd better stop," he said gruffly.

"Getting too close to something you don't want me to find?"

I'll say, he thought. Her hand was nearly patting his rear, which was awfully close to an area that didn't care that his only interest in Ms. Tinsdale was business.

"Aren't you just a tad overdressed for the occasion? Or maybe you ripped off the threads, huh? No, don't tell me. You're a hood who likes to make a statement."

Her fingers gripped his ankles, checking for a hidden weapon, then clamped onto his calves. When she made a quick glide over the back of his thigh, he groaned.

"Ms. Tinsdale," he said raggedly, "why don't you save us both some embarrassment and stop where you are?"

"How do you know my name?" She did stop, unfortunately, her palm resting near his crotch. "The door, of course. Ah-hah! Thought you could fool me, did you?"

She grazed the interior of his thighs, then went for the other leg.

"Ms. Tinsdale!" he said urgently. "*Enough.* I'm Rand Slick. I'm here for our appointment to discuss a missing person."

"Rand Slick?" she exclaimed. "Oh my gosh!"

Deciding he was in no condition to expose his front

side, he kept his position but lifted his head. His gaze collided with the most luminous green eyes he'd ever seen in his life.

A spark of recognition seemed to leap between them, and for a moment they stared at each other. Had he seen her somewhere before? Or maybe there was just something familiar about her that struck a chord with him.

Who was the more surprised, he couldn't have said. Ms. Tinsdale appeared speechless, embarrassed, and something else, something that mirrored his internal confusion. The situation had the feel of a tightrope, each of them tugging at opposite ends while the tension quivered through the charged air.

"Think you could put the rod away? I have an aversion to being on the wrong side of a trigger."

As quickly as the connection had been made it was broken. She turned and carefully put the gun in her purse. Rand was momentarily snared by the swish of long, vivid red hair, the sleek, poetic movement of her back twisting around, the exposure of slim ankle and white fabric riding up her thighs as she got to her feet.

She offered him her hand.

It was dry, but he caught a faint tremor. Or maybe it came from him. He must be having a belated reaction to the gun, because he sure wasn't some prepubescent kid—not that he'd ever been a prepubescent kid, exactly. But looking at her, full in the face— a face that seemed fresh but was arranged in sweet, provocative angles—he wondered just how old she was.

Apparently not too young to know how to handle a pistol.

With surprising strength, she helped him to his feet. Standing, she came just beneath his chin. Her own notched up. For something so delicate-looking, it sure had a stubborn set to it.

"Do you care to tell me what that little stick-up act was all about, Mr. Slick? I could've blown your head off."

"Sorry. I wanted to test out your reflexes. Not a good move on my part, I'm afraid."

She snorted her agreement, then nodded to a chair facing her desk. As they sat opposite each other, his respect for her climbed a notch. She looked composed in spite of the test that had gone awry.

Or had it? She was good. She was also one first-class frisker. He shifted in the chair, feeling an uncomfortable reminder of that.

"So tell me," she said, "do you make it a habit to hit people out of left field? Or was this just a lapse into…"

"Stupidity?" He chuckled. "I've been known to be unorthodox in my methods. But I get answers and results, one way or the other."

"Mr. Slick, I think we just connected."

No, Ms. Tinsdale, we connected on the floor. Had she read his mind? Was that why she was suddenly busy shuffling papers, why she'd quickly averted her gaze from his?

Rachel could feel his shuttered dark eyes boring into her. Something was happening here that she wasn't comfortable with. Growing up in the PI business had left her with fine instincts when it came to first impressions. Rand Slick had a polished quality that hid some dangerously rough edges.

He was handsome, for sure, but there was nothing

soft to balance out the stern planes of his face. His eyes, the color of slate, came close to matching his hair. He wore it a little long for an executive, brushed straight back from a well-shaped forehead. The severe style exposed several lines permanently creased into his brow; smaller lines edged his eyes. Great mouth. Nice jaw. Nothing weak about either.

For some reason he reminded her of Rocky Balboa. The kind of man who maintained an aura of the streets no matter how far he moved up in the world. Or maybe it was just those muscles of his, muscles that felt more brawler-tough than workout-lean.

"Okay," she said brusquely, "you tested me out and you're still here, so I take it I passed?"

"With flying colors."

"Then it's my turn. Before I take a client on I like to know exactly what I'm dealing with. We'll start with some questions."

"Shoot."

"I almost did."

Rand chuckled. Hard to stay tough with this guy, Rachel realized, struggling to maintain her objectivity. Just because he needed her services and had a terrific smile, that didn't make him an okay person.

"So what do you want to know?" he said, easing into a position that suggested comfort but struck her as guarded.

"Let's start with you. Harry Kline put us in touch, but he wasn't too liberal with facts. He said you're legit, you've got some mutual business interests and a personal reason to find someone who's missing. For knowing you a couple of years, he didn't seem to know much. I'd like to know more."

His smile dissolved into a thin, expressionless line.

"I didn't come here to discuss myself. Let's stick to business—and any information you need to find my sister." His voice was the flat tone of unquestioned authority.

Rachel felt as though she'd just slammed into a concrete rail after cruising along at a smooth speed. She'd picked up on his rough edges, but she hadn't been prepared for them to emerge so abruptly. Whoever Rand Slick was, he definitely was not a man people messed with. He had a way of turning the tables.

She didn't like it. It took a lot to unnerve her, but he did, with his tense posture and his sharp but strangely distant stare.

"Never let nobody know you're shook," she remembered her dad saying. "Look 'em in the eyeball, and even if your innards turn to mush, don't back down."

Rachel made herself sit straighter. Fortunately, the desk hid the foot she was busy shaking.

"In that case, tell me everything you can, no matter how unimportant it seems. Her habits, her hobbies, and especially the kind of people she hangs out with."

For a split second she caught a glimpse of something vulnerable in his expression. He quickly replaced it with the implacable mask. The unexpected reaction caught her like a velvet uppercut to the right before she'd recovered from the brass-knuckled sting from the left. Against her professional judgment, she found herself growing more curious about this quicksilver enigma than about the sister who had brought him here.

"She's seven years younger than me. That puts her

at twenty-six. I know next to nothing about her habits, what she does for kicks, or how she makes a living.''

''Do you have a picture?''

Again, that flash of unguarded emotion. Again, the disguise. He reached inside his coat pocket and handed her a faded black-and-white snapshot. He looked away while she studied it.

Rachel's heart softened on a lurch. There was a story in this picture. A very sad story. It wasn't so much the faded image of Rand Slick as a young boy, hugging a little girl who stared up at him adoringly. It was the creased texture of the glossy paper, the edges rubbed smooth from years of constant touching.

She struggled to appear unaffected. This wasn't a person who liked to expose himself, and any sympathy from her would be deflected with the same stony look he was now wearing. Besides, there was the cardinal rule: A PI never let himself get emotionally involved in a case. It wasn't professional.

''Nothing more recent?''

''No. We were separated shortly after this picture was taken.''

''How?''

''It doesn't matter. What does is that I've been tracking her for years. I've pulled strings, gone through litigation, and run into one dead end after another. The family she was living with died when their house caught fire. Any pictures there went up in smoke.''

''She got out?''

''They lived in the country, and I understand from the closest neighbors, she ran off a year earlier with a drifter who was passing through. She was a senior in high school.''

"There's an angle—high school. Did you check the yearbook? We could get a more recent picture there."

"I checked that out. Country school, and not enough students to go to the bother. Believe me, Ms. Tinsdale, I left no stone unturned."

"Do you think you'd recognize her if you saw her?"

"I do. I...I had occasion to see her twice. Once when she was ten, and then at fourteen. At least I thought it was her from a distance. A brother can spot his sister, no matter how many years pass."

"You didn't talk to her? Find out any facts we can use?"

"No. There were too many people around, and besides, I..." He passed a hand over his eyes, concealing what she suspected was some emotion he didn't want her to see. "It was an unusual situation. Don't ask me to explain. Please?"

That last word had seemed hard for him to get out, as though he were requesting a personal favor and asking favors didn't come easy. He'd kept his voice even, but there was no mistaking the undercurrent of something raw. If necessary, she'd probe later; for now she respected his need for privacy.

Rachel extended the photo to him. Their hands touched. They came to an understanding with that touch. She cared. He needed her to care enough to share his search.

They shared more. A distinct but disturbing current was passing between them. It was achingly personal, and something she couldn't acknowledge with a client. Especially not with a man as mercurial as this one.

"There's more." He pocketed the snapshot. "You

might as well know, five different detectives have worked on this case. I've got a thick file that you're welcome to look over if we can come to terms.''

"Go ahead and give me the rundown." She put pen to paper, ready to take notes.

"Sarah—my sister—moved around a lot after she ran away." He paused, and she sensed that some thought was troubling him.

"Do you know why she ran away? Could it have anything to do with why she stayed on the move?"

"I don't think so. The family she was with seemed pretty solid. Who knows? Maybe it was just a crazy whim, or an idea she picked up from…a bad influence." He cleared his throat and shifted as though the chair were a bun warmer and he wanted to get away from the toasty heat. "Anyway, I got pretty close several times, but either she had wanderlust or she was on the run."

"Any guess why?"

"My sources indicate the man she ran off with had some shady connections."

"Were your sources reliable?"

"They were shady enough themselves to make the connection."

Her pen stopped in mid-scratch. "Back up a minute. Are you telling me you're in with some undesirable characters?"

As he raked a hand through his back-brushed hair, light filtered through flecks of silver. How many of those flecks had been put there by his quest? she wondered. Didn't matter. Even if she sympathized with him, no way was she getting mixed up with the wrong crowd. Her reputation was more important than getting kicked out of this office because she couldn't pay the rent.

"Look," he said, sighing. "I'm clean. I've got no faith in the system, and I do know some people outside it who've gotten me information that money can't buy. I don't set myself up to owe favors, only to collect them. Relax. Whatever my connections, they're not who I am."

Rachel tapped her pen against the paper unconsciously and studied him intently.

"And just who are you, Mr. Slick?"

His jaw tightened; a muscle ticked in his cheek. Rand got up and leaned over the desk. Any vulnerability she had sensed in him before had been snuffed out. This towering man with the face of granite was intimidating the living daylights out of her.

She'd be damned before she let him know it.

"Since you seem as concerned with my background as you are with this case, I'll give you a little bio, and then we'll drop it. What do you want to know? The ID I can't give for my sister?"

Don't back down. If you do, he's out of here. You keep hitting a nerve, and now he's turning the tables. Again.

Rachel swallowed hard. "I like to know how my clients tick. If I'm risking my hide, you can't blame me for that."

His expression said that he could and did.

"Okay, we'll start with the fact that I find it grating when people tap their pens." He whipped the pen from her hand and tossed it to the desk. "As for habits, I brush my teeth two times a day and shower every morning. I drink moderately, avoid emotional entanglements and practice safe sex. My favorite hobby is making money, but I like to play racquetball and poker. I can't stand to lose, and it's rare that I do. As for palling around, I prefer to fly solo.'' He smiled without warning, and she was reminded of a barracuda contemplating lunch.

His turnaround bothered her as much as the thought that being devoured by Rand Slick had a certain frightful appeal.

''Now,'' he continued smoothly, ''since you know as much about me as the next guy, you can drop the mister and call me Rand. Turnabout being fair play, it's your turn, Rachel.''

Belatedly she realized she was staring at him, mouth agape. So much for being her father's daughter, master bluffer and A-1 private eye.

''What—what do you want to know?''

''Everything, actually. But for now I'll stick with some important specifics. Do you like to visit faraway places? Could you possibly endure being stripped in public? And, by some miracle, is your virginity somewhat intact? If the answer is no to any or all, can you fake the first two if I make it worth your while?''

''What?''

''You heard me.'' He gripped her wrist, his fingers biting urgently into her skin. His touch was compelling, even as it set off a shrilling alarm. ''I need a woman with guts and looks. You've got both. But they won't do me any good unless you're willing to stand on an auction block and go up for sale.''

''You've got to be kidding.''

''This is no joke, Ms.—Rachel. I need your skills, and I need your body.'' His gaze raked an incisive path from her head to her breasts. She was shocked to feel an electric reaction. Instinctively she crossed her free arm over her chest. "Good," he said. "The more innocent you appear, the better. If you've got the courage, I've got the in."

"What *are* you talking about?"

"The reason for this meeting." He fixed her with a level stare. "I want to buy you."

Funny, he didn't look nuts. Of course, Jack the Ripper probably hadn't, either. Her wisest move would be to humor him until she could buzz security.

"Of course," she said, forcing a smile and wishing her gun was in her hand instead of her purse. "Did you have a payment schedule in mind?"

"You can name your price. And quit fumbling for a way to flag the guards. Hear me out and I'll leave if you don't want to cut the deal."

"I think you'd better get to it."

"All right. I tracked my sister down, but I can't get to her without a special ticket." He leaned closer to her face. His breath was warm, and she inhaled the subtle fragrances of bay and night spice. "Three words," he said in a low, uninflected voice. *"White slave trade."*

2

"DID YOU JUST SAY 'White slave trade'?"

Damn, he thought. He'd let his desperation overcome his good sense. Hadn't he been turned down enough times without scaring this one off before she gave him half a chance?

Rand released her wrist, absently noting that he could easily break it. He was nearly twice her size. He also noted, and not so absently, that her skin was as soft as feather down and disturbingly pleasant to the touch.

"I think I came on a little too strong." He smiled apologetically, having decided charm might be his best tactic. "It's a long story, Rachel. If I can buy the rest of your day, I'll be glad to pay generously. No strings, just a chance to have you hear me out."

She was silent, probably weighing whether to take him seriously or question his mental stability. He caught her glancing at her purse before turning to an appointment book. She shut it quickly, but not before he saw that it was blank except for a space with his name. Rand looked away, not wanting her to know he'd seen.

"My fee is fifty dollars an hour."

"Why don't we make it an even five hundred for the day?" Rand shelled out the cash and laid it on her appointment book. "This shouldn't take ten hours, but I'd like to compensate for interfering with your schedule.''

She looked from the neat stack of bills to him, a startled expression animating her face before she quickly disguised it. Rand decided then and there that he had himself a good actress—a little unseasoned maybe, but lots of potential. He tucked the fact away for future reference.

"Well..." she said slowly, appearing to debate with herself. "I suppose I could break free, since this seems to be urgent. Have a seat, and we'll pick up where you left off."

"If you don't mind, I'd rather discuss this over lunch." Not that he was hungry, but putting her at ease in a relaxed atmosphere seemed a better way to lure her in. He didn't like to get overly personal with people, but from what he'd seen of Rachel, she might respond best to exactly that. "Tell me what you're hungry for and we'll head out." Rand went to the door, not wanting to give her time to balk.

When she hesitated, he twisted the knob. She made her decision, quickly stashing the money in her wallet and rummaging around for her keys. Five hundred dollars! Enough to pay the back rent and buy groceries for the month. If Rand Slick wanted to eat lunch on her time, she was in no position to quibble.

She just wished he'd quit throwing her equilibrium off, not to mention getting her sidetracked by the way he was waiting, his hands shoved into his pockets so that his shirt strained and his pants did the same. Lord, she hoped she looked calmer than she was.

"How about a sandwich at the corner coffee shop?" she suggested, relieved her voice was deceptively steady.

"How about a nice place on the other side of town? No offense to the neighborhood, but I prefer other surroundings. We can flag a taxi if you're uncomfortable driving in a car alone with me."

She was uncomfortable, but it came from the proximity of their bodies as they stood—too close—at the door. She could feel strange waves of energy generating an even stranger heat between them. It was as if radio waves were riding the air and tuning in on the fine hairs prickling on the back of her neck.

Rachel did her best to ignore it. He'd paid in advance, and the least she could do was show some good faith by allowing him to drive. Besides, in a taxi they'd be forced to share a cramped seat.

"Starting now, we're on your time, Rand. My office is officially closed for the day. Since my car's in the shop, we don't have to flip to see whose wheels we take."

He smiled, seemingly pleased, but the quirk of his lips only managed to make her awkward. At the moment, Cool Hand Luke she was not, and she cursed softly when her keys slipped from her grasp and clattered to the floor.

"I'll get them," he offered.

They almost knocked heads. Their hands connected at the keys. For breathless seconds, she couldn't move. Meaning to laugh the accident off and pretend there wasn't something so physically startling in the contact that it snuffed out her remaining composure, she slowly raised her face.

His breath was on her. There was a dark room behind his eyes, one that was as unchaste and ominous as it was lush with invitation. Leather and lace. Black velvet sheets and white silk curtains trailing the floor.

Haunting. Erotic. And so dark that she was momentarily blinded by his slate-eyed eclipse.

Rachel blinked, trying to get her balance. What was she doing? Decorating his bedroom and checking out his lighting scheme? Rand was way out of her range of experience, and this was a professional meeting, even if the roiling in her tummy insisted it was more.

She took an unsteady breath and managed a faint smile.

"Not a smooth move, huh?"

"I like the way you move."

Rachel quickly rose and shoved the key in. *Damn, why couldn't she get it to lock?* She was jiggling it frenziedly when he caught her hand. Her breathing was not normal. Nothing had seemed normal since he'd walked through this stupid door that she couldn't get locked.

"Let me." His hand glided over hers, working the key. It clicked. For several seconds they remained still, but then he broke the contact, and Rachel exhaled the breath she'd been holding so long her lungs shuddered with relief.

"Thanks," she said as Rand led the way, guiding her by the arm. His grip was polite but firm, and disconcertingly provocative in the subtle pressure of palm to elbow. "That's a testy door," she added, to fill up the taut silence. "It takes a special touch to get it to cooperate."

"Reminds me of some people I've known." He grinned devilishly, and Rachel felt as if she'd just tripped over something. She glanced down, almost expecting to see her heart doing a tap dance. "Take me, for example." He chuckled. "Believe it or not, I can get testy."

"Why, surely you jest." Rachel laughed, glad to break the tension. "And here I thought you were always laid-back."

"Laying back is something I could be tempted to indulge in—given the right person and circumstances."

Rachel looked at him sharply. If Rand had picked up her not-so-subtle reaction to him, he was certainly being forward about letting her know it. Or maybe she was just so shaken by it herself that she was getting her signals crossed.

"Why don't we talk about the circumstances and people in question? That is, faraway places and your sister."

"Here we are." He opened the passenger door of a Mercedes convertible. She got in without getting an answer. Rand lifted an edge of her skirt that was trailing the ground, then draped it over her lap. "Buckle up. I've got a vested interest in keeping you safe."

The door shut, and Rachel shook her head, hoping to clear it. For some reason, she'd never felt less safe in her life, or so aware of a man, as the one in question climbed behind the wheel. Rand put on a CD, surprising her with his selection. Strange music: dipping flute notes, the rippling, cascading sound of some exotic stringed instrument. Winding. Mellow. A musically sensual ache wisping round her mind with tantalizing images.

"Do you like it?" He glanced at her keenly as he negotiated the early-afternoon traffic.

"It's very…intriguing."

"Tell me what it reminds you of, what picture it draws in your imagination."

The low, mesmerizing appeal of his voice blended

into the hypnotic lull of the clear, undulating notes. She closed her eyes, and for a moment she was transported to a faraway world.

"I see...camels, people in long white robes, sand, palms." She laughed softly. "A hookah on a carved teakwood table next to a brass lamp that might have belonged to Aladdin. Persian rugs, dark rich silk. It's a scene from the *Arabian Nights.*"

"And do you smell anything?"

"Sandalwood, incense, and..." *Bay and night spice.* Rachel's eyes snapped open. Good heavens, she'd almost described his cologne! Feeling her cheeks grow warm, she rushed on, "My dad always did say I had a vivid imagination. I get carried away with it sometimes."

Rand stopped the car, and she realized they were parked in front of an exclusive establishment, the kind of place where she was afraid she might not know which fork to use. She'd just watch Rand and follow suit; she was good at bluffing when she had to be.

And now was one time she had to. The exotic setting she'd conjured was still with her, and she was caught up in the tendrils of the music. Rand was studying her closely, not making his expected move to get out. So why was she sitting here, mooning over some steamy, sensual and purely imaginary scene with a man who was, after all, nothing more than a potential client? Reminding herself that this wasn't a date, Rachel reached for the handle.

"Wait." He caught her hand. There was something very intimate in the innocent gesture. "Your imagination's more than vivid, Rachel. It's very close to reality. Have you ever heard of a small Middle Eastern country by the name of Zebedique?"

"No," she said quietly, acutely aware that he hadn't released her hand. Could he feel her small shake, the one that hummed to a sweet vibration through her nervous system? This was not appropriate to the situation, not in the least. Hadn't her father trained her better, taught her never to get involved with a client?

She willed herself to be immune, but failed. So she tried to withdraw her hand from his, because it felt too good holding hers. But Rand didn't seem inclined to let go unless she pried it loose.

"I'd like to tell you a little about Zebedique," he said, running his thumb over hers so lightly that she wondered if she might have imagined the brush. "It's very similar to the place you described. Rich, a little excessive, and hedonistic. I own a house there. Quite a bit different from my place in New York."

"A vacation getaway?" And what was he doing in Vegas, if New York was home? His sister, she supposed. The sister she'd almost forgotten about. Rachel winced, upset with herself. This was no way to start out her new practice.

"I guess it could be. But that's not why I bought it."

"You think your sister's there?"

He nodded. "I do. And I need a woman to get us connected. A very special woman who's savvy and brave and can pose as my—well, someone who has access to areas where only women are allowed. It's very segregated, and men can't approach other men's, ah…territory."

He watched closely for a reaction, and Rachel managed not to show her apprehension. He was choosing his words very carefully, obviously not wanting to scare her off. No need, she thought, she was scaring herself enough. Suddenly she realized that she was now stroking his thumb in a way that was not at all imaginary. With a mental slap of ruler to wrist, she stopped the nonsense.

"Go on, Rand. You're paying me to listen. I'm all ears." *And sweaty palms.* She felt his fingertips brushing over them, making her nerve ends leapfrog, then collide with each other. She needed to get her hand back.

She left it in his care. Rachel told herself that he was holding her captive with his grip. The fact that she was a willing prisoner was something better ignored.

"Okay, I'll be blunt. I have a plan that can get you in, as, shall we say, a desirable acquisition. No one would buy you but me, and once I did, no one else would dare touch you. You'd be considered my personal property."

"Your...personal...property?" Rachel stared at him hard. Surely her imagination was going berserk. All this illicit hand touching must be affecting her brain, shading his words with intimate overtones he hadn't intended. "You're not telling me that women are being sold there for sexual purposes to the men who buy them?"

"Not just any men. Wealthy men from around the world. I understand virgins go for a premium, due to supply problems, and American women are especially in demand because the slavers are afraid to risk many abductions. The ones they acquire seem to be without family to trace them. A local casino is where Sarah disappeared."

For a moment she was beyond speech. Then came

a surge of sympathy for Sarah, and her heart went out
to Rand.

"How horrible for you. You must be worried
sick."

"Worrying doesn't solve anything—action does. I
need you, Rachel. Once we're there and the transac-
tion's made, I can protect you, since you'll belong to
me." Something troubled and haunting was in his
gaze, and she puzzled over it, and then she puzzled
over her desire to soothe it away. "Experience has
taught me to take care of what's mine, whatever the
opposition."

"Sarah?" she said softly.

His nod was curt. She left it alone.

"You mentioned a house in Zebedique?"

"Where we'd live—the two of us. We'd have to
give the appearance of our expected roles." He
smiled that disarming smile of his that scrambled her
mental faculties and made her wonder what hid beneath the smiling surface. "You can act, can't you,
Rachel? It wouldn't be unpleasant. The house has
quite a layout. I've got an office already set up,
there's a pool, a sauna, servants around to do the
cooking and cleaning. You'd have your very own
handmaiden. I understand she used to be a masseuse.
Just think, in your off time you could get back rubs."

He patted her hand. If it was meant to be comforting it was anything but. Back rubs and strong masculine hands provoked other images.

"But our roles—what would they entail?"

Rand reached for his door; when she followed suit,
he caught her wrist.

"For one thing, it would mean I act like the sultan
of the house while you pretend to stroke my ego. If

you're half as good at that as you are in the hand-holding department, I'll be strutting for a month.''

Rachel flushed and jerked her wrist from his grip.

''Now,'' he continued, drumming her clenched fist with his fingertips, ''just in case we can strike a deal, what say we give it a little practice? You stay put, and I'll come around to get you. Then, once we're in the restaurant, I'll order for us both, and you look like you're hanging on my every word while I bore you silly talking about my arbitrage business.''

''Do I have to laugh if you tell a bad joke?''

''I understood all good concubines do.''

''Concu—''

His door slammed shut, and Rachel stared at it, mouth agape. Concubine? Hadn't that word gone out with the Old Testament? The CD had shut off, but Rachel was left with the uneasy impression that the music and the word went together strangely well.

As well as his hand and hers, and the lingering ripple that seemed to mesh warmth with a dark, forbidden thrill.

3

RAND TOPPED OFF their champagne flutes while Rachel excused herself and went to the ladies' room. He watched the alluring combination of slender ankles, shapely legs and hourglass curves that swayed in time with her gliding stride. He liked her walk. It had an attitude.

Fact was, there was a lot he liked about her. Maybe a bit too much. He'd have to be careful, or she might slip under his skin, which was more than any of the string of women who had passed through what he supposed was a personal life had ever done.

Rand sipped his champagne, mentally toasting his good fortune. If he was going to buy a woman, Rachel was definitely the one he wanted to own. He hadn't gotten her to agree yet, but he would.

If exposing enough of himself to evoke her compassion—and playing on the surprising physical tug between them—didn't work, money should do the trick. Then again, Rachel didn't seem to be all that interested in money. For some reason, that bothered him. Maybe because it made him feel devalued, reminded him of things he'd lost along the way—emotions he couldn't afford, and qualities that didn't have price tags.

"Now, where were we?" Rachel smiled, and he felt an unfamiliar throb penetrate his senses. Before she could reseat herself, he got up and pushed in her chair. "Imagine, a bona fide gentleman—and chivalry's supposedly dead."

She laughed softly, and it was as if effervescent bubbles were seeping into his pores. Natural. Wholesome. Lush. *Whew.*

"Imagine, a woman who accepts it as chivalry and doesn't growl 'You chauvinist.'" He saluted her with his glass, and she hit him with a hearty burst of laughter before he'd recuperated from the aftereffects of her full-lipped grin. "What's so funny? I haven't even told you a bad joke yet."

"When you said 'growl,' it reminded me of a silly toast my dad used to say." She giggled and sipped at her champagne. When she looked over the rim, her eyes were sparkling. Rand was startled to feel something jolt him dead-center like a bull's-eye zap into a runaway target that had never been hit.

"Now I'm curious." *And a little shook, and I'm juggling an arousal that's got nothing and everything to do with getting you to agree to share sleeping space with me.* "You were going to tell me about your dad and how you grew up anyway, so why don't we start with his toast?"

"I couldn't possibly say it in here."

"Why not?"

"Because this place is so classy."

She glanced around, and he noticed that she seemed ill at ease. He'd also noticed the way she had emulated his choice of fork or knife during the meal. Discreetly, with a PI's ability to play a charade, but he'd deliberately used an incorrect one, and she'd followed suit.

He knew. Rachel had a sharp eye, but a lack of

savvy when it came to protocol and etiquette. He could relate to that. Years ago he'd spent many a hard-earned dollar to order salad and soup in ritzy places like this. Watching. Assimilating. Mimicking the manners of the elite, then returning to his hole-in-the-wall to wolf down a substandard pizza or hot dogs with pork and beans.

No, she didn't fit here any better than he did, and it gave him a sense of something shared. Sure was a strange feeling, but he did find it a pleasant one. Comforting, even.

"Look, Rachel, you're classier than that highbrow bitching at her husband at the next table—and I'm a paying customer. I'd say that gives us the right to say anything we damn well please." Rand lifted his glass. "C'mon, indulge me. Then you can indulge me some more and tell me about your dad."

She shrugged. "We still have a lot to discuss. You're sure this is how you want to spend your time?"

"We will. I am. And let's hear it. Sultan's decree."

"In that case, touch your glass to your nose." Rand did as instructed, though his attention was on the cute way Rachel's nose turned up and crinkled as the tiny bubbles tickled it. There was a light sprinkling of freckles across the delicate bridge that made her appear younger than the twenty-two years he'd learned she was.

"Next you have to growl." She demonstrated, and he growled along with her. It was a low animal sound that provoked thoughts of similar noises in the heat of passion. His lids dipped to half-mast, and hers opened wide.

"Uh, that's...that's very good, Rand. A little ferocious, but definitely in the spirit. Kind of."

"Maybe you should show me again," he suggested, pulling his chair next to hers. Leaning in close, he inhaled her unique scent, a scent that was unencumbered by perfume. Money smelled good, but Rachel made money smell like dirt. "Growl for me. Soft, but deep in your throat."

Something that sounded like a faint squeak emerged.

"You can do better than that, Rachel. Once more, but with feeling. C'mon, I'll even do it with you."

He made a noise like an animal's mating call as it began to rut. She hesitated, then joined him, and this time he heard a sweet undulation shift into a kittenish purr.

"Purr-fect," he whispered. "What's that old saying, something about the cat's meow?"

She quickly reached for her champagne. Rand intercepted her and put the glass to her lips, raising it slightly so that a trickle escaped the side of her mouth. And what a mouth, he thought with a sensual pang. Made for kissing and kissing back until those lips were even fuller than they already were.

He felt his body shift, felt his tongue dancing against his teeth. Dying to lap up that stray drop, he bit down before he could act on the impulse. Quickly salvaging the napkin she was twisting in her lap, he dabbed the liquid away.

"Rand," she said in a strangled voice. "Rand, those people are watching us."

"Oh? Then let's do the toast, since we've hooked an audience. Maybe it'll give them something to talk about besides what they were arguing over."

"But it's for a noisy bar, or a party with friends."

"Then let's be friends and have our own private party." Friends. He'd like that with her, he realized. And then he found himself exposing his truer colors. Even as his mouth formed the words, he could scarcely believe he was lowering the guard that was his constant companion.

"Pretentiousness doesn't score many points with me," he heard himself say. "And, believe it or not, I'm more at home in a corner bar than hobnobbing with the likes of our fellow diners. I like you, Rachel. Just the way you are."

"Rocky," she said, almost to herself. He quirked a brow in question, and she claimed her glass. "Okay, here goes. Look out, mouth." His gaze settled on her lips. She wet them, and he managed not to try for a taste of her little pink tongue. "Look out, gums. Open up, throat—here it comes!"

Rand nearly choked on a growl, while a belly-deep laugh tickled his grinding lust. Oh, it did feel good to laugh. If Rachel only knew... It was like a gift tied with a bow of joy.

"Lady, you are dynamite."

"I am?" Rachel couldn't believe what she was hearing. "Open up, throat—here it comes!" wasn't exactly crème de la crème.

Whatever standards he judged people by, they sure weren't the norm. Then again, Rand was anything but the norm himself. They were a pair in some way she couldn't finger. Him, with his brutish but suave exterior; her, with her bungling attempts at sophistication, which only magnified how out of sync she was in this uptight, budget-straining joint.

As far as she was concerned, her Caesar salad was

wilted lettuce, this pâté de foie gras stuff was nothing but fancy chopped liver, and the beef whatever-you-called-it—bourguignon?—reminded her of Dinty Moore, with some Carlo Rossi stirred in for good measure.

"I think maybe you mean Rice Crispies, Rand. I'm closer to snap-crackle-pop than dynamite."

"Says who? You? Or some significant other I'd like to know about if there's one hanging around."

Rachel hesitated as his eyes narrowed on her. Rand Slick wasn't someone to toy or flirt with. If she was smart, she'd nip this in the bud, tell him she was heavily involved with someone who didn't exist. That was what she'd do—lie. Lie, and get this meeting back on track. Forget his dark charm, ignore the delicious push-pull between them, and settle for safety.

"No significant other." Rachel closed her eyes, angry with herself. She'd lied right nice, just to the wrong person. If the road to hell was paved with good intentions, she ought to be frying any minute.

"In that case, you are definitely dynamite. A lit stick that's giving me a charge I haven't had in...well, maybe never." A waiter appeared and took his plastic. "Now tell me how you turned out this way. I get the impression that dad of yours taught you more than a toast and how to frisk a hood making a statement."

Rachel laughed self-consciously, reminded of their hands-on intro. Those muscles of his were...better left unremembered.

"He raised me. My mother died before I was old enough to remember much about her."

"And did your mother have beautiful red hair?"

"She had red hair." Rachel smiled, greatly pleased

by his compliment. She touched her hair, then stroked her fingers through it before she realized what she was doing. Preening! She was preening for him, and wishing he was doing the touching instead of her. She jerked her hand away. Rand looked as if he longed to pick up where she'd left off.

"Anyway, Daddy did the best he knew how bringing me up. He signed me up for a softball team when I was six, and taught me to throw a punch when the boys said I pitched like a girl."

"Did he teach you to throw the ball, too?"

"You bet. Especially when I almost got kicked off the team for bloodying the biggest bully's nose."

He laughed, and she enjoyed the deep sound; it was a far different kind of pleasure from the illicit one she'd felt upon hearing his sexy growl. She liked to make him laugh. Maybe because she was pretty sure the faint lines fanning his eyes weren't caused by laughter.

"Was he protective when you started dating?"

"I'll say. He told me boys had one thing on their minds, and he should know, since he was one of them. He had this test for judging them. Handshakes. Said you could tell a lot about a man by the way he shook hands. A limp handshake? Wimp. A firm handshake meant guts."

As he chuckled, Rand stretched. Her gaze slid to his chest. When he didn't have his suit coat on, she could discern the width and proportions of his musculature. Again she was reminded of a street tough with a smooth veneer. Rocky. Slamming his punches into a side of beef instead of a punching bag. The underdog coming out on top, compensating for life's shortcomings with grit and character. She hadn't tested his handshake, but she was certain he had guts, and then some.

"I can understand his wanting to be protective. It's something I've felt in the past. The distant past." His expression let her know that he hadn't missed where she'd been looking and he rather liked catching her at it. "So. Besides playing ball, throwing punches, and screening your dates' handshakes, what else did you pick up from your dad?"

"Target shooting. Hanging around his office, learning the business. Sitting in on poker games with him and the boys while they drank beer and swapped jokes. If you were expecting fancy dresses and cheerleading practice, I don't qualify. Disappointed?"

Rand tapped a finger to his lips. She wished he'd quit doing that. It kept drawing too much attention to his mouth. In fact, everything he'd said and done had drawn too much attention to him as a man and to her as a woman, and too little to the real reason they were here. It should bother her; it bothered her that it didn't.

"Disappointed? Hardly. Intrigued? Very. But I can imagine it must have been hard growing up like that. Setting you apart from other kids your age." He hesitated, but then she felt his hand cover hers. "I know what that's like."

A small silence fell between them, one that was easy and yet not easy at all. She felt a sense that they were sharing a common bond, but she could feel him pulling back, as though he'd confessed more than he'd wanted to and was struggling to understand why.

The waiter broke into their tentative liaison before she could explore the lure of the unknown. How much of this man's exterior masked a self-protective nature, a nature born of a past that marked him as different from others? The question tugged at her, even as the marvelous sensation lingered that Rand found her intriguing.

As they walked to the car, he kept his hand at the small of her back. The light touch sparked a tingle at the base of her spine that shot out in all different directions. It felt like the lightest of kisses, traced by the tip of his tongue, and oh, Lord, why was she thinking such a thing?

Some PI she was. Her conduct in the restaurant had been anything but professional, and her thoughts had been even less. She felt miserable about it. Miserable and fantastic, what with this glow that packed the punch of ten hot toddies in a single gulp. It simmered, then expanded, as his hand shifted to settle at her waist. Then she felt a slight squeeze that was pure *mmm.... Magic. Madness.*

Distance. She had to get some distance, and quick. If she hit that nerve of his, maybe he'd keep his distance, since she couldn't seem to.

"You didn't tell me about how you grew up. Or how you came to lose your sister."

For a fleeting moment, something poignant, tortured, softened his features. But then he erased it, and his expression was as blank as a washed-down chalkboard. Rocky was transformed into a renovated high rise, all the cracks and damage disguised by plaster patches, fresh coats of paint and tightly sealed windows. One-way windows. The kind designed to let somebody look out but deflect the view of anyone trying to look in.

Funny thing about windows, she thought. They had

a way of getting broken or left open. Glass was fragile, and accidents did happen.

"I lost Sarah to fate, Rachel. As for growing up, my home was on the streets. Alone."

"And?"

"And arbitrage is a risky business, with big returns if you've got a knack for juggling two things at the same time. I buy and sell securities simultaneously when I detect a discrepancy in the going price. The way I operate is by getting rid of what I buy almost before I acquire it. In rare cases, I hang on to something for myself. If you're good, and I am, big profits are reaped. If you screw up, and that's easy to do, it's immediate death."

She frowned, disappointed with him for being so reticent, and for giving her the distance she needed. But most of all she was upset with herself for telling him so much and so freely, and for wanting more than she could possibly have.

"You think I told you nothing, don't you?"

"You explained your line of business but left out much of personal importance."

"Wrong. Read between the lines, Rachel. After all, you're a PI. You should be good at this." He waved her into the car, and she got in. Rand leaned in close, bay and night spice evoking images of exotic music. "While I drive, you can think me over. Who knows? Maybe you'll figure me out, which is more than anyone else has ever pulled off."

"I don't guess you're feeling generous enough to spare a hint or two?"

His lips thinned, and then slowly shifted to a sly smile. "Think of me as a Rubik's Cube. But even if you solve it, the colors won't quite line up, because a few slots are missing. Oh, and the hinges are stubborn, too. Comes from some jagged edges on the inside that've been there too long to budge from their old groove.''

As he drove, Rachel stole glances at his profile while she puzzled her way through the maze. Missing: Sarah. But what else? And what caused the jagged edges that he seemed to find more comfortable than exposing even a small bit of himself?

The music hovered between them again, slipping into the crevices of her mind and playing tricks with reality. She could see him dressed in a sheikh's flowing white robe, autonomous and mysterious, until he shed it and revealed all his missing pieces, rough edges, and multicolored hues to a special woman. She saw the woman in a long, flowing dress of white gauze, her arms open wide and trembling as he slipped away her veil.

Rachel couldn't see her face. Yet she couldn't deny that, more than anything, she wanted the woman to be her.

4

RAND STRETCHED, then leaned back into the cushions of Rachel's old couch, feeling an odd delight in simply being close to her after the way their first meeting had been cut short. He'd had to rush back to New York after their lunch to straighten out a potential mess in a high-stakes acquisition.

Two things had struck him in their three-day separation: For once he resented the intrusion of his work, finding the manic pace annoying rather than exhilarating. Moreover, he'd caught himself calling her on several occasions with tidbits of information that could easily have waited.

Truth was, he liked the sound of her voice, the kittenish freshness of it. But, most of all, that breathless little catch that made him think they were sharing this peculiar sensation of light-headedness—as if the earth had changed the rules of gravity, causing his jaded senses to be buoyed up on the air while his feet moonwalked New York concrete that had about as much substance as a marshmallow.

Staring at her bent head while she studied Sarah's file, Rand marveled at this internal out-of-syncness. He'd all but run to her front door, anxious and yet certain he was imagining the whole crazy thing. And then he hadn't been certain of anything, not even his name, because she'd knocked the supports out from under him with a single dazzling smile.

Whump! He'd felt the ground tilt as a soft, tingling blow clobbered him right between the eyes. He didn't know what the hell it was. Not lust; it went beyond that. And surely not love. He'd never been in it, never expected to be, and he most certainly didn't believe in love at first sight.

Rachel's brow was furrowed when she suddenly looked up.

"You're staring at me."

"Caught me. Want me to stop?"

"No—I mean, yes. You make it hard to concentrate."

"Do I? Sorry," he lied. Then he managed a half truth. "I'm trying to judge your reaction to what you're reading." He leaned over and tapped a well-thumbed page. "I see you've gotten to the meat of the matter."

"The investigator you hired did a good job. Several slavers operating under a single umbrella and shipping to one port. Zebedique." She tossed several photographs from the file onto the coffee table. "I thought you said you didn't have any other pictures of Sarah. I do assume this is her—or at least what I can see of her, covered from head to foot in the local costume."

"That's her. The men I hired to keep Sarah under surveillance managed to snap those before her guards joined her. As to why I didn't show you these before—two reasons. First, there's not much to see. Just a pair of eyes peeking out, and the rest of her face under a scarf. Second—"

"You thought it might scare me off if I got a gander at these too soon."

"Bingo. You do have to admit our first meeting was enough of a shocker as it was." Fearful of the effect the Polaroid images could still have on her decision, he tried to get a fix on their impact. "I felt the nature of these photos was more graphic than if she'd been wearing nothing. Maybe you can understand why I held out on you."

"I do, and it was probably a smart move on your part. Even knowing what I know now, I can hardly believe what I'm looking at. It's another world, and not one I'd ever care to be in. Imagine, living without the freedom to walk alone or even choose how you want to dress." Rachel studied the pictures a moment longer before replacing them in the file. She shook her head and said bluntly, "This is a very nasty business. It needs to be exposed, Rand."

"As soon as I've got Sarah. Any tip-off before then would implicate a casino manager who's rolling in dirty payoff dough. If I finger him now, and he squeals on his crooked buddies, any chance Sarah's got is snuffed."

"But this has been going on too long. Sarah disappeared months ago, and Lord only knows how many women were abducted before her. Surely there's another way besides the one we've discussed."

"Don't you think I've considered every other angle? I've kept round-the-clock surveillance in Zebedique since I traced her there. They've located the house—"

"Conveniently close to the one you bought when you went to check the country out yourself?"

"Of course. Unfortunately she's too heavily guarded to make a successful snatch. Unless you can come up with a better idea, I see no other way but to make the connection at the bathhouse she's taken to every Friday."

"Women only, right?"

"That's right. Massages, whirlpools, saunas. I understand from one of the servants I hired—the masseuse who would be your guard—that the concubines are left unattended in the sauna."

"They're not afraid their prisoners might escape?"

"Hardly. Not when they're naked and have to be covered from head to toe just to walk down the street."

Rachel tapped the pen she'd been using to take notes, and he stared at her hand, struck again by the delicate structure of tapered fingers he would love to feel sifting through his hair, flexing against his neck, reaching for his—

She abruptly stopped the tapping. And then he remembered his unbecoming little speech that first day. Abrasive. Typical of the man he'd become, who didn't quite seem to be the same man, the man within the skin that felt this inexplicable need for her touch.

"This handmaid, or guard…" she said.

"Jayna."

"How do you know she was telling you the truth? That she wasn't suspicious and might be setting you up?"

"Because she's under the impression I'm going to take up residence with a concubine of my own and I want to be sure said concubine would have no chance of escape. She's retired from the bathhouse, and I'm paying her well. Jayna has no need to be suspicious,

and every reason to want to keep a generous paycheck.''

''You've been thorough.''

''So have you.'' He smiled when she arched an
expressive brow in surprise. ''You checked up on me
while I was gone. Were you satisfied with what you
discovered?''

''I was impressed,'' she admitted. ''You're very
high profile. Respected. Successful to the point of embarrassment. But even the business magazines say
you're as much a mystery man as a boy wonder. No
one knows where you came from. There doesn't seem
to be a trace of your whereabouts until you hit the
arbitrage business eight years ago. You've been el-
bowing and plowing your way to the top ever since.''

''Surely you don't believe everything you read.''

''No. But apparently you found out I made a few
calls. I was left with the impression that you're not
necessarily liked by your competition, but you are
feared. Even by other cutthroats in the business. Mr.
Slick, you have a reputation for playing dirty pool.''

He usually regarded such a comment as a compliment of sorts. But when it came from her he felt a
sudden need to defend himself.

''I play to win, Rachel. It's the only way I know
to survive. And before you swallow someone else's
sour grapes, keep in mind we're all products of our
circumstances.''

''Meaning?''

''It's true I'm less merciful than most, but maybe
it's because I have reason to be hungrier than they
ever thought about being.'' He could see her weighing that, turning it this way and that and coming up
with something that might have been sympathy.

Sympathy for Sarah's case—that he wanted. Any other kind he wanted no part of.

"Sliding that around the Rubik's Cube? Careful of the jagged edges, Rachel," he warned. "My competition is, and they're ten times tougher than you."

He instinctively kept his expression challenging. And guarded. But the hardness he usually felt knotted in the pit of his makeup was struggling against an alien force. Something vulnerable. Something that was nudging his defenses with a persistent whisper that escalated into a cry for understanding. Acceptance. A distant but gripping need for a gentle and all-encompassing embrace.

Their eyes were locked in a revealing gaze. His were doubtless saying more than he could ever bring himself to admit, and the exposure, even unspoken, was tearing at years of protective masking he was urgently trying to slap back in place. Her returning gaze, asking for access to those hidden areas he hadn't even allowed himself to breach for so many years, was so soft that it began to hurt to look at her.

Rand glanced away.

She touched his hand. He commanded himself not to grasp it and bring her into his arms. Arms that felt so open and empty that he clamped them against his ribs to keep from filling the void.

"I hope you're not upset that I ran a check on you."

"Of course not," he said, more curtly than he'd intended. Steeling himself, he chanced another meeting of eyes, and found the gentlest shade of green. They could have been pastures of soft, dew-kissed grass, beckoning him to rest after years of ceaseless running.

"I wasn't trying to pry," she explained.

"I know. In fact, I would have been disappointed if you hadn't taken the precaution. You just proved you're careful and professional. Exactly the kind of person I need."

The person I need...I need...I need... Rand drew a deep and none-too-steady breath as his words came back to him with unsettling overtones that left him stranded between the need to yank her out of the chair and onto his lap and the urge to run for the front door and get the hell out while the getting was still good.

"I need to finish reading this file before we discuss whether or not I'm a willing candidate." She began to read, then muttered, "I can finish this sooner if you quit staring."

Rand managed to focus on her apartment, which wasn't easy since she held his attention as captive as he needed to hold her in Zebedique to free his sister.

And perhaps someone else. A boy buried so deep he'd been all but forgotten, but who seemed bent on putting in a belated appearance.

Was it the feel of easy comfort here that whispered to Joshua? His eyes settled on a nearby bookcase. How many women kept a can of Mace next to an old doll?

Shaking off the threat of memories, Rand glanced at his watch. It was getting late, and Rachel was turning the last page of the file. He anxiously scanned her face.

"So what do you think?"

"I think the findings seem accurate, and the plan you outlined for hooking the slaver—with me as the bait—would probably work."

"Then you'll do it?" He gripped the arms of the

chair where she sat—next to the couch that he wanted to pull her onto so that he could roll her beneath him. Chemistry wasn't new to him, but when had he wanted to hold a woman just to have her hold him back, give him some companionship so that he didn't have to keep going through this treacherous search alone?

"What you're asking me to do is infiltrate a highly dangerous society of pleasure seekers."

"I am." He took the file and tossed it on the coffee table. Grasping her hands, he forgot about his pride long enough to expose his desperation.

"I need you, Rachel. Five women investigators have already turned me down. With each 'no' I get, more time passes. Precious time, Rachel. I'm working against the clock. The slavers could move their operation any day, and then where would I be? Square one, scrambling to find their whereabouts, which could be fifty miles away—or fifty thousand."

"And meanwhile your sister remains prisoner."

"That's right. I've already invested more time than I can afford, working out of motels, burning up the phone lines, catching red-eye flights to New York to keep my business together. I can't do this indefinitely."

"But once you make it to Zebedique, how will you cope?"

"Hopefully we can move quickly. If it takes a while, I'm prepared. An office is already set up in the house. No need to fly out until the job's done." His jaw tensed. "I won't leave there without her."

"How much time have you spent looking for someone who'll agree?"

"Too long. That's why I need a quick decision

from you.'' He leaned in toward her, signaling his urgency. ''There aren't many women who can fit the bill for this job, and no one could be as perfect for it as you. I need you. Desperately. After everything you've read and heard about me, surely you realize those are words I don't use lightly.''

Rachel was experiencing a meltdown that turned her objectivity inside out. She felt for Rand, and for the sister she had caught glimpses of in the file. Black type had heartlessly translated Sarah into a statistic. But to Rand she was flesh and blood.

She felt Rand's warm human flesh pressing against hers, and the blood that flowed through his veins seemed to course into her own. Could she do it? Did she dare try to crack the slavery ring when simply holding his gaze made it impossible to think?

Just the facts, ma'am, she ordered herself. She was working hard to establish her reputation, one that wouldn't depend on her dad's and would transcend the liability of her age. Rand was in a position to help her get a leg up.

He was also capable of compromising her ethics. *No emotional involvement allowed.* As in a picture of a heart with a diagonal slash through it. Only her heart seemed heedless of the slash.

It pounded rebelliously as she looked at him now, the strong, enigmatic male, the caring, desperate brother. She tried to force away any outward softness while it was there, shifting, catching her up inside. If their first meeting had left her breathless, the dizzying momentum that continued to gather was enough to send her scrambling for escape from this emotional vacuum that was sucking her in. She couldn't see any exit except his arms. The very arms she needed to escape.

If only she could forget the case and search that dark place behind his eyes, a place that must have its roots in a faded black-and-white photo. If only...

Drawing on reserves of professional strength that denied the woman inside her who was reaching out for him, she confronted the stark, brutal facts that she could not ignore.

"You want me to work the casino, look lonely and lost. Hook up with the slaver, let him buy me a drink at the bar, lead him to think I've got no family and I'm sexually innocent. And I'd have to do this without even a gun for protection."

"The gun would raise suspicion, since they'd go through your things after getting you alone. But I'll watch from a distance. And we'll bring in another PI to tail you. If you've got a colleague you prefer to work with, we'll go with your recommendation, no question."

"Jack. Jack O'Malley. He was my father's best friend, and he sponsored me for the five years of training I had to put in before I could take the state exam. Jack's better than good, he's great. But no matter how savvy a PI is, there's no guarantee things will go according to plan. Even Jack might not be able to get close enough to switch drinks with me." Rachel exhaled a shuddering sigh. "I don't relish the thought of downing a designer drug, if it comes to that."

"And it could. Much as I hate to spell it out, you deserve the unvarnished truth. What it comes down to is that there's a good chance you *will* be drugged. If you are, they'll do whatever it is they do in transit, and getting through that just might be easier if you're flying high. If you manage to stay sober, you'll have to give the act of your life.''

''For how long?''

''The auctions take place every Saturday, so it depends on when the nab is made. Chances are you'll have at least several days of sheer hell when you'll have nothing to depend on but your wits. All I can promise is that once I get you off the auction block, we'll be in this together. Even when we're staging a performance for Jayna, or anyone else who might be listening at the bedchamber door.''

Rachel paused to consider the implications of that. Rand, enacting his role as her owner, master of her body. The body that, at the moment, was eager to get the show on the road.

Stop it, she ordered herself. Any hormonal urges or forbidden thrills she felt had no place at this moment, had nothing to do with his dire straits or her ability to make a rational decision.

''You're sure you're not being set up yourself? What if it's a fake invitation and you get hauled away to a foreign prison? What if I'm stranded and go to the highest bidder? I could end up just like Sarah, with no one there to get either of us out, since you refuse to go to the police.''

''It won't happen. My connections are paying back a debt that comes to a staggering sum. My seat's reserved, and I'll be watching you closely. Don't worry, I've made sure the invitation's legit.''

''I do worry. These go-betweens don't sound too ethical. What if they double-cross you?''

''Do you actually think I'd drag you into this without having some assurance myself? We're talking heavy leverage.''

"How heavy?"

"Let's just say that an unnamed third party has a sealed envelope with names, places and lots of incriminating evidence on its way to *The New York Times* if there's so much as a single screwup. My associates have plenty of incentive to make sure this goes off without a hitch."

This was definitely not a man to cross, Rachel decided. As tempted as she was to explore some things she was probably better off not knowing, a sense of self-preservation demanded she put up a final defense.

"It's dangerous."

"I'll protect you. That's one promise I won't break."

"You said I'd be stripped. Put on an auction block." *Stripped. Auctioned off.* Could she actually endure such a violation of her modesty, being bartered like a slab of human meat, while Rand sat in the audience with a clear view of her body? She shivered, imagining the ordeal.

"It's the only way. I'd never ask such a thing of anyone, and especially not a woman as special as you, but I have no choice." His grip tightened. "You can name your price. I'm willing to pay whatever you ask."

For some reason that hurt. He was reducing this to money. Then she hurt a little more, remembering the cash he'd laid on her desk to induce her to hear him out. Money talked; she'd listened to the seductive jingle of his coin.

"And what happens, Rand, if I say no deal?"

"Then I pay you some hush money and you promise not to leak a word about what you've learned here.

I'll walk out, and we won't see each other again—at least not under these circumstances.''

Money again. As much as she needed it, the thought of it had never been so distasteful. Just as the thought of never seeing Rand again left an empty ache in the region of her chest. Somehow, the idea of saying goodbye disturbed her more deeply than the idea of being stripped.

"But what would you do, where would you take this?"

He shrugged, a determined look spanning his face and radiating into the tenseness of his posture.

"I'd keep hunting until I found someone who would agree. I'm sure they wouldn't be half as intriguing or entertaining, or come close to being as tempting to look at as you. But I have a sister to find, and those are optional qualities that didn't enter the picture until now."

His laugh was short, humorless. "You know, Rachel, the too little time we've spent together, the conversations we've had when I called on any trumped-up excuse just to hear your voice…they've done something for me that money can't buy. I've actually found myself feeling something so good that work and Sarah weren't the only things on my mind. Even if you don't take the case, I'd like to thank you for that."

What those words did to her. Words that assured her that these topsy-turvy feelings that she couldn't acknowledge were alive and well in Rand's dark and vibrant persona, too. A persona that would have no choice but to go to another woman if she refused. One who would share his house. One who would take his case—and likely for the money she herself disdained.

None of these were reasons to agree, and yet she couldn't deny they were playing a crucial role in her decision.

"The ink's still wet on my license, Rand."

"Doesn't matter. You're good, Rachel. In fact, you're better than good. You'll be successful no matter what, but this case just might get you there a lot quicker. I have a certain amount of clout that I won't hesitate to throw in your direction if you say yes."

Rachel weighed the future ordeal, trying not to listen to the voice chanting in her head, *Say yes.* If she did, she could reunite a sister and brother and right a terrible wrong while she took a giant leap forward in her chosen profession.

Though, at the moment, her profession didn't seem nearly as important as the man waiting on edge for her answer.

Once she shook on it, there was no turning back.

She extended her hand.

"Put 'er there, partner."

5

"YES!" RAND shouted a victory whoop. His hand closed over hers. "Quite a handshake you've got, lady. Shows guts."

"I like yours, too." She returned his beaming smile, feeling buoyant inside.

"Wonder what your daddy would think?"

She glimpsed another window. No daddy for Rand Slick. But he was human, and he wanted approval as much as the next man.

"He'd think you were no mark. He'd like you, but he wouldn't trust you. At least not with me."

"I can understand that. Sometimes I don't trust myself."

"Why not?"

Rand shrugged. "Guess it goes back to certain promises I didn't make good on. Mistakes I've made along the way."

"We all make those."

"True, but some are more irreversible than others."

She wanted to probe, but his eyes told her this was private territory not to be investigated just yet. Best to stick with a more immediate concern. One her feminine instincts hearkened to while her business ethics demanded she avoid this part of the deal.

"About our roles, Rand. Think you could enlighten me a little more on just what they might involve?"

"Better than that, what say we give it some practice? Pretend I've just taken you into the master's chambers." He pulled her from the chair and onto his lap. Before she could stop herself, a small gasp caught in her throat, followed by a tiny purr. "This is the scenario—the servants are listening at the door, wondering how I'm going to stake my rightful claim. Do I seduce you with tender words that they don't expect to hear any more than I'm used to saying them?"

Wondering if this was truly a game, and too aware that she didn't want it to be, Rachel forced herself to back away from exactly what she wanted to explore.

"I'm not sure if this is such a good idea, Rand. Maybe we should forget this and ad-lib when the time comes."

"No. Rehearsal is part and parcel, Rachel." Her behind was anchored against his groin. He was... Sweet heaven, he was thick against her, large. *Aroused.* She felt an immediate, answering response that tensed her belly and tingled the tip of her womb, then reached up and increased the weight of her breasts. "God, you feel good in my arms. Where have you been all this time? And how can we have just met and fit together like this?"

"We can't do this." She said the words even as she felt herself settle deeper against him and realized she'd draped her arms around his neck. Her head rested against his shoulder, and she inhaled the marvelous scent of him. The light growth of whiskers at his jaw grazed her cheek. He was nuzzling against her, or maybe she was doing the nuzzling. "Please,

Rand," she said unevenly. "We have to stop this. Now."

"That would be an appropriate response. To which I would reply, 'We haven't even started.'" He locked his hands at her hips. "Then I'd add, 'How can you say we have to stop when I can feel you pressing deeper, deeper, and wanting the same thing as me?'"

A cry of need all but strangled her as she struggled to silence the instinctive sound.

"You want me to help you get your sister back, don't you?" She forced her mouth from his neck, his warm, strong neck, where she could feel the steady, reassuring beat of his pulse. "You have to understand, a private investigator can't get emotionally involved with a client. It can muddy their judgment, even leave them open to make mistakes."

"Is that a certainty? Be honest with me."

"It's a possibility."

"Anything's possible. Give me a concrete reason."

"Professional protocol."

"Protocol isn't something I bow to, and mistakes are possible no matter what the climate. Give me something, anything, to make me believe my holding you is going to jeopardize my sister. Facts. Examples. C'mon, Rachel. Remember, we're in Zebedique, and you'd better have some solid reasons to keep me on the other side of the bedroom door."

Was he testing her mental reflexes, just as he'd tested her at their first meeting? She didn't know, she didn't know anything, except that she wanted to forget possibilities and protocol and the missing sister so that she could embrace the brother, who had more facets than a crystal, more forbidden allure than she could possibly deflect.

"You're a client," she told him in a strangled voice. "A client. You're nothing more than a case to be solved and filed away once we're through."

"That's it? If that's the best you can do, then I must insist that you don't let the servants hear you say I'm nothing more than your client and you can't get involved for a mere technicality. Your flimsy protest would jeopardize our plan a lot quicker than any amount of involvement you might have to fake." He searched her eyes. "Or not fake?"

With one incisive look, with the sweet bite of his fingertips tightening at her hip, she felt more naked than she possibly could on the auction block. In self-protection, she denied the truth by emphatically shaking her head.

"You would still refuse me, the master to whom you belong? Then I would have no choice but to persuade you with logic." He traced her lips with a fingertip, then veered off to her throat. His smile was intimate as he monitored the rapidity of her pulse.

"This isn't logical, Rand," she said urgently. "This is not a businesslike position for us to be in."

"But it is business, and exactly the sort of position we will be in. And given that it's business, humor me so we won't have to completely wing it."

"Okay." She drew in a deep breath, needing some oxygen to clear her head. The oxygen didn't help. Reality and fantasy blurred together while she struggled to hang on to a fact she knew to be real. "I just told you, I won't have you, no matter what you say or do. It's impossible under these circumstances, and no amount of logic can sway me."

"That's good. Challenge me." He traced a pattern on her knee. She thought it was the shape of a heart, but he rubbed it away with the pressure of his palm before she could be sure. "What do you suggest I should say in a crucial moment like this?"

She shut her eyes while the world tilted to a skewed angle. "I think you should tell me that you like your women seasoned and sure, and that you're way out of my league."

"Am I now? You mean you can wave a pistol and likely hit your mark, bluff your way through a game of penny-ante poker and win with a pair of deuces. But you're off your turf when I'm hard and you're all but melting against me while we're both thinking of a dozen different ways we'd like to be kissing...and more. Oh, yeah, a whole lot more..."

He touched his forehead to hers. She could hear the mingling of their breath; they were sharing the air, and sharing the illusion he was weaving with consummate skill.

"Now it's your turn," he murmured. "Do you fight me? Do you succumb? Or do you simply fight yourself, because you want to believe this is only business, and business can keep you safe from the man who owns you and shares your desires—even perhaps, your bed?"

She'd been kissed. She'd been fondled. But she'd never encountered anything like this. Whether his words were sincere or not, he was right. She was off her turf.

She was also scared crazy, because she wanted to believe they could kiss a dozen different ways, and more. Lord, so much more. But to do that would dictate that she remain as emotionally removed as she'd have to in a relationship with a man who could hurt her with his distance if she let him get too close.

Then she remembered their earlier conversations: She always told him too much, while he returned little more than hints, dark looks that reached for her, only to retreat behind a shuttered window. *That* was the root of her resistance. His sister, yes—and that should be what had her drawing the line.

But it wasn't. When she finally gave her heart to a man, Rachel knew, she wouldn't be able to hold anything back. She needed a man who could return his heart just as freely.

Rand didn't seem to be that kind of man.

"Rachel? What do you say?"

"I would say that I'm not easy. And that succumbing to you, for any reason, is not going to happen. At least not until this case is over and Rand Slick's a mystery to everyone but me." A Rubik's Cube. How apt his self-description.

"But unraveling mysteries is your job. And while you're doing that, I'd have to give every appearance of trying to sway your judgment." He tugged at her hair and wrapped a strand around his finger, only to tease it to her lips, using the silky texture to arouse her. He did it amazingly well. Her breasts, pressing intimately into his chest, throbbed almost painfully, while her lips ached with wanting. "If tender words or logic didn't work, I would have no choice but to pretend force."

He tangled a hand in her hair and tugged until her neck was arched. It was a maneuver she'd never encountered, though his adeptness was that of a man very much in his element. His mouth grazed over her throat, and he whispered words that were rough, demanding.

"Fight me, Rachel. Just remember that whatever

you've uncovered on me doesn't even scratch the surface. So if you really want to escape, you'd better fight me tooth and nail.''

She pushed at his chest, while an unstaged cry of desire caused her to grip his shirt and begin to pull him closer, rather than thrust him away.

"Let me go. Get your hand out of my hair, quit rubbing against me, and leave me alone.''

"Not convincing enough. You don't say it like you mean it, and therefore I'm not buying.'' He jerked his hips forward and tightened his hold. "You're no match for my strength anyway, so fight me by telling me the real reason you can't be doing this. Don't use Sarah as an excuse, because you've told me involvement is a potential risk, not an absolute. Get me where it counts. Up front and personal.''

"It's you, Rand.'' Honesty, she decided, was her only means of escape. And if she didn't escape soon, she wouldn't have a chance. This time she pushed him away, with more strength than she thought she possessed.

"What about me? Specifics.''

"All *right*.'' She groaned, while her woman's needs screamed for more, more, more. "I can't afford to tangle with a man who lives on the edge and gets his kicks from outwitting the devil. A man who's probably had a lot of triple-X-rated nights but slips out before the sun comes up. Long on technique. Short on stayability. I'm sorry, Rand. As much as I wish otherwise, that's not the kind of résumé I'm in the market for. You're one puzzle I'd be better off not trying to solve. Jagged edges have a way of drawing blood.''

He released her hair and turned so that she couldn't

see his face. The silence was taut, distorting the seconds that passed into an immeasurable length of time.

"Let me tell you something, Rachel. You did a damn good job of reading between the lines, but maybe, just maybe, there comes a point in a man's life when he wonders if it's time to revise his résumé." He paused, seemingly caught by what he'd just said—and not quite able to believe he'd said it. "Guess that's an item I'll have to put on hold. After all, we're just playing. Aren't we?"

"I don't know," she admitted, then realized how ingenuous she must sound to him. "Yes, of course we are."

"Of course. But this game's left me with a very real problem. I've only got so much discipline, and at the moment it's too thin for my own comfort. Comfort, actually, is the last thing I'm feeling in our current position." He shifted, and a pained expression twisted his lips.

"You're right. This is uncomfortable. I'd better move."

"No, wait." He tightened his hold, but it was the softening of his tone that kept her in his arms. "You did give me some comfort tonight. A kind I didn't expect. It's something I'm not quite sure how to deal with." He seemed not to have finished. The clock tick-tick-ticked in the background, stretching out the elastic silence. When he spoke again, he rushed his words, as if to get them out before he could take them back. "I don't know how to deal with it, but I'd like to try."

"Deal with what—comfort?"

"Accepting it, that's what."

"I don't understand."

"Don't you? Tell me why you agreed, and don't play any games. Your answer's important."

Tell him, when she couldn't accept the reasons herself, couldn't even completely understand them? Reasons that reduced her to a refrain from *The Wizard of Oz: I'm melting, melting, melting... Ahhh...* It was the same tortured sound, the same sense of being thrust into a fantasy world that dazzled her even as she chanted, *There's no place like home...*

How could she tell him this, when her control was too precarious? If Rand had been dangerous before, he was lethal now. Holding her close, stroking her hair, letting her see inside just enough to touch the softness beneath the razor edges that could indeed draw blood.

Go ahead, Rachel, tell him, came the inner taunt. *You know it's about as safe as handing an arsonist a Bic. You're about to go up in flames as it is, with his mouth flirting with your neck. Don't you want to feel his teeth take a bite or two, before you find out how good his tongue feels slipping around yours? He's bound to be good at it. Maybe he'd even stick around long enough to teach you a few tricks to remember him by. Go to bed with him and get some more practice for the case. You can handle it. Right?*

Oh, God, so wrong. Her every instinct rebelled, but desperation demanded that she pull some of her own shutters closed before she could commit a very foolish and irrevocable act.

"Why did I agree? You promised to pay me well." How brittle her voice sounded in her ears. And as abrupt as his mouth jerked away from her neck. "My career's just getting started, and this is the chance of a lifetime to make my mark."

6

"No." Rand's fingers tightened, and his eyes narrowed to mere slits. He looked as if he wanted to shake her, and kiss her senseless, too. "You care. You're a good actress, Rachel, but not good enough to fool a master of the game. Whether you'll admit it or not, you do care."

He got up so fast she nearly tumbled to the floor. Then he grabbed his coat and slung it over his shoulder.

"I'll be leaving now. We can discuss details tomorrow. Call me at the motel if you need a ride."

Rachel smoothed her skirt with shaking hands, feeling too ashamed of what she'd done, and too unnerved by his sudden brusque demeanor, to look at him.

"That's okay. My car should be ready in the morning. What say we meet at 10:00 a.m., in my office?"

"Fine." He was leaning against the door, his chest filling her vision, when the smooth tip of his finger insistently lifted her chin.

Rachel stared into a face that was both filled with and devoid of emotion, a perplexing face that had upended her safe world in a matter of days. If this was what he could do in so little time, where would he leave her in a month, or maybe three? She shuddered to think.

"If it's a matter of money, Rachel, be warned—I always get the most out of my investments." He leaned in, his mouth hovering perilously close to hers. "Judging from your convincing performance, I'm certain that, whatever the price, you're going to be worth double."

She was still staring at his mouth, thinking of the threat it posed, when threat became reality—and from an unseen source. She felt the hard length of his leg slide smoothly between hers, felt the shock of her immediate moistening. She tried to protest, but no words would come, only a moan escaping her lips.

Into the wedge he lifted, shifting to a sure, steady rhythm. Slow and deep. Quick and teasing. She tried to move, but she seemed paralyzed, unable to tear herself away from his intimate stroking. Leg strokes that were so incredibly wonderful that her body turned traitor, her own legs parting, then clenching, now returning thrust for thrust.

She thought she must be half-crazed. Her breathing, so strange and choppy, quick rushes of it like gasps, and then no air at all. His palms were cupping her hips and urging her higher, faster. He was saying things that were disjointed and arousing, and she was trying desperately to hang on to his murmurings.

Beautiful... Yes, angel, that's it, so good... Feel the heat... But you're empty... Poor angel... Care... care...you do...

What was happening to her? She didn't know.... All she knew was this thing she was grasping blindly for, this thing that escaped her reach, while she was so empty she hurt.

She whimpered his name, knowing he held the

means to her release. He made a low, pleased sound, then quit moving his leg. Her own were trembling, and he gentled her frantic hips, which she couldn't stop from jerking against him. He soothed her with a touch that was generous and tender until she found a measure of control. And then his palms pressed tight on either side of her hips, stilling the last of her movements.

"You're okay," he said in a quiet, reassuring voice.

He kissed her forehead. Then he slowly moved away.

Rachel couldn't catch her breath. He thought she was okay? She could hardly stand. She was close to hyperventilating. She hurt between her legs, and she felt a frustration so terrible that a scream was trying to claw its way out of her throat. Did it show on her face? Was that why his held a mixture of kindness and male satisfaction that came close to smugness?

His gaze lowered and she suddenly realized what held his attention. Her skirt was hiked up to her panties. She glared at him and jerked it down with shaking hands. Actually, she was shaking from head to toe. In passion and passionate anger.

He turned to leave. She caught his hand at the doorknob, not knowing what she would say, because she was speechless. She only knew her pride demanded retribution for his blatant coup de grace. It staggered her, humiliated her, and worst of all, good Lord, it aroused her. *What kind of man was he?*

And what kind of woman was she to respond to him?

"What you just did— It wasn't fair, or appropriate, or—" She was sputtering, unable to string her feelings into a simple sentence. Rachel had never been so upset in her life; she silently counted to ten and took a shuddering breath. "Manipulative, that's what you were. You manipulated me, and I don't like it."

"Oh?" His gaze angled to the apex of her thighs. "Could've fooled me."

Her cheeks burned while her stomach bottomed out. Rand played dirty. Well, he was going to find out she could, too.

"Don't you dare try something like that with me again, or you'll be looking for another PI."

"Don't worry, I won't. You gave me the answer I was looking for. Too mad to ask? Since you're probably curious, I'll tell you anyway. I needed to find out if money was the only thing that's really motivating you. Now I can leave with the feel of you riding my thigh and know that at least that much was genuine."

She was compelled to disguise her weakness, to cover the shame of the lie that had caused this with another one.

"An impromptu performance. Nothing more."

"Are you up for an encore to convince me you're telling the truth?" He took a menacing step forward, and she quickly moved from his reach. He chuckled, apparently satisfied with her reaction. "Just kidding. You pulled out the big guns. I'll behave."

"You'd better. And don't even suggest another rehearsal. We have our roles down as pat as they'll ever get."

"Bravo. With an exit line like that, you deserve an Oscar." He winked. "Curtain's closed, angel." The door shut.

Rachel rested her forehead against the hard grain

of wood. At least it was solid, while she was coming
apart at the seams. She rolled her head back and forth.
Something wet slid down her cheek.

The tears of a clown, she thought. Some were for
Rand, alone in his ivory tower, where he knew how
to cope, and probably too well, even if he might want
more. But mostly they were for her, because she
didn't know how to cope when she needed more from
a man than he might have the capacity to give.

For all she knew, it had been nothing but a power
play, a well-executed performance on his part, or a
test of her stamina, to see how she held up under
undue duress. But not for her. She *felt*. Her emotions,
her words, the physical responses he commanded,
were very, very real.

Rachel wiped her wet cheeks with a determined
swipe of her arm. ''Get a grip on yourself,'' she
growled aloud. ''You're being ridiculous. He turns
you on. So what? He won't pull this crap again so
you're safe. Now quit crying. He's a client, nothing
more. Take his money, do your job, and you'll be
okay.''

You're okay, came the wisp of a voice, his voice.
She heard the soft reassurance again, felt his gentle-
ness when he could just as easily have taken her on
the floor without a protest from her. She still burned
for him to do just that. How in heaven's name was
she going to cope in Zebedique?

Exotic music. Palm trees and sand. Minaret swirling into an indigo sky. Sandalwood and incense
and...

Bay and night spice.

The image she'd conjured up in Rand's car that
first day was suddenly too vivid. She was there again,

could see the woman turning her head as Rand released the catch of her sheer veil.

Her fair skin was flushed with anticipation. She wore passion's maturity well, standing proud while he shed the fragile garment, and then naked as he leaned her into the bed with a mating growl.

Rachel swayed against the door, her legs refusing her their support as she stared into the vision. She saw the woman's face—and something more.

Fate winked, then vanished through a dark, steamy window.

RAND'S FOOT PRESSED DOWN on the accelerator, as though the faster he drove, the farther he could distance himself from what he'd spent nearly a lifetime outrunning.

Unfortunately, he just got himself to the motel that much sooner. Rand gripped the wheel, hearing his own harsh breathing fill up the silence. Claustrophobia pressed in on him. But he didn't move, didn't want to go to his empty room, any more than he wanted to sit at a bar alone or waste his time picking up a willing woman. He'd done it before, knew the emptiness of waking up next to someone he cared nothing about.

Care. He still couldn't believe he had the capacity to hurt as much as he had when Rachel had said she didn't. But he knew better; she did care, and nothing could have prepared him for the shock of realizing that he desperately wanted her to care. He'd actually called her "angel." He had always been miserly with endearments, and *angel* was the most treasured of all.

The sound of a couple laughing as they strolled through the parking lot arrested his attention. His eyes narrowed as they kissed and exchanged a verbal intimacy. A tight sensation stitched through his chest. He wanted what they were sharing—intimacy. A commodity that was rare in his life. Until now, the lack had been of his own choosing.

What was happening to him? How had Rachel filtered into the ice-water blood of a man most people considered little more than a moneymaking machine? He felt as though she had triggered twenty-odd years of gathered momentum that smashed his hardened heart with the grace of a two-ton velvet hammer.

It hurt. It felt damn good. A lot like doing emotional gymnastics after decades of no workouts. But was it worth riding out the pain to get to the gain? And how much hurt would Rachel have to endure while he bungled his way through?

He had to give this some careful consideration. Sarah was a commodity he couldn't risk—though there was a good chance she might resent him more than welcome him. What he had to know was whether Rachel had been honest about the potential consequences of getting involved. She could simply have been groping for an excuse to avoid exploring the boundaries of a relationship with a man as risky as him. He suspected it was some of both. That left the burden on him of figuring out the priorities.

He frowned as a final, crucial question emerged: Could he play his role convincingly and manage their proximity until Sarah was found? Even better, could he navigate a dual mission, save Sarah, and explore this compelling relationship with Rachel, too?

Rand flipped on the CD player, and music filtered through the whirlpool of his thoughts. Zebedique. An exchange of money and paper. Rachel, his possession, in a country that gave men absolute control over their women.

A slight smile tugged at his lips. Quite an amusing concept, really. That hair of hers was nothing compared to the fire within her. A fire that had challenged him to throw down the gauntlet before he'd had the good sense to leave. What he'd taken was a minor victory, the memory of her whimper, the sweet grip of her riding his leg.

He knew exactly where she'd been, could still feel the pulsing warmth radiating beneath his pants. He'd remember that tomorrow.

And remember was all he'd do. No more dress rehearsals. Zebedique would give them plenty of opportunity to walk the tightrope in a high-stakes game.

Rand came to a decision and shut off the music. Passing the lovebirds on the way to his room, he smiled. Funny thing about life, he thought. Just when a man believed he'd be happy if he could find his sister and make everything up to her, he discovered someone else that he'd nearly forgotten.

Joshua. Just as deserving as Sarah. Joshua, a poor kid who'd had his heart stripped out by his own childish misjudgment. He hoped Rachel wouldn't regret what she'd unwittingly done, peeling away his layers to expose some kernel of tenderness and need that belonged to a long-lost boy.

Rand, or Joshua, or whoever the hell he was, had to discover the truth: Was Rachel the key to giving Joshua a fair shot at the life he might have had if he hadn't run? And could Rand Slick stop running, after a lifetime of dodging the odds?

He made love to her in his sleep. When he awoke,

Rand knew that for once the sweat drenching his sheets was owed to a kinder source than the old demons who liked to pay their visits in a dream. One he jeeringly called See Rand Run.

SHAVE AND A HAIRCUT, two bits. Rachel glanced at her watch. Eight o'clock on the nose. Not only had Rand proved to be a man of his word, he was so punctual she could set her clock by him.

She couldn't get to the door fast enough, even though she was dreading the inevitable war of want versus will. Though she could look all she liked, Rachel didn't trust herself to touch him. The problem was, the more she looked, the more desperate she was to touch, to give up this farce of friendly allies pretending that that night a month ago hadn't happened.

But it had happened, and the memory was there, always there. Between them, and escalating, like the building tension felt by two estranged lovers riding in an elevator. Together but alone, separated by pride and more as they slowly inched up to the same floor while they stared anywhere but at each other.

Yet it didn't stop her furtive glances of longing. Or prevent her heart from deeply caring for him—at least as deeply as their slipping guards and their uneasy hands-off truce allowed. He was still a mystery to her. The better she got to know him, the more it seemed she didn't know.

Rachel took a deep breath and mentally snapped out an order to her nervous system to stop this crazy nonsense. And realized it was an exercise in futility the instant their gazes locked.

Rand let go a low, admiring whistle. "You could stop traffic in that getup."

"Let's hope it stops some trafficking. By the way, thanks for the lift. As soon as this job is over, I'm shopping for some new wheels."

"You could have caught a ride with Jack." He raised a brow in a silent challenge. When she refused to rise to the bait, he smiled warmly. "I'm glad you called me instead."

"Let me get my purse so we can get out of here," she said hastily, before he could press her for reasons she couldn't accept herself. "Jack's probably already at the casino. I hate to keep him waiting."

"Do you? You certainly haven't had any qualms about keeping *me* waiting. Do you realize this is the first time we've had a minute together since that night—"

"Don't be ridiculous, Rand." She wanted to cut him off before he could speak her own thoughts aloud. *Why had she set them up like this?* As if she didn't know. "Except for your quick trips to New York, we're constantly together. Planning, trial runs at the other casinos. And don't forget the two weeks running that we've laid the bait."

"Without a nibble. So what do we do? The *three* of us drink coffee till we're floating and swap jokes at some damn greasy spoon. I suppose you think that qualifies as time together, too."

"Of course it does."

"The hell it does. We're never alone. Jack's a great guy, but—"

"No 'buts' about it, he's the best backup your money can buy."

"Money." Rand snorted. "That again. Is it possible that for once, just this once, we could forget money and Jack and have an honest conversation about something that's been on my mind since before the first stakeout? We need to discuss it, and I want to do it *now*."

She wavered, on the cusp of giving in to the never-ending temptation to turn her back on her profession and confront head-on what always went unsaid.

"Later, Rand. Jack's waiting."

"Let him wait. This can't."

"Too bad, because it'll have to," she said sharply. Rachel was angry at herself for the weakness of needing some last, stolen bit of him to take with her as a talisman against the whims of fate. She turned, intent on a quick exit.

He caught her arm. She stared at the connection of his dark skin and her own pale flesh. Where his fingertips touched, she felt a glow. It spread until the room seemed to shrink in size and fill up with charged emotions and an energy that hummed of intimate whispers and hot sex.

"It's not too late, angel," Rand said quietly. "You can still back out. Do it."

Knowing how much his sister meant to him, she could only meet his probing stare with her own look of wonder and confusion. His brutally handsome face was softened by the same edge of concern she heard in the current of his voice.

"Do you actually think, even for a minute, that I would?"

"No. But I had to offer. I've got a gut feeling that tonight we'll hit pay dirt."

"I know. I feel it, too."

"Do you? Is that why I can feel you shivering like it's ten below zero instead of eighty degrees in here?" When she averted her gaze, he caught her chin and searched her face. "Is it?" he demanded.

"Of course," she said firmly, praying her eyes didn't give her away. "It's only natural to be nervous with stakes this high. But if anyone can pull some sleight of hand in the drink-switching department, it's Jack. And you'll be there, too."

"But not when you need me the most. Then you'll be on your own, without even a gun or a tracing device on you. I don't like it. Not one damn bit."

"We knew from the start that it's the only way, Rand. A hundred bucks and a false ID is my best insurance. They'll go through my things. They'll search me."

"I know." His grip tightened until she nearly winced. "When I think of what those bastards might—"

"Don't think about it. This is my job. It's what you hired me to do. I'm prepared."

"Yeah, right. The truth is, no matter how prepared you believe you are, it's going to be a nightmare, being helpless in the hands of strangers. A nightmare for you. A nightmare for me. When I first came into your office, you were a means to an end. Things have changed."

"This isn't a good time to talk about—"

"There's never a good time for us to talk, is there? You've seen to that. What are you afraid of? *Me?* When I haven't so much as tried to kiss you again?

You're my friend, or at least the closest thing to a friend I've let myself have for more years than I can count, and you won't even look at me. *Look at me.*'' He gave her small shake. ''That's better. Okay, *friend,* I'm giving you one final chance to back out. My instincts are almost always right, and they're telling me after tonight there won't be any turning back.''

As she stood there and filled herself up with his forbidden touch, Rachel knew to a certainty that there had been no turning back from the moment they met. Even if she could lie to Rand, she couldn't lie to herself.

She'd never been in love before, so she wasn't yet sure, but she was terribly afraid she was falling in love. In love with a man she knew, and yet knew not at all. She'd dated her share, had her share and more of kisses and heavy petting. But never had she met anyone like Rand Slick. And *never* had another man made her want, desperately want, what she couldn't have at this moment, and made her want it with nothing more than a look, a palm that swept to the small of her back, or a soft kiss pressed to her temple.

''Tell me you're off the case,'' he whispered sharply. His embrace was urgent as he kissed her again, only not so soft, because it was fierce and had trailed to her neck, where his teeth lightly scraped. ''I don't want you to go through with this. I'll find someone else, and—''

''Stop it, Rand. Stop it!'' Summoning up the core that was strength, belief in the rightness of what she was compelled to do, Rachel thrust him away. They stared at each other, both breathing in harsh, syncopated rasps. ''I told you we couldn't get emotionally involved. If this doesn't prove my point, nothing does. You have a sister who needs you, who needs me because I can get to her where you can't. And not only her—what about the other women who are at risk while you shop for someone to take my place?''

"I don't know those other women. I don't care about them. You I care about.''

"Don't," she snapped, flinching at her own sharp warning.

"Too late, Rachel. I do. Not that you seem to care that I…care.''

Steeling herself against the flow of something that felt like liquid nirvana coursing through her veins and making her head spin like a top, Rachel glared at him.

"Care later, Rand. Care when you can afford to.''

"When I can afford to?'' His harsh bark of laughter was derisive. "Here's another little tidbit to slide into the cube. Caring's the one thing I *can't* afford. Not yesterday, not today, not tomorrow. Sister or no sister. I won't be forgetting you threw back in my face what I'll never be able to afford. Just remember, I don't offer anything without the intent to reap my benefits tenfold. And I will, Rachel. *I will.*''

His gaze burned so hot it was freezing, rooting her to the floor and making the imprint of his hold on her arms chafe. But her heart he still held, held it so tight she could feel it squeeze out each erratic pump.

"If you're trying to scare me into backing off from this case, it's not working. I'm in, Rand. I'm in and I'm not bowing out until Sarah's safe and you're a file I've filed away. As, I suspect, you'll do with me once this is over. Case closed.''

Hardly was his silent response. Rand studied the stubborn tilt of her chin, which quivered ever so slightly, revealing her hard line as nothing but a sham from a woman of substance who didn't believe it herself. Who did Rachel think she'd taken on? Some horny kid who didn't know the difference between lust and whatever it was that she'd done to his insides?

Those insides balled into a hard knot, deflecting the blow of her rejection. One he couldn't accept, *would not* accept. He all but chortled because it was so obvious she *felt,* she *cared,* just as much as he did. It made her rejection a hell of a lot easier to handle than the fear for her safety that overshadowed his reason.

"Know what? I can almost pity that slaver once he gets his hands on you. Your tongue is sharper than any knife he might be tempted to cut it out with." His short laugh was accompanied by a sneer. It was directed at himself, fool that he was, for feeling too much. Not love, surely not, but something she called up inside him that kept growing and growing until he thought it might eat him alive. "Forget I ever said that I cared, okay? Like everything else between us, we'll pretend it doesn't exist, and maybe it'll go away. God, I hope so."

She hesitated, then touched his hand. Softly, a soothing brush of ruby-painted nails over clenched fist.

"I'm sorry I hurt your feelings, Rand. This isn't how—"

He knocked her hand away, and she covered her throat, as if he'd jammed a finger into her windpipe. Rand smiled coldly. Rachel was going to learn he didn't go down easy, and when he did he latched on to whoever dared tried to top him.

"Get your purse. And please, not the ugly one. The

one with black sequins should match that dress you
can hardly even breathe in. Maybe you'd like to
change into something closer to decent? You do seem
to be having trouble sucking in air and—why, Rachel,
your cheeks are turning such a lovely shade. They
even match your lipstick and nails.''

''What's the big idea, slamming the way I'm
dressed?'' she retorted hotly. Rand was perversely
pleased, quite certain that it was his refusal of her
touch, not his comment on her taste in purses or her
choice of dress that had her steaming. ''*You* picked
this out! Or don't you remember?''

He remembered and only too well. He remembered
his command: *''Turn around. Slow.''* His finger cir-
cling the air, while her feet pivoted on a platform at
a by-appointment-only designer boutique. His gaze
roving hungrily over her person, touching her with an
intimacy that his hands didn't share.

True to his promise, he'd kept his hands to himself.
All that day she'd modeled and he'd sipped champagne while drinking her in from his slouch in a
Queen Anne chair. He'd bought ten knock-'em-dead
outfits, though she'd insisted two should do.

What a joke. Everything she'd put on was transformed from cloth to class. The only urge greater than
to buy out the store was to strip her down to nothing
and drive into her so long and deep there was nothing
left of either of them.

''I remember, angel,'' he said smoothly. ''But that
was for my eyes only. I might be a lot of things, but
I stop short of scum. That's who you're peddling your
wares for tonight. He'll bite. Sink his teeth right into
that sweet, delectable top-dollar flesh of yours. I can't

help but wonder how much he'll sample before I buy up the leftovers in Zebedique.''

''They're not in the business to deliver damaged goods. Not if they want top dollar. And your dollars, no matter how ill gotten, are just as good as the next bidder's, Mr. Slick.''

He had to admire her grit. It caused him to quirk a brow and smile inwardly, silently acknowledging defeat. He couldn't let the smile reach his mouth, because it was impatient to crush hers with a lip-eating, tongue-thrusting, can't-get-my-fill hunger.

''But of course it is, Rachel. Money *is* the universal language, and it's the one I speak most fluently. Far better than English, so perhaps you can understand my lack of eloquence when I say—'' his gaze feasted on the swell of her breasts ''—pull up that damn bodice before you fall out. Your job is to lay the bait, not to feed the shark.''

She gave him her back and marched into her bedroom. But not before he saw the fleeting expression of hurt on her face. Then, sequined bag in hand and bodice a good two inches higher, she brushed past him with a haughty disdain he didn't buy for a minute.

With a brisk twist of the wrist, she locked up and stalked to his car. Rand beat her to the passenger door.

Instead of thanking him, she sliced him cleanly with a stony, madder-than-hell squint.

Rand guided the mean machine with a sweating palm over the leather-bound steering wheel. His guts turned to water just thinking about what might lie ahead for her once she was stripped of his protection.

The problem was protecting her from himself, once

foreign law gave him owner's rights and Rachel was handed into his own greedy keeping.

RAND SCANNED the crowd in the casino until his gaze connected with Jack's, who gave a small nod before moving to a gaming table a discreet distance from where Rachel stood.

It was tremendously difficult for him not to stare. In profile, she appeared to be enmeshed in a game of roulette. The black cocktail dress did indeed hug her too well in all the right places. It set off her red hair and green eyes so vividly that he was reminded of Christmas at night. Holidays were something he detested, since he had no family to share them with, but Rachel sparked images of youthful hope and a stunning feminine fire that crackled in a hearth called home.

She bent closer to the wheel, and his attention narrowed on her too-generous display of cleavage. Rand took a bracing swig from his glass, commanding himself not to go jerk the bodice higher, even as his fingers itched to plunge it down until her breasts tumbled free.

Rachel slid him a sidelong glance and smiled sweetly before turning the smile that was his on the man who sidled up beside her. The guy was wearing enough gold chains to put Fort Knox out of business, and he had a motor mouth that wouldn't quit. No way was this bozo their target.

The bozo rested a palm on a smooth ivory shoulder. Rand's grip tightened on the glass and he felt a distinct urge to hack the SOB's hand off at the wrist.

To his relief, Rachel cut the touchy-feely short and headed for a blackjack table. Jack cut his losses and moved in closer. Rand cut through the crowd, tailing her at a judicious distance.

His attention eventually focused on an elegant man in evening attire who approached her with a questioning smile and appeared to be confused as he asked her something. Then he shrugged expressively and shook his head, his smile so charming and sincere it immediately made Rand suspicious.

As the man continued to engage Rachel in what seemed to be an entertaining conversation, Rand bent down and pretended to tie his shoe, never releasing them from his peripheral vision.

Was it the too-smooth moves from the too-oily operator that caused his skin to crawl? Was it Jack's curt nod to Rand—he had a seasoned eye for a con— that made him shudder? Or was it the way Rachel was playing her role with a flawless finesse, appearing friendly and interested but not overeager, that had him swallowing against a dust-dry throat?

And then the man was gesturing toward the bar, and Rachel was appropriately hesitant before slowly smiling in agreement.

She dropped her sequined purse—the sign they'd hit the jackpot. The guy was good, so good Rand would've staked the cool ten mil he'd made on yesterday's coup that this was *it*.

He didn't give respect easily, but Rachel had won it, and it climbed several notches as he slyly observed from his post. She was reeling their mark in like a pro. If she was scared, she wasn't showing it, although his own heart was banging against his ribs and adrenaline was rushing through his system.

But as he followed them into the bar, an image of plump pillows, a feather-down bed, and Rachel his, all his, muted the apprehension clawing at his gut. Dear Lord, how he wanted to protect her, even knowing that if any woman in the world could protect herself it was Rachel.

Jack beat someone to the bar stool next to the one Rachel took beside the slaver. *It had to be the slaver.*

As Rand watched her doing her job, so incredibly well, even better than he'd dared hope, he did a double take.

For an instant he could have sworn she wasn't dressed to kill in black, but was naked beneath a loose, flowing gown of white gauze.

8

RACHEL'S STOMACH rolled over for the hundredth time in ten minutes. The cucumber cool she'd felt in rehearsal was nowhere to be found as she confronted the real thing. *Help, Rand! You were right! This is too scary, and I want out!* She battled the instinct to hightail it into his arms, which were less than twenty feet away.

Managing to stop her foot in midshake, she tilted her head so that the soft lighting would show her hair to its best red advantage.

"Beautiful hair on a beautiful lady," Maurice said. At least that's how he'd introduced himself. His voice dripped with enough culture for Barrymore and Olivier combined. He was so convincing that she might have bought it, if her trained eye hadn't spotted some subtleties that marked him as a counterfeit. His nails were clean, but needed clipping. When she'd dropped her purse, she'd noted that his shoes could use a shine. His cologne was way too strong. Little things, telling things. A man of true wealth and breeding would have seen to the finishing touches. And he sure as heck wouldn't be squirting his mouth with breath spray as she watched and forced a smile and gushed an ingenuous reply.

"I'm glad you like my hair. But really, Maurice,

such an outrageous compliment, it's enough to make a woman blush.''

''Don't tell me you don't get at least a dozen a day.''

''Are you kidding?'' She looked shyly away, her gaze brushing Rand's across the room, where he was making small talk with a woman who looked like a hooker. The momentary connection steeled her resolve and escalated her running pulse to a gallop. Her cheeks burned as she noted Maurice's quick, calculating assessment of her bosom. Rachel pressed an unsteady hand to her cleavage, hoping the material would absorb the trickling beads of sweat.

''Kidding?'' he repeated, laughing softly. ''My dear, I have never been more serious. You are, in fact, *exquisite*. I'm a worldly man, in experience, not to mention travel. But my acquaintance with women of your ilk—intelligent, divinely gorgeous, and most pleasant to converse with—is, shall we say, unfortunately limited. Surely you've had many men, besides myself, appreciate those attributes.''

''Oh, no! You see, I was an only child, and my parents were very protective, and—and I'm not exactly what you'd call, um, overly experienced when it comes to worldly men.''

At least if she didn't count Rand, whose compliments were often left-handed and unembroidered. Still, she'd take them any day over this stuff, which was so thick she wanted to gag. As for the protective parent, that much was true. Dear Daddy had run off many a boyfriend with his inquisitions and his bone-crushing handshakes. If he could see her now, he'd roll over in his grave and pound at his coffin lid to get out.

"You, inexperienced, when everything about you is the epitome of sophistication? You must be younger than you look. How old did you tell me you were?"

"I didn't." Her nervous laugh was genuine. "But I turned twenty-two last month. I hope you don't think I'm a baby."

"Rubbish. Why don't I buy us a drink, and we'll toast to your birthday?"

"That would be really nice. After all, I did spend it alone, and I would so like to share it with someone special." She paused for effect. "Someone like you."

"But what about those protective parents of yours? Surely they sent their love and presents, even if they were too far away to join you."

"Farther than that, Maurice. Mother and Daddy died in a car accident two years ago."

"How tragic. Surely you must have other relatives that miss you. Aunts or uncles or grandparents?"

"Unfortunately, no. My parents were only children, and my grandparents passed on when I was quite small."

"Oh, my dear, this *is* tragic." The glint in his eyes reminded her of matching fruit rolling up on a slot machine and spitting out a stream of silver to be fingered greedily. "Please accept my condolences, *and* my belated wishes for a happy birthday." He raised a single finger to the bartender, who had thus far stayed too busy to acknowledge them. "It seems the bartender is finally coming our way. What shall I order for you?"

Your slimy guts skewered on a toothpick umbrella and drowning in a Mai Tai for me to throw in your face, scumbag.

"A glass of white zinfandel would be wonderful."

"But not half as wonderful as you," he deftly insisted.

Rachel tugged down the hem that had ridden up her thighs an uncomfortable few inches. Maurice's appreciative note of the small act suggested that he more than liked her sense of modesty. He was lapping it up. The creep.

Refusing to consider the inevitable investigation of her body, Rachel managed to quell the queasy swishing of her stomach, and leaned back so that Jack was a few inches closer for the little while longer she would have him to count on.

Maurice placed their order, then kept the conversation running with an anecdote that she laughed at in all the right places. Stolen glances alerted her to the bartender's deceit. While he'd fixed her companion's Stolichnaya straight up in clear sight, he poured the wine, and took a half minute too long to do it, beneath the counter's ledge.

Drugged. The wineglass he set before her with a flourish and a smile was drugged. Rachel deflected her immediate impulse to recoil from Maurice and dump the drink in his lap. She could feel Rand's gaze on her back, and with it came the familiar prickling of the fine hairs on her nape. He was anxious, worried, and sending her a silent message that it wasn't too late to get out.

She reached for the wine, meaning to slide it a few crucial inches closer to Jack's identical goblet.

Maurice caught her trembling fingertips with his own. They were smooth, dry and insistent. He lifted her glass and inhaled the bouquet before gallantly handing it over.

"A sip and a toast. To you, my sweet, and especially to our most fortuitous meeting."

A quick glance to the left, and she saw their bartender disappear in a swish of ruby velvet doors. Her educated guess was that he had a fast call to make so that a driver would be meeting them at the entrance.

Rachel pretended to take a small sip, then set it next to Jack's, just as they'd planned. What they hadn't planned on was Maurice's quick retrieval of the glass, or his admonishing shake of the head as he urged the rim to her lips.

"Come now, you don't *really* consider that to do justice to your birthday, or to our delightful acquaintance, do you? Let's try this again. To you. To me. To a night we'll never forget."

Had Jack switched the glasses? Not unless he was faster than David Copperfield and Houdini rolled into one.

"Here, here!" Rachel faked another sip. Before she could land the glass on the bar and stall for a few precious seconds, Maurice caught her wrist and tilted, tilted...

Deciding that if she didn't drink up she'd risk blowing her cover, Rachel took several quick swallows. It had a slight bitter flavor, but otherwise there was no telltale taste.

From what she knew about the drug of choice, she could expect it to hit within ten minutes. *Let it hit,* she decided. Maybe she was better off drugged than enduring more of this hell that she knew was nothing compared to the hell awaiting her. At least this way she wouldn't have to fake the effects.

The effects kicked in before she could polish off half the glass. Something tickled the back of her throat and emerged as a silly giggle. Maurice was stroking her calf with the unshiny tip of his shoe, which had begun to gleam like Tinkerbell's wand in the shimmering darkness. And how agreeable she felt when he whispered that they should leave here and do the town in style.

Sounded good to her. But it shouldn't. Rachel frowned, then laughed as she scrambled for a wisp of comprehension. The room had grown hazy, and so had her brain. She reached for her purse and knocked it to the floor.

"I'll get it, my dear," Maurice offered graciously, swiping it up and leading her out on his arm.

If she had to be drugged, Rachel decided, this one—whatever it was—wasn't half-bad. She laughed gaily, feeling wildly uninhibited and loose. Everything struck her as funny. The way Jack was getting up and taking her glass along with him. And Maurice patting her purse, which he wouldn't find a gun in. Of course, in her current state of hilarious insanity, she'd have found it real funny to blow his miserable head off. She would have liked to say as much, but her tongue felt plumper than an overstuffed quilt.

As they made their exit from the bar, she was aware of an electric sensation stitching up her spine. Someone had touched her at the small of her back.

Even flying high, she didn't need to look to see who it was. Only one person had ever affected her like that. Rachel tilted her spinning head and caught a parting glance from Rand before he was swallowed by the crowd zooming in and out, then whirling round and round in kaleidoscopic Technicolor.

Unlike her, Rand hadn't been smiling. So what? she thought as another lilting giggle erupted. Those stern lips of his were made for kissing like crazy, and crazy as she was for him, she'd gladly return his dumb dough in exchange for a taste of that gorgeous, sexy mouth.

She hoped he hurried up and met her in—well, wherever the heck it was that he was going to buy her. Too bad it was going to cost him, when she'd gladly be his for free.

9

THE LONG WHITE ROBES fluttered against Rand's sandal-clad feet. He quickened his pace, sidestepping a peddler hawking gaudy jewelry from a brightly colored cart. A drunk, thrown through a tavern's swinging doors, landed in his path.

Rand stepped over him without a cursory glance, his mind locked on Rachel. A queasy feeling twisted his insides with each thought of what they might have done to her.

His utter inability to help her when she'd needed him the most was a bitter reminder of past failure. Shutting it out, he concentrated on the surroundings.

Zebedique. Just as he remembered it. Beggars and whores and stinking-rich sultans milled together in narrow cobblestone streets lined with casinos and massage parlors, opium dens and exquisite jewelry stores.

It was a twenty-four-hour party, as rich as it was sleazy. The thick smell of spice permeated everything. He caught himself sniffing his pores as he rounded a familiar corner.

He headed straight for a voluptuous building composed of stained-glass windows and swirling gold turrets that looked like butterscotch-dipped Dairy Queen cones. Rand adjusted the long, scarf-type hood covering his head.

"You are invited?" the guard said in broken English.

Luckily, English was the common language used by the international travelers who gathered here in Zebedique. Rand had had no reason to hire an interpreter, as many here did, or to pretend he was anything but what he was: a visiting American with enough money and contacts to grant him entry to this high-stakes den of iniquity. Even so, he'd studied up on the local dialect, and he could get by. Better yet, he could eavesdrop.

"I am invited. Do you wish to see my papers?" At the curt nod from the guard, Rand produced a letter of introduction and proof of an unlimited line of credit at a Swiss bank.

The guard waved him inside. As he took his indicated seat, Rand declined a drink and the sexual favors a servant girl offered. He scanned the crowd, aware that anticipation seemed to pulse through the air. Low murmurs filtered through the musical strains of a flute. Fat men, handsome men, old goats, fast livers, all lounged and drank and greedily fondled the girls who were in ample supply.

A loud clap sounded. The flute was joined by a stringed instrument, and a line of exotic, heavily made-up women took their places, then began to dance, to strip and undulate sinuously on the stage.

So this was how the slavers worked their customers up, he thought, almost dazedly. He wished he could say he was immune. But as he looked at the bronzed bodies glistening with oil, he could only envision Rachel, her fair skin, her flowing red hair, her lips, lush with invitation, beckoning to him to take her home.

Rand groaned, feeling the rush of his blood, the

rise of his sex. His groan was echoed by many, and
he wished to heaven they'd just get on with it.

He got his wish. The women finished their dance
and left. A dark, sinewy gnome of a man took center
stage. The room, charged with lust, now went silent.

"Bring the girl out." He clapped his hands twice,
and two men struggled with a dark, slender woman
who was twisting and screaming and trying to break
free of their hold, in spite of the rope binding her
wrists.

Rand was appalled. The rest of the crowd seemed
excited, judging from the murmur of approval sweeping through the room.

"She's spirited," noted the auctioneer. "A fine
Egyptian woman to warm a man's bed." He signaled,
and a large hook attached to a rope dropped from the
top of the stage. With practiced ease, the two assis-
tants looped the bonds on her wrists over the hook
and left. At another signal, the rope was raised until
she was balanced on her toes.

The woman was crying, and Rand toyed with the
notion of buying her just so that he could set her free.

He couldn't. There were going to be a lot more
women exactly like her, and buying all of them was
out of the question.

"You like her breasts?" said the gnome. "Then
see how you like the rest!" With a jerk of his hand,
he whipped the sheet from her body, exposing her in
full frontal nudity.

The woman shrieked, and the audience applauded.

"Unfortunately she is not a virgin." The gnome
caught her around the waist, the rope turning as he
pivoted. "But she's very tight, and why should vir-

ginity matter, with such beautiful buttocks, and thighs you can train to wrap around your waist?''

The bidding lasted several minutes, the auctioneer forcing up the bids, constantly extolling her merits.

She sold for the equivalent of fifty thousand dollars. The new owner claimed her. Amid polite applause, he carried her off the stage.

Rand wished he'd taken the drink he'd been offered. He needed something to get a hold on himself before Rachel was similarly disgraced. Something to dampen this sick anticipation. He couldn't bear the thought of seeing her so horribly handled, of these other men looking upon her while they fondled themselves and placed their bids.

While he would outbid each one and doubtless be filling himself up with the sight of her nakedness.

The thought left him with a load of self-disgust— and the familiar arousal that thoughts of her always evoked. By the fifth girl, those two warring qualities had twisted together with his gnawing anxiety: overt references to sex, nudity, and concern about Rachel bombarded his senses.

"And now, gentlemen, the most intoxicating beauty we have ever offered. American. Educated. And, best of all—" he clapped his hands, and Rand watched, numb and yet, as he had feared he would be, hideously enthralled, as Rachel was led onto the stage "—she is a *virgin!*"

Flanked by the guards, she held her head high and walked silently, dressed in nothing but a sheet and her attitude, to the center of the platform. Rand could see her scanning the crowd, eyes guarded but alert.

Lord, she was beautiful, standing proud and aloof from it all. He sensed the other patrons' anticipation as excitement swept them into a taut, hushed frenzy of lust.

Rand lusted, too. Her eyes caught his, and he knew she was pleading with him to end this quickly and take her away from this horrible place. He couldn't claim her soon enough, to whisk her away to the haven they'd share.

Something shifted in the middle of his chest, heaping sympathy and tenderness on the caldron of emotions he was struggling to control.

But then the auctioneer was teasing them, sliding the sheet from her breasts. One plump alabaster breast spilled out, her nipple haloed by a large, dark areola.

Feeling himself grow so stiff that he hurt, Rand told himself he was no better than any other barbarian here. How could he, a civilized man, be nursing this aching arousal, when it was Sarah's identical plight that had brought him here, to right a terrible wrong? He didn't know. But his need for Rachel was immense, and he'd never imagined being faced with such raw carnality before assuming his position on the tightrope.

Rand drew in a shuddering, hot breath, tasting spice and the anticipation of woman on his tongue. He commanded himself to raise his gaze again to her face and support her with that until she was his, only his, by virtue of his filthy lucre.

Nonetheless, this atmosphere was bad for a man's morals. And it seduced his to sink lower with each second that passed.

RACHEL LOCKED HER EYES on Rand. He was the only solid thing in the madness that had surrounded her since the minute she'd left the casino with the slaver.

She held fast to his presence, to the reassurance she read in his gaze.

But there was more. Something dark and earthy that permeated the room and was focused on her. She shivered and vowed not to cry or scream.

Or dissolve into hysterical laughter. The whole thing was so absurd, so bizarre, that she felt as if she were trapped in some B-grade movie, playing the starring role while another part of her observed, in disbelief, from a distance.

Distance. Maurice and company had kept their distance from her throughout the flight. Had, in fact, seemed eager to hand her over to this end of the business—which had, mercifully, proved to be *all* business. After a medical examination had established that she was indeed a virgin, she had been treated as if she were an investment to be handled with the greatest of care. She'd been bathed, massaged, manicured and pedicured, her hair washed and brushed so that it gleamed like the pennies she'd scrubbed with an eraser as a child until they'd glowed copper red and new.

An exclusive club for slaves in the making. No clothes allowed. She'd counted twenty naked bodies besides hers, and the treatment of each one had been so luxuriantly cavalier that she'd begun to feel oddly liberated by her own nudity. Her ingrained modesty, at home in the Western world, seemed a quaint, outdated custom in this anachronistic, backward society.

Rachel was strangely grateful for the five days that had passed since she'd been a free woman in Vegas. The time had allowed her to adapt to these foreign surroundings. She could deal with this, she told herself—no problem.

A sense of calm enveloped her. The guards departed, leaving her hands bound but unhooked. Why, she wasn't sure. Maybe it was her condescending glare, or the lack of struggle that accompanied it. Whatever, it apparently increased her value, judging from the mercenary smile the auctioneer turned on her. The terrible little man pried the wrapped sheet from one breast and then the other. The audience oohed and ahed their beastly approval. The auctioneer winked, and she managed not to spit in his face.

Instead Rachel thrust her breasts out, taking pride in her sculptured femininity. And it was more than pride. She taunted them with it, while Rand maintained his outward cool....

Which disintegrated before her stunned eyes.

Attuned as she was to his body language and to the silent support of his gaze, she was struck dumb by the metamorphosis in him. First, the steady rhythm of his breathing became agitated to the point of panting. Then the clear focus of his eyes on hers lowered to her upper nakedness and became transfixed so long that he appeared to be in a trance. His tongue snuck out, but rather than retreating, it repeatedly traced a hungry path, around and around, as if it were her inner thighs he was lapping at rather than his own dry lips.

Her savior was suddenly no savior, but the devil himself, considering the spoils of his ill-gotten gain. She was horrified to realize that Rand had relinquished his ally's support to stare at her breasts with a hunger unrivaled by that of his lust-in-the-dust colleagues.

A rope dropped down, and she felt the auctioneer lifting her arms to a hook.

"I can do it myself, you cheap little runt," she snapped, taking her anger out on the nearest scapegoat.

"So you can talk after all," he said in halting English. "Cooperate and I won't hurt your dignity."

"You can go to hell. Dignity's something you don't have to give." Warm air swirled around her breasts, and she ignored the agony of feeling more exposed than she had during the examination. Rachel raised her hands with a grace befitting a ballerina and defiantly notched her chin upward.

She shut out the rippling noise of the buyers, the drone of the auctioneer's wheedling voice. If only she could do the same with her hurt, her deep disappointment in Rand, looking at her as if he were even more crazed than the rest of them. After the time they'd spent together, the bonds they'd forged, bonds she'd believed to be of friendship, how could he turn into this—this animal? The fine edge of longing and unspoken emotions had never left, but never in her wildest dreams had she expected this kind of betrayal. It made her want to weep.

The hell she'd cry. Rand could destroy her illusions of him, and the disgusting men sitting with him could drool all over themselves while she was helpless to cover her near nakedness, but no one could strip away her pride.

Her body was another matter. Without warning, she felt the thin sheet whipped off. An outraged cry ripped from her throat before she could stop it.

"You sleazy little bastard, get your grimy hands off me!"

"A spirited virgin, gentlemen. And see the lovely

hair between her thighs, matching that of her scarlet head.''

''You stupid jerk, you despicable creep, you low-down, no good—''

''But let us not stop there.'' He yanked her around and stroked her buttocks.

Gone was her earlier calm. In its place came a flash-point rage. Rachel was on tiptoe, but she had her balance. With a quick self-defense move, she pulled up and kicked sideways, landing a blow to his groin.

He bent over, groaning and cursing and calling for a whip.

''One hundred thousand American dollars!'' came a shout.

''One hundred and fifty!'' echoed another.

Voices slashed her ears, dozens of men scrambling to outbid their competition with ruples, yen, pounds and marks.

By why wasn't she hearing Rand through the mayhem, while she dangled helpless, naked, and up for grabs?

The auctioneer was quickly gaining his footing, turning her around, gesturing to her breasts, her thighs, then stepping a safe distance away.

''Five hundred thousand American dollars from Prince Dominic,'' he said triumphantly. ''Do I hear a higher bid?''

Rachel stared in shock and fury at Rand. His eyes were almost glazed, and even from here she could see his labored breathing. What she saw was the look of a man in the throes of passion, but his passion was overlayed by the raw anger she saw in the clench of his jaw, simmering in his gaze.

Unlike the rest of the men, who had remained seated throughout the fanfare, he stood.

"One million American dollars."

Every head present turned at the commanding sound of his projected voice.

Then silence was followed by murmurs of speculation and respect for the amount of money.

The auctioneer called for silence.

"One million American dollars from the new member. Do I hear more? One million and a half?"

The question was directed to the prince. Rachel held her breath, or at least what she had left of it.

The prince shook his head.

"The beautiful woman goes for one million." The greedy slaver nodded to Rand. "Come and claim your prize."

She watched as he strode forward, his eyes fluctuating between her face and her naked body. When he gained the stage, he stooped and swept up the sheet. He positioned himself between her and the sea of watching eyes, shielding her from every view but his.

"You will enjoy taming her?" said the auctioneer with a sly smile.

"I will. But don't ever let me catch you touching her like that again, or you'll be using this sheet for a shroud. Beat it, and don't come back until we're gone."

Rand spanned the sheet wide between his arms, but he didn't immediately cover her with it. The spread of white muslin blended into his robe, the hood of it contrasting starkly against his dark skin. Her mind was spinning, casting him as Valentino in *The Sheik*. But he was no actor, he was a man she'd spent the past month with, craving the touch he withheld and wondering if she might be falling in love.

This was not the same man. This was a dark stranger more dangerous than the one who'd asserted his hold with a sexy ploy at her door. He whispered to her now, as he had then, saying, "You're okay, angel. I'm here, and I'll protect you."

He was protecting her, all right. Protecting her from prying eyes, only to devour her with his own. She bared her teeth, not trusting herself to speak.

His gaze hungrily trailed her body, and she was torn between fury and a quivering spark of—desire. No! How could she even think it? She wanted to tear his head off for daring to look at her like this, for subjecting her to such degradation, even if no one else could see.

"Remember the Oscar," he said in a low, gritty voice. Slowly he put the sheet to her back, his hands grazing over her fevered skin, relaying a proprietary feeling that spoke of the protection he'd promised. As he wrapped the covering beneath her raised arms, she could feel him shaking.

His fingertips hovered over the top of a breast, then slowly closed the distance, as though drawn by a force beyond his control. He touched the tip of a single nipple. His touch became a stroke. Once. Twice. A rolling, gentle squeeze that brought forth a tortured groan from him.

Rachel was appalled to feel both nipples harden and thrust out as if seeking more. Her legs shook, and her belly tightened. A tiny, mewling sound escaped between her parted lips in answer to his inarticulate murmurings.

Why wasn't she fighting him for all she was worth?

She didn't want this, not this way. She abhorred him for what he was doing, for making her acknowledge a shameless facet of herself in this obscene place, making his conquest in the privacy of her home seem trivial and pale.

She wanted to cling to him. She wanted to bolt and return to a time that was safe and familiar, when she was late with the rent and had never laid eyes on Rand Slick.

"Mine." The word was a thick whisper, and if she hadn't seen his lips move, she might have thought she'd imagined it.

Quickly, then, as though he didn't trust what he might do next, Rand wrapped the sheet around her twice and secured it between her breasts. She was still dangling from the hook when he pulled her insistently against him.

Even beneath the folds of his robe she could feel him hard, pulsing. He unhooked her arms, and she fell limp against him. The bindings stayed her from thrusting against his chest. Her bound hands caught between them. She squirmed to break free, but he subdued her by quickly shifting. Her fists pressed intimately into the harbor of their nearly joined groins. She was too close to hurt him, and too shocked by the stunning arousal the feel of him evoked even to try.

Vaguely she realized that the audience was craning for a better view as he fanned a palm over her buttocks and tangled a hand in her hair.

"What are you doing?" she demanded, fighting tears of horror and need.

"I'm sorry for what you went through. Dear God, I am. But I'd be lying if I apologized for this."

His mouth came down on hers. Greedily. Possessively. His kiss was compelling and tender and fierce. His lips slanted against hers, rubbed them, learned them, and ate from them. Then the tip of his tongue dipped into the groove of her lower lip before taking it into the warm haven of his mouth. Such was his wooing that her teeth unlocked, and with a pleased murmur he pressed between them, in a smooth glide that was so hungry it intensified her own mounting greed.

An absorbing, ravenous kiss. A shared kiss of mutual need held too long in check. He was making her crazy. Yes, yes, she must be losing her mind. Because if only her hands were unbound she would grip him to her, stroke her hands through his hair, wind her legs about his waist and—

And why had they waited so long for this rapture, this physical bond that felt like whispered words of a deeper bonding, an aching, unspoken vow? She couldn't remember—something about pride and manipulation and threats, a twisted part of the puzzle with the jagged edges.

Then she lost even that memory. He was kissing her madly, and she was opening her mouth, begging for more while she searched for the thread. *Pride, jagged edges, so twisted up...*

Through her moans, the faraway rush of rippling applause spread in her ears. It cut through, and she remembered where she was, and good Lord, if she didn't stop this insanity she wouldn't even care if he took her right here.

Rachel tore her lips from his and reared back. Eyes that lapped at her with dark, ominous fire stayed her from demanding the release she didn't want.

"Let's get out of here and go home," he said hoarsely.

She tried valiantly to keep something of her independence, pushed harsh words past her kiss-swollen lips. "First you call that pig back to give you a knife and cut me loose."

"So you can slap me? The answer is *no*." Rand hoisted her over his shoulder, one hand locked over the backs of her legs, the other cupping her behind with a possessive caress.

"Stop it," she demanded as the sound of music blended into the scent of spice and uncurbed desire. "You have no right to do this."

"The papers that are waiting say that I do."

"You don't own me. I don't belong to you."

"I guess that's something we'll both have to find out. I just spent a million bucks to have the chance, and from what I saw on that stage, the answer's going to be worth every dime."

"This isn't a joke, and I'm in no mood for theatrics. Put me down. Do you hear me? Put me down!"

He ignored her screams of demand, but as they exited to a standing ovation she heard him chuckle and say, "Once we're home, angel, we'll take our bows."

10

"DAMMIT, RAND, STOP! Let me walk!" Rachel hung over his shoulder, smacking his rear with her bound hands, since he had the rest of her in a clinch. They'd passed through the massive entryway of a house and been bowed to by servants who promptly disappeared; and now he was carrying her up a marbled staircase and through some kind of maze. She felt him shift, kick, heard a door slam.

"Did you hear me? I demand that you put me down right this instant."

"If you say so."

Suddenly she felt herself hauled upright, and then he was cradling her in his arms. Then he stooped low and let go. She fell a short distance before the softest sensation imaginable greeted her back.

Rachel sank into what might have been a pillow of clouds. A white canopy that was so huge it could have passed for a tent was fanned out overhead. A quick glance to either side informed her that she was lying on a bed, the likes of which she'd never seen before. Round, voluptuous, a gigantic silk pincushion.

Rand's face, still partially concealed by his hood, stared down at her. His dark brows were knitted together, making his eyes seem like twin obsidian stones glittering darkly beneath two horizontal slashes.

Rachel couldn't catch her breath and she knew it wasn't from the gentle fall. It was the way he was staring down at her, seeming larger than life from her vantage point, dominating the room with his powerful frame enfolded in the robe. A grand sultan in his domain. The torched expression he wore as he stroked her visually told her more than she wanted to know.

He wanted her. Now. And they were all alone.

Suddenly she wished for even the company of that disgusting crowd.

Rachel followed his gaze and realized the sheet had come loose. Her breasts were covered, barely, and so were her hips, even more barely. Her legs were exposed to her upper thighs and sprawled out in a most undignified way. She squirmed, trying to pinch them together. Her eyes dilated with alarm when she realized she'd succeeded only to loosen the sheet more. Her breasts were all but spilling out, and she could feel the rush of warm air tickling her feminine parts.

"Welcome home," he said in a thick voice. "I hope you find our bed comfortable."

"*Our* bed?" Her apprehension soared, as did her indignation that he was taking advantage of this. Staring at her with even more heated rawness than he had at the auction, and making no effort to disguise what it did for his masculine urges. "The audience is gone, Rand. You can drop the act."

"Hardly. The act's just begun." He thrust his hood back and sat on the edge of the bed. It gave under his weight and rolled her against him.

"You're a civilized man...aren't you?" she said desperately, fearful she might soon find out just how barbaric he could get. "Quit looking at me like that!"

"Like I want to strip what's left of that sheet off

in no civilized manner?'' he said in a booming, authoritarian tone.

"Stop it,'' she hissed. "I don't like this.''

"Good. Very good,'' he whispered, then returned to a forceful volume. "Whether you like it or not makes no difference. We play by my rules, woman, not yours.''

"*Your* rules!'' She struggled to move away, but he caught her upper arms and hoisted her upright until they were almost nose to nose, mouth to mouth. Her rapid, choppy breathing mingled with his, which was maddeningly deep and even. "Get your hands off me and take your rules right out the door with you.''

"I have no intention of leaving!'' he bellowed. "We're going to do this my way. Give me your hands and be quick about it!''

"Why? So you can loop them around a hook and dangle me from the bed while you rape me?'' She heard something that sounded close to hysteria rise in the pitch of her voice.

"Don't be ridiculous. When I choose to take you to bed, you'll be more than ready.'' His words were arrogant, but his gaze reflected an intensity of emotion she was too unstrung to decipher.

Again he spoke low. "Listen to me, Rachel. You weren't the only one in agony while you were being paraded on that stage. It practically tore my guts out to watch what they did to you. Every time I think about that creep touching you, I—'' His grip tightened, and his eyes took on a distant sheen. Was it anger? Frustration? "I've been in control for so long that—God, I forgot how it feels to be without it, to be helpless to protect someone that I—''

She whimpered as his fingers bit deep into her

shoulders. His vision seemed to refocus to the present, and he abruptly let go. "I didn't mean to hurt you." He swept a soothing stroke over the red imprint he'd left and murmured, "I'll do what I can to make up for what you went through, and I'd say that excludes rape. So relax. We're home. You're safe." Then he said brusquely, "The wrists?"

When she hesitated, he took it upon himself to place them in his lap. Working the fine knots, his fingers were deft and agile, belying their size and strength. Would she ever understand him? This paragon of mystery, whose touch veered from the harsh to the sensitive, while his expressions and words rushed in so many different directions she couldn't keep up.

For the moment, she was still too jangled from the ordeal to even try. All she knew was that he'd wanted to protect her, and as vulnerable as she was now, half-nude and responding to his gruff concern, she wanted to protect herself from her protector.

Distance. She had to get some distance from this dark edge of intimacy that she'd succumbed to on the stage with an abandon that she was too ashamed of to remember, even as she could feel it threatening to overtake her again as they sat, too close, on the bed.

"You might have hated it, Rand, but I was the one being terrified, disgraced and—"

"And you never showed it," he said quietly. "I was proud of you, Rachel. You should be proud of yourself for handling it as well as you did. Oh, and, by the way, great shot. Made me want to whistle and clap when you decked that munchkin."

"Are you as proud of yourself? The way you stared

at me, keep staring at me, makes you look as depraved as the rest of those slobbering heathens.''

''That's because I was.'' He flung the rope to the gleaming marble floor. ''And still am, though I imagine you gathered that with your hands in my lap. But as for your question, the answer is no. I wasn't proud of myself. I was ashamed. And more aroused than I've ever been in my life. Be honest, Rachel. Didn't you feel the same things, too?''

She didn't want to be honest with either of them, and so she looked away. He already knew, anyway. No need to give him the satisfaction of confirming their base bond.

Pulling her wrists to his lips, he kissed the abrasions marking her skin. ''I'll tend this after you have the bath I ordered drawn.''

He hadn't offered her an apology for his behavior, and so what if wanting one was hypocritical. She wanted him to say he was sorry, not make a statement that sounded suspiciously like a master's dictate. A solicitous one, but a dictate nonetheless. He'd said it so smoothly, with an ease of command that didn't expect to be challenged.

''You'll tend this? After I take a bath you ordered?'' She met him with a level stare, determined to assert some independence before he started taking his role to heart. ''I can tend myself and draw my own baths, thank you, Mr. Slick.''

''So the auctioneer didn't lie,'' he shouted. ''You are a spirited wench! Now get this, my virgin possession. I said *I'll* do the tending. And you will let me do it, like it or not. You will obey your master or suffer the consequences of your impertinence.''

He grinned. Rachel couldn't believe his audacity.

Why, he was actually enjoying this! Throwing himself into his part with relish, while the weakness of her position left her wide open to his whims.

"I'll most certainly do no such thing," she informed him sternly. "Leave, just leave before I scream loud enough to bring the servants running."

His low chuckle antagonized her. Her eyes blazed a path of outrage that he deflected with a spark of supreme delight.

"Why, you arrogant, pigheaded—" she sputtered. Pointing a shaking finger at the door, she gave an order of her own. "Get out! Did you hear me? Go away and don't come back until you can wipe that stupid smirk off your face. Do it before I scream these walls down on your head, you…you…*dictator*."

"Scream all you like, my hot-blooded beauty," he boomed. "The servants won't save you from the master of the house." He hooked a thumb in the door's direction, indicating there might be prying ears. "And don't forget I am your master, too. I own you, woman. Lock, stock and barrel."

"Why, you…you… Ooh!" She lunged at him, ready to punch him good for everything he'd done and everything she'd let him do. She aimed for his nose, which seemed apt, since he was rubbing hers in the situation that he had the nerve to gloat over.

She was fast and on target, but Rand reacted with the reflexes of a street fighter. He caught her raised fist and jerked her against his chest. The sheet fell away and Rachel's heart turned over. Her naked breasts were pressed into his robe.

"Scream again," he instructed in a low, rough voice. She tried to, but her voice was caught in her throat. "Then maybe you need some help."

He hesitated, then quickly loosened the folds of material to expose a large expanse of firm muscle and dark sworls of hair. His skin was warm, the color of coffee cream. Their nipples touched. Her breasts parted and rode against his. The way he held her to him rubbed their flesh together in a sinuous rotation, tight but shy of a crush.

"My way," he said in an intimate whisper. "Be careful, Rachel, or you might end up enjoying my way more than yours. Open your mouth and scream."

She did. She screamed in frustration, because he'd assumed his role so effortlessly, when she wanted something real and lasting. And then she screamed again, because perhaps if he thought she was pretending she could convince herself, too, and he wouldn't stop what he was doing, making her breasts grow heavy, weighted. A healthy dose of self-disgust spurred her on, the ease with which he could play her tasting like a bitter truth shoved down her throat.

Even as her cries faded, the tingle spawned by the brush of his hair spread in widening ripples.

"Perfect," he whispered. "Almost as perfect as your breasts gliding over my skin, so soft I could swear they're melting into my chest and you're feeling something more for me than you do for every other client. You do. Admit it."

"No," she said brokenly. "*No.* It's—it's what you're paying me for. You're a job, my ticket up. After today, I don't even know if we can still be friends."

"In that case, we should be safe, shouldn't we? You have no emotional attachment to me, and so even if I feel something very special and dangerous for you, we're both protected, and Sarah's future isn't threatened. Though more than ever I wonder if she's really the one at risk, or if she's simply a convenient excuse.''

Footsteps sounded in the hallway, and he shifted, hastily pressing her down into the giving cushion. His weight was on her, and their upper bodies were joined. And then he moved until he lay fully on top, his thighs hugging hers, his erection straining against the material of his robe to seek her out.

''Please, Rand...'' Pleading with him, pleading with herself because her instincts were screaming at her to part her legs and discover the dark secrets yet to unfold, to take them and the resulting risks without confronting the truth he had suggested. ''Get off of me. Get out. We'll pretend this never happened.''

''Pretending's something that we've been doing too long. Since the first day I walked through your door, we've skirted the edge, and it's been about the hardest thing I've ever had to do, keeping my hands to myself while all I could think about was touching you, and touching you a lot more intimately than this.'' He spread her hair out against the sheet. The tug of his fingers against her scalp shot downward, radiating to her belly, and to the place where she began to clench, to ache.

''You're forgetting about Sarah.'' It was her only defense. She didn't hesitate to use it, to cling to it like a cross that could ward off a vampire.

''No, angel, I never forget about her. Though chances are she's forgotten about me. Hold me. Help me to forget, too.''

He said it so gently, and with so much appeal in his voice, that she could feel her muscles go lax with the soothing flow of his words. And then she remem-

bered that he was most dangerous when vulnerable.
She tried to resist, but his lips were soft, feeling, asking for the comfort she wanted to give. She almost
reached for him; the urge to grasp his head, to kiss
him in reassurance and soothe him with loving
strokes, was so strong she hurt with the wanting.

But she didn't. Instead, she gave him a comfort that
was safer for her.

"Don't worry. I'll find Sarah. You'll get it worked
out. Then maybe you'll be the one doing the forgetting—about me."

"You're so wrong. We'll find Sarah, but together.
You and I, we're partners, Rachel, not adversaries.
And no matter what happens after we get out, I could
never forget you."

No, she didn't think he would. But chances were
he'd leave her. Patients did cling to their physicians
in their time of need, only to regain their health and
send a bouquet with a thank-you note once the crisis
was over. How easily it could happen with them. If
it did, she doubted she'd ever recover. It was that
threatening possibility that caused her to shove at his
chest rather than embrace him.

11

He bore down, all tenderness forsaken, demand spiking his tone.

"Don't push me away, dammit. You know as well as I do that what's happening now has been a long time coming."

"Nothing's going to happen except what we came here for. Get off me, Rand. You've been here long enough to satisfy the servants."

"The servants, maybe. But not me. I'm not leaving this bed until we've got a few things straight."

She renewed her struggles, frantic to avoid this confrontation. His hands were on her, grappling with her flailing arms until he had her wrists manacled above her head in a single hand, his grip firm but unhurting. She squirmed, but his body pressed insistently, pinning her down.

"Quit fighting me," he whispered sternly. His mouth was too close, so close that the heat of his breath fanned her face and she felt more drugged than if she'd inhaled ether. Then she quit fighting, praying he'd say what he had to and leave.

"That's better." Better? She could only hope it wouldn't get worse. "We've been hiding behind this case, because that's the way you wanted it. No more, Rachel. We're on new turf, and my patience with the sham has run out."

"I don't want to talk." She buried her head in the downy texture of a pillow. He took the access to her neck the position offered, running his lightly bearded chin against it, then soothing the slight abrasion with his tongue. "You're being unfair," she charged, trying to shift away, only to have him follow.

"I never said I was fair."

"I can't think when you're doing this to me."

"Good. Can I take that to mean that I am something more to you than a bank draft, a rung on the ladder you're climbing?" He released her hands.

"No." Her automatic denial was contradicted by her palms' refusal to obey her mental "Don't touch" message. They sought his bare skin, the flex of her fingers gripping his back tightly.

"Liar," he softly accused. "Admit it. You're more distracted by what you're afraid to confront between us than any amount of distraction that would be there if you risked confronting it."

His words rang of truth. She was desperate to escape them—and desperate not to. Once she owned up to them, there was no turning back, and that terrified her, because she knew her own fate could prove worse than Sarah's. Rand had the power to take more than her innocence. He could break her heart.

Rachel forced her hands away from the warmth of his skin, skin that she could easily grow addicted to touching, and played the trump card that was wearing thin from overuse.

"As much as you want to find your sister, that's a risk you shouldn't gamble on."

"Maybe I'm gambling on the fact that you're a woman of depth, who would stop at nothing if she was committed to a personal cause. One who would do her best if she's got an emotional stake involved.''

Rachel shut her eyes, feeling the bed beneath her, his weight so solid and so good covering hers. But his words, the ones just spoken, sparked a horrible suspicion. Oh, how it hurt to think it, that he might play her as heartlessly as he had his mean competition.

''If you're trying to barter my body and my emotions for a vested interest in your sister, you're not going to succeed. You can't manipulate me like I'm one of those commodities that you scarf up then liquidate to make your profit.''

''Is that what you think?'' he demanded. ''Dammit, quit hiding your face in the pillow and look at me.''

She shut her eyes tight. There was a sharp burning behind them, the threat of accumulated tears that she would not cry.

The insistent pressure of his grip at her jaw forced her face from the pillow. His breath was warm; she inhaled spice and the hint of bay. How could she compete with this? He was older than she in more than years, and she was floundering. No, worse than that. She felt as if she were staggering, banging into walls and sliding headlong into a revolving glass door that was going too fast for her to escape out the other side.

She reached for something, anything, to stop this crazy spinning that was more disorienting than any drugged wine.

''I'll tell you what I think,'' she said in a cracked voice. ''Once this is over, your old life will be waiting. A life that's as alien to me as mine is to you. You're a man who plays to win and bails out before he can sink. Anyone else on board had better be a good swimmer, because they'll be cutting through the waves you leave in your wake.''

He was silent for a while, and then he whispered, "You cut me, Rachel. You just cut me deeper than any insult that's ever been hurled in my face or any knife planted in my back. Including the one you drove in our last day in Vegas. You're still twisting the knife, and I'm still going against everything that defines my life to tell you I *do* care. *You* care. Don't deny it. Just tell me what it is that makes you want to.''

His genuine hurt touched her in a place that quivered in empathy. Her emotions weren't the only ones on the line, and his honesty deserved the same from her.

"All right. It's because caring does go against what defines your life. Maybe I am more than a means to heal your missing-person affliction or to gratify a mutual lust. But for me, it's not enough.'' She could feel his laser-sharp gaze against her still-closed eyes. She had to leave them that way to say what she had to. "You're driven by instincts when it comes to survival. Mine tell me that my ultimate lesson could come from you. I can't be a ship passing through the night for any man. And because I more than care, especially not for you.''

His curse was soft and curt. "You're right,'' he said roughly. "It could happen. But unless you can find the courage to take the chance, neither of us will ever know if you can teach me something I need to learn.''

"And what is that?'' she asked hesitantly, hopefully.

"It goes back to what you said about ships. After a long haul, they can run out of steam. Even the ocean liners, angel. Not an easy thing to accept when they like to think of themselves as autonomous. That is, until a sister ship comes out of nowhere and throws out a line."

He pressed into her. Deep and insistent was the grinding of his need. With a small cry, she arched upward, not meaning to, but somewhere, somehow, she had lost her own command.

Her eyes opened to search his, to discover if they were open and honest or simply those of a man in heat.

Steamy windows. Open windows, open as they had never been before. There was a depth there that she'd sensed, but sensed only. Staggering, yes, and frightful, because she saw him in all his darkness, beckoning her into his haunted, eerily vacant room.

"You know, Rachel, it's awfully disappointing when the line disappears before the captain can decide whether or not to take it. But I guess that's a moot point when the decision's already been made for him."

There was heavy disappointment in his statement, mingled with undisguised need. It touched her deeply, stoked a tender desire to share a mutual lifeline.

She touched his lips with her fingertips. His mouth drew taut with the stern clamp of his jaw.

"Who are you?" she whispered. "For once, Rand, tell me who and what you are."

"I'm afraid it's not that simple. In fact, since I met you, I'm not so sure myself. But I do know that at the moment I'm a man who's waging a real battle. You're innocent. I haven't been for a very long

time.'' A struggle was taking place inside him, one
she could feel in the sudden jerk of his hips, the si-
multaneous narrowing of his eyes. ''Right now I'm
wanting to take you somewhere that I don't think you
should go.''

Rachel's need to explore this unfamiliar path was
great; so, too, was her fear. She swallowed convul-
sively, her throat dry.

''You're probably right. But before you make that
decision for me, at least let me see the place you go.''

''It's a walk. A walk on the dark side.'' He smiled
without warning. A chilling smile that she sensed was
meant to frighten her away from the danger he posed.
She didn't recoil, as she knew she should, but stared
at him as though she were a doe paralyzed by a head-
light in the night.

''You really want to know who and what I am?
Then welcome, angel, to one very intimate facet of
me. If you're wise, you'll steal a glimpse and leave
it at that. Take my warning as a sign that you're not
a passing ship.''

Her palms bracketed his shoulders. She was
stranded between the urge to grip him to her—to rush
headlong, without looking back—and the realization
that she should heed his warning and shove him away
while she had the chance.

''Why do I get the feeling that you're trying to
protect me from yourself? That part of you is so good
it's the real danger. But that's another man who's
moving against me, tempting me to stay and take the
risk.''

''You see too much and you see too deep.'' His
lips bore down on hers, plundering in no polite way.
She responded before giving herself the option of es-

cape, letting him take her down, down, to a place where there was no light, just this blind spot where she groped for the feel and taste and smell of him. But then he was pulling back, done with his ravaging, and slowly shaking his head.

"Run, Rachel. Run while you can. Against everything I want, I'm giving you a head start. Take it. I'll catch up, but by then you'll be much safer, if not out of my sight. You deserve that much, even if it's more than I want to give."

"I see through you, Rand." She threaded her fingers through his hair; it was clean and thick and arousingly rich. "Heaven help us both, because I'm still here."

"So you are." The tempering she had sensed, had read behind the inky blackness, retreated, leaving a gleam of danger that both beckoned and menaced. "You're either very brave or very foolish, Rachel. Because I'm ready to give you a closer look at just who you're dealing with. A man who knows when a woman's aroused, and knows that you are in no small way. It would be so easy for me to touch you, just so…"

He insinuated his hand between their bodies and stroked her cleft. The teasing whisper escalated into a merciless vibration. She cried out. She arched, and her body shook as though in the grip of a palsied madness. His expression hardened with some purpose she was too far gone to care about.

"Help me," she moaned. "Protect me." And then she gripped his shoulders, the broad slope that loomed above her. "Ahhh…"

"That's right. I could have you right now, and well don't I know it." Swift and sure was the glide of his finger into her entry. The sensation was too great, and painfully unsatisfying.

"It's not enough. What you're giving me, it's not enough."

"No, angel. It's more than I've ever given any woman before." He began to thrust slightly. Gently. With guarded strength. "You said I was no different today than those other barbarians. But I'm going to prove to us both that you were wrong. That I can feel this soft heat inside you and leave it at that. Because there's so much more that I need, something you've got that I've lost. If I can manage this, then maybe, just maybe I can get it back. Believe it or not, I am protecting you now."

"Rand," she sobbed. "Please, Rand, I can't stand it. You're making me hurt inside. Where you're touching me. But even more, here. In my heart. Don't do this to me, not unless you can be what I need."

"Unless I know what that is, I can't give it. Tell me what you need, and don't hold out."

"You," she cried brokenly. "*You.* But I want it all, and I don't know if you're able to give it."

"Neither do I...yet." His strokes gathered momentum, now fuller, deeper, a tactile invasion that made her reach with each retreat and weep for his possession of her. "More than anyone could possibly know, I do care about Sarah," he said, in a voice ragged with frayed restraint. "But I also care about us. In fact, I care enough not to strip off my clothes and take what my body's demanding. I'm stopping this right now, Rachel, while I still can. Protection. From me."

He made to withdraw, and she grabbed blindly for his wrist.

"How can you leave me like this?"

"With great difficulty, that's how. But knowing that you do care, apparently more than you want to, gives me enough reason to leave you like this."

"You make me need you and then you leave? It's cruel, Rand. How can you say that you care and be so cruel?"

"Do you think what I'm doing is easy for me? Sweet heaven, Rachel, if you can't sense how close I am to the edge, surely you can feel me against you, so hard that I hurt. The way I see it, I'm not being cruel. I'm being kind."

"Damn you, Rand." This was kindness? This horrible, empty ache he had created yet again and was leaving unappeased was kind? It seemed the cruelest punishment a man could devise. "Damn you for inviting me inside just to slam the door in my face."

"Damned if I do. But more damned if I don't. You see, angel, there's more I need to know before we take this all the way. What I'm leaving you with is some time to think. As much about your motives as mine. We both deserve it." He shut his eyes, and she thought he sighed. A sad sound, a distant whisper.

"Joshua deserves it."

12

"JOSHUA?" How could he spin riddles at a time like this? His reasoning was madness, and his timing was even worse. She opened her thighs and wrapped them about his. Arching, all but begging, she clung to his waist, demanding that he not desert her.

Rand's head fell forward, and he stared down at her with more complexities in his expression than she could possibly interpret through her distress. She knew one thing, and one thing only: the instinct to mate with him, to bond.

"Joshua's very close to Sarah. Probably much closer to her than he is to me, though lately he's been paying me some surprise visits. But enough about him." His teeth clenched as he growled a final warning. "Unwrap your legs, Rachel, before I decide to finish what we've hardly started. My more honorable nature just clocked out, since it's already put in some overtime."

She shook her head in a stilted negation, more torn and confused than denying. His face discarded the wisp of tenuous discipline and bore down on her with carnal force.

She glimpsed something, something she couldn't quite define. It tugged at her, this nagging sensation of having brushed the gentlest core of him, only to have him jerk it away before she could touch it. Her physical need peaked and interlocked with the need to reach out, to go where he had withdrawn to. Her frustration was more than sexual; it came from being denied access to what made him the man he was.

"You're hiding something from me, aren't you? You managed to get what you wanted out of me, and now that I want something in return you're shutting me out. You're running."

"Be glad I'm offering to run. We're in a country that gives me absolute rights to your body, and those are some rights I'm way past being ready to claim. This is our bed. This our bedroom. It's only the possibility that we could have something we both need that's keeping me in check. But just barely." He thrust down. Up. Then down again. A hard, rolling grind. "Unlock your legs," he commanded. Then he snapped out, *"Now."*

She forced herself to release him. A sensation like glass shattering sliced through her extremities.

"It wasn't supposed to be this way." It sounded like an accusation, and at the moment she did blame him for all the terrible things she felt. "This wasn't part of the deal."

"Apparently the deal has changed. Seems to me we've both been guilty of lying to each other as well as ourselves."

He got up and adjusted his robe. She clutched at the sheet with shaking fingers. Rand caught her wrist and covered her himself. She glared at him, in outrage he'd dangled the bait, hooked her, and was leaving her floundering alone on a deserted shore. Her begging cries were still in her ears, and she winced at the memory of his rejection. He'd refused her body, her need to know him. One refusal was humiliating, the other hurt. She lashed out for both.

"Sounds like you've got it all worked out, Mr. Slick."

"Not yet, but I'm getting there."

"With your rules, right?"

"That's right. After I tend your wrists, we'll share a nice dinner." He paused, then gentled his voice. "I'd like us to enjoy a pleasant evening our first night together."

"Since you want it to be pleasant, I suppose I can count on you disappearing into another bedroom?" God, she hoped so. He'd found her out, and no amount of acting ability could disguise that.

"Another bedroom?" he shouted toward the door. "You will warm my bed, and that's final. Sultan's decree." He kissed the top of her head and murmured, "You and me, Rachel, in some ways we're one of a kind. Should be interesting to see what kind of bed partners we make."

"Something tells me you steal the sheets."

"And something tells me you're a natural cuddler. Can't wait to feel you snuggled into my backside."

"Don't count on it." Drawing on the remnants of her bruised pride, she sought to get back at him where it hurt. "This whole setup smacks of stacking the deck in your favor. Devious. Underhanded. Just the way you work your business. You've turned out to be just as much a shark in the relationship department as you are behind a desk."

"Maybe. But I wouldn't exactly call you merciful at the moment. I'd think you might be grateful. After all, you're in bed alone, aren't you? If I didn't have some morals, we'd both be screaming by now."

Rachel didn't want to be merciful, and she sure as hell wasn't shelling out any gratitude. Her fingers closed around the first loose pillow she could grab. She hurled it at him, and he caught it as neatly as a pro player handling a pass.

"Don't bother coming in here tonight. Just get out! Get out and leave me alone."

"I would have gone sooner, but those thighs of yours have quite a grip."

Her cheeks burned at the reminder. "That's right! Run for the control panel!" she screamed at him. "Hit the right knobs! Touch her breasts, blur the lines between what's acting and what's not. You, the master, so smug and full of his own power. But I know better, Rand. See how you run."

"Actually, I'd prefer to stay for a change, even with the nasty turn your temper's taken. And as for running, you're doing a good job yourself. Admit it, Rachel, your feminine ego's been pricked, and you'd rather throw me out than have me walk."

"Don't flatter yourself." Damn the man, standing there looking so insufferably sure of himself, while she felt more stung and discarded than ever in her life. "I wouldn't sleep with you if you were the last man on earth."

"As far as you're concerned, I am. You do belong to me, and we can't let anyone think otherwise," he said in a subdued, stern tone. "Therefore, you do sleep with me, Rachel. Sex or no sex. But judging from this little encounter, it won't be long until we're both too far gone to forget about pride, and who's right or wrong. I just hope by then I've got a few things resolved myself."

''What things?'' The question was out before her pride could intervene.

''Stick around and we'll both find out.''

''Do I have a choice?'' she retorted, miffed at his easy deflection.

''You have choices, and so do I. It seems we've both made some important ones already. By the way, there's a wardrobe in your closet. You will wear the white silk tonight?''

''Not if that's what you want.'' She'd wear black or green or purple. Anything but white silk or a muslin sheet.

''Suit yourself. They all end up on the floor for the servants to see anyway. Enjoy your bath, Rachel.''

''Go to hell, Rand.''

He stopped, his hand at the polished brass doorknob.

''Too late, angel,'' he said softly. ''I've already been there and back.''

A click sounded just before another pillow could hit its mark. Rachel dropped her head in her hands, vowing not to scream or cry, in case he was listening at the door. Taking deep, unsteady breaths, she realized the smell of spice was on her palms, mingled with the scent of bay. She sniffed her arms and realized she was covered with his scent. It was doubtless on her neck, her breasts, even in the haven of her thighs.

She hurt there, almost as much as she hurt in the twisted-up, inside-out span of her chest. What had Rand done to her? What had she done to herself? She didn't know. Hell, she didn't know anything except that she craved him, resented him. This lesson in emotional survival with Rand Slick had left her jarred, stunned and terrified of any brutal lessons he was capable of administering in their uncertain future.

If she'd had any doubts before, she had none now.

He did have the power to break her heart.

The sound of water splashing in an adjoining room was a soothing contrast to her chaos and turmoil. The bath he'd ordered drawn beckoned her to cleanse herself of the cloying musk that had tainted her at the auction. She would try to rid herself of the musk Rand had called from her own body, and wash away the hold he exerted, even now that he was gone.

"Your bath is ready." A weary, olive-skinned face peeked through the door that Rand had exited. "You may go through the side door in your bedroom. The master has given his permission."

"The master can die and rot before I need his permission to soak." Rachel felt bad when the woman ducked her head in a subservient manner—but not before a flicker of admiration and surprise flashed in her eyes. Accompanied by the trace of an approving smile. "Have you got a name?"

"Jayna."

"Jayna." So this was her guard. Rachel wrapped the sheet around her body as she rose to her feet, sizing Jayna up as she did. Trusting her gut instinct, Rachel decided she liked her. Maybe it was just that she was upset with Rand and Jayna seemed to sympathize. Whatever, if she had to have a guard, Jayna seemed like an A-okay one to have.

"Thanks, Jayna. I could use a bath. Maybe get my head on straight while I read a good book. Have you got anything around here I could read? Something the, uh—" make that *ugh* "—*master* would approve of?"

''The master left instructions to give you this.'' She smiled and extended a thick volume. ''It is in English so that you might read and gain knowledge.''

''Thanks. It's probably a travelogue, judging from his twisted sense of humor.'' Rachel accepted the book and headed for the side door. ''Take the day off, Jayna.''

''But the master—I cannot—''

''Sure you can. If Mr. Master has a problem, you tell him to come see me. I've got the only goods he's interested in getting under control.'' Rachel winced, remembering just how under control he'd had her goods. ''Now go on. I can see to myself. Go watch a soap opera or eat some lunch. Or better yet, go round up some cards and chips. I'll teach you how to play poker tomorrow.''

''You think to play cards tomorrow?'' She laughed behind her hand. ''It is not likely.''

''How come?''

''The master. He is young and strong. And his eyes, they glow darkly when he speaks of you. No, I do not think he has plans that you should play cards with me tomorrow.''

''You mean I need his permission for something as simple as playing cards?''

''Of course. He is the master. You are his bed slave. You would be wise to obey him.'' Jayna smiled sympathetically. ''Even wiser to please him and gain his favor. He is your master but he is also a man, no? Even a bed slave might have power over a man.''

If the auction and Rand's bedchamber performance hadn't driven home the absolute control he could wield over her in this perverse country, Jayna's observation did.

Shaken, Rachel grasped the gravity of the situation she was in the thick of, a danger far different from any she'd considered before.

"Thanks for the advice, Jayna. If you don't mind, I'd like to be alone and think on it awhile. Check you later."

"As you wish."

Jayna bowed out of the room, and for a long time Rachel stared sightlessly at the closed door. The rich mahogany took on the substance of iron, the engraved design resembling vertical bars. Shaking herself out of her trance, she looked around, absorbing the elaborately carved teak furniture, the walls draped in raw silk, the central location of the bed proclaiming its importance.

A gilded cage. And here she was in it, a woman in a country where a woman had to be covered from head to foot just to walk the streets. No freedom there, either, because she had to trail ten paces behind the man she was bound to—or, if a concubine, as Sarah was, and as she was, too, she was guarded by a servant of the master. Rand possessed a master's rights. She had none, other than those he chose to grant her.

The harsh reality of it hit her harder than the unreal memory of the kidnapping. Her hands clenched the binding of the book. By golly, he'd better be generous, or else... Or else what? What leverage did she have besides the tangled web of emotions they shared? Sarah? No bargaining chip there. This had become a personal mission, and she an avenging angel.

What it came down to, she realized, was her trust in Rand and his respect for her. *Talk about testing a relationship.*

Rachel padded into the bathing chamber and dropped the sheet. How could anything so decadent be for the purpose of washing up? Water spouted from a dolphin's gold mouth. She turned the handles—they were crafted in the shape of golden starfish—then got in. With a weary sigh, she leaned back.

The deep, sunken tub could easily accommodate four of her, which was good, since she felt trapped in one of those tri-fold mirrors, which multiplied her into a dozen different images. She shut her eyes, willing the perfumed warmth to ease away everything that had happened to her in these mind-boggling few days. She couldn't begin to piece it all together. She was too exhausted even to try.

In spite of her resolve to block it all out, images played in cinematic fashion behind her lids.

Rand in her office. Rand in her home. Desperate and sensitive, hard and mean. Rubik's Cube spinning on jagged edges until it blurred with too many colors, none of them matching. She felt as if she were screaming inside with frustration, and then in horror as the auction revisited itself. The velocity of it propelling her into the bedroom, where he made her feel too good, too weak, and then he was leaving her, leaving her still screaming, wanting, hurting....

Rachel grabbed for a nearby towel that had been draped next to something she thought was called a bidet. Pressing the thick cloth against her mouth, she gave in to the need to scream, purging her system with a long, agonized wail. The towel absorbed her volatile grief again and again. When her throat was too raw for her to do more than whimper, she thrust the towel aside and took in deep gulps of air.

''Buck up,'' she ordered herself. ''Quit wallowing

in what's past, hold out till you know if this is the real thing, and get your act together. Read a book. Maybe he left you P. D. James.''

Determined to escape her troubled thoughts, she fingered the bound volume on the marble floor beside the tub. She hoisted it up and flipped to a page halfway through the volume.

Her eyes bulged, or at least they felt that way. The green of her irises nearly tumbled onto a well-thumbed illustration. With a burst of frazzled nerves, she flung the book out the door like a spitball over home plate. Her aim was a little too appropriate, under the circumstances.

The *Kama Sutra* landed neatly in the middle of the silk-cushioned bed Rand had dictated they were to share. Sex or no sex, according to him.

Well, Rachel thought with a little huff, no sex, as far as she was concerned. She had a job to do, and Rand's earlier manipulation—and rejection—was too slick to be trusted.

But she wanted to trust him. She steeled her wayward heart against the flowering softness he commanded with shameful ease, and concentrated on how to go about getting the information she needed. The first questions were there already: Who was Joshua? And just what did he have to do with Rand, Sarah, and this relationship that was spinning beyond her control?

Rand could determine her physical responses, and he'd probed the tender emotions she was losing the battle to. But she'd felt the proof of his body's need, had glimpsed his deeper regions and felt his protective sensitivity. It put them on an equal footing of sorts. Their hunger cut both ways, and that meant she'd get her answers. Her dad had taught her a lot, but table-turning was something she'd learned from Rand.

And what of the lesson she'd learned from Jayna? *He is also a man, no? Even a bed slave might have power over a man.*

She was no slave, but Rand was all man. She had let him call too many of the shots, and it was high time she exerted some influence of her own. Feminine influence. Potent stuff.

That decided, she lined up her strategy.

Tonight. The bedroom. Answers.

A showdown. His turf.

But her way.

13

RAND PAUSED outside the bedroom door, hesitating as he remembered the volatile exchange that had marked his earlier exit. He'd won a minor but significant battle for Joshua—and, he thought, for Sarah—at the expense of Rachel's self-exposure. And, unfortunately, her wrath.

Listening, he heard nothing of her movements. Of course, she just might be standing inches away, ready to clobber him with something more substantial than a pillow. Like more slurs about his character. He was still licking his wounds. Rachel possessed the uncanny ability to hurt him, and the equally disturbing ability to summon Joshua's ghost from his past. Did she realize she held that power? Whether she did or not, he most definitely felt the internal struggle as Rand and Joshua slugged it out.

How vulnerable he felt standing here, dreading to enter, and so eager that adrenaline made him feel like a car shifted into park with the accelerator pressed to the floor.

He had to mask it. Taking several deep breaths, he gained his composure. He didn't want a power struggle, and if Rachel sensed the depth of his vulnerability to her he would feel even more at risk than he already did. And yet, when he'd allowed her a glimpse, she had responded with physical abandon and a tenderness he needed so much it made him ache.

It had stuck with him like a sweet lump of sugar wedged in the back of his throat. Likely the reason he'd given in and bought the two dolls he'd picked up, put down, then paced the marketplace for an hour before returning to buy. They were just bisque and cloth. Just sentimental memories.

Just his longing for the woman who held the key to reuniting him with his sister. One who was also unlocking some parts of himself he'd been stunned to discover still existed.

Keys. Locks. Doors.

"Do it," he commanded himself aloud.

His hand was poised to knock. But then he remembered his role, and that allowed him to solidify his hold under the pretense of acting his part.

His jaw clenching, he went directly for the knob.

His breath left him. She was facing the window, looking out at the indigo sky, her hand clenched in the voluminous drapes. The white gauze spilled through her ruby-painted nails and trailed the ground, blending into the white silk she wore. One shoulder was bare, the other half-covered by flowing, sheer fabric. Her back was partially exposed, revealing skin as rich and soft as cream icing on a cake. It contrasted with the cascade of her hair—a study in scarlet temptation.

He thought she must be driving him a little crazy.

Rand leaned against the door. She gave a small start before whirling around to face him.

Holy heaven above, what is she trying to do? Get ahead instead of even? He'd raised the stakes, but

Rachel seemed to have decided to make it all or nothing.

"I see you wore the white for me." Rand cleared his throat, since swallowing wasn't possible, with his mouth so dry. "I also see you've used something of a local touch."

"Do you like it?" Her voice was unsure, even anxious, perhaps. The curtain she was clenching appeared to have a case of the tremors.

"I don't know if *like* is the word." He advanced, and her kohl-lined eyes darted to the bed, then quickly back to him. Well, he thought with relief, at least he wasn't the only one feeling his feet slip on the high wire.

"I found the cosmetics laid out in the bathroom. I sent Jayna away, so I just used my imagination. They're not exactly what I'm used to." She wet her lips, which were glossed to a deep shade of wine. "I mean, the makeup I usually wear is different back home."

"I wish you'd try to think of this as our home until we get back to the States." He found her feminine uncertainty immensely appealing, especially since he'd never seen a woman look as desirable as she did now...standing there, wringing the curtain, afraid she'd put her makeup on wrong.

"Is it too much?" Her kohl-lined eyes, as mysterious as the Orient, glanced at him for reassurance. "I'm going to wash my face."

He caught her by the arm as she tried to leave and insistently pulled her to him. Twining a hand through her hair, he urged her head back. The tiny beauty mark she'd penciled into the low hollow of her left cheek dipped as her lips parted to accommodate a soft gasp.

"Leave it," he said, his voice a little rough. "You do realize, don't you, that you're the kind of woman a man wants to stare at to the point of being rude."

"I—I like it when you look at me. I always wonder what you're thinking behind those one-way windows."

"One-way windows?"

"Your eyes. Sometimes I peek in when you don't think I'm looking. That's when I see the most."

And how much had she seen today? How far had she looked when he'd been half out of his mind with desire to take her willing body, only to find that his moral fiber was stronger than his rutting instincts?

"Do you peek in while I'm busy staring?"

"I try to." She took a quick breath. "But usually they're too steamy to get a clear picture."

"Steamy windows... Hmmm... It does feel foggy in there sometimes. Especially when I imagine kissing you, wondering what makes you tick, and if you're as much of a hissing kitten in bed as you are out it. But the way you look tonight gives a whole new dimension to anything I've ever imagined before."

Her fair skin heightened in color, and she smiled nervously. She seemed to be blooming in enticing and unexpected ways. She'd lowered her guard earlier, but he'd forced that. Dare he hope that she was opening herself up to him freely? If she could trust him that much, then maybe, just maybe, he could trust them both enough to let her into his shadows. Shadows that wouldn't be so dark if she would share her light with him.

"Thank you, Rand. No one's ever said anything

quite like that to me. But I guess you're more familiar with flattering a woman than I am with being flattered.''

''The way you say that, I get the impression you think this is one of my standard seduction lines.'' He felt the faint tremor as her muscles tensed.

''Is it?''

''That's something I like very much about you, Rachel. Up-front and direct. I find that quality in a woman to be a rare and valuable asset. You don't go for deceit, or play the tease to manipulate a man to your advantage.'' She glanced away, and he caught her chin, forcing her to look directly at him. He searched her eyes. ''You wouldn't ever do that, now would you?''

''Of course not.'' Her eyes dilated and he felt her go from tense to stiff. Rand raised a brow, and his lips thinned. Feeling his hopes threatened, he searched for the familiar hardness of self-protection. It seemed to have moved, because he couldn't find it. Suddenly he was desperate to get rid of Joshua's interference and cling to what he knew.

''No, of course not,'' he said flatly. ''You're above that. Just as I don't resort to flattery to entice a woman into my bed. Seduction under false pretenses isn't my style.''

''But buying a woman under false pretenses is. You are using this situation to your personal advantage, aren't you?''

How easily she'd tripped him up. He should have known better than to take her appearance and the sensual bent of her words for what he wanted them to be. Damn Joshua for putting him through this. Damn him for insisting he accept the blow because he deserved it, when Rand Slick was champing at the bit to silence her pert mouth with a punishing kiss.

He waited a full minute before one of them gained the upper hand.

"I asked for that, didn't I?"

"That. And more."

"You're right. Why don't I make up for my earlier advantage-taking and show you around our house before dinner?"

"You mean I'm actually free to tour the premises?"

"Not only tour, but have the run of the place. Just as long as you don't get this disrespectful in front of the servants." *Whew.* That was close. Too close. Before he could stop himself, Mr. Slick demanded some retribution. He was squirming uncomfortably and wanted some company.

"Don't forget where we are, Rachel," he said sternly. "I'd be expected to punish you for such a sharp tongue. If I didn't give a proper show of taming you, we'd raise suspicion. Do us both a favor and don't put me in that position."

"Tame me! Punish me! With what? One of those whips the auctioneer was screaming for? Or maybe you've got some chains or leather bindings stashed away, along with a black face mask."

"Actually, no." A grin tugged at his lips, but he squelched it. She was riled enough as it was, though he did find the flash of her eyes, the agitated heave of her breasts, very much to his liking. "I'm adventurous, but more status quo than kinky. The servants would think everything was aboveboard if I simply hauled you into the bedroom and made you scream."

"I'd bite my tongue off before giving you that satisfaction."

Rand traced her mouth, sliding his thumb over it, savoring its glossy texture. The internal war raged on, as did the voice demanding that he take her lips, kiss them until they were too swollen to talk back and she simply accepted that he needed her spirit, her acceptance—and if she could find it in her, even perhaps something called love. *There.* He'd let himself think it. *Love.* A four-letter word he was compelled to explore for himself, Rand, because no matter how much of Joshua was left, he would still be what life had made him. He wanted her to accept all of him, the good and the bad. Wanted? Needed. Desperately, just as he needed the security of knowing she couldn't run away from him here.

More important, neither could he. Rachel seemed to think she was a prisoner of sorts. The truth was, he was more a prisoner than she, cut off from all the avenues of escape that were so plentiful back in the States. He found these walls a comforting sort of prison, and Rachel, its sweet warden.

If only she knew how close to the mark she'd come today, tearing out his insides with her accusations. *See how he runs!* He'd wanted to defend himself, to tell her that old habits, even destructive ones, were hard to break.

He hadn't then. He couldn't now.

"Temper, temper, Rachel." He made a clicking noise, a reproving tut-tut. "You wouldn't really want to bite off your tongue, would you?" He stroked the supple interior of her lower lip, careful to avoid her teeth. "Judging from the sample I had earlier, I'm certain that would be a terrible waste."

"You are *the* most impossible, infuriating man I've ever met in my life. Maybe chivalry *is* dead, since chauvinism is apparently alive and well."

"I'll take that for a compliment, since I'm not in the mood for *The Taming of the Shrew* as a prelude to dinner. But I always did enjoy cherries jubilee for dessert. There's something about a room with muted lighting and a dish going up in flames against a white cloth that appeals to even the most jaded connoisseur."

Rachel was doing a slow burn. "I won't even dignify such a lewd insinuation with one of the many names I'd like to call you at the moment."

"I'm disappointed. Names can tell a lot…angel."

"I agree." She fixed him with a level stare. "Who's Joshua?"

14

HIS THUMB TENSED, but then he commanded himself to go about his sensual play as if she hadn't struck a nerve.

"Joshua's a boy who grew up the hard way. He's a mutual acquaintance of mine and Sarah's. I've seen him more recently than Sarah, but I'm sure she remembers him well. Once you locate her, that's the password to clue her in that I'm here."

"Why not use your own name?"

"Because…" He should tell her. And yet the thought made him feel more exposed than he already did, and this was torture as it was. Later, perhaps. When he had his footing. Or in a moment of intimacy, when Rachel was as defenseless as he. "Because this way my identity remains a secret. Anyone who might overhear could inform Sarah's owner and blow the cover we have to maintain until we leave."

The room felt claustrophobic, cloying, as memories rushed back to him, memories he'd relegated to a lockbox long ago, because that was the only way he knew to survive. And how well he'd done it, slamming the lid shut before the past could injure him further.

He abruptly turned for the bathing chamber, leaving his lockbox behind, only to feel it being dragged after him on some invisible chain.

"I thought I saw some ointment in here earlier. Let's get those wrists tended to, then go for that tour. Big place. Could take an hour to show you around, and I'd hate to ply you with an overdone dinner."

"Rand?" She stood at the door, and he kept his back to her as he rummaged through a drawer full of household supplies, his mind shunning the unwanted baggage and casting about for an avenue of escape. He found it in an unexpected form.

Girl stuff. Opening a tube of salve, he waved her to the sink while his attention focused on the cosmetics she'd used. Her things. How would his things look next to hers? Lipstick next to a shaver. Panty hose draped near his bathrobe. Strange to imagine, but he found the idea unaccountably appealing.

"Let's have a look at those wrists." He scowled as he gently smoothed the healing balm over the abrasions. "Bastards. I'd like to strangle them for this."

"I need to ask you something, Rand. I wish you'd look at me, because it's important, and I want to see the truth in your eyes. None of those shutters you're so good at drawing."

Her voice was soft again, as it had been before she'd gone for a confrontation. As much as he wanted to trust it, he feared to. Undoubtedly she was resorting to her initial strategy since he hadn't taken the bait. Maybe Joshua's tempering influence was good for something.

"What do you want to know?"

"I keep wondering something." She winced, and he kissed the thin red lines at her wrist. He was indirectly responsible for this. It gave him a sick feeling.

"And what something do you keep wondering?"

''What would you have done if the prince had agreed to pay a million and a half?''

If they were going to get closer, he knew he had to start letting her in. There was danger in that for both of them, and he didn't want her to get hurt should his demons decide to race out. But this seemed a safe place to start. Rand risked letting her have more than a peek.

''No shutters, Rachel. Look inside and tell me my answer.''

She searched his eyes, and then she smiled.

''You would have bid two, wouldn't you?''

''I don't stoop to haggling.'' Rand tipped her chin up and darted his tongue between her parted lips. ''I would have bid five. Where my personal portfolio's concerned, you're one investment that's invaluable. Case or no case.''

She fairly glowed as she shook her head in amazement.

''You must be about the richest man I've ever met in my life, Rand Slick.''

''If it's money you're counting, I do okay. It tends to buy respect and fear and favors. I've got plenty of all that, but I've learned there are some things that money can't buy.''

''My dad used to say it couldn't buy love.''

''Your dad was a smart fella. Money can induce people to fake emotions for the person carrying the money clip, but it doesn't guarantee genuine feelings.''

''That's shallow. Only someone with a lack of character would pretend to care for another person just because they've got something to gain from it.''

''And you have more character than anyone I

know. Maybe that's why I never believed money was the reason you agreed to risk yourself for me.''

The look they shared was one of rushing memories—her earlier insistence he was a client, a paycheck, and the way he'd twice called her bluff. Rachel had every right to resent his methods, but it just wasn't in him to be sorry for having touched her intimately. Those moments had changed the course of their relationship, those hot, precious moments when he could forget everything but what touching her did to him.

The memories arced between them, and he wondered if she would turn away, rather than confront his unspoken need to let what was between them flow and not fight it anymore. He had to fight himself enough, without her fighting him, too.

She touched his shaved cheek, and he felt a surge of tenderness. From her. And in him. It left him off balance, wavering between the bittersweet lure of the contents of his lockbox and a quick dive into his concrete bunker.

''I know what I said that night at my home, Rand, and today. You found out for yourself that I was lying, but I'd like to take it all back just the same. Lies don't sit well with me, and the truth is, even if you were poor I'd still...''

He waited on edge while the four-letter word beginning with *L* flirted with his senses.

''Yes, Rachel?''

She seemed unable to go on, as though she'd painted herself into a corner and was frantic to find a way out. How well he could relate to that.

''Because...'' She wet her lips, and her eyes darted about, looking at the sink, the tub, the ointment, any-

where but at him. "Because even if you were poor
I'd still think you were a beast, and wonder why I
was crazy enough to take your case," she said tartly.
"No doubt you would have smuggled us in and we'd
be sharing dinner out of a can while I posed as a
masseuse in that spa I'm supposed to get greased up
in to find Sarah."

"I can think of worse things than having to spend
the day getting massaged and relaxing in a sauna."
He managed a faint smile, masking his disappointment at her retreat.

"I'll still be on the job. All the massages in the
world can't take the tenseness out of asking the right
questions while your insides are upside down."

"You'll do fine. And don't forget, Jayna will be
there, too. One word and she'll come get me. If you
even sense a threat of danger, I'll be there. I give you
my word."

"No, Rand. You could make a bad situation even
worse. You can do your bit after I make contact. Until
then, you stay scarce. It's my job. And my neck."

He touched the neck in question. The pad of his
thumb rested over the thrum of her pulse, which both
of his personas would protect at all costs, whether she
liked it or not. Without Rachel, neither he nor Sarah
stood a chance.

The urgent need to rescue Sarah, and the gut-deep
drive to solidify this bonding of man and woman escalated to a dizzying pitch. Both hinged on protecting
the neck he longed to put his lips against, to taste and
suck until she bore his mark. His, and only his.

"I thought we had this settled. We're a team, Rachel. Don't try to take back what happened today.

You should know me well enough to realize I don't give up ground I've gained.''

''You weren't very ethical about gaining it.''

''Ah, now it comes back at me. Well, let me tell you, lady, you gained some ground of your own that was hell for me to give up. Between the two of us, I hope we can win more than one war.''

''There's one war we're going to win for certain.'' Her chin got that stubborn little look to it that he found so appealingly saucy. ''I've come to realize how imperative it is to get Sarah out. After walking in the other woman's shoes, I want more than anything to give her a new pair.''

Shine your shoes, mister? It hit him out of left field, jarring loose the lockbox. He tried to close it again so fast he stung from the snap.

''It could take awhile, Rachel,'' he said in a vague voice while he shoved and kicked at the contents trying to slither their way out. ''Even if it's the most popular hangout for the elite concubines, you can only spend so much time making small talk in the sauna.''

''I'm sweating already. If this takes longer than a few trips, I'll start looking like a prune.''

''Not once your skin's anointed.'' He passed a hand over his eyes, praying that when he looked again he'd see nothing but her, that the unwanted garbage had packed up and gone home. Home…

I'll come back when I've got lots of money. Then I'll buy you and me a brand-new house… Whenever you feel sad, just think about that.

''Anointed, huh? Then I'll be a prune with zits. Should be a real experience, dehydrating then getting my pores clogged with perfumed butter.''

She laughed, and he felt the memory subside. Thank God for Rachel. Even now she could make him want to smile. But he didn't. He considered her, and this elixir effect she had on him, at length.

Rachel's laughter trailed off, and she began to fidget.

He continued to stare; she fidgeted some more. The staring and the fidgeting had a way of taking his mind off the little monsters. *Well, well, Mr. Slick, the wooly bullies seem to be gone for now, but watch where you step, 'cause there's some smushed guts laying around. 'Nough to slip on.*

He could feel himself begin to relax as Rachel's discomfort with his perusal gave his jagged state a sense of companionship. And he did like her company under any circumstances.

Deciding to go for the rose at the expense of a few thorn pricks, he chuckled. "Perfumed butter? Don't you mean oiled and prepared for your lover?"

"Whatever, but I suppose getting it slathered on is better than being the one working it in."

"I wouldn't mind working it in."

"Rand!"

"The oil, of course. We could take turns practicing and slide all over each other like a couple of greased pigs oinking their heads off at the county fair."

Rachel's throaty hoot of laughter washed over him. Just what he needed to forget the threat of slippage. He was okay now, his gut emotions all stuffed safely away.

"I like it when you talk my kind of language. It's a lot more comfortable than that hoity-toity way you can act sometimes."

"Oh, I can get down and dirty when I want to.

Comes from having too much practice at eating out of cans.''

Her teasing expression softened, and he read a hint of the pity he had learned to abhor in leaner days.

Taken off guard by it, he cringed inwardly. With nothing more than a sympathetic look, she'd managed to shove him back into the same dark place that her laughter had momentarily banished.

"Are you feeling sorry for me?" he demanded.

"A little. Maybe because you don't feel sorry for yourself.''

"Don't do it," he warned. "Laugh with me. Fight with me. Work and possibly even make love with me. But don't ever let me catch you pitying me. I won't have it.''

"But there's something inside you, something that's marked you for life. I don't know what it was exactly, and I'm positive it wasn't fair. But if pride goeth before a fall, then you're very close to the edge.''

"You're right—I am close to the edge. One that you'd better back away from. Let it lie, Rachel, because the pride in question sure as hell doesn't need your sympathy.''

He turned, determined to cut her short before he could undo the progress he'd made. If he didn't get out fast, he feared he'd slip and come down on her like an avalanche.

Rachel caught his arm and yanked him back with surprising strength. He glared at her, silently warning her not to persist.

"Quit running, Rand. I've got something to say that I think you need to hear.'' She leveled a stern gaze at him that he admired, even as he cursed her foolhardy courage. "The kind of pride that refuses a sympathetic ear is false pride. Why don't you talk about it for a change? What happened to you, what made you this way. If you got it out of your system—"

"I don't want to listen to—"

"You'd feel a lot better for it. Stop hiding from things you can't change. Your roots are permanent, whether you like what they are or not. Share them with me. I know it must be bad, and if I feel sympathy for what you went through, just try to accept it. Accepting compassion won't make you any less of a man. Maybe it could even help you accept yourself."

He felt as though she'd slapped him with her concern, caring in a way he didn't want her to care, trying to make him confront the past by jarring his lockbox wide open. And she wouldn't let him shut it. It was as though she were reaching inside and searching through the muck to find some hidden treasure. It was like being stripped of all the power and prestige he'd earned, to be thrust back into a soup-kitchen line.

He wanted to lash out at her for serving up his insides on a hellish platter, compliments of her compassion.

In reflex, as automatic as deflecting a blow, he thrust his hand into her hair and leaned her back against the sink. He hit the handle. Water spilled from the faucet. He cupped it and quickly poured several handfuls onto her chest, wetting the silk until it was transparent and clinging to her breasts.

"What are you doing? Rand! Rand, please, you're scaring me. Please, stop it!"

"We're going to play a game, Rachel. It's a simple game. I get you wet, and than I get you hot. You've 'got beautiful breasts, did you know that? And your nipples look— Oh, poor things, they look so cold the way they're puckering. I think I need to mouth them, warm them a bit for you. It's the least I can do, since I'm the one to blame. Just out of compassion, you understand. Because I feel so sorry for you.''

''Rand—''

''I'd rather you call me a beast. You called me that before, and I'll take it over your pity any day. Again, Rachel. Let's hear it. *Beast.*''

''Beast!'' she sobbed. ''Beast!''

In that moment, he loved the beast within him, clung to him, because he was invulnerable, and strong in his weakness.

''Much better. How can you pity a beast like me? Do you still want your beast? I hope so, because he does want you. Now let's cut the crap, because we both know this is no game.''

He palmed a breast, bent on his self-serving mission, the eradication of her hurtful compassion, and the assuagement of his never-ending lust. He'd almost succeeded in burying Pandora's legacy when he realized she was crying.

He stopped cold. He stared at her, unblinking. And then, as if he'd stepped outside his body, he saw the ugly scene as an onlooker might, with a sense of disbelief.

Was this what he'd become? This monstrosity that passed itself off as human? This creature that had squelched the man who was capable of heart and depth, the man who deserved this rare woman?

''Heaven help me,'' he groaned. ''What have I done?'' Rand's hands were shaking as he traced the path of her tears, the kohl streaking black down her cheeks. The makeup she'd put on so painstakingly and then anxiously wanted his approval of was being washed away by the proof of her hurt, compliments of the man who owned her—a man who was no prize himself.

No prize, but you've still got your precious pride. Satisfied, Slick? The stupid pride that he wore as protective armor had been penetrated by the strength of her softness, her acceptance. The very things he craved, and yet he'd punished her for offering them unconditionally. Money he understood, but something this priceless he had smashed, then ground to dust.

"Sweet Jesus—" His voice cracked. He turned off the water and lifted her, oh, so tenderly, until she was burrowed, limp and sobbing against his chest. He stroked his hand, the one that had so cruelly turned against her, into her hair and then gently rubbed her bare back. He made a shushing sound, a long *shhh, shhh* of comfort that hadn't passed his lips since the day he jumped the boxcar. He kissed the tears from her face until she was done crying.

"Angel..." he whispered. "Angel..."

Rachel latched on to his wrists so hard her fingernails bit into his skin.

"Why did you do it, Rand? If you won't tell me anything else, tell me that. Help me understand."

His neck felt stiff as he jerked out a shake of his head. He didn't want to go back into that dark place, that place that had driven him to this belly-scraping low.

"I can't tell you, Rachel. I don't know why."

"You do. Somewhere, somehow, you have to."

For her, he forced himself to peer inside the stash of jumbled treasures and trash. Plowing his way through, he fingered the priceless, smashed down the ugly filth, and emerged with something of value: the truth.

"All right," he said unsteadily. "You're dealing with someone who's gone a hard path, and he's afraid of what you're doing to him. Worse, what you can do. It's like waiting for the other shoe to fall, and feeling it hit can't be half as bad as fearing the blow."

"But what am I doing? What did I do to deserve this? I don't know what I've done, what—"

"You dug too deep." He pressed his lips to her forehead while he grappled with an emotion that tore through his insides like a runaway train. "You let me know you would have eaten out of the same can as me."

15

"MORE WINE, RACHEL?"

"No, thank you, Rand." Uncertainly, she watched out of the corner of her eye as he concentrated on his own glass. The purple garb she had changed into matched the grape of the vintage.

"I could call for white zinfandel. I know that's your favorite."

"This is fine, really. It's much better than any wine I've ever had before."

"You must have a discerning palate. Some people can't appreciate a fine wine."

They continued their meal in a stilted silence. Rachel forced herself to sample the exotic fare on her plate. Not that she was hungry, with her stomach tied up in knots, but she'd been taught that wasting food was sinful when others went without. Now she had cause to wonder just how many meals Rand had gone without.

What had life done to him? How had it twisted him so? Doubtlessly with brutal jabs and blows he'd learned to return with an ugly finesse to survive.

She shivered, wondering if she had the stamina to survive him. The problem was, she was already in so deep her heart was hocked to the limit, and he was holding the pawn ticket. It was too late to get it back. She saw only one way to emerge intact. She had to

find enough inner strength to get through the emotional land mines he had buried in more places than
the government had warheads—and shatter his one-
way windows.

"You didn't say much about the house. I'd hoped
that you would find it to your liking."

"It's very...opulent," she said tactfully.

"But you don't like it."

"No. No, it's not that. I'm just accustomed to more
lived-in surroundings."

"You could decorate it however you want." He
caught her hand on the elegant tabletop of white linen.
"Jayna could take you to some of the local dealers.
Friday's six days away, and there's always the chance
we could be here awhile. I'd like you to be comfortable, however long the stay."

She stared at the dark fingers grasping hers in what
felt like earnest hope. Or perhaps a silent apology. It
would be easy to turn that against him, to spite him
for what he'd done; and yet she sensed he had suffered more than she, and the price he was paying was
the vulnerability in him now.

Remembering her own survival strategy, she decided to take a step forward, hoping she wouldn't hit
one of those land mines of his.

"I'd rather you go with me instead, Rand. Maybe
we could take a day to go to a market and find some
things we both like. You know, some knickknacks,
souvenirs." Her smile was hesitant. "We could even
buy a few more pillows for me to throw at you."

"Sounds like a plan." He squeezed her hand, and
she took it as a thank-you. "I'll work it into my
schedule."

"When?"

"Soon. I have a lot of business to take care of in the next few days. But maybe you gathered that from the mess in my office."

Rachel thought of the high-tech apparatus, the whirring computer with staggering numbers on the screen, the neat stacks of paper and printout sheets piled high. There was a clinical starkness to it that she hadn't liked, the only indication of warmth being the faded snapshot of two youngsters hugging within the protection of a gilded frame that sat prominently on his massive desk.

It seemed typical of him, this picture, out of sync with the tools of his trade, which allowed him to pay megabucks to buy a woman. A woman he'd said he would have given any amount for, case or no case.

Maybe it was a good time to try out Jayna's sage advice and see if she couldn't influence his decision.

"I'd like to go tomorrow."

"Why tomorrow?"

She took a deep breath and leaped. "Because I want you to give up working in your office so you can spend time with me. It goes back to what you said about my feminine ego being pricked. I hate to admit it, but you were right. This way I can tell myself your priorities suit me, even if nothing else you say or do makes any sense yet."

Rand chuckled. "You're a pistol, lady. The first day we met you should have warned me you always end up on the other side of the trigger." He scooted his chair out and patted his lap. When she didn't move, he said quietly, "Please, Rachel. I just want to—well, to hold you while we talk."

Risky. Damn risky when he could easily yank the ground from beneath her feet and bring her to her knees. The emotional strain she'd endured in a single day had bled her dry, and though she'd survived— barely—she wasn't sure she could manage a repeat performance.

"Do it? Please, angel. For me."

In his own way, she realized, he was reaching out to her. She could refuse and remain safe, but with that came the very distance she longed to bridge. Drawing a steadying breath, she complied, but managed not to drape her arms about his neck.

"Okay, I'm sitting. Now, how about making that date for tomorrow?"

"Done. Now, how about me telling you something a lot more important?" He cleared his throat, and she felt his hold tighten. "I'm sorry, Rachel, deeply sorry, for what I did to you tonight. Apologies are hell for me. If it tells you anything, I've been rehearsing this one all through dinner."

His guard was lowered; she tested the chink in his defenses.

"I could make this difficult for you."

"Indeed, I've left myself wide open for a quick jab, if not a devastating blow. You could even go for the jugular, and I wouldn't blame you. You've got every reason to wash your hands of me after this. But I'm asking you, please don't."

She searched his eyes and saw his honesty, his anxiety. She was moved to the compassion he'd refused earlier. She wouldn't speak it, though something told her he wouldn't spurn her offering this time. Letting her actions speak for her, Rachel draped her arms about his neck and tentatively stroked the tense, corded muscles. She thought she heard a relieved sigh just before he laid his head against her breast.

"I can hear your heart beating," he said gruffly.

It beats for you, Rand, she thought. *It beats too fast and too sad and with too much hope, because you are who you are—the man who can either love me or leave me with nothing but shattered glass.*

"It took a licking, but it's still ticking," she said around the squeezing sensation inside her chest. His low, throaty chuckle vibrated against her, and she felt her heart accelerate at his intimate touch.

"So's mine," he whispered. "It's not too steady or reliable yet, but..."

She urged his face up, compelled to see through what she thought just might be the beginnings of a broken window.

"But what, Rand?"

"Hang tough, Rachel. When a rusty engine gets a jump start, the going's usually rough before all the gears remember how to work." He shifted, and she realized there was one piston that was sure as heck in working order. "You look tired. What say we call it a night? You can find out for yourself if I steal the sheets."

Oh, Lord, she wasn't ready for this. Not yet. Not until she felt sure she wouldn't make a fool of herself again, not until she was better able to handle whatever lessons Rand might dish out. The core. She had to get to his core, because there she'd find protection and heart and him.

"What say we have another glass of wine first?" she suggested. "I'd like to talk. Tell me what your favorite pastimes were when you were little."

"Popping tar bubbles with a stick. Racing on my bike. Braiding Sarah's hair." He latched on to the bottle, then got up, still holding her in his arms.

"Grab the glasses, angel. No? Okay, we can forget them. Drinking straight from the bottle isn't so different from open cans."

His directness surprised a smile out of her. "I believe you're letting your rough edges show, Mr. Slick."

"Goes with the package. Your feminine ego should be flattered that I'm not making my usual effort to cover them up." His stride was decisive as he took the stairs. "I just hope you don't already regret it, or end up disappointed when the mystery man's exposed for what he is."

When the mystery man's exposed. Not *if*. Could it be that something had been jarred loose by the nightmarish scene of water on silk? Taking the gamble, she dealt him the unvarnished truth.

"I don't think I could possibly be disappointed. But I am afraid there's a price attached. One that's so high it scares me."

"And that is?"

"That you'll take a part of me with you that I'll never get back."

"Works both ways, angel. I'm a little afraid for myself. You've already taken a part of me that I know I'll never get back, and Lord knows I've got too many missing pieces as it is. Maybe that helps? Knowing you have that power over me?"

"It does." She rested her head against his shoulder, feeling the strength of muscle, and the inner strength his admission built within her.

"Then are you still afraid?" He stood at their bedroom door.

"No," she said, willing herself to believe she didn't fear what might await her there.

"Prove it. Open the door," came the soft command. "Open it, and give me the chance to put your fears to rest."

Her hand was visibly shaking, and the brass slipped in her grip twice before the door yawned open. She gasped, amazed.

"Who did this?"

"I left instructions to have the bedroom made ready. I understand it's the custom, but I took the liberty of requesting a few personal touches. You like, or no?"

"It's…breathtaking. There must be a hundred candles lit, and is that music I hear?"

"Sound familiar? Seems like you said it evoked images of *Arabian Nights* and a brass lamp that belonged to Aladdin." He leaned into the door, a click sounded loudly like a hollow gong announcing their absolute seclusion.

Rachel tried to wet her lips, but even her tongue was dry. "I thought you were going to put my fears to rest."

"I didn't say which ones." He settled the wine bottle on a bedside table, then slid her slowly down his length. His hands strayed over her back, wisping and teasing her flushed skin to a prickling chill. She shivered and tried to move away, trusting herself less than him.

"Tell me your worst fear, the one making you pull away from me when I simply want to hold you. Is it me? Did I hurt you so deeply tonight that you don't want me to touch you?"

"You did hurt me," she admitted. She searched his eyes and found remorse there, a need for acceptance in spite of what he'd done. She gave it, slipping her arms about his waist.

"I want you to touch me," she said. "But even more, I want to touch you. Inside, where you wouldn't let me in before. That's my worst fear, Rand. That you'll close me out and I'll die from the cold."

He hesitated, his lips pursed. Then he sighed heavily and embraced her, resting his cheek against the top of her head. She felt the tenseness of his muscles, the faint shake as he tried to force them to relax.

"The ice is part of me, Rachel. It probably always will be. But you've been thawing it out. I feel like I've been slipping and sliding through dark tunnels I can't see my way through anymore, while I keep straining to reach a faraway light. You're holding it, and I just pray to God I don't snuff it out before I can hit the finish line. Be patient with me. Be strong when I stumble, like I did tonight. If you can do that, you'll be saving someone besides Sarah." He tilted her face upward. "That someone is me."

16

SHE REACHED OUT, daring to touch the flame that could both sear and warm.

"Rand," she whispered, touching his lips, desperately needing to touch them with her own. But the moment was ripe for a deeper discovery, one more urgent than the need to kiss. It was the need to *know* him. "Tonight I hit a tender spot with you, and we both suffered for it. Maybe I'm a glutton for punishment, but I don't think so. Tell me what you wouldn't before."

"It's not pretty," he warned. "You might not like the answers you get. I know I don't."

"I'm not asking for anything pretty, or a dressed-up truth. And as far as liking your answers goes, they can't be half as bad as I feel not knowing."

His pause was a terrible timelessness as she waited...and waited.

"All right." His nod was curt. "Stay here. I have something for you."

He kissed her quickly, then disappeared into a connecting room she'd learned was his dressing chamber. On edge as she waited for whatever it was he might bring back, she knew the victory of courage, of having endured the hurtful and emerging with the prize of his willing exposure.

The hypnotic leap of the candle flames, their white

tips dancing to the tune of the soft breeze billowing through the open window, was a seductive companion in his absence. It wisped through her heightened senses, while she listened to the ripple of music enhancing the scent of spice and...

Bay. She turned.

No robe. His chest was bare. Loose black silk pants rode low on his waist, revealing the indentation of his navel. It was garb befitting a dark, powerful genie, but he looked to her more sleek and dangerous than that.

A savage in silk.

Her legs took on the substance of no substance. She tried to swallow and almost choked on the immediate surge of unadulterated desire that followed.

"I have two things for you. Give me your hand." Rand folded her fingers over a vial, keeping one arm behind him as he did. Her palm touched glass. The shifting weight of liquid. Liquid in the glass; liquid between her thighs.

"What is this?"

"Your freedom of choice."

Rachel held the vial to the candlelight and saw that it was the color of burgundy.

"This looks like blood."

"When the cook wasn't looking I drained it from an uncooked lamb she'd stored in the refrigerator. It's a little thin, but it should serve the purpose."

She guessed the purpose and its emotional significance. Rand's show of respect for her rights induced her to trust him implicitly.

"You're offering to let me keep my virginity. When you have every legal right to take it here, and you want to, you're not." Rachel rolled the vial between her palms like the talisman it was. "The blood of a lamb."

"A sacrifice on my part, believe me." He glanced down at the front of his silk trousers. Rachel followed his gaze and inhaled sharply. She did indeed believe him.

"A stained sheet is expected by the slavers tomorrow," he explained. "It's the custom for the slave to show proof of her virginity, if she is so sold to her master. A great store is put on that, especially since an owner can demand the return of his money if he has reason to think he's been sold used property."

Forcing her attention back to his face, she could feel her own grow warm. With pleasure. With an answering arousal. And with a little embarrassment that he'd caught her staring
at him with undisguised interest.

"You're a man of many colors, Rand Slick. Every color but black and white."

His face darkened a shade, and he said, "Put the vial aside. I'm going to give you a piece of my past. Just remember what I told you. When the ice melts, I tend to slip."

"I'll catch you," was her soft vow as she laid the blood beside the wine.

"Just so I don't crush you when you do." He took a deep breath and slowly brought his arm from behind his back. He extended a delicate doll to her, and she took it. As she did, she felt the quick retreat of his hand as he rid himself of it.

She studied it, unable to imagine why anything so sweet and comforting to hold would affect him as if he thought it vile. He turned and passed his finger through the lapping flame of a bedside candle. Several times he repeated the motion, as if he'd rather court a burn than face another, deeper pain.

"I bought that for you today," he said in a tight voice. "I almost didn't."

"I'm glad you did. I'll treasure it as much as the doll I have at home. My dad gave it to me. Maybe that tells you how much this means to me." She closed the small distance and tried to see his eyes. Flat. Turbulent. Resentful. Tender. Emotions merged together as his fingertip descended again and again.

She gripped his hand and forced it away from the dancing heat. He shook off her hold and reached for the wine bottle.

"I bought one for Sarah, too. Santa gave her one a long time ago, but I doubt she's still got it." He laughed; it was a bitter sound that jarred her with its harshness. Rand took a long swig, then swiped his forearm over his mouth before offering Rachel the bottle.

She took it and drank as a comrade might, while she clung to the doll as if for protection from the beast she knew he could be and feared might emerge with a vengeance. Courage, she told herself. And then she acted on it.

"Tell me about Sarah's doll."

"Not much to tell. Just that that's all I left her with when she needed a brother." He turned to her, his eyes glittering with fury. At himself. At her, for making him relive this. Rachel forced herself not to shrink back.

"Did you run away?"

"Oh, yeah. I ran. I was so damn good at it I can't seem to stop."

"Why did you run?"

The sound he made was close to a snarl. She drank some more, needing some borrowed courage. He jerked the bottle from her hand and helped himself.

"It's like this, Rachel. See, we had a home. Not a rich one. Fact is, we were probably on the poor side by most folks' standards, but me and Sarah never knew to care, 'cause we had plenty when it came to what counted. Then our old man croaked. Penniless. No insurance, so you might as well forget a will. You got any idea what happens to kids without parents? Kids that got no money, so their white trash relatives don't wanna take 'em in, since they're nothin' but extra mouths to feed."

She felt as though he'd struck out at her with each hateful word. Words that he spoke in a dialect as foreign to his usual speech as the language of this country. But it was the picture that he'd painted with broad, slashing strokes of black that stunned her into silence. She saw the tight swallow he made, saw the watery shimmer in his eyes that seemed closer to acid rain than tears.

"Tell me." She wanted to shed the tears that he refused himself, but she didn't, knowing he would refuse them from her, as well. "Tell me what happens to kids who are left like that."

"They get split up, that's what. One gets sent to a stranger's home, the other gets railroaded to an orphanage. Unless he tucks his sister in nighty-night with her doll, climbs through a window, jumps a train and never keeps his pro—" He choked on the last word.

"Oh, Rand. I'm so sorry." She made to lay her palm against his cheek, and he slapped it away.

"Keep your pity to yourself," he snapped. "I've had enough of it for one night."

"Not pity, Rand. Caring." *Love*.

"Yeah?" He snatched the doll from her grasp and flung it on the bed. "Then why don't you kiss me and make it better?"

He raised the bottle to his mouth, then slammed it down on the table. She was staring at him, loving him, shaking with fear of what he might do next.

He jerked her against him. He crushed her open mouth with his lips. Rubbing them hard, as if to punish her for his exposure. She whimpered. And then she embraced him.

Stroking his back, she tried to soothe away something she knew she couldn't make right, while he thrust against her belly as though he could find release that way and flush out all that was ugly inside him.

His thrusts gave way to a gentle bump and grind, and then he was moaning, opening his mouth and giving her the wine that he hadn't swallowed, so that it swirled warm and rich over her tongue, trickling sweetly down her throat.

"Rachel," he groaned, "you're killing me, tearing down what it's taken me a lifetime to build."

"Build again. Build with me." As her eyes beseeched him, she thrust forward to topple his last defenses.

"I want to. God, I do, but I'm empty. Used up. Right now, I've got nothing left to give. You deserve more."

"I'll make up for it. I can give enough for us both."

"That's not my idea of a relationship." He fumbled for the vial and raised it between them. "This

is.'' He uncapped it with his thumb and set her away
from him.

Rachel watched as he drizzled the blood onto the
pristine sheet and then strode to the window. He
hurled the vial down to the street beneath, then braced
his hands against the windowsill as the tinkling shatter of glass sounded below. His head hung forward
as he took deep breaths of air.

She came to him, wrapped her arms about his bare
waist and pressed her cheek to his back.

''You amaze me, Rand. You may have some missing pieces, but you make up for them in the most
unexpected ways.''

''Do I? I'm selfish, Rachel. What I just did was
selfish, because I'm hoping it makes you want to give
even more than you already have. Manipulative of
me, don't you think?''

''Maybe. But this time I rather like it.''

She pressed a kiss to one of his vertebra, and then
another. He sighed raggedly and clutched at her wrist.
Expecting him to disengage her arms, she was taken
aback when he flattened her palm against bunched
muscle and male chest hair. Hair that gave way to a
thinning as he led her hand down, down, until he
slipped it just beneath the drawstring of his pants and
then let go.

''I'd like you to manipulate me for a change.
Whether you do or not is up to you. But I am asking
you to touch me. I need that much from you, if you
can give it.''

What she felt was trepidation, excitement, and a
need that mirrored his. She slowly inched her way
down, her heart pounding against her ribs to drum
against his back. His abdomen was flat, taut, and one

or both of them were quivering as she reached to grasp him.

Air sluiced through her lips. "My God," she whispered. *"Rand."* His flesh was sleek, and so warm it was hot. But what she hadn't expected was his pulse filling her palm, this part of him assuming a life of its own.

"Stroke me?"

"I—" She began to pant in time to the movements she was making by instinct. "Am I doing this right?"

"The mechanics don't matter, angel. The truth is, I've never been touched by a woman this way before. What you're doing is better than right. It's so right it's a little scary."

He moved his hips, guiding her uneven strokes into a smooth, perfect rhythm.

"It could be more right," she whispered as she kissed his back, tracing his spine, so curved and deliciously salty, with her tongue.

"I can't make you any promises."

"Then don't."

"But you want them."

"I want you."

"Then take the only thing I've got to give you tonight." The evenness of his speech shifted with his groan as he cupped her hand over the plump end of his flesh. And then his fingers were interlocked with hers and he was pulling her hand away.

"No," she protested. "I want more."

"That's what I'm giving you, angel." He kissed the hand that had stroked him, then wrapped it about his neck. His embrace was gentle, desperate, and so very encompassing. They held each other tightly, for how long she didn't know. And then he lifted her chin and pressed a deep kiss to her mouth.

"Thank you, Rachel. For everything. I hope I can make it up to you someday."

He released her and started for the door.

"You're leaving?" How could he leave after this? *I'm so good at running, I can't seem to stop.* His confession came back to her with a clarity she didn't want to acknowledge. She wanted to tear at it, to rip it to shreds and burn it for the waste it was.

"As the master, Rachel, I can sleep wherever I choose. And until I can give something back, I choose not to sleep with you."

"Did it occur to you that just maybe I'd be satisfied with a warm body for the night?"

"Don't devalue yourself like that. Hold out for something more substantial." He softened the gentle rebuke with a gaze that held both kindness and heat. "Sweet dreams, angel. With luck, maybe I'll have some for a change, too."

When he'd denied her before, she'd felt angry, rejected. But this denial was worse. She had touched him. Reached inside him and grasped his being in far more ways than the physical. And that was what made her heart contract now, and her unfilled body do the same.

She could beg him. She could possibly seduce him with her minimal skills.

She could let him go and wait for him to come back—a different man, perhaps. But still a man who held her captive more surely than money or the laws of Zebedique could ever guarantee.

As he made his way across Persian rugs and marble

floors, she watched the departure of two very different people sharing the same body. Two men, not one...

It was a flash, one of those stark insights that come out of nowhere but emerge clear as a conspiratorial whisper.

His hand was on the brass doorknob when she stopped him with a single word.

"Joshua," she called.

He paused while her recognition echoed in his head. *Joshua, Joshua, Joshua...*

How many years had passed since anyone had called him that? Sarah had been the last. And here he stood, hearing the past roar in his ears as loud as a freight train flying by.

Joshua waved to him from a boxcar, a memory resurfacing and demanding his due. But he wasn't Rand. They were both tied up in him, struggling to reach a compromise.

"Joshua's at an impasse, Rachel. As soon as I can manage it, I'll introduce you. Something tells me the two of you would have a lot in common."

He left then. Went straight to his office and a bottle of bourbon. It kept him company, but not very good company. It wasn't Sarah. And it sure as hell wasn't Rachel. Rachel, who had recognized his dual identity, who continued to summon the remnants of Joshua's spirit.

The thick, ribbed glass that held the whiskey was infinitely more satisfying and more true to his real nature than a crystal glass. Tonguing the bottle's mouth, he pretended it was Rachel's virginal lips, the warm liquid inside the nectar of her arousal, the boozy nirvana sensations those that her strokes had evoked.

They hadn't made love, and yet it had been the most sexual experience of his life. Maybe because she'd given and asked for nothing in return. There was a word for that, wasn't there? *Selflessness*. Or was the word *love?*

Rand considered the word, or rather the actions that spoke it. He thought she loved him, selfish bastard that he was. But now he had cause to wonder if maybe even selfish bastards could fall in love, too.

Messages flashed on the computer screen. Probably important, but for once he didn't give a tinker's damn.

He wasn't drunk yet, but his mind was racing so fast his head was spinning. Love. Could it be that he was in... Was it possible that his refusal to accept her offer meant that...

Rand got up and rummaged through his desk. As he put pen to paper, he decided that getting sauced and staying put sure beat the hell out of shutting windows and running.

17

A LIGHT TAP SOUNDED at the bedroom door. Rachel peeked over the top cover, wondering if it was Rand. Her heart accelerated. She scrubbed at her cheeks and wiped at her puffy eyes, hoping her crying jag didn't show. The doll that she'd held on to in the night lay on the pillow, where Rand's head should have been. She quickly and carefully shoved it underneath the bed.

"Come in," she said shakily.

"Good morning, mistress. The master requested that I bring you breakfast. He said…" Jayna averted her gaze as she rolled a table next to the bed.

"Yes?" Rachel looked at her hopefully as she clenched the sheets, wrapping the top one about her and wishing for her granny gown back home.

"He said you should eat well to keep up your strength, since he had exhausted your favors."

Rachel understood the double message. He'd kept up the front while secretly extending his regrets to her.

"Um…Jayna… How was the master when you saw him this morning?"

"Not well." Jayna flashed her a discreet smile. "He looked to be a man with favors more exhausted than yours."

So, Rand had had a bad night, too. She wasn't surprised, but there was comfort in knowing he'd shared her misery.

"Did he say when he would visit me again?"

"You are eager?" She gestured to Rachel to get out of the bed and began to strip the bottom sheet. As she studied the bloodstain, she shook her head. "This is surprising. He is kinder than most masters, I think, but I would not guess it from this."

Rachel ducked her head, embarrassed by the implication and by being privy to the deceit. He is kind, she wanted to say, in his hidden places he is kind. Places, she thought with a private smile, that he had let her into.

As Jayna took her leave, the sheet tucked neatly in her arms, Rachel came to a decision. Enough of this sleeping in separate beds while she cried into her pillow. Rand meant well, she knew, but her woman's instincts insisted that last night's protectiveness had only kept them apart.

"Jayna!" she called. "About what you said yesterday, you know, about even slaves being able to influence a man? Well, I thought about that, and it reminded me of something. Have you ever heard you can catch more flies with honey than vinegar?"

Her brows drew together. "It is not familiar. But there is an old truth each concubine knows in the harem. If the master is good, and she desires he lie with her and not another, she lures him with the scent of jasmine oiling her body, and promises him the greatest pleasure with the slant of her eyes, the tight binding of her robe."

"Seems to me that those gals in the harem know a lot about flies and honey. Think you could come in here and oil me up before dinner, maybe help me out with some makeup and get that robe bound real tight?''

''With pleasure, mistress. It is what the master requested, as well.'' She paused, and then she winked, catching Rachel off guard. ''No cards today, mistress. He has ordered you to be made ready to shop after you bathe.''

Rachel smiled as Jayna bowed out of the room, feeling very differently about his dictates from the way she had only twenty-four hours ago.

He'd sent her breakfast. He'd even taken the time to order her bath drawn. He was taking her shopping!

Rachel laughed at herself. Even here she could still get excited about going shopping. Maybe after they were back in the States, she and Sarah could become friends and go shopping together. They could exchange Christmas and birthday presents, watch as Rand opened up a box with a tacky tie inside...

She stopped herself from taking the image further. Her thoughts had implied permanency. And then she knew. She had lied last night, lied to them both. Because she did want promises. She wanted forever. As in a wedding ring and children who would never be subjected to what he'd gone through.

Be patient with me, he'd said. *Be strong when I stumble.* He'd also said he hoped he didn't crush her when he fell, or snuff out her light before he hit the finish line.

Her excitement dampened, she felt the threat of a loss she couldn't bear. *Courage.* Her jaw clenched, as did her fist, and she scrambled under the bed for the doll he'd given her.

Rachel hugged it to her, along with an unwanted truth: No woman could force a man to love her or

commit to her, especially not a man who admitted to
compulsive running.

*If you love something, let it go. If it comes back to
you, it's yours. If it doesn't, it never was.*

The old cliché had never held so much meaning as
it did now. But she'd learned a lot from Rand, and
her latest lesson was about finding the courage to take
personal risks.

A month ago, even a day ago, she would have held
out for the promises she wanted. She wanted them
badly enough to give him her all and pray he could
come to love her as much.

Setting the doll in a chair opposite the table Jayna
had left, Rachel tried to take her mind off her borrowed worries by playing her favorite childhood
game.

"Would you care for tea?" she asked the doll.
"No? Then perhaps you'll join me for…" She raised
the stainless steel globe off a steaming plate of some
interesting-looking items. "Well, I'm not sure what
we're eating, but it smells good. And just look, Jayna
left an orchid floating in a brandy snifter. How did
she know we have a weakness for flowers and—"

Her conversation with the doll was cut short when
she spied an envelope peeking out from beneath the
glass. Quickly tearing the seal open, she scanned the
bold script on the parchment.

"Listen to this," she told the doll confidentially.

"Dear Rachel,

"Old garbage has a way of piling up when
ignored, and I haven't aired out the house for a
very long time. You told me that I'd feel better
for it, and you were right. Long way to go, but
thanks to you I'm getting there."

Rachel paused, a warm smile brimming from her lips.

"You know," she confided to the doll, which she'd named Sarah sometime in the long, lonely night, "it's not so scary to let someone go when the scales are tipped in your favor."

Clearing her throat, she continued reading.

"It's very late, and I'm not exactly sober. I can't sleep, because you're keeping me awake. Maybe if I just keep writing I can keep from acting on what I want to do to you now. I can see you in bed. I'm imagining you in it without any clothes…"

Rachel stopped reading, her eyes wide, her breathing shallow. "I'm not sure if you should be listening to this," she said to Sarah while she fanned herself with the hot sheet of paper. "Cover your ears."

Scanning the lines, she went on.

"I'm very affected by this little imagining. It arouses me. In fact, I'm damn close to throwing down this pen, barging into our bedroom and taking back what I gave. But as long as I can put one word in front of another I can keep myself from acting too soon.

"I'm pretending that I'm with you now, that I've pulled away the sheets and you're sleeping on your back. I like you this way, uncovered, unconsciously responding to my hands as they take what they want without asking. I can feel your bare skin hot against my palms; your breasts are wet where my tongue is teasing them.

"I know it's wrong to take advantage of you this way, but that doesn't stop me from doing it. But you don't want me to stop, do you? I can hear the sounds you're making as you slowly come awake, realizing I'm kissing my way down, until my mouth fits between your legs. How good you taste, Rachel. And I do love the feel of your hands gripping my head to you.

"Are you hot? Do you want me inside, angel? God knows I want to be there. But I'm not, and I think I know why. It's the reason I left you when more than anything I wanted to stay. For once in my life, I don't want to take, but to give.

"What I'm sharing with you on this page has very little to do with sex and a lot to do with something I'm not too familiar with. It's called lovemaking. A mutual possession.

"You haven't asked me for promises, and I'm grateful for that, because promises are something I have a problem with. But I will make you one now: I'll never make a promise to you that I won't keep.

"Our days are numbered before the plot thickens—let's make them count. Sleeping without you, well, it does leave something very much to be desired. I hope that soon we'll wake up together sharing rave reviews."

"Good Lord," Rachel moaned. Rand had said she was thawing him out, but he was doing a doozy of a job of turning the thermostat up to scalding. Was she hot? As far as she could tell, hell couldn't compete with the fever she was in.

Rachel glanced at the doll. Then she reread the letter. Two gifts from the same man. The man who'd signed off with "Love." She studied his signature, realizing he'd written Rand over something he'd whited out.

Rachel began to scratch. She almost tore a hole through the parchment, but she managed to uncover a thin, blurred word. Holding it up to the light, she smiled slowly. She pressed her lips to the name, then held it to her breast.

"Love, Joshua," she whispered.

She ate breakfast in a dream state, sharing her hopes and dreams with her Sarah doll but keeping her libidinous thoughts to herself. A walk on the dark side, indeed, she thought. Rand had crooked his finger, or pen, and summoned an anxious companion. Her. At least she thought it was still her. She was changing. But so was he.

When Jayna tapped on the door and announced that her bath was drawn, Rachel floated toward the scent of jasmine emollient. She realized, belatedly, that she should hide Rand's—or rather Joshua's—note.

With a womanly sigh of delight, Rachel reached for a book and tucked the letter inside.

"Just thought I'd read what the master sent yesterday," she said to Jayna, who nodded her approval.

Climbing into the tub, Rachel set about gaining some knowledge from the *Kama Sutra*.

JAYNA ADJUSTED the veil covering Rachel's face, leaving just enough room to peek out with her kohl-lined eyes.

"How do women around here stand to wear so many clothes?" Rachel tugged at the full-length crimson silk robe, checking out the gold brocade fasten-

ings that ran from her neck to her sandal-clad feet.
"This getup is ridiculous. I'll bet Zebedique holds the
world record for heat rashes in women."

"You will grow used to it." Jayna shook her head
with a weary sigh. "I have."

"And I thought panty hose were a drag," Rachel
muttered.

"It could be worse." Jayna fussed with the head
covering, then nodded her satisfaction. "You please
the master, and he is treating you well. Many concubines are not so lucky."

"No concubine is lucky, Jayna. Everyone deserves
the right to freedom."

"I agree." Jayna covered her mouth as though
she'd spoken treason. "But we must keep these things
to ourselves."

Rachel reached for her elderly hand and patted it,
carefully choosing her words. "Maybe someday,
Jayna, you and I can play that game of poker and I
can tell you what you're missing out on. What would
be even better would be if we could play it where
we're both free to call our own hands."

Jayna shook her head. "I, too, was a concubine,
many ages ago. My master was not kind, and I tried
to escape. Do you wish to see what he did to me?"
She lifted her robe and exposed two burn marks on
the inside of her thighs. "These are signs of shame.
But that is not all. A man may be made a eunuch,
but a woman may be cut, too." Her mouth trembled,
then grew hard. "In ways that make her no longer a
woman."

"Oh God, *no!*" Rachel choked, nearly gagging on
the sickness in her throat. Her vision blurred, and she
clasped Jayna to her. "I hurt for you." She could

hardly get the words out, her horror and compassion were so complete.

Jayna patted her back—oddly, the one who was offering consolation.

"You must not cry for me. My next life will be better. And yours can be good now." She held Rachel away then, gripping her by the shoulders. "I tell you this so you will be warned. But if you should ever be foolish, as I was, I will turn my back when I should be guarding." She gave her a small shake. "Tell no one of this talk."

The desire to tell her all was great, but Rachel knew better. Too much was at risk, and Jayna had suffered enough without being dragged into this, too.

The bedroom door opened without a knock of forewarning. Jayna quickly stepped away as Rand entered, looking as powerful and demanding as his role dictated he appear.

"Leave us, Jayna. I wish a few words with my bed slave."

Jayna bowed out, catching Rachel's eye, then touching a finger to her lips in warning.

As soon as the door shut, Rand's stern mouth gentled into a smile. If she hadn't been so upset, she would have been struck by his almost-boyish charm.

"Hi, angel." He quirked a brow. "How did you sleep last night? No better than me, I hope."

Rachel shook her head. "Rand, we have to talk."

He frowned. "What's wrong?"

For a moment, she was too overcome to speak. He opened his arms, and she sank into them, grateful for his solidity and strength and moral substance.

"We *have* to get Sarah away from here."

"Of course we do." He lifted her veil and brushed

a soft kiss to her lips. "We're walking to the market so that I can point out her house and you can get a feel for the general territory. It's a good excuse to time the distance."

She gripped his robe in both her hands. "It's not just that. We *can't* fail. If we do, what could happen to her would be worse than if we'd never come at all. This country is vile. Slavery isn't even half of it."

"Explain."

She did, feeling his own grip tighten with each appalling word. His expression revealed shock, grinding anger, and something else, something she hadn't expected. A protective intensity.

"Forget the shopping and get packed. I'm calling for my plane."

"What?"

"You heard me."

"But Sarah—"

"Sarah means the world to me, Rachel. But so do you. Having one woman I love at stake is bad enough, and I'm not going for double or nothing. Now get packed, while I get ahold of the men I've had watching her house. We'll just have to come up with a plan to abduct her. You're leaving."

Rachel knew a momentary dizziness, one part of her mind sifting through what he'd said about not going double or nothing with the women he loved, turning it this way, then that, afraid she'd misinterpreted it. Meanwhile she grappled with the realization that he was sending her away. What if he failed? What if Sarah's owner caught them? This was far riskier than their original plan. Sarah could be mutilated while Rand rotted away in one of this stinking country's many prisons.

"You can't do this, Rand."

"Watch me. It's my decision to make, and it stands."

"But you already told me how she was guarded, how your men couldn't make a successful snatch. It's why you hired me. I can get to her where you can't. Don't do this, Rand. Don't do it to Sarah." She yanked the robe at his throat and brought his eyes even with hers. "Don't do it to *me*."

She saw concern slowly replaced by an implacable hardness, a calculating expression.

"Why? I'll still pay you in full."

She almost slapped him. Instead she gritted her teeth and tore aside her veil, making sure he could see that she wasn't put out. She was livid.

"Oh, no, you don't. You dragged me in too deep to expect me to swallow that line of tripe. As far as I'm concerned, you can stuff your stupid money where the sun doesn't shine. Forget the plane, because I'm staying. Either we all leave together or we don't leave at all."

"Sounds like you've got it all worked out, Ms. Tinsdale."

"That's right, Mr. Master. I'm not going anywhere today but shopping with you."

They had a staring contest that was a draw until his flat gaze softened and he sighed heavily. "I'm only trying to protect you, Rachel. I'd never forgive myself if anything happened to hurt you."

"The only thing that could hurt me now is if you sent me away. Let me stay and do my job. We're partners, remember? I can't go back without you, because I—"

She caught herself. Were her eyes giving her away,

she wondered frantically, while his own narrowed, probed, ascertained?

"Because…why, angel? I'm waiting."

What few defenses she had left were crumbling, crumbling, leaving her like so much raw wood he could torch, then leave in ashes for the wind to scatter.

Rachel shut her eyes and prayed for courage.

"Because I love you. That's why."

It was out, and she couldn't take it back. She had the sudden compulsion to run, and she felt a strange empathy for Rand's nonstop flight from emotion and commitment.

She forced herself to look at him, and wasn't sure what she saw staring back. He was unblinking, too still. As if he were absorbing, considering, making some decision.

She couldn't stand the taut silence, the churning inside her head and in her stomach while she wondered if she might just have given him the impetus to run faster than he ever had in his life.

Rachel beat him to it. She spun away, ready to dart for the door.

Rand grabbed her wrist and jerked her back, so fast her breasts collided with the ungiving width of his chest, pushing a soft gasp from her lungs.

"Where do you think you're going?" he demanded, whipping the covering from her head and thrusting what seemed an uncommon number of fingers against her scalp, twisting her hair round and about them so that she had no choice but to stay put.

"I'm going shopping," she said between a gasp and a pant.

"I don't think so." His mouth was against her

neck, and then it was busy drawing an earlobe slowly between his teeth as he growled, "Neither of us is running this time around, Rachel. You left yourself wide open with that enlightening bit of news. We're going to explore just how far it goes, and find out if I can manage a return on the same emotional investment. Let's get started with a promise from me to you."

Trying not to hope for too much, Rachel focused on simply getting her vocal chords to work. "What kind of a promise?"

Her heart was in her throat, the throat he was nuzzling and sucking, while the brush of his fingers connected with her skin as he impatiently worked the brocade fastenings, slipping them free, then tugging and snapping them loose when they didn't obey. Somehow her own hands began to make themselves useful, pushing at his robe, searching for his bare chest.

"I'm going to make love to you, and take my sweet time doing it. By the time we're through, we'll be too exhausted to crawl to the door. You'll be my slave and I'll be yours, both of us slaves to our mutual pleasure. Angel, that's a promise you can take to the bank. Or, better yet, to bed."

18

SHE LOVED HIM. As unlovable as he'd been at times, she had still said the words. His mind was reeling with them, even as he feared to believe them. What if she changed her mind? What if she took it all back once she knew everything there was to know about him? To lose this after having had it would be worse than never having it at all.

His hands worked in fevered tandem with his thoughts, her soft little moans making it hard to think clearly. *She loved him.* His filthy lucre carried no weight with her. *She loved him.* He'd exposed the beast he could be, and she'd soothed him, helped him reach out to Joshua.

Rand came to a decision, a manipulative decision, but one that her love meant enough for him to make. He'd bind her to him with the senses so thoroughly that she'd keep coming back for more. He'd use that to solidify the love she professed, let her touch that part of him that retained a tattered nobility, the ability to love her back as much as she deserved. By the time she saw him in all his unglory she'd be in too deep to retract the love he ached to have.

Nobility. He called on it now.

"You love me," he whispered. He was on his knees now, flinging her sandals away and taking a soft bite from the inside of her leg. "Even the unlovable, you love."

She seemed too busy grabbing at his hair and urging his face against her, then arching back with a tormented wail that might have been his name, to grasp the importance of what he was demanding to be reassured of.

Rand gritted his teeth and forced himself to rise. Soon, he told himself. Soon he'd lose himself inside her and, he hoped, find that part of his soul that continued to play hide-and-seek. But not until he had a promise from her that, more than ever, he craved to return.

He backed her against the cool silken wall and stilled her thrashing head with his forehead pressed against hers, all the while making soothing noises and stroking her hair.

"You want me."

"Yes, yes..." she murmured.

The hot silk of her panties came into contact with his fingertips; unable to stop himself, he slid around the thin barrier and rotated her cleft as he repeated himself in terms that left no room for doubt.

"If you do love me, Rachel, heaven help you, because I can't help what I am. You said once that you wanted it all, but damn, I want it, too. Joshua can make love to you, hold you, and be what you deserve. Rand can screw you until you can't walk, hurt you without blinking an eye, and manipulate you, because it's his stock-in-trade. You asked who I was, and there's part of the answer. But you have to want them both. There's no having one without the other. Tell me you understand."

Her eyes were so glossy he thought she might be

close to fainting. But there was a spark of cognition that showed she had grasped the essence of what he had said.

"Can you love me like that?" he demanded. "Choose your words carefully, angel, because I won't let you take them back in a saner moment."

"I meant what I said. I love you. I've never said those words to a man before." Her palms rubbed, pressed and slid from his cheeks to embrace his neck. "Much less to two men sharing the same body."

Her kiss was severe. It was the sweetest heat he'd ever taken, and the sweetest he'd ever been given back. He was staggered by the totality of the acceptance she offered. She, a woman who had left herself so vulnerable to him that he could easily destroy her. And yet he felt he was the one being destroyed, torn apart and put back together with her touch.

Her hands didn't have the practiced feel of expertise, but held an urgent and emotional sincerity that was so much sweeter, so much better, and infinitely more arousing, than anything he'd ever experienced before.

He wanted to tell her that he loved her, and he tried to push the rusty words past his lips.

"Rachel, I—" Stuck. The words hurt, echoing the rigid hurt in his groin. She made it worse by tilting herself against the remaining barrier of the thin pants he wore.

"Walk with me, Rand. Lead me through the dark side."

With a groan, he dropped to his knees and urged hers a generous distance apart. Against her panties, his mouth breathed the heat of promises he longed to make. His tongue bathed them until they were wet—

or perhaps it was her own arousal he could taste through the silk. The barrier of the soaked cloth became intolerable, and he slid the panties off, then hooked them over his wrist. A medal of sorts, they seemed, a trophy of her yielding, and of his claiming.

Each darting lick was a message, a message of loving sensitivity transmitted from his heart to her very core.

She screamed. He had no mercy left to give her. Her body was a vessel for murmured words, words that said all the things he ached to make true but needed time to make a reality. But he was making it so now, wasn't he? With each second that passed, wanting only to give, he created a new reality in himself.

She cried out to him, cried two different names, and he made her weep for more. He gave it to her, and felt her rippling thrill as though it were his own.

She climaxed against his mouth, and as she did he heard his own tortured sounds mingle with hers as emotions too long dammed up were released in a rush.

"I...love..." he murmured into the wet haven of her juncture. Then, with an ease he hadn't expected, he said the rest, whispering against the shudders from her womb, "I love you."

Without further prelude, and with his vow and her sobbing cries of the names still singing in his ears, he rose and tore off his pants. Her legs were shaking uncontrollably, and he caught her as they gave way.

He absorbed the remnants of ecstasy contorting her tear-streaked face and lapped the salty liquid with his tongue. It occurred to him then that he had triumphed, that for once he had given without taking. And he felt wonderful, better than he would ever have believed possible, even with his own body gripped by this grinding ache.

She covered his face with kisses, whimpering as though she were distraught. He'd never seen a woman so... He searched for words to describe what he was seeing. What he was seeing touched him deeply, because it was something he'd never witnessed before in a woman. Fragmented, that was it. She seemed fragmented. While he had never felt so whole.

"Are you all right?"

"No. Yes." She sniffled, and he wiped her nose with the panties dangling from his wrist. "I don't know."

"You're beautiful standing there like that. All flushed and weepy. I can still hear you screaming my name. It was sweet. Moving." His kiss was tender. "Orgasmic."

"You were listening." She cast her gaze downward. "God only knows what I said. It's frightening, losing all control. I had no idea. I feel...I feel like I'm in a thousand pieces."

"I wish you'd look at me." He lifted her chin, and he looked into the eyes of Woman. Woman discovering the enormity of passion's price—the total forsaking of reason and self. And she was awed by the discovery. But the discovery wasn't hers alone. A possessiveness gripped him, so intense that his vision momentarily blurred, and he knew he'd die before ever letting her go.

"It's powerful, Rachel. People have killed in the name of passion. We haven't even hit the tip of the iceberg...." He smiled slightly, for once enjoying the thaw. "Already I know there's a part of me that wouldn't hesitate to kill any man I found daring to touch you like this.''

His palm fit over her mound, and he cupped her, using their mingled moisture to prepare her for discoveries yet to be made.

Rachel gripped his wrist. She was panting; her eyes were wide and uncertain. Her reaction thwarted him; it created a determination to go on without stopping, to trample down whatever the hell was holding her back, to cement his feet to the floor if that was what it took, to bind her to him for good.

''What's wrong?'' he quietly demanded. ''I gave you a taste of what's to come. It's time for the feast, and I'm starving.''

''I'm scared, Rand.''

''If it's the pain, I'll ease it. I want this to be good for you. Trust me.''

''Not the physical pain. I'm shattered, and it terrifies me to think of how deep it can go after we make love.''

''Ah, I see. Fear of the unknown. Don't worry.'' He kissed her reassuringly. ''I'll know when you fall, and I'll be there to catch you when you do.''

No, Rand, she wanted to say, you don't see at all. His windows were open, and he was waving her inside, but the courage she'd found earlier was deserting her when she needed it the most. Nothing could have prepared her for this. She felt bound to him more completely than she could ever have dreamed. She quaked with the knowledge he could hold her here, inside him, and then cast her out again as soon as Sarah was found.

How she wanted promises. Promises that he would never do that. Because she wouldn't be able to survive. At least she didn't think so—and she had no desire to find out.

"What happens after we go to bed, Rand?"

"Maybe take a bath together, rub each other with oil."

"But what happens to *us?* Once we're out of Zebedique?"

His eyes were dark with wanting her, and sharp with sudden understanding of her question.

"We are talking forever, aren't we? As in—" he cleared his throat, as though the word wouldn't come "—marriage?"

She nodded, the short jerking movement cutting off the air in her throat. At least he'd gotten the word out, which was more than she'd hoped for.

"You want a commitment from me that I'd sever my right arm to make. But the truth is, you're going to have to be a little more patient. I'm close, Rachel. Closer than I ever imagined was possible for me." His face clouded. "And, too, you deserve time to learn some things about me before you make such a long-term commitment yourself. Now enough about that. We've got plenty to deal with here as it is."

He wrapped her fingers around him, and she felt his hips jerk as her hand sheathed sleek, turgid flesh.

"We can do this one of two ways," he whispered. "We can make love, which is an act you can never take back. Or you can tell me to leave, and remain intact. If that's what you want, you'd better tell me quick, before I lose what little control I've got left."

Rachel was stunned that he would still offer the choice. It told her a lot about him as a man, about his principles. It told her that he might return her love, though he hadn't spoken it.

The silence lengthened, and she felt his hands fan over her buttocks, felt his intimate strokes as he lifted her up, wrapping her legs about his hips. The wall was cold against her back, and she so wanted to feel it against her while he pressed deep inside her. The image of him entering her begged to be embraced, begged her to forget any promise but his body's offering.

"Think of my letter," he urged. "Think of me doing all that and more to you." He pressed himself lightly against her entry. His touch was flirtation and tantalizing temptation. "Does thinking about it make you hot, make you want me now?"

"You're manipulating me." She knew it, accepted it, and found she wanted more of the same.

"You're right, but it's not manipulation the way I could take this. I could tell you that if you pressed me into you, I'd give you that commitment you think you want. Or I could seduce you, and after it was over remind you that you wanted it as much as me and promises weren't part of the bargain. But I'm not going to do that. Instead, I'm offering you the truth— I want forever, and it's just beyond my grasp. Take me inside, and it might help me get there a little quicker. My fear is that once I'm there you may decide you don't want me."

Her breasts rode against his chest, urging her to mate their nipples, to bear down and plunge him inside. *Courage.*

"Love me," she pleaded. "Say it. Just say it once."

"I...I..." His breathing was shallow. "I love you." The words spilled from his lips in a rush. And then he said them again, slowly, with feeling. "I love you, Rachel. Now choose."

"There never was a choice, Rand. Even if you hadn't said it, I'd want this. But hearing the words makes the risk a lot easier to take." Her fingers were unsteady as she closed the tiny gap and sought to fit him against her. It was not unlike a sprung cork seeking to reenter a wine bottle's mouth. "Rand." His name was a gasp. "Help me?"

She expected him to bang her against the wall. She expected an immediate and forceful invasion. What she couldn't have counted on was his withdrawal, the feel of his arms scooping her up and holding her against his chest as he carried her to the bed with haste and decisiveness.

He knelt over her there, his palms bracing her knees apart, his phallus positioned to enter what begged to be entered, and his face above hers. Dark passion was illuminated by a spark of light. He appeared to be not only in the throes of heated passion, but also…happy? Pleased with himself?

"I want to practice," he said. "I love you. There. I said it. And it didn't hurt one bit. In fact, it felt so damn good I'm saying it again. I love you, Rachel Tinsdale."

"And I do love you, Rand. Both of you."

"Don't ever try to take that back. I won't give it up."

His hands began slowly working her over, finding erogenous zones she'd had no idea even existed.

Do you like this?

God, yes.

Touch me this way, angel…. Ah, perfect… Your

eyes, what are they saying? Tell me what you want…just say it….

I'm hurting. Please make the hurting stop.

I don't want to hurt you. Let me do this…. There, isn't that good? And you do feel so good to me, angel. Relax…relax…that's my girl. Damn, you're tight. Wet. Now feel me just this little bit inside you.

You're making it worse. You're teasing me.

I'm not teasing. I'm caring. And I'm loving you enough to go slow. But…stop that. Did you hear me? Dammit, Rachel, be still. Quit—Oh, Lord! Hold tight to me!

Her cries he took within his mouth. So soothing, his murmurs of possessive consolation. So sheltering, the arms that gathered her in ultimate possession.

Pain became a memory, and then all she knew was bliss. Rachel returned his careful thrusts, her improvised movements meeting with his whispered approval, delighting her and giving her an ample taste of what it meant to be a woman with power, heady with the knowledge that she pleased her man.

Then patience fled, and tender lovemaking became a primal rutting. She should be shocked, came the distant thought, yet she found it stunning. Their coupling was beautiful, because it was who they were, the guts and the grit of what they felt for each other. She lost all thought of caring about promises she was more desperate than ever to hear, about what sounds she made, about whether she was losing all pretense at dignity as they rolled and wrestled and mated without any manners at all.

She was hanging half-off the bed when he begged her to come, to meet him in that dark place where he would catch her if she would please, please, just fall.

She shattered like glass, her body battered and lush, as she felt his liquid release. It was tingling and hot and not where it should be, but upon her belly. They slid over each other, covered with sweat and the scents of bay and shared ecstasy.

For a long time, their murmurings made no sense, and yet all the sense in the world. When she shivered, he pulled the tangled covering about them, stopping to scowl as his hand searched the bottom sheet for blood—human, not lamb.

Rand groaned. "I was rough. I'm sorry, angel."

"I'm not." She exhaled a languourous sigh, that of a woman who was well loved and well bedded. "No matter what happens, I'll always remember this as one of the most amazing moments of my life." She touched his cheek, feeling a wondrous bonding, a deep and abiding affection that nothing he could ever do would steal. But he was frowning, concern etched on his brow. "What's wrong?"

"A couple of things. You weren't protected." He rubbed his hand over her belly. "I've never skated so close to the edge before, tempting fate like that. I promise to be more careful in the future."

A promise. One that signified his wish to protect her. One that raised a question that she hadn't considered.

"What happened to you, Rand—has it made you turn against ever having children?"

"I've never wanted children. I'm not sure I'd exactly be a good role model."

"But what if—"

"What if I didn't pull out in time, and you're pregnant?"

She nodded. She had always wanted children. But that wasn't the issue, was it?

"I get the feeling you want to know if I'm the kind of man who'd get you pregnant, push for an abortion, and then, if you wouldn't go for one, salve my conscience with an offer of money instead of assuming the responsibility."

"I didn't mean to imply... Don't look at me that way."

"Like I'm angry, hurt? The fact that you had to ask just goes to show you still have a lot to learn about me." He stroked back the hair clinging to her face, and she saw a depth in him that was honor, a refusal to shirk duty. It was a surprising turn of the Rubik's Cube. His unscrupulous reputation might be valid, but he held to some very traditional values.

"I'm sorry, Rand. I didn't mean to offend you or question your principles. I wish I could take it back."

"We're learning, that's all, angel. But your question does bring up something else that's bothering me." His kiss was lingering, persuasive. "I want you to leave. It's not likely that you're pregnant, but if you are, I don't want to risk our baby. If you're not, I don't want to risk you. Go home, take this memory with you, and wait for me to come back."

Our baby. He might not want children, but that one word told her how far a commitment from Rand would reach. It augured well for the future, and it told her that the question of children could be worked out in time. It strengthened her resolve to stay, to lessen his and Sarah's risks, even if her own was increased.

"No, Rand. The answer is an unequivocal, flat-out *no.*"

"Trust me to come back."

"This isn't about trust. You have mine, won with a vial of blood." She traced his lips, lips she wanted to touch when they were surly and tight, soft and open, old and drawn. "What it comes down to is this. Even if you can't commit yet, I have. For me, that means we're in this together and there's no way I'm leaving when you, and your sister, need me the most."

"I don't like it."

"I'm not asking you to." She offered him a smile that he didn't return. "Take me shopping tomorrow and show me Sarah's house. We *will* succeed, Rand. Trust me."

"You're a hardheaded woman, you know that?" He sighed heavily, giving in, but not gracefully. "All right. We'll do it your way. After I have mine with you." The sure glide of his palm from breast to cleft moved on to the bedside drawer. He slipped on a sheath, and without further ado he was inside her.

"I love you," he said, the rhythm of his words matching the gentle rocking of his hips. "Strange, how it gets easier to say every time."

It was a promise of sorts, she decided. One that was hers to treasure, to climax yet again upon, and forever keep.

19

As SHE WALKED ten paces behind Rand, Rachel was glad the veil covered her mouth. It wouldn't do to be seen in the open market wearing the euphoric smile of a woman supremely sated after two days of alternately tender and ravenous lovemaking. She was, after all, expected to play the role of a just-bought bed slave getting a public lesson in submission.

A sigh of relief filtered through the thin cloth. She was glad for this taste of limited freedom, and even more glad that Rand had bowed to her judgment.

He'd been anxious to walk past Sarah's house en route to the market, and his anxiety worried her. It made her nervous. One screwup was all it took, and no matter how in control Rand thought he was, one chance glimpse of his long-lost sister could set off some dangerously instinctive reactions. It had taken some doing, but Rachel had won. Today's destination was saved for last. At dusk, when the shadows would mask their faces and the hired surveillance team tailing them at a discreet distance wouldn't be as easily noticed.

That had been her reasoning, though in truth it was more a gut feeling that something could go wrong, a feeling that she couldn't have justified. The feeling was still there, but Rachel shook it off, determined to enjoy this bit of sight-seeing while she could. Friday would come soon enough. Today she'd savor.

The descending sun slanted into the huge canvas tent as they filed down one row and then another, Rand the leader, she the chattel, and Jayna bringing up the rear as her guard. Jayna had kindly, but sternly, laid out the rules. A slave was not permitted to speak to her master unless spoken to first. A slave was not to make eye contact with any man but her master. A slave was to keep the expected distance at all times, unless signaled to trot to his side should he want a quick fondle, then fall back the required ten paces once he was ready to move on.

To break any of these rules was to risk a public whipping.

Trinkets and fabrics and hand-carved wood all vied for Rachel's attention. She paused to admire an ivory necklace. Jayna gave her a gentle push.

"Hurry, hurry," she urged. "The master walks on."

"But I want to know how much this—" A high-pitched wail stopped short her protest. Rachel searched for the source.

She gasped. Close to where Rand stood, a good twenty paces ahead, was a spectacle that caused her stomach to lurch and her blood to boil. A fruit vendor was grappling with a dirty, urchinlike child, who dropped a banana as the man shook him.

Acting on impulse, she began to run toward the child. Jayna grabbed her arm and spun her around.

"Do not be foolish, mistress. Else you suffer a beating."

"But that man, he can't abuse the poor child! Somebody has to do something. Let me go!"

Jayna's grip tightened as Rachel struggled to intervene.

"You can do nothing. It is sad, but common, to catch hungry thieves. The child will be punished. I do not wish for you to be punished, also."

"Punish a starving child for stealing a banana? That's inhuman. What's his punishment, a spanking?"

"His hand will be cut off. It is the price all thieves must pay."

Such was her shock that Rachel stared dumbly at Jayna, and then at the weeping boy, who was begging for mercy. *What could she do?* She had to do something, anything, to stop this atrocity.

Rachel broke free of Jayna's hold and rushed forward. When she was just shy of the fruit cart, Rand confronted the merchant. She was close enough to hear his halting speech in the Zebedique tongue, which the other man replied to with a rabid snarl and another shake of the wailing child.

Just when she was ready to join the fracas, Rand held out a thick stack of local currency and gestured to the fallen banana. The merchant hesitated. Rand withdrew the bribe.

Before Rachel could yell at him to give the man however much money he wanted, the child was dumped on the hay-strewn floor and a bunch of bananas thrust into his grimy little hands by the vendor—who quickly held his own out, palm up.

Rand shelled out the payoff. The child kissed his feet and, hugging the fruit to his skinny, bare chest, darted from sight. His savior appeared to take no notice. Rand's gaze had turned on Rachel, and she saw mirrored in his eyes the distress, anger and compassion she herself felt. She stood only a few feet away, far closer than she was allowed.

"Woman!" he bellowed, and raised his hand as if he meant to strike her. "Will you never learn your place? Get back where you belong. Ten lashes await you at home."

He was so convincing that she instinctively fell back two paces and collided with Jayna. Several passersby shouted their hearty approval, no one needing an interpreter to know that she'd just been royally admonished by a most masterful master.

She caught his playful wink as he turned and studied the vast array of exotic fruit. The rat. The stinking, naughty, marvelous, sweet rat. Rand was the only man she'd ever wanted to cover with kisses and slap senseless at the same time. He had a hard heart, she knew that, but it was just as big and gentle and good as it was hard.

She did love him. She loved him so much that her throat constricted and her mouth trembled beneath the veil while she watched him select an assortment of cherries and figs, dark grapes and ripe persimmons. When he offered the vendor a handful of coins, the man refused payment and tumbled the fruit into a thin cotton sack.

Rachel assumed it was Rand's generosity in exchange for the child's hand that had earned him the freebies. But she was wrong, she soon realized. The man pointed at her and laughed, apparently impressed with Rand's hold over his concubine.

Rand slapped the man's back, as if they shared similar philosophies on the treatment of women. She knew better. Though he smiled a tight smile, Rand's jaw was clenched, and so was his fist around the sack.

He looked mighty close to shoving the vendor's face into the wagon of fruit.

Fearful that he might give in to the urge, Rachel stepped forward. Jayna clamped a firm hand on her shoulder.

"Do you wish for twenty lashes, mistress, not ten?"

"For heaven's sake, Jayna, Rand wouldn't—" Rachel bit her tongue. She'd slipped, just like an amateur—or a woman in love standing up for her man. Amateurs and women PIs falling for their clients were not mutually exclusive. It was too late—from the beginning it had been too late to fight the inevitable—but she rushed on to salvage what she could. "What I mean is, the master seeks his own pleasure. He'd rather make me pay up in bed than beat me to a pulp."

"Yes. I think this, too." Jayna's soft laughter was that of a wise old woman who'd endured enough pain to recognize love, no matter what its form or its disguises. "Do not make him shame you again when it is not his wish. Be still, child, for he comes."

Before she could utter a single questioning word, Rachel was staring up at Rand's madder-than-hell face. He gripped her wrist and shoved the sack into her hand. If not for the soothing rubbing of his thumb over her pulse point, or the apology she read in his eyes, even she might have bought his act.

"Carry this," he commanded harshly. "You will feed it to me later." And then, to Jayna, he said, "How long before the sun goes down?"

"One hour, perhaps."

"Shit."

His impatience relayed itself with a yank of the

clasp at Rachel's temple. Thrusting the still-attached veil to one side, he immediately took her mouth, which was open in an "Oh!" of surprise.

His kiss was immediate, greedy and rough. It was a long kiss, so long she wondered if he meant to make out until dusk set in. Not that anyone around here took notice of such matters, judging from the activity that bustled around them.

Staying as true to her role as possible, Rachel refrained from gripping him close, though she returned his kiss with a fervor equal to his. He was her lover, her friend, and her only link to Western civilization. Their kiss was confirmation of all three, and his lips left her with no doubt that he needed this bond as much as she did.

In this place, this evil place, they kissed with a madness they both clung to for their sanity. These people weren't right, not right at all, but in their midst was rightness. Call it love, call it lust, call it truth.

Whatever she called it, it was *them*. She and Rand, two strangers in a too-strange land. His hands were kneading her buttocks, and her own were clutching the bag between them to keep herself from returning his show of possession.

His mouth was still open when it skimmed her cheek and settled beside her ear.

"I hate this country," he said, so quietly that even Jayna couldn't hear. "I'm close to hating myself for being the one who got you into this. But, Rachel, there's no one else I'd rather be with."

"Me, too," she whispered. "Me, too."

"Good enough. And so was that kiss. It'll get me through sundown. How about you?"

"I'll make it, but I'm counting the minutes till

we're home.'' While she still had the chance, she reminded him of her earlier warning. ''Don't forget, if we see Sarah or her owner when we pass their house, you *have* to keep going. Don't stop. Don't even look their way.''

''Gotcha. In the meantime, I think it's a good idea if you pretend I'm that jerk by the fruit stand who's watching us. Get uppity and give me a reason to play your master. Who knows? Maybe he'll toss me a pineapple or two.''

It was almost as hard not to snicker as it was to let Rand go. Rachel wiped the back of her free hand against her wet mouth and refastened the thin cloth. Indulging a grin, she cherished their moment of shared humor.

Rand's sardonic laughter echoed through the tent.

''Just a taste of what's to come, wench! Wipe your mouth again and I'll slap it.''

He turned on his sandaled heel and didn't glance back. She waited until Jayna gave her a nudge.

Only Rachel heard her low chuckle. Only Rachel and the patron saints of harmony and justice and love.

TRAILING EVEN A PRETEND master home should have rankled, but it didn't. She knew they were equals, and just as important, so did Rand. In fact, as they approached Sarah's street, Rachel was all too aware that she was his professional superior when it came to this kind of risky business.

The nagging apprehension she'd felt earlier came closer to an alarming unease with each step toward their destination. She told herself she was being ridiculous, that nothing could go wrong simply because they passed the place where Sarah was kept.

Even so, Rachel said a silent prayer that they'd make it home without incident. She shifted the assortment of packages in her arms while she kept her gaze locked on the back of Rand's head. An elegant black car whizzed past and turned into a driveway two houses down. The houses were mansions, and she and Jayna were a good half block away. Rand sped up.

She might have been the perfect concubine, instead of a sweaty-palmed PI, the way she immediately matched his accelerated pace over the redbrick sidewalk.

Her heart kept time with her feet, beating faster, faster. The swish-swish sound was so loud in her ears that she didn't hear Jayna panting as she rushed to pick up a fallen package.

"You carry too much, mistress. Let me help."

"Thanks, Jayna," Rachel muttered distractedly. She thrust the bulk of her load into Jayna's arms, hardly aware that the elder woman was struggling to grasp it all, while she herself now carried nothing but a bag of fruit.

For a split second, Rachel chanced a backward glance. The hired men, dressed in Zebedique garb, were making tracks behind them. They appeared to be deep in conversation, but she was certain from their quickened pace that they were aware of the sudden switch in what had been an innocuous walk home.

"Damn," she groaned, cursing herself for taking her gaze off Rand for even that little bit. And then she silently damned him for sprinting ahead at an aggressive saunter. He was closing in too fast, but, thank heaven, not fast enough to beat the wrought-iron gates that swung shut behind the car.

He stopped in front of the gates. He stood there frozen, so still he might have been an ice sculpture. The driver got out and opened the back door of the car.

What in the world did Rand think he was doing, calling attention to himself like that? It was exactly what she had feared. He didn't know what he was doing, wasn't capable of thinking past the need to reach for, to rescue, his sister.

By the time she'd regained her ten-pace distance, a man and two women had emerged from the back seat. Rand was leaning forward, his own hands reaching for the bars and his mouth opening.

"You bastard!" Rachel dug into the sack and hurled a soft persimmon as hard as she could. *Smack!* The juicy orb splattered against his upper arm. Rand's mouth snapped shut, and he whirled around. "You son of a bitch, who do you think you are, expecting me to bow to you?"

Fruit began to fly. A handful of cherries hit his chest, zapping the target like buckshot. Next she launched an attack of grapes, from his face to his crotch, screaming insults at his genital endowment as she advanced. By now the car's occupants had turned to observe what appeared to be a mutinous slave turning her owner into a living work of abstract art.

Several figs landed between Rand's stunned eyes before she pounced and knocked him on his butt. Rachel punched at his chest and kicked at his shins. She wrestled in earnest, until he had no choice but to flip her on her back, sprawl over her and lock her in a stranglehold, unless he wanted the stuffings beat out of him.

Once his face was within inches of hers, she wheezed out in a whisper, ''Get a grip, Rand. Get it fast, or you'll blow the scam. Hurry up and apologize to our audience for your wayward slave, and let's get the hell home while the getting's still good.''

He shook his head, as if to clear it. Rachel pushed him off and sprang to her feet. There had to be a God in heaven, because Rand had regained his senses enough to follow suit.

He shook her hard, then thrust her away with ample momentum to send her stumbling backward into Jayna and the two hired men, who'd caught up.

While Rand made a stilted apology to the small gathering on the other side of the gates, Rachel insinuated herself between Jayna and the hired guns, hoping against hope they passed for locals enjoying a cheap thrill.

''Scram,'' she hissed at the two men. ''Get the hell—''

They took off, laughing as if they'd just gotten their jollies for the night.

These guys that Rand had brought in were good, really good. But not as good as Jayna—gentle, wise Jayna—who sized Rachel up with a withering glare before scourging her with a string of scalding epithets, throwing down bags and shoving her to her knees.

Her hands pressed against her charge's shoulder blades, then moved to urge Rachel's face to the ground, until her forehead rested by Rand's foot in humble, beggarly fashion.

Once the onlookers retreated to the house, Rachel

felt Jayna's soft pat of reassurance and then Rand's tight grip as he pulled her to her feet.

The trek home was made in silence. Rand, ten slow, deliberate paces ahead, as if he had to struggle against nature to take each step. Jayna, just behind her, murmuring a litany that might have been a lullaby or a prayer.

And she, Rachel, thanking the stars for their narrow escape and cursing, yet understanding, Rand's near fouling of their master plan.

And while she thanked heaven, she thanked Jayna in silence. Jayna deserved better than what she'd been born to, and Rachel was ready to go to the mat to see that she got it.

But why stop there? Why not go for broke?

Rachel wanted it all. Freedom for Sarah and Jayna. The screws put to this country and the slavers who benefited from its twisted mass psyche. They'd earned her enmity, and she wanted their heads. And Rand. She wanted Rand. With all his secrets, his flaws and his darkness and his marred beauty, she wanted him. No other man would do. They all faded in his shadow. Here, there, anywhere, she loved him. Would always love him.

The question was, once this nightmarish dream was over, would he still feel the magic, too?

20

RAND DIVIDED THE LENGTH of Rachel's hair into three portions, rubbing the inviting texture between his fingers as he began to braid.

"Only two days left till Friday," Rachel said, snuggling her backside between his open legs on the bed. He nudged his hips forward and was rewarded with a girlish giggle.

"No thanks to me, Friday's still on. I still can't believe I almost blew it yesterday—and Sarah wasn't even one of the concubines that got out of that car. I owe you, Rachel, I owe you really big."

"You owe me nothing but a back massage tonight."

"You're too easy on me, angel. I'd feel a lot better if you'd slug me, instead of being so nice and understanding about my major-league screwup."

"It's easy to go easy on you. After all, you've been so hard on yourself, you've saved me the trouble." She caught his hand, which had strayed to her breast, and brought it to her mouth. Even his knuckles responded to her gentle bite, sending an immediate message to his groin. "C'mon, Rand, give yourself a break. You're human. You acted on instinct. There's no crime in that. And besides, no harm was done."

"Thanks to you. You tried to warn me, but it's like I heard and didn't really listen. If you'd been me—"

"I would have reacted exactly the same way. She's your sister, not mine. And that's why, no matter what, once you drop me and Jayna off at the bathhouse, you don't budge from the car until you see the whites of our eyes."

She kissed his palm, giving him the reassurance he needed, the trust she still had in him when he'd lost it in himself. He loved her. Lord, but he did. He loved her so much that fear for her safety was gnawing away at the pit of his stomach. If he ever lost Rachel, he'd never find himself again. And Sarah, sweet little Sarah—who had long ceased to be little, even if that was how he remembered her—she needed Rachel just as desperately as he.

They were bound, the three of them, parts of a whole, Rachel, the crucial link. Without her, Joshua would forever be missing. He gathered her as close as he could, nuzzling his cheek to her neck, his hands cinching her waist.

"I'm scared, Rachel. I'd never admit it to another soul, but my skin's crawling just thinking about you walking into that bathhouse without me."

"Don't borrow worry, when chances are it won't even come. We've got our backup, a plane on standby, and maybe even an ally in Jayna, if push comes to shove. A week from now we could even be back home…Joshua."

He felt her slight stiffening and knew it came from her reference to home and promises he hadn't made. Promises of marriage. The word was an ominous one, but he'd begun repeating it to himself in silence, as if by doing so he could make himself immune to the punch it packed. It held a strong and heady lure for him, being one of the few things he'd never compromised his standards on.

In his mind, marriage was a sacred union, binding, irrevocable. Divorce, as far as he was concerned, was breaking a promise—and that was something he'd done one time too many.

He asked himself how he could be so deeply in love and even think about divorce. Maybe it was because most everyone he knew had been divorced at least once, though they'd probably never even considered it as a possibility. Rachel was like that. She saw only what they had now. It was a naive, seductive part of her nature—part of what he loved about her.

Marriage. What a concept. Rachel needed time more than he did, though she had yet to realize it. Marriage to him would not be easy. Marriage to him would be for life.

She was so everything he could ever want that it made him go gentle on her hair and absorb the utter delight it gave him to hear her sigh again, "Joshua."

"You've taken to calling me Joshua. Why?"

"Because it makes me feel good. Joshua Smith. A boy who ran away, shined shoes, and became Rand Slick."

"Rand Slick," he repeated with a laugh. "Right out of a comic book or a gangster movie."

"I wonder if that's where the real Rand Slick's parents came up with his name."

"Damned if I know. Dumb luck finding the same name on a local gravestone with a close enough date of birth."

"You never told me how you got his birth certificate."

Rand continued his braiding and shook his head at

the memory. "Amazing what kids can learn from watching the tube. I wrote to the county department of records and asked for a copy, since the original had been lost. Five bucks for the fee, and Rand Slick I officially was. Wish I'd chosen better, but after I got it on a social security card, it was as good as engraved in granite. The government doesn't seem to know I've been officially dead for twenty years. Selective memory, I suppose, considering what I've paid in since."

He could have finished the French braid twice by now, but still he took his time. Rand absorbed the domesticity of their easy companionship; it reminded him of the days he'd braided Sarah's hair. He was getting much better at peering into his lockbox. Lifting the braid, he kissed Rachel's nape and thanked her silently for giving him such freedom.

"Had you paid your first visit to Sarah by the time you managed to change your name?"

"No. That was two years later." Memories. This was one he didn't like, and he told Rachel so.

"Remember it anyway. Tell me why you didn't approach her then, or the second time, either."

Rand hesitated. He hadn't slipped recently. Maybe it was a good time to test how much progress he'd made.

"It's simple, Rachel. I was ashamed. I can still see her when she was ten, coming out of the school, laughing, talking to some other wholesome-looking kids. And what was I? Just this vagabond who survived on the streets. I wanted her to remember me the way we parted. Her big brother who hung the moon, not the hardass I'd become."

"But what about your second visit?"

"I was twenty-one and didn't even have a high school diploma, much less the home I'd promised to give her. I was working odd jobs, making ends meet and putting aside a dollar here and there. She looked happy, and I had nothing that could compete. So I decided leaving her was the most loving thing I could do. As it turned out, turning my back when I didn't want to was the incentive I needed to get where I'm at now."

"But how did you get there? That's a mystery you still haven't spilled."

"You'll be disappointed. And I hate to destroy the last of my mystique." He tied a ribbon in the middle of her back, then swished the scarlet tail over his lips.

Rachel turned, and they locked in an embrace that was almost too good, to all-encompassing, to be true. So good he was afraid it was too good to last.

"Indulge me," she said. "I won't be disappointed. Everything else you've told me's been better than a Saturday matinee. But it has more daring and courage, more twists and turns than a movie could ever pull off. It's human. It's you. I'll love it. Guaranteed."

If she loved him, really loved him, it had to be warts and all. Rand took a deep breath and braced himself to expose a few that, though he'd tried to cauterize them, were there to stay.

"Okay, it's like this. I got mad. At life and myself. I'd worked hard, been honest. It got me minimum wage and little else. The only thing I could do better than a Wall Street executive was play pool. I had two hundred dollars saved and took it to a pool hall to hustle nickles and dimes."

"You must have racked up quite a bundle."

"Enough to take to the racetrack while I devoured

every finance book, money magazine and *Wall Street Journal* the public library had to offer. I got lucky and knew when to cut my losses before my wins took a dip. In six months I had twenty thousand smackers. I was ready for higher stakes.''

''The stock market?''

''Commodities. They pay off bigger and faster than stocks. Twenty grand turned into a hundred. A hundred to a million. In three years I had my nest egg. By then I'd hooked up with some professionals who didn't play by the rules and found out I had a knack for arbitrage. I had what it took.''

''You mean a self-taught profession, and lady luck.''

''They got me started, but that's about it. I had the instincts of a shark, the ethics of a snake, and the hunger of—well, the street kid. I'd been so poor that I couldn't get enough. A million, ten million in the bank, and every morning I expected to wake up in a roach-infested shack and find out it was all a dream. For years I've put in sixteen-hour days and slept more nights in my office than at home in bed. That's been my life since I last saw Sarah.'' His smile was no smile. It was a grimace.

''Everything you heard about me from my competition is true. I played dirty pool, bet on fixed races, and came out on top at the price of my morals. And by the time I could offer Sarah a good life, she was nowhere to be found. So here I am. With so much money it's indecent, tracking down a sister who has every reason to hate me, and holding a woman in my arms who's crazy if she gambles on the likes of me.''

''The likes of you?'' Rachel kissed him softly. ''The likes of you are very special, Rand. You shouldn't beat up on yourself for doing what you were driven to do."

He stared at her hard. "Were?" he repeated. "You used the past tense. But we're in the present and wondering about our future. You've asked me what happens to us once we get out of here. That depends a great deal on what you can accept and what you can't. I've cleaned up my act some, but—" He gritted his teeth and took the plunge. "Rachel, I still play dirty pool. Barring a miracle, chances are I always will."

He waited for her to recoil, or at the very least judge and hold him in contempt.

"C'mon, angel," he bit out, unable to endure her silence. "Aren't you impressed with the secret of my success?"

"Are you?"

"Impressed? Hardly. Sorry for it? Absolutely not."

"Then I suppose we see eye to eye, to a point. I don't like how you've gotten where you are. But I understand your motives. Maybe that's why, even knowing what I do, I can respect what you've accomplished. You did it the only way you knew how. Life dealt you a dirty hand and you just learned a little too well how to deal it back."

Considering her entrenched ethics—the kind of ethics he now wished he'd never traded away—her reaction was a lot to swallow, despite his need to drink it up. He had to test her. Besides, he might learn something new if he watched her real close.

"You could make a load of money yourself if you wanted to give an exposé. I'm sure the money magazines, and maybe even the reigning rags of trash, would love to get the scoop."

"Shut up, Rand." She shoved him down on the

mattress, her braid whipping against his chest. "I've always known you played dirty. But you've changed even more than me, and I imagine that's something you're going to take with you when we get back. Whether you stick around for me or not."

He felt a little mean, and a whole lot threatened. But Joshua tempered his words, even as Rand slipped and struck back.

"And you're just champing at the bit to find out which direction I head for once we escape, aren't you?"

"You bet I am, Mr. Master. But for the time being, you're not going anywhere except to bed with me."

"You still want to sleep with me after this? Lord, Rachel, either you've got a worse case of lust than I gave you credit for, or you give new meaning to love being blind."

He waited, on edge, her reaction so important it somehow seemed to be the very key to the future.

"You idiot," she said softly. "How dare you even suggest such a thing? I resent the hell out of your ugly implications, and I've *never* had blinders on when it comes to you." She kissed him full on the mouth. "You've sold yourself short, Rand, but don't try sharing the wealth. I could never love you less for showing your life to me."

She proceeded to chastise him with velvet lashes, strokes of acceptance that touched him down to his roots.

Deep into the night, Rand stared at the canopy overhead, while Rachel's even breathing soothed his savage breast. It seemed he was still learning lessons from her. She was young but wise. And she was strong and sharp, cutting into him as cleanly as a surgeon's blade with her uncompromising acceptance and her uncanny insight.

He wondered what she would think of the insider trading information that had arrived earlier that day. He hadn't stooped to that lately, but this deal had been too sweet to pass up. She'd hate it if she knew. But he didn't think she'd leave him for it. Unbelievable. That a man like him could marry a woman of her substance...

It made him want to deserve what she offered. It made him think of who he'd been and who he wanted to be while the words *marriage* and *divorce* jousted in his head.

The night wore on, and eventually he got up. Rand went into his office and hit a button on his phone that immediately connected him with the other side of the globe.

"The deal's off," he said flatly. "From now on, I don't know you and you don't know me. Keep any future information to yourself, unless you want a visit from the SEC."

With that, he hung up and fed a pile of papers that spelled pay dirt into a shredder. A smile of supreme satisfaction curved his lips as he watched the equivalent of millions of dollars swirl into the trash can, like confetti raining down on a hero returning from war.

RAND JERKED to a sitting position. Sweat-drenched sheets clung to his skin. For heart-palpitating seconds, the stubs of flickering candles guttered into the dregs of his nightmare.

Only the dream had a new twist this time. Or was it prophecy?

Rachel. His disoriented gaze locked on the form huddled by his side. Peaceful, sweet. She reached for him.

"Rand?" she murmured groggily.

He was breathing fast. Was she really here, or was this the dream and she was climbing a flight of stairs while he fell straight to hell?

His hands were shaking as he cupped her face. Her skin was smooth, and warm, and reassuringly *there*.

"Rachel," he groaned. "Rachel."

"Is something wrong?"

"Bad dream."

"Tell me."

He didn't want to relive it, not now, when he needed more than anything to assure himself that she wasn't an apparition, that she was truly real. He was so afraid of losing her, just as he'd lost Sarah.

Her gentle strokes down his chest were comforting. In his naked need, her touch was fire in barren, dry grass.

"Rachel," he said, his voice ragged against her mouth. "Hold me. Hold me tight."

His kiss was desperate. She draped an arm about his neck, and her free hand clasped his. Their fingers interlocked.

"I need you, Rachel. Tell me you need me, too."

"I do need you. Both of you. All of you."

"Then take me. Help me to forget."

She sheathed him with an intimate assurance and followed his entreaty, mounting him with feline grace.

"Tell me about your bad dream," she urged.

"It's a nightmare I've had forever, and you're a dream chasing it away. Get rid of it, angel. Ride me."

"Is it about Sarah?" She followed the direction of his grip, rising and descending in time to their words.

He didn't want to relive the awful thing, but maybe, just maybe, he could kill the old monster if he shared it with Rachel. At the least, it was sure to lose some power with her by his side.

"It was always Sarah. Until tonight. You took her place behind a glass wall. I saw you but I couldn't get to you."

His upward thrust was urgent; her downward reply met it, stripping away the scene replaying in his head. He felt her cloaking him in the darkness, her empathy so strong it was palpable, giving him the strength to go on.

"I tried to break the glass until my fists were bleeding, but it was no good. The black fog came, and when it lifted you were gone. Harder. *Harder.*"

"Where did I go?" She met him with rapid strokes, her breasts rising, then crushing against his chest.

"Up the stairs. Out of sight. I ran through the endless tunnel while a train chased me down." His breathing accelerated as though he were a marathon runner in the race of his life. "Elevator," he gritted between his teeth, then gnashed out, "I make it to the elevator just before the train eats up my feet. No way but down with...with..."

"With what? Who? Oh God—"

"No God. A demon. He's winking at me. Taking me... My feet leave the floor. My—my head's striking the ceiling." His movements echoed the sensation. "I've lost you."

"No," she whispered sharply. Her nails bit into his tensed shoulders, and oh, how he loved the sharp bite

of it. So real. So good. "No," she assured him. "I'm
here."

"Make it true. End the nightmare." His plea was
desperate, his hips were locked, up, up, and fixed.
"Drive it away. That's it, angel. Love your beast.
Ride him to dust, break his dream like glass."

She obliterated the horrid vision in front of his wide
open eyes. Her own were pinched shut, her neck was
strained back, and her mouth was stretched in an oval
cry of...

"Joshua."

Her convulsions gripped him, taking the hated
dream into her. He ejaculated, and knew not only the
sweetness of soulful release, but also the regret that
it was a condom and not her that he had spilled himself into.

Nightmares. Marriage. Children...

In that telling moment, he knew he could want
them with her. There was so much he wanted, and so
little time before this woman he loved too much
would put her life on the line to make up for the grave
mistake he had made. To help him keep his promise
at last.

She collapsed on top of him, using what strength
she had left—very little, he sensed—to stroke his
face.

"I hate your nightmare," she whispered. "I hate it
for hurting you."

He pressed his lips into her palm, then studied the
ring finger of her left hand in the muted light.

"I hate it for making me feel what it would be like
to lose you."

"But I'm here. Feel for yourself that I am here."
She rocked slowly forward.

"I feel it, all right." He felt a lifting of his heart from nothing more than her pleased smile. She rubbed her cheek against his chest in a soothing back-and-forth movement that reminded him of a kitten brushing figure eights about his legs. Such a contrast to the woman who had practically ridden him into his grave. "You ride me well, angel. You love me even better."

Her chuckle was soft, a welcome sound that challenged the mean, dark demon. Rand joined her, chuckling until it gained momentum and he laughed aloud at the nightmare. It was just the same as spitting in its face. It felt good. No, it felt *damn* good.

He kissed her soft. He kissed her hard.

"This time, ride me," she demanded. "Ride me until we're both too tired to move or even dream...."

21

"READY, ANGEL?" Rand tucked a stray curl beneath Rachel's headdress. She caught his hand and kissed it. He realized they were both shaking.

"Ready as I'll ever be, master."

He tried to chuckle at their standing joke, but the sound caught in his strained throat, and he groaned in distress.

"My guts are like water." Pulling her close, he felt the pooling of their strength.

"You'll be okay, Rand."

"It's not me I'm worried about."

"I know." She patted his back. "I know."

"I don't want to let you go into that bathhouse alone. It's hell already, and we haven't even left yet."

"Jayna will be with me. Just remember that, while you stay posted in the car. With luck, I'll be hustling Sarah out with me and we'll all be on the plane before her guard can find her owner and sound the alarm."

"With luck. Backup. And no delays on the runway. I just hope if we pull this off Jayna doesn't get punished for our success."

He caught a spark of determination in Rachel's eyes. He knew that look and guessed what it meant.

"You want to take Jayna with us, don't you? Rachel, she doesn't have a passport, and we're going to be running for our lives as it is. She's old. She could slow us down.''

"To hell with a passport. We're bypassing check-in and customs anyway, and our own government won't have the heart to send her back.''

"No government, not even ours, has a heart. If we get caught, they're going to be more worried about the political situation and keeping Zebedique's oil than getting us out.''

"But you have that contact, the official you said you could count on to throw his weight around if need be.''

"The men following us have orders to get to a phone fast if we run into problems.'' He snorted with a wry kind of humor. "My guess is, our ticket out would be the tasty bit of dirt on Zebedique and American slavers that my lawyer would turn over to *The New York Times*. Wish I could've just done that to begin with. But there was no way, with Sarah caught in the middle. Her owner might have gotten rid of the evidence. Permanently.''

Rachel nodded. "You did right. It does make me feel safer, though, knowing that if the political machine lets us down the public will raise enough Cain to get some action.''

"I imagine so. A high-profile citizen incarcerated for trying to rescue his sister sold into slavery? Front-page news, sure to incite some good old-fashioned moral outrage.''

"And speaking of moral outrage...''

"Jayna.'' Seeing what this meant to her, and aware of his own reluctance to leave Jayna to the wolves, he relented. "Okay. If she wants to go, we'll take her, and I'll use my clout to make sure she doesn't get sent back.''

"Thank you, Rand.''

"Thank Joshua. Better yet, you can thank them both properly, once we're out of here.'' A weary sigh sifted through his lips. ''You know, you've got this damnable way of stirring up my conscience. I just hope to hell you haven't done irreparable damage. I could end up out of business if the competition senses I've lost my edge. They'd love to pick my bones.''

The sound of her soft laughter as he exposed this very real possibility would have ticked him off at one time. Instead, he took it, savored it, and slowly smiled. At the moment, the idea of his financial demise did seem a petty consideration, hardly worth considering.

''You could retire today if you wanted to and leave them to tear each other apart. Besides, if you did lose your money, you'd still have me. And Sarah. We could all sit around and pass the cans at dinner. Maybe see who won the spoon in a hand of poker.''

The quip was light, but the question of where their rapidly accelerating future was heading was still there.

''I guess it could be romantic. Sharing cans. Sharing the spoon.'' *Sharing lives* came the persistent thought. On the heels of that was the other one that continued to nag at him. He'd changed in a very short while. Her mention of open cans even gave him a warm glow. But how much of it would stay with him once they were back in their old reality and away from this artificial scenario?

He saw himself plunged into the manic pace of New York. He saw Rachel returning to her Vegas home with the kind of reputation that would keep the phone ringing forever and a day. And Sarah, free again, free to decide whether she wanted to have anything to do with her black-sheep brother.

He didn't like any of it. He wanted to ask Rachel to marry him and let the dice fall where they might. Only...what if he couldn't retain what he'd gained here; if he slipped too far, could Rachel handle it? And he had a promise to keep, the professional boost she had earned. He wouldn't renege on that promise, though it might prove his undoing. She could get caught up in the fast-track life and decide that a future with him was more thorns than roses.

Rose-tinted glasses. He jerked them off and knew what he had to do. The answer was as incisive as a paper cut: When they returned, he'd keep his business promise and withhold the vow he ached to make. They'd see each other on weekends, until he found out if Rachel's lessons would stick or if she would see him in a different light. This place affected their judgment, and marriage—a forever marriage—left no room for mistakes.

"We need to go, Rand. How about a kiss for luck?"

"Luck's something we're going to need, Rachel. Let's make the kiss good."

As his mouth savored the open invitation of hers, he felt the taint of his decision. An ugly feeling that he was hurting them both in the name of rationalization tore at him. He felt he was reducing their relationship by evaluating it as though he were cutting a high-stakes once-in-a-lifetime deal, rather than relying on the emotions and trust he'd learned from Rachel.

Did this mean he was regressing already? The fear relayed itself in the urgency of his kiss. Crushing her lips as if he could extinguish the unwanted thoughts, then pressing his tongue deep inside, he groaned his need for her understanding as she held him within the haven of her mouth's womb.

Time weighed heavily upon them, its tick-tock-ticking a suffocating pressure. Did she feel his tumult, he wondered? Then he knew that she did, because her own embrace was desperate, and held a fear that went beyond their immediate danger. In this silent understanding they reached for a fleeting comfort.

He hiked up her robe and pushed down her panties. Her own hands were equally frantic to expose just as much of him as was necessary before they fell to the floor together.

It was not a graceful coupling. She parted her thighs, and he sank into her without foreplay. His thrusts were quick, deep and urgent. As she took him, they stared at each other in silence. No words were needed. They both knew what this was. Their need to cling to what they had, to put off the inevitable, while girding themselves for it with this raw act.

Not more than two minutes had elapsed, but somehow what had passed between them in those two minutes seemed to bind them in a way that marked them for life. He felt her contractions, though she didn't blink or utter a sound. He was near to coming himself, fully aware he'd ignored the wisdom of a condom. Rachel knew, too, he was quite certain. And neither of them was pretending it was an oversight made in the heat of the moment.

This wasn't heat. It was desperation.

Rand made as if to pull out. She gripped his wrist

and moved for the first time, raising her hips from the floor.

He hesitated, then gave a final jerk—but not in the direction of prudence. The act was done. A decision made, based on anything but rational judgment. Why had he done it, he wondered? Was he manipulating himself now, taking out some future insurance that could spell marriage no matter how far he backslid?

The touch of her palm at his cheek was comforting, though her gaze told him she was wrestling with similar questions of her own.

He offered her his hand, and she took it. They held that between them, this thing that they'd done. Then, breaking the contact, neither of them knowing where it might lead, they adjusted their clothes and exited their bedroom of memories.

They left hand in hand, without a backward glance, and without a word having passed between them.

RACHEL SAT CLOSE to Rand in the back seat of the Mercedes limousine that he'd bought—and planned to leave behind, along with his home, once they shook the dust of Zebedique from their feet. He didn't seem concerned about losing his assets in case the country confiscated them after they escaped. She couldn't imagine shrugging off a loss of those proportions as if it were nothing more than a dime rolling into the gutter.

She couldn't imagine a loss of the proportions she stood to lose herself. Was it the uncertainty of where they went from here that had caused her to do what she'd done? Had it been a last-ditch effort to keep something of Rand if stateside reality tore them apart?

She'd been foolish; she knew she'd be foolish again in a heartbeat, given the choice.

But what if they were caught? How horribly selfish of her to bear a child here. But it wouldn't happen. She knew it in her bones. They would succeed. And if they didn't, the hired men trailing two cars behind them had their instructions. They'd get out—whether it was clean or messy.

Rand reached for her hand and stroked it over and over. "We're almost there, angel."

Jayna, facing them on the opposite seat, watched them shrewdly, though Rachel couldn't interpret what she might be thinking, because her face was covered, as was her own.

The driver, one of their hired men, parked a discreet distance from the bathhouse entrance. Rand's slight smile of encouragement was forced and tight.

I love you. He mouthed the words. She nodded and gave him a thumbs-up sign as the driver opened her door and she got out, Jayna in tow. Rachel could feel his gaze upon her as she walked away, intent on her destination.

She wished he was going with her, as partner and friend. She wished she'd had another good-luck kiss. Anything to put off this awesome undertaking that had her trembling from the inside out.

But as she stepped through the pair of shiny brass doors, Rachel sensed the strength he willed her, sensed his tough love protecting her even now. It acted as a catalyst for her courage, creating a gritty resolve to see this through. The time had come to do her job. She'd do it right.

Rachel blinked in the soft light of the interior after the brilliant sunshine. The entry itself was immense, and thankfully cool, giving way to columned arches, golden urns housing lush palms, and decadent rooms smelling of jasmine. Groans of pleasure from cushioned massage tables reached her ears, as did murmurs of conversation in various tongues, and the universal sound of laughter.

"You will like it here," Jayna said. She pushed aside her headdress, and Rachel followed suit. "It is a haven. An escape."

Rachel's glance was incisive. Jayna raised a brow and smiled conspiratorially.

"Let's hope so, Jayna."

"For many years I was a masseuse in this bathhouse. It is where I learned to speak your language." She paused, and Rachel experienced the full effect Jayna seemed to intend. "American concubines who were lonely taught me."

"I don't suppose there's a chance you know of some hanging around lately, besides me?"

Jayna's eyes darted quickly in either direction, seeming to ensure they wouldn't be heard.

"Two Fridays past I came to visit old friends. One friend was guarding her slave. American. She reminded me of the master. Not dark, but there is something they might share."

Holding her breath, Rachel whispered, "Blood?"

"Yes." Jayna's smile was kind but sly. "But not of a lamb."

"You knew."

"An old woman learns much from pain and years. It is good to see honor before passion."

Of course, Rachel thought, mentally slapping her forehead. The sheets were changed daily, and the second night would have been evidence enough, even if

Jayna's intuition—or eavesdropping—hadn't tipped her off already.

"You're a good person, Jayna. I hope I can help you out one day." She thought she could trust Jayna; she knew she needed her. Time was of the essence. "If I can find the master's sister, you could play that game of poker with me soon. As a free woman."

Jayna waved the offer aside, though her gaze was wistful. "It is too late for me. But not for younger souls. I must be careful, but I will help if I can." The sound of approaching feet had Jayna moving them toward a dressing area. "Now, quickly, undress. I will ask my friends if they know of the American woman while you are tended."

"But what if they—"

"Shhh." Jayna silenced her by efficiently stripping Rachel of her heavy garb and thrusting her arms into a thin silk robe. "They are my friends. They, too, hate bondage."

Before Rachel could question the safety of the ploy, Jayna hustled her to the outer room, where a massage table awaited.

Cries of greeting were shouted to Jayna, who returned them in the native tongue. She shoved a cold glass of sparkling water into Rachel's hands after removing the flimsy robe and helping her onto a cushiony table. A quick wink, and Jayna disappeared to an adjoining room that seemed to be where the workers took their coffee breaks.

The masseuse made grumbling noises as her ministrations failed to work the tenseness from Rachel's bunched muscles. Finally giving up, the attendant took her to the next phase, while Rachel's eyes darted about for a glimpse of anyone who might be Sarah. She fretted over Jayna's whereabouts.

Upon entering a huge chamber, Rachel was greeted by a sight that momentarily stunned the worry out of her.

"Good Lord," she muttered. "What is this, Hugh Hefner's old home away from home?"

Naked female bodies of all sizes and ages appeared to be in a state of nirvana as they soaked in a massive communal tub. It bubbled like a vat of champagne, curling about Rachel's toes as she climbed down the marble steps and seated herself on a vacant ledge.

The water was the perfect temperature, and there was a cool swish of air from overhead fans. It should have been soothing, but she hardly noticed it, every sense she possessed honed to pick up any possible clue.

With half-shut eyes, she leaned back and did her best to blend in as she scanned the assembly. She studied faces, decided who looked friendly and who didn't. She listened for even a single word of English. All the while she stayed alert for the scent of potential danger, the feel of an unseen threat. So sharp was her attunement, she turned at the sound of Jayna's footfall, picking it up over the sound of gurgling water.

"Mistress," Jayna whispered urgently. "You have the luck. Come."

Rachel forced herself to rise nonchalantly while her pulse galloped and blood pounded between her ears. As Jayna wrapped a Turkish towel about her, they exchanged more furtive whispers.

"What did you find out?"

"She has just entered the steam room, this woman I believe you seek."

"Is her guard with her?"

At this, Jayna smiled. "She stands outside, waiting. My friend, Montage, has been tortured as I have been." Her lips thinned. "The master she serves is not so kind as ours. He is a cruel man, but she needs money, and so she plays guard. She does not like doing this to eat. Should she have food, shelter from someone kind, then…"

"You think she might be for sale?"

"For freedom. A place where her master cannot punish her for treason."

Yes! Rachel stayed herself from raising a victorious fist in the air and whirling Jayna in her arms.

Anticipation forced adrenaline through her veins until it was all she could do not to rush them both to their destination. Once they were there, Jayna nodded to an elderly woman, who began speaking to her in hushed tones, though no one else was around to hear. Rachel couldn't understand the language, but gathered from their quick hug that they had come to some understanding. Rachel saw the gleam of excitement and hope in the other guard's eyes, just before she made a curt bow.

"It is done, mistress. I have told Montage your word is good. For freedom, she will do this." Indicating the arched door of the sauna, she said, "Enter. Be quick. We will guard, and call if someone comes."

"Be ready to hightail it out of here as soon as I come out. But tell your friend we have to be discreet. You and I, we'll lead the way, and they'll follow until we get to the exit. Then we walk to the car, real easy, like we're taking an afternoon stroll. Got that?"

"You…you bet." Jayna's attempt at Western slang

coaxed a tight smile from Rachel as she took a determined step and then another, striding into the
chamber, from which puffs of steam were billowing.

The door closed behind her, and a quick survey
informed her that two dark women were enmeshed in
a private conversation, while another one, blond and
very pretty, lounged on a marble bench near the back.
Her eyes were closed, but Rachel discerned dark circles of fatigue beneath them. A purplish bruise rode
high on her cheek.

Fists clenched, Rachel wasted no time in closing
the distance between them. As she drew closer, the
impact upon her was immediate and forceful. She
didn't need a recent photo to know that this had to
be Sarah. This woman bore such a strong resemblance
to Rand that there was no room for doubt they shared
a family heritage.

"You look like an American," she said quietly.

The woman raised herself up and looked her full
in the face. She smiled tiredly, as though the spirit
had been beaten out of her, then indicated that Rachel
should sit.

"Welcome to the club." She made a derisive
sound. "Been to any good auctions lately?"

"Yeah. A man by the name of Joshua bought me."
Rachel took note of the immediate flicker of hope in
her eyes, which was immediately snuffed out, as if
the woman had given up on her brother a lifetime
ago. Rachel kept her voice low, but her tone was urgent. "Tell me, does the name Joshua mean anything
to you?"

This time the flicker sparked to life. Rachel touched
her finger to her lips.

"Just nod, yes or no." She got her answer. "How are you, Sarah?"

"I—I'm…" Her voice trailed off, her mouth working but no words coming.

"Just listen, and listen close. I'm sitting in for your brother. It seems there's a promise he came here to keep. He's waiting in a parked car nearby. A car that's headed for an airstrip where a plane's idling, ready to take off."

"Joshua," Sarah whispered in a faraway voice. She choked back a muffled cry. "I can't believe it."

"Believe it." The two dark women continued to talk, and Rachel hurried on, fearful of an intrusion. "We have to move quickly. What I want you to do is count to one hundred after I leave, then get up and follow me out. Everything's set. All you have to do is walk."

"But my guard…"

"You only have one, right?"

"Several," Sarah said. She appeared to be battling shock. Rachel felt a sudden sense of alarm. "But today, just one came. Montage. She's kind to me. She tends me when I'm beaten."

"She wants out of here, too." Rachel sent a thank-you to heaven, at the same time feeling a thirst for brutal revenge against Sarah's owner. "Just do your best to stay calm, Sarah. All you have to do is leave after me, go with Montage to get dressed, and the two of you follow me out the front door. After that, we're on our way. Think you can do it?"

"Joshua." Sarah was crying. *"Joshua."*

"Stop it," Rachel hissed, cringing at the necessary sharpness of her warning. "Please, Sarah. Blank out everything except my instructions. Pulling this off depends on you getting yourself together. Come on, I'll start counting with you. One...two...three..."

"Four...five...six..." Sarah continued the numbers as she swiped at her cheeks.

"Good girl." Rachel squeezed her hand and got up. She nodded amiably to the two other occupants of the room, who sent her a cursory greeting and continued their gossip. At the door, she stole a look at Sarah, who gave her a tremulous smile.

Fifteen minutes later, Rachel and Jayna stood at the entrance to the bathhouse, waiting, on edge, for the anticipated swing of the door. It came with a swish, and they started walking while a quick glance assured Rachel that their company was close behind.

She recognized the nondescript car with their cover about to pull out as she heard the limousine's engine start and purr. The back door opened when she was less than five paces away. Her heart quickened when she spotted Rand's drawn and expectant face. She realized he was assuring himself of her safety. At her nod, he craned for a look at his sister.

It was then that she heard the sudden shout. A cry of outrage, while the sound of running feet sounded too close behind her.

22

RAND'S GAZE WAS FIXED on Sarah—God, could he believe it was really her?—when he heard the man's harsh voice.

"Stop!" His robe was flapping and rolls of flab bounced up and down in time to his agitated jogging. "Stop, you stupid bitch! Where do you think you're going?"

This repulsive insect of a man had to be Sarah's owner. Rand's blood ran hot, and an impulse to mutilate the bastard who was daring to slander his sister had him out of the seat before he could think on their safest course of action.

He grabbed Rachel and shoved her into the limo while Sarah ran close behind. Any thoughts he might have had for a warm reunion fled as he thrust her in the same direction and barked, "Get in!" Her headdress covering came loose, exposing a large, ugly bruise. He fought the urge to kiss it and make it all right.

Rand caught a flash of an elderly woman close behind Sarah, but his eyes remained locked on the unbelievable sight of Jayna hurling herself at the greasy-looking slave owner while she screamed, "Go! Go now! Flee…"

Teeth clenched and bile in his throat, Rand rushed to Jayna as she reeled back from the fist that had caught her in the face. He disentangled the old woman from the enraged brute who had hit her and pushed her to safety.

"Get in the car. Get out of here, and don't wait for me."

With that he jerked Sarah's owner by the robe at his throat and shook him like a mouse caught in a cat's mouth. They were in the middle of the street, and a car whizzed past without stopping. It seemed that in this country a public brawl was nothing out of the ordinary.

In spite of his girth, the man managed to twist free and land a blow to Rand's jaw. Amid spitting curses and the man's screams for "Police! Police!" Rand's street smarts took over.

He fought dirty. He fought mean. An uppercut to the right, a fist to the gut, and a knee in the groin that should have castrated the bastard. It should have been enough. But it wasn't. He wanted to kill him.

"You filthy son of a bitch." Another brutal jab. "That's for beating up on my sister. How d'ya like it, huh?" He grabbed him by the hair and nodded his battered face up and down. "Feels real good, don't it? Big man like you, so tough you go hitting old ladies. How'd ya like a taste of your own medicine?"

He might have literally beat him to death, heaping murder on top of any other charges he might have to face, but for the sudden grip on his shoulder, pulling him off. He whirled around, ready to push the intruder aside. But it was Rachel. She caught him by both arms.

"Rand! Rand!" She shook him hard. "Oh, God, Rand, please stop. He's not worth it. We've got to get out of here while we still can."

He had trouble focusing, he was so blinded by his vengeful purpose, but she was pulling at him, pleading with him, and then raising her own fist as if she might knock him out and drag him away herself. Rand was suddenly aware that a crowd had begun to gather, some placing quick bets and shouting "More! More!" while others called for the police and an ambulance.

He caught Rachel by the waist, and they began to run, almost staggering over their robes and each other's feet in their haste. Somehow they made it into the car. Before the door was shut, the driver was already peeling out.

Rand was breathing raggedly, the fight still in his blood, and blood on his face, his robe. Then he felt a shaking palm cover his hand.

"Joshua?"

As he stared at his sister, who sat by his side, the years rushed in reverse. All the rehearsed words of apology and reunion deserted him and he blinked against an unfamiliar stinging in his eyes.

Big boys don't cry… Big boys don't cry.…

"I finally kept my promise, angel." His voice cracked.

Then Sarah's arms were around him, and his around her, and they were clinging as tight as the day they'd said goodbye.

"I always knew you'd come back for me," she said brokenly.

"I guess better late than never?"

"In the nick of time, Joshua. Daddy would be proud."

Rand used the edge of his sleeve to dry her tears and wipe her nose.

"I got ya something, angel."

He reached across the seat and discovered that Rachel was holding his gift in her hands. They connected, hands touching, gazes meeting in a silent understanding. *Bless you* was the message his eyes sent. *Bless you for giving me Sarah back.* Rachel's chin quivered, and out rolled two big tears. Rand's throat tightened; he knew she was shedding the tears he couldn't because big boys didn't cry.

Placing his offering in his sister's lap, he said, "I thought you might want to hold your doll on our way home."

"Home," she repeated, stroking the doll's curls. Her eyes met his, and he knew they would make it back there together. And then the words that had haunted him in his nightmares, spoken behind a glass wall he'd finally broken through, were spoken aloud. "I love you, big brother."

RACHEL AND RAND WALKED side by side down the corridor to her office.

"That was some trip back, huh, master?"

"Nothing like getting shot at while you're climbing into an airplane. Good thing those local police weren't too handy with their pistols. They could use a few lessons from you." His chuckle was strained.

Rachel knew they were both trying very hard to keep a lightness in their conversation as their impending departure rushed near. He had a plane to catch, work piled to the ceiling in New York and Sarah waiting for him at his home.

In the month since they'd returned, they'd hardly had a minute alone, what with paperwork for their defectors, statements, bringing in the big guns. Not to mention him getting Sarah settled with Montage, and Jayna moving in with Rachel in Vegas.

Rachel's stomach lurched when they stopped at her door. She made herself busy, refusing to look at him while she rummaged around for her keys.

"Anyone ever tell you that you've got terrible taste in purses?"

"Jayna. And you."

"How is Jayna? Is she adjusting okay?"

"She's fine. Getting Americanized. She threw her old outfit into the trash after I took her shopping."

"Is that why you look so tired? Shopping till you drop?"

Rachel tensed. "No. It's just all this business with the authorities. Exposing slavers is hard work. But now that they've caught one in the act and he's spilling his guts, I think things should calm down."

"Not with all the business that's coming your way. Every time I call, the phone's busy. I guess you're up to your armpits in cases now that you've managed that leg up you worked so hard to get. You deserve every bit of your success, Rachel. I'm happy for you."

"Thanks," she said, too abruptly. "I'm real happy for me, too." Happy? She'd never been such a wreck in her life.

He pushed a hand through his back-brushed hair, and she commanded herself not to run both of hers through it. She feared that if she did she'd break. The tension in her was brittle, with so much unresolved, and no promises for the future. His window-glass eyes were wide open, and what she saw there hurt.

He loved her. But he wasn't going to offer marriage. Not yet.

"I want you to know how much I appreciate what you've done. If you hadn't come after me, I could be cooling my heels behind foreign bars."

"It's nothing. Just doing my job." Her fingers were so icy they were numb. The keys clattered to the floor.

"I'll get it," he offered politely. Too damn politely.

Their fingers touched when they reached for the keys. Neither of them moved. Rachel slowly lifted her face. His breath was on her, and she inhaled the scent of spice and bay.

"Are you pregnant?"

She knew she could keep him simply by telling him the truth.

"Rachel, I asked you a question. Did I get you pregnant that last day in Zebedique? Are you carrying our baby?"

If you love something, let it go. If it comes back to you, it's yours....

She let him go.

"No, Rand. I'm not pregnant. Case closed." Rachel rose and shoved the key into the damn door she couldn't get to unlock.

His hand covered hers, and he leaned toward her, too close.

"Rachel. We can't leave it this way."

She pressed her forehead against the etched-glass door, refusing to let him see the overbrightness of her eyes.

"So how do you want to leave it? What do you propose?"

The last word fell between them like a window that couldn't make up its mind whether to open or close while it shuddered from a storm brewing on either side.

"I need some time, angel. Be patient with me?"

Angel. He'd called Sarah that, she now knew. The endearment meant as much as hearing him say that he loved her. But not as much as a lifetime commitment.

"My patience is wearing thin, Rand. You either want me or you don't."

"Of course I want you. I love you."

"Do you? Do you love me enough not to run away?"

"I'm not running. I'm coming to terms with myself. And the future."

"But your terms don't include me."

"My terms have everything to do with you. Look, I've been thinking it's going to get old fast, jetting back and forth to see each other. How do you feel about…" He tapped his lips, and she shuddered. With so much need to kiss them; with a terrible premonition of what he was struggling to say.

"I'd like you to move your business to New York, use an extra office of mine. There's plenty of room in my penthouse for Jayna. And you. I think it would be a good idea if we lived together for a while before—"

"Don't insult me with some half-assed commitment," Rachel snapped, tears springing to her eyes. Rand reached for her, and she shoved him away. They stared at each other, her eyes glittering with hurt and fury, his dark with apology and a plea for understanding.

She wanted a fight, a fight that would make his Zebedique street brawl look like a schoolyard tussle.

Apparently sensing how close to ugly this confrontation was getting, Rand backed off, spreading his hands in a gesture of defeat.

"I'm sorry, Rachel."

"I didn't ask for a character reference."

He winced. Rand hesitated, then took an envelope from his coat pocket and pressed it into her palm.

"Here's your fee, as promised. Remember, any promises I make to you, I'll never break."

"I don't want the stupid fee." She thrust it back at him. Rand's controlled expression was suddenly jarred.

"It's a million dollars."

"And you think I care about that? Keep your damn money. It's not what I want from you." She pushed the door open.

"I'm coming in. We need to talk."

"We're through talking, Rand. And don't you dare step through this door again until you've got your own mind made up one way or the other. Don't call me. Don't write." She stepped over the threshold and faced him point-blank. "In fact, I don't want to see your face again until you've got a ring in your pocket and you're ready to head for the altar."

"But, Rachel… Angel…"

"No ifs, ands or buts. Those are my terms. And in this case, my terms stand."

She shut the door in his face. And then she waited…and waited. It didn't open. And while she slumped against the wall, her face buried in her hands as she heard his retreating footsteps, she repeated over and over, "Big girls don't cry…. Big girls don't cry…."

"FULL HOUSE, MISTRESS! I win. Hand over the loot."

"Criminy, Jayna, you're wiping me out." Rachel shoved a pile of pennies over her desk.

"Just call me, how you say, Cool Hand Luke? Or is it Minnesota Fats?"

"You're watching too many movies on the VCR, Jayna."

"I know. So yesterday I went to the casino. All that fruit running around made me hungry. So I ate a hamburger and drank a shaked milk. The commercials say you can't drink the water."

"Lord," Rachel groaned. "Now it's the slots and junk food. Heaven only knows what comes next."

"Once the baby is here, I promise to—" Jayna's brow furrowed. "Oh, yes. Clean up my act."

The mention of the baby, now two months in the making, brought a sudden catch to Rachel's throat. A month since she'd seen Rand. A month spent straddled between the never-ending need to see him, touch him, while she stroked her still-flat belly and remembered...too much.

Jayna's gnarled hand covered hers. "Call him. Tell him of the baby you carry. He will come."

"No. Absolutely not."

"But you are so sad."

"Heartbroken, Jayna."

"And stubborn." The kindness of her eyes contrasted with the chastisement in her voice. "You foolish woman. Why must you be so proud? The master, he loves you."

"No one's my master but me. And as far as I can see, he's guilty of being too proud himself. Pigheaded, that's what he is." Rachel snorted, even as her heart nosedived. "He's had a month to come to his senses, and he hasn't shown his face yet. Guess I'll have to rack up my losses, no matter how much it hurts, because it's all or nothing, and I'm not backing down.''

"His sister, she calls you much. You say she is worried about him.''

"Sarah's a good person. But her brother has to make his own decisions, not her.''

"Montage says he sits alone in the dark. He sleeps with your white robe. She finds it when she changes his sheets.''

In her mind's eye, Rachel saw sheets stained with lamb's blood. Her robe on the floor, lying next to his. So much they shared. So much he was cheating them of.

"The way I look at it, if he wants to sleep with more than a robe, he knows how to get his butt to a jewelry store. Some trade-off, huh, Jayna? Him in the sack with a wad of cloth, while I cuddle with a doll.''

Rachel had to cling to her hard line, because that was all she had. Except for memories—and an unborn baby. And a love that was so strong it took everything she had not to hop on the first plane to New York and settle for no promises and Rand's arms holding her tight.

How she hurt for him. How she hurt for herself. And for the baby that they shared, keeping her company while he remained alone except for his sister.

"Why don't you go cash in those pennies for some quarters and go for the jackpot, Jayna? If it's all the same to you, I'd like to nap on the job.''

"As you wish, mistress.''

"My wish is that you'd quit calling me that.''

"Okeydokey…Rachel.''

"You're a gas, Jayna. Oh, and thanks for the shoulder. It helps to have you around, especially since Rand's not."

"Small tomatoes, right?"

"Potatoes, Jayna. But, no, you mean a lot to me. Making sure I eat right and get my rest. You'll be a great nanny when the time comes."

"It is time you should rest now." She drew the curtains together, then pulled down the shade at the door. Just before she took her leave, she turned. "Call him, Rachel."

Once Jayna left, Rachel squeezed her eyes tight, fighting the moisture that was trying to leak out. Reaching beneath her desk, she latched on to the doll she always kept close. Her sleeping with a doll, Rand with a robe. There was no sense in it. Jayna was right—she was being stubborn, and prideful.

She eyed the phone, her hand shaking as it hovered over the receiver. She laid her head on the desk, listening to her heart pound, putting off the inevitable a few moments more.

The door opened and shut. She thought she heard a click of the lock. Jayna, no doubt, playing guard, locking up for her safety. Footsteps. Maybe if she pretended to be asleep Jayna would decide to go on to the casino rather than watch her snooze. Then she'd make the call.

"I'm looking for a missing person."

Rachel's head snapped up from the desk. Eyes the color of slate pinned her where she sat; a faint whiff of bay and spice tempted and teased. Some Middle Eastern instrument played a distant refrain while Rocky's theme surged in the background.

"His name is Joshua Smith, and I understand

you're just the person who can help me find him. He loves a woman. One he can't live without. Rachel Tinsdale is what she goes by, but her alias is Angel.'' He withdrew a black velvet box and flipped open the lid. A diamond so large it was gaudy winked into her stunned eyes.

''Allow me to introduce myself. Rand Slick. A rose by any other name probably smells ten times better, but if you'll have me, I've got a car idling. Its destination is the courthouse. My mission is marriage.''

Before she could absorb the head-spinning, heart-thudding magnitude of what he'd just asked, he was behind the desk and hauling her into his arms.

''I love you, Rachel. I'm no bargain, and life with me won't be a bed of roses. But if you can handle that, I'll spend the rest of my life doing my damnedest to deserve you.''

''*Rand.*'' She plowed ten fingers into his hair and laid a kiss on him that torched them both to ashes, ashes, all fall down....

''I've been so miserable without you.'' She was crying, not caring if her mascara was running or even her nose, because he was there, making promises she knew he'd never break. He pulled out an embroidered handkerchief and wiped away her tears.

''I've missed you like crazy, angel. It's just no good without you. I can't work, can't sleep. I can't do anything but think about how right it is with us and wonder why the hell I ever thought keeping us apart was in our best interests. The truth was staring me in the face, and I couldn't see it.''

''And what is the truth, Rand?''

''I'll never be perfect. You'll never quit loving me

because I'm not. We're meant to be together. It's that simple.''

"Took you long enough to figure that out.'' She sniffled as she stroked his chest, absorbing and exulting in the solid feel of him, the quickening beat of his heart against her palm. "I've been crying myself to sleep every night. I haul your doll around in my ugly purse along with a bottle of your cologne. I sniff it, close my eyes and pretend you're there.''

"I'm here, angel. I'm here. Now, I want to do this right....'' He knelt, one knee on the floor, the other crooked, in a formal, gallant pose. Taking her left hand, he held the ring at the tip of her finger. "Will you marry me, Rachel? Think about it before you answer, because marriage to me is for life.''

"I wouldn't have it any other way. The answer is yes, Rand. And it's yes again, Joshua.'' Her hand was shaking; why, even her finger had the tremors as he slipped on the ring.

"For better or worse,'' he said in a gruff voice. "Though I'm afraid I'll get the first and you'll get the second. But maybe the richer or poorer part will help even things out. Especially since you threw that million bucks in my face.''

He pressed a kiss to the ring and got up. Rachel's eyes darted from him to the rock on her hand, unable to decide whether she was closer to tears or laughter. She gave in to both.

"You idiot. You know better than to even mention money. Like my dad said, it can't buy you love. You've got mine, and it's free for the taking.''

"And I need you enough to take it. I want forever, Rachel. I want the fights when I slip, I want your arms to be there when I fall. And I want babies. The whole nine yards.''

Rachel's gaze froze on the ring. Had Jayna interfered? Was Rand here because he knew about the baby?

''Did Jayna call you?'' she demanded.

''Call me? About what?''

''Being a father-to-be, that's what.''

Any pretense Rand had to suave sophistication gave way as his jaw dropped in a *Duh, say again?* expression.

''I don't believe it. You said you weren't.... I'll be damned. You lied, didn't you?''

''You bet I did, Mr. Master.'' She smiled smugly. ''I let you go, and you came back.''

''Why, you little sneak,'' he growled. He tried to pull a stern face, but all he came up with was an ear-to-ear grin. With a quick swipe, he shoved the phone and papers and playing cards from her desk. They thudded to the floor as he leaned her back and ran a hand up her thigh. ''I think I need to dole out a lesson to my concubine for keeping secrets from me.''

Rachel yanked him down by his tie, bringing his mouth a whisper from hers. Angling for a heated kiss, she murmured seductively, ''You're a savage.''

''And angel, you're silk.''